Speak My Language, and Other Stories: An Anthology of Gay Fiction

Torsten Højer

ROBINSON

ROBINSON

First published in Great Britain in 2015 by Robinson

3 5 7 9 8 6 4

A CIP catalogue record for this book
is available from the British Library.

ISBN 978-1-47211-997-1

Typeset in Great Britain by Hewer Text UK Ltd, Edinburgh
Printed and bound in Great Britain by CPI Group (UK) Ltd,
Croydon CR0 4YY

Papers used by Robinson are from well-managed forests and other natural sources

Robinson
An imprint of
Little, Brown Book Group
Carmelite House
50 Victoria Embankment
London EC4Y 0DZ

An Hachette UK Company
www.hachette.co.uk

www.littlebrown.co.uk

This book is dedicated
to the memory of Peter Burton

Contents

Foreword
Stephen Fry

Most young gay people today would, I think rightly, be grateful to have been born into an age of greater acceptance and tolerance. We may not as a society be there fully but, my word, how things have changed from my own schooldays back in the 1970s.

And yet . . . let me tell you a little about my upbringing deep in the Norfolk countryside where we were, in the words of the eighteenth-century wit Sydney Smith, simply miles from the nearest lemon. Television at our house was not precisely banned, but only brought out for special occasions like the funeral of Churchill, the increasingly common assassinations of prominent Americans and, more happily, the moon landing.

Insomnia, especially on hot nights, was one of the chief miseries of my childhood and youth. Therefore, the only answer in lieu of television was to read, which in itself presented an absurd problem. If I opened the windows to cool the room, it would soon fill with huge moths, May bugs, June bugs and all kinds of simply terrifying arthropods peculiar to Norfolk which, like crazed winged lobsters, would carom and careen straight to my bedside lamp and flicker, bang and buzz about inside the shade. I happen to be horribly afraid of moths – an utterly irrational fear, I am quite aware, but agonizingly real.

Somehow I managed, despite these abhorred fluttering distractions, to get through hundreds of books a year. My parents had many of their own, most of which I had soon consumed more than once. I further supplemented my reading matter at first from a large grey mobile library, which arrived every other Thursday at the corner of two lanes not far from the house.

One Sunday afternoon, aged perhaps thirteen, I watched on the little television that was pushed into a tiny corner of our huge Victorian kitchen Anthony Asquith's film version of *The Importance of Being Earnest*. I vividly recall sitting on an uncushioned wooden kitchen chair, face flushed, mouth half-open, simply astonished at what I was watching and, most especially, *hearing*. I had had simply no idea that language could do this. That it could dance and trip and tickle, cavort, swirl, beguile and seduce – that its rhythms, subclauses, repetitions, *clausulae* and colours could excite quite as much as music.

When Algernon says to Cecily, "I hope, Cecily, I shall not offend you if I state quite frankly and openly that you seem to me to be in every way the visible personification of absolute perfection?" I wriggled and giggled and repeated the phrase to myself in disbelieving bliss. Enough times to commit it to memory there and then. I would repeat it solemnly to our (faintly bewildered) cook.

"Oh, you do go on with your nonsense. How that drives me crazy."

My repeatedly telling her that I hoped I would not offend her if I stated quite frankly and openly that she seemed to me to be in every way the visible personification of absolute perfection might have flustered her a little, but she was used to my behaviour, which was at times so frantic, fanciful and foolish that it would today quite certainly be diagnosed as Attention Deficit Hyperactivity Disorder.

Wilde's phrase, and many others from the film – "I never travel without my diary. One should always have something sensational to read on a train" – took hold of me completely. In an age before video recording, the best I could do was imagine myself inside the world of this extraordinary motion picture which turned out, my mother told me (after patiently enduring the matter of her too being the visible personification of absolute perfection), to have been based on a play – a copy of which she was sorry to say was not in the house.

The following Thursday I stood then, the only customer (lender? User? What was the word then?), at the corner of the lanes, fretfully waiting until the battleship-grey mobile library hove into view. The driver lurched the van – of the kind that I think used to be called a pantechnicon – to a halt, came round to open the door and lower the steps, and tousled my hair and patted my bum as I ascended (as adults were quite rightly allowed to do in those days without being hauled up before the courts and having their houses set fire to). The librarian, a becardiganed, multi-beaded old dear, was also apt to ruffle my hair. She often told me that I read so many books I would soon grow into one. For a child to read books, especially in the summer, was looked on as very peculiar and, of course, unhealthy – something I had always been used to being considered, on account of my loathing of all forms of organized games and sports.

"Have you," I asked her breathlessly, "ever heard of a play called *The Importance of Being Earnest*?"

"Why yes, my love, that's just up there, I think."

It was far from the largest drama section you have ever seen in a library. A smattering of Shaw, Priestley and Shakespeare, but also marvellously the collected comedies of Oscar Wilde. She stamped the book out with that splendid springing, spanking sound that will never be heard on these shores again. The previous stamp showed me it had last been lent in 1959. I thanked her, dismounted in a bound, flew up the lane, round the rear of the house, up the back stairs and into my bedroom.

Lady Windermere's Fan, *A Woman of No Importance*, *An Ideal Husband*, *The Importance of Being Earnest*. I read them all again and again and again until a fortnight later, when I found myself once more restlessly pacing the corner of the two lanes.

"Have you anything else by Oscar Wilde?"

"Well, now, I aren't rightly sure . . ." she lifted her reading glasses from the delicately linked silver chain that hung round her neck, pushed them to her nose and came around the desk to inspect the shelves as if for the first time. "Ah, now, there you go."

The Complete Works of Oscar Wilde. This was more, so much more than I could possibly have hoped for. Once again I flung myself on my bed and started to read. Some of the dialogues written in the Socratic style in essays like *The Decay of Lying* and *The Critic as Artist* confused me a little, and parts of *The Soul of Man Under Socialism* were quite beyond me. The poems I frankly disliked, save for *The Ballad of Reading Gaol*, which seemed an odd subject for such a glamorous and flowing lord of language to have chosen. The stories for children made me weep, as they do to this day, and *The Picture of Dorian Gray* touched a part of me that I couldn't quite define, but disturbed and excited me very deeply indeed. *De Profundis*, too, I found beautiful, but puzzling. I wasn't sure what the allusions to "prison" and "shame" and "scandal" and so on were supposed to mean. Indeed, I assumed the letter to be a work of fiction that held some allegorical meaning beyond my reach.

I kept this collection for four weeks, and the cosily obliging librarian waived the late-return penalty of sixpence when I at last brought it back to the mobile library. I asked if she had anything else by this Oscar Wilde.

She pointed at the book. "If that says *The Complete Works*, then I should think that's the complete works, wouldn't you, young man?"

"Hm." It was hard not to see the justice of this. "Well, do you have anything *about* him, perhaps?"

Her soft, powdered cheeks pinkened a little and, in a rather quavery voice, she asked me how old I was.

"Oh, I'm a very advanced reader," I assured her. Being tall and with a voice that never broke but slowly deepened, I could usually pass as older than my real age.

"We-ell . . ." she fossicked about the lower shelves and came up with a book called *The Trials of Oscar Wilde* by an author called H. Montgomery Hyde.

The book was like a kick in the teeth. A kick in the gut. A kick in the groin. A kick most especially in the heart. After reading about the character of this brilliant, engaging, gentle, exceptionally kind and quite remarkably gifted Irishman, to discover the truth of the sudden and calamitous third act of his life – the three trials (it is often forgotten that, following the legal action he foolishly took against the Marquess of Queensberry, there were not one, but two criminal trials against him, after the first ended in a deadlocked jury), the exile and the squalid and unhappy travels and subsequent penurious death in Paris – all this was almost more than I could bear.

Yet.

Yet it also confirmed in my deepest heart something that I had always known. That he and I shared a similar "nature", as he would say, or "sexuality" as we would call it today.

My heart was wrenched by the story of Oscar. The mobile library was no longer enough. The only place for me now was Norwich City Library, twelve miles away. Sometimes I had the energy to bicycle, sometimes I took the daily coach that stopped at that same meeting of lanes at twenty to seven every weekday morning.

Before the Internet and Berners-Lee's miraculous World Wide Web, the closest you came to metadata or hyperlinks were the bibliography and the index cards in the wooden drawers of a library catalogue.

I started by seeing what else this Montgomery Hyde had written. *The Love That Dared Not Speak Its Name* was one book. *The Other Love* was even more astonishing. I found myself endlessly in Norwich City Library, scribbling down names from the bibliographies at the end of each non-fiction book and then haring to the catalogues to see if the library might hold a copy of anything related to a newly acquired lead to the world of forbidden love. Through such means, I learned about the infamous Baron Corvo, aka William Rolfe, and his eye-popping, trouser-shifting "Venice Letters", Norman Douglas, T. C. Worsley, "Y" (an anonymous gay autobiographer), Robin Maugham, Angus Stewart, the scandalous Michael Davidson, Roger Peyrefitte, Henry de Montherlant, Jean Genet, William Burroughs, Gore Vidal, John Rechy and dozens and dozens of others. It was the equivalent of clicking on web links – more cumbersome and time consuming, of course, but breathlessly exciting. Along the way, as a happy accident, I acquired a kind of alternative literary education that ran in parallel to the one I was receiving at school. You cannot read Genet or about him without encountering (the entirely heterosexual, so far as we know) Jean-Paul Sartre, and you cannot brush up against Robin Maugham without making the acquaintance of Paul Bowles and the Tangier set. Burroughs leads to Denton Welch, Corvo to the Bensons, Ronald Firbank, Stephen Tennant, Harold Acton and so on until, by fortuitous and serendipitous circumstances, fuelled by inner erotic curiosity and stimulation, I found a world of artists and writers, straight and gay, who were their own reward.

Suppose I had been born in the 1980s? All the vindication and support I might ever have needed to make me comfortable about my sexuality could have been found in television programmes like *Queer as Folk*, by the pioneering gay kisses on *EastEnders* and *Brookside*, in Pride marches along the streets of London and in the billions of pathways, savoury and unsavoury, offered by the Internet. The fact that my childhood, youth and early manhood preceded all of this diversity, freedom, tolerance and openness I, of course, regret to some degree: the brave new gay world would have saved me the doomed feeling I had that my life was inevitably to be one of secrecy, exile, seedy sex shops and the police courts. But I am very, very glad that the only available route to a proud acceptance and endorsement of my gay nature should have come through literature. I think I would always have loved Shakespeare, Keats, Austen, Dickens, Tennyson, Browning, Forster, Joyce, Fitzgerald – what the bluff English master of one of the private schools I attended called "the big hitters" – but I cannot thank my sexuality enough for giving me, in my particular case, a love of all reading and an introduction to the gay identity that offered so much more than Gay Tube and xhamster.com.

So it is for you now to read with pleasure the stories laid out before you and feel with me, if you can, that there is something special about literature, high or low, that addresses our innermost sexual and amatory selves. Whether they be light in tone, intensely erotic or lyrical, gay stories offer us vindication, fellowship, validation and a sense of shared identity that we need now as much as ever.

Introduction
by Torsten Højer

———

I admit that, for good or for ill, I am addicted to my Facebook feed. It lurks as I work, perpetually pinging up popular stories from not only my chums, but also the gaggle of gay news outlets that now exist. Among the multitude of muscular men in minuscule briefs are the good, the bad and the downright ugly gay stories of the day: joy as the United States legalizes gay marriage; despair as HIV infection rates increase; the horrifying situation for gay men in Uganda.

As relentless consumers of tidbits of gay information from around the globe, we find ourselves instantly informed as the extremes of equality and inequality trend; the latest news from Kansas is as accessible as that from Kampala.

Reflecting on our appetite for knowledge of gay experience both at home and abroad, I left the premise for stories within this collection entirely open – bar requiring a gay element – preferring to approach authors writing from a kaleidoscope of ages, locations, political climates and cultures. Indeed, the youngest contributor is in his twenties, the eldest in his eighties. The stories here are set in countries including Australia, Cuba, England, Greece, Italy, Kenya, Portugal, Russia, Somalia, South Africa, Spain, Sri Lanka and the USA.

Another desire was for a mix of contributors ranging from emerging talent to established, award-winning and sometimes pioneering authors. This is in part a continuation of the work of journalist, editor and writer Peter Burton, to whom this book is dedicated, who tirelessly championed gay literature throughout his fifty-year career – and right up to his departure in 2011.

I'm honoured to include stories from celebrated authors such as

Neil Bartlett, Damian Barr, Patrick Gale, Francis King, Vestal McIntyre, Joseph Olshan, Diriye Osman, Felice Picano and Rupert Smith. I'm also privileged that Stephen Fry has written the foreword.

Equally, I'm thrilled to include stories from emerging writers such as Michael Carroll, Cliff James, Joseph Lidster and Joshua Winning.

To my knowledge, this is also the first time the British poet David Robilliard has been published by a major publisher.

Thanks are due to Duncan Proudfoot, Georgie Szolnoki, Emily Byron and all at Constable & Robinson/Little, Brown Book Group; Rose Collis; Danny James; Simon Coulson; Sarah Rushton-Read; Rikki Beadle-Blair at Team Angelica; Louise Jameson; Lisa Dowdeswell and Kate Pool at the Society of Authors; John Byrne; Ron Robertson; Vickie Dillon and Bill Hamilton at A M Heath; Cathy Rosenberg, Claire Conville, Jo Crocker, Marigold Atkey at David Higham Associates; all of the contributors to this collection (especially those who shared contacts and suggested further writers); my family and Robert Common, with whom I look forward to enjoying this gay life.

———

Torsten Højer
Brighton, 2014

This is Serious
James Robert Baker

Excerpt from tape recordings made by Dean Seagrave in his car, as he hunts down his ex-boyfriend, Pablo Orega, in Los Angeles, on 24 June 1996.

OK, I'm out of here. Oh, man. I think I blew it. Let me get out of here. Fuck. I don't think they'd dare call the cops though. I'm probably OK.

Hold on. Let me make sure I'm getting out of here. What the fuck street is this? Romaine? What's this up here? It must be Highland. Fuck. OK, I'm running the light. Fuck it.

That wasn't smart. But I guess I'm OK. Shot, I've still got a hard-on. I think I'm insane.

Man, I'm still shaken. I really thought it was him. That poor guy. I think I scared the fuck out of him.

So OK. So I go in the door and there's a window. I have to show ID and all that, which is fucked. Because of course they've got my name now. But I really can't see them calling the cops. They've already been hassled. I mean, these sex places are kind of controversial. Even though they've sprung up all over now. And gotten progressively bolder in their gay-rag ads. Instead of being the guilty secret they were a few years ago. Now they're almost proudly proclaiming: *Yes, we spread HIV through multi-partner cocksucking and unprotected buttfucking. Won't you please join us on our fabulous death boat, the SS Jonestown. Special college-boy discount rates. Just show us your uninfected buns and student ID.*

Of course, if you say anything, if you point out that these places are mass-suicide parlors, they call you sex-negative. Which no self-respecting PC queer wants to be. And the health department, the liberal supervisors who are all taking fag money – nobody gives a shit or does anything. They're probably thinking: "Fuck, we give up. If those fags want to kill themselves, why should we try to stop them?" You know what? They've got a point.

Anyway, I show the guy at the window my license. And I can see him noting the birth date, then checking me out, making this judgement call. That OK, I may be thirty-eight, but I don't look *that* old. Or I won't anyway under a 20-watt red light bulb. Because it turns out that most of the guys inside are young. In their twenties. The new sex-positive nineties seroconversion set.

So I get my card, all that, he buzzes me in. It's very dark, of course. My geriatric eyes need time to adjust. So the first thing I notice is the music and the smell. The music is the U2 song, "One". Which I really like, but it's a strange kind of moody, grief-riddled, heavily Aids-coded song, which seems like a very bleak *comment* on this scene. Like this incredibly moving, re-humanizing, de-objectifying *comment*. But I get the feeling I'm the only one who's taking it that way.

It's this labyrinthine place. Guys wandering around through the plywood cubicles and corridors. Glory holes everywhere. Smell of piss and stale cum. Some guy back in one urine-scented booth, hunched in the shadows, squatting on a toilet that doesn't work. He's emaciated, like he's got maybe three T-cells left, and he sticks his tongue out. I don't think he wants to blow me. I think he wants me to piss in his mouth. Last call.

Another guy, with a honey-blond beard, is kind of listlessly jerking off back in a barred, jail-like cubicle. Like Vincent Van Gogh on crystal. So fried, he's kind of talking to himself. Like muttering sex talk to himself. He worries me. Like I half expect him to flash a straight-razor or something. Cut off his ear. Or his dick or something. He looks just like Kirk Douglas in *Lust for Life*. Except the more fitting title is *Lust for Death*.

The whole place reminds me of the old Basic Plumbing. Which got to be so mean I quit going there way before Aids, just because of the attitudes, the evil, callous way guys treated each other. So I'm having all these flashbacks about things I haven't seen or felt since 1981.

I mean, it's crowded but nobody's really doing that much. Just walking around, like bored rats in a maze. Like the bigger the selection, the pickier people get. So there's this thin air of frustration. This sense of judgement, of tense restraint. It doesn't seem very warm-hearted. That's the term that LA Weekly moron used in his PC propaganda piece a while back. "Unlike the sex clubs of yesteryear, the new sexual anarchy is warm-hearted . . ." Something like that. Maybe I'm missing something, but it seems about as joyful as Buchenwald.

I see one guy with a goatee, which makes me quake for a second. Till I notice the hair on his forearms, which Pablo doesn't have. So I make the rounds a few times, feel a few looks of interest, which is cheaply reassuring. I finally see some action. Three or four guys around another guy, who's down on his knees. But it feels disembodied for some reason. Like the first time I ever went to a bathhouse, in the early seventies. Even though there were other times, later, when the same scene – say at the beach – might have turned me on. Like I'd get a hard-on and join the crowd. But this doesn't thrill me. It's like looking at a porno photo that no longer turns you on.

Speaking of porno, that's my next stop. The room that's like a lounge with a TV monitor showing a tape. But I don't stay there long. This tape's completely insane. It's like four or five guys in this intense frenetic scene. Like this rough sex scene where they're yelling abuse. "Suck his cock, you cock-hungry pig." But that's not what bothers me. It's the pitch the film's maintaining. The frantic, borderline hysteria. Like some abject fiend on the edge of coming. Except it never stops. There's just this sense of frantic violence that goes on and on. And the sound's also fucked up for some reason, distorting. So you hear these garbled yells of: "Suck on it! Choke on it, you pig!" And it seems very clear that sex is not enough, that they don't want to fuck, they want to fucking kill each other. So you're starting to feel: why don't they just cut the shit and *do it*! Forget about their dicks, whip out a goddamn machete. Let's see some fucking *blood*! That's what you *want*!

So I have to get out of there. I feel like this tape is ridiculing me.

Turning what I feel, what for me is very serious, into a cheap porno conceit. As if the culture, the gay consumerist culture, wants to defuse and neutralize me.

So I kind of stumble down the corridor, feeling panicked, even paranoid. Like everyone sees me as some floridly short-circuiting, pathetic loser who isn't cold enough to function in this scene. Like I should be stuck in the dumpster out back like a broken, discarded *replicant*. So I duck into one of the cubicles, just to get away from all the eyes.

It's like a stall with a door on a spring. So I hook the door and try to collect myself. And I can smell marijuana smoke in the air, which I've smelled since I came in and that reminds me of this joint I lifted at Reese's. Guess I haven't mentioned that until now. Not especially proud of it. But there was a box on the coffee table, filled with maybe two-dozen joints. Didn't think Reese would miss one. I thought it might help bring me down from the speed, when I needed to do that. I stuck it in my pocket a second before Stan came in.

Now feels like the time to bring myself down some, so I fire up the joint in the cubicle. And it's odd. This other strange song starts to play. I mean, strange for the setting. That Frente! acoustic version of "Bizarre Love Triangle", which is one of my two favourite New Order songs. I mean, it was weird the first time I heard the Frente! version, since I've been singing that song to myself for years. My own acoustic version in the car, in the shower, idly walking around the house. I like the chorus especially. Where you get down on your knees and pray . . .

Which is maybe what I should be doing right now. Praying. If I knew who to pray to or what, but I don't anymore.

And so for a while I was gone. I mean, the dope was good, very good, and for a while I was lost in the sad lost world of that song. Like I could write a whole novel, a Proustian novel, about everything that went through my mind in those two minutes.

But then the song was over and there was nothing for a moment. And that's when I heard these two guys, these two guys talking in the next cubicle. Like having a conversation after sex. And I reel because this one guy is saying, "So my friend John goes: 'I don't know why you keep attracting these guys who always get obsessed with you.' And I go, 'John, it's because I have a kind of sexual magnetism that I can't turn off . . .'"

So it's him. It has to be him. It's his voice, his phrasing, it's him.

Except I'm buzzed now, from the dope, so how can I be sure my mind isn't playing tricks? That's when I notice the peephole. I turn down the light in my cubicle, and crouch down and look through the peephole. Meanwhile, the other guy's talking, all very low-key, about his boring job as a claims adjuster or something. So I look through the peephole and there they are, on a small cot. I can't see a lot at first in the weak yellow light. Their crotches mostly. They've taken their clothes off. You can see their limp dicks, their hands holding cigarettes, as they go on talking. But I'm sure it's him.

"I'm working on this paper now. It's really been exhausting me," he says. Playing grad student on study break.

Then he reaches over to stub out his cigarette and I see his moustache and goatee. I see his Auschwitz buzz cut, as predicted. So I have no further doubt it's him.

The other guy gets up, pulls on his pants, says he has to take a leak.

Pablo says, "So, you're going back on Tuesday?" Like the guy's from out of town. Like Pablo wants to spend some more time with him. So I know I have to act now, before the guy comes back and they leave together.

I don't have time to think, or to savor the anticipation. Which is somewhat disappointing, that the moment is coming so fast. I take out the Glock, hold it under my T-shirt as I step out. I press the door to his cubicle. It's unlatched. I enter, pulling out the gun. He jumps as I say, "Don't make a fucking sound."

That's when I see all the hair on his chest and stomach and I know it's not Pablo. I still don't want to believe it, though. I was so sure. I keep looking at his face, as though his body could be lying. Like he's grown hair on his chest to fool me, to fuck with my head. Which is crazy, I know. But my mind really wants to be right.

Finally, I have to admit it. It's not his face, either. This guy's nose is too long, his cheeks too sunken. So I say, "Look, sorry. I thought you were someone else."

So that's when I leave. And then this strange thing happens. Except it's not so strange, which is why I'm very concerned now. But as I step outside, into the bracing night air, I suddenly get an erection. Like for no apparent reason. Except I think at first it's maybe some weird form of relief. Like I've been in this hellhole of death, this stinking, suffocating prison, and now I'm busting free, embracing the fresh night air and life or something. I don't want to admit yet what's really going on. It's too horrendous.

But I'm admitting it now. Because I've still got a hard-on. It's been a half hour now and it still hasn't gone down. I can't wait any longer. The stakes are too high. It's the hemp that did it. My doctor warned me about that. It can cause this kind of side effect. Smoking dope when you're taking Desyrel. I thought about it at Reese's when I lifted the joint. I guess I just didn't believe it. Or maybe I was thinking, when I smoked in the sex club . . . Maybe I was thinking, if I'm really honest, that as foul as the place was, if I got a killer hard-on, I might just – who knows? – get all this sucked out of my system. But I'm in trouble now. I'm in deep shit, I can tell. It's a different kind of hard-on. Like an *extra-hard* hard-on. But the problem is this. I'm not thinking about sex. And I can tell I could think about anything – Pat Boone, Rush Limbaugh naked, Nancy Reagan's twat – *and I would not lose this erection*.

Which may sound funny. Or like a highly desirable state. Boy, you could fuck all night, ha ha. But here's the thing. If I don't do something now, this could permanently damage me. Make me impotent. Which is really no joke at all. That's why I'm closing in on Cedars-Sinai Hospital – right now.

———

OK, I'm back. It's about eleven. A lot's been going on. I'm moving, as you can tell. I feel OK now. Leveled out. Just did some more speed. I kind of had to. They hit me up with something at Cedars. Valium or something. They could tell I was tweaked. But right now I feel perfect. Wired out but not frantic. In control.

Which is good. I feel like this is it. I'm closing in. It's going to happen. I've never been more sure of anything in my life.

So I go into Emergency. Which, for starters, is painfully bright. And I've got my T-shirt out and all that. But it's not completely covering my crotch. So I'm very self-conscious. Like some teenage kid with a boner who has to share it in front of the class.

The waiting room's not crowded, fortunately. Just this elderly Jewish couple. I kind of walk to the window half-turned away from them. The guy at the window turns out to be the problem. This icky young queen who reminds me of Calvin. Calvin pre-Aids. So he asks me what the problem is and I tell him I've got an erection.

He says, "We should all be so lucky."

And I say, "No, look, this isn't a joke. I'm taking Desyrel, this anti-depressant, and this is one of the side effects. It gives you a permanent erection and if you don't do something about it, it can physically damage your penis."

I realize this old Jewish couple can hear me. And this queen is kind of smiling. And I'm starting to feel like no one's going to believe me. Like no one here is going to know what I'm talking about.

"How long have you had it?" the guy asks.

"I don't know. Forty-five minutes."

"You mean, constantly?"

"Yes."

He's looking at me like he thinks I'm a nut case. Or like if the Jewish couple weren't there in the waiting room, he'd ask me to show him.

I say, "Look, this is serious. I need to see a doctor immediately."

So he finally takes my Blue Cross card and all that. Then he says, "Why don't you have a seat, Mr Seagrave? It'll be a few minutes."

So I say, "Look, man. You're not getting it. I know this sounds silly or something, compared to the gunshot victims and people having heart attacks. But it's a very real thing! If I'm not treated, damage will result. I'll be impotent, man! Don't you get it? Maybe you don't give a shit, but it's my fucking life! I want to see a doctor and I want to see him now!"

So he goes and talks to someone, and this nurse comes and gets me. She leads me back into one of the examining places, and I have to tell her all over again what's going on. Then finally the doctor finally comes over, this young Jewish guy who I recognize immediately from a local news show. Like he's this doctor who always does the medical reports. So I explain for a third time what's going on and he wants to see. But this nurse is still there, and I know she's a nurse, but I say, "Do you think she could step out? I'm shy, OK?"

So she does, and I show the doctor my boner, which is totally huge and dark red. I mean, the color freaks me out – it's so dark, like all the blood in my dick is clotting or something.

And the doctor says: "Are you sure you weren't just stimulated?"

And I almost say: "No, I was just at this truly vile sex club that if anything had the opposite effect." But I decide not to mention that, in case he's homophobic or something. But I'm already getting terrified, since I can tell that he doesn't know anything about this. He's got this expression like he's thinking: "This is a puzzler."

I say, "Look, I knew this could happen. If you smoke marijuana. My doctor gave me that warning. I just didn't take it that seriously. But I know there are drugs you can give me that will counteract the effect."

I didn't want to say anything more. Because I knew, I remembered this conversation with my doctor that seemed like a joke at the time, that if the drugs didn't work they had to do surgery. Cut the blood vessels or something. Which will also result in permanent impotence. That's part of why I don't want this guy to know I'm gay. He might say, "Sorry, Bud. Only one way to deal with *this*."

But this guy looks baffled. Then he goes and uses the phone. Which seems to take forever. Getting through to some other doctor. I can see him from the examining room. At one point he laughs into the phone. And I'm thinking: "Man, chat it up some other time, dude. This is fucking *serious*, you asshole!"

Finally he comes and gives me a shot of something. As he does it, he says, "If this doesn't work, we may have to perform surgery, which could leave you impotent."

I say, "Oh, man. My girlfriend will shit."

Not taking any chances, since I'm kind of at his mercy.

Then he says, "Your pupils are dilated. What else have you taken tonight?"

So I tell him I did a couple of lines of crank, since I was working on a project. That's when he calls for the Valium shot.

Then it's like this waiting game. This big suspense scene. Like if it's going to work, it should work within minutes. So the doctor's there and so is the nurse. And other people are kind of watching from further back. Like everyone in the ER knows what's going on.

I'm just sitting on the table at this point. My pants are up, my shirt's covering my crotch, so everybody's watching my face, like I'm supposed to tell them if there's any change.

I'm really thinking: "If this doesn't work, I'm going to kill myself. Since I can't see living if I can't fuck."

Then, the tension gets unbelievable. Not that I care a lot, since I'm kind of peaking on Valium. But on another level, I still know what's at stake. The doctor keeps looking at his watch. I half expect him to say, "OK, I feel something. It's going down. Yeah, it is."

The doctor wants to see it again, so I make him draw the curtain. Like I don't need an audience watching me lose my erection.

And it's OK. It's going down. Way down. Until my dick's so shriveled up it looks like it was dipped in ice water. At which point I get panicked. I say, "Look, this isn't permanent—"

He says, "No, no. You'll be fine in a day or two. But you should definitely avoid re-stimulation."

Re-stimulation? Like he still thinks I was probably fucking.

Anyway, that was it. They wanted me to stay there and rest for an hour or so, just to be sure. They didn't try to have me admitted, like I thought they might. But I left after about forty minutes, because I suddenly realized where Pablo will be tonight – it suddenly hit me. I'm almost certain I'm right this time. And it's been a long day. I just want to find him and kill him and get it over with, so I can go somewhere and get a good night's sleep.

Dead Air
Joshua Winning

———

10 p.m.

Adam Fox drew the microphone closer and used his best radio voice: the husky one that had earned him so many fans in the halcyon days of prime time. It helped that he'd just downed a cup of scalding coffee.

"Hello, creatures of the night. This is Adam Fox, checking in for a long-haul flight to dreamland. For the next seven hours, I'm all yours." He clicked an icon on his desktop screen and a horror-movie cackle filled his headphones. "But before we slip into something a little more comfortable, let's catch up with those news headlines. Don't go anywhere."

Another click and the Mantrap FM jingle played, followed by a recorded news bulletin. Adam slumped back in his chair, stretched his arms above his head and yawned. After three months working the graveyard shift at the radio station, he thought he'd have acclimatized, but the opposite was happening. The bags under his eyes were deepening, becoming more permanent. He was pale, too. The kind of pale that looked sickly, malnourished. He slept all day and worked all night, which was doing nothing for his complexion – or his sex life.

The door behind him clicked open and Adam swung his chair, freeing one ear from his tin-can headphones.

"I'm out," said Giles, an adorable twenty-something DJ who wore a parka and an earring. If only their shift patterns were more compatible.

"Sayonara," Adam said, stifling another yawn.

"I brewed a new pot for you," Giles said. "Looked like you needed it."

Considerate, Adam thought. *Too considerate? Something somebody with a vested interest might do?*

"Thanks. Hey, off anywhere exciting?"

"Bed."

"Sounds exciting to me."

"You're on."

"Huh?"

Giles pointed to the screen.

"You're on," he whispered, slipping out of the dark studio and closing the door.

"Shit." Adam pulled the headphones back on.

Click.

"How about that news, huh?" he purred into the mic. His gaze went to the viewing window, where Giles pretended to fall asleep while standing up, then laughed and waved, his slight frame disappearing down the hall. Adam was alone again. He'd be alone for the next six-and-a-half hours until Twig came in for the breakfast show. Cocooned in the shadows of his studio, Adam could be the last man on Earth. If aliens attacked or a nuke went off, he doubted he'd hear it through the soundproof walls.

He cursed his manager, Dale, for roughly the sixtieth time that week. This time last year, Adam had been on prime-time radio, damn near the star of Mantrap FM – or as much of a star as a radio personality could be nowadays. He went to movie premieres and interviewed the stars as they glided down the red carpet. Now he was being squeezed out the arsehole end of the schedule – and all because he'd pissed Dale off at the Christmas party. Adam couldn't even remember what had happened that night. It was a sozzled blur of liquor and cigarettes. But in one fell swoop, Dale had killed both his career and his social life.

Thirty-two and sharing air with the alkies and the crazies. Just shoot me.

"It's that time of night when I put on my therapist's hat and help all you hopeless romantics," he said into the mic. "Caught in a bad romance? Got a mystery itch down there? No matter what the problem, the love doctor's here to give you a hand. Give me a call on 0800-MANFIX and I'll see what I can do. Oh, and I come fully lubricated. It won't hurt a bit. Unless you want it to."

It was the most popular portion of the night, just early enough for the lovelorn to still be sufficiently sober to form a sentence, and late enough for salacious dilemmas that wouldn't usually make it past the watershed. Within five minutes, the board had lit up like a disco floor and Adam put through the first caller. Ordinarily, he'd have a producer to field the calls, but budget cuts had resulted in yet more restrictions on the station's staff. Adam had a feeling Dale was behind that, too.

Fuck you, Dale.

"Hey caller, who are you and where are you from?"

"Hey, it's Harry from Finsbury Park."

"Nice place."

"It's a shithole."

"What can I help you with, Harry?"

At least this one sounded sober.

"Okay . . . Uh . . . Well, basically, I'm seeing this guy, but he has this sort of fetish, I guess."

"Sounds kinky. And you have a problem with this?"

"Well, it's just . . . He loves *The Lord Of The Rings* and he wants me to dress up as Gandalf . . ."

11 p.m.
Adam hit play on the extended news bulletin, which gave him five minutes to dash to the toilet and then refill his coffee cup. He hung the headphones over the mic and hurried down the corridor. The fluorescent lights buzzed as he went into the toilet. As he pissed in the urinal, he chuckled at some of the calls he'd received. A young guy who thought his nose would cave in like Danniella Westbrook's because he'd snorted poppers. Another who'd lost his douche somewhere unpleasant.

Turn out the sun and the weirdos emerge. Don't these people have any common sense?

Zipping himself up, Adam went into the poky kitchen and filled his mug, then headed back towards the studio.

He stopped. Listened.

For a moment, he was sure he'd heard a noise. A shuffling from further down the corridor. But there was nobody there. He was alone at the station. Giles had locked him in when he left, like he always did.

Adam checked his watch and hurried back into the darkened studio.

"The next hour is all about smooth tunes," he breathed, unleashing his best husky. "Got a request? Give me a call on 0800-MANFIX or send a text to 8465."

He spun a few tunes for the next thirty minutes, took some requests from callers – one of them a regular who always flirted down the phone line. It had been entertaining at first, but Adam was sure he could hear a baby in the background, which was a massive turn-off. Didn't stop the guy phoning in every couple of nights and requesting the same song. Always "Gimme Shelter" by the Rolling Stones.

The last track played out and Adam noticed that there was a caller on line one. He placed a bet with himself. Smooth tunes generally meant Hot Chocolate, Aretha or Texas. Somebody had requested Enya once and he'd laughed them off the air, slinging on Sinéad O'Connor instead.

Click.

"You're live on Mantrap FM. Who's this and where are you from?"

Heavy breathing huffed into his headphones.

"You have to help me!"

Adam sighed. He hadn't had one of these for a while.

"Very good," he said. "If you raise the Bat signal, I'm sure—"

"*Please!*" the voice screamed and Adam jumped. "I don't know what to do!"

The hairs on Adam's arms prickled. Was this for real? The voice sounded familiar, though he couldn't place it. One of his friends playing a prank? None of his friends listened in, though. They took great pains to sound surprised when he talked about his "little show".

Our celebrity, they oozed, flapping their hands and flicking their hair. *A-list Adam just loves a celebrity shindig.*

No. This was different. He could hear panic in the caller's voice. Hoarse, rasping desperation.

"What's wrong?" he asked, sitting up straighter.

"There's somebody after me. I—"

The line went dead.

"Hello?" Adam asked.

Shit.

He tried to get a handle on his nerves. Leaned in to the mic. "Caller, if you can still hear me and you're in trouble, please, the best thing you can do is to call the police." It was all he could do. The caller's number hadn't shown up so he couldn't give it to the authorities. "That goes for anybody who feels unsafe out there, no matter where you are." He let out a deep breath. "Let's . . . all just chill out with a little Miles Davis, shall we?"

12.10 a.m.

Adam's hand shook as he raised the coffee mug. Annoyed at himself, he tried to blame the caffeine jitters, but he knew that wasn't the reason. He couldn't stop thinking about the call. Who had it been? Was it a prank or had somebody really been in trouble?

That wasn't the only reason he was shaken up. The voice had sounded so familiar. Almost like . . . but that was impossible. Harris was dead. There was no way he could be calling the station. Not unless technology was getting *really* good and, in this shithole of a radio station, that was about as likely as it raining men.

Adam put a hand to his headphones. Under the news bulletin, a strange sound was coming through. It was so quiet that he had to strain to listen. Frowning, he realized the sound wasn't coming through the tin cans at all. He freed one ear and listened.

Tap, tap, tap.

Tap, tap.

Adam spun in his chair. His own pale reflection peered back at him from the viewing window. But nothing else. He was alone.

Must've been an electrical tick, he told himself. The building was old and riddled with peculiarities. *Electrical tick*, he repeated in his head. *That's all*. He willed himself to accept the explanation, as if the tapping hadn't sounded exactly like somebody skittering their nails against the glass.

With a start, Adam realized the news bulletin had finished and he scrambled to click the mic on.

"Uh, hey all," he said. "Next up, we have a bit of a treat for you. Remember the docu-exposé we aired a few months back about the secret life of bodyguards at gay clubs? Here's your chance to enjoy it all over again. And remember to keep those song requests coming in. 0800-MANFIX. Call me."

Click.

Adam tugged the headphones off and rubbed his eyes. The night shift really was getting to him. He'd never imagined hearing things before. And that call . . . The more he thought about it, the more the voice had sounded like Harris. He'd know that voice anywhere. They'd been together for six years. Six ridiculously good years.

An image of Harris's blood-drenched face flickered before his eyes and Adam grabbed his mug, easing himself out of the chair. In the kitchen, he leant against the counter and stared into the dark orb of the coffee pot.

He tried to ignore the ache. The belly-deep darkness that leeched through him in those quiet moments when there was nothing to distract him.

You have to help me, the voice had pleaded.

Help with what? And how could Adam help? He was a DJ hidden away in a remote part of North London. Why would somebody call him?

The shriek of twisting metal rang in his ears. The sound of the car folding up around them. And Harris screaming. Screaming, then suddenly silent. His eyes fixed on Adam's.

"Shit," Adam muttered, pouring himself another coffee. He was getting to the end of the pot, which meant it would taste bitter but strong. Strong enough, hopefully, to yank him out of this torpor. He had loyal late-night listeners he couldn't disappoint.

Yeah, right. I'm king of the gay truck drivers and the hopeless insomniacs. They're my army of nocturnal no-lives.

There were still twenty minutes left on the documentary, so Adam wandered the halls of the station. He might as well check he really was locked in alone. If somebody was trying to mess with him, he'd find them quickly enough. The station was one floor and seven rooms. There weren't many places to hide.

In the cramped reception area, a graveyard for wilting pot plants, the front door was locked securely. Adam went back down the corridor. He stopped at one of the doors.

Dale Dixon – Station Manager.

Adam went in there sometimes. Dale had made his life a misery, so it was only fair for Adam to return the favour. A month ago, he'd hidden a square of cheese down the back of one of the desk drawers, noting the gradual ripening of the air every time he came in for the graveyard shift. It must have driven Dale crazy.

He tried the door. Unlocked. He went inside.

Dale's office was meticulously organized. In the darkness, Divine shrieked at him from her frame on the wall and a dust cover had been placed over the desktop computer. Adam wandered further inside, noting the photograph of Dale with his boyfriend and their irritating little yappy dog. He put the picture in Dale's "out" tray. The "in" tray was full of freebies that were sent into the station. An invitation to some soiree hosted by an ex-Spice Girl. Glow-in-the-dark condoms. A cardboard mask of Liza Minnelli.

Boring.

He wondered what Giles was up to. He was probably asleep by now. Adam found himself filled with sudden yearning: for a new life and for Giles. The younger DJ had started working at Mantrap FM five months ago and, before his banishment to the night shift, Adam had been responsible for showing him the ropes. There had been eye flirting and nervous blushes. Adam thought maybe they'd kissed at the Christmas party, but he couldn't remember, and then he'd been made king of the witching hour.

Guilt polluted the yearning and Adam left the office. He headed back towards his studio, then froze.

Through the viewing pane, he glimpsed a dark shape.

Somebody was standing perfectly still in the centre of his studio.

"What the—" Adam began. He threw the door open.

The studio was empty.

Adam checked behind the door and under the desk. He was alone.

Rattled, he closed the door and set his mug down. Something strange was going on.

"Baby Jane's got nothing on you," he muttered under his breath, if only to hear his own voice, hear how sane and put-together he was. Definitely not somebody who saw man-shaped shadows and heard mysterious tappings. Though wasn't talking to yourself the first sign of madness? Or was it the first sign of loneliness?

Adam checked over his shoulder to make sure he was the only one in the gloomy studio, then ordered himself to stop being ridiculous. He was over-tired and the phone call had frayed his nerves. He had to sort his shit out. There were still four and a half hours of the show left – if you could even call it a show – and he couldn't lose it.

The coffee was comforting and he felt instantly more alert.

He checked the counter on the documentary. Still four minutes left.

A light flashed in the corner of the desk. The office phone, on mute for when he was on air. Who'd be calling him at this hour? Dale? He'd done it before. Called in at some ungodly hour to tell Adam he was doing a great job, just awesome, he was *so* pleased he'd given him the night shift.

Adam picked up.

"Adam here."

"Please," a voice choked.

Adam nearly dropped the receiver.

"Who is this?" he demanded, his voice quavering. "How did you get this number?"

Strangled sobs came down the line.

"I did something and I can't take it back."

The voice was so familiar. A tortured whisper. But it couldn't be Harris. No chance in hell it was Harris.

"Please," Adam said. "Who is this?"

"It's so tight! I can't stand it! I can't breathe! Please tell someone to take it off!"

A chill shot down Adam's spine.

It sounded so much like Harris.

"Listen to me," he said. "I can only help you if you give me more information. Is somebody hurting you? Where are you?"

"I'm so alone."

The line went dead. The dial tone hummed in Adam's ear and it took him a moment to notice the cramp in his hand. He was crushing the receiver. Shakily, he replaced it.

It couldn't be Harris, but it sounded so much like him. If Harris had been whispering and in pain.

I'm sorry.

Before he died, he whispered two words. In the mangled ruins of the car. Adam had lain beside him for thirty minutes before they were cut free. It had felt like an eternity. And not long enough. Adam had spent those thirty minutes talking to him. Reassuring him.

Reassuring the corpse.

Adam lurched out of his chair and barrelled into the corridor, stumbling towards the toilets. Bile burned the back of his throat and he made it into a cubicle just in time, vomiting violently into the bowl.

A few moments later, he gripped the basin unsteadily, then splashed cold water onto his face. Rinsed his mouth out. Spat.

His wan reflection was a mockery. All colour bled out of the room and Adam felt like he was falling, drowning in the darkness of his reflected eyes. He'd been useless after the crash. Harris's sister called him a couple of times, but Adam couldn't talk to her. He drank too much and refused to visit the grave. He'd escaped with nothing more than a broken clavicle.

Harris's skull had been crushed.

Adam wiped his face and swallowed the memories. The grief collapsed into anger. Somebody was trying to get under his skin. Whoever it was had a twisted sense of humour. None of Adam's friends were capable of such maliciousness. Who was responsible?

Dale.

No, Adam told his reflection. Dale was an idiot, but he was professional, for the most part. He wouldn't play a prank live on air.

Harris.

Impossible.

Somebody who read the story in the papers.

That was the most likely explanation. Was it one of his regulars? If it was a total stranger, though, why call now? Adam had been working the graveyard shift for three months. The accident happened eleven months ago. It was another month until the anniversary. Why target him now? Why target him at all? It didn't make any sense.

With leaden legs, Adam staggered back to the studio.

The audio monitor on his screen was flatlining. The documentary had finished. All that was circulating was dead air.

"Christ."

Adam rushed to his desk and pulled the mic up.

Click.

"Adam Fox here. Apologies for the silent treatment, we're having a slight technical issue this end, but we're all good now. I'll be right back after this."

He dropped Madonna's latest tune into the playlist and heaved a deep breath, running a hand through his hair.

I hope Dale didn't hear that.

1.45 a.m.

Usually, the silence was comforting. An escape. Tonight, it suffocated. As the minutes struggled by, Adam became more and more aware of it. It became a roaring wall of static. When he removed the headphones during breaks, it crashed in his ears.

He imagined the silence groping inside. Electrical currents snaking through him, welding onto his bones until he became nothing more than dark, vibrating energy. Invisible. A memory. A hole in space.

"Tonight, we're discussing unusual jobs," Adam said into the mic. He could hear the strain in his voice and hoped the listeners couldn't. "So far, Paul's the clear winner. If you're just tuning in, Paul used to be a water-slide tester at a resort in Florida. Lucky sod. If you've got anything weirder, give me a call. We can't let Paul win this. The fucker. Sorry, Paul."

Adam checked his mobile. He'd texted his friend Alisha. She was a writer and sometimes pulled all-nighters, mostly because she liked leaving things until the day before deadline. She must be asleep, though, as she hadn't replied. For a moment he contemplated texting Giles, but it wasn't like they were best friends. Besides, Adam sort of regretted messaging Alisha. Somebody was trying to rankle him and it was working.

Get it together, he told himself.

The call board blinked at him and Adam eyed it uneasily.

One of them could be his taunter.

Click.

"You're live on Mantrap FM."

"Hey Adam. Big fan of the show."

"You have impeccable taste."

"Uh, yeah, so I'm Luke and I'm from Brighton, but I live in Clapham now."

Tell us your life story, why don'tcha?

"Cool. Why'd you leave Brighton, Luke?"

"Seagulls the size of dinosaurs."

"Who needs *Jurassic Park*, yeah?"

"Pretty much."

"So, Luke, what's this crazy job you do? Give us some clues and we'll see if we can guess what it is."

"Okay. Well, I use my mouth."

Flirt.

"Interesting," Adam said. "Next clue."

"Uh, it sort of involves fur. Sort of."

"I'm gonna ask for one more clue before my mind starts going to really dirty places."

"Okay. Uh. My taste buds are important."

"What the hell kind of job is this, Luke?" Adam teased. Luke's laughter filled his headphones and Adam felt as if a small weight was lifting.

"It's weird, man."

"Okay, mouth, fur, taste buds," Adam mused. "Callers, any ideas? I'm trying not to picture you as some kind of fur-eating dungeon keeper, Luke."

The laughter again. Adam caught himself smiling.

"Okay, I give up. Luke, what do you do?"

"I'm a dog-food taste-tester."

The lights went out.

"Uh, hello?" Adam tapped his headphones, but no sound came through. He sat in the pitch dark. The computer was dead, which meant he was off-air. He waited. Supposedly, there were precautions in place in the event of a power cut. The back-up generator should kick in any second.

Adam counted to thirty before he realized the generator was dead, too.

He pulled the headphones off and fumbled around for his phone.

Then he heard it. A sound like rope being twisted between gloved hands. It was so close that Adam imagined he could feel the rope hairs grazing his skin.

Panic bursting in his chest, he clumsily drew his mobile from his pocket and pressed a button. A blinding white glow bathed him. Adam caught his reflection in the viewing window and every hair on his body stood on end.

Something else was reflected beside him.

A skeletal face with sunken eyes. The sound of twisting rope filled his ears.

Adam screamed and hurled himself at the studio door. He tumbled out into the dark corridor and ran blindly. His phone sent ghostly white shapes flickering ahead of him and Adam charged into the station's main reception, crashing against the exit doors.

They were still locked.

He felt in his pockets for his keys, then remembered with a sick feeling that they were in his bag in the studio. He tossed his head back and howled, then clamped a hand over his mouth. Whoever had been in the studio was still here with him.

His gut contracted in terror. His palm was sweaty against his mouth.

That face. That awful, bony face.

Adam sank to the floor, his back against the doors. From there, he could see down the corridor that led to his studio. Solid darkness filled it, but at the far end the studio door was cast in the red glow of an emergency light that had finally blinked on. The door stood ajar and the studio looked empty.

You're not going back in there.

As he raised his mobile to call the police, there came a crackling sound like a needle being dropped onto a record. Adam peered up at the speakers behind the reception desk. Shows often aired live through them during the day. A haunting refrain began to play. A ghostly voice pined.

Adam hunched where he was, too scared to move.

"Oh, a storm is threat'ning, My very life today . . ."

He knew the song.

"If I don't get some shelter, Oh yeah, I'm gonna fade away . . ."

"Gimme Shelter" by the Rolling Stones.

He should still be scared. He should be worried that a maniac was loose in the station. Instead, Adam frowned, his mind working. The caller. The flirter with the wailing baby in the background. He always requested this song. Was he in the station? Was he stepping up his obsession?

Adam got to his feet slowly. A feeling like relief flooded through him. He wasn't losing his mind. He hadn't been imagining things. Somebody had been locked in the station with him the whole night. They must have hidden in the toilets and waited for Giles to leave.

Not Harris. It wasn't his voice on the phone.

He remembered the creak of twisting rope and his confidence quailed. He wasn't going to die here. Not on the shift that fucking Dale had assigned him to. He dialled 999 and waited.

"Please state the nature of your emergency."

"I'm at Broadcast Towers in Muswell Hill," Adam said. "I'm locked in with somebody. I think he wants to hurt me."

"Okay, sir. Please stay calm. Officers are on their way. If you can find somewhere safe to hide, I advise you do so. And keep your phone on you."

Adam hung up. He stared down the corridor.

Silence had returned. There was no sign of his visitor.

His phone vibrated in his hand and Adam jumped. He looked at the screen. It was his number – the number of his studio phone. Confused, he peered down the corridor again. He could see the phone sitting on his desk, bathed in the sickly red glow of the emergency light. Nobody else was in there.

He answered. "Hello?"

"Hey, hot stuff."

"Who's this? Giles?"

"Got it in one. How's the show going?"

"Where are you calling from?" Adam asked.

"I couldn't sleep so I thought I'd check in on you. Is that okay?"

Adam checked his phone again. It was definitely his office number. His phone must be glitching.

Just my luck.

"You still there?" Giles's voice asked.

"Yeah, I'm . . . Things are sort of . . . There's somebody in here with me."

"In the studio? You bad boy."

"Seriously," Adam said. "I think I'm in danger."

"Shit. Get out of there."

"I can't. My keys are in the office."

"Try the toilets. There's a window on a latch in there. You can climb out."

"Okay."

Adam went to the door hesitantly. The corridor looked clear. The toilets were three doors away. If he ran, he could probably make it.

"Shit," he muttered to himself. "Stay on the line, okay?"

"I'm here."

Adam checked the corridor again, listening for any sounds. All he heard was the soft, quick flutter of his own breath. He had to move fast. Balling his fists, he hurried down the corridor, moving as quietly as he could. He ducked into the toilets and pushed the door shut.

It was even darker in here than the rest of the station.

Adam jumped as he caught his own scared reflection in the mirror. Then his blood froze.

A face was reflected behind him. It was swathed in shadows but the eyes drilled into him. Black and penetrating.

A strangled cry erupted from his throat. The figure leapt at him and they crashed to the floor. Adam's phone spun across the tiles and he felt gloved hands at his throat. They squeezed.

Bright spots bobbed in Adam's vision. He couldn't breathe. He thrashed beneath the weight of his attacker, but he was too weak. He couldn't fight him. He pounded the tiles desperately and bucked with all his strength. The hands slipped and Adam threw his attacker off.

He scrambled away, gasping air through his crushed throat. Propped up against the wall, his gaze wheeled to his attacker and Adam thought he had finally lost his mind.

Sunken eyes stared at him, pale skin shimmering like ice.

"No," Adam retched, refusing to believe it. He felt around on the floor for his phone, his eyes locked onto the impossible thing in the shadows. His fingers scraped his phone and he clenched it tight in his fist.

The thing in the shadows reached for him again and Adam screamed, lashing out with his legs. His attacker stumbled and hit the floor.

Adam staggered to his feet and bowled out of the toilets. A sob rose through him as he saw that the office number had tried to call his phone three times. Giles must be worried. He hit 'call back' and staggered towards the first door he saw. He fell into the room beyond and slammed the door behind him, throwing his weight against it.

He was back in his studio.

Shakily, he raised the mobile to his ear.

A few rings and then – *click!*

"You're live on Mantrap FM. Who's this and where are you from?"

"You have to help me!" Adam wheezed, though the voice on the phone didn't sound like Giles. His throat throbbed painfully.

"Very good," the voice on the phone said wearily. "If you raise the Bat signal, I'm sure—"

"*Please!*" Adam screamed. "I don't know what to do!"

"What's wrong?" the voice asked.

"There's somebody after me. I—"

And then he realized who the voice belonged to. Who the radio host was. With trembling hands, he hung up.

"No," Adam whispered to himself. It wasn't possible. He stared around the dark studio. He was alone in here, but he'd just spoken to . . .

He went to the desk, grabbed the office phone. It was dead.

He turned around and stopped breathing.

A body swung by its neck, reflected in the glass of the viewing window. Sunken eyes met his.

Adam glanced up and remembered.

The rope. He'd found it in the caretaker's cupboard. Adam looked down and felt the rope in his hands. He twisted it until it creaked. Tears made tracks in his cheeks.

He'd been alone on the night shift. Feeling guilty because of Giles. The crackling silence had suffocated and Harris would never understand.

As if in a dream, Adam drew his chair into the middle of the floor and climbed onto it. He couldn't stop himself. He knotted the rope onto the pipes above his head and drew the noose around his neck. The rope hairs bristled against his skin.

Somebody had requested "Gimme Shelter" by the Rolling Stones. And he'd forgotten. How could he have forgotten? The song playing in the car as it toppled across tarmac. The sound of shrieking and guitars and lives being wrung out.

The loneliness became a thing. Like the silence, it filled every room. It weighed everything down until Adam decided to weigh himself down.

He'd played the song. Just as the caller requested. And then he'd taken the rope and fitted it snugly. And he'd succumbed to the darkness, watched his own skeletal reflection in the viewing pane as he slipped away.

He still remembered his final words. Two of them.

I'm sorry.

10 p.m.

Adam Fox pulled the microphone closer and used his best radio voice: the raspy one that had earned him so many fans in the golden days of prime time. It helped that he'd just scalded his throat with fresh coffee.

"Hello, creatures of the night. This is Adam Fox, checking in for a long-haul flight to dreamland. For the next seven hours, I'm all yours." He clicked an icon on the screen in front of him and a horror-movie cackle reverberated through his headphones. "But before we slip into something a little more comfortable, let's catch up with those news headlines. Don't go anywhere."

Shadows
Damon Galgut

The two of us are pedalling down the road. The light of the moon makes shadows under the trees, through which we pass, going fast. Robert is a little ahead of me, standing up in his seat. On either side of his bike, the dogs are running, Ben and Sheba; I can never tell the difference between them.

It's lovely to be like this, him and me, with the warm air going over us like hands.

"Oh," I say. "Oh, oh, oh . . ."

He turns, looking at me over his shoulder. "What?" he calls.

I shake my head. He turns away.

As we ride, I can see the round shape of the moon as it appears between the trees. With the angle of the road, it's off to the right, above the line of the slope. The sky around it is pale, as if it's been scrubbed too long. It hurts to look up.

It's that moon we're riding out to see. For two weeks now, people have talked about nothing else. "The eclipse," they say. "Are you going to watch the eclipse?" I didn't understand at first, but my father explained it to me. "The shadow of the earth," he says, "thrown across the moon." It's awesome to think of that, of the size of some shadows. When people ask me after this, I tell them, "Yes." I tell them, "I'm going to watch the eclipse."

But this is Robert's idea. A week ago he said to me, "D'you want to go down to the lake on Saturday night? We can watch the eclipse from there."

"Yes," I said. "We can do that."

So we ride towards the lake under the moon. On either side, the dogs are running, making no sound in the heavy dust, their tongues trailing wetly from the corners of their mouths.

The road is beginning to slope down as we come near to the lake. The ground on either side becomes higher, so that we're cycling down between two shoulders of land. The forest is on either side, not moving in the quiet air. It gives off a smell: thick and green. I breathe deeply, and my lungs are full of the raw, hairy scent of jungle.

We're moving quite fast on the downhill, so we don't have to pedal any more. Ahead of me, I see Robert break from the cut in the road and emerge again onto the flat path that runs across the floor of the forest. A moment later I do so too, whizzing into the heavy layers of shadows as if they are solid. The momentum is wonderful, full of danger, as if we're close to breaking free of gravity. But it only lasts a moment. Then we're slowing again, dragged back by the even surface of the road and the sand on the wheels.

The turn-off is here. I catch up with Robert and we turn off side by side, pedalling again to keep moving. Ahead of us, the surface of the lake is between the trees, stretched out greenly in the dark. The trees thin out, there's a bare strip along the edge of the water.

We stop here. The path we were trying to ride on goes straight and even, into the water. That's because it used to lead somewhere before they flooded the valley to make the lake. They say that there are houses and gardens standing empty and silent in the currents below. I think of them and shiver. It's always night down there at the bottom of the lake; the moon never shines.

But we've stopped far from where the path disappears. We're still side by side, straddling the bikes, looking out. The dogs have also stopped, stock-still, as if they can smell something in the air. There's a faint wind coming in off the water, more of a breeze really. On the far side of the lake we can see the lights of houses. Far off to the right, at the furthest corner of the water, are the lights of my house. I glance towards them and try to imagine them: my father and mother, sitting out on the front veranda, looking across the water to us. But there are no lights where we are.

"There," says Robert.

He's pointing. I follow his finger and I also see it: the moon, clear of the trees on the other side. It really is huge tonight, as if it's been swollen with water. If you stare at it for long enough, you can make out the craters on its surface, faint and blue, like shadows. Its light comes down softly like rain and I see I was wrong – it makes the water silver, not green.

"We've got a view of it," I say.

But Robert is moving away already. "Come," he says. "Let's make a fire."

We leave our bikes leaning together against the trunk of a tree and set out to look for firewood. We separate and walk out by ourselves into the forest. But I can still see Robert a little distance away as he wanders around, bending now and then to pick up bits of wood. The dogs are with him. It isn't dense or overgrown down here. The floor of the forest is smooth. Apart from the sound of our feet and the lapping of the lake, it's quiet here.

There isn't much dead wood around. I pick up a few branches, some chunks of log. I carry them from behind where the bikes are. Robert has already made one trip here, I see from a small pile of twigs. I don't much feel like this hunting in the dark, so I delay a while, wiping my hands on my pants. I look out over the water again. I feel so calm and happy as I stand, as if the rest of my life will be made up of evenings like this. I hear Robert's whistling coming from behind me out of the dark. It's a tune I almost recognize. I start to hum along.

As I do, I can see Robert in my mind's eye, the way he must be. When he whistles, small creases appear round his lips. He has a look of severe concentration on his face. The image of him comes often to me in this way, even when I'm alone. We've been friends for years now, since I started high school.

Sometimes, late at night as I lie trying to sleep, a shadow cast in from outside will move against the wall and then he breaks through me in a pang, quick and deep. We've been friends for years now, since

I started high school. It's often as if I have no other friends. He has, though. I see him sometimes with other boys from the school, riding past my house in a swirling khaki pack down the lake. It hurts me when this happens. I don't know what they speak about, whether they talk of things that I could understand. I wonder sometimes if they mention me. I wonder if they mock me when I'm not there and if Robert laughs at me with the rest of them.

He comes down now, carrying a load of wood in his arms. "Is that all?" he says, looking at what I collected. "What's the matter with you?"

"Nothing," I say and smile.

He drops his wood along with the rest and turns. He's grinning at me: a big skew grin, little bits of bark stuck to his hair and the front of his shirt.

"Do we need any more?"

"No," he says. "That should do fine."

We build a fire. Rather, he builds a fire and I sit against a tree to watch. It always seems to be this way: him doing the work, me watching. But it's a comfortable arrangement; he doesn't mind. I like the way he moves. He's a skinny boy, Robert, his clothes are always slightly loose on him. Now as I watch, my eye is on his hands as they reach for the wood and stack it. His hands are slender and brown. He's brought a wad of newspaper on his bike. He twists rolls of paper into the openings between the logs.

Like me, the dogs are sitting still and watching. They stare at him with quiet attention, obedient and dumb.

He lights the fire. He holds the burning match and I'm looking for a moment at this white-haired boy with flame in his hand. Then he leans and touches it to the paper. Smoke. He shakes out the match.

The fire burns, the flames go up. In a minute or two, there's a nice blaze going. We're making our own light to send across the water. I think of my parents on the wooden veranda, looking across to the spark that's started up in the darkness. They point. "There," they say. "That's where they are." I smile. The fire burns. The flames go up. The heat wraps over my face like a second skin. The dogs get up and move away, back into the dark where they shift restlessly, mewing like kittens.

In a little time, the fire burns down to a heap of coals. They glow and pulse, sending up tiny spurts of flame. We only have to throw on a stick now and then. Sitting and staring into the ring of heat, it would be easy to be quiet, but we talk, though our voices are soft.

"We should camp out here sometime," he says. "It's so still."

"Yes," I say. "We should do that."

"It's great to be away," he says. "From them."

He's speaking of his family, his home. He often speaks of them this way. I don't know what he means by this: they all seem nice enough. They live in a huge two-storey house made out of wood, about half an hour's ride from us. They're further up the valley, though, out of sight of the lake. There are five of them: Robert, his parents, his two brothers. I'm alone in my home. I have no brothers. Perhaps it's this that makes their house a beautiful place to me. Perhaps there really is something ugly in it that I haven't seen. Either way, we don't spend much time there. It's to my home that Robert likes to come in the afternoon when school is done. He's familiar to us all. He comes straight up to my room. I know the way he knocks on my door. Bang-bang, thud.

My mother has spoken to me about him. At least twice that I can remember, she's sat on my bed, smiling at me and playing with her hands.

"But what's wrong with it?" I say. "Everyone has friends."

"But lots," she says. "Lots of friends. You do nothing else, you see no one else . . ."

"There's nothing else to do," I say. "Other people bore me."

"There's sport," she says. "I've seen them at the school, every afternoon. Why don't you play sport like other boys? You're becoming thinner and thinner."

It's true. I am. When I look at myself in the mirror, I'm surprised at how thin I am. But I am not unhealthy; my skin is dark, I'm fit. We ride for miles together, Robert and me, along the dust roads that go around the lake.

"It's him," I say. "Isn't it? It's him you don't like."

"No," she says. "It isn't that. I like him well enough. It's you, you that's the matter."

I don't want to upset them, my parents. I want to be a good son to them. But I don't know any way to be fatter than I am, to please them. I do my best.

"I'll try," I say. "I'll try to see less of him."

But it doesn't help. Most afternoons, I hear his knock at my door and I'm glad at the sound. We go out on our bikes. This happens at night too, from time to time. As now – when we find ourselves at the edge of the lake, staring at the moon.

"D'you want a smoke?" he says.

I don't answer. But he takes one out of the box anyway, leaning forward to light it in the fire. He puffs. Then he hands it to me. I take a drag, trying to be casual. But I've never felt as easy about it as Robert seems to. The smoke is rough in my throat, it makes my tongue go sour. I don't enjoy it. But for the sake of Robert, I allow this exchange to take place, this wordless passing back and forth, this puffing in the dark. I touch his hand as I give it back to him.

"Are you bored?" he asks. "Why're you so quiet?"

"No," I say. "I'm fine." I think for a while, then ask, "Are you?"

"No," he says.

But I wonder if he is. In sudden alarm, I think of the places he might rather be, the people he might rather be with. To confirm my fears, he mutters just then:

"Emma Brown—"

"Why are you thinking about Emma Brown?" I say. "What made you think of her now?"

He's looking at me, surprised. He takes the cigarette out of his mouth. "I was just wondering," he says. "I was just wondering where she is."

"Why?" I say.

"I just wondered if she was watching the moon."

"Oh," I say, and smile bitterly into the fire. I don't know what's going through his head, but mine is full of thoughts of her, of silly little Emma Brown, just a bit plump, with her brown hair and short white socks. I remember a few times lately that I've seen her talking to Robert; I remember him smiling at her as she came late to class.

"I was just thinking," he says, and shrugs.

I finish the cigarette. I throw the butt into the fire. We don't talk for a long time after that. I can hear the dogs licking each other, the rasping noise of their tongues. I begin to feel sad. I think of my anger and something in me slides, as if my heart is displaced.

He reaches out a hand and grazes my arm. It's just a brief touch, a tingling of fingers, but it goes into me like a coal. "Hey," he says. "What's the matter?"

"Nothing," I say. "Nothing." I want to say more, but I don't like to lie. Instead I say again, "Nothing." I feel stupid.

The fire burns down to a red smear on the ground. Across the water the lights have started to go out. Only a few are left. I look off to the right: the lights in my house are still on. My parents keep watch.

When I look back, Robert is on his feet. His head is thrown back. I don't stand, but I gaze over his shoulder at what he's watching: the white disc of the moon, from which a piece has been broken. While we were talking, the great shadow of the earth has started to cover the moon. If you look hard enough the dark piece can still be seen, but only in outline, as if it's been sketched with chalk.

We stare for a long time. As we do, the shadow creeps on perceptibly. You can actually see it move.

"Wow," he says.

Sensing something, one of the dogs throws back its head in imitation of us and begins to howl. The noise goes up, wobbling on the air like smoke.

"Sheba," says Robert. "Be quiet."

We watch the moon as it sinks slowly out of sight. Its light is still coming down, but more faintly than before. On the whole valley, lit weirdly in the strange blue glow, a kind of quiet has fallen. There is nothing to say. I lower my eyes and look out over the water. Robert sits down next to me on his heels, hugging his knees. "You know," he says, "there's times when everything feels . . ."

He doesn't finish.

"I know," I say.

We sit and watch. Time goes by. The trees are behind us, black and big. I look across to my home again and see that the lights have gone out. All along the far shore there is dark. We are alone.

"It's taking a long time," he says. "Don't you think?"

"Yes," I say. "It is."

It's hot. The dogs are panting like cattle in the gloom. I feel him along my arm. A warmth. I spring up, away. "I'm going to swim," I say, unbuttoning my shirt.

I take off my clothes and drop them on the sand. The dogs are staring at me. Robert also watches, still crouched on his heels, biting his arm. When I am naked, I turn my back on him and walk into the lake. I stop when the water reaches my knees and stand, arms folded across my chest, hands clinging to my ribs as if they don't belong to me. It isn't cold, but my skin goes tight as if it is. One of the dogs lets out a bark. I walk on, hands on my sides now, while the water gets higher and higher. When it reaches my hips I dive. It covers my head like a blanket. I come up spluttering. "It's warm," I say, "as blood."

"Hold on," he calls, "I'm . . ."

As I turn, he's already running. I catch a glimpse of his body, long and bright as a blade, before he also dives. When he comes up, next to me, the air is suddenly full of noise: the barking of dogs as they run along the edge of the lake, the splashing of water, the shouts of our voices. It is our voices I hear. I'm surprised at the sound. I'm laughing. I'm calling out.

"Don't you," I say, "don't you try—"

We're pushing at each other, and pulling. Water flies. The bottom of the lake is slippery to my feet. I feel stones turn. I have hold of Robert's shoulder. I have a hand in his hair. I'm trying to push him under, wrenching at him while he does the same to me. He laughs.

Nothing like this has taken place between us before. I feel his skin against me, I feel the shape of his bones as we wrestle and lunge. We're touching each other. Then I slide, the water hits my face. I go under, pulling him with me, and for a moment we're tangled below the surface, leg to leg, neck to neck, furry with bubbles, as if we'll never pull free.

We come up together into quiet. The laughter has been doused. We still clutch each other, but his fingers are hurting me. We stand, face to face. While we were below, the last sliver of moon has been blotted out. A total darkness has fallen on the valley, so that the trees are invisible against the sky. The moon is a faint red outline overhead. I can't see Robert's face, though I can feel his breath against my nose. We gasp for air. The only sound to be heard is the howling of the dogs that drifts in from the shore: an awful noise, bereaved and bestial.

I let go. And he lets go of me. Finger by finger, joint by joint, we release one another till we are standing, separate and safe, apart. I rub my arm where he hurt it.

"Sorry," he mutters.

"It's okay," I say. "It doesn't matter."

After that, we make our way to shore. I wade with heavy steps, as if through sand. By the time I reach the edge and am standing, dripping beside my clothes, the moon has begun to emerge from shadow and a little light is falling. The dogs stop howling. I don't look up as I dress. I put my clothes on just so, over my wet body. They stick to me like mud.

I wait for him to finish dressing. As he ties his shoelaces I say, not even looking at him, "What do you think will happen?"

"What d'you mean?" he says.

"To us," I say. "D'you think in ten years from now we're even going to know each other?"

"I don't know what you mean," he says.

He sounds irritated as he says this, as if I say a lot of things he doesn't understand. Maybe I do. I turn away and start to walk back to the bikes.

"Hey," he calls. "What you . . . don'tcha want another smoke or somethin' before we go?"

"No," I say. "Not me."

I wait for him at the tree where the bikes are leaning. He takes his time. I watch him scoop water over the coals. They make a hissing noise, like an engine beneath the ground. Then he walks up towards me along the bank, hands in his pockets. The sight of him this way, sulking and slow, rings in me long after we've mounted our bikes and started back up the path.

By the time we rejoin the dust road a little way on, the soreness in me is smaller than it was. One of the dogs runs into his way and he swears. At this I even manage to laugh. I look off and up to the left, at the moon, which is becoming rounder by the minute. Its light comes down in soft white flakes, settling on us coldly as we ride.

Men Without Men
Vestal McIntyre

———

Every Tuesday evening, the members of our little group converged from points across the bottom half of Manhattan onto East Thirteenth for two-for-one draft beers, or as we called them, "two-fers", at the Phoenix. But this frosty February night was special, because Eric had returned. On the way to the bar, we picked up little welcome-home gifts that fitted into our jacket pockets and searched our reflections in shopfronts, wondering if we had aged in the eighteen months since Eric's job had taken him to London.

The steady red glow of the Phoenix sign lit an otherwise dark block lined with parking garages and grated storefronts. It was ten o'clock when I passed under it, and most of the others were already inside. I gave the international *shhhh* gesture so I could approach Eric unseen, took the fringe of my scarf, and touched it, just barely, to his naked neck below that fine cap of wavy hair.

Eric was the hub of the group that had continued to meet in his absence. If any of us had ever thought ourselves in love with him, we soon realized he wouldn't love us back – couldn't love anything right under his nose, because proximity made things repulsive to him. Boyfriends were many and short-lived – a few even made it to the Phoenix before Eric discovered some microscopic tic or blemish that he considered monstrous, unmanageable and grounds for dismissal.

Once, years ago, he had taken me to a Bryant Park fashion show he had to attend for work. At the party afterward, he asked me, "Do faces ever gross you out?" I looked around to see which face he might mean, but they were all beautiful. "No," he said, "just *faces*, the fact that humans have this ball riding on top of their body, and the front is flattened out, and there's an opening for you to pour champagne down, and a ridge down the middle with holes on either side for you to breathe through . . ."

Eric was lucky. His ball was flattened in pleasingly square angles and embedded with two eyes that managed to be both black and twinkling. As for his ridge, it had been broken in a high school lacrosse game and now turned at a barely detectable angle from the lump between his eyes. This fantastic nose, this reminder that Eric had flourished in the straight world where others of us had withdrawn, gave him the air of a wounded bruiser, a prizefighter in decline. How we wanted to save him from that next round!

"No, that has never occurred to me," I had said.

I was able to get closer to Eric than anyone, only because I, a born quantifier, had made a mental measuring stick of just the distance he required, and always kept it in place.

Now he twitched, brushed the touch of my scarf-tassel away from his neck, saw the smiles and turned.

"Buttons!" he said, taking me by my shoulders.

"Eric!" I said.

A moment passed between us, slowly and in great detail. Eric's eyes were already steeled against me. No sooner did I wonder why than I had my answer: a bit of the beauty of his face had fallen. There were dents under his cheekbones and a dome shape to his mouth – all so subtle you might not notice unless you had studied that face as I had. A decade before, I might have said that this slight sinking distinguished his face with a severe new maturity. But in the years that concluded the last century and began this one, my eye had become accustomed to *lypoatrophy*, a condition caused by prolonged use of antiretroviral drugs. In an instant, I knew that Eric had HIV and had had it for years. How could he not have told me, of all people? Then, with a sensation of free-fall, I remembered what he had said that afternoon when he showed up shivering on my doorstep having pissed himself on the bus, and understood it.

Eric noticed the shift in my expression. He had already witnessed five different versions of the same shift as our friends arrived, saw him, then *saw* him – five sets of eyes snuffed out then re-brightened with a false light as five minds scrambled: *Why didn't he tell me? Have I ever said anything insensitive?* They all came up with something. Josh, for example, remembered referring to a former boss who had fired him as a "riddled old titty monster", which at the time Eric had answered with tommy-gun laughter: "*Ha! Ha! Ha! Ha! Ha!*"

I, on the other hand, always thought so hard before speaking that I never said anything untoward. I tended to contribute to conversations when the guys had already moved on, winning me a round of pitying, affectionate looks. Now, for once, being slow on the uptake had served me well.

"Welcome home," I said, and Eric responded by placing me, still by my shoulders, onto a bar stool someone else had pulled up.

Why hadn't one of my friends gone to the bathroom and texted me, *Eric has HIV*, so I would have met him poised and prepared? For that matter, why didn't I text Archie, who arrived next, shedding his jacket as he approached in order to show off to Eric that he had lost ten pounds?

"Welcome home," Archie bellowed and, sure enough, when Eric swiveled toward him, his face froze.

"Archie! Look at you!" Eric looked him up and down mock-approvingly, then asked, "Have you lost *hair*?"

Archie stood, a gasping, happy-sad little fish.

"So, Eric," someone asked, to break the tension, "how was it, living over there?"

"London, London. What can I say about London? Puddles. There were puddles in my street that hadn't dried since the reign of Queen Victoria. Little plaques told you so. On the upside, though, you don't have to laugh at jokes that aren't funny. That's what separates *them* from *us* – all our desperate, showy laughing."

Our laughter dipped in volume. It was a difficult situation, and I suppose Eric felt he had to turn the critical eye on us, punish us a little.

He went on describing London, and I scanned our ranks to see who had yet to arrive. Only Trevor, and this was a relief, since Trevor was an actor and, like most actors, performed his life, controlling the shape of his face at all times. The summer before, he had fallen asleep on the train back from the beach and had worn a look of perfect, blissful rest: Exhausted Swimmer Nodding with Rail Rhythm. We all giggled and whispered until he stirred, smacked his lips and gave a big, orgasmic gorilla-yawn. No need to text Trevor, I decided. His supersmile would stay intact.

But no. Trevor's enhanced ability to emote actually worked against him. He arrived and Eric faced him, and you've never seen a grin of such dismay (other than, maybe, on Polynesian war masks).

"For Christ's sake," Eric said at last. "Yes, Trevor, I've got The Aids." There was silence, and Eric looked to us with an expression that was actually *kind*. "I've got The Aids, guys. Sorry I didn't tell you before."

I waited for his eyes to light on mine with emphasis, significance – "*especially you*" – but he could keep me waiting forever. Eric was back from London, and I'd have to re-learn those lessons.

Anyway, that broke the spell. We had failed the test, but he loved us still. Now we could reveal our little gifts and drink and burp and bicker about what songs to play on the jukebox. But I couldn't help wondering if he knew that I now understood what he had said that day.

A couple of years earlier, Eric had gone through a wild phase with crystal meth and God knows what else. He found himself one Sunday morning strung out amid the debris of a very scary sex party in Astoria. His clothes were near the door, but his wallet was gone. He actually had to steal a MetroCard from someone else's pocket just to get downtown. This took two hours of navigating the subway system with all its altered weekend routes. Halfway home he vomited, and people moved to the other end of the train car. When he finally emerged out of the Delancey Street station, the sky was screaming, sunlight was falling in white sheets, and he desperately needed to urinate. He was about to head home when he saw a bus idling outside the station with its doors open. Eric, in a state nearing psychosis, got on. He was obeying a command from God, a punishment for having sinned. He cowered in his seat, squeezing himself with both hands to keep from peeing as the bus started making its way slowly back uptown. The bus driver was watching Eric through the mirror. Then Eric had a startling realization: this driver was actually a priest from his parish back in Maryland! How had he not aged? And these grannies on the bus with him, pretending not to watch him – they had gone to his church, every one of them! What kind of trap was this? He was so terrified his abdomen tensed and the piss began to leak from him, then flow, heating his hands, flooding his seat.

The Eric I found on my doorstep was gray-faced, hollow-eyed, frightful to look at. He scratched at his wrists, which were speckled red almost to the point of bleeding, and told me about how he narrowly escaped his childhood congregation on the bus.

"Maybe you're just imagining this?" I suggested.

He gave me a look with real fear in it and edged toward the stairwell.

"Or maybe not." Quantifying his need to be believed over his need to be released from the nightmare, I let him continue. Then he paused, stopped scratching, took out a bottle of Visine and, with shaking hands, squeezed out droplets onto his wrists.

"Eric, what are you doing?" I asked.

"There's antihistamine in this stuff," he said.

Gently, I took the Visine from him and screwed its tiny lid back on and put it on the little table beside my door, next to the change bowl. Eric closed his eyes and kept his arms at his sides. I put my arms around him. We stood like that for a while. Every few breaths, Eric was seized by a violent shudder.

"I n-n-n-need . . ." *Breath. Breath.* "I need you to tell me I'm not going to die."

Not until the night of his return would I know what he had meant. He had wanted to tell me he had HIV, but he was too afraid.

I gave Eric a Valium and put him to bed. Every so often, he stirred and whimpered, "It feels so bad!", pulling the pillows around his head, and I'd climb in bed and hold him for a while.

I washed his jeans in the bathtub and hung them out the fire escape to dry. I slept beside him that night, called in sick the next morning, rented DVDs from Kim's Video, made him a grilled-cheese sandwich, slept beside him again the next night.

I wouldn't trade those two days for anything in the world.

————

A new phase in Eric's life began, when a door that had been locked swung wide open, all because of a medicine that had caused a few ounces of his face-fat to be displaced. One morning we met for breakfast, then decided to call in sick, both of us, and go to museums. Eric cupped his hand around his phone to keep out the restaurant din. "Hi, it's Eric . . . No, the other Eric. Aidsy Eric."

He never referred to his condition as anything but "The Aids," as if that distancing, old-ladyish, capitalized article "The" conveyed everything he cared to say about his relationship to his condition.

"It's not so easy to find a boyfriend when you've got The Aids," Eric said at two-fers a month or so after his return.

What do you say to that?

"It's not like that," Archie said. "Guys these days don't care."

"There's a website for positive guys to meet each other," I said.

Eric gave these responses a huge eye-roll. He could roll his eyes all the way around the world.

"Or you could go to one of those meet-and-greets at the Center," Josh said. Josh had HIV too – had had it much longer than Eric – but we tended to forget about it because he seemed at peace. And Eric tended to forget about it because it served his purpose.

"*Mnyeh-mnyeh-mnyeh-mnyeh*-Center-*mnyeh-mnyeh*," Eric mimicked with wrinkled nose and head a-bobble.

"I think it has less to do with The Aids and more to do with the fact that you're a horrible old tortoise without a bit of air or light or love in your little green heart," Trevor monologued.

"Fur*real*?"

"Uh-huh."

Eric's face was warmed by a rare and dazzling smile. What he wanted from the world was so specific and so much in flux, he never knew himself what it was until someone plopped it into his lap. Apparently, at that moment he had wanted to be told to fuck off.

Then Bendiks said, "I know someone you'd like."

Eric's smile dropped.

Bendiks was the newest member of our little group and the youngest – still in his twenties, a lovely, broad-boned, honest-eyed little man. Josh had invited him over to talk to us one night and, like a little orphan, he had stayed. Having emigrated to the US as a teenager, he still squeezed his vowels a little, still maintained a Soviet paleness at his core and a defense against snow and oppression. We all wanted to kiss him, every one of us, even those who didn't know it yet.

"His name's Greg. He lives in my building. He actually reminds me of you."

"I don't like people like me," Eric said.

"I've been meaning to bring him around anyway. You don't have to think of it as a set-up."

Eric sat stumped, and the rest of us gloried in the fact.

Greg, as he appeared next to Bendiks in the Phoenix doorway the following week, was a thin, handsome black man whom we had never seen there before, but who seemed to have read a manual on how to dress for the place: baseball hat slightly askew on shaved head, an undershirt worn to a state of near-transparency, jeans that were frayed at the hem and colorful sneakers that Josh later told me cost around $200. He took off his hat inside, which struck me as gentlemanly. Bendiks made the introductions, and Greg laughed as he shook our hands, as if there were some joke we were all already in on. "I need a drink," he then said. "I've had the shittiest week so far. I just got back from Argentina on Sunday, and my kitchen was full of ants. In everything. Like, the glass container I keep my cereal in? Ant farm. There were tunnels through the granola, little ant highways. They had made rooms."

Eric narrowed his eyes. "Why were you in Argentina?" he asked.

"I was between jobs. I work freelance. So I just decided to go. If you're going to do nothing for a couple of months, it's cheaper down there."

"Buenos Aires is fun," Trevor said.

"I've always wanted to go to Buenos Aires," I said.

"I've always wanted to go to the Bronx," Josh said.

"I've heard there's a zoo up there," Bendiks said.

"You know what I've always wanted to do?" Archie mused. "Slap someone across the face with a fish."

"Alive or dead?" Eric asked.

"Dead, I think. Heavy. Yea big. Right across the face."

"Who?"

"No one in particular. It's not an aggressive thing, purely sensory."

"Mmm."

Then we all turned to Greg again, blinking expectantly.

He hesitated with an open-mouthed smile. *Am I being attacked, or is this just how these assholes communicate?* He forged ahead: "Yes, Buenos Aires is the best. The absolute best. The Malbec is dirt cheap and drinkable, and all these artists and writers are living there. Everyone tangos. It's the new New York."

Eric dropped his head forward and tilted it to the side. It was a gesture somewhere between that of an old man trying to hear with his good ear and an angry bull pawing the dirt. "The new New York?" he said.

"Kinda," said Greg.

Eric scanned our faces, as if to quickly register that each of us agreed that Greg had just said something ludicrous. Then he said, "Buenos

Aires was the new New York, like, five years ago, then Montreal became the new New York, and then everything came back around here. New York is the new New York."

"Really," said Greg. "I guess I'm still living a few New Yorks ago. Oh, I'm vibrating." He jumped up and took out his phone. "I know it's rude, but I have to take this call. It's about a job." He went outside.

We all told Bendiks how handsome we thought Greg was. All except Eric. He started talking about the canker sore on the tip of his tongue. "It's a big one, see?" He opened his mouth, extended his tongue into a pink taper, and crossed his eyes to see the tip where a white ulcer was circled in red. Then he retracted his tongue and said, "It's impossible to eat anything spicy or interesting. I'm in hell."

"I get those sores sometimes," said Bendiks.

"It's a pain you can't ignore," said Eric. "Kind of like when you get . . ."

"A zit inside your nose?" said Greg, who reappeared beside Eric and pushed a button on his phone. It played a little shutdown tune as he dropped it into his pocket. "Oh, it's so awful, the Zit Inside the Nose. I always wish I could transport the pain to my fingertip or my butt or something. The closer a pain is to your brain, the harder it is to ignore. That's the scientific rule, I think. Women in the 1800s got toothaches so bad they'd throw themselves out the window. It was the leading cause of suicide, actually. Not those oppressive marriages, not the whale-bone underwear – toothaches."

Eric was quiet, and I wondered what he had planned to say before he was interrupted, if it was something more droll than what Greg said, or less. Bendiks twisted his little flower hands. His matchmaking wasn't going well.

To take things in a different direction, Josh asked Archie, "Who's been around the office lately?"

"Let's see. Lindsay Lohan, Richard Gere . . ."

We were all intentionally slovenly, but Archie was the only actual slob. His hair and beard were straggly, he had a beer belly that only recently had shrunk from second to first trimester, and often, when he slipped between us to order a drink, we got a whiff of curry and knew that he had stopped on Sixth Street for a big meal of cheap Indian food on his way to the Phoenix. We could almost have told him what he had ordered, so strongly did his bodily oils trap a meal's bouquet. But Archie also had the highest-paying job. He was an agent at a company that represented actors, singers, all manner of stars.

"Who's Lindsay Lohan?" Josh asked.

"I hate Richard Gere," Eric said. "He copied my trick!"

"What do you mean, he copied you?" Bendiks asked.

This was a story I had heard before – most of us had – but it was a good one.

"Well, it was when I first moved to New York. I was working at the Strand, and here comes Richard Gere, making a big show of buying all these books on Buddhism . . ."

"Richard Gere copies everyone," Greg said. "That's what he does."

We were all surprised that Greg had interrupted Eric's story.

"How exactly, pray tell, do you know this?" Eric said. "I suppose Richard Gere copied one of your tricks, too."

"It's common knowledge. Oh, I'm vibrating—" And, again, he stood up and pulled out his phone.

"You are *not* vibrating!" said Eric. "You turned your phone off ten minutes ago. We all saw you."

Greg put his phone back in his pocket, opened his mouth and released a few bars of throaty laughter. "That's it. That's the thing Richard Gere copied from me. I do that all the time when I want to get out of a conversation. I say, 'Oh, I'm vibrating,' and take out my phone. The best is when I don't even have my phone on me. I take out my wallet and look at it and say, 'Oh, I have to take this call.' Complete dis. Richard Gere saw me do that at a party, and now he does it all the time."

"You just made that up!" said Eric. "You're good, but I'm better. I totally busted you."

"Nigga, please!" Greg said merrily. "If I'm going to make something up, it'll be less banal than Richard Gere coping my trick."

Eric sat back with a complicated smile. He had just been called "nigga" by a black man. Should he feel insulted or flattered? And how to respond? What trumps "nigga"? Furthermore, Greg had implied that Eric's Richard Gere story was banal. As Josh said the next day when we gossiped over the phone, "That Greg had a lot of tricks up his sleeve for someone in an undershirt."

"Does anybody *like* you?" Eric asked Greg.

"Those with sophisticated palettes find me irresistible. Truffles Limburger would be my drag name. And you? Does anybody *like you*? Oh wait, let me guess. Everybody's drawn to you, and you beat them all away."

Eric gave a shrug of assent.

Greg broke into song: "*I hate everything I love-ah!*" He flashed jazz hands and made it a Broadway musical. "*I hate everyone I love-ah! The oldest story in our homosexual world-ah. Singit!*" He lifted an imaginary top hat.

"Okay, you want to play a guessing game," Eric said. "It's my turn. Everyone has always underestimated you. All your teachers, everyone. As a result, every sentence out of your mouth is an effort to prove your wit. Just like how you wear those clothes to *prove* you're not a thug. Just like how you mince, just a little, across subway platforms to *prove* to the white women you won't mug them. Isn't it exhausting? Oh wait, wait, I get one more guess. I guess that you've never dated another black man. You like lording it too much."

"My turn? Oh, goody. First, let me guess your age, and don't tell me I'm wrong, because I'm always right. You're . . . one hundred . . . and fifty . . . three. Yes, one-hundred-and-fifty-three, and you were born with Venus rising and the moon in the House of Prick. Let me add here, just parenthetically, that I dated a black man for *five years*, who is still my best friend and with whom I share a dog. Who is much more clever and charming than you. *The dog*. But back to our game. You've gotten by on your looks so far. Well, *Sugah, you ain't dat pretty no mo*'! The stars say that you will fade away lonely and alone, having lived your life a porcupine who jabbed everyone who got close – jabbed even himself – couldn't jerk off your pokey little porcupine penis for all the jabbing. So yes, honorable son," (here Greg pressed his palms together), "you were born during the Year of the Masturbating Porcupine. Many happinesses." He gave salaam.

We all sat trembling with fear and titillation. Would it come to blows? The Phoenix had never seen a fist fight. It wasn't a lesbian bar, after all.

But Eric stood up and shouted, "You are a worthy opponent!"

Greg responded in the same voice, "It is a good day to die!"

"*Kaplá!*" they both shouted. They flung back their arms and jumped up against each other, thumping chests.

"What the fuck was that?" Archie asked me.

"Klingon war cry, from *Star Trek*."

"Christ."

"Yep."

Bendiks had made a match – a different kind than he intended, but a match nonetheless. He had given Eric someone who shared his sci-fi obsession, and the rest of us were invisible now as the two talked *Trek*. I joined another conversation, but couldn't help noticing how animated Eric became, how he'd jump off his bar stool to make a point. He bought a round – not for us, just for him and Greg – then Greg bought the next. Finally, the beer had its effect and Greg went off to empty his bladder.

"This *Greg's* a total fraud," Eric said, his eyes barely grazing me. "I'll beat Bendiks silly for bringing him. Did you hear that *shit merchant* talking about Buenos Aires?"

"Ridiculous," I said.

"Everyone knows that Buenos Aires is totally over. It was the new New York *years* ago."

"Wait," I said, "you were serious about that?"

"What?"

"All that *new New York* stuff. I thought you were making fun of him for using that phrase."

"I was making fun of him for saying Buenos Aires is the new New York."

"Oh," I said, allowing myself a little giggle.

Eric shot me a friend-or-foe look. Then he said, "Anyway, I got him *good*."

"Fur*real*," I said, and this time Eric gave me a stare of true suspicion.

"Fur*real*" was one of his trademarks, and I had meant to use it in homage, as a demonstration of solidarity, but it had the opposite effect. By Eric's stare, I could tell that it had sounded like I was mocking him and, although mockery was the keystone of his other friendships, it wasn't the keystone of ours.

But now the shit merchant was back, and Eric could barely contain his excitement. The two started arguing about the Bajoran–Cardassian conflict, and I moved away. But I didn't leave. I stayed until the end, as usual. No human or animal was waiting for me at home; at work, most of my talents were employed in creating the sense that I was necessary. Only here, on Tuesday nights, was I truly needed – even if only as an audience.

———

I don't know if Eric ever gave Bendiks the sound beating he had promised, but if he did, it didn't take. Unencumbered by the memory of the stunners Eric had dated in an earlier phase of his life and the ease with which he flitted from one to the next, Bendiks brought to this problem the earnest, icy attention that he gave all important things, and that made you want to take him by the shoulders, kiss him and say, "Lighten up and enjoy being beautiful."

Without announcing his intentions, Bendiks brought Hal the next week.

"Hal, this is Josh, Archie, Buttons . . ." We all half-rose from our barstools to shake his hand, which felt like a big, firm sandwich. He wore tailored clothes. Maybe he was required to dress that way for work, but you changed into some old T-shirt with a logo before you came to the Phoenix. Hal was dressed for success, we for irony.

Eric happened to be in the bathroom during these introductions. From where I sat, I could see him now emerge and head toward us. Then he saw Hal, and slowed. I could see him put two and two together, and narrow his eyes. Then he straightened up and marched over.

"So this is two-fers," Hal nodded. "Thanks for having me."

"Do *not* go into that bathroom!" Eric said, fanning the air as he joined us. "*Phew!* Give it, like, an *hour*. I just made a *crappuccino* with extra foam. Espresso beans everywhere. Oh, hello! I didn't see you there. You certainly are tall."

"Eric, this is Hal," Bendiks mumbled.

"Sorry if my hand's wet."

"Eric. I'm pleased to meet you. Bendiks has told me all about you."

"Did he tell you I have The Aids?"

"No," said Hal without missing a beat, "and I wouldn't expect him to. He told me about your personality, your qualities."

"What did he say? You can paraphrase. It'll be like that game, Telephone, or Chinese Whispers as the English call it, though that's a bit racist. My friends here can judge how close you come to the truth."

Bendiks squirmed and twisted his petals, but Hal wouldn't be deterred. "Well, to paraphrase, it sounds like you're an orange." Hal said this breezily, then saw from our blank stares he would have to explain. "Oh, an orange has a thick skin and a soft center. Your inside is segmented. This isn't an insult, just a mode of description. I'm an apple. Thin-skinned and firm. Bendiks is a kiwi, I think, though he says he's a banana."

"Oh my God," Eric said, "you're in *est*! This is *est* talk. I haven't heard it in years."

"I'm not in *est*," Hal said.

"What is *est*?" Trevor asked.

"A self-help brainwashing thing from the seventies," said Eric.

Bendiks intervened: "It's Milestone Workshop. It has nothing to do with *est*."

"*Nyet*, Bendiks! Not you, too! Has he dragged you to a seminar?"

"That's where we met," said Bendiks.

"Quit, now!" said Eric. "It's extortion. A pyramid scheme. They get you hooked, then they take your money, fur*real*."

Hal smiled patiently. "Milestone is empowerment training. We have major CEOs at our meetings, judges, Congressmen. There's no extortion involved."

"Seriously, guys," Eric insisted, "they beat you into submission at these marathon meetings, convince you you're worthless, then build you back up into one of them. They don't let you go to the bathroom. Right, Bendiks? They made you hold your pee."

"No," Bendiks said with great seriousness. "They gave me lunch."

"Oh, just you wait," Eric said. "At the next meeting, they'll make you hold your pee."

"Eric," said Hal, still amused and patient. "I like your passion, and you've got a great way of expressing yourself, but you really have no idea what you're talking about."

"You like my passion?" said Eric. "Oh, that's rich. Am I a passion fruit now? *Passion fruit!*" he cried, turning a delighted *Get it?* expression on us.

Much to our relief, Greg arrived at just that moment, crying, "It's me!" from the doorway.

"Oh, God, not that one," Eric muttered; then, loudly, to Greg: "Do you ever enter a room without throwing up your hands?"

"*La-la-laaa! Tee-hee-heee!*" Greg ballet-danced across the room.

"Get over here and sit down!"

With the gentle, liquid instinct of an amoeba, our group divided in two, separating Eric from Hal. I think Eric repeated his tirade against *est* to Greg, but I was in the other circle, where Hal was politely asking people about themselves. He had perfect features – intense green eyes, a straight arrow of a nose, an earnest, out-turned bottom lip – but there was a millimeter too much or too little space between the features, a disharmony which made me wonder about the nature of handsomeness itself.

Eventually, the others in my circle went home or joined Eric, leaving me alone with almost-handsome Hal. But I didn't mind, because I was enjoying our talk. Hal listened to every word I said. He asked me about my job, and my answer must have been lackluster, because he asked, "But what do you *want* to do?"

"I guess I'd like to get out of human resources and into recruitment," I said.

"But what do you want to *do*, ultimately?"

"Move to head office?" I answer-asked.

He nodded in a way that was not judgmental, yet made it clear that I had a problem.

Then, later: "Why do they call you Buttons?"

"Oh, Eric named me that. It was the name of his cat when he was little."

"Do you find that a little insulting?"

"No?"

This stranger cared more about me than I cared about myself. Was that *est*?

Later, when Hal made his polite good-nights and left, Eric said, "There goes a man who has never in his life said one interesting thing."

"He was nice," I said.

"And here is another!" Eric said with a hand-flourish, as if he had just conjured me from thin air.

Something unexpected hit me: the urge to weep.

Eric must have seen it, because he softened. "Let me buy you a beer, Buttons."

I should have said no. I should have gone home, maybe joined *est*. But I didn't. I stayed – till the end again, when everyone else had gone and it was just Eric and me, drunk. We decided to go to Bereket on Houston Street for some 2 a.m. falafel. As we turned onto First Avenue, still ablaze with cabs, drunks, fluorescent light spilling from bodegas, Eric said, "That Hal was awful. I wish Bendiks would spare us this nonsense. I've told him to stop, but he won't listen. Have a talk with him, will you, Buttons?"

With cool air in my lungs, I felt like a new beginning. I said, "Do you ever think it might be appropriate to call me by my name?"

"Yes, Buttons. Always."

"My real name. I do have one, you know."

"Buttons!"

"Chris. My name is Chris. Why do you always call me Buttons?"

Eric heaved a sigh of boredom that, at its crest, threatened to burst his chest. "It was the name of my cat when I was little."

"And why do you feel the need to call me by your cat's name?"

"Because you once claimed to be able to lick your own ass?"

"I did not."

"That's the way I remember it."

"No, Eric, it's because you have to treat me like a pet so I'll always be docile and you'll always have mastery over me."

Eric stifled a falsetto cough of embarrassed laughter.

"What?" I said.

"You waxing psychoanalytical – it's a bit like Miss Piggy speaking French, isn't it?"

I spun around and walked away, up the avenue.

"Buttons, come back. I was kidding!" Eric hollered. "Buttons! Wait! Don't be a wanker!"

But off I marched.

As good as this felt – making demands, naming myself, marching – I didn't call Hal and go to a seminar. I went back to my life and, to be honest, I can't remember *what* I did until Eric called that Sunday (which happened to be Easter) offering to treat me to brunch as an apology for the Miss Piggy comment. I accepted, then watched Eric avoid the use of either of my names – a task that became more and more difficult with each successive Bloody Mary. Then we went to the Phoenix, where the management had put baskets of Easter candy out on the bar. By this point, late in the afternoon, all the chocolate had been eaten and all that remained were Peeps. We had barely started our drinks when Eric grabbed one electric-yellow chick-shaped marshmallow and threw it at a man who was making out with another man at the bar. "Oi!" he shouted. "Not here!"

This was the Cockney *oi*, not Yiddish *oy*. Although Eric had resisted picking up an accent in London (we would have slaughtered him for any such Madonna-ese), he did employ British words he considered superior to their American counterparts. Bathrooms were now *loos*, one occasionally *fancied* a *snog*, and I, when I stood up for myself on First Avenue, was a *wanker*.

The Peep bounced off the head of the offender, a muscular man with a military cut. "What the hell?" he said, rising.

"No snogging at the bar! Where do you think you are?"

"What's your problem?"

"It's not that kind of place."

The man approached, followed by his companion. "I can kiss my boyfriend wherever I want. Understand, asshole?"

"That's not how it works."

Eric and the man stood face to face. The man wore a tight polo shirt that said Abercrombie & Fitch across his considerable chest. Eric said, "I can tell by the way you've decorated your *ridiculous* bosom that you're from the other side of Broadway. So let me be your guide to these eastern wildlands. This is not Splash or G or wherever you're used to lurking about, this is the Phoenix. We don't listen to music *spun* by a deejay," (he gave *spun* the dizzy, wide-eyed treatment), "we listen to *rock songs* our friends put on the *jukebox*. We don't drink *cosmos* or *metros* or whateverthefuck, we drink *beer*. And most importantly, we do *not* practice oral surgery on each other out in plain view. We *chat*. With our *friends*. There are plenty of places for *your* type of behavior. In fact, I'll probably be at one of them later. But! Not! Here!"

"Eric, sit the fuck down and shut the fuck up." It was Gary, the bartender, who on quiet Tuesday nights often joined our group. "Guys," he said, "ignore this jerk. If you go back to your seats, the next round's on me."

"Yes, boys, drink up! Vomiting gives you great abs."

Gary leaned over the bar to pull Eric onto his stool while some other patrons shepherded the other two back down the bar.

"It is a truth universally acknowledged," Eric said to me, "that any fag anywhere in the world can be bought for a drink."

I gazed at him patiently, yardstick in place.

"God, I'm sick of the sound of my own voice."

"Maybe we should go have a coffee," I said.

We went around the corner to Alt Coffee, where a man with tattoos on his face served us satisfyingly huge lattes – annoyingly, in handle-less bowls. We sat in the front window, which looked out on a bus stop. Every few minutes a new group of riders nodded their stone faces in unison with the lurching of a bus – a quiet, collective *yes* – before continuing downtown. Eric still had a trace of the mean drunk in him, and before long was bitching about our friends. At least his targets now were safely offstage, and there was no candy to throw, so I played along. Self-righteous Josh, sloppy Archie, maudlin Trevor. Bendiks was conspicuously absent from the list.

"You know what the worst thing about this *Greg* is?" Eric said. "He laughs at his own jokes."

"So do you," I said.

Eric looked at me as if I grossed him out, as if my face was suddenly reduced to an arrangement of ridges and holes. "No, I don't."

I silently conceded that he was right. I suppose I had meant only that, like Greg, Eric joked constantly. But it was true that he never laughed at his own jokes; rather, he scattered them like breadcrumbs to pigeons, never partaking of them himself. They served a purpose more complex than his own enjoyment.

But what I said was, "Oh, come on, Eric. Don't complain about Greg. You get so excited when he shows up. We can all see he's your new best friend."

"I suppose you're right," he said.

Not wanting Eric to see me look stricken, I turned away. Greg was his new best friend? A group of bus riders nodded, *Yes.*

On he talked, but I wasn't listening anymore.

Finally, I interrupted. "So let me get this straight: you think Greg would skip work to take care of you if you needed him to?"

"What?"

"Well, that's what you're saying."

"Buttons, I don't know what you're talking about."

"You don't, do you? You really don't remember what I did for you."

"What you did for me *when*?"

"Well, if you don't remember, I'm not going to help you out."

"Christ, what's wrong with you? Lately you've turned into such a nag."

I stood up. "Enjoy him," I said and, for the second time in a week, marched away.

I decided to take a few weeks off from two-fers. In my absence, I kept tabs on the guys. Trevor and I went to a Peter Lorre festival at Film Forum, Archie and I met for curry, Josh and I shopped for his boyfriend's birthday present. I called Bendiks, feeling a little shy, since we had never been phone-friends. Maybe, away from the others, a get-together would become a date. Why shouldn't it? Who said I didn't deserve his serious, light-eyed sweetness to myself? I could be funny. I could make him smile. But the profusion of meaningless obstacles between us, the impossibility of finding a time to meet, made it apparent that he loved me not.

I jogged in the mornings. I went to Boston for the weekend. I got in touch with old friends and went out for drinks with the girls from work. But I was always the first to call it a night and head home.

Humbled by the extent to which my social life depended on two-fers, I returned. "Buttons!" they cried, "where have you been?" – then didn't wait for a response.

"Just one beer for me tonight," Archie said. "I have a date."

"Ah, anxious to get slapped around?" Eric asked. I never knew if Archie was actually an insatiable masochist or if this was just Eric's invention. "Which master will you be serving tonight?"

"I serve myself," Archie said.

"You serve yourself up on a platter with an apple in your mouth. Which master?"

"My lips are sealed."

Eric inhaled, paused to consider it, then said, "*Too easy*."

Eric looked different. A month ago, he had told us he was starting a new treatment to fill in his cheeks. It was working. Also, a business trip to San Diego had flushed him with sun. I wondered if there would be a new phase to Eric's life, where his beauty would be made whole again. Then I wondered why Eric's life got to happen in phases while mine seemed to be unrolling in a much more even and featureless manner. Like toilet paper.

"Speaking of butt plugs," Eric went on, even though we hadn't been, "Josh's phone number, when he lived in Brooklyn, used to be 718-buttplug, didn't it, Josh? Wait, where's Josh?"

"He didn't come tonight."

"Why not?"

"He has bronchitis," Trevor said, "so he figured he'd better stay in bed till it's through."

"Oh, right," we all said.

Eric could sniff out any slight. "It's so unfair! Just because Josh doesn't have *this*" – with his fingers, Eric dragged his skin down into a saggy-eyed *Frankenstein*-face – "everybody forgets we have the same disease."

"That's because you *don't* have the same disease," Archie said.

"Whah?"

"Yes, Josh has HIV, but it didn't drop into a pre-arranged little slot in his psyche. Admit it, Eric. You were *so* ready to believe your jizz is poison."

"*Archie!*"

Even Greg gasped.

"You fat fuck!" Eric began to rise.

Trevor held him down by his shoulder. "It's not that, Eric. It's just – Josh doesn't make a fuss."

"A rare gift," Greg said.

"What?" I asked.

"Fuss-free-ness. Contentment. It's something you're born with, not something you achieve. One of my aunts has it. We all fight to be around her, then forget that she's there."

"Eric," said Bendiks gravely, "I might bring my karate teacher next week. I think you'd like him."

"Bendiks, you are getting on my last . . . gay . . . nerve."

"I only—"

"Stop laying your friends on the altar. You'll run out."

"Yes," said Archie. "Let *me* lay your friends on the altar."

It was a lame joke, but succeeded in pointing out that Bendiks wasn't finding mates for the rest of us, who were varying degrees of single.

"Fatty's right for once," Eric said. "Leave me alone. Bring someone for one of these guys." He indicated the lot of us with a dash of derision.

"Just give him a try! He's cute!"

"Why, Bendiks? Why do you insist on doing this?"

"Because I love you."

Bendiks said it the way a nurse says, "Step on the scale," but it was as if Eric had been punched in the chest. He recovered and said, "Look. I don't know how it is in *Lapland* or wherever you come from . . ."

"Latvia."

"But we don't throw that word around willy-nilly here."

"But I do. I love you."

Eric grabbed Bendiks by the ear – *by the ear* – and dragged him across the room to the corner. Bendiks whimpered, "*Ow-ow-ow-ow!*" all the way.

There was a short silence before we all laughed low, guttural, dirty-joke laughs. Then someone asked, "Who's been around the office lately, Archie?"

Archie started telling his stories. I resisted the urge to look over my shoulder – resisted, that is, until Archie's voice ceased and his jaw just hung.

I looked. We all did. In that darkened corner, Eric and Bendiks were locked in an embrace as if they meant to squeeze the breath out of each other. As if they could step into each other. Their faces mashed together. They were snogging.

"I can't believe this!" I said. "What's going on?"

"Kind of obvious," Archie said.

"No! They can't . . . Somebody stop them!"

"Stop them?"

"He's out of control. He's completely lost it. Eric's been going crazy lately. On Easter Sunday, he – hey, Gary, tell them what happened on Easter Sunday!"

Gary, who was polishing the bottles, came over. "Oh yeah, it was hilarious. These two gym queens were making out and Eric started throwing marshmallows at them."

"It was not hilarious! Eric was being totally aggressive. Seriously, you guys, doesn't it seem like Eric's been out of control lately?"

"Buttons, don't be J," said Trevor, who often reduced unpleasant words to their initial.

"My name is Chris and I'm not jealous. Eric *is* out of control. On Easter Sunday he almost got in a fight. Gary had to make him sit down. And that's only the beginning. He's always going off. You should hear how he trashes you guys, every one of you!"

"He's spitting!" Archie giggled, referring to me.

"Leave him alone," Greg said quietly. "Can't you see he's hurt?"

"Who's hurt? I'm just trying to tell you—"

I turned again, and they were still at it, feasting. "Hypocrites," I said, though words and their meanings were peeling apart. "Fuck! I can't—"

Everyone was watching – me, not them. I grabbed my coat and left.

———

This is what I came up with at about two o'clock in the morning, lying in bed with my slide rule and protractor and spirit level: Bendiks, lucky in his stupid youth, had said, "I love you," at just the right moment, and had slipped into Eric's arms. Eric, in taking him aside rather than hashing it out in front of us, had slipped into Bendiks's. Anyone could love anyone. It was a matter of timing, of coming together in that second between not knowing each other well enough and knowing each other too well. A life of lunging blindly till you pinned the tail on the donkey. Or, better metaphor: in a war of archers, two arrows in an arrow-filled sky can meet point to point and split each other with a kiss and fall to the ground together, locked. Those arrows are lovers, darlings of chance.

To Bendiks and Eric, though, it seemed like destiny – a collapse after resisting the inevitable for so long. While I was mapping out my theory alone, they were lying, looking into each other's eyes, hearts aflutter, adrenalin surging in the thrill of intimacy – a lovers' game of chicken. Minutes passed, and it seemed that Eric's black eyes would close, or Bendiks's light eyes would look away. But they met each other now – and now – and now – courageous, until tears of happiness welled.

They cried together. How do I know? Because Bendiks told Josh, who told me in a phone conversation a few days later. Home with bronchitis, Josh hadn't witnessed my outburst at the Phoenix, so he thought he was giving me good news. But it felt like a colony of termites were gnawing themselves a new home in my chest. I knew I should end the call, but I had to hear every last thing.

At times that night, Eric and Bendiks tried to put words to what was going on, but their voices sounded oddly harsh in that silent room. So they stopped trying and said everything that could be said, made every promise that could be made, with their bodies and with their eyes. *I will hold you when you're scared and make you grilled-cheese sandwiches. I will tell you that you're not going to die.*

"Well, Josh" – I managed to hammer a smile into my voice when he finished telling me – "sounds like someone finally shut Eric up."

I know, I know. My sarcasm, like my theory, was nothing but ice – bags of ice to pack around my heart and keep it solid and intact. Any fool could have told me what I really wanted. The problem was, at that time, in New York, I didn't know any fools.

Nelly's Teeth
Nigel Fairs

_____

Her lips had melted easily, as Mr Dawkins suspected they might, but now he was having real trouble with her jawbone.

"The problem is that Dawkins Jr is getting too good at his job," he muttered as he gave the darkening skin one final blast with the blowtorch.

A swift tug at the obstinate stitching, meticulously finished off by his son only two days ago, and Nelly's mouth dropped open, revealing his target: her gleaming golden teeth.

Quite where communication had broken down regarding the teeth was a mystery. Mrs Dawkins, in her warm but professional way, handled that side of the business. There was always the possibility that she'd been having one of her "purple days" and that the blame lay entirely with *Dawkins & Son* (hence this business with the blowtorch), but Mr Dawkins thought it more likely that, in all the emotional and practical upheaval surrounding a death in the family, the teeth had been forgotten.

As it happened, they hadn't. At least not by Nelly's husband.

And if he'd taken more interest in the funeral arrangements, perhaps he might have been able to communicate his wishes to the rest of the family a bit earlier, Nelly's nephew reflected, helping his mother shuffle up the aisle towards the family pew at the front of the church.

"He's not coming then?" a distant cousin enquired, her face contorted with concern.

"Flu," Nelly's nephew explained, shaking his head.

"Poor love," the contorted cousin sighed, "Maybe we'll pop in later with some grapes and a *Daily Express.*"

"Don't want to catch anything!" Contorted Cousin's husband said gruffly. "We've got the Donkey Derby at the Boys' School on Sunday."

Nelly's nephew was about to sit down when he noticed Ralph Dawkins beckoning him over from the vestry. Satisfying himself that his mother was settled next to his wife (pregnant but pristine in a black crimplene trouser suit), he nipped across to the sallow figure, who immediately thrust a package, neatly wrapped in brown paper, into his hands.

"The teeth!" Dawkins whispered.

Nelly's nephew nodded conspiratorially, and, unsure quite what to say, settled for a polite, "Thank you."

"I had quite a job, you know," Dawkins continued. "The old bird was frozen solid! Had to take a blowtorch to her in the end!"

Nelly's nephew stared at the peculiar little man for a moment or two, then pulled a ten-bob note out of his jacket pocket.

"Oh no!" Dawkins protested, "I didn't mean to . . ."

"Have a pint after the service," Nelly's nephew insisted, "and thanks for the extra effort!"

"Very kind, very kind," Dawkins said, acquiescing, and, slipping back into the vestry, he tipped his hat and murmured, "Sorry for your loss."

"Everything all right, dear?" his mother asked as he sat down.

"Just a little memento for Uncle Freddy," he smiled, popping the package into his pocket.

"How kind of him," his mother sniffed. "That'll probably be her rings. Fred said something about wanting to keep them, but I had a feeling the message hadn't got through when there was all that fuss about choosing her frock for the . . . you know."

His wife shot him one of her looks, knowing full well that "all that fuss" had arisen because there hadn't been a single frock left to choose from for the coffin; Uncle Freddy had had a bonfire the morning after Aunt Nelly died. She'd been boxed up in an almost new Mary Quant that his wife insisted would be "horribly out of fashion" by the time she'd be able to wear it again. As for the rings, they'd disappeared before Aunt Nelly's corpse had even been taken to the mortuary.

Quite why Uncle Freddy had detested his wife so much was difficult to fathom, though his nephew had always assumed that it was all down to what the family always referred to as "That Business in Blackpool". Exactly what "That Business" had been remained unclear. His wife was convinced that Aunt Nelly had been found *in flagrante delicto* with a lover, but he wasn't so sure. On their honeymoon? Somehow it didn't quite ring true. On the contrary, Aunt Nelly had always seemed rather uptight, even frigid. The thought of her making mad, passionate love with anyone at all (even Uncle Freddy) was quite absurd. And somehow the possibility of him being a Lothario was even more ridiculous. So what else, then? A secret gambling addiction that had come to light in the penny arcades on the Golden Mile? A horrific murder buried deep in one of their pasts, revealed over toast and marmalade in the Seaview B&B? Or did the frock pyre have some other strange significance? Was Uncle Freddy secretly Aunty Freda?

He snorted, despite himself, and pretended to be lowering his head in prayer.

———

Nelly's sister patted her son's knee comfortingly. Bless him for trying to disguise his tears as laughter. He'd always been such a brave little boy, but that was mainly down to his father's strict sense of decent, manly behaviour and proud working-class values. "Be a man or be done with you!" was his response to a grazed knee or hints of bullying, "Little boys should be seen but never heard."

He'd hated Fred on sight. "I knew men like him at the Front," he'd said, "Always managed to keep one step away from the white feather but by God they never so much as got their boots dirty!"

"I thought soldiers were *supposed* to have clean boots!" she'd teased him.

"You don't know what I mean," he'd sighed, "but then how could you, my sweet, innocent little darling?" and kissed her on the forehead.

Not as innocent as you think, she'd thought, but said nothing, of course.

Gone now.

His had been the last funeral they'd been to, barely a month after Nell had got back from her honeymoon. She'd turned up at the bungalow with a mouthful of golden teeth. "Freddy's wedding present to me," she'd gleamed: her only smile of the day. It was only after two cigarettes and a large sherry that she'd weepily confessed that the teeth had been less of a present, more of a fawning apology. Fred had drained almost exactly half of his savings.

"An apology for what?" she'd asked Nell, not because she wanted to know really, which was just as well, as the reply had been an enigmatic, "Oh, just some business in Blackpool."

Typical of Nell to make the day all about her, she'd thought, and hadn't probed her for further details, simply to spite her.

Everyone in the family had their own theory about "That Business". Nelly's sister was almost certain it was something to do with money, based on the Miss Marple-like observations that Fred had arranged to meet Mr Jones, their bank manager, on the second Saturday of their honeymoon, and that, on their return, Nell and Fred had changed from Lloyds to Barclays. Not only that, but Nell had insisted that the whole family change their allegiance as well. Her sister thought that was a shame; she rather missed "Jolly Jones", as she'd christened him after a very amusing Christmas Eve do at the bank. Even her husband had grudgingly confessed to a liking for "that Jones fellow". "Most comical turn of phrase, he has. More importantly, he knows exactly what to do with our pounds, shillings and pence."

"And it was *very* kind of him to give us all a mince pie and a glass of stout," she'd added.

"Keeping the customers sweet, my darling!" he'd cooed. "He knows which side his bread is buttered! And I know a decent man when I see one!"

"What a shame he's not married."

"Married to the bank, he is! That's a good worker if ever I saw one. We'll stick with him. He'll see us good, that one."

At the time of the great migration from Lloyds to Barclays, her husband had been slipping away in the hospital and unable to raise any objections. She'd never seen Jolly Jones again, although, a year or so later, she'd noticed in the local paper that he'd married a very pale girl called Wendy. *The type of girl that works in a library*, she'd thought, *how funny, a handsome man like him marrying such a plain Jane. Nell would have eaten her for breakfast at school.*

A respectful silence fell over the church and everyone stood as Nelly's coffin moved slowly up the aisle.

———

"Did you know her well, um – sorry, what was your name again?"

"Wendy."

"Wendy. Yes, sorry, I'm terrible with names."

"No, not at all, actually. My husband corresponds with her husband."

"Pen pals, you mean?"

"Sort of. They were in the War together."

"Oh yes, I see. Is he here?"

"I don't think so. Somebody said he has the flu."

"No, I didn't mean Alfred, I meant your husband."

"Oh, sorry, no. William's had to go into the bank this morning. He's the manager."

"Oh really? Which one?"

"Lloyds."

"I'm at the National Westminster. Alfred told me all about his War days at camp. Awful business."

"Camp?"

"Boys' Brigade. We shared a tent."

"Of course. I thought I recognized you. My Stuart came to you for a while."

"Not Stuart Jones by any chance?"

"Yes, that's right. He had to stop coming because of his asthma."

"I remember. Funnily enough, Alfred and I were talking about him just last week. Because Stuart is Alfred's middle name, did you know?"

"No. I didn't."

"He was a real little character. He'll go far. Mind you, that mouth of his could get him into some real scrapes if he's not careful!"

"And out of 'em again!"

"Beg pardon?"

"Oh, sorry. Just something my husband says. I think Stuart takes after him, really, as far as the humour goes. He gets the asthma from my side of the family, I'm afraid."

"Ah. How's he doing, young Stuart?"

"He's very well, thank you. Though if he paid as much attention to his schoolwork as he did to his transistor radio set . . . Oh goodness, I'm starting to sound like William again."

"Who?"

"My husband."

"Oh yes. Terrible with names, sorry. Well, please send your boy our regards. Look, here she comes!"

Wendy smiled weakly and pretended to lower her head in prayer as the coffin passed, inwardly cursing the fact that she was trapped next to this ghastly man and that, far from confronting the grieving widower as planned, she would now have to endure the whole service. Blood pounded in her ears. She felt like crying. For the corpse, for herself, for her beautiful, oh-so unhappy son.

————

"Did you get them?"

"Yes, Uncle Freddy."

His nephew placed the brown paper package onto the table between them. Freddy pocketed it and smiled, adjusting his tie in the mirror. The Red Lion buzzed around them.

"You're feeling better then?"

"Oh yes, much more my old self," Freddy replied. "You're a good boy, handling everything for me and your mother like you did. I'm sure she was very grateful. She and your Aunty Nelly were always as thick as thieves. Do you know, once all the unpleasantness is over, I think I might take a little holiday?"

————

"Will you be partaking of a Seaview Special tomorrow morning, Mr Jones? Because if you are, the missus will be buying in some fresh kippers. We know you like them."

"I think I might," William twinkled. "Never could resist a Seaview Special!"

"Oh good! Off for a perambulation? Or a trip up the tower, maybe? Lovely views today."

"I'm meeting an old pal from the War actually."

"Ah."

A knowing nod.

"One of the lucky ones?"

"Two of the lucky ones."

Another twinkle.

————

The white October sun sliced through the café window and for a moment Freddy's face was illuminated like a movie star's, his eyes even bluer than William remembered them. He opened the smart black box and smiled.

"It's a pen, Billy," Freddy said, still one to point out the obvious. "Real gold."

Shoga
Diriye Osman

My grandmother worked my roots with the vigour of a woman who meant business. She dug her fingernails into my 'fro and when she discovered dandruff she pulled out her clippers and said, "Waryaa, fix up! Hadiikale, I shall shave you cleaner than a baby's ass."

"Ayeeyo, I want to be braided, not be given a bloody sermon."

"Hododo!" She clapped her hands. "You've mastered the art of backchat. Now learn the basics of hygiene."

"Ayeeyo, man!"

"Is it not true? And furthermore, this business of me braiding your hair has to stop! You're a boy, not a lady-boy!"

"You know you love me," I smiled. "Besides, what's wrong with being a lady-boy? It's a good look."

She pulled my hair and said, "Waryaa, if you grow up to be gay, walaahi I will do saar."

"Saar" was a brand of Somali exorcism. Those "possessed" – which was code for the mentally unstable – were put through their paces. Healers would beat drums to release spirits from them, and they would shimmy and shake. If they got too frisky, they would face the kind of beat-down usually reserved for criminals. Such superstition has always been rife in the bush, and my gran, a country gal through and through, knew its effectiveness at deterring unacceptable behaviour.

I smiled as she flexed my follicles. My grandmother did not know that I was gay. I've always loved being gay. Sure, Kenya was not exactly Queer Nation, but my sexuality gave me joy. I was young, not so dumb and full of cum! There was no place for me in heaven but I was content munching devil's pie here on earth.

I was seventeen and I specialized in two things: weed and sex. And there was only one person in my neighbourhood who served both those dishes on a steaming plate for me.

Boniface.

But I've missed a beat, my bambinos. A narrative without a backstory is like meat with no bone: there's no juice to it. So let me take two steps back.

My family moved to Kenya in '91, after my dad hauled our asses from Mogadishu. I don't remember much about Somalia – I was only a toddler when we fled – but over the years Mogadishu assumed mythical status in our lives. It could only truly flourish in selective memory. It was years later that I learnt the precise term for what my family and millions of other Somalis had experienced during the war: post-traumatic stress.

But my father was not one for wasting time. He got to work and started amassing a small fortune by selling blankets and medicine to NGOs headed for Mogadishu. My mum did her bit and became a pharmacist in Hurlingham. While baba na mama made money, my gran took care of home.

All that changed in '94. My parents were driving home from Trattoria Restaurant one night when they got stopped by the police. The cops ordered them to get out of the car, but my dad refused. Kenyan police are the shiftiest crooks this side of the Sahara. If they want to extort you, nobody can stop them. If they want to make you disappear, no one can prevent it. My father knew this, so he refused to get out. Without missing a beat, the police fired three shots into his head. Then they blasted my mother's brains out when she started screaming. Their bodies were found floating in Athi River the next day. I was seven years old.

While my gran's peers were settling quietly into old age, she now had to support both of us. We owned our small maisonette, so housing wasn't an issue. My parents had taken out life insurance, but it wasn't enough for us to live on. My grandmother took half the cash and invested it in a small import–export business she ran out of our living room. The rest went into my education.

As the years passed, Gran decided she needed help around the house. She found it difficult to bend over and clean floors and cook three meals a day, raise a teenager *and* run a business. She didn't want another woman in her home. She wanted a man who was strong enough to cook, clean and carry water to the tank. She wanted a man to protect us from burglars. Basically, she wanted a budget superhero.

Enter Boniface.

Boniface was from Burundi and my grandma dug this. She dug the fact that he was a refugee like us but I was more impressed with his muscle mass. While she saw enough brawn to carry three sacks of bariis at once, I saw prime beefcake. Papi was beautiful and he looked like he was packing. I licked my lips and locked and loaded.

Every day, I'd go to my window and watch him wash clothes outside. When it became humid, he'd remove his shirt, fold it and place it on the ground. His pectorals would be slick with sweat. Whenever he saw me, he'd smile and wink. I'd stick my tongue out. He'd make a fist and pretend to punch himself. I'd flip him the finger.

"I'll tell Ayeeyo!" His eyes glinted.

"Tell her," I laughed.

"She shall thup you," he warned.

"And I shall thup *you*!"

"Bring it!" he said, flexing his muscles.

"Ever tasted the flying fist of Judah?" I asked.

"More like the flying fist of foolishness!"

"Are you challenging me?"

"I believe I am," he said.

"Then it's on. Tonight. Backyard."

He laughed. "We shall see who thups who."

We sneaked into the backyard that evening. My grandmother was asleep so we tried to keep it quiet.

All I wanted was to feel his body against mine and, if it took a wrestling match to achieve this, I was game. I thought he'd go easy on me but he lifted me up like a ragdoll, ready for a literal smackdown.

"Put me down!" I yelled, wriggling in his arms.

"What do you say?"

"Fuck you!"

"Now, now," he said, tightening his grip. "I'll let you down on one condition."

"No dice!"

"Are you sure?" he asked. "It involves a treat."

My ears pricked up. "What kind of treat?"

He put me down and reached into his pocket. He removed a spliff – purple haze. I eyed it greedily.

"I never smoke alone," he said. "So I was wondering—"

"Yes!" I said quickly. "I'll puff with you."

"But if Ayeeyo busts us, you take the blame."

"Toka!" I scoffed.

"I know you want some." He dangled the spliff.

I wiped my drool and said, "It's a deal. But I get to light it!"

We went to his quarters and smoked up. Boniface's room used to be a storage space, but he'd transformed it with paint and posters. There was a cassette player and a stack of bootleg tapes on the bedside table. The cassettes were by artists like Koffi Olomide and Papa Wemba.

"Don't you have any hip hop?" I asked.

"Hip hop is shit," he said. "Check this out." He pulled out a cassette, opened the tape player and slid it in. He then sprawled on the bed and passed me the joint.

The weed hit me the moment the music started playing. It was an old soul record. The singer had a tone that made me feel slinky. I got up and snaked my hips. Boniface looked on. He smiled and stroked his chest. I walked over and lay next to him. He didn't inch away. Instead, he examined my face, ran his calloused palm across my cheek. I noticed a beauty spot under his right eye. I touched it. His skin was soft.

I placed the joint on a nearby ashtray. I pulled my T-shirt over my head and slid out of my shorts. He kissed me, tongue tasting of weed. He broke the kiss to unbutton his shirt. His abdomen was cut like slabs of chocolate. He removed his trousers and wasn't wearing underwear. His thighs were thick, dick hard. I bent down and deep-throated him. He smelt of soap. He pushed his hips back and forth. I stopped to come up for air. He helped me out of my underwear and spread my limbs, licked every inch of me until I was sex-funky. He then reached for the joint and took a long pull. He blew the smoke in my mouth. I was open.

That night we fucked until the bed threatened to collapse. After we came, we went into the kitchen and made Spanish omelettes and tea. We wolfed the food down and went back to his room to smoke some more.

As we puff-puff-passed, I considered what had happened. Sure, I'd fooled around with boys before, but this was different. Boniface was a man who fucked like he ate: greedily. I relished the thought of him feasting on me again. I went to bed dreaming of bubbles that would never burst.

After school the next day, I ran inside the house to find Boniface making dinner. Ayeeyo was in the kitchen, smoking sheesha.

"What's this haraka business?" she asked. "Usually, I have to drag you in by force. What gives?"

"I just wanted to see you." I kissed her.

She gave me a look that said, "Wacha mchezo." She continued filling up the kitchen with smoke. Boniface glanced at me and I smiled. Ayeeyo noticed but said nothing.

"Boniface, serve this boy his dinner. He needs to do his homework."

"Yes, mama," said Boniface. He piled pasta onto my plate. He was wearing tight shorts and a Beasties T. As I admired his legs, my grandmother watched me. She kept quiet. Boniface poured sauce on my pasta and gave me the plate. I sat on the veranda and waited for Ayeeyo to leave the kitchen.

She didn't leave until midnight. By then, I had given up and gone to bed. Boniface had also retired to his room. I could hear Ayeeyo playing

Ludo alone, dice clacking against board. I knew she was afraid to go to sleep, afraid of being haunted by nightmares. She had clung onto my parents because they were all she had. It was years after their deaths before she finally accepted her loss. I had come to take their place. She was afraid that once I left home for college, I too would never return. I tried consoling her but she didn't want pity. She wanted a guarantee. I couldn't give her that.

Eventually, the dice stopped rolling and she went to sleep. That's when I heard a tap on my window. I jumped up and opened the curtains. Boniface was outside, grinning. I told him I'd meet him in his room. When I got there, he was sprawled naked on his bed, puffing a joint. I bent down, kept his dick wet. He pulled me up, laid me on my back. I unbuttoned my shirt, loosened my belt. He opened me up using lips, fingertips, tongue tricks. He grabbed some Vaseline, slipped on a condom and fucked me until I was sticky with sweat. After we came, we wiped ourselves clean and continued smoking.

"Boniface," I said, "what do you dream about?"

"Leaving Kenya," he replied.

"Where would you go?"

"Somewhere exotic like England."

"But what would you do there?" I asked.

"I'd become an engineer. That's what I studied in Burundi. I could use that degree."

"You have a degree?" I asked.

"Yah man, I did three years in college before the war began," he said.

I imagined Boniface as an academic. He'd do well in England.

"Na wewe?" he asked. "What do you dream of?"

"Love," I replied.

"But you *are* loved," he said. "By your grandmother, by me—"

"You don't love me!" I smiled.

"Haki! Otherwise I wouldn't be thinking of you kila siku."

I played the coquette. "Hata mimi nakupenda."

"Course you do!" he grinned. "It's hard not to!"

I punched him lightly. He hugged me tight. I left his quarters high on happiness and heat. As I tiptoed to my room, I noticed that Ayeeyo's light was switched on, her door slightly ajar. I went to bed, praying that she didn't know what had happened.

I woke up the next morning to find Ayeeyo making breakfast. I greeted her, but she didn't reply.

"Where's Boniface?" I asked. "He usually makes breakfast."

Ayeeyo didn't look at me. She silently added pepper and tomatoes to the eggs in the frying pan. When she finished cooking, she turned off the stove, slopped the eggs onto my plate and said, "Eat up. Your bus will be here soon."

Her voice dripped with contempt. I knew better than to say anything, so I took the plate and ate the eggs. Ayeeyo waited for me to finish. When I was done, she gave me a napkin and told me to go.

"Ayeeyo—" I began.

"You'll miss your bus," she said.

I grabbed my backpack and left the house. I couldn't concentrate at school that day. I was petrified that Ayeeyo had discovered my affair with Boniface. What would she do? Had she fired him? Would she kick me out of the house? By the time I returned home that afternoon, I was a wreck.

I walked into the kitchen to find Ayeeyo cooking dinner. I was afraid to ask the obvious, but I had to know.

"Where's Boniface?" I said.

"He's not here," she replied chirpily.

"You sound happy about that."

"Of course I am. The man was a thief!"

"What did he steal?" I asked.

"Something that can't be replaced," was her reply.

"Like what?"

"Does it matter?" she snapped. "The fact is the man is a thief and I don't tolerate thieves in my house. Or drug addicts, for that matter."

"Boniface is not a drug addict! What the hell are you talking about?"

She looked at me and smirked. "Then why were the two of you smoking weed in his room last night? And the night before?"

My stomach dropped. "We weren't smoking!" I said. "We were just listening to music."

"I can forgive a little marijuana, but the two of you were doing something else in that room. Something that makes me want to retch!"

I was about to shit a brick but I kept my ass in check. "Tell me, Ayeeyo, what *were* we doing in his room?"

She steadied herself on the sink, as if literally gagging on the words. "I will not let a fanya kazi corrupt you. You will *not* become a . . . a—"

"Go on, Ayeeyo, you can say it," I snarled. "I will not become a khaniis? A shoga? A faggot? Well, tough luck! My ass *is* a khaniis. I am a shoga, a faggot."

She smacked me so hard across the face that I lost my balance and fell onto the ground. I got up and said, "I will leave this house one day and you will die a lonely, embittered old woman."

She looked like she had been punched. Her eyes welled up but she wouldn't allow me to see tears. So she left the kitchen and went to her bedroom. She didn't come out for four days.

My relationship with my grandmother was never the same again. She stopped speaking to me altogether and we became two strangers bound by blood and bad history. When I finished high school she didn't show up to my graduation ceremony. When I got a scholarship to Central Saint Martins in England she didn't congratulate me. On the day I was leaving for London she didn't wish me luck. She didn't whisper comforting words or urge me to come home soon. I got on that plane with a suitcase of painful memories and little else.

I called Ayeeyo regularly from London, but she never picked up the phone. I began to be afraid that something might have happened to her. I called Nairobi every day for four years and there was never a response. One day, I called and a woman picked up. I jumped with excitement.

"Hi, I'm looking for my grandmother," I said. "Is she home?"

"I'm really sorry, son," the woman said. "Your grandmother passed away a week ago but we only found her body last night. She's been taken to the morgue. I was her nurse."

The air felt like it had been sucked out of the room. I sat down on the ground and breathed slowly. "How did she die?" I asked.

"She had a stroke. I'm really sorry."

"But you were her nurse!" I shouted. "Where were you?"

"Your grandmother told me to take the week off."

"Are you serious?" I screamed. "You left a sick eighty-year-old woman by herself?"

"I'm sorry."

I wanted to strangle her, but I was more livid with myself. I was the one who had hurt my grandmother. I was the one who had abandoned her. She had died alone and it broke my heart. After I spoke to the nurse, I contacted some relatives in Kenya and asked them if they would bury her. In Islam, the funeral has to happen immediately after the person's death. I wired my savings to my relatives and they buried my grandmother that afternoon.

The next few months were spent in a self-destructive haze of alcohol and weed. I skipped classes, missed assignments and almost got expelled. I took a leave of absence from college and got a job as a bartender in a dingy club in Soho. It was there that I met Ignacio, a Colombian émigré who taught me how to make caipirinhas. We spent every evening after work in his bedsit, sipping cocktails and sucking cock.

One night, Ignacio played an old-school soul record that made my heart skip a beat. It was a melody from another time and place. It was the song that Boniface played for me when we first made love.

"What's this tune called?" I asked Ignacio.

"'All I Do,'" he replied, lighting up a joint. "Stevie Wonder."

I took the joint from him, lay down on the bed and opened my legs wide. Ignacio smiled. As he fucked me, I closed my eyes and imagined Boniface in his place, working me, tightening me like a knot before giving me release. I imagined Ayeeyo in her grave in Nairobi. I imagined my mother and my father. I imagined our modest home in Nairobi: the baobab and jacaranda trees in the backyard, the quiet veranda at the front. My whole life zigged and zagged in my head. When I came, I cried. Ignacio asked me why.

I didn't tell him about my loss. Instead, I said, "Insha'Allah, everything will work out." He looked at me quizzically. But I kept repeating this statement louder and louder until it created an incantatory effect. I repeated this statement until it became something I could hold onto, something I could believe in; until it shifted from mantra to fact.

David Robilliard
Tonight's Hope Shattered-Never and other poems

―――――

Tonight's Hope Shattered-Never

Read more of "Lace" in bed the next morning
and at tea time over drinks, drank sherry.
Then later on when everyone had gone
and I was getting very bored
and in need of company,
I went to the pub where I discovered two charming sayings.

1. Twinkle twinkle little rectum
Big dicks come when you least expect 'em.

2. Last night's trade is tonight's competition.

Waiting for Nothing

We're all waiting for
someone to arrive
to brighten up our lives.

Dream Man

Nobody finds a dream man
till they're asleep.

Help

Either the body's right
and the mind's wrong,
or the mind's right
and the body's wrong.

Fashion

Is just a flash in the pan
when you're standing next to a naked man.

The Cat's Pyjamas

Dancing till dawn
and then another night is born
you got ripped
and the night got torn
for better or worse
you spent every penny in your purse
you put a few beers
and a few chips
through your lips.

Fuck Off

Woken up next morning
by a sad and lonely person
clawing at you
oh how could I?
and the discomfort of the hangover
makes you want to say
please leave immediately

give me a break
don't stay for breakfast
you're irritating
my search for . . .
isn't loneliness a bore?

Nothing

Nothing
is better
than second best.

Eating Out

You're like a potato.
You'd go with anything.

Ish

The traditional sex colours are pink and blue.

Intense Desire

The thing that thrilled them
was the thing that killed them.

Memory of a Friend

A burst of tears
from all your friends
the end.

W.G.
Tim Ashley

Part I

When I had friends, I was known as *W.G.*, an abbreviated version of my
initials. The *W* stands for a boy's name with which you will be familiar.
It has resonances of bravery, power and tragedy – or of foolishness,
ambition and failure, depending on which historian you favour. In
either case, you will note that it does not end well.

The *G* represents a name so egregiously famous, so long associated
with extreme wealth and privilege, so omnipresent in the annals and
journals of Europe from the 1500s through to the mid-1970s that if you
are of a particular generation, you will recognize it immediately even
though you are unlikely to have heard it of late.

These days I am known, to my very few acquaintances, as Schmidt.
This may be Herr, Mister or Monsieur, depending on the where and the
when of our meeting. I cannot say that I greatly miss *W.G.*, though at
first of course I did, but only out of habit. It took just a short while for
me to let him go.

Let me clarify: in my youth I was handsome and wealthy beyond
measure. I was educated at the best universities and knew only the best
people. I lived, first with my family and then for a while independently,
in the sort of grand residences to which payment will never gain you
entry. During these years, I had enormous fun. My parents were loving,
if often absent on business or duty, and my lack of siblings was no
obstacle to my happy engagement with suitable playmates; I had (still
have, I believe) a plethora of cousins and, as a family known as much
for its grace and kindness as for its wealth, we had a great number of
hangers-on.

As an undergraduate, away from the eye of parents, governesses and tutors, I traded on my wealth and looks in pursuit of a great deal of pleasure: a certain amount of recreational drug use; the best food and the very best wine; sexual pleasure, with girls and boys and sometimes both. We, my entourage and I, travelled as rich people do, constantly, leaving used things in our wake. Our pleasures were felt by some to be a plague but we experienced them with the intensity of youth and we had no regret.

It was during this period that I first came to realize the caveats and exceptions to the privileges of wealth and beauty. Females aspired to marry me; males hoped to feed off my wealth or my connections. Even the cousins who travelled in this circus with me proved often not to be genuine or profound in their affections.

Poor little rich boy! Everybody wanted a "piece of the action" but few could be trusted. You will not be surprised when I claim this – and quite possibly there will be no sympathy – but please believe me when I tell you: even the wealthy have hearts and souls; even the beautiful suffer doubt; even those who can have anything sometimes fear that they may be worth nothing.

There was only ever one person I could trust and therefore love, absolutely. Let us call him *K.J.* His wealth and popularity matched my own and his beauty exceeded all. The chances of our meeting were high but the probabilities of our being so perfectly matched were infinitesimally small, and yet . . . and yet it happened, and we were blessed beyond any riches by this great gift of fate.

He died. Of course! Of *course* he died! Why did I not see the inevitability of that twist in the narrative? No one person can possibly have so much and keep it – and so naturally the fates called back their gift, taking from me the one thing that could never have been purchased and could never be replaced. We were both in our mid-twenties when this happened. It was in the Alps, off-piste at my behest. An avalanche. I saw it happen and I hold myself to blame. I will not describe it.

After this, realizing that my one mate and match had come and gone and that no other would ever be found, I became greatly unhappy for a while and I withdrew. At this time, pulled apart by beauty and tragedy, I ensconced myself in a residence owned but rarely used by my family in Florence, a city I did not know well until then. There, I gradually became drawn in by the richness of the city's art and, from the Baptistry through the Uffizi to the Vasari Corridor, I found at first a solace and then, to my quiet surprise, the beginnings of a slow replacement for the beauty I had lost. Through these cool halls and rooms I wandered alone, but never quite alone, for the works themselves began to speak to me, to reveal their secrets in unexpected ways. I began to love again.

Soon, however, I learned that *Firenze* is a city where so much that is perfect and lovely has been carelessly treated: a city where great works of art that should have been timeless were stored in the flood path of the raging, rising Arno and allowed to be consumed by the filthy rushing water, to be thrashed about like so many logs in a muddy jam. It became clear to me, with the protective instincts of a lover, that this was a city which could not be trusted with its treasures. The more I learned of this story, the more I came to dislike my temporary home, and soon enough I left, for Paris and Rome, for New York, Amsterdam and London; I left for anywhere I could find the works of art that were now becoming my obsession. I wandered alone here too, through galleries and museums, alive again, my love turning to a great passion for framed and frozen beauty.

As a child, of course, there had been a quantity of art in our homes but, being a child, I had largely ignored it, save for the pleasurable game of learning from my mother the names of the ancestors whose haughty portraits stood guard over our fortunes.

As an adult, increasingly learned in the field, it quickly became clear to me that there was no point in visiting the commercial galleries and auction rooms. The fact is that truly great art is rarely made in modern times: the glory days are over and we are largely offered a conceptual swill of tampons and diamonds, of videos and installations, of tripe and of offal. The art of painting people and places, the art that became my second passion after the death of *K.J.*, is out of fashion and untaught other than in certain dull studios, where people learn merely to ape the style of the greats rather than to develop their own. Not only is great art rarely made, it is very rarely available for purchase. Nearly everything of real and enduring value is already in a museum somewhere or other, and so my great and growing wealth – my parents were now gone, and I had inherited – was of little use to me. I could not buy the fabric of my dreams.

In 1914, long before I was born, a rabid woman chose, for some "political" reason, to enter the National Gallery in London with a cleaver and slash at the *Rokeby Venus*, the great work by Velázquez. The painting was said to have been "successfully restored" in time, but in truth no restoration is fully successful and no public museum or place should be trusted with the guardianship of treasure such as this. Whether it be an enraged suffragette, an iconoclast member of the Taliban with a lorry load of TNT, or a lazy and stupid Florentine flood-defence "expert", the world's most precious treasures should never be put in the way of risk of any kind. Go into any gallery and look around you: milling herds of potential vandals, guards who peer into the middle distance or read a book or even, as I have sometimes seen, fall asleep. These people, these places, are not to be trusted. They rarely shut the stable door until the horse has bolted.

This matter came to vex me greatly and then, one day, I read in the newspaper of an attack on Michelangelo's *David*. A madman with a mallet. I became, once again, greatly unhappy.

In those days, I had largely become distanced from the people I knew. But it so happened that one day, in the Isabella Stewart Gardner Museum, a Japanese man I had known briefly in my youth happened to recognize me. Knowing that his family had a great and discrete collection, I flew to visit him in Japan some weeks later in order to see a certain Monet. Takashi (not his real name) allowed me to wander freely amongst his works for a while – the Monet alone was worth the trip – and then honoured me with an impressive meal of local delicacies.

As we chatted, I learned two things that filled me with horror: firstly, that his home had some years previously been subjected to the very significant impact of an earthquake, and during this indignity a Greek vase of great value had been slightly damaged; secondly, that he was planning to lend a particularly important Rokotov to the Hermitage. The Hermitage! In a city notorious for its thieves and bandits, contained within a country famed for sieges and revolutions! One might as well put *The Last Supper* out to air on the streets of Naples. I hid my disgust, politely, but at that moment it became concrete in me that some works of art would be better being kept perfectly safe, for ever, even if they were never seen again. It is the things themselves that matter.

Dining alone in Beijing the next evening, I remembered something that K.J. had once said to me, something he had heard his father mention: the existence of a certain organization, of use to Machiavellian and corrupt heads of state, the extremely wealthy and criminals; known as *Concierge*, it could arrange anything. Murder, abduction, hijacking – and theft.

I quickly realized what I must do.

It took me a long time, some two years, to make contact with *Concierge*. As an organization it does not hide, either in secret or in plain sight. It simply does not exist until you know about it and need it, and then, like a face in the fog, it emerges.

It is a key element of all dealings with *Concierge* that the client has absolute deniability, always. The request is phrased in the form of "wouldn't it be nice if 'X' happened?" and is then processed with no visible or traceable connection whatsoever. It is absolutely watertight. It has to be. The cost is vast, the discretion complete. And loyalty is also guaranteed: it is known that the best way to avoid falling victim to the activities of *Concierge* is to subscribe to its services. This gives one assured immunity, a thing of great value. No client of *Concierge* can ever commission it to act against another.

Before I availed myself of the service, I had to make complete my disappearance from the world. Surgery, in Korea, changed my appearance: it was not a restoration – I had no remaining vanity – but a painting of one image over another so that no hint of the palimpsest remained. Discreet bankers and lawyers arranged for my transition, and that of my now-liquidated and consolidated assets, to the identity of Schmidt. My family name had long since faded from frequent mention in the press and now it was gone. I was gone. No one would hear of W.G. again.

Part II

Schmidt drives slowly down a grey street in a small, largely modern town not far from Bern. The town is not picturesque. It has little history, few diversions and no function other than as a dormitory and a place where elderly people come to be. The architecture is nondescript and the streets are clean and mostly straight, but the view of the mountains is, in every direction, magnificent.

He stops at a small convenience store, parking with care, to purchase milk, eggs, bread, nothing fancy. Some cigarettes as an afterthought. He hasn't smoked in years but sometimes feels that he might want to. Then he gets back into the small car and continues through the town until it dissolves into a stretch of well-spaced roadside bungalows. He turns left after a few hundred metres, then right. Left, right, left, and straight on, losing himself in the inert sprawl of anonymous houses in the chill, settling dusk. He winds slowly up a small hill and then descends into a dark valley. There are fewer houses now, each set in half a hectare of land or more. As the land starts to rise again on the other side of the valley, he turns left between trees onto a barely metalled road that leads, soon enough, to an L-shaped two-storey house of modest proportions. A garage opens, automatically, and he drives in.

The engine stops and Schmidt reaches to the side of the dashboard, where the press of a button causes the luggage compartment to open with a soft hydraulic sigh, revealing a flat rectangular package wrapped in brown paper. He takes this gently into the house before returning for his provisions, which he places in the kitchen before taking the parcel into a downstairs bedroom at the back of the house. The room, nudged into the rising hillside, is dark and plain. At the back of it is a wall of built-in wardrobes. Schmidt opens one of them and steps inside, closing the door behind him as a fluorescent tube flickers into life in the interior. Behind a rail of clothes there is what looks like a gun cabinet – not unusual in these parts. He dials the combination and, as the door swings open, a panel lights up. He presses his thumb to a pad, enters a code, awaits a series of confirmation lights and then enters another code. The panel swings, giving way to a dimly lit staircase that descends a few steps before entering a passage, hewn deep in the rock. After twenty metres, another door and another code give access to a vast space, hidden in the flank of the mountain. It is gently, beautifully lit and it has further passageways, galleries in fact, leading to further rooms. Music comes from somewhere hidden. Chopin is playing for now but later, on a month-long loop, other pleasures will follow.

This series of chambers and passages was originally a nuclear shelter, again typical of the region. Schmidt's agents acquired the site on his behalf some years before and, with the correct permissions gained, had the house built on it. All sign and memory of the shelter itself have now faded from memory and the property appears to have passed through two subsequent owners, making it easy for Schmidt to feign ignorance if the need arises. The original entrance to the shelter still exists, should any bureaucrat come snooping, but it is at the back of a cave outside and has been deeply filled with concrete. Schmidt's entrance through the wardrobe is new and off-record.

In the centre of the first room is a large and sturdy oak table, covered in soft green rubber. Schmidt places the brown paper package on it and with great care cuts the twine that surrounds it. Inside, having removed several layers of acid-free tissue paper and a pair of protective boards, he reaches the prize: a little-known but perfect Botticelli, oil on copper. It sits in a gilt frame, and even in this quiet light it glows as if alive. Recently liberated from a private collection in Rome, it is now his and his alone, and it will stay here, deep in the mountainside, forever. The temperature will never vary, nor will the humidity. It will live mostly in darkness until, for brief and carefully measured periods of time, it is exposed to light and the sight of Schmidt himself, and at such times it will spring instantly and perfectly to life.

He already has a space picked out for it, in a gallery that runs straight off the room in which it has been unwrapped. Schmidt takes it carefully through and hangs it, illuminated by a perfectly shaped rectangle of LED light. He returns to the first room and selects a bottle of Grande Année from a rack. It will be somewhat too warm, of course, but he cannot risk having a refrigerator in here: refrigerators pump out heat and might even have an effect on humidity, which simply would not do. He will suffer for his art.

Pouring himself a moderate glass, he returns to the Botticelli and proposes a toast to it. The subject matter is a saint, half-naked and muscled, with skin that has but one imperfection, which is the point at which the torso is pierced by a spear. Schmidt, in his rush of love and with the alcohol entering his system, reaches forward as if to touch the wound, as if to heal it, but he pulls his fingers short of the panel because this is how it must be. No touching, ever, however much his desires direct him otherwise. His relationship with these things of beauty is, and must always remain, chaste.

However lovely, this new addition is not quite the finest on the list of treasures in Schmidt's cave. Monet's *Waterloo Bridge, London* and *Charing Cross Bridge, London*. Raphael's *Portrait of a Young Man*. Caravaggio's *Nativity with St. Francis and St. Lawrence*. Works of astonishing rarity and value by Van Eyck, Matisse, Picasso, Michelangelo, Turner, Hokusai, Cézanne, Manet, and a host of others. Looted by the Nazis, stolen from homes and museums, abducted from the workshops of restorers, these pieces are all presumed lost or destroyed. The world does not suspect that they are all now in the immaculate and perpetual care of Schmidt, who was once the famous *W.G.* and whose inner world is filled with beauty.

After a few minutes, he returns to the house carrying the rest of the bottle, his half-empty glass and the paper and boards from the Botticelli. Lights are extinguished and doors are locked and his beauties return to their slumber.

He makes an omelette, eating it while sipping champagne. Then he sits in his favourite chair in front of the television and begins to watch a film. Almost dozing, he is disturbed by a knock at the door. Unexpected though it is, this can mean only one thing: *Concierge*.

On his doorstep, seen through a video-entry system, stands a man dressed in dark colours and wearing a hat, his back to the door. Schmidt presses a button and speaks.

"May I help you?" he says, taking his Glock carefully from a locked drawer and tucking it into his waistband.

The man turns to face the camera. It is not Lafarge, his "usual". Instead, a younger man's lightly bearded face shimmers in the spotlight that illuminates the step.

"*Concierge* for Herr Schmidt," he says flatly.

"Password?" replies Schmidt.

"Chiaroscuro Ondaatje Judenburg," the stranger answers.

"Mornington Cassiopeia Transvaal," Schmidt responds, pressing another button to open the door.

The young man steps into Schmidt's hallway, stamping his feet on the mat and reaching as if to remove his coat. Schmidt raises his hand to stop him.

"This is not acceptable to me," he says. "My next meeting was due with Lafarge in Zurich on 8 January. That is over one month from now. No one but Lafarge is authorized to visit me here. Kindly explain."

"Lafarge is dead," the young man says. His voice, slightly tinged with an Italian accent, seems dead too. "He fell during a job. My code is Vrony."

He takes off his hat and his hair, neatly tied into a ponytail, tumbles out like a skein of flax. Schmidt notices that his eyes are green. Vrony stands with his feet a little apart and smiles, the cold formality replaced by a sudden bolt of charm. This is not what Schmidt has come to expect.

"Take off your coat and come in," says Schmidt. "Here, let me help."

Over Vrony's shoulder Schmidt sees, through the door as he pushes it closed, that thick and unexpected snow has started to fall, the first of the season.

For reasons he cannot explain, Schmidt – dimly aware that he should be conducting their business in his study – lights the fire in the kitchen and offers Vrony coffee. Vrony accepts only water and sits, alert and upright, on the edge of his chair. He looks younger now that his coat is off. Not exactly thin, but slim in an athletic way. There is no age in his bones, no tiredness looking for release in a slump or a sigh.

"So," says Schmidt.

"So." Vrony sits for a moment, looking around as if for a prompt. "I am here to introduce myself as replacement for Lafarge. *Madame* thought it best. He . . . Lafarge and I worked on many jobs together. Possibly some of them for you, Herr Schmidt, though I would not have been told and would never ask."

"Some things, one should not ask," says Schmidt. "But I would like to know. How did Lafarge die? He worked for me over the course of many years, you know. I cannot say I knew him at all in terms of personal matters but, well, I came to respect him greatly. His abilities and his good sense. His advice on what was possible and what was wise. Was I fond of him? I cannot say I was not, despite our personal knowledge of each other being limited. So, I would like to know how he died and possibly if there is anything I might offer to *Madame* in the way of help for any . . . dependants he might have had?"

"He died quickly, very quickly, doing the thing he loved," Vrony replies slowly. "He fell from a ledge and he died immediately on impact. I . . ."

Schmidt notices the strangest thing. A hint of moisture at the corner of Vrony's eye. At first he thinks it best to ignore, but it quickly swells into a tear and begins to roll downward. This is very unexpected in an operative from *Concierge*.

"Excuse me," says Vrony. "Please forgive me, Herr Schmidt. This only happened yesterday and he . . . Lafarge and I, we were very close. We worked on many things together. He was my teacher and my friend. And . . . to answer your question, he had no dependants."

Schmidt stands to reach for a box of tissues and then pours a small glass of brandy, handing each to Vrony in turn. "I will ask no more," he says quietly. "But I am very sorry indeed to hear of this."

Vrony takes one sip of the brandy and then pushes it politely away. He takes the tissue and rubs his cheek quickly, once, and the tear is gone. He smiles.

"To business," he says. "*Madame* would like to inform you that the Titian job is not possible. She is not able to say why this might be but asks for your trust and understanding."

Schmidt has heard this before, has often wondered if this phrase should be taken to mean that the owner of the desired artwork is also a client of *Concierge*. There have been occasions when, later on, he has been informed that an impossibility has been transformed into a possibility. Some technical advance in the work of the thief, perhaps? Or possibly a client not renewing his *Concierge* subscription? For whatever reason, Schmidt knows that he will trust, even if he does not quite understand. He cannot have the Titian. It is quite a blow: he has already chosen a space for it.

"But there is good news too," Vrony goes on. "News worthy of . . . should I say, an enigmatic smile."

Schmidt's heart stops.

"It cannot be."

Vrony gives a simple nod before continuing.

"As you know, the authorized version of events is that Vincenzo Peruggia stole the *Mona Lisa* from the Louvre in 1911, keeping it hidden for two years whilst trying to find a way of returning it to Italy. And that around the same time, De Valfierno had also planned to steal the painting. But De Valfierno's plan was more ambitious: six forgeries already made by Chaudron would each be discreetly sold to private collectors such as yourself, the claim being made to each collector that they were the only one being offered the "original". Peruggia was eventually caught trying to sell the original to the Uffizi, and during the two-year period before the painting was recovered in this way, De Valfierno took his chance and deceptively sold each of his "originals". End of authorized version."

"And the unauthorized version?"

"No one ever tied these two stories together correctly," replies Vrony with a broad smile, before continuing. "Lafarge's last great discovery was that neither story is completely true. Peruggia *did* steal the painting, but he did so *for* De Valfierno – and only one *perfect* copy was made, after the theft, by Chaudron. The other six copies, made before the theft, were certainly superb but each, in its way, not quite *absolute*. It is the perfect copy that now hangs in the Louvre. The museum knows that they have a fake but, well, every face must be saved, and Chaudron's fake is so accomplished that the world has never known the truth: that the fake and the original were switched *before* the attempted sale to the Uffizi."

Vrony pauses and pulls the half-drunk brandy back towards him, draining it before he continues.

"Before you ask, I cannot tell you how Lafarge discovered this. Nor can I tell you where the item is now except to say that it is in Italy. The owner is a client of *Concierge* but he is very sick. He is burdened by the weight of this painting, a weight that he, his father and his grandfather carried all their lives. But he does not want to return it: rather, he wants to assure the financial security of his heirs, who do not know of its existence. In short, he is ready to sell, and he has asked us to find a suitable buyer."

There is no blood in Schmidt's face as he pours himself a large brandy. He is visibly shaking, in fact, and the brandy almost splashes down his chin as he drinks. The ultimate prize, the greatest ambition of his life as Schmidt, is finally within his grasp.

"I have two questions," he eventually says. "Price and provenance."

"Provenance you must decide for yourself," Vrony replies.

"Naturally, there is little documentation. We will arrange for you to view the piece. You must make up your own mind. We can offer no guarantees, though Lafarge was quite certain. He was to have brought you this news himself. He was looking forward to it."

"And price? What price could ever be put on the *Mona Lisa*?"

"As you would expect," says Vrony. "It will not be inexpensive."

"Hmmm," Schmidt replies, smiling. "Look. I would like to talk about this in more detail. Are you hungry? Would you like an omelette?"

While Schmidt prepares food, the men discuss plans. Schmidt will travel to Italy where, in the back of an armoured vehicle, he will be given time to examine and assess the picture. Then, all being as hoped, a deal will be struck. Vrony will, payment having been made, deliver the *Mona Lisa* to the place of Schmidt's choosing.

At one point, while he is sliding the omelette onto a plate, Schmidt looks across the kitchen towards Vrony, who smiles. He smiles in imitation of the *Mona Lisa* herself. And then he laughs. This is so unexpected, so not in the mould of Lafarge or of *Concierge*, that Schmidt suffers a moment of confusion: he feels for a moment that he is with a friend rather than a contractor and, with his already heightened emotions, he finds the moment hard to bear. This has not happened for a very long time, this moment of contact, this moment of humanity, so, having deposited the omelette in front of Vrony, he excuses himself from the room to gather his thoughts.

Soon enough, he returns.

"The snow has come down hard outside. Do you have winter tyres or chains?"

"No," replies Vrony. "The forecast was for rain."

"You had better stay the night here. It is early season snow, quite unexpected, and the roads will be impassable until morning – the ploughs will not be up here until then. They will concentrate on the main roads."

"But *Madame* . . ."

"*Madame* will understand. I will explain that short of sleeping in the car, you had no option – and that I insisted you be my guest. Please. You will stay."

Schmidt is surprised at how he and the young man fall to drinking. There is a certain sense of celebration, with toasts made to the *Mona Lisa* – and of sadness, with toasts drunk to Lafarge. The boy, as Schmidt quickly comes to think of him, has none of Lafarge's reserve. He is friendly, he smiles, he is witty. At first this feels subtly wrong: *Concierge* in general and Lafarge in particular have always been resolutely businesslike. Polite, superbly well-informed and capable, but professional rather than personal. For many years, this has suited Schmidt very well, being perfectly attuned to his mood and his single-minded focus. Vrony, by comparison, is a person such as Schmidt has not encountered, but who is quickly recognizable to W.G. He is handsome, he is young, he is energetic and charming and alive. He is Schmidt's first guest in this house and he is increasingly seen, through the appreciative eyes of age and brandy, as a marvel and a pleasure.

At midnight, Schmidt shows the boy to a hitherto unused guest room next to his own. He makes up the bed and supplies the bathroom with toothbrush and paste, with soap and towels. He also offers pyjamas, which are declined. And then he leaves, allowing Vrony to undress in privacy.

Schmidt does not sleep. Not a wink. He lies awake all night, caught between the rigours of Schmidt and the appetites of W.G. He sweats and turns and frets and burns with confusion and, yes, with desire. He becomes, in his own estimation, quite unprofessional in his feelings.

At dawn, which comes quite late at this time of year in the valley, he gets up and peeps through the boy's bedroom door to see if he is awake. No. He lies with his hair loose now, curled upon the pillow, his body covered only by a sheet – the room is hot – and his outline is clearly visible beneath the cloth. Quietly, Schmidt closes the door and goes to the downstairs bedroom, letting himself through security in order to view his collection. But in the cool of the rooms and passageways, he finds no pleasure: the lustre of the oils seems dull after the sight of his sleeping guest, and the beauty of the subjects seems flat and unreal in comparison. An old hunger is returning, edging out the new, but Schmidt knows, for the first time in many years, that in life there are some things he must not, and very likely cannot, have.

He closes the gun cabinet and heads for the kitchen, makes coffee and takes it upstairs. Vrony is half awake now and looks gratefully towards the steaming mug, hugging the sheet to him in a yawn as he does so. There is a lazy erection outlined by the fabric and Vrony's eyes follow Schmidt's to it.

In this frozen moment Schmidt, who is so close to reaching forward, waits a second too long until whatever chance he might have hoped for is gone. Vrony sits up, holding the bedclothes to his chest and hiding his groin from view.

"I had better be going soon," he says, gently. "*Madame* will be expecting me to check in."

Part III

Over the next months, Schmidt speaks to Vrony on the telephone from time to time but finds it impossible to meet him in person. The Italian owner of the *Mona Lisa* is too sick to be contacted, then he is too well, too full of life, to progress the transaction. There are any number of obstacles, small and large, all temporary of course, in the way of the new acquisition. At first Schmidt is full of energy: he plans to employ Vrony more than he ever did Lafarge, finding works to acquire at a rate that will create opportunities for him to visit. Schmidt chooses low-hanging fruit, of course, items that are relatively easy to steal and which will put the boy in the way of no real harm: a small but moderately significant Picasso; a Da Vinci cartoon; some exquisite Dutch miniatures; a Fragonard of indifferent quality and dubious provenance. Each will need to be briefed and planned and received, but on each occasion *Madame* regretfully informs him that Vrony is not available, or that the acquisition of the artwork in question is for one reason or another "not possible for the moment".

Schmidt now knows himself to be in both love and lust. Absence has made his heart not simply fonder, but fixated and frustrated, and his collection gives him little pleasure compared to that he imagines he would draw from even the sight of Vrony. But the impermeability of *Concierge* remains absolute. Slowly, he falls into an old and familiar despair.

Suddenly, in August, Vrony sends a message. The "Italian deal" is on and Vrony, being the only *Concierge* operative known to the owner of the *Mona Lisa* aside from the dead Lafarge, is to be present at the viewing.

They meet on a plain in Tuscany, early one morning. The armoured vehicle, which looks from the outside to belong to a delivery company, is air-conditioned, comfortable and well lit. At first Schmidt barely has eyes for the *Mona Lisa* because here, finally, is Vrony.

Schmidt has often remarked to himself that the first viewing of a work of art is never sufficient to penetrate its depths. Certain nuances of technique, certain textures and tones and details, cannot be quickly taken in; symbols and metaphors are missed or misinterpreted, meaning is elusive. Distance is required – an absence of the thing itself from view, in order that it might, when seen again, reveal more. In order to appreciate great beauty in full, one must first look away. And so he finds it with Vrony: there is a tiny mole below his right eye, overlooked on their first meeting; his chin is squarer than Schmidt remembers it; he is a little taller and more well-built across the shoulders. His hair is shorter and more businesslike now, forming tight waves that frame his face like that of a Roman statue. He seems to have aged, a tiny bit, more in attitude than in appearance; there is a new assurance to him, a gravity, perhaps.

Schmidt realizes that he must be seen to give his attention to the great painting in front of him, so with Vrony, the subject of many a stolen glance, sitting quietly at his side, he spends over two hours examining the image. In the end, he can find no reason to doubt its authenticity but he is not yet prepared to admit this.

"I cannot yet be quite certain," he says to Vrony. "I need to digest what I have seen and then I need to see it again, tomorrow. After that I will be able to decide."

"Herr Schmidt," replies Vrony, "with respect we simply cannot do that. The painting must be returned to the secure keeping of its owner tonight and that place is far from here. Neither the owner nor *Madame* would countenance any deviation from this. I wish it were otherwise but it cannot be done."

Schmidt sighs and appears to be thoughtful, but in fact his plan has been clear for the past hour or so.

"This is my suggestion," he says, giving the impression that he is thinking it through as he speaks. "I will, in the next hour, arrange the transfer of the agreed sum, via the usual route, to arrive today into the hands of *Madame*. I trust her to hold it in escrow. The painting will remain in the lorry overnight, guarded by your people. If anything happens to it then *Madame* is authorized to take her fee from the sum so deposited and to remit the balance to your counterparty. This is the only option. If it cannot be agreed I will, regretfully, be forced to walk away. This is both the most famous and most famously forged painting in the world and I need, I insist on having, more time."

Schmidt attempts to fix Vrony with an icy glare but, aware that the ice will rapidly melt, he looks away and awaits a response. Vrony does not reply for a few moments and then, very slowly, he reaches for the exit-code pad.

"Herr Schmidt," he says, a click of heels in his voice, "if you will be pleased to wait in your car for a few minutes I will speak to *Madame*."

Thus it is arranged. The lorry will be taken to a secure warehouse overnight and driven to a new meeting place the following morning. A reservation is made for Schmidt at a discreet local hotel, nothing fancy but comfortable and with reputedly excellent food, and it is announced that Vrony will remain overnight in the lorry.

This last obstacle must be overcome. "I cannot have that," says Schmidt. "The humidity from your breath and sweat."

"But the vehicle is air-conditioned and humidity-controlled. We were in it for two hours or more today, you were not concerned then."

"That is precisely why I am concerned," says Schmidt. "I felt the moisture rising in that time. I am very sensitive to it. The system is good but not good enough. This was one of the reasons for my requiring us to continue tomorrow, to allow the air in the lorry to be fully filtered, replaced and dehumidified. You are aware that the *Mona Lisa* is painted on a poplar panel which is already warped and slightly cracked as a result of changes in humidity over the years. Please trust me."

"But *Madame* . . ." Vrony's voice trails off. He looks at his shoes, a diffident boy once more.

"Yes?"

"*Madame* was not happy, at all, last time. When I stayed as a guest in your home. It is . . . *verboten.*"

"You will not be staying at my house and for all *Madame* knows, not that it should concern her at all, we will not be in the same hotel. Again, I am sorry to say that I must insist. As you know, the customer is always right. Besides," he lies, "I consider you to be almost as knowledgeable as Lafarge. He taught you well. I need the help of another qualified head with which to consider the authenticity of the painting."

"I work for *Concierge,*" replies Vrony. "It is in our interests that you decide to purchase the painting. You cannot consider me impartial."

"Then you must act as Advocate, and I as Prosecutor. It seems a sensible solution. Now go! Make a reservation at the hotel. We will dine separately just to be sure and meet later, in my room."

Schmidt eats quickly that evening, drinking one glass from the bottle of Montepulciano he has ordered. As he gets up to leave, he catches Vrony's eye across the room then departs, taking the bottle with him. Fifteen minutes later, there is a knock at his door.

What follows is torture for Schmidt. Vrony retains his new-found formality throughout: he is polite and restrained, reasoned rather than passionate in his arguments, but the smile that Schmidt craves has gone, completely. Worst of all is that Vrony seems always to be examining Schmidt's chin, ear, mouth or nose, but nothing will provoke him to make full eye contact – nor will he accept any wine.

"It must be *Madame*," thinks Schmidt. "She has dressed him down, called him to order. He is no longer allowed to be himself."

Eventually, he can bear it no longer.

"Vrony," he says. "I must ask you a delicate question. *Madame* has clearly had words with you about the etiquette of overfamiliarity but . . . please, be your own man for a while. I greatly appreciate your skills, your diplomacy, your discretion, but honestly I felt more comfortable with you the first time we met. It is easier to trust a person rather than an operative. Please," he adds, reaching for the bottle, "trust me. Now have some wine and relax."

But Vrony does not take any wine. "How do you know that this has anything to do with *Madame*?" he asks, his tone almost disdainful. "In fact, it does not. It is not you that I do not trust, Herr Schmidt. Nor is it familiarity itself." He looks around the room, then down at the floor, and finally he mutters, as if to himself, "It's probably more that I don't trust myself."

With this unfathomable comment Vrony rises suddenly and excuses himself, claiming tiredness and the need for an early start, but he turns as he is leaving the room, smiles the long-desired smile and says, "Good night. And please forgive me; I may not be cut out for this job."

That night, for the second time after an evening spent in the company of Vrony, Schmidt finds it difficult to sleep. The room is warm and, lying in his bed with the window ajar, he turns and sweats and thinks, round and round, about what Vrony can have meant. Eventually drowsiness comes, followed by a restless and dream-filled slumber.

Suddenly he is awake. A slight sound has alerted him that someone is in his room. He reaches instinctively for his Glock, but it isn't there and so he lies frozen with fear, trying to discern threat from shadow.

"Don't worry, it's me, Vrony. Shhh. Don't turn on the light."

Schmidt stares into the incomplete darkness. He can just make out the shape of a man in the chair near the bed, beside the open window, but he cannot tell what he is wearing. He sits up and Vrony stands quickly and walks over, perching on the side of the bed. Schmidt smells alcohol. Suddenly, unexpectedly, miraculously, Vrony takes his hand.

"You asked me a delicate question earlier," says Vrony. "And I answered, honestly. Will you answer me one in return?"

"Of course. Anything. Ask me anything you like."

"These paintings," says Vrony, "I don't want to ask where you keep them but I would like to know what will happen to them. Eventually. When . . ."

"When I die, you mean?" answers Schmidt.

"Yes. When you die."

"They will be kept somewhere safe, for ever."

"Will people be able to see them?"

"No," says Schmidt. "Sadly, if people were able to see them they would by definition not be safe in perpetuity. The two things are incompatible. Sad, but true."

"Does it matter if they exist at all, when no one can ever see them?" asks Vrony.

"Yes. Yes it does."

"Ah, that great question of philosophy!" Vrony replies with a slight slur. "Berkeley, Schrödinger, Bohr and Einstein. The tree that falls in the forest, the invisible moon. I see it, I don't see it. It exists, it doesn't exist. Which? Which is it, Herr Schmidt?"

Without waiting for a reply, Vrony leans forward, takes Schmidt by the shoulders and kisses him firmly in the middle of his forehead. Then he stands and leaves the room.

The next morning the two men check out of the hotel separately and, in their separate vehicles, travel to the new rendezvous. Wordlessly, they enter the lorry. Vrony looks tired, thinks Schmidt: the air seems to have gone out of him and he seems slow, distracted, a little slumped.

Schmidt makes a great show of rechecking the painting, examining the surface of the panel with an LED torch and a loupe, from every imaginable angle, referring what he sees against his notes: the faintest signs of an acid attack by a lunatic; the tiny scar where a rock was thrown in protest – the signs of the *Mona Lisa*'s life post her 1913 return that only an expert could detect. All this expertise is deployed for show, however: he no longer cares if this is the genuine *Mona Lisa* or not, though by now he is quite sure that it is.

After a while he runs out of things to scrutinize and he turns to Vrony. He is about to speak, to ask about their conversation (or was it merely a dream?) in the dead of night, but Vrony makes a tiny gesture to indicate that the interior of the vehicle is monitored.

"Have you decided, Herr Schmidt?" he asks, his formality fully returned.

"I have. I'll take it. When can you deliver?"

Later, outside the lorry, Schmidt is not able to catch Vrony alone before he leaves. There is security discreetly present and the lorry driver hovers. They part without further unguarded words but again, as Vrony gets into his car, he turns to Schmidt and smiles. This time it is not a warm and open smile but a faint, distant, beatific one – a Renaissance crucifixion of a smile, as if looking to God in anticipation of deliverance from pain.

Schmidt knows at this moment that Vrony is lost to him. He would throw a thousand *Mona Lisas* on the fire for this not to be true, but he knows that it is and he feels as if his heart will break.

Part IV

There is much to be arranged. The door to the downstairs bedroom is already reinforced but the bars on the windows must be checked and checked again. Shackles need to be installed, attached to chains long enough to reach the bathroom but not quite as far as the door. They also need to be positioned so that they cannot be seen when passing casually through the room. The bathroom is internal, backing into the hill on one side and onto further rooms on the others. Again, the integrity of those walls must be assured and all ventilation ducts examined to ensure that they cannot be used for escape. Nothing must be overlooked. Schmidt will be having a friend to stay for quite some time, and his guest must be comfortable yet absolutely secure. Perhaps some sedatives might be useful, at first?

The great day arrives. Schmidt is as nervous as a boy before his first date. He dresses, for the first time in years, in jeans – he still has a fine figure – and puts on a new and beautiful shirt. Comfortable but elegant loafers, a touch of cologne. The mirror, several times. Dust off the shoes. Shirt tucked, untucked and re-tucked. The second hand on his Patek ticks; the minute hand crawls at taunting pace.

The doorbell.

"*Concierge* for Herr Schmidt."

It is not Vrony, that voice, that unpleasant face and figure on the porch revealed through the video system. Instead, a squat, toad-like man waits outside, clutching a parcel.

"Where is Vrony?" barks Schmidt. "This was supposed to be delivered by Vrony."

"Vrony is not available. *Madame* begs your understanding."

Schmidt wants to scream, "Fuck *Madame*. Fuck her! I am the client and I was promised Vrony. I want VRONY!" but instead he says, flatly and in sure defeat, "Password?"

The *Concierge* man quickly gone, Schmidt feels himself to be in a daze. He takes the package through the downstairs bedroom and automatically enters the series of codes required to gain access to his system of caves. The sounds of *Tosca* seep from the walls as he carries the *Mona Lisa* down the long corridor to the easel he has readied for her, lit by a single spot, and undresses her before hoisting her up before him and allowing her to rest. He hates her. Hates her mocking smile, hates her complacent certainty, hates what she has cost him and how utterly futile she has turned out to be. He is glad that she will sit here, for ever, unseen and giving pleasure to no one. He will turn the music off later: she will be interred in silence.

Unbearably angry, needing some form of release, he finds himself craving, for the first time in years, a cigarette. Yes! A cigarette. The bitch *Mona Lisa* has no bulletproof glass over her, no attendants, no smoke alarms. He is going to blow smoke in her smug face. He is going to go to the kitchen, find that stale packet of Winstons and blow smoke right into her unprotected face.

Just as he locates the pack, a headlight strafes the kitchen ceiling. It is a matter of seconds before the doorbell rings.

The video screen shows, clearly, Vrony. No password required, the door is open, and Vrony rushes in, bedraggled and excitable. He is clutching a bottle of champagne but he puts it down and grabs Schmidt, hugging him while kicking the door closed behind him.

"I thought you were 'unavailable', Vrony!"

"Well, here I am! I was on a job, quite a rough one, then I had to rush to get here. Sorry for the state I'm in, but I had to be here with you – had to share this moment with you. Where is she? Can I see her?"

And in this moment of insane pleasure Schmidt says, "Yes, follow me."

The bedroom passes in a blur. The passage beyond is a rushing tunnel of musical echoes and suddenly, there, on the easel, is the most famous face in the world.

Before Schmidt has the slightest chance to consider what will happen next, whether Vrony's presence is a sign of love or merely the excited success of a young art thief reaching his peak before his prime, before he has given any thought to the question of the planned captivity of this most beautiful of things, Vrony grabs him and holds him close, kissing him on the forehead once more, held in the tightest imaginable embrace.

Schmidt does not realize that the bottle is still in his beloved's gloved hand – does not notice when one of the embracing arms breaks briefly free, and does not hear the rush of the bottle towards his head. His last moments of consciousness are spent in a state of bliss.

Breaking News: 1 November 2015
Smiling Lady Found at Scene of Crime

In a bizarre twist to the long-running and dramatic story of Leonardo da Vinci's *Mona Lisa*, police in the Swiss canton of Bern received last week an anonymous email leading them to a modest and secluded house in a valley near the city of Bern itself. There, they found the body of local man Vassily Schmidt lying in a vast, decommissioned nuclear shelter behind the house. He had been killed by a blow to the head delivered by an unknown assassin; his lair contained a large number of long-lost works by some of the world's greatest artists, the most famous of which appeared at first to be the *Mona Lisa*. Experts at the Louvre have examined the painting and declared it to be "a very fine copy", probably by the early twentieth-century forger Yves Chaudron. This was carefully compared to the original, which has been temporarily removed from the gallery for the execution of previously scheduled restoration work. The head of the museum's Department of Restorations has told the BBC that he hopes the restored painting will be "brighter, fresher and more splendid than at any time since it was first acquired". The Louvre has also suggested that if no owner can be traced, the "extremely accurate" forgery should be given to the *Galleria degli Uffizi* in Florence as a gesture of thanks to the museum for having alerted the Louvre to an attempted sale of the original, subsequent to a theft, in 1911.

It is believed that this Swiss "Aladdin's Cave" also contained long-missing works by Caravaggio, Michelangelo, Manet, Monet, Picasso, Raphael, Van Eyck and others, though sources are currently unclear as to the full extent of the haul. Some of the paintings are on the "wanted" list of insurers worldwide, and delicate negotiations with the original owners of the works are expected to take many months.

A spokesman for the Swiss Federal Department of Justice and Police told our correspondent that the stolen works were in "pristine" condition, having been kept in an environment that "matches or exceeds the standards provided by the finest museums in the world". He added that no video-surveillance material was found on the property and that feeds from an extensive network of cameras were routed directly into the "dark net", to a destination that cannot be traced.

The anonymous email was also routed via the dark net and therefore untraceable. Aside from the information leading police to the haul, it is believed that the sender made only one further comment: "Only I could let the cat out of the box."

Meanwhile, the famously enigmatic *Mona Lisa* remains the only witness to a crime that might prove impossible to solve. She's still smiling after all these years, and we may never know why.

The Gang
Sebastian Beaumont

———

My name is David. I didn't get my first taste of the gay scene until 1985, when I was eighteen. I'd been yearning to see what it was like for a couple of years before that, but I happen to be blessed (or cursed, depending on how you look at it) with extremely youthful looks. My peers at school called me "Billy" (as in Billy the Kid), which I didn't really mind, or "baby face", which I did. In my last year, I was still only five foot two and could easily pass for fourteen if I wore my old shorts.

On my eighteenth birthday, I ventured out to a bar – The Aquarium – down near Brighton seafront. I was supposed to be doing last-minute revision for my A-levels, but had taken an evening off one Wednesday to come down from Haywards Heath, on the pretext of seeing my older sister. She was working as a secretary at American Express at the time and was living in a flat up by that pub that used be a morgue. I walked down from her place to The Aquarium and was nervous as hell, and felt as young as I looked.

I wandered round the block more times than I care to admit before I summoned the courage to open the door and go in. I had, however, rehearsed the moment well. There were to be no timid requests for lemonade from me. I walked straight up to the bar and, in my best "authoritative prefect" voice, asked for a pint of lager.

The two other men at the bar turned to look at me. The barman smirked in disbelief and said, "Pardon?"

I pulled out my passport and slapped it on the bar and said, "I'm eighteen. A pint of lager, please."

The barman studied the passport for a while, then laughed. "Happy birthday," he said and pulled me a pint.

I took the beer and went to stand in a corner, where I kept sipping it in that neurotic way that people have when they are nervous and want something to do with their hands. I guess you can imagine that for someone of my stature (slim as well as short) a pint of lager is, proportionally, far more than it would be for most men, and by the time I'd finished it I was feeling halfway drunk. I leaned against the wall and watched the others in the bar as they chatted. There weren't many there – half a dozen or so. It was only eight o'clock, after all, and I hadn't yet understood that gay men go out later in the evening than straight people. All but one of the men I saw in that bar had moustaches. I didn't know at the time that I had stumbled across *that kind* of pub, and assumed that all gay men wore moustaches.

I left after only twenty minutes, without talking to anyone, and took the train home, feeling decidedly affected by the alcohol. But I was also affected by the atmosphere – by that intense *frisson* that accompanies our first experience of seeing men together like that, of seeing the casual way in which a man can lean towards another and say something quietly, with an utterly assured intimacy and carelessness – and I knew, then, I *knew* that I had experienced something that would change me for ever.

The next few weeks were taken up with my exams, which went OK-*ish*. After they were over – on the day I left school, in fact – I stopped shaving my upper lip. It took about a week before anyone noticed. My mother leaned over, at breakfast one morning, and pointed at my lip and said, "What's *that*?" as though it might have been some strange fungal growth. I think I blushed. In fact, I'm sure I did. But I knew better than to say anything and remained silent. My brother, three years younger than me and already taller, grinned and said, "I think it's supposed to be a moustache, Mum." My dad grunted and looked disdainful. My thirteen-year-old sister, both proud and self-conscious of her incipient breasts, seemed even more embarrassed than I was at the mention of a secondary sexual characteristic.

My moustache continued its imperceptible growth, and at the

end of the following week we went away to East Anglia for our annual holiday – a fortnight of windy walks and home cooking with my uncle and aunt at their cottage near Hunstanton. I got into that terrible cycle of looking at my lip every morning in the mirror and not seeing any difference. Still, by the time we got back, my moustache was nearly four weeks old and, with the aid of a little of my mother's mascara, looked almost passable.

I ventured out to The Aquarium once more, on a Friday evening at around nine-thirty – a much more sensible time. I'd arranged to stay the night with my sister and, when I told her I wanted to go out on my own, she smiled conspiratorially and slipped a fiver into my pocket and said, "Have fun."

This time I walked straight into the bar and, not wanting to make the same mistake twice, ordered a half-pint of lager (I never drank whole pints after that). I was served by a different barman that evening and had to go through the whole passport business again before he would serve me. There were more people there that evening and I drew plenty of stares as I stood on my own, sipping my beer, catching my reflection every now and then in the metal edging of the cigarette machine. I thought I looked like some kind of preppy twelve-year-old wearing a stick-on moustache. But I was incredibly proud of it so I didn't care.

After a while, a man sauntered over to me and said hello.

"I saw that business with the passport," he said. "I expect it's a real pain sometimes – to look so young."

"Yes," I replied.

"I used to be like that, too," he told me. "I hated it. I never had the nous to use proper ID. When I was eighteen I was always getting chucked out of pubs for under-age drinking, whilst other boys who couldn't have been more than fifteen looked on. It *is* a pain, now, but you'll think of it as an advantage in a few years' time, believe me. I'm thirty-five, though under most circumstances I don't admit to more than twenty-seven."

I held out my hand.

"I'm David," I said.

"Please," the man smiled, "don't be so formal. I'm Mark. I'm waiting for The Gang. There's nothing quite so desolate as hanging around in a bar on your own when you want company, is there? I'll introduce you around when the boys turn up – if you want."

So that was how I met The Gang. They were loud, jokey, sexy and almost all moustached. I seemed to strike a chord somewhere, because they took to me immediately. They did all those things that I would have taken offence at if they had been done by other people – they patted me on the head, cuddled me as though I was a toy, teased me and joked about my height and extreme youth. They got away with it because it was all done with affection. That was the great part of it. They teased me, but they teased each other, too, about everything – appearance, domestic habits, sexual tastes . . . No one was let off, and so we all laughed together.

They called me the Half-pint Clone and I loved it. I loved it, but there was something sad about it all too, because one of the reasons I'd come out to this bar was so that I could find someone with whom to lose my virginity, and although they liked me, they didn't want to sleep with me. They stood around and laughed, and talked about the sex they'd been having, and I listened, and I longed.

I mentioned this to Mark, who seemed the most approachable member of The Gang, and I remember his sympathetic look as I stammered out my wistful yearning to him, and he said, "You should find someone your own age for that, David, or maybe someone older who's into younger guys. It's not really our scene. If you went to the right place, and met the right people, you'd have more offers than you could deal with. If this was five years ago, rather than now, I'd suggest you went down to the bushes for a hearty, breathless encounter in the moonlight. But you must have heard about this thing, this *disease*? It's changing everything."

His words had a curious, echoing ring to them, and I later found out that that was the night the first member of The Gang was diagnosed as unwell – his name was Joe and he was a travel agent from Hove who held the kind of parties that we'll never see again. I went to one or two, but latterly they became so tinged with absence that it was hard to dance with a smile.

I met The Gang down at The Aquarium every Friday night that first summer and, when I started at Sussex University, even more often than that. They bought me my half pints, took me to their parties, made me laugh. They lectured me on safe sex, too. In those days, everything was potentially unsafe – there was even a debate about kissing.

It was at around that time that I met Gareth. He was only five foot five and so I didn't feel quite so small when I was with him. He was dark, with plaintive dog-like eyes and a straight mouth that made him look as though he was permanently being taken aback. His swarthy looks complemented my paler complexion and together we were light and shade, somehow. He had sure hands, too, and a gestural openness that made me trust him. He was in his third year of a media course, whilst I was doing computer studies and playing around with early ideas of artificial intelligence. We met at a Gay Soc evening and went out for a drink afterwards, each admitting after our third beer that we were virgins and worried way beyond rational explanation about the potential deadliness of sex. We skirted the subject of doing it with each other for some time and, after a month or two of scheduling and rescheduling the event, we finally managed a hesitant mutual masturbation, after which we fastidiously and warily cleaned up our own – virginal and therefore untainted – bodily fluids.

We became boyfriends. I felt that I might be falling in love with him, though it was hard to tell. I had intense flashes of tenderness for him, and I enjoyed his company, so I *assumed* that it was love. We slept together most nights and, because I was so relieved to have lost my virginity, I didn't question the restricted nature of our super-safe sexual repertoire – which in those first few months meant basically tossing each other off.

I removed my moustache then, because I realized it made me

appear ridiculous. Also, I'd found out that it wasn't the ubiquitous sign of homosexuality that I'd first imagined it to be. So I became clean-shaven once more and went back to looking like a fourteen-year-old – well, perhaps fifteen by then. At the end of the year, Gareth graduated and found a job in a PR firm in Brighton. He took a mortgage out on a flat and persuaded me to move in with him. I grew another inch that year, which strangely seemed to make all the difference.

Setting up home together seemed so adult and final. I loved feeling secure and wanted and *enveloped* by my new domestic life. Gareth turned out to be a habitual television watcher, which didn't bother me at first. Sitting watching TV with my lover had been one of my "what life will be like one day" fantasies that I'd had when I was a teenager. But I can only watch so much television and, if it hadn't been for my regular socializing with The Gang, I would have become bored. My life settled into a comfortable routine where Gareth fulfilled most of my needs and The Gang provided that all-important outside influence.

Gradually, more and more sexual acts became passed as safe by HIV experts, but Gareth remained steadfastly unversatile. He was the only lover I'd ever had, and vice versa, so you'd think that we'd have been happy doing *everything* to each other. But he didn't trust me, not deep down, which I found painful. He didn't trust me because of The Gang, with whom he refused to socialize. He avoided them as much as possible, though we often bumped into one or another of them in the street and I would talk to whomever it was, or go for coffee somewhere and sit around gossiping, whilst Gareth sat silently, smiling one of his "I'm not really interested" smiles.

When I met The Gang for drinks, I went on my own. When I went to their parties (which I did less and less frequently), I also went alone. Later on, especially when I began to visit them in hospital, Gareth would treat me as though I was infected myself. I was always confused about this side of his personality because in other respects he was open, trusting, generous and affectionate. He clearly loved me, and was happy that I was with him, and pleased that my course was going well. But there was this one area in our lives that gave rise to conflict. Sex.

I had always wanted to take his penis into my mouth (I had always wanted to be fucked by him, if I'm honest, but *that* was out of the question). It was one of my fantasies, to give a really good blow job, but Gareth couldn't bring himself, even after we'd been together a couple of years, to let me do that. I once persuaded him to put a flavoured condom on, but at the approach of my lips, he sort of shuddered and pushed me away, his Adam's apple jittering up and down as though he was desperately trying to swallow a dry biscuit. I began to realize, belatedly, that he was suffering from a severe case of Aids panic. But I didn't press the point. At least we were having sex of a kind and, whatever else may have been true, I never had to bother about whether or not I was putting myself at risk.

I began to observe Gareth's responses around the whole area of sex and became aware that he was actually *unable* to make love to me on the days that I'd been to the hospital to visit a member of The Gang. This was crazy, but even a peripheral mention of the subject would send Gareth into a weird anxiety in which he would actually thrust out his hands as though warding off a physical presence. And so I decided to lie whenever I could, and go to the hospital on the sly.

At one point, there were three members of The Gang in Ward 6 at the same time and it would sometimes get so that it was one big party, with all of us laughing and joking and making fun of the nurses and sneaking dirty videos in, and the odd beer, too. And one day, when I was sitting with Mark in the kitchen area and laughing so hard I thought I was going to be sick, I thought to myself, *They've had so much fun!*

Of course, laughter only took up a part of this time. There was all the other stuff that goes with illness, too. It was so hard to watch it happen, sometimes, especially when, in the middle of something hilarious, I would be hit by the thought that it was all so unfair.

I hated the funerals. Gareth never came with me to any of them. Not one. He was sympathetic in his way, I know, but just to think of that particular disease made him go into a still, silent area of dread, and there is no greater reminder of illness than death. So, he never saw the solidarity with which The Gang dwindled. He never saw the brave laughter, the sudden tears, the overwhelming sorrow of it all, and because he didn't see it, he didn't know how to give me the sympathy I needed.

I graduated from university in 1988 with a good degree. I could have chased money up to London, or abroad, but I chose instead to work with a small, personal company in Brighton that did not pay well, by industry standards, but which didn't demand long hours and which allowed me to stay on with Gareth. We sold the flat and bought a little house between Western Road and the sea, and moved in on 5 November that year.

In almost all respects, my life was going well. My family accepted us. My job was gay-friendly. The work I was doing was interesting. I had been with Gareth for nearly three years. I should have been content. But The Gang had decreased to only seven by then, and Gareth still treated my sperm as though it was radioactive.

I knew our relationship was dull, no matter how safe. But that was my fault, too. In saying that Gareth was the one who suffered from Aids panic, I'm not trying to imply that I was in some way nonchalant about it. I watched my friends succumb to this terrible illness and it made me shudder inside to realize that it was only a quirk of timing that was preventing me from following suit. It gave me a sense of responsibility for myself. If there was one thing I could learn from The Gang, it should be how to survive. That's why Gareth was, in many ways, the perfect haven. OK, so what if our life together was dull? Who said survival was going to be fun? Also, it was seductively easy to allow our life together to continue as it was, rather than make an effort to do anything about it. I was spending a lot of energy, that first winter in our house, just getting used to my new job. I kept looking on the plus side of things: I was in a town that I loved; Gareth and I were getting our home organized. And when I felt bored or restricted, I could always go out with The Gang.

It was all self-perpetuating and easy and managed to keep me going, without question, for a further two years.

Gareth came to accept, in his own limited way, my nights out without him. That is to say, we'd agreed not to talk about them, so I had to keep my wonderful times to myself, as well as my sad times, and gradually this came to seem to be for the best. Not sharing these things with Gareth made them seem precious to me, somehow, and I hoarded my happy memories, and nursed my sorrows as best I could. I would come in from the pub, or a party, or just a quiet night in watching a film and drinking tea, and he would be asleep in bed with the duvet pulled tightly to his cheek, and I would hug him briefly and he would smile and kiss me without really waking.

In January 1991, five-and-a-half years after I met him, Mark went into hospital. He was the last member of The Gang alive by then and it was the most extraordinary experience for me. He was the first member of The Gang that I'd met, he was my closest friend, and even when the other members succumbed to illness, I still never expected Mark to get It. I can't think why, now.

When I visited him, there was no lively group to laugh with him, no one to make black jokes about his symptoms, no one to make the ward into one great house party. There was just me. He smiled often when I saw him, and held my hand, and, towards the end, he whispered to me, "You've grown up, you know. You look nearly adult now. Actually, I quite fancy you – at last."

I was twenty-three.

That night I cried in front of Gareth – for the first time, I am ashamed to say. He hugged me and told me that he loved me and he said what a relief it was that it would all be over soon.

I asked him what he meant.

"This blight," Gareth said, "this blight of illness that has affected you ever since we met. At last, it is almost finished."

I couldn't believe that he could say those words. As he continued to speak, I realized that all these years, all this time, he had seen The

Gang as a terrible imposition on our life together, and somewhere in his mind – not consciously perhaps – he had been ticking them off as they died, making the assumption that when they were gone he would finally have me to himself.

This made me go into a kind of shock that I had never experienced before. It was a sort of calm numbness that allowed me to act as if nothing was wrong. I developed a habit of testing Gareth out, by talking about The Gang in the past tense, and I noticed a kind of smugness in him that I found hateful. He seemed to be saying "At last!" under his breath whenever my friends were mentioned, and I felt the great, smothering cloak of his dullness closing around me, getting more and more suffocating every day. It was only then that I fully realized what a compensation The Gang had been – how they'd made my life with Gareth bearable because they'd provided such vibrant relief from it. Gareth didn't notice this change in me, and nor did my work colleagues. Nor, it seemed, did Mark when I visited him in hospital. It seemed impossible that I could feel so changed inside without people noticing.

I managed to continue to make love to Gareth, in our half-hearted way; I managed to cook when it was my turn; to eat; to sleep. I also managed to hold Mark's hand when I sat beside him on his bed in Ward 6, and to smile and laugh with him.

The day before he died, he said, "At least you've survived, David. I'm so pleased you've been spared all of this. You have a lover. I so envy you your future."

And I looked at him and thought, *The only life I've EVER experienced, the only emotion that I have felt that has been truly worthwhile, has been experienced with YOU and with the rest of The Gang.*

"What am I going to do without you?" I mumbled, and he squeezed my hand, and cried when I cried, and managed to make me smile before I left. And when I went back to the hospital the next day, he had died.

The funeral was well attended by family and friends. The only thing I could think of during the short service was that Mark had said he envied me. Me! I was the one who'd scuttled into a relationship out of fear of illness. I was the one who was so fettered by inhibition that I refused to let myself go in anything like the fearless way The Gang had – experiencing only through them, rather than with them. I was the one who'd never *lived*. I was too busy protecting this future of mine that Mark envied so much; too busy not doing things, so that I never really had a present, let alone a future. And the future was beginning to look frighteningly bleak and empty without The Gang around to give it emotional depth. OK, there had been too much sorrow along with the fun, but there had been love as well, in abundance. In everything The Gang did, and felt, and expressed, there was an intensity that gave it meaning.

I walked home from Mark's funeral that afternoon quiet inside, and calm. But no longer numb. Gareth was there when I got back. He was cooking dinner and he couldn't disguise the relief he felt that The Gang were gone. He hugged me briefly – a moment of dispassionate human contact.

"It's over," he sighed.

I stood in the doorway and watched him cooking, watched the calm sureness of his movements – the utter *separateness* of his being. And I thought of Mark, and the others, and how they would never have put up with the life I was leading for more than a weekend at the very most. Probably not more than an afternoon, and only then because it could be laughed about later. It suddenly astonished me that I had justified my inertia by blaming it on fear of illness. And as I stood, it struck me that the greatest lesson I could learn from The Gang was not survival, but the need to make the most of the life I had, however long or short. Perhaps I owed it to Mark to have a future that was worth envying . . .

I left Gareth to finish off dinner and slipped upstairs. I took my car keys from the bedside table and my wallet with its credit cards from the drawer. I looked down at the bed we had slept in for more nights than I care to remember, and I felt no emotion whatsoever – or rather, I realized that feeling nothing was a kind of dreadful emotion in itself.

I crept down the stairs to the hall from where I could hear the sound of frying and the chink of cutlery, and let myself out onto the pavement.

Gently pulling the front door closed behind me for the last time, I whispered:

"Yes. It's over."

Imaginary Boys
Paul Magrs

David Taylor was walking home from sixth form college, through drifts of orange leaves during the season known as autumn. He was seventeen, of medium height and build, with brown hair that needed cutting. His eyes were downcast and dark as stewed tea. He wore a blurred, vague sort of expression as if his thoughts were far away.

It was starting to get dark and David kept looking over his shoulder as he hurried back to the council estate where he lived with his female parent.

This seemed like the most stressful week of David's life. Besides everything going on at home with his mam, there was Lawrence as well. The new boy in the sixth form. Awkward and hanging on the sidelines and always there. David had felt watched by him these past two weeks. Was he imagining it?

"Why are you walking along with me, Lawrence? I never asked you to."

David stopped walking and Lawrence almost bumped into him.

"And will you stop . . . narrating me?" snapped David. "It's driving me mad."

I'm sorry about that, David.

"Are you trying to wind me up?"

I can assure you I am not. It's a compliment, really.

"To have you following me around?"

Lawrence could see that David was at the end of his tether.

"Just get lost, will you? Leave me alone."

But this is where I'm meant to be.

"You what?"

I'm doing my job. And it's all to do with you, David.

"I mean it – shut up. And go away!"

There was a slight pause.

I'm sorry if I seem like a "weirdo" to you, David. That is what you think, isn't it?

"I don't think you're a weirdo."

I'm Lawrence. I'm new in town.

"I know, you're in my class. Where are you from?"

Verbatim 6.

"What?"

It's a small planet about 300 light years from here. I'm your Novelizor, David.

David looked unconvinced. "Okay." He frowned. "Bye, then!"

David turned and walked quickly away.

————

His mam was watching a quiz show when David came home.

"Where have you been?" she called from the front room. "Your tea's all black in the oven."

He shrugged. "I'm not really hungry."

"Here. Have one of these. I've left you all the soft centres."

He peered at the mostly empty box of chocolates. "Have you finished another box?"

"I can't help it."

"I'll get you some more when I'm in town."

"Are you all right? I usually get a lecture about how my cravings are no good for me."

"I'm fine, Mam, really."

"No one's been picking on you or anything, have they? Or giving you any trouble?"

"No, no. Nothing like that. Just some strange lad on the way home. New guy in our year . . ."

"Cos if those rough lads are bothering you again I'll . . ."

"Mum, I'm seventeen. I can look after myself."

She watched him carefully as he went to leave the room. "Where are you off to now?"

"Up to my room."

"Yeah, don't whatever you do spend any time with your poor old pregnant mother who's been sat here alone all day."

Lawrence was watching this unfold from outside. He was crouching down by the window, in some bushes. He hadn't been invited in yet. He wasn't close enough to his subject. Not as close as a Novelizor needs to be.

Through the window he could see a room with a large television screen and sliding panels of glass that opened onto a flat concrete area with green moss growing on it and plastic chairs. He saw the distended form of the female parent supine upon a settee that was decorated with a floral design. She was fabricating a tiny pair of shoes out of strings of coloured twine using two metal rods that made an insistent ticking noise. Then she left the room and walked upstairs.

She knocked on her son's bedroom door.

"Can I come in?"

"No," he said.

She opened the door.

"What are you doing?"

He was on his bed. There was a bunch of old books from the library on his duvet, as usual. "Reading poetry," he said, holding one up. "Keats. 'Ode to Autumn'. 'Season of mists and mellow fruitfulness'."

"Oh yes?" she laughed at his put-on poetry voice.

He went on: "Close-bosom friend of the maturing sun . . ."

"Sounds a bit saucy. Bosoms in poetry."

"Mam!"

"You and your poetry," she said, rolling her eyes. She wanted to sit down with him. Ruffle his already-messy hair. "You've had to be the man of the house since your dad went. But you have to be even more so now, with the baby nearly here."

"I know that, Mam."

"It's a long time since I went through the agony of giving birth to you and it's scary just the thought of going through it again."

"I'm here, Mam."

"There's all the bringing up baby, too. I'm going to be what they call an older mother."

"We'll manage."

"I suppose you'll be swanning off to university soon and I won't see you any more . . ."

He burst out: "Oh, give it a rest!" Then he took a deep breath. "Sorry, Mam. I'll be home to visit."

"I was used to being a young mother. With you, I was sixteen and I got all the catty remarks. I had to fight everyone to keep you."

"I know, Mam."

"It's always been me and you, David."

"You and me against the world."

"Your dad never really fit in, even when he was here. He was always so bound up in his bloody police work. We hardly even noticed him gone last Christmas, did we?"

"Cos we still had each other."

"Oh, come here. Give your old mam a hug . . ." Just then, a funny look went across her face. "Oh . . . !"

He sat up quickly. He was on his feet. "What is it?"

"I think . . . I think it's coming . . . the baby's coming!"

"Are you sure?"

She looked stricken. She was grabbing hold of the bedroom door. "David, call an ambulance!"

"You know what happened last time."

She was holding onto the door, shaking her head. "Ow! This is really it. Owww!"

"You're sure this isn't another of your false alarms?"

"Call it," she shouted. "Call them up, David, now!"

————

For the third night that month, David and his mam raced to the hospital prematurely. Another late night while the doctors looked at her and felt her all over and told her the baby wasn't ready yet, and she should get herself home. Another ride back home in a taxi.

Next day, in the sixth-form common room, David seemed to be prone to opening his mouth and making sudden, wordless noises and then looking embarrassed. This, Lawrence discovered, was "yawning".

Then David went off to somewhere called the "Boys' Bogs" and Lawrence followed him for a quiet word.

He stood outside the cubicle David was in and gave a polite knock.

David?

"What?"

It's Lawrence.

"Can't I get some peace?"

I wanted to explain something.

David flushed the toilet and came out of the little room, banging the door.

"Yeah?" he snapped. "You can explain why you're following me about for a start."

It's my job, David. This is what I'm here on Earth to do.

"Yeah, yeah . . ."

I've come a very long way to see you, David. To watch your early years here. It's all very interesting.

"Did anyone see you follow me in here?"

The thing is, David, I'm only in disguise as a new pupil. This isn't who I really am at all. My job is to collect stories and keep a record of interesting lives. And, well, I chose you.

There was a long pause.

Then David asked, "You chose me?" He frowned and stared at Lawrence. "What for?"

Said David, his heart rate increasing and his pulse pounding in his ears.

"And why do you keep on doing that?!"

Narrating, you mean? I have to keep an account of your actions.

"I really don't need this right now. Just stay out of my way, okay?"

He started to leave the "Boys' Bogs".

Aren't you going to wash your hands first? I believe that is the custom.

———

The following morning at breakfast, David's mam was fixating on the idea that her son might put another person – an undetermined female person – in a condition she described several times as "the pudding club".

"Mam, seriously, I'm running late. Can't this wait till later?"

"All I'm saying is, you're seventeen now, and I don't want you getting caught out like I did."

"Yeah, well, I won't."

"You don't know what girls are like."

"You're right about that."

"I'm just saying. You've got to watch out. Don't chuck your life away like I did."

"Thanks!"

"You know what I mean."

"Mam, I'm not going to get caught out, as you put it. When would I ever get the chance, even if I wanted to?"

"Don't get smart," she snapped.

Their late-night false alarms and ambulance trips ensured they were both over-tired and cross almost every morning.

Then the front door went.

"Who's that knocking at breakfast time?"

"I'll go," David said.

It was me! Lawrence the Novelizor from Verbatim 6. I had decided to take things to the next level in my campaign to get closer to my subject, and had learned of these things called "friends". I had decided that I would become David's, and to that end I had brought a small offering.

"Lawrence! What are you doing here?"

I want to become closer to you, David.

Mam was shouting from the kitchen. "Who is it? It's not religious, is it?"

I've brought you an offering, David.

"Oh! I don't really want . . ."

Here!

"What is it?"

It's a journal. You have to write in it.

"Okay . . ."

You've always wanted to be a writer, haven't you? These empty pages are for you to fill with all your secrets and dreams and ideas.

"Right," said David. "Thanks."

David looked – as he would put it – "freaked out" by the whole thing.

"Do I look freaked out?" he asked.

Of course. But you're getting used to me, I think. Can I walk to college with you?

"Go on then. Hang on. I'll get my bag." He yelled back at the kitchen: "I'm off now, Mam!"

She yelled back: "Aren't you going to kiss me goodbye?"

"See you tonight!"

The boys walked in silence for a while across a building site and then Lawrence said that he thought David should have introduced him to his "mam".

"I don't think so," said David.

But I need to know everything about you. She gave you life, didn't she? She was one of your progenitors.

"That's why I can't introduce you to her, Lawrence. You'll go saying something like that."

I think I'm getting the hang of life on Earth.

David pulled a face. "I wish I was."

David and Lawrence climbed through a broken fence and across damp playing fields to get to the low, blocky buildings of the school. As they joined crowds of younger human beings, Lawrence sensed David draw away from everyone else. He really seemed happiest when he was being most distant. In his classes he sat on his own. Which was good, because this made space for his Novelizor to pull up a seat alongside him. He did this in every classroom David went to and, eventually, David seemed all right with that. Do you mind if I sit here?

"Fine. As long as you don't describe everything I do."

Said David.

Sorry. Couldn't resist.

————

David had another friend called Robert, who was into "bands" and was very keen on football as well. At the end of that particular day at college David was walking alongside Robert, and Lawrence lagged along behind, listening in.

Robert was describing something he had seen happening during a game of football. Apparently somebody involved had "nutmegged the defender" and "planted it in the top corner".

David appeared to follow the meaning of this about as much as Lawrence did. "Wow! Great. Er, is that good?"

But then Robert had noticed who was following them down the street. "Don't look now, Davey boy, but your mate's following you again!"

"Oh," said David. "Yeah."

"Do you want me to have a word?" Robert asked him. "Or something a little harder?"

Lawrence gathered that Robert was offering to do something violent. David was alarmed. "No, it's okay. He's all right." He stopped and turned round. "Lawrence? You can walk with us if you like."

Pleased, Lawrence hurried to catch up with them.

"What are you doing?" said Robert.

"He's all right. Give him a chance."

Here we all are then! Walking home through the dark streets of the estates and the deep autumn leaves and talking about . . . what are we talking about?

"Football," said a glum-looking David.

"And I was telling David he should come and watch the match down the Turbinia," said Robert.

Should he?

"I can't," said David. "I should be getting home for Mam."

Robert was keen for his friend to come to the pub and see the game. "Come on. You should come down. We'll get leathered."

What is "leathered"?

David told Lawrence: "He means drunk."

But David is only seventeen. It would be against human law for him to consume alcoholic beverages.

Robert looked at the Novelizor incredulously. "Just . . . forget it."

Lawrence turned his attention to his subject. I can't help noticing that you're dawdling, David. Won't your "mam" be worrying?

Robert looked from one to the other. "What is it with you two? It's like he's got some sort of hold over you, Davey."

Lawrence nodded eagerly and happily explained how, in the old days, Novelizors used to have a literal hold over their subjects and if anyone tried to escape their brains would be burned out. Very nasty. Of course, it wasn't like that nowadays.

Robert tried to pull David aside. "What the hell's he on about?"

Embarrassed, David said: "Just some science-fiction thing. Lawrence is into sci-fi."

"Oh, he's a geek as well, is he? Fine. I'll leave you to your boyfriend."

"Shut up," David said, looking cross.

Lawrence shrugged. I am indeed a boy, and I'm his friend. What of it?

Robert was bored with the pair of them by now. There was something funny about the way they were going on and he didn't like it. "Look, I've got better stuff to do. See you tomorrow, maybe."

"Robert, wait . . . !" David called, but it was hopeless because Robert was already running off and turning the corner at the end of the street.

David was left walking along with Lawrence, who grinned at him.

Robert seems nice. What would you like to talk about? Shall we continue that very interesting conversation from our English class? About Woolf and the Brontës and how every human relationship seems, in your opinion, to be ultimately doomed to failure?

"No," snapped David. "It's fine. I'll see you later, maybe. I ought to be getting home . . ."

"Hey, buggerlugs," Mam said. On the telly, someone was taking something out of an oven really carefully while a couple of other people watched on. "Come and watch the Cakey-Bakey show with me."

"No thanks."

"What's the matter with you?"

"Oh, I'm just knackered, that's all. Too much coursework and . . . stuff."

"Stuff?" Mam pressed the mute button on the remote. "I thought as much. Is it . . . a girl?"

"No!"

"Huh – I know troubles in love when I see them. Oh, come on, David, you can confide in your mam!" She reached for her box of Celebrations.

"It's nothing. It's just . . ."

"What?"

"Dad was . . . he was your first, wasn't he?"

She laughed bitterly, fishing around in the chocolates. "Yeah, first and only – and look how that went!" She stared at him. He looked so awkward standing there. "Hey, you're not worrying about ending up like him, are you? You're more like me than him. You've got my nicer nature."

"Yeah, so I've heard." He rolled his eyes. She'd been saying that stuff for ever. "So . . . if you could go back in time, would you . . . would you change things?"

"Of course not! It was worth going through every moment of those eighteen years with that stupid tosser. Because out of all of that I got you, didn't I?"

David smiled. "Thanks, Mam."

"Think nothing of it. My best years were wasted, my confidence was ruined and my looks have gone to pot, but you make it all worthwhile, son." She gave him a great big smile and then she turned the sound back on, just in time for judges' comments.

———

It was a few days later that David next saw Lawrence at college. The Novelizor had been minding his own business, observing David's world. David found him sitting alone in the common room.

Lawrence thought he would sit here quietly, trying to blend in.

"I want to ask you something . . ." David said.

Have you started writing in your journal yet?

"Listen, I've got a free afternoon so I came to ask you if – you wanted to . . ."

It's important that you start writing quite soon. You've got a lot of work ahead of you, you know.

"I've an afternoon off. And actually, I was going to ask you . . ."

Yes? What were you going to ask me?

"If you wanted to come to Darlington on the bus with me. There's a place I'd like to show you."

Lawrence could hardly believe it.

I would be delighted, David.

"Really?" David grinned. "Great!"

David and Lawrence caught the 723 bus to Darlington. In the marketplace they visited a small shop. David led the way inside, as if it was a place of worship. There were pale wooden shelves and a long table in the middle, with paperbacks laid out in luridly colourful rows.

The air was scented with exotic spices and that was apparently because these were foreign imports. These books had travelled from far afield.

David said, "I brought you here because you like sci-fi."

Do I?

"This bookshop is the best. They're all American remainder copies. And comics, too." He started poring over the stacks, and picking up particular books that caught his attention. "Have you read this? *The Grisly Space Fandango* by Penelope Faith Conquest? Or this series, *The Eternal Mayhem Chronicles* by Everard Donat." He stopped and looked at the close confines of the shop around him. "I've been coming here for years . . ."

Lawrence studied everything that David pointed out to him.

Some of these illustrated covers are very interesting, David. The being on this one who is strangling the Earth astronaut has a look of my fifth eldest aunt on my female parent's side.

"What?!"

That was me joking. She has far too few secondary sexual characteristics.

"Right . . . Oh, look: *Entrails by Moonlight* by Marcia Sopwith."

Lawrence peered over his shoulder.

I like finding out what you like.

David was pleased to hear this. He'd never had anyone share his enthusiasm for books like this before. "Come and take a look at the Paranormal Romance section! Some of these are brilliant!"

Lawrence frowned.

What is . . . Paranormal Romance?

"It's where people fall in love with unsuitable beings," David explained. "Vampires, werewolves, shape-shifters and stuff. And it usually all goes wrong."

I myself am a shape-shifter. Have I told you that?

"Er . . . no."

I can turn into just about anything.

Later, in the café next door, David and Lawrence had organic cheese scones and Lady Grey tea and David talked once more about the futility of human love.

David started quoting: "'I am the only being whose doom / No tongue would ask, no eye would mourn.'"

Lawrence stirred his tea.

Pardon? Could I have the sugar, please?

"Emily Brontë," said David.

Ah, yes. A very nice lady. I did some of my early fieldwork in nineteenth-century Yorkshire, probing into the psyches of the Brontë sisters.

"Right . . ." David said. He supposed he was getting used to Lawrence's strange sense of humour. "I guess she was saying that we're, like, all on our own in the end."

Novelizors can't stand being on their own. Lawrence frowned and examined his scone. We begin to lose our faculties if we have no one to observe.

"I actually think human beings are made to be on their own," said David. "We're better off being solitary. Everyone ends up falling apart otherwise. Look at Mam and Dad. And Mam and my nanna. It all goes wrong. Even Mam and me are falling out more lately."

Not good examples there, David, since the common denominator is your mam. Might it just be that she causes rows with everyone?

"She's had a tough time!"

David was cross whenever Lawrence criticized his mother.

"I'm all she's got since Dad walked out, just after she told him about the baby. And she had me so young. I owe her so much. She was like sixteen and her own mother chucked her out and wouldn't even visit the hospital . . ."

Is this why you read such sad poetry all the time? Because of your guilt and attachment to your mother? Perhaps you are identifying too heavily with her view of the universe?

"I . . . er . . . don't know about that . . ."

I haven't been on planet Earth for very long, but I will venture an opinion. I don't think quite all human relationships are doomed.

"I feel like mine are," sighed David. "It's like I've grown up wrong, somehow."

Lawrence was surprised to hear that. He thought David was probably okay, actually.

David looked up at him, surprised to hear this. "Erm, thanks."

They stopped to look at each other over the table. Lawrence suddenly thought that David's eyes really did look like the very dark, very sweet tea he favoured.

David took a deep breath. "You know . . . I think I might fancy you. A bit. Is that okay?"

Lawrence wasn't sure how to react to that.

"I've never said anything like that to anyone before."

This was obviously a big moment in David's emotional development. It was most interesting.

"Right," said David briskly. "Well, let's just forget it, shall we? I never said anything."

Lawrence made a note of it.

"Just forget it!" snapped David.

———

That night, David started writing in the journal Lawrence had given him.

I kept a page-a-day diary when I was a kid, years ago. I stopped because I thought nothing was happening in my life. It was all about what was on TV and having pizza for tea and Mam fighting with Dad and everything they said.

Maybe now is when things start to happen. I feel jumpy and tingly, like my whole body knows something. Does that sound daft? Maybe I should write this in cipher. I know Mam goes through my stuff when she's bored. And if you're reading this, Mam, don't try to deny it . . .

I met this boy called Lawrence. He says he comes from a world called Verbatim 6. He says that he has chosen me.

———

The following evening, Lawrence was following David home as usual, looking forward to another of their chats.

"Oi!"

But then he saw David get stopped by an older boy called Simon Grainger – and his spotty mate, whose name David never knew.

They were bored and dizzy after an afternoon spent drinking a local beverage known as White Lightning.

"Hey, it's that posh git. You. Yes, you."

David tried to move past them. But they planted themselves either side of him.

"Excuse me."

"Listen to his manners. He sounds like a puff."

The spotty friend laughed at this. Lawrence stood watching from the top of the hill as Simon shoved David and he fell down in the mud.

"Whoops – look out. You've slipped on the leaves!"

David tried to tell him to leave him alone.

"Come on then, you faggot. Fight back, won't you?"

David couldn't get up.

"Where's your boyfriend today, then?"

"He's just a mate, that's all."

Lawrence realized they were talking about him.

"You ought to watch out. We don't have queers round here."

"Get off me!"

David stayed on the ground. They kicked him. And they spat on him. All the shouted words were blending into one then. Faggot. Puff. Queer.

They kept kicking him.

The bigger boy was shouting, "Come on! Get up!"

The other one noticed that kids were gathering round and taking pictures of the fight on their telephones and posting them on social networking sites and getting "likes".

The Novelizor watched all of this from the top of the hill. He was making careful mental notes. He wondered if David was getting hurt.

This had to happen. He knew that it did. It was a part of the story.

There was such a lot going on. A small crowd had gathered. Some girl was calling the police on her phone.

And then the two aggressors both turned and ran away.

Lawrence came to join his subject. His face was bleeding. I saw what happened. Are you all right?

Lawrence tried to help David up, but he was shrugged off angrily. Kids were still staring, fascinated. Then the last of them ran off.

"Why didn't you do something?"

Did they really attack you because you are a queer puff?

"It's because you hang around me, making them think you're my bloody boyfriend. It's all your fault and when I could do with some help you're not even there!"

I am a Novelizor. I can't get involved. I can only watch and narrate.

David looked at him in disbelief. "You what? Oh, just piss off, Lawrence. Leave me alone."

David picked himself up and limped home. He was winded from having his balls kicked. And I – Lawrence the Novelizor – followed him home. Always a few steps behind.

"Piss the hell off, Lawrence."

———

Lawrence wanted to see that David was safely home. His mam was so shocked by the state of him that she almost went into labour there and then. But she didn't. She did something even more disturbing.

She went and phoned David's dad, who David hadn't seen since he moved out the previous year.

"I know you don't want to see him – neither do I! He made both our lives a misery."

"Then why did you phone him?" He was horrified at the idea of his dad turning up.

"He's a copper. He's got power. He can get them – those animals – who did this to you."

"I'm all right. Phone him again and say we don't need him."

"You're not all right. Look at you."

"Just cuts and bruises."

"You were lucky to get away. And where was that friend of yours? That so-called best pal?"

"Lawrence?" David shrugged. "Lawrence didn't want to fight, he . . ."

"Some pal he turned out to be."

"It wasn't his fault."

There came an abrupt knocking at the front door.

Mam squeaked. "That'll be your dad. I've got to get changed. Answer it, will you?"

"Why are you getting changed?"

"I want to show him what he's missing."

"What?!"

She was halfway up the stairs. "Just answer the door."

David took a deep breath before opening the front door. And there was Dad. In his work suit. Looking more or less the same as ever.

"David. God, look at you. What the hell happened?"

"I've been beaten up."

His dad gave a mirthless laugh. "I can see that!" He stepped forward. "Can I come in?"

"I guess."

Dad led the way to their front room. "When your mam phoned the station she was lucky to get me. I should be in Sunderland right now." He turned to study David's face. "That's a nasty shiner you're going to have there, son."

David looked away from him. "There's not much to make a statement about . . ."

"Young thugs can't go round attacking people like that. I understand that's what happened." He sat down heavily on the armchair and tugged his trousers neat. Then he fetched a little notebook and pen out of his jacket.

"It was unprovoked," David told him. "They got me on the way home from school."

"Did they say anything?"

"Nothing. Just laid into me."

"And do you know who they are?"

"Simon Grainger and some mate of his. They left school last year."

"I see," said Dad. "There was a lad hanging about outside the house when I pulled up."

"What?"

"Blond lad."

"Oh. That's just Lawrence. He wasn't involved."

"Okay," said Dad, as David came back from peering through the net curtains. "Now, you are going to tell me the details slowly and I'll write them down and then yourself can sign it and we'll see about getting these lads picked up tonight, all right? I'll get them. They can't do this to you. Not to my son."

"They already have."

"This wouldn't have happened if I was still here. I could . . ."

"It would have happened anyway."

His dad looked cross with him. "I could have taught you better how to stick up for yourself. I should have . . ."

Mam came breezing in, wearing a floaty aqua-print maternity dress. She looked glamorous with her hair down. She gave off a kind of carefree vibe.

"Oh!" she said, looking at them both in the middle of their interview. "There you are . . ."

Dad nodded at her. "Mary."

"Have you seen what those scumbags have done to your son?"

"We'll sort it out." He looked her up and down briefly. "You look nice, Mary."

Her eyebrows shot up. "Me? I'm in my rags. And I'm huge. The important thing here is David. Your son. Have you forgotten about him, eh? Look at him. You've not seen him since before Christmas. Not so much as a card!"

"Look, Mary, I've got to get this statement done and then . . ."

"Oh, you get on and do what you have to. I remember all your bloody 'procedures' and paperwork. Nothing ever changes with you, does it? I suppose you'll be wanting a cup of tea."

"Milky. Lots of sugar. For the shock."

Mam laughed. "He's the one who's had the shock!"

"I meant him," said Dad.

Mam waltzed off to make tea.

So David made his statement to his dad, who laboured over it, scribbling away. David was dismayed to see his words being changed, simplified, misspelled. His mam brought the tea and went on sitting there in her colourful frock the whole time, with the best china out and French Fancies on a plate. The telly sound was down and she was shooting glances at his dad.

When the statement was all taken, Dad stood up again and studied Mam. "And you, Mary. You must be . . . close to time now."

"Yes."

"You'll let me know, won't you? When the baby comes . . ."

"Will do."

"I could be there . . ."

"I'll let you know. If you're that interested. Look, if you've finished taking his statement, just go, would you?"

Lawrence the Novelizor had been waiting outside. He waited until the policeman left and drove off.

"Er, hullo. Is David home?"

Mam wasn't impressed by Lawrence standing there on the doorstep. "Oh, so this is your mate who didn't help you, is it?"

David let him in. "Mam, it's fine. Come on, Lawrence. We'll go to my room."

David flopped down on his single bed and let out a huge sigh. He lay on top of scribbled essay notes, paperbacks and his new journal.

"That was awful."

Lawrence had never been in David's bedroom before. It was messy and dark and musky-smelling.

"Just shut up, will you, Lawrence?"

Lawrence sat down carefully on the desk chair.

I was interested to see your male parent. Will you look like that when you are older? Balding and blotchy?

"I don't even know why I'm still talking to you."

I believe it's because you don't have many other friends in your peer group. Tell me more about your reunion with your male parent. This is a very significant moment.

"He wanted to know what names they were shouting at me. Not how I was getting on at college, or how Mam and I are doing without him. Just what words they chose to use when they beat the crap out of me. And what was I going to say? Puff? Queer?"

Did you?

"What do you think?"

Lawrence thought about this. He thought about everything that had been happening during the past few, interesting hours.

He seemed like a nice man, your father.

"No he didn't. And then he said – he said . . ."

What?

"He said I needed a proper man's influence in my life. That I'd been missing having him around all year and it was doing me harm."

Is that true? Do you miss him?

"I don't know. Not really. But . . . I end up actually feeling guilty. Because I haven't been in touch with him either, have I? I agreed to go out on Saturday with him. To the shops."

You are going to spend "quality" time with your male parent.

"He's offered to help me choose a suit for my university interviews."

You don't look very pleased about this.

"I just want to die."

I'll come with you, if you like.

"When I die?"

I meant in the car with your dad. To the shops. On Saturday.

"No! Absolutely no way. No!"

————

Lawrence looked out of the car window at the motorway, streaking by.

I've never been in a police car before.

"It's not a police car. It's a Mondeo," said David's dad, keeping his eyes on the road. Next to him, David was being very quiet. "What do you think of this suit I'm wearing, David?"

"Very smart, yeah."

"I thought we'd get something like it for yourself."

"Great".

Lawrence had noticed that David's dad would use the word "yourself" instead of "you". It sounded strangely formal and oblique, as in: "I'm taking yourself to the biggest shopping mall in Europe!" and "Can yourself drive a car yet?"

"What's your friend saying back there?" Dad frowned.

"He often talks to himself, don't you, Lawrence?"

"I don't mind bringing him along, even though it's literally the only time we've had together in months."

"Thanks," said David.

"Do you see much of that Robert Woolf still? He was a good lad. Still into his football, is he? He had a natural talent, I always thought."

"We've kind of drifted," said David. "He hangs around with a dodgy crowd."

"That's not good."

"Yeah."

"Your mother's looking well. I hope you'll both cope. Just the two of you."

"We can manage."

Dad shot a glance at him. "Not fair on a young lad like yourself, though, is it?"

"It's okay."

"I would have stayed, you know. For the little one. And for you, as well. It's just . . ."

"What? It's just what, Dad?"

"It would have been worse if I'd stayed. You know that. Me and your mam, you know, it just couldn't go on like that . . ."

David wasn't sure what he was supposed to say to all of this. "Well, it's better now."

"That's how you feel, is it?"

"But it is, isn't it? Your life is better too. Away from Mam."

"Yes . . . you'll be away soon as well, won't you? Which universities are you applying to?"

"Lancaster, York, Middlesbrough . . ."

"You'll look the part in your new suit. I could drive you there, to the interviews and stuff."

"Yeah?"

"What are dads for?"

David bit his tongue.

At the shopping mall, Dad made him try suits on and David was mortified by styles, prices, by the things his dad said. By the matey way he had of going on.

"What you want is something that will last for years. Quality, not something trendy . . ."

"I suppose."

Dad's favourite menswear shops weren't appealing to David very much.

"You needn't spend a fortune to look stylish and smart. Are you listening, son?"

But David had seen someone.

"Oh no."

"Isn't that your mate? Robert? Go and talk to him, David. He's waving you over."

Robert Woolf was hanging around with some girls, next to a fountain.

"Davey," Robert greeted him.

"You remember my dad?"

Robert nodded. "Mr Taylor."

"Hello there, Robert. What are you up to, then? Shouldn't you be at football practice? I remember yourself being a smashing centre-forward at one time. Do you still play?"

"A bit. When I can."

"We're getting David kitted out with some new gear."

Robert grinned. "Gear, eh? And what about his pal? Are you kitting him out as well?"

The two girls giggled, and everyone turned to look at the Novelizor.

"That's Lawrence," Dad said. "He's David's new friend."

"Yeah, I know," Robert said. There was something funny about his tone of voice. "His 'friend'."

David was turning away. "Look, can we just go now?"

Dad chuckled. "He's just in a bad mood."

Robert called out: "You could hang out with us if you want, Davey."

Lawrence piped up.

David is going to the Terrace Café for high tea with his father and his friend, Lawrence. That's what's going to happen now.

"Uh . . . right," said Robert. "Go on then. Do what you want."

David, Dad and Lawrence moved away from the small party by the fountain, in the direction of the food court.

"You should be nicer to him," Dad said. "He's just a pleasant, normal lad."

David didn't look convinced.

Dad snapped, "Would you stop butting in all the time, son?"

"Leave him alone!" David said, louder than he'd meant to.

Dad was getting angry now. "I'll tell you what you've got to learn to do better, David. And that's mixing in more. There's all types of people in this world. Don't be getting ideas about yourself."

David had had enough for one day. "Can we . . . can we just go home now?"

———

So they didn't choose a suit in the end. They went home empty-handed. All the way home Dad talked about his police work.

"When you're in a position like mine, you've got to be sure about things. I banged up a vicious cross-dresser from Ferryhill who was abusing his foster kiddies. There's no shades of grey in a case like that. It's stark black and white. He's the baddy and I'm literally the goody."

He was playing them his Simply Red CD.

Are we nearly home yet?

"I think Lawrence is feeling carsick," said David.

"We're almost back," Dad told him. He didn't really care if Lawrence felt unwell or not. "Look, did they really call yourself a puff?"

"Who?"

"Your assailants. They admitted in their own statements that they used terms of homophobic abuse and all that." There was a pause then, and David stared at the green fields sliding by, and clouds that looked to him like galleons. "Look, son. You can tell your dad anything. If yourself has anything to say . . ."

"I've got nothing to say."

It was like a police interrogation.

"I'm just asking."

"Well. Okay," said David.

"Cos if yourself has any worries on that score – they are wrong. Those lads. You're just sensitive and clever, like your mam used to be. That doesn't make yourself a homosexual or anything. You needn't worry. You can still be a normal lad."

"You what?"

"I don't think you've grown up wrong and perverted. I really don't."
Now they were pulling into their town. They were almost home.

"Oh. Okay. Thanks," said David. Then, a few minutes later, they
were parked outside David and his mam's house. "Bye, Dad."

"Bye then, son."

The car raced off again.

Lawrence thought he preferred David's female parent.

"You're not the only one," David told him.

That night was the night David's female parent went into the throes
of the state known as labour – and this time it was real.

"What?!" David gasped.

––––––

They could hear Mam screaming in the front room, even before David
got the front door open. The pair of them went running through. She
was on the settee and the cushions had been flung all over. Her knitting
and all the remotes were on the floor.

"Mam! What's happening?"

"What do you bloody well think is happening?"

Lawrence the Novelizor had been quite correct in his earlier
assessment of the situation.

"Lawrence, just stop! Mam?"

Mam was gasping with pain. "You've been too busy running about
with that pig of a father of yours."

"Oh God," said David. He was frozen in the doorway.

"Can you . . . phone an . . . ambulance . . ." Mam panted. "I
couldn't find the cordless – nnnnnggh – bloody thing . . . or my . . .
flipping mobile . . ."

"Will an ambulance get here in time? Mam!"

David's mother was hauling herself onto the settee with her legs up.
Her "waters" had apparently broken and her knitting was ruined.

Mam was struggling to sit up. "Your father spoiled – nnnnnggh – both
our lives. Aaagghh. I hate bloody men. Don't just stand there, David!"

For a few moments he couldn't move. He couldn't even think straight.

"David, man! It's going to happen right now. What did he say about me? Nnnnnggh. Your so-called father? Aaagghh. Slagging me off, I suppose?"

"What do I do?"

She was trying to get both her legs onto the settee, grunting and breathing hard. "Did he buy you anything? Nnnnnggh."

"Shut up about Dad. He doesn't matter."

"He's useless. AAAGGHH."

David seemed to come back to his senses. "Hot water and clean towels. That's what we need."

Lawrence wasn't sure what you did with the hot water and towels once you actually had them. Neither was David.

"Mam, can you wait until the ambulance comes?"

"AAAAGGGHHHH!"

"And shouldn't you be doing your special breathing or something?"

"NNNNGGGHH! What special bloody breathing?"

It was getting very noisy in their sitting room by now.

Mam had both hands on her huge belly. "This won't wait for the ambulance."

David was worried in case it was like the boy who cried wolf and the paramedics had stopped believing her.

"Lawrence, shut up!" David shouted at his friend. "Stop saying stupid stuff and help me! Boil the kettle and I'll phone."

Lawrence stared at him, trying to be calm.

I shouldn't interfere. I'm not supposed to.

"Just do it! You have to help! You can't just stand there!"

Lawrence just stood there, feeling unhappy and torn.

You don't understand, David!

"I do. You're scared. I'm scared. But you have to help."

But Novelizors aren't supposed to get involved! You saw me! I just stood there, didn't I? When they hit you and kicked you?

"It doesn't matter about that now," David told him.

Lawrence stared at the carpet and the sopping bundle of knitting.

I tried so hard not to get involved.

Then Mam started shrieking: "HURRY UP! NNNGGHH!"

"It's really true, isn't it?" said David, in an awestruck tone of voice. "It's really going to happen. On our settee."

Lawrence nodded.

She is going to give birth to another person, yes. A smaller one.

David was at the sideboard, fumbling with the cordless phone.

"Maybe it'll take ages," he said. "They sometimes do, don't they? Maybe the ambulance will have time to get here . . ."

Mam was screaming at the top of her lungs by now.

Lawrence shuddered.

It could put you off for life, this.

Mam's screams ebbed away for a few moments and she caught her breath. Her face was bright red and wet with perspiration. "I wish I'd bothered with more of them classes now. I thought I'd remember everything from last time."

"That was seventeen years ago," David told her. "Do your breathing!"

"You popped out easy as anything," she told him.

"Mam! You have to remember! Your breathing! Do it!"

"I can't!"

"Mam – look, I don't know what to do. I . . ."

"Nnnnggggghh! Aaaaaaaagh!"

David turned to his friend for help. "Lawrence . . . I . . . I can't . . . What do I do?!"

Lawrence the Novelizor from Verbatim 6 took a huge breath and made the biggest decision of his life.

Stand back, David.

"What are you doing?"

I'm taking off my school tie. And I'm rolling up the sleeves of my shirt.

"But what are you going to do?" David shouted.

I'm getting involved.

Mam yelled out croakily: "I'm going to die."

No, you're not.

She had her hair plastered all over her face and gently, Lawrence helped her brush it aside.

Can you push?

"I don't know. I'll have to take my pants off."

"Oh God," David said.

Mam screamed and David stepped backwards, watching in horrified fascination as Lawrence took over looking after his mam.

"Listen," Mam grunted. "Listen – if I die . . ."

You're not going to die.

"Women die in childbirth all the time," she pointed out, her voice full of panic.

Lawrence considered this.

I suppose they do in novels. In the Victorian ones that David loves so much.

"Lawrence!" David yelled, thinking his friend was getting distracted.

Mam was shrieking again. She looked wildly at David. "Who is this bloke, David?"

David swallowed. "He's – he's . . ."

"He's your friend, it's fine," Mam said.

More than that, really.

"Yes," David agreed. "More than that."

I'm his Novelizor.

Mam couldn't really get the gist of what they were on about since she couldn't stop howling. "What?"

"Never mind that," said David, steeling himself. "It's about time I told you, Mam . . ."

"AAAGGGHHHH!"

"I'm . . ."

Mam screamed at him: "Can we leave this till later?" Then she lapsed into a frantic burst of panting.

Lawrence stepped in, speaking as calmly as he could.

Breathe, Mrs David's Mam!

Mam tried her best to breathe properly.

In the relatively peaceful pause, David spoke up. "I'm gay, Mam. That's what."

"What?" said Mam. And then she was racked by another wave of pain that had her screaming, fit to burst.

Push, I think, Lawrence told her. I believe this is the time for pushing.

"Did you hear, Mam?" shouted David. "What I said? I'm gay."

Mam screamed back at him, through gritted teeth: "I already knew!"

"What?"

"Mothers always know!"

Then her screams reached a crescendo, and pretty soon after that, the ambulance arrived again at their door.

————

At the hospital, David and Lawrence found a coffee machine and drank soupy lattes. Then they had Twixes and Twirls – splitting them to be fair – and Lawrence decided they were the very best kind of food he had eaten since arriving on planet Earth.

"What if she's not all right, Lawrence?"

She will be. Lawrence was sure.

"What if they both die and it's all my fault?"

Lawrence was amazed how long and complicated this human childbirth could be to accomplish.

"Stop pretending that you're not human!" David was glad that the waiting room was empty apart from them.

But I'm not, David! I'm not human. I'm here with a very particular job to do, and I've already compromised that.

"Whatever."

Do you want to hear how Novelizers are born on Verbatim 6?

"Not especially."

"We begin as the merest inkling, and then someone says . . ."

"Listen!"

Suddenly, there was all this noise of doors opening and closing, and a baby crying. A nurse appeared before them. David and his Novelizor were gently asked to enter a room, from which the most unearthly racket could be heard . . .

———

"Come on, don't be shy . . ." Mam said. "Say hello to your baby sister."

David peered close at the little bundle. "Oh. Wow." He stared at the bright pink squidgy face. It was easy to believe the baby was already having her own thoughts inside that tiny head.

Lawrence took a long, thoughtful look at the baby, too.

She has really long feet.

"She's amazing," said David.

"Thanks for your help, boys. I'm sorry it was so fraught."

David was entranced by the baby. Her black scrap of hair, her red fists, which were punching the air, like in triumph.

"I'm calling her Katherine," Mam announced. "After your nanna, even though I hate the blummin' woman."

David nodded. "Lovely."

"Pick her up. Don't be scared."

David did as he was told. He lifted the baby so carefully. "She's heavy!"

Mam laughed. "Tell me about it."

David held the baby up to Lawrence, too.

Greetings, small human. Greetings from Verbatim 6.

"Ha!" sighed Mam. "What's he like?"

"He's hilarious." David rolled his eyes. Then he said, more quietly: "I texted Dad. Just so he knows . . ."

"I wish you hadn't." Then she glanced at him again, curious. "Any reply yet?"

David shook his head. "Not yet, but he's probably at work. I'm sure he'll come by later."

"I'm not sure I want him to."

"But look at her," said David. "Look at Katherine. He's missing all of this."

"He walked out. We've got our own lives to get on with. And you've got yours, too. With your university stuff."

"That can wait. I'll take a gap year, or something; stay and help with the baby."

"Don't you dare!" Mam said crossly. "I might be what they call an 'older mother', but I'm not geriatric."

"We'll see."

"It's your life, David. You have to make sure you live it."

He chuckled. "Is this the gas and air talking?"

"I mean it. You do what you want to with your life. And if you do, I'll feel I've done a good job of bringing you up right. And it's true, you know."

"What is?"

Mam met his stare. "I already knew about you."

"Oh, right."

"About being a puff."

"Let's talk about it later."

"I like him. That daft lad. Your boyfriend. That's what he is, isn't he? He's a bit odd, I suppose, with the way he goes on."

Lawrence was only half-listening. He was busy trying to communicate with the newly born human.

David said awkwardly, "Well, he's not really my . . . my . . ."

"I think he is, you know," said Mam decisively. "Now go on, take him home. Get some rest."

David smiled. "Thanks, Mam."

As they left the hospital and went out into the cold to catch the early morning bus, Lawrence was dwelling on the thought that he was now far too close to his subject.

Boyfriend. It was a strange word. Wrong, somehow. But nice. Nicer than Novelizor.

———

A familiar Ford Mondeo pulled up at the bus stop in front of them.

Dad called out of the window, "Hey, lads!"

"Dad, what are you doing here?"

"You yourself texted me with the news . . ."

"I never thought you'd come." It was freezing out on the pavement. Dad had Simply Red playing on his car stereo again.

He said heavily, "I literally still care about you both, you know."

Lawrence beamed at him.

Thank you, Mr David's Dad!

"Not you, daft lad."

David told his dad, "She's sleeping now. But she's got a little girl."

"Lovely."

She has extremely long feet, Lawrence pointed out.

"Still got your mate with you, I see," Dad sighed.

"He's not just a mate, Dad," said David, with sudden resolution. What did he have to lose? "He's my boyfriend."

"Oh!" said Dad, taking this in. He looked at them both and went slightly pink. "Right! I see." He nodded. "Well, I guess you'll both be wanting a lift home, yeah?"

———

Twenty minutes later, Dad dropped them off and the boys went straight upstairs to David's room. It was early morning and everything was very quiet and still.

Lawrence watched as his friend and subject flung himself down on the bed.

"I could do with a hug," said David, softly.

Novelizors from Verbatim 6 aren't really trained to give hugs.

"Just give me a hug, will you?"

———

There were a few moments of rustling then, as Lawrence lay down awkwardly on the bed. They tried to work out who was lying on top of the duvet and who was getting under. David pulled off his jumper and shirt and, after a moment of hesitation, unzipped and shucked off his jeans. Lawrence watched all of this, wondering whether he ought to get undressed too. He wasn't sure what the protocol was. In the end, he lay down stiffly, fully dressed, on top of the duvet, quite close to David. He could smell the milky coffee on his warm breath.

You've got a little sister.

"I know. It's amazing."

Lawrence thought about that for a bit. Still, your planet is horribly over-populated. I hope your mother puts a stop to her reproductive urges now.

David shoved his shoulder. "Can't you drop the space act now?"

The what?

"The space act: saying you're from space." David looked straight into his face and Lawrence felt uncomfortable for a few seconds. "It's like a neurotic thing. A way of deflecting attention somehow, away from who you really are . . ."

But this is who I really am.

"Oh – if you can't be serious about anything . . ."

I am serious. This is as serious as it gets.

"No, it isn't." David smiled at him. Suddenly he felt daring and conscious of all the covers between them. "Come here."

They kissed.

It took several hot moments and a few delicate manoeuvres.

Oh.

"Wow," David whispered. It was like they were in a bubble of secrecy. "That was my first kiss. I've never . . ."

Yes. Um.

"Is that all you have to say about it?"

Um.

"You!" David laughed, but he was becoming slightly annoyed too. "You're never lost for words! You never shut up! Now look at you."

Er, yes.

"Is that it?"

Lawrence realized that they had crossed a line. This had gone too far.

"What are you on about?"

Lawrence was seized by a sudden idea. He sat up in the bed. "Come with me, David. There's something I want you to see . . ."

———

Minutes later, David was fully dressed again and they both had their coats and shoes on. They were out in the early morning light, hurrying together over the rubble and rough terrain of the building site.

Lawrence was leading the way to the edge of town and the wasteland.

"What are we doing out here?" David shouted at him.

Come on, and don't ask questions.

"It's the crack of dawn, Lawrence." David was stumbling over heaps of bricks and sand and scrubby plants.

Maybe it was a mistake to come out like this but the Novelizor had been seized by this sudden, mad impulse.

"When you said you had something to show me . . ."

Sssh. This is secret.

Eventually, they came to a halt. Lawrence waved his arms about and they stood stock still. Then Lawrence crouched down in the undergrowth and David joined him. Lawrence started pushing aside the overgrown vegetation.

"There's nothing here," said David. "What are you looking for?"

I'm going to prove to you, once and for all, who and what I am.

"You don't have to," David told him. "You're Lawrence. That's all I need to know . . ."

We've gone this far. I might as well show you everything.

"Lawrence. It – it . . ."

He could hear it before he saw it. There was a wonderful chiming noise that filled the morning air. Then there was all this multicoloured light glittering about, and all at once, something appeared before them.

Something that was as big as a council house, that hadn't been there a moment before. It was a grand and futuristic vision.

David stared at the rainbow lights at the heart of the wasteland.

"What . . . what is it?"

My spacecraft. It's been hiding in hyperspace. Sort of tangential to this dimension, you see. Here but not here. I thought it was time to show you. What do you think?

"I . . . I don't know what to say."

I used to know the future. I thought I knew how you'd react.

"It's magnificent."

They're quite common, where I come from, but this one . . . this one is mine.

As if on cue, as if responding to the pride in Lawrence's tone, a hatchway opened in the side of the ship and a shining ramp extended to meet them.

"It's opening," gasped David. "Does that mean . . . Are you . . . ?"

I don't know how things are going to turn out any more. For the first time ever I don't know the end of the story!

A louder bass note accompanied the chiming noise. It sounded very much as if strange and powerful engines were gearing themselves up.

Lawrence the Novelizor turned to his subject.

Will you come with me, David?

"Uh . . ." David was flabbergasted. "Where to?"

Into space. It's all true – everything I said. I come from your future. I fell in love with your books.

"My books?" This brought David up short. His books?

They were why I came to this place to find you. All this way. I was meant to just observe, but then I changed things and we kissed and now . . . will you come with me?

"I write books? What are they called?"

I can't tell you.

"But . . . what do I write about?"

All kinds of things. Time. Friendship. Love. How to keep people together. Learning to love them.

"And you want me to leave Earth?"

Will you?

David had to think hard about this.

"Lawrence, my family needs me. I've got a new sister. And my mam gets panic attacks when she can't get a supermarket trolley through the revolving doors. And I write books, do I? And I get . . . I get published?"

Fully activated, the semi-sentient ship from Verbatim 6 began to signal its readiness to depart.

I've said too much already, David. We shouldn't even really be in the same story. I used to know how it all worked out. The future was set. But I got too involved.

David took hold of him. "I do want to go with you, Lawrence. But I can't. I've got to stay here. I've got stuff to do in this world . . ."

But you can write in space. Just think what you might see out there!

"I have to stay. For Mam. And Katherine . . . Besides, you said you loved my books. If I'm not here to write them, then you'll never read them, and you won't come back to see me, will you? We'd never have met."

Lawrence knew that he had messed things up. Now everything had changed.

David shook his head. "Do you know what? I reckon it all changed when you first gave me that journal."

The ship's noise and brightly shining lights were intensifying now, as if it was eager for the off.

Lawrence made you want to write?

"You did. Mission accomplished, I reckon."

But I was sent to observe! Not to change your life.

"But you have!" David grinned. "You've changed it, for ever, I think."

It's only been a couple of weeks . . .

"Maybe that's enough." David hugged Lawrence hard, and felt him relax into it at last. "Will you come back, then? One day?"

If I can, I will. I promise.

Then Lawrence kissed David, and stepped away.

Goodbye, David.

"Goodbye, Lawrence. I'm really going to miss you . . ." David had to shout to be heard over the spaceship engine noises. "And thank you!"

For what?

"You've read my books – you tell me!"

Lawrence turned and hurried away into his beloved ship. David watched as the ramp slid back and the hatchway smoothly closed. Then the ship seemed to glow in a satisfied kind of way before lifting off, gloriously, into the brightening air of the morning.

———

Home again, later, David went back to writing in his journal:

When I turned seventeen I didn't really know who I was, or what I might become.

And then, all of a sudden, I did.

I knew exactly who I was.

And I knew who it was I was writing for. And I knew that, when he read it, he would love my story.

Ghost, Come Back
Jerry Rosco

Ron was not really someone who believed in psychiatrists, and professionals can sense that right away. The tall, fifty-ish, pleasant-looking psychiatrist didn't know what to think of the young man who had made this appointment with a doctor's referral, with only the complaint of "bad dreams." His first-time patient was well dressed in a casual way, his blond hair very curly but cut short, his face pale but handsome, his arms folded tight across his slender chest as he sat straight up on the leather sofa. No way in hell would he lie down on that sofa, they both seemed to think at the same moment. The man looked down at his preliminary notes and saw no clue. Ron was in his early thirties, he worked in real estate, he was in good health and was engaged to be married.

In those first awkward moments, Ron glanced at the man's broad, friendly face. He thought he looked intelligent. He didn't really think he needed a psychiatrist, he just wanted an opinion. He'd hated asking his doctor for the referral but that was the only way to have his insurance cover it. Ron didn't have any problem with money, he just hated spending it. He wasn't just a broker; he'd also flipped – bought and sold – half a dozen houses at a big profit. He'd lived in his parents' house until now. In five months, he'd marry his fiancée, Kate, and they'd move into the house he was now having refurbished. Everything was set, his life was good. The only problem was one thing in his past.

The psychiatrist went back over these facts, or statements, just as a way to make Ron relax. Then he asked about his health, whether he was sleeping all right or had anxieties. When that checked out okay, he just leaned back in his chair, looked at the younger man directly and said, "Well, what about the bad dreams?"

"There really aren't any bad dreams," Ron said, getting ready to get to the point.

That didn't seem to surprise the man at all. "All right," he said in a soothing voice. "What's going on?"

Ron unfolded his arms and ran a hand through his hair and over his face. This is what he, or the insurance, was paying for. Finally, he could say this. "I come from a big family. About twenty miles away in Newburg, my father's brother has a big family. Growing up, I spent a lot of time at my uncle and aunt's, and we kids were all close." The man kept looking at him and nodding and seemed to just jot down a word or two.

Ron cleared his throat and the words he'd held back for so long came easily. "Out of all my cousins, I was best friends with John, who was a year younger than me. We saw each other a lot through high school years, but not much in college when he moved out of state to an art school. Then, after college, I got busy in real estate and he got a job and moved away to New York." Ron leaned back on one arm. His body was relaxing and he could almost lie down now. "Then three years ago he got real sick." He paused and didn't say more, and the man deliberately did not interrupt. Ron started again. "John came home to his parents for his last months. I only saw him three or four more times. It was tough. He was brave. Then, when he passed, I went there with my parents for the funeral. There was a wake on a Friday night and the funeral in the morning. After the wake that night, the whole family got together for drinks and food. One of my cousins put me up at her house for the night."

The psychiatrist noticed that Ron was staring intensely ahead as he spoke. "During the night, I stayed up. I was in an upstairs room and it was about 2 a.m. That's when John came into the room. I was sitting up and awake. It was him. He was standing by the bed. He looked at me and touched my shoulder. All the closeness we felt as kids, it was there.

He told me not to cry or he'd leave. But I couldn't help it; I started to cry. He moved away and he started to disappear at the same time. I mean, I could see through him to the wall. Then he was gone and I was sitting there alone. I couldn't sleep until near dawn. I told people the next day, and they seemed to believe me. But once time passed, people didn't want to hear that." He laughed. "And I'm sort of left alone with it."

The therapist put up his hand. "Before we go further. That was three years ago. Did it ever happen again?"

"No."

"When he touched you on the shoulder, did you feel it?"

Ron thought for a moment. "No."

"Okay. You haven't experienced anything like that again. You're in good health. Your cousin John was only in his late twenties when he became sick. Can you tell me more about him?"

Ron physically cringed. But this part was totally beside the point. He shrugged. "Well, you know, he was an artist. I know he had a boyfriend in college, and one later on in New York."

"And you?"

Ron's face flushed and he looked up angrily. "Not."

"All right," the man said, and scribbled a few notes, his face impassive. There was the sense that he wanted to ask more questions along that line, but with an uncomfortable new patient it was too soon. He made a note to himself. There was a silent moment.

Ron felt he'd walked to the edge of a cliff and was left standing there. "What I'm saying is, I really saw him. That happened. I mean, I'm not the type to imagine things. I have a nice, normal life, but I can't get over him coming to me, and can't talk about it to anyone. What do you think?"

The man put his notes on the desk next to his chair. "Well, I know how powerful the memory and emotion must be for you. But in cases like this, the first thing is the fact that you were in bed. There's such a thing as a waking dream. The conscious and subconscious merge for seconds or minutes that seem much longer. You were emotionally upset. You'd also been drinking, which complicates things even more." He looked over at Ron's fixed expression.

Ron was not surprised, and he would consider everything. He wanted an opinion and he got one. But he still believed what he saw and knew it to be real. Soon, their time was up and the psychiatrist suggested they meet again, "to examine the trauma of your loss," he said as they both stood up. Then he added, "I mean, the issue isn't whether it was or wasn't your cousin, but what it meant to you." Ron nodded and said he'd think about it, but didn't make an appointment.

That night, he stayed at his fiancée Kate's apartment as he did at least twice a week. Under the covers she slept close to him, silky smooth but fit and athletic, and he loved it when she slept naked as she had tonight. He couldn't resist running one hand lightly along her body. An hour ago, they'd made love and Ron was already looking forward to the morning when they'd do it again. He knew she didn't like to be woken in the middle of the night for a second round, which was frustrating but made him smile. It embarrassed him that he hadn't had much experience with women before Kate, but now it just kept getting better. He loved how much she turned him on but he also liked that she had a good job and was independent. That's what a partner should be. She drove him crazy with the wedding plans but that was pretty normal. Everything is fine, Ron thought, I have everything I need.

But then his mind drifted to that one thing he could not forget or leave alone. He did not tell Kate or anyone about seeing the psychiatrist and would be mortified if they knew. He did not like how the man dismissed what he said, but it wasn't a waste of time to get someone's opinion. A small television across the room flickered soundlessly. He realized something. Now that he'd finally done something about the night he saw John, after three whole years, he wanted to take it a step further. Just being curious was reason enough – curious about the most disturbing thing that had ever happened to him. "Don't cry or I'll leave," John had said. When he remembered those words, even with Kate asleep beside him, he felt all alone in the world.

It was a week later when Ron had a free afternoon and some quiet time to make a phone call. He'd searched online for the website of the Mid-Atlantic Paranormal Research Center. They seemed like a legitimate group that studied and investigated incidents like his, and listed case histories. They gave a phone number and hours to call. He dialed and someone named Stewart answered. His name had been on the website. It wasn't an office, he could tell, just the guy's phone.

Feeling his face flush, Ron said, "I want to report something that happened to me a few years ago and get your thoughts about it." He described what he remembered as quickly as he could.

Stewart's questions got right to the point. This only happened once? Nothing else in that room or anywhere else? Any static electricity? No one else reported anything in that house? Finally, he said, "We wouldn't investigate that."

Ron felt the same flash of disappointment and anger he'd felt at the psychiatrist's office. "So you think it was, what, my imagination or a dream?"

"Oh no," Stewart said. "I just mean there's nothing to investigate as far as bringing equipment to the house to record sounds or video of activity. That's what I do myself in some cases; that's what I'm trained for. But if you tell me where you are, and I have your phone number, I'll have someone meet up with you in the next week or two, to take a report and talk about what you experienced. Okay, Ron?"

That at least was something, maybe the most satisfaction he could get. He thanked the guy. At least someone took him seriously.

Over the next two weeks Ron was busy with work, and helping Kate find a hall for the wedding, and checking on the house he was having refurbished. After plumbing and electrical work, it would be ready for painting. He was disappointed that the paranormal researchers hadn't called, and was close to calling them again. But first he had to get away for a weekend.

He drove to Philadelphia for a two-day real-estate conference, something he did once or twice a year. He had a room in the same hotel as the conference, in the busiest downtown area. Clothing shops, grocery stores and fast-food places lined the crowded streets. When he left the parking garage and walked to the hotel entrance, he noticed the little storefront with candles in the window and a sign that read, "Psychic Medium – Spiritualist – Crystal Gazing Clairvoyant". Gypsies, he thought, in this day and age? The sweeping statements on the sign made him laugh. But it also stayed in his mind.

During the day, he saw two young brokers he knew in one of the conference rooms and that night they went to dinner. He knew they wanted some of his success to rub off on them, but he liked the company. The truth was that Ron didn't have many friends and it was good to have a few drinks and talk about sports. Then the two guys took him from one bar to another. But he couldn't keep up with the drinking. By midnight, he was walking the few blocks back to the hotel. As he walked he took out his cell phone and called Kate. She laughed at the sound of his voice. He was not a drinker and it was obvious when he'd had more than a few. He promised to be home by the next evening.

At the corner where he would turn for his hotel, he stopped in his tracks. Two college-age girls were talking loudly as they stepped out of the fortune teller's storefront. Ron looked through the window to the candlelit front room, and saw a stout middle-aged woman sitting before a small table, gathering her Tarot cards. She looked the part, wearing a flowery print dress, with her black hair tied back. Ron knew he was drunk or he would never do this, but the word "clairvoyant" drew him. As he stepped inside, the woman's dark eyes fixed on him for a moment and she wrapped the Tarot cards in a piece of cloth; she knew he was not there for a reading. She extended her hand, with rings on three fingers, and he sat in a metal folding chair across from her. For just a moment Ron had a feeling of vertigo, maybe from the drinking and the flickering candles all around the room at different levels. But he recovered and pulled out his wallet. Knowing he was greatly overpaying, but this was the time for it, he slid two twenties across the table to her. From the back of his wallet he carefully took out a small, worn photo of John and placed it on the table, facing her. He spoke slowly, not sure of her English. "This was my cousin and friend, John; he died three years ago."

She looked at the picture for a long moment, then slid it back to him. "John," she said. "He was of your mother's family?"

Ron didn't understand, then thought: mother's side of the family. "Yes."

She looked at him with narrowed eyes. "What do you want?"

That stopped him for a moment. He didn't want to focus on seeing John, not yet. Instead, he said, "I want to know if he's okay."

A green velvet cloth was covering something on the table and she removed it to reveal a small crystal ball on a wooden base. She reached over to rest a hand over his. "Think of seeing him," she said. "Don't think about him, just see him, like a picture, as you remember him." Ron didn't like this idea, but he closed his eyes. Random flashes of John, just moments, without thoughts. How he looked the time Ron drove to his college dorm to visit, with curly black hair, happy; and the time in high school when he won an art award, though he was pouting about something that day, his face more round, his hair long; and in the last days, thin, pale, lying under a blanket on his parents' sofa. The woman drew her hand away. Then she looked into the crystal for a long time. All Ron could see in the glass was a moving, white vertical light, maybe a reflection from the candles.

The medium spoke in a low but clear voice. "He was very sick. He had a bad time." She looked up. "But he is all right. That is what you asked me." She did not seem sympathetic. Her right hand was pointing a finger at the crystal and it moved like the dial of a compass toward Ron. "I see only you. Maybe . . . you have other questions and you have to keep searching." She put the velvet cloth back over the crystal.

Fighting sleep, fighting alcohol, Ron didn't want to try to say any more. He stood, a little unsteadily, and thanked her.

Just minutes later, far above the noisy streets in his quiet hotel room, Ron wondered if he was a fool for going to the psychic. Probably. She could have guessed the little she said. But he laughed at the thought that she did say more than the psychiatrist. Maybe, he thought, it was time to put the business with John out of his mind . . . though he'd tried before.

After a long, hot shower, he dried himself and fell naked across the oversized bed. It was too late to call Kate again. Too bad she was so strict about getting sleep; it would be fun to fool around over the phone. His mind drifted. There was a girl in her twenties at that day's seminars who was hot. He loved Kate's tight, fit body, but this girl's curves were extra sexy. And her tits were definitely more full than . . .

He stood up and faced the large mirror. There was something about hotel mirrors. Against his smooth, lean torso and flat abdominals, his hard cock always looked really impressive. He turned to the left, then the right. When Kate saw him fully naked, the sight of his erection really got to her. He could see it in her eyes and it made a difference in their fucking. Those were the times, he knew, when she really felt lust, and acted like it. He started to remember one of those times, at a beach cottage that summer. Now he backed up, onto the bed, and lowered the bedside lamp light.

———

Days later, back home, Ron deliberately focused on his work, and tried to put that last memory of John back in the past. But he realized something. Talking to a few people had stirred up some feelings, as if he were standing outside the door of the room where he slept that night, and the door was opening. He pushed away those thoughts more than once.

After showing a couple younger than himself a bargain house that needed work, he was about to drive home when his phone rang. A guy named Paul apologized for not calling him sooner. He was from the Paranormal Research Center and was driving by the area tomorrow. Ron almost called off the meeting, but didn't. He suggested they meet late afternoon at a diner near the thruway.

The next day, they sat across from each other in the booth at the nearly empty diner. Ron just had coffee while Paul got a sandwich. Except for his long dark hair and being in his late thirties, Paul looked like a lifeguard, with square-jawed good looks – not what Ron had expected. He said he was a car mechanic and like the others at the research center he volunteered his time.

Once again, Ron repeated his story about seeing John two days after he died. Paul had a few notes on paper from Stewart and added a few himself. He needed dates and addresses. With repeated glances, he seemed to be studying Ron. He put down his pen.

"Our guy Stewart who you talked to is interested in what they call 'residual hauntings'. That's when there's a scene, an image or noise that keeps being repeated in a particular place, like something recorded. It could be footsteps. It could be energy. If there is a presence, it does not interact with you. Stewart will investigate a residual haunting with an electromagnetic meter, video and audio."

Ron had read brief summaries of some case histories on the website. He asked, "Have you ever gone along? Have you seen any of that?"

Paul laughed. "Yes, and yes. Not that often, but definitely. I'm a parapsychologist. I'm interested in psychic phenomena, like telepathy, psychokinesis, and clairvoyance."

Ron mentioned the storefront psychic and what she said.

Paul shrugged. "She might have felt or seen something. But what I want to know is if you just saw your cousin in the corner of your eye. That's a common kind of sighting."

"No. I saw him full-on."

"What was he wearing?"

Ron thought. "White. He wore all white. And when he was leaving I could see through him."

"But you were in bed. You know, there's such a thing as a 'dream visitation'."

"I was sitting up the whole time, my feet on the floor. I'm sure I was awake."

"Did you feel ill?"

That was one of the emerging memories that were coming back to him in recent days. "I felt, I guess . . . dizzy."

Now Paul was writing full sentences on his report. "To me, this is a more rare thing, called an 'intelligent haunting'. There are different reasons why the person wants to come back to a certain place, but the obvious one here is a strong connection to a place, a thing, or person. You. To communicate something. From my experience, it was a one-time thing, and that's it. This is a good case study."

Paul was getting ready to leave. "But I'd like you to do one thing, Ron. When you can, spend another night in that same room. I doubt anything will happen, but your memory may bring back more, more than just, 'Don't cry or I'll leave.' If there's anything you learn, please get in touch."

Finally, Ron was satisfied. Someone believed him, and now there was a record of what he had experienced. Driving home, he thought that Paul had seemed really professional – he was not some weirdo. But the idea of sleeping in that room again seemed very unlikely. Less than a month later, that changed.

One day, Ron was checking the listings of available houses and he saw a good deal in his cousin's hometown. Laura was John's older sister, ten years older, and now she was divorced, with a daughter away at college. Ron would need two days to make the house deal and she said she'd love his company.

The evening he arrived at Laura's place, he saw right away that she was using a different room for guests. The room he slept in three years ago was now filled with boxes of clothes and other stored items. They had a long dinner and a bottle of wine. He mentioned John a few times, but she wanted to talk about his wedding plans and his parents.

Late that night, Ron was wide awake and still dressed in the guestroom. The house was quiet. Barefoot, he walked down the hall to what was now the storage room. A hall light made it easy to see in there and he stepped inside and sat on a large box that was about where he'd been sitting on the bed that night. He tried to remember how it had been.

That night, the memorial wake and his many relatives had worn him out. But he saw himself as the strong one. He'd closed the door to the room but he was in no rush to get undressed and go to bed. He sat there, tired but not sleepy. The house was quiet and the room was partially lit by a standing lamp in the corner to his left. Gradually, a feeling came over him. He'd told that guy Paul that he'd felt dizzy, but it wasn't that exactly. He felt uneasy, uneasy right through his body.

Ron closed his eyes and remembered how he'd looked up and there John was, directly in front of him, against the wall and facing him. Then he seemed to glide forward – he didn't walk, he somehow moved closer. Remembering, picturing him again, Ron saw that John wasn't really dressed in all white, but in what he'd been wearing during his last twenty-four hours . . . a tight white T-shirt with a rock band logo, and pajama pants, white with a light blue pattern. Now he recalled that John's eyes did not look at him; they stared straight ahead in an eerie, fixed way. But he had come back only for Ron. At that moment, they both were aware of how close they had once been. Intensely close. Before John went off to college. Throughout their high-school years they found ways to be together, especially when Ron got a driver's license.

John's hand came down on his shoulder – he didn't feel it but he saw it. The message, the whole feeling, was about how close they'd been. John wanted to remind him, just remind him. And now, in present time, the missing piece came to Ron. It wasn't the college years that ended their close bond. It was himself, he knew. The part he never wanted to think about, what he thought didn't matter – but it did matter. Through several years there had been their secret – sex. It was no big deal, the teenage Ron had thought. It was what John wanted, and what Ron allowed. But, before he was experienced with girls, he didn't mind. And, if he admitted the truth, he liked the feeling of power he had over John – that's what was a turn-on to him. In fact, he realized now, that's where he learned the thrill of showing-off: in those unspoken, secret, late-night moments of lust with John. How hot to be desired so much. How passive his cousin was, and how pretty. Their French-Canadian heritage really showed in John's teenage years – such a beautiful boy. But it had to end. By last year of high school, he was dating girls. He cut John off, made excuses not to see him. Only now did he realize that those times fooling around had a much greater meaning to John.

More than that. As John had stood there by him in that room, his unspoken message had been just to remember their closeness. It was more important than sex. Ron had betrayed it. But somewhere beyond time it still mattered – how close they were, their love. They should have remained close. But John forgave him. He only wanted Ron to remember.

He did remember. He did agree. It had been special between them.

That night three years ago, John's voice seemed strange but real enough: "Don't cry or I'll leave." Ron did cry and John backed away and vanished against the same blank wall Ron looked at now. Sorry for the past but, with a glowing feeling in his chest, glad to understand now, Rob sobbed quietly, and said, "I'm sorry, John. I'm sorry."

A Night with Mr Goldstein
Colin Spencer

———

"There must be some heterosexuals who are patrons of arts," Jane pronounced. "So why don't you ever manage to find them?"

"But we don't know about Mr Goldstein," Matthew answered, trying not to let the irritation creep into his tone. He was thinking: don't make difficulties, please; we desperately need the money. Jane had stopped working, for she was in the final stages of pregnancy, so they now relied upon the sale of Matthew's paintings and drawings in order to live.

Jane knew that her husband had had a somewhat promiscuous and homosexual life before they had married and her personal insecurity fastened upon this as the reason for any strife and unhappiness they suffered.

"I don't know why you must always leap to conclusions," he added with a slight note of bitterness. He watched Jane's face as she smiled with that self-righteous superiority that always infuriated him. "It could mean a lot of money," he said, raising his voice and staring at her defiantly.

He had been commissioned to do a series of drawings of different aspects of a large Victorian country house which was owned but soon to be pulled down by a property millionaire who wished to build in its place a more suitable abode for the times, made out of reinforced concrete and glass. Mr Goldstein had extensive property interests in London and a chain of new hotels, which were all built in the ubiquitous and aggressive modern style. It had been pointed out to Matthew by Mr Goldstein's private secretary that there could easily be many future commissions for him in painting murals in the hotels. He was informed by those in the upper hierarchy that clung around Mr Goldstein that the millionaire did not like to be crossed, that he had difficult moods, but that he wished eventually to be publicly known as a discerning patron of the arts.

"But is he?" Matthew asked.

The private secretary, Rex Whitehead, both lank and elegant and smelling powerfully of lime toilet water, raised his eyebrows and said: "No, of course not. We choose what he buys. That is why . . ." he inclined his head to one side so that one fair wavy lock of hair fell down over his forehead, "we can help you."

Matthew looked about the spacious office, murmuring: "Ta, ever so." He stared at the paintings that now hung on the walls. They were all safe choices: two early Sutherlands, a Henry Moore shelter drawing, a still life with eggs and frying pan by William Scott, a relief by Ben Nicholson and a sub-Calder mobile. Mr Whitehead stood in the middle of the room observing Matthew's reactions, then he said, flapping his arm: "Oh, it's the crème de la crème in here, but down at the house we're far more adventurous. There's some enchanting work by younger painters. A Keith Grant that's absolutely super, so Icelandic it gives me the shivers, so chilling, so cold . . ." Mr Whitehead went on with gruesome expansiveness.

The commission meant that Matthew would have to go down to stay in West Sussex for a long weekend.

"Well, I see I'm not invited," said Jane, "so obviously they don't like women down there."

Matthew shrugged. "It's a matter of business, that's all." He rose to go to bed and heard her say, as he climbed the stairs, "Just you wait. I can smell 'em a mile off." What a tiresome woman, he thought, but as he climbed into bed he looked forward with pleasurable anticipation to the weekend ahead, where there was sure to be plenty of excellent booze and delicious food. It would make a change from the penury of their present existence.

That Friday, he arrived by train and taxi and was shown immediately into the drawing room of Westingcote. It was carpeted in dove grey, the windows were draped with sage green velvet curtains and the armchairs and sofas upholstered in smoky blue silk. There were half a dozen other young men awaiting the arrival of Mr Goldstein. Matthew could not help thinking that Jane had a truer instinct over these matters than he did, for there was not one young man assembled in the room who did not have a perfect profile, nor hands empty of rings, nor necks unscented, and a thought passed through his mind that he may have been chosen not for the value of his work, but rather for the regularity of his features. A large Keith Vaughan of nude bathers reflected all the colours of the room; indeed, as aspiring patrons do, misjudging caution for taste, the painting had been bought first and the drawing room furnished in the same colours afterwards. Matthew carried on a vaguely polite conversation with Rex who was showing him the consideration due to a stranger, but as Matthew glanced about the room, staring at its inhabitants, the thought occurred to him that there ought to be a descriptive noun for such an assembly. If there is a gaggle of geese or a swarm of bees or a shoal of fish, couldn't one have a cuttle of queers or a swoop of sodomites? But into these reflections came suddenly an awed hush that fell upon the room – all heads were turned expectantly towards the door as the master-millionaire's progress was discerned through the house. "Mr Goldstein," Rex whispered in muted tones, "likes us all to wait for cocktails until he arrives."

Matthew glanced at his watch and murmured: "He's about three-quarters of an hour late for me."

Rex gave him a glance that seemed to ask for caution, warning Matthew that he may be on the way to violating the hidden rules of the house. Suddenly, framed in the doorway, was an extremely short gentleman with white hair and dressed – impeccably, but in colour mercilessly – in a metallic blue of unfortunate stridency; his tie was the perfect choice for the English gentleman, navy blue with white spots, but his shoes, two-toned white and brown, gave both his foreign extraction and his monetary affluence away. On closer inspection, everything was hand-sewn and his smile, when grasping Matthew's hand, was of warm yet abrupt docility, as if he were Matthew's servant and had not even heard of the words "power" and "property", or was not aware of the concept of a financial empire. Matthew noticed that he treated all of the young men similarly. Then Mr Goldstein gave an almost imperceptible snap of finger and thumb and immediately a butler walked in carrying a tray of iced martinis.

They sipped their drinks and Mr Goldstein returned again to Matthew; he held his arm and drew him away to one corner of the room, nodding to a sculpture. "This I bought two days ago," he said, with his slight Polish intonations. "What do you think of it? You are a young painter, I would like to have your private opinion." He said this small speech with more harshness than Matthew thought absolutely necessary; the charm and docility had gone, gone now because he was on uncertain ground and he desired to protect himself.

Matthew said truthfully, recognizing the work to be by Elisabeth Frink: "I like her work. This is a fairly good example – she is both figurative and expressive," and then smiling at Mr Goldstein and with the barest hint of a bow, added: "I think you made a wise choice."

But Mr Goldstein was still carefully debating in his mind the import of what Matthew had said, and after a moment's consideration he swung round and cried out to Rex Whitehead: "Only fairly good. Mr Simpson says this is only fairly good." And he walked swiftly across the room to where the alarmed Mr Whitehead was quickly finishing his martini and snatching another. "Why do you waste my money? Why is my money thrown away on works of art that are only fairly good?"

Rex, in his agitation, swallowed the olive in his glass and, staring for a moment with spite over his angry employer's shoulder at Matthew, said in a voice of disdain: "It was not the opinion of several excellent judges of Miss Frink's work." Matthew had also crossed the room, distressed by his inadvertent remark and horrified at the change that had come over his host.

"You really must not be concerned with what I said. Rex is absolutely right, I know very little of her work and am in no position to judge."

Mr Goldstein looked slightly mollified. He took out a white lawn handkerchief and patted the suffused pinkness of his cheeks and forehead.

"I have to be on my guard," he murmured. "You do see that. I have to be on my guard."

The rest of the time before dinner was without incident for Matthew who, warned by this exposure to Mr Goldstein's sensitivity, was extremely careful only to admire and congratulate his host on the various *objets d'art*, even when they were of the utmost vulgarity and in the most bizarre juxtaposition.

Dinner was served upon a long black marble table, the legs of which were green and carved in the shape of cherubs, their podgy stomachs and limbs glittering with emerald brilliance. The room was lit by three-coloured glass chandeliers of recent Murano make, and upon each of the two walls that had neither door nor windows hung what Mr Goldstein referred to as his "old masters", one of which seemed to be yet another representation in shades of turd of a platitudinous Holy Family, the mother of Jesus draped with a Spanish shawl that might have been more suitable for a flamenco dance than for holding the Son of God; the other painting was of more interest, being possibly the School of Rubens and exhibiting three fat ladies with gargantuan thighs and bottoms playing ring a ring o' roses.

Matthew had noted that the house contained only one female – a Mrs Biggs, who was both cook and housekeeper and had appeared momentarily when they had entered the dining room. She was impassively large and glowering, wearing a starched white overall, her grey hair pinned tightly back beneath a cap, and appeared to Matthew rather like the sternest possible matron commanding a lunatic asylum.

He had also noticed yet another change come over his host. To make things seem like a social occasion rather than a business exploit, Mr Goldstein was addressed as Bernie and showed a side of himself full of jollity. All the young men now relaxed into incessant, tiresome chatter and gossipy anecdotes about people that Matthew was not familiar with. Until Bernie suddenly, as a frog does when it croaks, puffed out his tiny metallic-blue suited self and cried: "My house will be the most modern, the most up-to-date, the most efficient streamlined house ever built this century. Why live in a museum," and he looked about him, "like this?" Then he shrugged. "What do people see in old houses? They're draughty and cold. They were never built for people like me and my needs."

Rex leant over the table towards Matthew and said: "After dinner you must see Bernie's suite of rooms. They're at the back and are the beginning of the new house."

"I have the best view of the county," Bernie cried from the other end of the table. "No windowpanes, just one great big piece of glass and the whole of the county at my feet." Exactly where he would like it, thought Matthew.

Following their host, who was still in the midst of the diatribe against any house built before the present year, they all trooped after him up the stairs to where a heavy baize door was unlocked. For them it must have been the twentieth time they had seen these rooms but they all behaved like children, excitedly chattering as if on a special school treat. As Matthew went through the door into the rooms nothing indeed could have prepared him for the shock. It was insane science fiction.

The first stimulus on one's eyes was of bright shining light and areas of silver metal but, as Bernie moved about the room pulling switches, pressing black knobs and turning small silver handles off and on, extraordinary things began to happen; to the sound of a slight whirr a white wall contracted to one side, revealing the late evening landscape, a smooth rolling lawn edged by shrubs and finishing in a ha-ha then progressing through long grass down to the lake fringed with forest and more clumps of giant oak trees and rolling hills now misty and grey with the dusk. The quiet beauty of the English landscape outside made Matthew even more acutely aware of what was happening inside.

In the middle of the room there hung what one might have supposed was a form of electric light, but as Bernie explained: "And what do you think of my Dolmech-Doon?" A large plastic egg pierced by various steel pins with three different-coloured balls rotating inside. "He is the rage in New York," Bernie said proudly then, swinging around, he pressed another switch and the third wall groaned, caved outwards, and a large black bed on its oiled hinges swung out from the wall. It was completely round and Matthew paused to reflect how bewildering it might be not to know where your head or feet ought to be. Then Bernie took them into the sunken bath in marble, onyx and gold; Bernie's love of Hollywood glamour having obviously got the better of him here. Then from the bathroom he entered his dressing room and, at the touch of a switch, walls opened to show rows of suits and overcoats, piles of laundered shirts, rows of well-polished shoes. To cries and exclamations of how brilliant and clever Bernie was, the party returned to the Victorian side of the house where coffee and liqueurs awaited them. It was while taking these that Rex crossed the room to Matthew and said: "As you were so delighted with the modern suite, Bernie would like you to sleep there tonight." There was a horrified silence.

Matthew said: "Not in that bloody bed."

Rex looked as if sacrilege had been spoken and with an air of hushed pain announced: "If you should wish it, there is a separate bed, but that's really a matter between you and Bernie." Rex swung around, leaving him alone. Matthew went towards the window and pulled the curtains aside, looking out at the dark countryside. It was ten miles to the nearest station. Should he make a fuss? He felt furious about the whole establishment, furious that in employing anyone they should think they have the right to his body as well. Then, suddenly smiling a little, he turned and went over to Bernie, who was in the middle of a crowd of several admirers. "Oh, Bernie," Matthew said in a loud voice, "I hear I'm sleeping with you tonight."

Bernie looked up with his most ravishing smile, nodding.

Matthew went on: "I think I ought to warn you that I suffer from epilepsy. Strange beds in the dark often bring on an attack. If this should happen, don't be alarmed, don't bother to call a doctor – the worst of it will be over in a matter of hours and I sleep very soundly after one."

Bernie did not look as put out as Matthew had wished. He simply said airily: "Oh, I'm sorry to hear that," and went back to continuing his former conversation.

Matthew thought grimly: I'll get the rich old sod; he's going to have a night to remember.

The party broke up and went to their various rooms; Matthew yawned and murmured how tired he was. He and Bernie went through the green baize door and to Matthew's extreme distaste he noticed that Bernie locked it after him. The round bed was down and in position, its covers turned back.

"Rex said that there was another bed."

"Oh, far too small," Bernie muttered.

"But if I should have an attack," Matthew cried, thinking that he really didn't know quite what epileptics do except go into violent spasms and froth at the mouth.

Now Bernie's gestures took on the air of a predatory animal as he flung off his coat and undid the zip of his trousers. He eyed Matthew warily, much as, Matthew thought, an owl in a tree staring down at a field mouse. Matthew appeared to be unconcerned and indifferent and began to whistle the waltz tune of Baron Ochs. He undressed, keeping a pair of black underpants on, and got into bed and closed his eyes, only to open them again with a terrible shock a moment later as he heard Bernie squeak: "Oh, my little lovely, my fair blond dearie, can't you love your uncle a little?"

"No," Matthew said vehemently, beginning to draw back from the two pink podgy hands that stroked his hair. But to draw back on a round bed is merely to circle the bed, and as Bernie's naked form, covered in grey hair, advanced over him he wondered whether he might start an epileptic fit that very moment, but somehow his emotional resources were not ready.

Bernie's imploring cries went on: "Oh, my little saucy-faced lovesome, don't be a naughty, wicked boy to uncle when uncle's so rich and will give you everything you want," and he flung himself at Matthew and lay panting with his teeth irritatingly stuck to Matthew's right nipple.

Really, this is too much, Matthew thought, the wretched man was gnawing at his chest like a dog at a bone. With a lurch he flung himself round the bed, rushed across the room and went into the bathroom. Bernie was in hot pursuit and to Matthew's horror no doors had any locks on them because they were all electronically controlled. So now, with the taste of wild adventure within him, every knob and switch he saw, Matthew pulled, pushed and turned. He was immediately deluged with a jet of hot water that Bernie, running into the bathroom, got the full force of. Matthew went on into the dressing room, touched a switch and hid himself behind a row of suits. Bernie entered, nude and streaming wet, crying out: "I can play games too." Matthew peeped from behind a crimson velvet dressing gown and saw his predatory host advancing with a whip in one hand and a chain in the other. This, he thought, was getting beyond a joke. He pushed the bar holding twenty Savile Row suits out from the cupboard so that it swung into the room, knocking Bernie down onto the floor while Matthew ran into the smaller bedroom. There, just for the fun of it, he pulled every switch he could see and discovered that he was standing on a glass floor that had suddenly become lit from beneath and was filled with an aquarium of miniature fish.

"I am getting angry," Bernie cried. "I will not be trifled with."

Matthew ran back into the first large bedroom, into the centre of the room, and taking the large Dolmech-Doon egg from its steel thread, he threw it at Bernie, saying: "Here, catch."

"My egg," Bernie squeaked, making a sideways leap in football style to catch the hideous flying object. To Matthew's surprise, not only did he catch it, but he threw it back. Were they going to spend the night playing a form of rugby with the Dolmech-Doon? Matthew threw it again and it landed on the bed, where Bernie was crouched, having somehow lost the chain, thrashing the bedcovers with his whip and crying: "Very well. Now you will pay for it," as if the bed itself was animate.

Matthew was delighted with the excitement of the switch-pulling, and continued, only aware that the bed had withdrawn into the wall, taking its owner with it, upon hearing a strangled gasp of: "Help, help."

Matthew was not certain whether to be horrified or pleased. As long as the muffled cries for help continued, he felt that at least he couldn't be charged with manslaughter, so he dressed, noticing that the jet of hot water was now seeping in from the bathroom and running in a long, glistening puddle over the white marble floor. He unlocked the green baize door, opened it, looked both ways and ran down the empty corridor. He opened the first bedroom door that he could find, fumbled for the light switch, flooded the room with electric light and looked at the large double bed, in which were two naked forms heavily entwined. Both sat up abruptly, cursing. "I'm looking for Rex," Matthew said.

One of the young men began stuttering and pointed: "The third door on the left."

Matthew turned, put out the light, said: "Do carry on without me," and began his journey down the corridor, hoping that the muffled cries for help had not yet stopped. He opened the third door on the left, switched on the light and surveyed the marble eyes of Mrs Biggs, her hair in curlers.

"I do beg your pardon," Matthew stuttered. "I'm looking for Mr Whitehead."

Mrs Biggs gave him a look of thunder and pointed to the door. He found himself bowing and even walking out backwards, such was the august presence of this lady. He closed the door behind him and reflected that he was nowhere near finding the usually ubiquitous Mr Whitehead. He decided to try the door opposite and this time knocked before entering. He switched on the light and with relief saw that Rex was asleep, his face shining with moisturizing cream. Matthew shook him and Rex's sleepy voice said: "What do you want? I've just taken sleeping pills."

"Bernie's locked up in the wall," Matthew cried.

"Wall?" Rex echoed.

"The bed in the wall. Bernie's in it. You get him out; I'm sleeping downstairs on the sofa."

Rex groaned and slowly heaved himself to a sitting position. "Oh no, oh no! What have you done with Mr Goldstein?" he cried piteously. "You haven't left him in the wall?" Slowly, he rose out of the bed, his pale pink nightshirt rucked up to his thighs. "This is the end," he wailed, "for us all. Not locked in the wall?" He went out into the corridor calling the names of the Goldstein sycophantic group: "Gerald. Julien. Andrew. Tony. Matthew's locked Bernie in the wall. He might be dead by now. Come and help." His dismal pink figure trailed down the corridor, swaying sleepily from side to side, and slowly rising in the house were the murmurings of distress, sounds of commotion and unrest, as svelte, pale, rose-skinned, half-naked young men began to fill the corridor. Matthew left them, went downstairs, opened the sideboard drawer, found a white damask tablecloth and, taking that for a blanket, a glass and a full bottle of Scotch, he retired to the drawing room sofa.

He awoke early in the morning with a disgustingly bad head and debated what he might do. The price of the first drawing had been agreed as £2,000. He decided to rise early to do that drawing and be paid for it, and then to leave. It was about ten-thirty – he was halfway through a line drawing of the absurd mansion with its turrets, battlements and decorated chimneys – when he observed Mr Whitehead delicately walking on his toes over the dew-sodden grass, carrying with him a small slip of green paper that flapped in the gentle breeze. Matthew did not look up from the drawing, but murmured: "Good morning." Rex laid the cheque upon the white paper and said icily: "Mr Goldstein wishes you to have this and to leave immediately."

Matthew said: "I'll leave when the drawing's finished."

"That will not be necessary," Rex said. "We do not wish for this drawing."

"Bugger your wishes, mate. You're getting it."

Rex moved away in silence.

On his return home, Jane asked him how the weekend went, for Matthew had not gone back immediately, but spent the Saturday night in London relating to a friend the absurd and incredible events of the night before. Matthew told Jane that Mr Goldstein was the kind of person that would bring on anti-Semitism in even the most liberal and kind-hearted. He implied to her that he doubted whether there would be any more commissions and she, sensing again the world that threatened her, asked him no more.

Best Tasted Cold
Felice Picano

———

It had all begun back in 1968, that very special year of chaos and fun: political chaos all over the world and political madness and, well, personal madness too. So Victor shouldn't have been too surprised at the way the whole affair began. Or turned out. On the other hand, he *was* still a young man that year and, while a little battered and slightly bruised from two previous failed affairs with men, still pretty naive. Worse, yet, he still had hope and somehow or other that must have actually shown. Hopes seem to exist only to be crushed, don'tcha think?

Well, anyway, he and Todd met in an astrology class that Victor attended once a week, right after his work in a bookstore a short subway ride away – I did mention that this happened in 1968, right?

Victor had met the astrologer, Randy, through a friend because she knew that the two of them – Victor and Randy – were both learning to read Chinese: Classical Mandarin. Victor was also learning to write it, too, with an ink-brush, on rice paper, both of which he'd bought for too much money at Takashimaya, a specialized Japanese-only products shop on Fifth Avenue near the main branch of the New York Public Library.

Randy was an Aquarian, a big, healthy, outgoing, optimistic, brown-eyed, brown curly haired, straight-acting Western Ohio guy who would have been the life of the toga party of any alcohol-soaked and weed-crazed, self-disrespecting jock fraternity – except for the fact that he was happily queer and was always hungry for guys.

Victor and Randy began having sex, and the Chinese language that had first brought them together was totally forgotten. And, while Randy was really a lot of fun, he was really just into Victor for a toss in the sack once a week; in rotation, Victor worked out, with another half-dozen guys. Which was fine by him. There was little in the way of anything beyond a sexual *frisson* between them; Randy was about as romantic as a freight-train boxcar, and even for young Victor he was physically unsophisticated – a kind of Slam-bam! Thanks, man! bed partner.

But one evening, between bouts, he mentioned to Victor that he taught astrology classes and he was starting up a new one, and he said that Victor might sit in, at half the usual fee – as long as they continued to occasionally have sex, natch. And, since Victor was horny all the time in 1968, and Randy had charted them and done "synastry" (i.e. looking at their birth charts placed together), he'd come to believe (which Victor didn't need synastry to *know*) that there was no possibility of a relationship ever developing between them. So it all seemed clear and easy, an all-round good deal.

Most of the others in the class were earnest, young straight women (and one older one) who'd taken the course not for pure knowledge as Victor had, but for more practical reasons. They wanted to know more deeply or complexly about themselves – keep in mind that this was an early era of Serious Feminism – and they also wanted to know about their relationships: chiefly boyfriends, but also lovers, and there might have even been a husband knocking about.

There were maybe nine altogether in the class, although the actual number varied from week to week in its make-up from six to sometimes twelve. They met in Randy's not-quite-Chelsea area Manhattan loft, a big well-heated space that you reached via a clackety old industrial elevator or by several tall, narrow stairways, high up within a beat-up old building with sweatshops on its lower floors. The loft had been furnished pretty much off the nearby Manhattan streets, chiefly via the unintentional largesse of the NYC Sanitation Department's policy of "Throwaway Thursdays", but also from thrift shops, with a few clearly from-home (if unexceptional) pieces. The only item bought new was Randy's king-sized waterbed – quite sensibly, as he got so much use out of it.

The pupils would sit around on not-quite-tattered sofas or bean-bag chairs or on a wooden floor barely covered by carpets and Randy would lecture from a rolling blackboard at the front of the living room, upon which he'd draw and mark up chalked-in and pinned-up colored paper astrological charts.

The year or so that the group met, they were taught the "basics" of astrology and they worked on sample birth charts. But because those times were so filled with assassinations, wars, and media-grabbing crimes – the famous Manson Family murders, for example – Randy would also bring in "horary" charts, i.e. horoscopes about specific events, especially for the more knowledgeable students: in effect, detective work.

That was fun and, while Victor found the group to be intermittently interesting, he also learned enough there to give himself a very reliable groundwork in this occult art (or science; or better yet, symbolical language) to last the rest of his life. It also ended up being a great help for a young writer to look at people's birth charts and analyze how various aspects of a specific personality were linked – and/or *not* linked – together. In the next few serious years of his writing career, whenever Victor found himself "stuck" figuring out who a major character actually was, he would simply construct a date of birth for him or her, or make up an astrological chart, and then delineate it, as though analyzing a real person's birth chart. He found that helped.

Among the other regularly attending men in the astrology class, there was Lars, a travel agent and former airline steward, who had pretensions toward the arts of some never clearly specified nature. Lars was blond and slender and Nordic-ly handsome – a type that Victor was instantly drawn to, and he guessed that Randy was fucking Lars too. Even so, despite only being in his early thirties, Lars's looks were going fast. He would look middle-aged for a very long time.

Then there was Todd, a sleek, solid, well-built fellow who was a close pal of the group leader, and about the same age; although not, Randy said, a fuck buddy, as they were "too alike". According to Randy,

Todd had been a sort of whiz kid at Harvard University, where a play of his had been put on by the acclaimed Drama Department. He'd then won some sort of drama award and the play had been produced for a commercial run at the Mark Taper Forum in Los Angeles – all by the age of twenty. A considerable achievement.

Supremely confident, extremely comfortable in his large, well-muscled, attractive body, Todd seemed to be the kind of man Victor had come to learn to avoid in postgraduate life. From his suave, well-oiled, FM radio-announcer's bass-baritone voice to his apparent sense of his own importance while issuing questions to Randy and the group, there was an aura about Todd, an ineffable sense of having been a prodigy and of still being a golden boy, a privileged youth, part of the *jeunesse dorée*, that made Victor wary – and a little contemptuous.

Perhaps it was Victor's poorly hidden scorn that drew Todd toward him. God knew, Victor did nothing *consciously* to attract Todd, besides – of course – his inability to help being young and cute. Yet, from the very first class meeting at that overheated Twenty-seventh Street loft, Victor felt that Todd was after him. For proof: right after the initial meeting, Victor found Todd rushing to catch up to him along the street, asking Victor to join him and a woman, who called herself "Tanya", also from the group, barely able to keep up behind, for "coffee and discussion".

Victor said he couldn't; he had another appointment – a total lie. The truth was, he didn't trust Todd and he didn't like the look of the woman. She was tall, with slender waist, wide hips, very well dressed (a fur! compared to the general poverty of the rest of the working-class students in the class) – and she had too much astray long strawberry blond hair and, even more than Todd, an air or attitude of privilege Victor couldn't quite put a finger on. Worse, he didn't like the two of them together. They had sat side by side, a little away from the others during that first class, on a distant sofa, and had murmured and confided. He'd kept hoping that Randy would tell them to shut up and pay attention but he hadn't seemed to care.

Before the second class meeting began, Todd came early enough so that he could ask Victor out after again. Randy must have told him that Victor would be there early – having sex with Randy, in fact, though he was sure Randy hadn't told Todd *that part*. Again, Victor said he had to be somewhere afterward and couldn't join Todd. Another lie, even though Tanya wasn't present.

This went on for weeks, and since by early spring, Victor had discovered without particularly wanting to that Todd, (1) was born under the sun sign of Taurus, and thus known to be persevering to the point of unrelenting, and (2) had remained in class while Tanya had totally dropped out, proving to be more palatable on his own. One day, Victor at last gave in to Todd's repeated blandishments, and had coffee with him after class.

This turned out to be what Victor's best friend Gilbert characterized as a "Classic Major Mistake" the next day – and Gilbert had not even *met* Todd.

Alone, one on one, Todd was charming. Todd was modest. Todd was a perfectly modulated, utterly unthreatening, off-hand kind of guy. Todd was intelligent. Todd wasn't *half* the jerk Victor had assumed he was. Unlike those at Victor's stupid bookstore day job who looked at Victor as though he had three heads whenever they would see him at lunch or on coffee break reading his giant, carmine-covered Mandarin Chinese primer, Todd was encouraging.

In fact, Todd himself practiced Zazen meditation and, like Victor, he was a budding Buddhist. He said he would help Victor try "sitting contemplation" and perhaps, in turn, Victor might help him learn the art of calligraphy, a revered Zen art. As for Chinese, Todd also studied it. And more. So much more.

An older Victor would have seen all this as the life trap it clearly, in retrospect, was. Whenever anyone is that perfect, there's got to be a hitch, right? Right!

A week later, Victor let himself be talked into going to dinner with Randy and Todd at a wealthy friend of the astrologer's town house. Afterward, as the three walked home, well fed and especially well wined, toward the subway station, Todd threw an arm over Victor's shoulder with studied casualness and kept it there. He had recently revealed to Victor that he was bisexual and had last been dating, but had stopped seeing, Tanya. Even so, Victor found himself surprised, and he had to admit – this was 1968, remember, pre-Stonewall – even impressed by this minor, yet expressive, openly physical demonstration of homoeroticism.

Victor was equally surprised the next time they went out to dinner by Todd's sudden and passionate kiss at the subway entrance. From there on, it was only a matter of days until Todd had finagled Victor inside his little studio apartment off Central Park West.

In those days, this area was not the overpriced yuppie fiefdom it's since become: a boutique-ridden, logo-shop-filled outdoor city mall. Instead, it was a blessedly empty, if not quite forlorn, residential neighborhood, inhabited mostly by hetero singles needing cheap rents in newly remodeled buildings, interspersed with larger, uglier, slightly less old, un-remodeled tenements, literally chock-a-block with Puerto Rican immigrant families. There were very few food stores or other convenience shops, and all of them were mom and pop-type establishments, chained up and locked by sunset, some with inadequately leashed, oversized Alsatians trained to leap at you with bared, drooling fangs.

As a result, of course, the neighborhood proved to be dazzlingly romantic, certainly for a twosome wanting to be left alone, since the Rican domino and card-players didn't even blink seeing guys arm in arm. This setting had been partly responsible for Victor letting down his guard enough so that Todd could woo him, break down any possible remaining resistance, and jump his bones.

Their sex together was not great. Not really even good. Kind of fumbling one moment and deeply passionate the next. Then fumbling again. At least the first few times. They were both more or less "tops", even if Todd was a larger and more aggressive version. Victor thought this should end matters between them quickly. But Todd was a persevering Taurus, after all, and he persisted, and so after some weeks of relentless battering, hints, suggestions, pleading, dirty talk, blowjobs – not to mention rim jobs – Victor relaxed, and then Victor relented, and finally Victor let big Todd in the back door.

But it was by no means a conquest in any definition of that term. After, and for some weeks after, Victor thought he could take or leave Todd in an instant. Having spent months getting to know Victor, more months wangling Victor into bed, and another few getting Victor beneath himself, Todd seemed at last happy, at least for the moment – maybe because he did actually see Victor as an official "conquest". Whoever knows what men are really thinking in these situations – straight or gay? Victor never would know, and for the record, he only counted himself an adult the day he stopped trying.

All the more of a surprise, a rather terrible surprise for Victor, one morning a few weeks later, as they rode the subway from Todd's studio to their respective workplaces after a night together, when Victor happened to suddenly realize that he'd been seduced more deeply, more thoroughly than he'd suspected, or had wanted, or, truthfully, more than he would admit.

Victor remembered the awful moment all too well: Todd was eating a piece of celery and looking up at the subway's placard ads around them, oblivious of Victor. And Victor looked down and saw that he had a boner and he thought: Oh hell! I'm in love with this guy.

He kept this fact to himself. But men like Todd somehow always intuit when this critical stage has been attained; even if the other party does not alter his behavior one jot. From then on, Todd began to be more cavalier around and towards Victor. Vic's slightest feelings, once catered to by Todd as though Victor were a Habsburg Grand Duke, were now, little by little, ignored and at last traduced. All tiny matters, but increasingly consistent. Plans they'd make would be changed by Todd at the last minute, and by phone. He began to drop by Victor's flat with women he'd dated, or perhaps was about to date, without phoning in advance – and one time with a guy in full leather, also a playwright.

Victor could never figure out if Todd was sleeping with any of them, just sleeping with them, or what precisely he was doing with them.

Todd had long wanted Victor to meet his sister, younger and with a history of emotional problems, and Victor at last did. She verbally reminded him of those scars on Todd's wrists. Those scars, she said, were from when Todd had attempted to commit suicide, when the first love of his life, sophomore year at Harvard, had dumped him. Todd had almost died.

So Victor had even been *warned* about this guy. But did Victor pay attention? What do you think?

One weekend, Todd left Victor waiting somewhere a little too long and Victor got tired of the constant mistreatment and took off. Todd's phone call that evening was five minutes of apologies. He wanted to come over and make it up to Victor – instantly. Victor made up an excuse why that would be impossible. The next day, Todd didn't phone as he was supposed to. Nor the next. Nor the next. Nor, naturally, did Victor. On the outside, at work, among friends, Victor was a wall. Inside, he'd slowly begun dying: lovelorn dying, the worst, and even then he knew, the tackiest.

The week worsened. This was the era before faxes, emails, instant messaging, texting, or even common phone-message machines. Missed calls were missed, period. Or, more likely, they hadn't been made. Victor waited for a phone call from Todd.

Finally, one Sunday evening, Todd phoned. In the background Victor heard a public announcement about various flight-departure times.

What Todd said was simple enough: he thought they needed time apart. He knew *he* needed time alone. In an hour, he was flying to Athens, and from there taking a boat to a Greek island he'd talked often of them visiting together. Only now he was going alone. He didn't know how long he would remain there, probably until his money ran out. That might be six months.

Why go into details about exactly how Victor felt receiving that particular phone call? Victor did recall being polite, never once raising his voice, and then – well, Victor couldn't recall more than that – and not a lot of the ensuing seven months, either. Except that he got through it alive and in one piece. He also recalled walking home from some gathering at a friend's that he'd left early, feeling unwell, and once home and indoors, literally falling face forward onto the carpeted stairway of his building, feeling that his heart had been driven into, as though by a spear point. Who knew that a person could actually, physically, experience heartbreak?

Following that ghastliness, Victor went to bed for four days and when he returned to work he looked so awful that his store manager – a crude person of no apparent sensitivity before this very moment – sat him down in his office for an hour and kept asking if he needed an ambulance. When Victor refused, the manager at last got them a taxi and took Victor home himself and got him into bed. He held the job open for two weeks. But Victor never returned to the bookstore, although he eventually did get out of bed.

By the time Victor heard that Todd was back in Manhattan, the news came from one of the women he'd earlier brought by Victor's place, with whom Victor had become a little friendly of late. She and her roommate were giving a party and she mentioned, just as Victor walked in the door, that she thought Todd might show up. She waited for his response. There was none. So she and Victor danced to the Rolling Stones as Mick Jagger yelled out, "Brown Sugar!"

Victor did see Todd enter, with a man. Victor vanished into the flat's single bedroom. Todd came looking for him. He acted as though nothing had happened – ever – between them. Victor tried to flee the bedroom, and when Todd made the egregious error of trying to stop him, Victor drove Todd against the wall hard and said, very, very quietly and very, very close to Todd's right ear: "This city isn't big enough for the two of us. If you want to stay healthy, I suggest you leave." Victor then split the party himself.

Years went by. Victor heard from Randy that Todd had taken his advice and moved to faraway Southern California. Randy the astrologer moved to Northern California. The mutual female friend visited Todd in Santa Monica. She offered little info and Victor asked for none but, over time, although Todd kept on plugging away at play after play, it at last became apparent that no one was interested: as a playwright, he'd been a one-shot wonder. Not one of his new scripts was produced, although that first one was done several times more, by ever-smaller and more-distant companies.

Then, at long last, Victor's first novel was written and published and, to his utter astonishment, it sold paperback and book club rights, foreign rights, and then was shortlisted for a brand new, very prestigious literary award.

From their mutual female friend, Victor heard that Todd now had a younger live-in lover, and that they occasionally visited New York City. Then Victor's second novel was published to even better reviews, better sales, and more subsidiary rights than the first. A year later, in paperback, *Justify My Sins* became a national bestseller. Walking through a subway train on the way uptown to meet his publisher – Victor no longer worked regular hours anywhere, of course – he was astonished to see a dozen people in three cars reading his book.

Meanwhile, it was rumored that Todd had stopped writing altogether and had gone into social work. Before they'd met, Victor had been a social worker for two years, right out of college. Now, somehow, their lives had become sort of exchanged: it was downright weird.

In the years in between, Victor had of course thought of revenge against Todd. Whenever Victor had free time in his increasingly ridiculously busy life, he would sit down and plot out elaborate schemes and plans. He was of Italian heritage, land of the Sforzas, Borgias and Machiavelli, and Victor felt it was almost an ethnic duty to seek retribution for how badly he'd been wronged by Todd, a man who may not have become a well-known writer like he was himself these days, but who, after all, still existed on the same planet – a fact that by itself simply *had* to be an outrage.

Victor's third and then fourth novels were published to increasing national, and even international acclaim. With *Nights in Black Leather*, Victor decided it was time to become open and so he went on a national book tour as an openly gay writer – not all that common in 1979, Victor would assure you.

He began in the Northridge Shopping Mall, the center of SoCal Valley Girl suburbia, and, after circling the country by jet, he ended the tour in downtown Los Angeles. Victor found himself feted by readers and famous writers. The Sunday *New York Times* hired a famous, closeted, mystery writer to vilify his new book – and instead, it sold even more copies and was taken up by a major book club as an alternate selection. Victor was written up in newspapers and magazines, interviewed on radio and TV. Harold Robbins threw a party for him. John Rechy asked to meet him. Victor was housed in the Beverly Hilton Hotel, with a chauffeur. Film studios phoned daily, although he'd as soon eat glass shards on toast as trust any of them with gay material.

For a couple of years, Victor was the most famous gay writer in America; you would have to have been illiterate, a gay living under a rock, to not know about him. So Victor assumed that Todd also knew.

Now you've got the backstory. Let's cut back to week number four and a half of Victor living in Beverly Hills as a Frank Perry (*Mommy Dearest, David and Lisa*, etc.) contracted screenwriter.

And, of course, back to Jared the horny roofer man.

It was Mark Chastain, Victor's lover, of all people, who insisted that Victor meet with Todd. Victor had told him the story once, years ago, early in their relationship, and now he reminded Mark again of some of the worse aspects of it all. But Mark was On the Road to Sainthood (an unsavory route Victor would only find out about quite late and to his everlasting chagrin) and it was Mark who mentioned that Todd had called at the West Village duplex several times, leaving a message saying he'd heard Victor was in LA and nearby, and it would be a "real shame" if they didn't meet.

"He sounded nice," Mark said.

"Everyone sounds nice to you, because you're nice," Victor tried explaining.

"Maybe Todd's joined one of the ten-step programs and he's trying to compensate. Don't they have to make nice to everyone they harmed?"

"'Overcoming Egomania' is not covered by Double-A. At least not that I'm aware of."

"Come on! What'll it cost you? Half an afternoon of being polite? Think of it this way," Mark the lawyer in training tried, "What if Todd were me?"

"You're light years apart," Victor assured him. "To begin with, you actually possess a soul."

"So just say to yourself, 'This is Mark who was young and stupid and screwed up once,' and it'll be easier."

"Why? Why? Why? Why? Why?"

"Vic, you're why-ning again."

"Very funny."

"Come on, Vic, you're forgetting important stuff. To begin with you're living in an oversized house with a view, in the 90210 zip code, that someone else is paying for. Next, you are so very close to the top of the world, with two new plays under your feet, four novels out and selling worldwide, *and now* working for Perry doing a film of one of them! While Todd's writing career is utterly nowhere. Tell the truth – will there ever be a better time for you to be seen by this guy?"

It was tempting. Mark then went on for so long and in so many different ways, with variations on that theme, as though he were Vaughan Williams with a string orchestra, for crissakes, that at last Victor relented. Admittedly, he relented just so he could re-meet Todd and then, when Mark *next* called, he could tell him how wrong he had been and what an utter, indeed what a *supernal* schmuck Todd remained.

But Mark was half right. If at any time in his life, Victor was perfectly ready *now* to be seen by Todd. Victor certainly did not expect an apology, never mind an explanation of Todd's past behavior, nor *anything* of the sort. In fact, he was certain the subject would never come up. If it did – on Todd's part – Victor would act like one of those royals in the Duke of Saint-Simon's *Memoirs*, being so ultra-courteous in denying any of it as in any way damaging that Todd would end up thinking none of it had even happened: hemusta'gottenitallwrong!

After all, Todd would be arriving in what he'd told Mark was a "broken-down VW bug", coming from the tiny, leased studio apartment their woman friend had once described, and he would find Victor where? In Mulholland Drive, Hollywood Hills splendor, with balconies and views and a hot new Z Coupe outside. It might not be the vengeance Victor had hoped and planned for but, given it was all happening so fast, he had to admit it would do nicely.

Then fate intervened and, as often occurs in such a case, it soon went from nice to something quite special.

When they'd briefly spoken, Victor had invited Todd over "after work", which he assumed would be sometime after 5 p.m. Todd had accepted the invitation, and so when Alabama-bred Jared showed up after his roofing work for a little fun *out* of the sun, at 3.55, Victor figured they had plenty of time to play.

In fact, they'd already had sex and had hopped into the shower and out, and the roofer was in fact in the act of chasing Victor around the lower bedroom floor of the house, snapping a towel at his luckily unburnt backside, when the doorbell chimed.

Who in the world?

Victor peeked through the side window, couldn't see who it was, grabbed the towel from Jared, and wrapped it around himself, shoving Jared away, down the corridor toward the bedroom. Victor thought he'd take off to find another towel.

Victor then opened the door to – *not* a UPS guy in brown shirt and shorts, *not* the mailman – Todd, a bit older, smiling, his quite nice-looking, undented, crimson VW parked in full sight on the curb of the cul-de-sac.

Todd looked over Victor – who knew he looked stunning, if

perplexed, at this moment – with a smile in which, as T(ough) S(hit) Eliot once put it, surely, memory mixed with desire.

He said: "I came a little early. I hope you don't mind."

Victor had just barely caught his breath from the race around the lower floor and was now about to say, "Wait, you're an hour early," or some other reasonably un-lame reply, when he was suddenly aware of Jared stepping in behind him.

Tall, gorgeous, hung like a mule, and still naked, Jared placed his huge hands around Victor's waist in the classic pose of total sexual possession, leaned forward so his blond ringlets brushed Victor's cheek and asked in that honeyed voice of his – an absolutely perfectly butch Southern construction-worker's bass, redolent of outdoor fish-fries and overlong NASCAR races, of Friday night bar-fights and skinny-dipping in ferny ponds – "Who is it, hon?"

Todd stammered, and immediately after he'd offered to come back on time and before Victor could say a word, he had driven away.

Only to return an hour later, at the appointed time, by which the wonderful Jared had once more been sexually gratified and was gone and Victor was all dressed, dry, and fluffed: ready to be taken to the Hamburger Hamlet.

Once they were seated in those comfy burgundy leather booths facing Sunset Boulevard, Jared was, naturally enough, never once mentioned. Todd and Victor were both by then sufficiently distracted by many other matters than him or even their own long-ended relationship for that to become a topic of conversation. Then, of course, to add insult to injury, halfway through dinner there were Victor Regina fans hovering nearby – a waiter came up to them and asked would he mind terribly? – and Victor simply had to excuse himself and go sign an autograph or two.

In the ensuing hour and twenty minutes, Todd and Victor remained unfailingly courteous, breathtakingly well-mannered: two old friends playing "catch-up" in the most superficial of superficial manners. No trouble, no dirt, nothing that could possibly cause a flicker of a hint of pain to each other ever dreamt of arising. Todd did reference one of Victor's gay stories that a friend of his had read and "thought good", but Victor didn't take up the dropped glove, didn't even recognize that he had been obliquely approached by such an object. Instead, smoothly, he turned the tables and said, "What you're doing with those runaway kids is so terribly, *socially*, important," so that even that cattiest of Ethicists, the Duke of Saint-Simon, would have approved.

A few years later, he told their mutual friend about the meeting and she uncharacteristically pursed her lips, so as not to utter an iota of an adjective, giving Victor the impression that he – and big-dicked Jared – had indeed made the appropriate impression.

And remember that guy in college that Todd slit his wrists over? Victor met him a few years after this event. Slept with him a few times, led him on some months longer, then dumped him quite publicly on the Twelve West dance floor . . . and, of course, he made sure Todd heard all about it.

But that hardly counted. For years after, Victor continued to wonder, really wonder, if he could have purposely prepared a better retaliation than how it actually happened, and he arrived at the conclusion that really, imaginative as Victor could be, *he couldn't have*.

He would never forget, and neither would Todd, Victor believed, that image: Victor in nothing but a tiny hip-slung towel, standing in the sun-flooded foyer of a multi-million-dollar home, with Jared buck-naked behind, holding him possessively, slightly kissing his ear, while he asked that oh-so-innocent, totally devastating question, "Who is it, hon?"

"No one, hon," Victor wanted to have said back, if he only had the sense then. "*No. One. At. All!*"

Eric in Retirement

Robert Cochrane

A car dealer since "National Service",
Eric in retirement
got in touch with his feminine side
with a vengeance.
Two sons, two wives, one bigamously.
And then alone,
he introduced his inner woman to a startled world.
She favoured long black wigs with eye-hiding fringes,
although they were concealed by "Jackie O" shades,
a red padded jacket, black mini-skirt and tights;
dark canvas boots solved his problem with shoes.
For added eccentricity where none was required,
a pale grey military cap suggested
the oldest "Heavy Metal" widow in the west.
Gnarled hands,
a skeletal disposition,
with a face the texture of old grapes
completed this creation,
the final prop, a baby's push-chair,
guided with clumsy incompetence
down supermarket aisles and into charity shops,
causing real old dears quite a turn.
"I can't go into hospital," he explained to one
in a voice suggestive of pints and dominoes
"Who'd look after my birds?
The doctors say I must and these days I do feel awful."

So decomposed when found,
the cause of death could not be ascertained,
he even made the local press.
"Cross-dressing Bigamist Leaves Thirty Thousand Pounds"
and his sons,
the reluctant heirs,
were mentioned without names
as being "emotionally fragile".
Caged and because of his concern for them,
the songbirds also died,
small feathered forms of silence and decay,
perhaps they sometimes sang after he had slipped away
in his council flat like some old pharaoh,
entombed with his glad-rags, handbags,
diamonds, gold and cash,
but in which guise he'd died
the paper didn't say.

The Halfway House
Cliff James

———

In the beginning, the world behind the kitchen door was a foreign place for Brân. He knew nothing of the sedge that had overrun the banks of the sluice and taken possession of the borders. He knew nothing of the reed sweetgrass that had claimed the ruins of the old toolshed and cast armies of plundering roots out to take the lawn. And he knew nothing of the yellow balsam, the *Impatiens noli-tangere* or touch-me-not, whose sensitive seedpods erupted explosively at the slightest caress, firing ripe kernels into the sky and colonizing the dank soil along the riverbank with saplings.

In all the years that he had lived in this house on the edge of the fens, all his life in fact, Brân had never once unfastened the bolt on the kitchen door or stepped outside to gather buddleia blossoms from the butterfly tree. For Brân, the land behind the kitchen door was inherently threatening.

The house itself was neither here nor there; it existed in a liminal space. Some said that an old straight track or ley line passed through its walls and marked the ancient boundary between the realm of human habitation on the one side and the treacherous marshland on the other. Whereas the rear of the house had been reclaimed by rushes and creeping reeds, the front door opened out upon orderly pavements and kerbs. Across the road was the concrete shelter where Brân caught the bus to the library five mornings a week. Beyond the bus stop, a Norman church and cemetery was shielded behind a stone wall. Lampposts had been stationed at regular intervals down the street to cast an unbroken ring of light around the town, protecting the terraced houses from the elemental darkness of the fenland night. Brân's house, however, was on the far side of this road; it was only partially touched by the reach of these streetlights.

Belonging to neither the town nor the wilderness, some said that the house had been built on a thin place. It was also mostly a quiet place. It remained hushed and undisturbed until the evening of Brân's twenty-third birthday, when an October storm stripped the last leaves from the trees and brought a man in a black leather coat to his doorstep.

Resting his suitcase on the pavement, the man knocked once and waited. The leaves swirled around his legs and flicked against his cheeks. He brushed them aside, swept the curly blond horns of his fringe out of his eyes and scowled at the rainclouds until Brân opened the door. For a moment, they eyed each other uncertainly and then exchanged a brief smile.

"Kearn," Brân said at last. Relishing the sound of his visitor's name, he spoke it again, warmly. "Kearn, you came."

"You begged me often enough," the other replied, only half-teasing. "Will you invite me in? Or am I to stay out here all night?"

"Of course. Come in." Brân took the suitcase from the pavement and gestured for Kearn to follow him inside.

"Is this going to work?" asked Kearn. He stepped over the threshold and glanced doubtfully down the unlit hallway.

"We'll make it work."

"You think so?"

"Of course we will," Brân replied and, surprising them both with an awkward kiss that landed on Kearn's ear, he closed the door against the storm.

———

The following spring, a wayward honeysuckle felt compelled to cast its tendrils around the recently cracked pane in the bedroom window. Inside, copper moths nested among Kearn's shirts and jeans, which hung idly in the wardrobe. His frayed trainers still stood paired and pointing towards the unmade bed, and his leather jacket still sagged from the broken hook behind the front door. But the scent of his cologne was already receding, his toothbrush was less often seen in the bathroom mug and the echo of his raised voice was fading from the hallway.

On midsummer's day, the honeysuckle cupped a spiral hand against the window to eavesdrop on Kearn's parting curse that thundered through the house. The butterflies abandoned the buddleia tree when Kearn swung his suitcase and cracked a bone in Brân's left leg. As Kearn slammed the front door irrevocably on their relationship, the honeysuckle flinched. In the back garden, the sensitive seedpods of the yellow balsam erupted at the noise, showering the sky with jejune seeds.

———

Over time, the house returned to its customary state of hushed decomposition. The relentless advance of the sweetgrass continued unabated. When the reeds reached the house, they chafed against the kitchen wall and grazed the brittle mortar between the masonry. The honeysuckle folded its limbs over the windowpanes, resting its yawning yellow flowers against the sills. Within the house, bruises appeared on the bedroom ceiling; rings of ochre and lilac rot manifested miracle faces in the bathroom wall. Sheets of wallpaper slipped like lolling tongues onto the floor where flocks of silverfish scuttled for cover. The copper moths emerged from cocoons in the mottled carpet and threw their bodies against the light bulbs. As the unpaid bills piled up on the doormat, Brân cultivated a sombre black beard that engulfed his slender face.

———

On the morning of his thirty-third birthday, Brân received an unexpected letter. Leaning forward in his wicker chair until something cracked, he scraped together enough loose tobacco strands from the desk to fill a thin cigarette. Being composed mostly of paper and dust, the roll-up flared when he lit it, kindling an equivalent flame in his sea-blue eyes. He stared at the window for some time, at the pink stem of a vine that curled against the pane, and re-read the letter.

There had been no word from Kearn since he had given Brân an oblique fracture in his left tibia and stormed out of their relationship. When the front door had slammed all those years ago, the world had softly closed in upon Brân. After the first month of his absence, the library discharged him of his shelf-stacking duties and kindly requested the return of an overdue book, or else fees would be accrued. As Brân no longer recognized hunger and saw no purpose in currency, he was unconcerned.

After a year, the gas pipe was disconnected and there was no more hot water or heating in the house. Shortly afterwards, the light bulbs flickered a cryptic code of farewell and expired when the electricity was cut. As Brân no longer washed and the rain dripped serendipitously into discarded cups around the house, he could not say when the water supply was switched off. Sometimes a man or a woman with a clipboard, presumably from the council, paid visits to his front door and peered through the slit in his curtained windows. Brân stared impassively back from his chair and remained unseen, his presence indistinguishable from the threadbare furniture. Eventually, the civil servants departed with a shrug, making stern remarks on their clipboards.

The copper moths, having time on their wings now the light bulbs no longer provided fatal entertainment, danced on Brân's fingers and nested in his beard. That was all the company he needed, he thought, until the unexpected letter arrived on his birthday. He held the paper in a thin shaft of sunlight and read the message again.

Dear Brân,
I suppose you delete my emails before opening them. That's just the kind of behaviour I would expect of you, so I thought I'd write the old-fashioned way. Do you still have my leather jacket? I must have

left it at yours. If you haven't burned it by now, I need to pick it up sometime. Write to me.

It has been a long time, hasn't it?

Kearn.

Limping from the fracture that had never healed, Brân walked into the hallway to look at the jacket, now speckled with mildew, which still hung on the broken hook. Every morning that he pitched himself out of bed and climbed down the stairs, he glared at the jacket and thought about hacking it into shreds with a kitchen knife, feeding its remains to the moths. On those evenings that he could face returning to his empty bed, he cast a backwards glance at the jacket's lifeless form and longed, guiltily, for Kearn to fill the absence.

This morning, the arrival of the letter had unbalanced his routine. The prospect of writing anything to Kearn – or, more unthinkably, of Kearn being present once again in this hallway after ten lean years – flashed through Brân's mind. The hairline crack in his left shinbone tingled and roused an unaccustomed agitation in his stomach. Backing away from the jacket, he retreated into the kitchen. Instinctively and without knowing why, he opened a cupboard that was empty except for a scattering of oatmeal crumbs, and licked the shelf clean.

———

The pathway through the cemetery was lined with veteran horse chestnut trees. Being late October, most of the nuts had fallen to the ground. The glossy conkers had already been plundered by squirrels and schoolchildren, and now the spiky, empty shells lay discarded among the graves. Although the sun was hidden behind a delicate cover of cloud, there was a rare luminosity in the air that cast a bronze light upon the bare branches, the fallen leaves and the grey stone wall.

Walking lamely down this path that he had not travelled for so long, Brân considered how little he had recognized of the town. His memory of the streets was disjointed and dreamlike. After a few wrong turns, he had found the market place where the sight of red apples on a greengrocer's stall provoked another unfamiliar surge of hunger. He was surprised that it had taken all of the coins in his pocket to buy just two bags of fruit. Ten years ago, he could have bought twice as much for that same handful of coppers.

When he reached the cemetery gate, he stopped to look across the road at his house. Decaying gently on the edge of the fens, it seemed to Brân that the walls bowed and the roof buckled in the grip of the creeping vines. Beyond it, the level plains of peat, sedge and water-logged marsh stretched as far as the sea on the horizon. Inside the house, hanging on a broken hook beside the door, was the leather jacket. Even from this distance, Brân could sense the coat waiting for him like a living presence.

As Brân considered the option of never returning home, one of his paper bags split and the apples tumbled out over the grass. His eyes followed the escaping fruit towards a gravestone, where they came to rest at the bare foot of a seven-foot seraph.

The creature glanced down. He – it was unquestionably male – swept a lock of red hair out of his eyes and frowned at the fruit. But for the expanse of swanlike wings that twitched intermittently behind his shoulders, the being could have been human: an exceptionally attractive human with an unusually round nose and toffee-apple-red hair, but a human nonetheless. It was peculiar, thought Brân, not just that a live angel was standing a few metres away from him, but that it was wearing a pair of faded denim jeans and a checked shirt with rolled-up sleeves.

The seraph looked at the apples for some time, before he raised his face and changed Brân's life for ever.

"You smell like vinegar," he said matter-of-factly. The creature's voice was a rich baritone that contained the slightest hint of a Celtic inflection. He sounded neither offended nor disrespectful, but was simply stating a truth.

"I do?" Brân asked.

"Like vinegar," he confirmed.

It was not the fact that the creature had spoken that transformed Brân's life. It was his eyes. For that flickering instant that he held the angel's gaze, he experienced an intense pulse of bodily pleasure. Immersed in those rings of unutterable colour, Brân encountered something sweet and dark and carnally addictive. He became conscious at once that a universe of unchartered sensations existed beyond his own blunted experience. At length, the angel glanced away, but the damage had already been done.

"I could always give you a hand with those," said the angel, "though they say you mustn't eat the wind-fallen ones." He touched one apple with the perfect tip of his big toe. Brân imagined what it would feel like to sink his teeth into that particular fruit.

"Would you mind?" Brân could have said. "I live in that house over there, the one on the other side of the road. I live on my own, but this is the first time in years that I've been outside. In the hallway, there's a black coat that hangs behind the front door. It's waiting for me to return; I simply cannot face it alone. Would you mind?"

But Brân said no such thing. Taking care with his lame leg, he sank uneasily to his knees and collected the apples at the angel's feet.

"As you will," the creature said. He shrugged and returned to his original pose, scowling at the flat horizon beyond the cemetery gates.

Brân struggled to retrieve the fruit. No sooner had he recovered one apple than another rolled wilfully out of the bag and returned irresistibly to the angel. Even as Brân realized how pathetic his performance must seem, some secret, indecent craving compelled him to stare at the seraph's beautifully sculpted feet. He resisted the urge to stroke the tufts of downy red fur on the toes.

"You're doing a grand job down there, I must say," the angel said, still gazing at the horizon.

"Would you mind, after all?" asked Brân. "I live in that house over there."

"On the other side of the road?"

"That's the one."

"You live on your own?"

"I do."

The angel twitched his wings. Without another word, he reached down and gathered the unruly fruit.

"No worries," he said, holding six apples in the palm of one large hand.

"This really is very kind of you," said Brân. They were now standing unnervingly close to each other, but Brân lacked the courage to glance into those magnificent eyes a second time. If he looked again so soon, he thought he would go blind. He was conscious only of the angel's brilliant hair that burned like a halo around his shoulders, the curly red down on his muscular forearms and the scent of warm honey on the air.

"Are we done here?" the creature asked.

"I should have told you that I don't believe," Brân exclaimed unexpectedly, fixing his gaze on the angel's Adam's apple, "before you were kind enough to pick up the apples. I'm sorry, but I simply don't believe."

"Believe in what?"

"You know," Brân floundered. "The supernatural."

"Yes?"

"No, I mean, a prime mover. A higher power. Celestial things."

"Me neither," the angel shrugged and stretched his colossal wings. "What's that to do with the price of apples?"

"I thought you should know."

"Am I missing something?"

"I just thought I should tell you."

The angel shrugged again and said, "Are we done?"

Limping beside his companion across the road, Brân felt intensely conscious of his own inferior height, the absurdity of his feral beard and the dullness of his own blue eyes. Worse still, he could think of nothing to say. He wished that one of them would break the silence.

"You do smell like vinegar," the angel said, seeming to answer his unspoken request. "Why do you smell like vinegar?"

"I'm sorry," Brân apologized. "I suppose I haven't been looking after myself recently."

"Who usually looks after you?"

"No one," said Brân as they reached the front door.

For the first time, Brân saw the angel smile and caught a glimpse of the sharp, flawlessly white teeth behind his lips. Brân felt an overwhelming urge to kiss those lips, but he unlocked the door instead.

"Would you like to stay for tea?" he asked as he stepped inside. For the first time in ten years, Brân forget to notice the leather jacket that hung behind the door.

"That an official invitation, is it?"

"I suppose it is, if you like."

"Don't mind if I do." Folding his immaculate wings, the seraph followed his host over the threshold.

In the sitting room, Brân tugged the dusty curtains open and let the auburn sunshine flood over the tattered furniture. When he turned around, he was alarmed to find himself alone. For a moment, he feared that the creature had departed – or worse, that the entire afternoon had been a figment of his disintegrating mind. He looked in the empty hallway, glanced up the stairs, returned to the sitting room and then heard, with such relief, the clatter of crockery at the back of the house. He found the angel straightening a cloth of white linen over the kitchen table.

"I know what you're thinking," the angel said without looking up. "I'd make somebody a mighty husband one day."

Brân was actually wondering where the tablecloth had come from. He also thought that he had brought only apples back from the market. He could not think how it was possible that the angel was now laying plates of orange marmalade, salted butter and toasted currant buns on the table.

"Dig in," the seraph said, seating himself at the head of the table. "I'm not waiting on you to say grace."

As he ate, Brân realized how much he had forgotten about food, and how good it was to taste melted butter on warm buns. As if in accord, the angel's wings gave a quiver of pleasure.

"I suppose I should confess," Brân said tentatively, "I'm not one for miracles."

The angel laughed, again revealing his brilliant teeth. A morsel of half-chewed bun fell out of his mouth and landed on the tablecloth. Brân eyed the lump of dough enviously. He considered how he could put it on his tongue without being observed.

"What now with the miracles?" cried the angel. "Is this like some kind of game, is it? Are we playing non sequiturs? Do you get a kick out of playing non sequiturs?"

"No." Brân shook his head and decided that this would be the last time he would mention it. "I thought you ought to know."

"You should play non sequiturs. You'd be the high king of non sequiturs."

———

After tea, they moved into the sitting room. Now the curtains were open, Brân felt ashamed of what the sunlight revealed. Screwed-up tissues, dirty socks and underwear littered the floor. The silverfish glittered busily through the carpet and sporadic ears of orange fungus sprouted from the walls. Nonetheless, the angel nodded approvingly.

"Homely," he said. "You've been here for some time."

"I was born here."

"You read a lot." The angel bent down for a closer look at a row of books on the mantelpiece.

"Not for a long time," said Brân. He lowered himself onto the sofa and found himself admiring the flawless curve of the angel's buttocks.

"Read something to me now," the angel said. Turning abruptly, he cast his direct gaze upon Brân who was struck once more by an indescribable rapture. It was as though the angel had taken Brân in his arms and licked his face with his warm, currant-scented tongue.

"You want me to read to you?"

"Sure, read something for me." The seraph grabbed a slim paperback from the mantelpiece and threw it playfully onto Brân's lap.

"It's an odd thing to ask."

"So's picking wind-fallen apples in a graveyard."

"I haven't read in years," said Brân. The paperback, he noticed, was the library copy of *The Tempest*, which he had never returned. He wondered vaguely how much ten years of accrued fees amounted to.

"We'll take it in turns, if you're shy," said the angel. He joined Brân on the sofa and stretched his swanlike wings at full length behind them. Although he pretended not to notice, every pore of Brân's skin was attuned to the angel's solid thigh, barely a hair's breadth away from his own knee.

Between them, they agreed to read alternate lines of the play. It was an unconventional proposition, but Brân soon realized that it enabled them to trade sentences without ever drying up or saying the wrong thing. Sometimes, he was so beguiled by the angel's softly lilting voice that he missed his own cue. Occasionally, the creature interrupted the flow of dialogue to ask a question: "what's a *boatswain*?", "what's a *cloven pine*?", "why does Prospero drown his books?", all of which Brân explained as best as he could. They read to each other until the sun dipped behind the waterlogged fens and they could no longer see the writing on the page.

The angel made no mention of leaving and Brân did not want to frighten him away by asking him to stay the night. After some time spent sitting in silence, Brân realized that the angel had fallen asleep. His exquisite head had drooped onto the arm of the sofa and he purred faintly as he breathed. Brân gazed at the silhouette of the creature's impeccable nose, at his pronounced Adam's apple and at the red eyelashes that twitched as he dreamed. Behind the kitchen door, the flowering tips of the reed sweetgrass whispered in an autumn breeze.

Hours later, Brân decided to leave his companion where he lay sleeping on the sofa and to head upstairs to his own bed. As he rose stiffly to his feet, he found himself leaning towards the angel's beatific face and he caught again that unmistakable scent of honey. For a stolen moment, as the sweetgrass hushed and the moth wings wavered, Brân thought how simple it would be and how harmless to kiss the creature goodnight.

"Not yet," the angel murmured without opening his eyes.

"I'm sorry," said Brân. "I didn't—"

"You don't even know my name. It's Belenos. Bel-en-os." Within seconds, the angel was purring in his sleep again.

"Belenos," said Brân, tasting the otherworldly strangeness of the word on his tongue.

Later that night, as he lay under the blankets in his bedroom, Brân mouthed the name like a bedtime spell in the shadows.

———

The next morning, Brân awoke from enigmatic dreams of honeyed dough and knew instantly that something was missing. It was not only the stench of vinegar that had disappeared in the night – an odour he finally noticed because it was no longer present – but something more profound. As he lay in bed and listened to the ravens calling across the fens, he realized that he was experiencing the absence of absence itself.

When he came downstairs, he found Belenos in the sitting room, frying eggs over a makeshift grill in the fireplace.

"Man cannot live on apples alone," the angel said by way of explanation. "I know you don't mind. I had to use whatever was at hand to get this damn fire going."

Brân followed the angel's meaningful glance to the empty writing desk. The letter from Kearn was nowhere to be seen, although he knew he had left it there the day before. At the time he had opened the envelope, the sight of Kearn's name had thundered through his bones. It had been a monumental event, but now Brân looked at the fiery-haired angel bending over the fireplace, frying eggs for their breakfast, and he forgot all about the letter. He said, "I'll lay the table."

"Good man."

In the kitchen, as Brân straightened the linen and laid clean plates on the table, Belenos called out for him to open the back door.

It was not an unusual request. The smoke from the frying pan had filled the sitting room and was drifting up the stairs. Unthinkingly, or rather thinking of other things, Brân unfastened the bolt on the kitchen door and pulled the handle.

"Sedge," said Belenos, standing beside him. Brân had not heard him come into the kitchen. He did not know how long they had been looking out together over the hushed wilderness of rushes and reeds, at the sweetgrass that bowed silently at his feet and the level marshes that stretched as far as the pastel sea.

"Sedge," Brân repeated.

"Sure, sedge and reed. Dry them out; they'll make a sound thatch for the roof. Keep the rain off your ridiculous beard."

Impulsively, Brân turned to embrace the angel, but Belenos pushed him gently away.

"I told you," he said, "not yet."

———

Without ever mentioning the fact that it had happened, Brân and the angel were now living together. It was not quite as intimately as Brân would have desired, but it was together all the same. Belenos, it turned out, was a jack-of-all-trades. Within days, he had plumbed three water barrels into the guttering to provide a supply of fresh rainwater. The ruined toolshed he reclaimed from the sweetgrass and rebuilt as a chicken coop. When a bitter wind swept in from the sea, he laboured without a shirt in the garden, never seeming to feel the cold, and harvested whole sheaves of sedge for the thatch. "Before that sky falls on our heads," he said. Brân gathered the severed stalks and hung them over the fireplace to dry, all the while stealing glimpses of the curves of the angel's powerful torso.

Belenos was also the bringer of firewood and intriguing objects.

Returning home from unexplained excursions, the angel would appear with another curiosity in his arms: a hen for the coop, a copper kettle, a Victorian wine press and, once, even a Saxon helmet. Whether he excavated these artefacts from a landfill site or pilfered them from antique shops, Brân never knew.

In the evenings, they would take turns to read to each other in the firelight. Sitting close together on the sofa, Brân's knee would invariably find a way to make contact with Belenos's warm thigh, resting there until the angel shifted his legs away and stretched his feet under the coffee table. The touch might have been subtle and lasted less than a heartbeat, but it was enough to set Brân's pulse on fire.

———

One particular midwinter morning, Belenos was unearthing potatoes from the rich, black soil along the bank of the sluice when he heard the faint stirrings of thunder. Looking out across the fens, he could just make out the figure of Brân struggling with a wheelbarrow of cut peat on the bleached horizon. Beyond and above him, an immense mass of rainclouds advanced inland from the sea. As the angel returned to his digging, he was interrupted again – this time by an insistent knocking on the front door. Belenos frowned, flexed his immense wings and took the shovel into the house.

Kearn was not expecting the angel to open the door to him – that much was evident from his reaction. Lightly brushing the curly blond fringe out of his eyes, he blinked disapprovingly at the angel.

"Is he in?" Kearn asked.

Belenos did not reply.

"He knows why I'm here," Kearn continued, folding his arms. "I've written to him enough, he knows I have."

Belenos still did not reply.

"And you can tell him from me I'm not leaving without my leather jacket. Tell him that I'm not going anywhere."

Casually, Belenos leaned back to take the full measure of Kearn's legs. He glanced down at the iron blade of the shovel that he was still holding in his fists, and then he looked up into Kearn's widening eyes and smiled, revealing a set of brilliant, sharp teeth.

―――――――

When Brân returned to the house in the afternoon, he failed to notice that the black leather jacket had disappeared. Belenos, he found, was in an exceptionally good mood.

"You've ploughed the vegetable patch," said Brân. Exhausted after cutting peat all day, he relaxed onto the sofa beside the honey-scented seraph. "Was there much to dig up?"

"This and that," Belenos replied. "But I tell you, next year's crop will be a right bumper. So, what do you say we read tonight?"

―――――――

After many more harvests, some abundant and some lean, more than half a century after he had first gazed into the unimaginable eyes of the angel, a silver-bearded Brân closed the book he had been reading and lay it on the grass. Sitting in the shade of the buddleia tree, the blossoms around him flickered with crimson butterflies. Behind him, the house that had been built on a thin place, halfway between the town and the wilderness, was now engulfed by the abundant honeysuckle. At his feet, Belenos lay stretched on the lawn. Unlike Brân, the creature had barely aged a day.

"You reading no more?" Belenos asked, opening one eye.

Brân did not reply immediately. Recently, he had been experiencing pains in his chest. He was not in agony, but he knew that a change was coming.

"Why were you there?" Brân asked after a pause. "That day in the graveyard, what were you doing?"

Belenos rolled onto his side and loosened the belt in his jeans.

"I was listening."

"To what?"

"To the chorus of worms. It's a soothing sound. Not distressing at all. It takes patience and not a little courage, but I tell you, it's worth the wait."

"What does it sound like?"

"Now that's a question." Belenos laughed and casually unbuttoned his checked shirt. "Like everything and like nothing. Like a perpetual storm of fireworks permeating the soil. Like a thousand neurons exploding in the infinite cortex of time and space, a kaleidoscope of stars dancing around an unending dream. It is beautiful."

"You are a poet," Brân gasped as a charge of intense pain tore down his arm.

"You taught me poetry," said Belenos, "and my profit on it is I know how to love."

The angel slipped out of his remaining clothes and stood for the first time fully naked in the sunlight, more magnificent than Brân could ever have imagined.

When Brân cried out, the creature knelt down and embraced him, cradling their bodies together within the folds of his glorious wings. Brân kissed the warm honey of the angel's skin and closed his eyes as the unimaginable ecstasy ruptured his heart.

At that sound, the seedpods of the yellow balsam, the *Impatiens noli-tangere* or touch-me-not, erupted explosively, firing ripe kernels into the empty air.

What You Left Behind
Nick Alexander

———

Mark sits staring at the blank screen of the switched-off television. Since he got back, he has been feeling numb, unable to do anything except sleep, drink and eat. In fact, even eating and sleeping are proving to be challenging.

He fiddles with an app on his iPhone and music starts to play from the hi-fi speakers. iTunes shuffle has selected a track by Faithless. It's a bit upbeat to be an *ideal* soundtrack for this specific moment in Mark's life, but perhaps that's a good thing. Perhaps it will cheer him up, if such a thing is possible. He stares at the dead TV screen a little longer, at his own reflection upon it. He's probably still in shock, he figures. But then, who wouldn't be after *that* holiday?

They (that is, he and Jonathan) had been in the Greek islands when it happened. They had only been together for six months, it was true, but everything had been going well up until that point. Or so Mark believed. Naxos and Kos had been wonderfully relaxing, the weather had been fabulous, the food was great, the locals were welcoming, the bed comfy, the sex good, and they had been about to jump on a boat and move on to the most beautiful island of them all – Santorini.

Because Mark was a little sunburnt from the beach the day before, they had chosen to spend their final day in Kos apart, Mark reading on his Kindle beneath a poolside parasol and Jonathan heading off to their favourite beach, a mile to the east. One day apart. That was all it had taken.

By the time the evening came and Jon returned, something had changed. Jon seemed jumpy and distracted. He also unexpectedly declared that he wanted to go to Mykonos next rather than Santorini, even though they had planned to go there from the very beginning, even though Santorini was always meant to be the climax of the trip.

Though Mark had his heart set on Santorini (where his best friend Emma said the most beautiful sunsets on the planet were to be seen), in the face of Jonathan's rigid insistence that Mykonos would be more "fun", Mark had capitulated. *I don't actually know Jonathan that well*, he had thought for the first time ever.

Once they got to Mykonos, things went from bad to worse. Jonathan spent what little time he deigned to pass with Mark either fiddling with his phone or sleeping, and the majority of the day inexplicably absent. Mark had ended up wandering around the island on his own. He *tried* to enjoy himself, he tried to sightsee, to browse, to shop . . . but the truth was that he hated the place. With its luxury shops and fashion outlets, its rainbow flags and sex clubs, it was everything he had wanted to escape when he had suggested the Greek islands in the first place.

On the second day, he got home to find Jonathan sitting on the balcony, looking serious. "We need to talk," he said, followed less predictably by, "I've met someone new."

"I know this is going to be a bit tough for you, but I'm afraid it's something I need to explore," he continued, earnestly. "It feels important to me. It feels like love – like *real* love."

"Tough" didn't really cover how Mark felt and, by the end of day three, the atmosphere between them had become intolerable. Jon was sleeping elsewhere, presumably with his new Air France boyfriend, while Mark, for his part, was barely sleeping at all.

On the morning of day five, unable to take any more, Mark packed his bags and headed to Mykonos airport, where he purchased an outrageously overpriced last-minute ticket to bring him home. He did not fly with Air France.

Home, where he finds himself now. Home, alone, in his flat. Home, surrounded by Jon's possessions. And all he can seem to do is stare disconsolately at the switched off television – also Jon's – as he tries to understand what went wrong.

The relationship hadn't been perfect, of course. Jon had always been unpredictable. He had always liked his drugs to be stronger and more copious than Mark did. He had always partied harder and later and more often than Mark, too. At fifty, Mark felt that he had pretty much explored all that the club scene had to offer, while as an ex-straight guy, Jon was only just starting out. All *Mark* really wanted these days was to cook a nice meal and eat it in front of the fire, or to spend a day with Jon and his granddaughter Mia playing happy families. So not a perfect pairing, no. But they had fun together all the same. They enjoyed each other's company. They had good sex. There was nothing that could have presaged this car-crash of an ending.

Mark sighs and heads to the kitchen where he fills and switches on the kettle. He pulls the French press from the cupboard and attempts to blank out the memory of buying it with Jonathan in IKEA. Little Mia had been strapped to his chest and Mark had discovered with surprise that a mixed-race baby was an efficient man-magnet. Never had he been smiled at so frequently, nor chatted up so easily. And when he and Jon had jokingly placed Mia on top of a pile of stackable IKEA storage crates, no fewer than six hot, admiring men had gathered around them to watch the photo being taken.

He spoons coffee into the pot and pours on the boiling water. He should probably throw it away it after this cup of coffee; he should probably buy himself a new coffee pot. *And* a new television. But then they all leave something behind, don't they?

He glances through at the lounge and sees Fred's designer armchair sitting in the corner. That had been a surprise for his fortieth birthday. Ten years he's had that chair! Frederic had led him outside to where a Transit van was waiting, and inside the van had been a whole bunch of friends with booze and a sound system, and behind them, all wrapped up, the armchair. A whole birthday party delivered in a van – now there's a good memory. There's one to hold on to.

A less agreeable surprise had been when Frederic walked out just a month later. He too had met someone else. "I'm sorry," he said, "but

I realized that I just never really loved you." So what had the birthday surprise been about? Why the expensive chair? Why go to so much trouble? Mark has never been able to convince himself that Frederic didn't love him back. But he does believe that, for whatever reason, Fred had needed to *convince* himself that he didn't.

He pushes on the coffee-pot plunger and looks around the kitchen. His eyes settle on the Rothko print he bought at the Tate Modern with Scott. Beautiful, sexy, Californian Scott, the man with the softest skin ever to walk the Earth. A sensory memory of the feel of Scott's powdery skin fills his senses now, the sweet smell of him too. God, the sex had been good with Scott! He remembers, now, the curved arc of his back, the yielding joy of his muscular behind. Scott had been travelling, had been halfway through a world tour when they met that Saturday in Compton's. Essentially, by paying for everything, Mark had persuaded him to stay in London for three months instead of three weeks, but they had both known that he would continue on his way eventually. And they had both suspected that they would never keep in contact once he did.

Mark's eyes glide from the Rothko print down to Krzysztof's pottery vase on the shelf below it. Yes, even the three-week relationships liked to leave their mark. What had the phrase been? What was it that Mark had said to detonate the bomb that would end that particular flash in the pan? He wrinkles his brow as he tries to remember.

"You're too clever to be working as a cleaner."

Yes, that was it. That was all it had taken. Krzysztof had become irritable and bitchy after that and, because he kept on and on quoting that innocuous phrase (intended to be flattery), Mark knew that this was where the problem originated, even as Krzysztof emphatically denied it.

"I'm leaving to that job I'm too clever for," he said every morning as he left for work. And when he got home in the evening and Mark asked how his day had been, he would say, in his thick Polish accent, "My day in job I am too clever for? Fine, thank you very much."

On the fourth morning, Krzysztof had taken his toothbrush from the jar and his vodka from the freezer. And that, as they say, was that. Had it lasted three weeks, or four? Mark can't even remember.

And this is the problem with dating in your forties and fifties, Mark thinks. Virtually every guy you meet is hiding some shattering insecurity and, no matter how carefully you tread, at some point you're going to step on the landmine that blows everything up.

Mark pours his coffee and heads through to the lounge where he sinks onto the sofa. He stares, anew, at his blurred reflection in the TV screen and tries not to imagine Jonathan running his fingers through Ms Air France's hair.

iTunes shuffles and a Metronomy track – "The Look" – starts to play, prompting Mark to think, *Jesus! The exes are even lurking in my iTunes library!*

He remembers Ewan now. Beautiful, sensitive, fed-up Ewan. Ewan who so hated London, who so *despised* everything to do with London that Mark started encouraging him to leave, started pushing him, for his own good, to return to Edinburgh.

He had met Ewan on Grindr, but unusually, uniquely, Ewan had offered him not a sex date, but a Metronomy concert date – a concert that had been utterly brilliant, and during which Mark (hearing Ewan singing beside him) had fallen head over heels in love. The singing had never stopped the whole time they had been together. Ewan sang in the shower, in the car, on the Tube, while he cooked, and even occasionally during sex. And he sang beautifully.

Yes, the Metronomy concert had been the best first date ever. And it had been followed by the best two months ever, as well. Except that Ewan was out of work and fed-up. Except that Ewan hated London with the kind of passion that people usually reserve for Tony Blair or Nick Clegg.

And Mark had loved Ewan so passionately that he had chosen to encourage him to leave, had insisted that for his own good, he really *should* return to Edinburgh – THE best city in the world, as Ewan kept saying.

Mark sips his coffee and glances out at the shiny rooftops of the house opposite. From sunny Mykonos to rainy London, from ouzo to coffee, from partnered to single . . . Yuck. He hadn't been expecting any of it. Or at least, not yet.

He remembers how it rained when Ewan was here with him. Mark had loved those rainy Sundays – the first time he had ever *not* minded the rain in his entire life.

And these, of course, were the other things these guys left behind, the non-material things: the memories, the habits, the discoveries, the life lessons . . .

Fred had taught him to enjoy cooking, and Scott had taught him some American sign language. And Ewan, well . . . Ewan had taught him so much that it was hard to know where to begin. He had taught him to enjoy rainy Sundays in bed, and to sing and dance when alone, simply because it felt good. He had taught him to think about where his food came from, that it was not irrelevant whether an egg came from a hen spending its life in a cage being pecked to death or from a healthy, happy chicken clucking around a field. "You can taste happiness," Ewan always said, "and you can taste unhappiness too. You just have to choose which one you want on your plate."

Ewan had taught him that it was possible to refuse to think about things that make you angry or upset, as well. He had explained that it was possible to guide the mind towards thoughts that make you happy, to tell it to stop thinking about others that make you sad. Like thinking about Ewan right now, for example. Like *not* thinking about Jonathan with his Air France trolley dolly.

Yes, there are plenty of good memories lurking in these objects as well as plenty of bad ones.

For most of his life, Mark had been jealous of his straight friends' lifelong marriages. But Ewan, again, taught him to see that just maybe this life of his – this life of many lives – was denser, was richer, was less monotonous than the monogamy he pined for.

"Don't underestimate the hours of boredom, the hours of irritation, and the hours of regret that go into most lifelong marriages," Ewan had said, memorably. Short stories had their own intrinsic value too, he insisted. Yes, they were more painful sometimes, but they were also sharper, sweeter, more intense.

It's strange really because, in the midst of his devastated summer holiday, in the midst even of this catastrophic break-up, Mark is discovering that he misses overweight, "beary", singing Ewan much more than he misses gym-built Jonathan, and he realizes in this moment that he probably loved Ewan more than any of the other men he has dated. And let's face it, there have been plenty.

He tries to remember why he didn't just go to Edinburgh *with* Ewan. Because surely that would have been the obvious solution.

Of course, the timing had been wrong: Mark had recently been promoted at work, had just signed up for the mortgage on this flat, too. And at the point when Ewan had decided to leave, they had only been together for six weeks. But all the same, he should never have let the pain that he felt over their separation become such an impenetrable barrier between them. He should never have lost touch so completely, not with singing, dancing Ewan – not with the gentlest, wisest, most generous man he had ever met.

He wonders what Ewan is doing these days. He wonders if he's still fed-up or if Edinburgh really did fix that for him. He wonders if he's single. It's been two years, so probably not. He wonders if he's still bopping around the bathroom to Metronomy, still singing into a toothbrush, and reckons that he probably is. He smiles at the memory of Ewan's crazy dancing.

His mobile rings, so he swipes it from the coffee table and looks at the screen.

A surprise: it's Jonathan calling.

He will have just got back from Mykonos. He probably wants his stuff back. Or perhaps his holiday romance is over already, in which case perhaps it's *Mark* he wants back.

The Metronomy track comes to an end and the god of randomness that is iTunes chooses to play "Air War" by Crystal Castles. Mark snorts at the irony of the choice. Because "Air War" had been Ewan's favourite track back then, and it's still one of Mark's favourite songs today. Ewan had played it on a constant loop the entire time that they were together. Even once they had filled his tiny, rusty Fiat with boxes, he had driven away with this same song drifting ever-more faintly from the open windows.

Yes, Crystal Castles is still Mark's favourite group, and "Air War" is still his favourite track, and Ewan, he has to admit, is still one of his favourite lovers – no, his *absolute* favourite lover. Ever.

He wrinkles his nose at the phone. It's still ringing.

"I don't want to talk to Jonathan," he murmurs to no one in particular. "I want to talk to Ewan."

He pulls a face, surprised at the revelation and, when finally Jonathan's call goes to voicemail, he hits "contacts" and, with a lump of expectation forming in his throat, with a sense of fear and hope and everything else in between, he begins to type. E-W-A . . .

"Hello?" Ewan's voice says, and Mark finds himself momentarily unable to speak.

"Mark?" Ewan says. "Is that you?"

"Yes, it's me."

"Och, that's weird," Ewan says. "I was just thinking about you."

"You were?"

"Aye. They were playing Metronomy in Starbucks, and I was remembering that concert we went to. D'you remember that?"

"I do," Mark croaks.

"Was that not the best night ever?"

Déjeuner sur l'herbe
Matt Harris

———

The canal looked picturesque at this time of year. During the colourless winter months, this particular strip of scummy liquid and its environs was best left to quick-footed joggers or their assailants, but the sun was now high, the leaves were out and the warm air was fresh and promising, as yet untainted by London's dusty summer smog. There was even a gaily painted barge out for its first trip of the season. However, there was still something irredeemably melancholy about parks and other green spaces in London, Jasper felt. And this one, which was rarely used for the joyful recreation intended, was no exception.

He sighed and blew his drugs-ravaged septum carefully into his monogrammed cotton handkerchief and scanned the slope.

Here, not far from Regent's Park proper, the towpath fronted a small patch of, not woods exactly, but a substantial patch of scraggy-looking trees that bordered a modest council estate on the far side. Not so large to entail too much walking and not so small to necessitate too much skulking around in public view. It wasn't a problem now spring had sprung. You could go about your business screened by the ample foliage.

A middle-class couple pushing an over-designed pram strolled by (there were also some charming Regency terraces nearby) and Jasper pretended to look up into the canopy at some feature of natural interest, theatrically shielding his eyes against the dappled sunlight. They weren't convinced and proceeded to walk just a little more briskly on. When they were out of sight, Jasper left the narrow path for the undergrowth.

What was he doing here? A quick fumble? Looking for a boyfriend?

Here? He did want someone. He was sick of being alone. True, he had more quirks than most but everyone said he was a bloody good catch. He was rich, tall and fit. He was blond.

The trouble was, no one ever lived up to expectation and, if they didn't live up to expectation, well, they didn't live.

Jasper headed out of sight from the canal. There were sundry used condoms and their wrappers glinting on the ground. Discarded Kleenexes, once wet, were now papier-mâchéd over the shrubbery. His heart sank. Filthy bastards.

It was unusually quiet. Jasper was about to turn back when he heard a contrived cough coming from nearby. In a well-trodden clearing just a few yards further on Jasper was greeted by the sight of a man with his trousers around his ankles, wearing a black leather harness and lowering himself onto an old-fashioned glass milk bottle.

The skinny, obviously drug-addled skinhead looked up and stared vacantly at Jasper. Formal greetings weren't required. Jasper stared back just as vacantly while he tried to evaluate what response was required of him. Was he supposed to just watch, impressed? Give marks out of ten? It never ceased to amaze him how indifferent he was to what people got up to for the cause of sexual gratification.

His last boyfriend liked to be beaten. There really were no boundaries. He liked to be slapped hard across the face until his eardrums burst, then on from there, culminating in a rough fucking whether he was conscious or not. Always eager for more, his dopey eyes would light up like an expectant puppy when they got together. The relationship had its moments but it was no challenge. Ankles tied. He had to let him go. It was, he was sure, what he wanted.

The skinhead grinned then beckoned him over. He was old – he must have been fifty at least. Not much potential there, then. Yes, Jasper was casually ageist. He was in many respects a conventional young homosexual. He studied the man's features. He would have been about the same age as Eddie when he'd finished with him. This was probably what he'd got up to, too. Edward was his first.

Jasper had known Eddie since Westminster School. Apart from French and English, Eddie had taught Jasper, the precocious schoolboy, many extracurricular facts of life. They had progressed through a brief, covert affair and onto, for no other reason than their families knew each other, semi-platonic friendship. Eddie was old-school queer. His identity, defined by others, was shackled to shame. The result was a penchant for risky, guilt-ridden sex for which he longed to be punished. In the end, Jasper couldn't resist giving him what he wanted and he died as he had lived. At the mercy of his self-loathing libido. And Jasper discovered an identity all of his own in the process.

He moved in just a little closer. Feigning nervousness. Jasper calculated he could do anything with or to this creature. But what?

Jasper crouched down to his level. Much like David Attenborough would in front of some giant tortoise in a documentary. There was a faint whiff of faeces. It made him flinch. The skinhead's white polo shirt was lying, dirtied, on the ground. Did he have no standards?

The creature kept grinning deviantly then dropping the expression temporarily with each doubtful thought about the scenario. This inner dialogue playing across his face irritated Jasper, who winced at his stained teeth and looked down from his face, only to be met by his ravaged nipples. It was patently clear. What had once been a relatively attractive, vital "bit of rough" had aged into a weak and over-used sex object, a parody of anarchic skinhead vigour.

Jasper stared at the disappearing milk bottle and decided exactly what he wanted with him.

He stood up straight and touched and caressed his own crotch in oft-performed ritual. To egg him on. The skinhead dutifully pulled on his pale, flaccid dick as the bottle went deeper up his rectum. Jasper moved closer, his healthy rower's physique towering, flawless, over him. The skinhead, increasingly excited by Jasper's proximity, half grunted and half moaned a come-on to touch. Jasper looked back towards the path to check for possible witnesses. It was too easy to get caught up in the moment in these situations and forget where you were.

Once, Jasper had been asphyxiating a married man in a chalk wood in West Sussex, not far from Arundel (he had been to a wedding at the castle). He was about to give a final squeeze to the trachea when he looked up to see a rambler staring at them. Luckily, he was too fixated on the main picture to notice the darker details and marked the experience under "too much information" before moving swiftly on.

"Name?" Jasper demanded. He often liked to know. The skinhead stopped, confused. He was almost never asked such a personal question in these situations.

"Er, Dave," he lied. He didn't have to. He would have nothing to hide by tomorrow.

Millimetres from him now, Jasper pressed firmly down on his angular shoulders, prompting the crouched figure to alternately snarl then simper. The bonehead seemed to be attempting some sort of role-play. It was rather theatrical and frankly embarrassing. Any real sense of danger was lost on the skinhead as he went further into his drug-induced reverie.

Jasper stood back and stripped to the waist before replacing his fingers on Dave's head. He ran them lightly over the skull's hot, bristly, scabby surface. Revolted, he retracted his hands and cupped them lightly over the creature's ears instead. They felt waxy and cold in contrast with his head.

I'm actually messing around with a zombie.

He pulled Dave's head on to his crotch, squashing his nose. The man groaned and panted as he clawed passionately at Jasper's firm, chino'd buttocks. Very annoying. He pulled the soiled hands off and stepped right back again.

Looking at the red combat trousers around Dave's ankles, Jasper rehearsed the next move in his mind. Satisfied with his plan, he stripped down to his pristine white underpants and placed his neatly folded trousers in the fork of a small tree. It pleased him to see the skinhead's grateful excitement rising. Pre-cum bungeed off the end of his now fully erect cock into the leaf litter.

Jasper looked up as if for some divine inspiration. A blackbird dashed overhead at high speed, cackling noisily.

He bent down over Dave's slight body and grabbed a handful of trouser material. With a sporting bellow, he yanked upwards with all his strength, causing Dave to twist and sprawl face down in the brambles as his feet left the ground. He barely let out a gasp as his addled brain tried to figure out what had just happened. The milk bottle was still up his arse, the rectal vacuum holding it firmly in. He tried to turn and face upwards but Jasper pressed his foot on his upper back.

"Stay there!" He commanded, slapping his flabby buttocks hard. Dave complied, hoping, but not quite convinced yet, that this was a harmless, if unusually rough, scenario.

"Aw, yeah."

Jasper then spread the skinhead's legs as far apart as the combats would allow and leant over him. He put his lips next to his ear: "D'you like that?"

"Aw, yeah."

"Aw yeah?" Jasper asked.

"Yeah . . . Aw, yeah."

"What do you mean?"

"Fuck, er . . ."

"What? You want to get fucked?"

"Fuck . . . I mean fuck me. There's poppers in my pocket."

Dave pointed to the thigh pocket of his combats. Jasper reached inside and grabbed a small, brown bottle of amyl nitrate, unscrewed the cap, threw it on the ground then held the open bottle up to one of the man's nostrils. He inhaled deeply, gratefully, while Jasper deftly shoved the milk bottle further into his arse at the other end.

"Ah! Gently."

"Got a boyfriend, have you?"

"You what?"

"You have, haven't you?"

"Yeah, so what?"

Then Jasper whispered in his ear, "You sick, vile creature. Stop making it difficult for the rest of us here. Eh, Dave."

"What? What did you say?"

Jasper couldn't conceal a hateful expression any longer. The skinhead's sense of danger surfaced too late as Jasper pressed his head, side on, into the muddy ground, causing him to protest too loudly.

"No. Get away. Please—"

Jasper rammed mud and leaves into his mouth before he could finish, breaking some of his teeth in the process. He whined as Jasper emptied the rest of the poppers into his ear and one of his eyes.

"Now, you're fucked!"

Before the burning fluid had any time to register pain, Jasper stood erect, brought his right leg back and, with as much force as his close proximity would allow (he would have liked a run at it), kicked the end of the milk bottle as hard as he could. The skinhead's skinny body cannoned forward with the force and there was a muffled crunch as the glass shattered inside him.

Jasper was on his way. Dave was paralysed with shock.

"I haven't got a bloody boyfriend!" Jasper's scream was fuelled partly by adrenalin and partly by the very real exasperation at this fact. Mud and blood vomited out as Dave opened and closed his mouth like a landed fish. Jasper calmed down and grinned triumphantly at more blood running out of Dave's ear and eye. He considered his next move.

"Help . . . me." He held out a hand. "Please." Though his voice was strangulated, Jasper was sure he wasn't addressing him.

Horrified, he looked over, in the direction of the pleading. Somebody was standing there, behind a tree, smoking. The smoke spiralled quietly around the large, smooth trunk.

"Who's there?" Silence. "Excuse me. Step out."

A man stepped sideways into view. "I'll finish my fag, if you don't mind."

While the skinhead tried to gesture for help, no one said anything. They just stared at one another. Looked deeply into each other's eyes.

The skinhead lost consciousness and the tableau held for what seemed an age.

The man smiled a beautiful smile. "Name's Craig, mate."

Jasper noticed various features of interest. He was much shorter than Jasper and broad, but very lean. Like a footballer. He wore white Reebok track pants and a red nylon vest to back up the impression. He held his cigarette in the macho style, between thumb and first finger, and had straight, dark, slightly greasy hair. Being fair, Jasper loved the contrast of dark hair against his own. The thick, long eyelashes cantilevered out over wide deep-set eyes and the hair in the middle of Craig's chest, arms, the back of his hands and on each finger joint was dark and shiny, like an insect's. Only sexy. It framed his stark white musculature. The stranger had a cold, dangerous energy about him, no doubt born to a life on constant defence or offence. Jasper imagined he lived on the nearby council estate. The thought immediately thrilled him and a pulse of attraction surged through his body, causing his downy cheeks to flush.

"Do I know you?" Jasper sounded petulant, like he was rebuffing a gatecrasher at a party, not a witness to a violent crime. "Are you going to tell?"

"What d'you fink?"

Craig started purposefully down the slope towards him. Jasper tensed.

"You gotta keep 'em awake for it to be fun."

"Sorry?"

"Are you deaf or what?"

Christ. A confrontation could only ever be a few sentences away with this one. Jasper backed readily out of his way but Craig nonchalantly stepped over Dave and stamped on one of his outstretched arms. It snapped like a twig.

The skinhead jolted back to life. Between the pain, the drugs and his increasing immobility, he was now completely disorientated. He was, however, perfectly able to take in the gravity of the situation.

Jasper gasped at Craig's bravado. First with surprise then with relief, then pleasure.

"They all behave the same, don't they?" Craig deftly flicked his fag stub away.

"Well. I suppose . . ."

Dave began shivering, then fitting.

"They never run. Do you fuck 'em, first?"

"I wouldn't touch that with a barge pole. I'm just . . . experimenting." Craig's hand lingered subconsciously near his crotch. His package was increasingly visible, Jasper noticed.

"I used to play football," Craig announced.

"Oh, yes?" Jasper replied, amused at this left-field statement.

"Semi-professional, yeah. But I got an injury. Anterior cruciate ligament."

"Oh? Bad luck."

It was. It was Craig's only socially normal activity, a good discipline to counter his mainly solitary existence. He was a natural player. Bold and fearless. His captain always pressured him into doing just one more season for the Harvey's Building Contracts League and Craig always relented. Until last season, when his injury made his decision for him. It was just as well. The changing rooms continually put him in the way of petty temptation. He was afraid one day, one solitary moment of weakness would send him rifling through the jackets and trousers and holdalls and rucksacks and God knows whatever other possessions his trusting team members cared to leave around. It was time to move on.

"We gotta stick togever. You and me."

"Really?" What a sweet, brave thing to say. Jasper smiled, revealing white, even, upper-class teeth in healthy pastel-pink gums.

"I hardly know you."

"It's okay. This stuff's practically legal again now."

"What d'you mean?"

"Wiv all the mosques and that . . ."

Jasper nearly hooted with laughter. He couldn't hide his amusement at Craig's reductive take on the new moral zeitgeist. He couldn't hide undressing Craig with his eyes either.

"You're laughing at me."

"No. I was just thinking of something."

"Don't beat around the bush. I can tell you like me."

There was a definite electricity. A connection.

Craig admired Jasper's athletic, flawless torso. He imagined him playing on stately winter rugby fields and rowing on mist-laden home-counties rivers. He was a fantasy.

"Show us your cock."

Japer was taken aback again by Craig's confidence. "Look, are you always this forward?"

"Well, if you don't wanna talk wiv a real geeza . . ." He pretended to leave.

Gosh, he had a charming innocence. If nothing else, Jasper relished the possibility of his lively banter. "Not at all. I'm used to talking down to people like you . . . Chav."

"Yeah. That's funny." Craig admired his confidence in turn. He knew his currency.

"Here it is." Jasper unfurled his cock from cotton briefs that gave no clue to his dick's size. Craig was genuinely surprised.

"Fuckin' hell. A baby's arm. You cunt!" Craig looked on aghast as Jasper moved his grip back and forth on his pound of alternately wrinkling then smoothing flesh. Craig pulled at his nipple, provocatively, not taking his dark eyes off Jasper. They narrowed quizzically as he concentrated on the action. Jasper slapped his cock on his open palm for added effect.

"You can fuck me later, if you want." And, despite his obvious bluntness, there was something by turns coy and honest about Craig's manner, which was refreshing. Jasper imagined escorting him back to his house. Probably in excited silence while he decided what they would do together. He imagined walking him through the front door and holding him in his hallway for a moment while Craig chattered, while he decided whether to take him upstairs to his bedroom or downstairs to the cellar. It was all a matter of chemistry. Then Dave started moaning. Breaking the moment. They both stared reverently at the crippled figure lying on the ground.

"I 'ate the bloody gay scene. Don't you?"

"Yes. It's awful."

"How many have you done?"

Jasper thought for a second. "I'd like to do more."

"Me too." The birds seemed to stop singing as Jasper and Craig approached their victim.

Panicking, he tried getting on all fours, but failed.

"Mind the broken glass. It's a bit slippery now," Jasper said considerately as Craig rooted around for a small stick. He found one about a foot long and snapped it in half.

"Let's do one eye each." Craig handed one length to Jasper.

They crouched down either side of Dave's head. He started wailing so Jasper slapped his cheek. "Shut up! Just shut up!"

On the count of three, they stabbed the skinhead hard in both eyes. He let out a guttural sort of howl and tried to scrabble away, only to get caught blindly in the brambles.

"Oh. I thought they'd pop."

"Me too." Jasper and Craig laughed at catching one another's disappointment. They were two little boys just playing in the woods, completely comfortable with each other. They stood up straight. Jasper, tall and tumescent, seemed to fill Craig's view.

Craig liked that. Jasper clasped Craig's shoulders and sniffed in his clean, salty smell. He felt strong yet so impressionable. And he couldn't honestly say what the power balance between them was. Was he at risk of being condescending?

A truly terrible thought occurred to Jasper: could he just be nice to keep a boyfriend?

Was this idea a revelation? Really? He knew, technically, you had to be. Did he? Unless they liked it otherwise, which was ultimately boring and fatal. It was such a quandary. Craig seemed different, and something felt different.

"I want to know all about you," Jasper said softly, tracing a bloody finger over Craig's pneumatic pecs.

"Yeah? I'd have brought a picnic if I'd known."

"Ah. *Le déjeuner sur l'herbe.*"

"Wot?"

"Oh . . . nothing." Jasper blushed. Craig drew Jasper's face down to his and kissed his full, velvety lips. Jasper pulled back. He looked troubled. "I'm sorry. I won't do outdoor sex."

Disappointment registered on Craig's face. "Mate. I can do beds."

Jasper smiled. "Are you busy later?"

"Flicks. West End." Craig wanted to appear busy. Just for a second. He did indeed have more power than Jasper gave him credit for. He knew "the rules". "Never mind. Another time—"

"No. Come wiv me."

Jasper smiled, then relaxed. He looked at the skinhead twitching and squirming for attention.

"Sure. I have a few more things I'd like us to do here first."

The Man Who Noticed
Francis King

From time to time, Rick – reticent, modestly handsome and always smiling – would say of himself, "I'm really a pretty ordinary sort of a bloke." Usually the claim would be diffident; but on rare occasions, a hint of boastfulness would irritate his colleagues in the council-housing department. Those colleagues liked him, since he so readily accepted even the most preposterous of their decisions and volunteered for even the most tedious of jobs. But the sad truth was that they had little real interest in someone to whom so little ever happened. From time to time one of them would speculate, not all that concerned with getting an answer, along the lines of, "Do you think our Rick might be gay?", "Do you think our Rick really spends every evening watching the box?" or "Has our Rick ever entertained anyone in that pad of his?"

However, although he seemed so ordinary to everyone who came into contact with him, there was one respect in which Rick was extraordinary. He possessed not the slightest flair for either fiction or detection, but he did have the obsessive powers of observation essential for any successful novelist or police officer. He was that rare thing: someone who noticed without being noticed.

Propped on three pillows, to relieve the acute breathlessness that was one of the symptoms that had brought him in an ambulance to the hospital, he watched the ancient patient on the bed opposite and his numerous visitors so surreptitiously that they were totally unaware they were under his observation. They had the air of being a closely knit group long familiar with their surroundings and therefore so knowledgeable about every aspect of the frenetic life there – the geography of the bathrooms and loos, the names and nationalities of the nurses, the times of the consultants' rounds – that they now felt totally at home. Did they even have a home, a real home, of their own, he sometimes mused fancifully, as one of them would briefly vanish to reappear with a plastic bag stuffed with what would soon become their next meal in the course of a day spent almost entirely at the hospital. Meals were also routinely brought to the patient by two middle-aged Nigerian catering assistants – twins, Rick surmised – but when the old man jerked his head fretfully away from the food, closing his eyes as though it were something at which he could not even bear to look, the three children would then jump off the floor and get to work on whatever was on offer, with a lot of argument as to who was entitled to gobble what.

The children were well-groomed and well-behaved, keeping their voices low so that, to his irritation, Rick could not always hear what they were saying. They never rushed around as so many of the child visitors tended to do out of boredom and restlessness. There was a middle-aged woman, clearly the children's mother, with shoulder-length straggly hair, brown streaked with yellow, and low-heeled shoes that clacked noisily whenever she dragged herself about with a weary, worried expression on her round face. There was also another woman, an emaciated ferret with a small moustache and long, surprisingly dirty fingernails, whom Rick confirmed must be the sister of the mother when he heard the children addressing her as "auntie".

Rick, who since his adolescence had had an abiding, unconfessed interest in the Pre-Raphaelites, thought that the emaciated old man, so rarely shifting on the bed or uttering a word, looked like a Christ, painted by Burne-Jones or Rossetti, who, instead of being crucified in his prime, had lived on into old age. His long, wispy white hair and white beard floated, rather than flowed, over the waxen flesh revealed by a pyjama jacket, the top buttons of which had not been fastened. Suddenly, on one rare occasion, he had opened his eyes and, alarmingly, intercepted Rick's gaze with a strangely severe, even threatening one. At once Rick had looked away. *The noticer must never be noticed*: that was the primary rule of the game. But Rick had had time to see that the eyes were of so pale and misty a blue that they each might have been sealed by a cataract were it not that one of the children, a daughter, had identical eyes.

The old, obviously dying man interested Rick more than any member of his family; but he did not interest him as much another person, clearly an outsider. This was a burly, fiftyish man, with muscular, tattooed arms revealed by rolled-up shirtsleeves, and straw-like hair closely and inexpertly cropped. He never joined the others in reconnoitring for chairs or, if that quest met with failure, in squatting on the floor. He merely shook his head with pursed lips when one of the party held out the plastic bag bulging with food and drink. He rarely spoke, and then only in the hoarse whisper of laryngitis, inaudible to Rick, however hard he strained to hear. For most of the time he would merely stand and stare down at the patient from the far end of the bed, clutching its rail and leaning over it, with a look that, oddly, expressed exasperation – why the hell are you dying? it seemed fiercely to demand, more than any other emotion.

After three days, there was a crisis of some kind. "But where are they going to take him?" one of the daughters, no more than six or seven in age, demanded of her mother. Rick heard that clearly and the response: "Oh, somewhere private. On his own." "But why? Why, Mum?" The mother now had a haunted, despairing look on her face. "Oh, he'll be better like that. It'll be easier for him." "When are they going to move him?" "Oh, you and your questions, questions, questions! Tomorrow. That's what that one from Trinidad said. Tomorrow morning. They expect a bed to be vacant by then." Rick knew that meant that the staff were expecting an overnight death to free the bed of its present occupant, so that the old man could take his turn to die in it.

That evening, with the exception of the tattooed interloper, who always seemed to Rick to deliberately keep a distance, the little party began, with a weary sadness, their usual task of picking up empty bottles, books, playing cards, toffee papers and sandwich wrappers before their departure. The tattooed man made no attempt to help them, merely watching them with the same intensity with which Rick was watching him. The old man remained motionless, eyes shut, as the children each stooped over him to fulfil their last duty, urged on them by the mother, of kissing him goodnight. "Sleep tight, darling," the mother said. Her sister said nothing, barely putting her thin lips to his shiny forehead. Then, in a military column, the mother their leader, they shuffled out in single file. The tattooed man, his trainers squeaking on the linoleum floor, went last. For a moment, he halted and glanced over his shoulder. Frowning, he gave a little shrug.

A few seconds later, to Rick's amazement, the man was back. Alone. Again the trainers squeaked, as he went over to the nearest side of the bed. He stared down at the old man, whose eyes never opened. He took the frail hand in his powerful one and gripped it tightly for a few seconds. No response. Eventually, he lowered his head to whisper in the old man's ear:

"I *did* love you."

It was a whisper of such passionate intensity that Rick was certain that he had heard every word. But what was the meaning of the declaration? Rick could only guess what precisely had been the nature of the cord that had bound together two men so totally unlike each other.

The tattooed man seemed to be awaiting some response. Then he stepped back, glanced across at Rick for a second, and hurried off.

Throughout the night that followed, Rick's sleep was shallow and intermittent. Repeatedly, waking as though he had been suddenly yanked up from the recesses of some icy, dark pool, he would silently say to himself the words *I did love you*. But his curiosity, an insatiable yearning, remained unsatisfied.

Early in the following morning, while all the other ancient inmates of the ward were still asleep, a nurse with a flat, Oriental face stood on tiptoe to jerk together the curtains round the bed. Rick had been watching the old man, but the pale-blue cloudy eyes never opened even during this disturbance. Perhaps, Rick thought, he was now in a coma. Perhaps – yes, it was possible – he was already dead.

Later, the family arrived. The mother let out a wail and her sister then remonstrated: "Now, Emily! Be brave! Remember the children!" One of these, a boy, was whimpering, a fist pressed to his mouth. Another, a girl, was standing on tiptoe in what looked like ballet pumps, as she lifted a curtain flap to peer behind it.

The tattooed man was not there. Rick awaited his reappearance with an excitement that made him feel that the tachycardia for which he was being treated was about to recur. But he never came. That "I *did* love you" must have been his last farewell.

Later, after the body had been wheeled away by two obviously Eastern European orderlies chattering cheerfully in a language that Rick decided must be Polish, he once again repeated over and over to himself, "I *did* love you." Had the two men, so totally unlike each other, merely been relatives? Or colleagues? Or father and son? Or lovers some time in the past and perhaps even in the present? Rick longed to be told that the last of these suppositions was the right one. But he was never to have that confirmation.

––––––––

Hurrying past his bed with a trolley of medicines, the emaciated, middle-aged Irish nurse Dilys, whom unrelenting activity seemed to be consuming like some fatal disease, skidded to a halt.

"You're back in that bed again!"

Rick looked up at her in silence, smiled amiably, lowered his eyes and then turned his head aside.

"I keep telling you – get up and sit in a chair. Otherwise, take my word, you'll never get any better."

Head still turned aside, Rick remained silent. He wanted to reply, "I *am* getting better," but he always shrank from confrontations.

"We want that bed. And to have that bed we want you out of this ward and out of this hospital. This isn't a rest home."

She hurried off.

Bitch! Rick got off the bed with a sigh and settled himself on the bedside chair, so uncomfortable with that diagonal crack, like the serrated edge of a knife, across its leather seat. He picked up the copy of the *Daily Mail* that he had purchased the day before from a white-haired female volunteer, who had told him, "Somehow, I thought you'd be a *Telegraph* man," before confiding in him that she had a toothache – "This seems to be a place where everyone has to suffer," she had sighed.

Later, Rick's consultant, whose youthfully plump cheeks were covered in a blue-and-red network of fine blood vessels, halted with his entourage. Rick, observant as ever, had noticed that a girl with a head too large for a body so wispy always walked and stood close to the great man, the large head cocked to listen to everything that he might utter in his wisdom.

"Why do you sit in that chair all the time?"

"Sit?"

"Yes, sit, dear chap. Sit. You've reached a stage when you ought to start walking. We want you out of here – enjoying all the pleasures that this rather dull and dreary suburb has to offer."

Rick pointed at the machine beside him. "But how about this?"

"How about it? It has wheels. You push it. Not heavy. You must have discovered that on your journeys to the loo."

The Irish nurse, Dilys, hurrying down the ward with a loaded bedpan, had paused to listen. "Yes, doctor," she confirmed, "I'm always telling him he must get up and about."

"Why not try our terrace café? It's a beautifully sunny day," the consultant suggested over his shoulder as he began to sway off down the ward, the large-headed girl at his side and the others behind him.

Ah, well, Rick decided, he'd better descend to the terrace. Otherwise they would go on bullying him. He staggered to his feet and all but fell. He gripped the shaft of the drip, the hot flesh of his palm finding the cold metal oddly comforting, and began to push it. It always seemed far lighter than he had expected; on this occasion it all but shot out of his grasp at the first thrust.

Every table in the café was occupied. But then a solitary woman with knobbly knees and frizzy grey hair jumped to her feet. "You could have this table. I'm on my way." She gave a brief, cheerless laugh. "Unless you want me to join you."

As so often, Rick's response to this kind of flirtatiously jocular suggestion was no more than that brief silence, slow smile, lowering of the eyes and turning aside of the head.

He sank into a chair with a brief groan and looked around for a waitress. Then he heard a high voice, raised in exasperation, from the next-door table: "No, no! *Not* another lump. What's the matter with you? You know I never take two lumps. Oh God, Philip, what's the *matter* with you? Do you purposely do these things to irritate me?"

Rick strained to listen to everything that followed. But he did not look across to the next-door table. *The noticer must never be noticed.*

The man incensed about the second lump of sugar had long, thin, slippered feet crossed at the ankles, and long, thin hands clasped in his lap. His hair, a lock falling across a corner of his forehead, was silky and so pale a yellow that Rick had first thought it had gone prematurely white. His features suggested an agitated bird's at the approach of a predatory cat. Hovering about him, now handing him a biscuit and offering to pour him some more tea ("I promise that this time I'll be good about the sugar lumps"), was the man called Philip, heavily built, with a wide, full mouth and small eyes with long eyelashes. Rick thought him attractive; his type, he told himself.

"I feel rather giddy," the man in the wheelchair suddenly announced. He bit into a biscuit. "Oh, dear! I was just about to enjoy myself."

"Would you like me to push you back to your room?"

"No, sweetie, you're not going to get rid of me as easily as that." He gulped for air and stared into the distance, face contorted, as though he had just mouthed something unexpectedly bitter. Then he turned back and wailed: "Oh, I so much long for you to put your arms around me."

"Shhh!" The other man blushed as he peered around to see if anyone had heard. Then his eyes focused on Rick and he briefly gave him a smile of complicity. "I'll be putting my big, strong arms around you as soon as I get you home."

"Oh, I sometimes just give up on the thought of that ever happening!" Rick caught the despair in the man's carefully articulated, almost falsetto voice. He experienced a pang of pity. "The only reason I don't want to leave this bloody world is that I don't want to leave you."

"Oh, please, please! Everyone can hear you. You've no idea what a penetrating voice you've got." Again, Philip gave Rick a glance of complicity followed by a quick grin.

Rick lowered his head to look down into the overgrown garden below the terrace. All at once, he realized, "Oh, God, I've got to pee." It was that furosemide, dripping remorselessly down into his arm from the machine beside him. They had that morning raised his dose from 40 mg to 80 mg a day.

He got to his feet, placing his *Daily Mail* on his chair. He all but asked the two men if they would keep an eye on the chair for him in his absence. Then he decided to take his chance.

Rick had a dislike of using a urinal rather than a cubicle. But, since both cubicles were occupied, there was nothing else for it. With difficulty, he manipulated the spindly crane of the drip so that it did not get in his way. He fumbled inside his pyjama trousers, suddenly shocked at the realization that, after three days of wear both day and night, they smelled badly in need of a change.

The door of one of the two cubicles opened with a shrill squeak and a bear-like man lumbered out. It was too late for Rick to change from urinal to cubicle now. Besides, the floor of the cubicle – he had just noticed – was awash with pee. The bear-like man might have been a horse.

Someone had entered from the corridor. Out of the corner of his eye, Rick made out the features, heavy and rough, of the oh-so attractive Philip. Brazenly, the newcomer grinned, sidled into the stall next to

Rick's and began to pull down the zip of his trousers. "Hi, fellow – well met!" he announced in his deep, resonant voice. "I couldn't keep my eyes off you. I hope my partner didn't notice. He's terribly jealous and he notices everything."

"No, no, I'm the one who notices everything," Rick wanted to say. But he merely smiled and turned to the business of shaking his cock.

"Why not let me do that for you?"

Rick cowered against the side of the stall, as far away from the other man as possible.

"Oh, come on! A little of what you fancy can't do you any harm. That's what I always say."

"No. No! Sorry."

The man in the wheelchair watched Rick as he emerged and made his way over to his table. "I kept it for you," he said, long fingers fiddling with the lock of almost-white hair drooping diagonally over one corner of his forehead. "A *very* persistent foreigner – Italian, by his accent – demanded it but I kept it for you."

Kept it? Kept what? For a moment Rick was bewildered. Then he realized. The table. "Thank you," he said.

"He's my partner." The enunciation had become even more precise than ever. "Eleven years. Think of that. We met at school. I adore him. There's never been anyone else – for either of us."

Rick thought: Why are you telling me all this?

The man peered down the corridor towards the lavatory. "He's taking an age. He always does. He has trouble getting started."

Rick put his hand out to the crane holding the drip and gave it a gentle push. "Well . . . I must be on my way. It's getting chilly."

"*Chilly!* I was just thinking how warm it is."

Rick shuddered involuntarily. "I find it chilly."

———

The head rent officer, with her generously deep but far from inviting cleavage, brought Rick a tin of shortbread and lolled on his bed. Mr

Zeiss, who was about to retire as the boss ("And about time too!" his staff repeatedly remarked to each other), presented Rick with an M&S bag full of tattered and long out of date copies of the *New Yorker*. A newcomer to the department, easy to mistake for a disgruntled, ageing spinster, although in fact she was in her early thirties, handed him a Madeira cake that she claimed, mendaciously, to have baked herself. None of these or the other few visitors came more than once and, always observant, Rick sensed both their restlessness soon after they had arrived and their relief that he did not urge them to stay when they had prematurely made some excuse like, "Well, I must let you have a rest now," or, "I've got to get back to the office, so many staff are off with this dreaded swine flu."

In contrast to these transients clumsily doing their duty, Rick's friend Laurence, a civil servant, came often and on each occasion stayed for far longer than Rick would have liked. Rick had once loved him and now had an affection for him, but, well, he could be so *embarrassing*, with the result that Rick always resisted the suggestion that he should move from his drab little West Kensington flat into Laurence's ostentatiously sumptuous one. Neither Laurence's voice nor his manner was camp and his appearance – portly, moustached, hair close-cropped over his oddly pointed ears – often made people decide at a first glance that he must be some sort of military man. But it never took such people long to cotton on to the truth.

"Shhh! Don't boom like that!" Rick now hissed. "Why d'you always have to make yourself so conspicuous?"

Laurence giggled, in no way offended. "I've brought you a lot of lovely goodies from Fortnum's. I know your favourite chocolates are Bendicks Bittermints but they now have a new line – Bendicks Bitteroranges. Marvellous! You'll love them."

"You've forgotten that I have an allergy to orange."

"Oh, you and your allergies!"

"I've asked you before – please, *please* don't raise your voice like that!"

"No one's paying any attention."

"Of course they are. There's no one but you to whom to pay it."

"You always make out that I'm *obvious*. I'm not. Not at all. No one in the office has an *inkling*. If they did, Brenda would never have pinned that other bugger's effort on to my proud bosom at Buck House."

"Laurence. For God's sake! Please!"

As soon as Laurence had gone, Rick, who had been so eager to get rid of him, began to miss him. He was someone with whom he always felt *safe* – and of whom else in his life could he say that? He dug into the plastic bag for one of the *New Yorkers*.

Suddenly that emaciated Irish nurse, Dilys, scuttled past, pushing her trolley of pills. She halted abruptly and turned. "I saw that he was here again just now," she said.

"Who?" He feigned puzzlement. "Oh, that friend of mine, you mean? Yes, he works only a few streets away so it's easy for him to come by."

"Well, that's nice." But from her tone it was clear that she did not find it at all nice. "Have you been together for a long time?"

"We're not *together*. Just friends. His mother and my mother . . ."

"Were mates. Pull the other one, dear." She blinked, the corners of her mouth sagging in a bitter grimace. "Well, anyway, he's generous, I will say that." She picked up the box of Bitteroranges. "Can you believe it – the mother of that boy at the far end over there has brought him only one present since he came here more than a week ago. A box of Quality Street – on offer for £4 at Tesco. Imagine! Yet always dressed up to the nines. With all that jewellery." She stooped over him. "You two been together for some time?" All at once her mouth had thinned cruelly, and her eyes had a steely look in them.

"We're not *together*. I told you that. We were just at school together." This was a lie to which Rick often had recourse. In fact, Laurence had gone to Eton, whereas he himself had been at a grammar school, highly regarded but hardly posh.

"I wasn't born yesterday. In this line of work one sees things –

everything. Oh, nothing shocks me now. I was an innocent little girl from County Clare once upon a time, long, long ago. But now . . ." She gave a snorting laugh. "You won't believe this, but when I was in my teens one of my brothers spent all his time in the company of this older man, a priest. I never guessed what was going on, not for one moment, until there was a scandal and my poor little brother had to give evidence – which was the last thing he wanted to do, the publicity and shame of it all." She peered. "How's the drip? Still dripping?"

As she walked away, Rick thought: Just you wait. From now on it's *you* that I'm noticing.

————

Fiona, the nurse who, diminutive and with the smallest of breasts and the closest cut of springy brown hair, looked like a pubescent boy, was having trouble with replenishing the dripper – sighing, scowling and screwing up her eyes as she attempted to do so. From the far end of the ward, Dilys hurried over. "What's the matter, Fiona?" she asked. Her voice, usually so hectoring on such occasions, was almost wheedling in its concern. "Oh, you *have* got things into a mess, you poor thing. No, you don't unscrew *that*. Just leave that alone. The one you have to go for is the one next to it . . ."

"Oh, sorry, sorry." Fiona sounded mortified.

"Nothing to be sorry about, dear. Just let's get it right next time. Yes?"

As the two women completed the operation, there followed a lot of giggling from Dilys, and a lot of grateful sighing and batting of the eyelids from Fiona.

"So that's how it goes," Dilys concluded. "D'you think you've got the hang of it now?"

"Oh, yes, thank you, Dilys, thank you."

"The great thing is not to get yourself fussed. Remember that."

As the two woman walked away, laughing together at something that, inaudible to Rick, Dilys had uttered, he watched them, while still struggling in vain to hear them.

––––––––

Yes, from now on I've got both of you under observation.

The idea, as always, gave him a feeling of almost supernatural power.

All through that day he waited and watched. On one occasion, bustling about their tasks, the two women halted, Fiona with a rolled-up bandage in one of her small nail-bitten hands, and had a little chat – inaudible to him, unfortunately. On another occasion, he saw them exchange smiles first across a bed and then across a wheelchair that Dilys was helping Fiona to push, which was filled with a vast purple-faced man slumped, eyes closed. At one moment Rick heard from Dilys, "Oh, you naughty girl!" but that could not have been intended in reproof since both of them burst into laughter.

The noticer was not being noticed, Rick was sure of that. The two women were too busy rapturously noticing each other.

Just beyond the door of the lavatory to which, from time to time, Rick would have to shuffle along in his slippers, pushing the drip ahead of him – oh, that bloody furosemide – there was another door marked "Staff Only". When both women suddenly moved to night duty – could it have been at their own request? – he at once noticed how, when the patients were all asleep, the two women would slip through this door, either one after the other or together, leaving the now unattended ward reverberating with its eerie cacophony of snores and farts.

Eventually, having yet again seen them both whisk into the room, first Dilys boldly and then Fiona scuttling in after her, head lowered, he eased his leaden body out of bed with a groan, slipped his swollen feet into the new slippers that Lawrence had given him on his last visit, and began to push the crane of the drip noiselessly ahead of him towards that "Staff Only" sign. He halted outside the door, listening. Then, all at once, he heard a high-pitched gurgle of laughter – clearly

Fiona's – followed by a delirious, "Oh, that's the way, girl! Yes, *yès!*" from Dilys.

Heart scurrying, he put out a hand and pushed the door open, revealing a long, narrow room lit only by a low-wattage lamp at the far end of it. It was crammed with cardboard boxes, untidily piled on top of each other, and broken items of furniture. Beside the dim lamp, there was a wrought-iron bed, with nothing on it but a mattress – and two vague forms.

From the mattress, the two women stared up at him in shock and, yes – there was no other word for it – terror. The skirts of their uniforms were rucked up to their waists; one of Fiona's tiny, pointed breasts glimmered, exposed.

"What are you doing here? This is 'Staff Only'." Dilys's voice quivered; it had none of its usual blasting tone.

"Oh, sorry, sorry. I thought the loo was here. The corridor light's so weak. It's one further on, isn't it? I'm so sorry."

He was the noticer; they were the noticed. He felt triumphant. He had them where he wanted them – and where Dilys always wanted her patients and fellow nurses, abject and humiliated.

———

Rick waited not in the terrace café overlooking the garden but in another one, on the ground floor beside the main exit from the hospital, that consisted of a long bar with a huddle of tables and chairs before it. Laurence was due to fetch him and, despite his protests, to take him back, not to the grim little West Kensington pad, but to his own house, where he could spend his first night of freedom.

Rick had already drunk two cups of milky coffee and eaten a stale doughnut. Laurence was late. "Sorry, darling," he said when he eventually called Rick on his mobile to tell him, "but madam is in the foulest of moods. I can only suppose it's her time of the month. I simply must do a hundred things at the last moment for her before getting to you."

"Oh, don't worry. This place by the revolving doors is hardly cosy but at least I get the smell of freedom instead of farting."

Other people at the tables were also waiting – the patients with suitcases and carrier bags stacked around them, and their rescuers constantly looking at their watches for some occupation to hasten the time.

"Excuse me, sir. Please, sir." It was a young man with dark, languorous eyes, hollow cheeks and a small goatee, little more than a black, bristly tuft under his full lips. Of course, by dint of surreptitious peeps rather than a full, frank look, Rick had already observed him in every detail and decided that, apart from that ridiculous tuft of hair, he was really rather appealing. Italian? Spanish? No, Arab seemed far more likely. That clumsy gold ring with its huge "diamond" (surely not the real thing) suggested prolonged bargaining in some Middle Eastern *souk*.

"Please, sir. May I borrow your sugar?"

"Of course. I don't take it in coffee." Rick proffered the bowl.

The man bowed. "Thank you, sir." Then he returned to his chair, beside a pram of dimensions that evoked generations of Norland Nurses seated under trees in Kensington Gardens. He placed a brown hand on its handle. Momentarily peeping, Rick had already noticed the baby asleep in it. "I wait. You wait. Everyone wait. We are all waiters. Not a good job." Clearly he intended a pun. He pulled out a cigarette packet from the top pocket of his green silk shirt, and then sighed, shook his head and pushed it back in again.

"Yes, this is really not the hospital café, as everyone calls it, but its waiting room."

"My wife is always late. English. Before I come to England, I hear English are never late. But . . ." He shrugged his narrow shoulders and laughed. "Not true." Head on one side now, he queried: "You also wait someone?"

Rick nodded.

"Also your wife?"

"No, not my wife. A friend."

"My little baby here – not well. You know asthma?"

"Of course. I'm sorry."

"We are lucky. Famous professor look after her."

At that moment a girl with a harassed expression on her plain face began to thread her way between the tables. In the uniform of a junior nurse, she was carrying some files under a plump arm.

"Nina!" The young man half rose as he called out the name.

With obvious reluctance she approached. "Oh, Hamid. It's so nice to see you."

"Please sit! *Sit!*" The tone was peremptory, as to a disobedient dog. He patted the chair beside him. Rick realized that he had now become invisible. He liked it like that. It was the invisible that always noticed most.

"Oh, I can't. I'm so sorry. The prof wants me to do an errand for him." With a podgy left hand, she indicated the files under her right arm. "You know how tiresome he is."

"To me – and the little one" – he indicated the baby – "he is always kind, kind, kind."

"It's possible to be tiresome as well as kind." She turned away. "Well, I must be on my way."

"I brought you present."

The news was clearly far from welcome. "Oh, dear! I do so wish you wouldn't! I've so often told you that."

He put his hand in his pocket and took out a little package wrapped in pale-blue tissue paper. He held it out to her, with a look of entreaty.

"But I can't. Really, I can't."

"Please. To make me happy. Take, take!" He pushed it towards her.

"But what is it?"

"Never mind! Just take!" Suddenly he was angry. Saliva flecked the corners of his mouth, the rapidity of its appearance amazing Rick.

Reluctantly, she took up the package and pushed it into the pocket of her blouse. She squinted down at him with small, pitying eyes. "Oh, I wish . . ." she sighed. Then with angry emphasis: "I don't *want* your presents. Ours is not that sort of relationship. Can't you get it?"

But all too clearly to get it was beyond him. He was smiling up at her. "You will like it," he said. "I promise."

As she hurried off, he stared after her until she had disappeared from sight.

"She is such a beautiful girl, yes?" He sighed. "My wife is good woman. Good mother. Very good. But . . ." He shook his head. "Not beautiful. No, not beautiful. And getting old."

Rick almost asked what it was that he had given to the girl. Then he was glad that he hadn't. Often the best way to get the answer to a question is not to ask it, he had long since decided.

"I give her beautiful present," the young man was already volunteering. "When she opens, she will be happy. Very happy. Ring like this. Exactly same." He held up his hand, moved it towards Rick and then turned it sideways to reveal the ring that he was sporting on his middle finger. "From Marrakech. Lots of money. But I am happy for her to have such a ring – so expensive. Very happy."

Suddenly, Laurence was arousing everyone's attention at the café as he boomed across it: "Rick! Rick!" Absurdly, he raised his furled umbrella and brandished it back and forth, as though he were greeting a friend from the other end of a long station platform. Then he hurried over, to arrive snorting through the nostrils of his short, blunt nose. "Sorry, sorry! I'm afraid you must have got terribly bored, waiting here all alone for me."

Rick got to his feet. "Not at all. It's really quite interesting to watch all the comings and goings."

"I managed to find a parking place just a little way up Church Road."

"Oh, good."

"I didn't want you to tire yourself unnecessarily."

The Arab, leaning forward in his chair, head tilted upwards, was clearly expecting Rick to say goodbye to him. But there was no goodbye as Rick, leaning on Laurence and gripping his arm, ventured one unsteady step and then another.

"Goodbye, sir! Goodbye!" the Arab called after him, a note of desperation in his voice.

But Rick, swaying and staggering back into his old life, genuinely did not hear him.

There was even more desperation in the Arab's voice as he again called: "Sir, sir! *Sir!*"

Then the baby, so long silent in its vast pram, emitted a piercing wail.

———

"Oh, Rick, it's so lovely to have you back," one of the female secretaries declared with obvious insincerity. She and Rick had never got on.

A group of them were seated together on sagging, soiled armchairs or hideously uncomfortable wooden upright ones, sipping their mid-morning coffee.

The head of the rent office, her deep cleavage chapped from recent autumn winds, rattled her teaspoon in her cup, as though to express her annoyance. "Hospitals have really become horrendous places these days. What has become of the personal touch? I felt so sorry for you when I visited you among all those snoring and farting old gaffers."

"We must now try to spoil you for a little," the boss, Mr Zeiss, put in, leaning forward to pat Rick's knee with a solicitude that he rarely displayed to anyone, Rick least of all. "Please, don't try to do too much. You're always so conscientious."

At that, a pale, skinny accountant said: "If only we still had some of those magnificent Gorgons marching around as matrons. I was shocked at how dirty the floor was around your bed. I even think I saw a drop of dried blood." He gave a little shudder.

Rick laughed. "Not mine."

"That makes it even worse."

Rick looked around him. Then he said: "This'll probably surprise you all. But, you know, I really enjoyed myself."

"You *enjoyed* yourself?" That was old Mrs Pearson, who rarely enjoyed anything. "In that horrendous place? You must be joking, dear Rick."

"Not at all. It was all so interesting. The most interesting time I've had for, oh, years and years. Truly. I mean that."

Astounded, they all stared at him, as though he were a stranger who had confessed to some unmentionable crime or disease.

He responded to them as he usually did: first with the brief silence, followed by the lowering of the eyes and the slow smile, and then the gentle turning aside of the head.

But on this occasion he also finally said something: "There was so much to notice."

Royale with Cheese
Joseph Lidster

I open my eyes and I can't see.

Total darkness. I feel around to the left of me and my hand hits something hard. A wall? A door? I feel to my right and it's the same. There's something soft underneath me, some kind of material. But there's something hard underneath that.

My heart is pounding in my chest. It's all I can hear. I try to call out but there's no sound. I try to think. Think calmly. Not panic. I know that where I *think* I am is, well, it isn't possible. It isn't. Unless it's a dream? Maybe I haven't woken up? That makes sense because this, it's always scared me. Always. I hardly watch horror films in case it happens. So yeah, it could be just a dream. But I'm thinking that it could just be a dream and that's not what happens in dreams. But it can't be real. I'm too young. I'm far too young to die. I'm only thirty. That's too young. It feels ancient but it's young. I can't be dead. I mean, I'm not dead. I didn't die in my sleep and I haven't woken up in a coffin. This is not a coffin. It just simply absolutely can't be a coffin and, fucking hell, am I in a coffin? I know all I have to do is raise my arms, just a bit, and if they hit something then . . . fuck. Oh fuck. Please. Okay, maybe I won't raise them, then I won't know and I'll just be somewhere else and my life won't be over before I've even started. How much air do I have? Should I try to hold my breath? Will that just prolong it and . . . Okay. I'm going to raise my arms. Just . . . raise them and . . . okay . . . slowly . . . holding my breath and slowly raising them and fuck! What's that? Oh God, it's a . . . it's . . . it's a coat-hanger!

I raise my arms fully and they clatter into a bunch of coat-hangers. I'm in a wardrobe. A fucking wardrobe. And I'm a fucking tit for thinking I was in a coffin.

Except. I definitely went to bed last night. My own bed. I hadn't even been drinking. I had a couple, maybe three glasses of wine but not proper drinking. Why am I in a wardrobe? And whose wardrobe is it? It's not mine and . . . FUCK. Where's my phone? Why haven't I got my phone? Okay. I'll find out where I am. Someone's just moved me here for a joke. Which is clearly hilarious. So I just need to open the door and find out where I am.

I push open the door and obviously I fall out. Dignity is my middle name. I'm in a hallway, which is an odd place to put a wardrobe, and I can hear music. Someone's playing . . . the Scissor Sisters? And it sounds like they're having a party. Maybe I didn't go to bed last night? Fuck, have I really blanked out a whole party? I don't even recognize the place. Okay, really going to have to stop drinking so much. There's funny memory loss and then there's downright terrifying memory loss. Time to man up and see where I am. And who I'm with.

"Look who's awake!" Behind me. A voice. I don't recognize it.

"Eddie! Want another shot?" The voice knows my name. So I guess I must know her. And this, kids, is why we don't do drugs. I force an "I'm not too out of it really" smile and turn to see a zombie. And not just any zombie. It's a girl dressed as Pope John Paul II. The zombie.

"Yeah?" she says, waving a bottle of something red. It's a bottle of . . . Aftershock? Do people still drink that? I nod at Zombie Pope as she approaches with a drink. Naturally, I knock it back and the taste makes me suddenly feel very nostalgic, although I panic at how many calories might be in it.

"You all right now?" asks Zombie Pope Girl. "You were well out of it."

I shrug. "Yeah. I'm fine." I shrug again to emphasize just how fine I absolutely am.

Suddenly, Zombie Pope Girl leans in. "You do know, if there's anything you want to tell me, it's okay, yeah?"

And the world lurches. Because that. I remember that. I remember years of people saying that. Years of people trying to basically say,

"Look, I know you're gay and it's fine and you can tell me and you can just say the words and it'll be fine." Years of me pulling a confused face and saying, "Sorry, what? I'm fine! Ooh, let's have another shot!"

And rather oddly that's exactly what I say to Zombie Pope Girl. I mean, I tumbled out of the closet years ago. Well, I was pushed out of it. Long story. So why wouldn't I tell Zombie Pope Girl? And who was Zombie Pope Girl and why did she remind me of . . . thingy . . . Susan Wotsit. From uni. Susan.

Susan who once went to a fancy-dress party as the zombie of Pope John Paul II. Susan who once went to a fancy dress party as the zombie of Pope John Paul II just a few weeks after Pope John Paul II had died.

The party where I got so drunk so quickly and someone, I never found out who, thought it would be funny to put me in the wardrobe.

Okay, so I haven't woken up in a coffin but I have woken up in the past. Ten years in the past. That's the only explanation. Either that or it's a dream. It might be a dream. Again, it's odd that I'm aware I'm dreaming but let's go with it. Fuck it, what else can I do?

I realize Susan has poured me another shot and she's knocking one back herself. I swig mine and hold out the glass.

"Someone's keen," mutters Susan as she pours me another. Just then, Prince Charles and Camilla stagger out of the hallway. And I know. I remember. It's Peter and . . . fuck . . . her name . . . Lucy! Peter and Lucy. And they've come dressed as Charles and Camilla and she's about to . . .

Lucy falls out of Peter's arms, staggers into the wardrobe and yells, "Who's after putting a wardrobe here?" in her thick Dublin accent. Just before throwing up all over where I'd just woken up. Lucky escape. With a resigned sigh, Peter pulls her out and continues half-carrying her upstairs. Susan and I laugh, then she heads through to the living room. I go to follow but then I remember there's a mirror in the kitchen. And I need to see.

I open my eyes. God. I mean. Ten years. You don't think ten years is much. You don't think you've aged. Thanks to Instagram you don't look like you've aged. But ten years. I mean, I'm only thirty. No grey hairs yet but . . . twenty-year-old me? My face is so much younger. And less red. I look like a pale white waxwork. I haven't discovered tanning moisturizer or how to grow a beard. My eyes seem brighter. My hair is . . . well, the hairstyle was ill-advised even then. But it's darker. My hair's darker and glossier, my eyes are brighter, my skin is cleaner and . . . no lines. There are literally no lines on my face. I look innocent. I look like a sodding twink! Oh, and I'm dressed like Christopher Eccleston's Doctor Who. Yeah, cos I obviously looked really cool in a leather jacket. I suddenly smile, remembering. I'd loved Christopher Eccleston's Doctor Who. Him and Billie Piper having those fun adventures back in the days of Aftershock and fancy-dress parties. And then it got all complicated, and sexy, and dark. I realize I could go through to the living room and tell everyone what would happen over the next few years. And then I remember that most of them wouldn't be remotely interested.

I lift up the front of the jacket and my T-shirt . . . No abs. Fuck.

And then, there's like this explosion in my head as I remember who else is here. I remember him. The boy who *was* interested. The boy who was interested in me. The boy who, ten years ago, knew what I was, knew what I wanted, knew everything . . . I close my eyes and I remember him. I can't remember his name or why he was there or anything like that. But I remember *him*. I can remember how I felt. How my stomach churned. How I desperately, desperately wanted to be with him, to kiss him, to hold him, to do anything he wanted but . . . how I'd laughed and said I had a girlfriend back home and thanks but no thanks.

And now I'm here. I'm here again. And it might just be a dream. It's probably almost definitely just a dream but . . .

"I could say yes." I open my eyes and I stare at myself. "I could say yes and I could be with him and things would be different."

I take a deep breath and all I can hear is my heart pounding once more. I walk out of the kitchen and through the hallway, past the wardrobe and into the living room. A calm, measured walk. I'm fine.

Into the living room and everything looks so strange. I mean, everyone's in fancy dress so that's bonkers enough but nobody has an iPhone in their hand. There's a few old grey plastic Nokia things dotted about but nobody's looking at them. Nobody's on Twitter. Nobody's on Facebook. No Grindr, no Tinder. Nobody's taking a selfie to prove they're here. It all seems unreal yet more real maybe? I don't know. It's just fucking weird. Some bloke even has a camera. A real proper Boots disposable camera. I briefly wonder what'll happen to his photos. Where will he put them? Everyone's talking and dancing and getting off with each other. And God, loads of them are smoking. I mean, really, loads of them. Pretty much everyone in the room is smoking. You're lucky to meet another smoker these days. We're a dying breed, ha-fucking-ha. And yet everyone looks so alive and fresh and colourful and young. I know a few of them, like Susan from uni, but there's one bloke I don't know. I think he's Susan's cousin or something. I can't remember. But I remember exactly where he was sitting and I slowly turn to look over at the window.

And there he is. Leaning against the windowsill and – oh, he's young. I mean, yeah, I guess he would be. When I saw him ten years ago he was about five years older than me which back then just seemed so much older. He'd seemed so confident and cool and perfect. Now, he seems more . . . human. I mean, he's still beautiful. I can't not stare at him. He's dressed as a soldier, which is clearly, obviously, blatantly hot. Hair is a sort of gingery blond. Not over-styled. In fact he's quite scruffy-looking, which doesn't go with his costume at all. He's wearing glasses but he doesn't look like a hipster. They're just glasses. He's got really broad shoulders. He doesn't look like he works out but he's just . . . broad. He's a mass of contradictions but it works. He's just perfect. The most perfect man I'd ever seen and the most perfect man I've ever seen.

And suddenly, he's looking over at me and he's smiling. It's funny but, ten years before, that smile had seemed so confident. The sexiest, most confident smile in the world. A smile that beamed, "You do know, if there's anything you want to tell me, you don't have to because I know and I don't care and we don't need to say anything because I just know and you don't need to be scared." Now . . . now I'm older and he's younger, I realize it's simply nothing more than a friendly smile. He's alone. I'm alone. So he's just smiling hello at me.

And, I'm realizing, I'm older. I'm older than him. I can do this. Christ, there's been enough men over the years. I'm not that in-the-closet twenty-year-old any more. I can just talk to him like I talk to any bloke. I can change things. And yeah, if somehow this is real that'll change history but, frankly my dear, I don't give a fuck. I want him and I know already, I remember, that he wants me. Already, this is so much easier than Grindr. You're looking for *friends*?

I push through the dancing and just stride towards him with a big grin on my face – making sure I don't look drunk, keeping to that straight line, just staring ahead – and, just as I'm a couple of feet away, some bugger falls into me and sends me crashing into his arms. But I'm not going to panic. Because actually, come to think of it, I think that's how it started ten years ago. And who needs an opening line when you're already in his arms. Sorted.

"Hi," I say.

"Hi," he says.

"I'm Eddie," I say.

"Nice to meet you," he says before pushing me back onto my feet. He takes a sip from a mug of wine. "Caspar."

"What?" I say, very nonchalantly leaning against the windowsill next to him.

"My name's Caspar."

"Like the—"

"Yeah. The ghost. But I'm not a ghost. Obviously."

I laugh. But I hate myself for saying what clearly everybody says to him when they hear his name. Funny thing is, he *is* a ghost. From ten years ago. But this time, things are going to be different.

"So . . ." and what? I'm struggling to think of what to say! Normally, if I'm chatting to a guy in the real world, as opposed to online, we'll talk about music and telly and shit, but I can't remember what was out ten years ago. What were we watching? What were we listening to? I need Wikipedia. But I don't have my phone so I can't Wikipedia and I don't even know if Wikipedia exists now. Fuck! What else do you talk about?

"So . . . how do you know . . . who do you know here?" I ask him.

"I'm Susan's cousin. Just visiting." He takes another sip of wine. And then another. Actually, he seems a little nervous. Which isn't how I remember it at all.

"Oh yeah, I'm on her course. We used to live together in Halls but then we moved to different houses but we're still friends, obviously."

Seriously. What the actual fuck am I saying? I need a drink.

"Cool," he says. "I never went to uni. Wish I had. The parties are good."

"Yeah, they are."

"So you and Susan never had a thing?" He's deliberately not looking at me.

"What?"

"No? I know she's been with a few blokes since she's been here."

I laugh and nod. And I suddenly remember having this late-night conversation with her about how people had been calling her a slut. Christ, what would they think of me if they could see me now? Well, now now. Not the now I'm in now. God, this is confusing and while I'm doing all this thinking, I'm not doing any talking and he's going to lose interest and . . .

"No, not me," I reply. "What about you? Seen anyone you like?"

He shakes his head, smiling, which breaks my heart. I pause for a lifetime before saying, "I'm just off to get a drink."

He smiles again and I notice his teeth are crooked. "Can you get me some more wine?"

He wants me to come back?

"Yeah, sure," I say, playing it cool. Then I turn and try to push through the crowd. And I look anything but cool.

In the kitchen, I start searching through the half-open bottles of wine. There's got to be at least one that cost more than a couple of quid. As I do this, sipping from each bottle, I think about what I'm doing. About how ridiculous this is. Yeah, Caspar's fit and yeah, I'd always regretted not going for it with him but I hadn't been out back then. I hadn't been really sure what I was. And it had been ten years ago. But then why was I here? What was all this about? A second chance? A chance to put things right? But – it's not as if my life's bad. It hasn't gone wrong. I've got a decent job, decent flat, decent shags. I don't need a second chance. Yeah, I regret not coming out until I moved to London but I've more than made up for it since. Seriously, I've got over 400 followers on Instagram.

But it's him. There's something about him. He meant something. He was perfect and he meant something and we were meant to do . . . I don't know what but we weren't meant to just have some brief encounter. These days, we'd have added each other on Facebook and chatted and flirted and made plans to see each other. But back then, back . . . now, we can't do that. So that's all this is. A time-travelling dream-Facebook-friend request. I keep sipping from the different bottles.

"Did I see you chatting to Caspar?" says a voice. Susan. I turn to look at her. It's funny, I haven't thought about her in years. I think she ended up getting married. I know I got a friend request from someone who looked a bit like her but I didn't recognize the surname. And, obviously, she wasn't a fit bloke so I never bothered. But I'm looking at her now and I'm suddenly remembering just how close we'd been. I'd been so shy at uni but she'd insisted that I went to parties and that. It's only looking back that I can see just how much she cared about me. Ah well, I guess that's life. You lose touch with people. But suddenly I hug her. Which surprises her. Cos we never really hugged in those days. Actually, it surprises me too. Guess I'm pissed.

She laughs. "You okay?"

I nod and pull back. "Yeah, yeah, I'm good. And yeah, I was chatting to him."

"He's a nice guy," she says. "A really nice guy."

Nice guy. Can't remember when I last met a *nice guy*. He's not a bear or a twink. He's not a gym freak. He's not asked me how big my cock is. He's just a *nice guy*. Christ, do I really want to shag a *nice guy*? "I'm just getting him a drink. Cos, you know, he doesn't really know anyone."

"Cool," she replies. And her smile is so desperate. It's desperate for me to man up and deal with what I am. It's desperate for me to be happy. And fuck, I've missed that smile. I want to cry. I actually want to cry. She reaches behind me and grabs a bottle.

"He's drinking this," she says, handing it to me. "It's called Pinot Grigio."

I laugh. She says it like it's a foreign language. I remember how back then we only knew "white", "red", "pink". And as long as it was cheap and did the job, that's all we cared about.

"I know," she says, laughing. "Pretentious twat."

She smiles again at me and she's close to telling me to go for it but she knows it would scare me so she just grabs another bottle and heads out. And, with the bottle of cheap Pinot in one hand and a chipped mug in the other, I head back through to the living room.

"Is This the Way to Amarillo" is playing. God, is that really ten years old? Everyone's dancing to it. Even Caspar. Well, he's more . . . bopping along. And again, I suddenly see this different side to him. When I saw this ten years ago, I remember thinking how cool he was. He wasn't one of the gang, he was doing his own thing. Now I realize he's just a bit shy. He doesn't know anyone and he's half-heartedly trying to join in. He's waiting for someone to invite him in. Well, that's what I'm here for, bitches.

I push through everyone and go to join him.

"Pinot Grigio all right?"

He looks at me surprised then grins. "Yeah, actually it's what I'm drinking. Cheers."

I pour some into our mugs and we each take a sip. Christ, it's vile. It tastes like Wetherspoons. Quickly, I drink some more, hoping if I gulp it down I won't taste it.

"I . . ." I start to say, determined to take control.

"I . . ." he says, at the same time.

We both stop.

"Listen, I can hardly hear over the music," he says. "You want to go outside?"

Do I? Of course I do. I want to be with him. I want nothing else. I'm going to change things. He's going to be mine. This time, he's going to be mine. I'm going to change who I am and how I got here and I'm going to change everything.

Wait? I want to change who I am? When did that happen? I don't want to change.

It's cold outside, but we're both drinking and smoking so we don't really notice. And we're talking. Well, he's talking. I'm trying not to say much. What with coming from the future and all that. He's telling me about how he's just got back from travelling around Europe with his mates. And I'm just listening, taking it all in. Amsterdam, Venice, Rome. He's telling me about the sights, the museums, the people, the clubs, the bars. He's laughing because he had a Royale with cheese and a beer in McDonald's in Paris. I can't remember why that's supposed to be funny, but I laugh along with him as if I know what he's on about.

"You don't say much," he says, but he says it like it's a question.

Back then I'd been shy but now? I just want to listen. I'm becoming aware that this is the first party I've been to in years where I haven't taken a shitload of coke, which is probably why I'm happy to sit there in silence.

"I like hearing your stories," I say. Which I think is what I said last time but never mind. I'll change things shortly. As he talks, I realize just how sweet he is. A nice guy. Yeah, he's got an air of confidence about him but he seems so young and hopeful. I know it's because of how much I've changed. I've done so much more in my life than he has. And yet, actually, I don't feel like I've done half as much. If you asked me to summarize the last few years of my life . . . well, yeah, career's gone well and I go out all the time but other than that? I've never had a Royale with cheese and a beer in a McDonald's in Paris.

And then he's telling me what he wants to do. How he wants to see the whole world. He's got this dream of hiring a van and just travelling the world. Which I don't think is particularly viable but I just nod and smile.

And I wonder, what did he go on to do? He had so many dreams, so many choices. We all did. Ten years ago, we all had so many choices. When did that change? When did we run out of choices? But, for all I know, he might have died a week later.

"And then, I guess, at some point I want to settle down," he says. I don't push him on it. I know he means with a man. And he knows I know. And he's looking at me. He wants to kiss me. He wants me to say something. But I can't. I want to. I want to say something. I want to kiss him. I want to change things but I can't. I literally, physically can't. I'm back in time and I can't change anything! What's the fucking point in that? I want to cry. I wanted to cry back then. Nothing's changed except the reasons why. So we just sit there and he's thinking about his future and I'm thinking about my past.

I'm thinking about how I moved to London. About the coke and the parties. About the guys on Twitter with their beards and abs. About the perfect smiles and perfect teeth. And about how I'm one of them. I'm just another one of them but Caspar, Caspar isn't. Caspar was different. Caspar was fit because he didn't fit. And then I'm remembering my reflection in the kitchen mirror. And I'm thinking about how, here and now, I don't fit. My coat's too big. I've got bad hair. No beard. I couldn't even grow a beard back then. We didn't go to the gym. We didn't know what Pinot Grigio was. We didn't know anything. And even though I'd been in the closet, I'd been happy. Because I remember what I said to Caspar. And I say it again.

"Yeah. I'd like to do that."

I'd wanted to go travelling. I'd wanted to see the world. I'd wanted to one day settle down. But I didn't. I didn't do any of it. I moved to

London and I joined a gym. I got a job at an advertising agency and I grew a beard. And, yeah, it's been great, and I love it, and I love the parties and I fucking love the men but . . . I'd wanted something different.

I want something different.

And I realize that I don't want Caspar. Because it wouldn't be like it would have been. It would have been hot, obviously, but it would have been naive and messy and silly and fun. I don't think I know what that is any more. And even if we could, I worry that I'd change him. I worry that I'd ruin him. I don't want to spoil his hope for the future. I just want to get mine back.

So I say sorry, and I tell him I've a girlfriend at home and he knows I'm lying but there's nothing he can do as I walk away from him. And I walk back into the house and I walk straight through to the hallway and I stand in front of the wardrobe and again I wonder why it's there. I'm about to climb inside it but Susan's running up to me.

"You okay?" she asks.

I just nod.

"It's never too late," she says. Before smiling her beautiful sad smile and stumbling back into the living room.

And she's right. It isn't. I can't change what happened but I can change what's going to happen.

I climb into the wardrobe. And I curl up. And it should be a powerful cathartic moment but it's full of Lucy's sick so that kinda spoils things. But I close my eyes.

And when I open them, my eyes are open.

Caesar's Gallic Wars
Neil Bartlett

———

At ten past three on the afternoon of June the twenty-fourth, at the hottest hour of the hottest day of the long hot summer of nineteen hundred and seventy-four, a boy with glasses is sitting in a school gymnasium on the edge of an undistinguished small town in the south of England. He is not alone – but he might as well be, since all the other heads in the gymnasium are bowed, no one whispers, and no one looks up at anyone else. Only the movement of pen nibs across paper scratches at the edges of the room's sunlit silence. The boy is absorbed in completing the peculiar task of transcribing, by hand, and in ink, an English translation of an 800-word long passage taken from the ending of the seventh book of Julius Caesar's account of his conquest of Gaul. The seventh book is the volume in which the last of the rebellious Gallic chieftains, Vercingetorix, is captured, humiliated and led in chains through Rome before his execution.

The doomed Vercingetorix and his captains are wild and bare-chested; they fight and die half-naked and screaming, painted, each of their necks clasped in a gleaming gold torque. All of these details are catalogued by Caesar – the boy has committed them to memory – but needlessly, as it turns out, for they do not feature in the particular passage that the examination board has chosen this summer. The passage that they *have* selected is easy to recognize, much to the boy's relief. It features a word that is memorable chiefly by virtue of the fact that it has no English synonym or translation; a word that the boy feels sure he will never have reason to write again once this exam is over. The word is *quincunx*, which, as the notes to the boy's school edition of Caesar explain with the aid of a simple diagram, is the alignment of five like objects so that four are set at the corners of the square and the fifth is at the exact intersection of the two diagonal lines bisecting the same square from corner to corner. The *quincunx* was the formation in which the despairing Vercingetorix and his captains, stealing a trick learnt from their attackers, drove sharpened wooden stakes into the earthen ramparts of their final citadel, the points facing out and down, aimed viciously at the chests of the first men in the inexorably advancing Roman cohorts. To no avail: the breast-plated cohorts trampled their pierced and fallen colleagues as they clambered upwards; the citadel was taken, the bare were vanquished by the armoured, and the wildness of Gaul was over for ever.

At ten past three, with twenty minutes to spare, the boy looks around, and is not a little satisfied to see that he is the first to have finished his paper– and not a little relieved to see that no one seems to have noticed the unnatural swiftness with which he has completed his task. For two years now, he has clumsily but successfully concealed his inability to understand Latin grammar or translate an unseen Latin text by blushing and bluffing his way through every lesson; every evening for the last four weeks of those two years, he has devoted a whole, secret hour to memorizing from a paperback translation the entire seventh book of Caesar's *Gallic Wars*. His only fear (the palms of his hands are still sweating with it; his index finger is calloused from holding the pen so tight) was that he might, flustered by the silence of the examination room, have transcribed – with faultless accuracy, but in complete error – a passage other than the one set. That one ridiculous word, *quincunx*, the word on which Vercingetorix pinned his last hope, the word that betrayed him and all his captains, has saved the boy. It only occurs once in the book, unmistakably placed at the opening of the description of the very last battle between rebel and ruler, and it has enabled him to select the appropriate string of sentences from his memory and so execute his fraud to perfection.

At half-past three, when the two hours of the exam are over, the master who sits at the front desk will call out, "*Put your pens down now please*"; but the boy does not wait for this instruction – he lays his pen down early. This is no small gesture, for this is the very last afternoon that the boys will be assembled in the school gymnasium in this way. Once this paper is over, the summer will be over. And when it's over, he'll almost be fifteen.

He lays down his pen, and he looks out of the window. Sixty-two boys bend their white-collared necks over their exam papers, but the sixty-third lifts his head, turns it, and stares.

The school gymnasium has tall, metal-framed windows which reach from floor to ceiling, four of them. Between them are the racks of wooden wall-bars on which this boy, together with all the others, has clambered every Tuesday afternoon of the summer term. The bars are empty now of bare, sweaty gym-lesson arms and legs, and quiet. The windows are all shut – despite the heat – to keep out the sound of any passing plane or traffic. Beyond them is a stretch of black playground tarmac, turning oily in this heat, and beyond that are playing fields, kept empty on this particular afternoon, and the turf is brown and the earth cracking where the groundsman has shaved the pitch too close. There are no long grasses for the hot wind to move, no gulls even; the playing fields are as quiet as the ramparts before a final attack. Only one thing is moving. Coming slowly up the drive, which bisects the playing fields and leads to the playground, is a car; a big, dark, shining and silent car.

The boy is instantly and unreasonably sure that the car is coming for him. Quite sure. The car halts, engine running, in the middle of the playground, and there it waits – waits, as a lion might wait. Oddly, none of the other sixty-two boys raise their heads, which they might have been expected to do when they caught sight of it stopping – after all, no group of boys of that particular age could be expected to concentrate quite that hard on anything written in Latin. One smoked-glass car window slides down, issuing an unspoken invitation. The boy looks round to see if the supervising master has noticed what is happening, but apparently he has not. A rear door swings open now as well, revealing a glimpse of a dark, expensively upholstered interior. And now comes what is perhaps the oddest detail in this admittedly odd story: earlier in the afternoon the master has been very strict about insisting that none of the boys move either to or from their desks before precisely the allotted time; but now neither the master nor any of the boy's classmates attempt to stop the boy as he rises neatly from his desk, leaves his blazer hanging forgotten on the back of his chair, moves towards the second of the four windows, climbs the wall-bars, levers open a panel in a metal window frame, climbs through it, drops to his hands and knees so as to break his eight-foot fall onto the baking tarmac, gets to his feet, walks across the empty playground and then gets into the empty back seat of the car. The entire action is as unhesitating, as easy – and as private – as a dream.

In retrospect, we can be sure that this boy had had, that summer, many such dreams – he was, after all, nearing the end of the final summer of his adolescence, and any boy capable of memorizing the translation of an entire book of obscure Latin prose clearly has a capable and inventive mind. He surely, once the car door had closed, would have recognized as familiar from his adolescent fantasies the dark eyes of the driver gazing at him in the rear-view mirror – recognized the elegantly powerful hands on the wheel (one gloved, one ungloved), the quiet surge of the engine, the unhurried smoothness of the ride down the drive – and the distinctive sound of the smoothly obscene voice which now began to tell him what was in store for him once he had been driven safely through the streets of his home town behind the car's darkly smoked glass windows. The voice reassured him that no teachers, no parents and no neighbours would see him. That no one but the man now glancing up again to watch him in the rear-view mirror would see the smile which broke slowly across his face as he felt the leather of the seat sticking slightly to his back now that his white school shirt had been unbuttoned, crumpled into a ball and thrown to one side.

And now, many years later, we may be sure that this same boy has in fact done all or almost all of the things that he ever imagined doing on that final hot afternoon of his fourteenth summer. He will, now that he is older, have seen many men bare-chested, jewelled and captured; men humiliated, and men led in triumph. On several or perhaps even many nights in the course of those intervening years he will (we may be sure) have reached over his chosen partner to turn the bedside light back on so that he can once again enjoy watching the exact transition from defiance to surrender pass over a man's face. But still, even after all these years, there is something about the memory of that late June afternoon and of that half-remembered drive that catches in his mind like a fish hook – like a fish hook will catch in the fleshy part of the hand at the base of your thumb, if you're careless.

It's a fierce pain, shocking. Almost unbearable, should the fishing line suddenly pull tight. It can hurt so much that you want to get a knife and cut it out.

So much, that you want to get a knife and slice yourself open.

The boy – now grown – cannot quite account for the power of this memory of his past self, no matter how often he replays it. Sometimes he feels sure that the key to it lies in that one untranslatable Latin word, the word that is explicable only by a diagram, the word he learnt at fourteen but has never used since. He feels sure, also, that the meaning of the memory is something to do with the fact that he was never caught; that no one ever knew that his perfect marks for that translation paper were earned by his having memorized a set of words which he never actually understood – no one, not his parents nor his teachers nor any of the adults who had so eagerly queued to assure their prize pupil that his future was bright. He recognizes now that it is a lesson that has stood him in good stead, this trick of remembering what you have never really understood, of reproducing with perfect conviction the meaning of words that are meaningless. He also knows now that the driver of that car, whoever he was, knew how to do something that he himself has since learnt, but which none of the other boys nor their teacher not his parents seemed to know: how to pick the right boy. How to pull a fourteen-year-old out through a schoolroom window without a sound. How to do it just by waiting – waiting, on the hottest afternoon of the year. How to do it so that no one in the whole of that small, quiet town suspected what was being done right under their noses. How to do it so well that it is without a single sound except for one grateful and astonished sigh that a now fifteen-year-old boy helplessly arches his back, some six weeks after that particular afternoon, arches his back and lets his head fall, lets it fall and then again at the last moment lifts it and looks up at the other man he is with and comes and comes and comes and comes – and now, now, all of these years later, looks at the clock, and sees that it is ten past three, and smiles, and lays his pen down.

How the Story Ends
Hugh Fleetwood

———

"Mum, Stefano and I are getting married!"

Lying on her hospital bed, June looked at her daughter. How beautiful she was – and how shrill, how strained her voice. "Are you, dear?" she said. "That's nice." Then, because she realized that "nice" wasn't really adequate, she smiled – smiled tenderly, sadly – at poor Soops, who had been a difficult child all her life, and managed to hold out her arms.

Her embrace was almost as awkward as the way Soops leaned forward and rested her head on her mother's much-diminished bosom. But at least I have the excuse that I'm dying, June thought. Whereas Soops – even as a baby she didn't know how to come to my breast. She would scream and scream to be fed; and then, when I offered her my nipple, she would push it away as if it were infected, or chew on it without drinking. Lizzie fed naturally, but Soops – it was always a struggle. Maybe it was my fault. Maybe she felt I disliked her, and that was why she refused me. But I don't think I did. I think, just because she was always in such a rage, I loved her still more than I loved Lizzie. I thought I understood her anger, and even if I didn't, realized that unless she overcame it her whole life was likely to be a battle. Poor little mite, I thought. And the fact that you're so beautiful is going to make it worse. People will look at you and think, aren't you blessed? Blonde hair, blue eyes, perfect skin – you had them at one, you still have them now. But at one you already had that shrill, strident voice, and that terrible sense of unease.

Later, you would try to explain it: the early death of your father, the state of the world, the fact that you felt you had too much and most people had too little. But the truth is, you were uneasy first; the justification came later, and if it hadn't been the state of the world it would have been something else: your legs would have been too long, or you would have felt that other people had more than you, and *you* were one of the deprived. Admittedly, that might have been difficult, since as well as beauty you had brains, and you have always been more than comfortably off. But I expect you would have managed if you'd put your mind to it.

And now, June thought, will marriage and maybe motherhood make you more comfortable? I doubt it. Oh, you'll pretend – for a while, anyway. You'll put on an act so that those who don't know you well will think the fairy tale continues: lovely Soops, who got a first at Cambridge and then a job with the BBC, is now going on to marry her handsome prince.

Those who know you better, on the other hand, will hold their breath, put a hand over their mouth, and whisper to themselves, "Oh no," as they wait for the inevitable crash. Their only hope will be that it isn't too painful; that no one gets permanently injured.

Oh my poor, poor Soops, June thought, and realized she was crying.

"I'm so happy for you, darling," she whispered, wondering whether her tears would make Soops think she meant it. Probably not, but they might help her to forgive her for lying.

"We're doing it for you," Soops said, gracelessly.

"For me?" June couldn't help exclaiming, hearing that she sounded shrill herself, now. Then, since she supposed Soops was trying in her way to be kind, she managed to say, "Thank you dear, that's sweet of you" – before rushing on, again unable to keep silent, "But you really shouldn't marry just for me."

"We're not marrying just for you!" Soops snorted. "Of course we're not! We would have married anyway, sooner or later. It's just that – we thought we'd do it sooner, so you'd be able to come. I mean be in reasonable health. Otherwise . . ."

You might make arrangements and I'd mess them up by dying on the very day you planned to get married, June this time succeeded in not saying.

Nonetheless, in case her daughter had read the unsaid in her expression, June repeated, "I'm very happy for you dear, and – thank you."

"Thank Stefano," Soops murmured, aware, even as she spoke, that now she was being just too sour. She tried to get out of it by adding, "I mean – I wanted to tell you that we were *going* to get married. That we were engaged. I thought maybe the fuss and palaver of a wedding might be too much for you. But Stef said no, it would give you something to – look forward to." Soops had been intending to say "live for".

"Stefano's a sweet boy," June murmured.

"He is, isn't he?" Soops agreed, somewhat speculatively, as if she had her doubts. Or as if sweet wasn't necessarily a quality she prized. "Anyway – it's going to be in exactly four weeks. On 24 June. I spoke to the doctor and he said you can go home tomorrow—"

Because there's nothing more he can do for me and he told me I've probably got another three months.

"And that as long as you take it easy and don't try to do a thing yourself you should be in fine form. So – all you have to do is buy an outfit—"

Because although it's a bit of a waste under the circumstances, all the clothes you have would hang off you and make you look like a scarecrow, and we don't want you letting the side down. I mean, aside from the immediate family, there's no need for anyone to know you've *got* terminal cancer. You can just be the pale and interesting mother of the bride, who looks as if she's taking the loss of her elder daughter rather hard.

"And leave everything else to us. Stefano's mother's going to let us use one of her barns for the reception, and the wedding will be in the local church."

"In Yorkshire?"

"Of course in Yorkshire," Soops snapped. "And – either you and Ada can come up the day before with Lizzie, or if she's coming straight from Cardiff and Ada doesn't feel like driving, we'll arrange to have a car bring you both up."

"Oh, we can take the train, darling."

"Of course you can't!" Soops practically yelled now. "Who's going to carry your bag? You're *sick*, Mum. And Ada's not too strong herself. It would just mean more trouble and anxiety, and—"

Getting control of herself, Soops went on more calmly: "No, we'll have you driven up, driven everywhere, and then the day after the reception, driven home again."

After which I assume I will not see you again.

"Stef suggested we wait till – we wait a few months before we take a honeymoon. But I've got this new project starting in the autumn and I might not be able to take any time off then, so – if it's all right with you, we're going to go to Patagonia for a month."

In the hope that no one will be able to reach you there, and by the time you come back, I shall not merely be dead, but buried – having, your wedding over, absolutely nothing left to live for.

Well, I shall try to oblige, June conveyed with a smile to her daughter. Frankly, at this stage, a few weeks more or less . . .

"Yes, of course you must go. You've always wanted to go to Patagonia, haven't you?"

"Yes." Soops became suddenly gentle, even wistful. "It's always struck me as the furthest away anyone could get from England. The end of the Earth."

"My poor love," June said, and patted her daughter's hand – a hand that was not immediately withdrawn. Indeed, the rare moment of communication continued with Soops leaning over and kissing her mother again, on the forehead. Then she got to her feet and was herself once more. "Well, I must be getting on with it. Lizzie said she's coming up tomorrow, so she'll be able to see you home, won't she, and – when's Ada arriving?"

"The day after tomorrow."

"And she's sure she can stay?"

"As long as is necessary," June said, making her meaning plain.

"Good old Ada," Soops muttered, with only slight contempt.

"Yes, she is good," June felt bound to retort, she hoped not too censoriously. "She's nearly seventy, you know."

Soops would not be reproved at all, however; and to be reminded of other people's charity was more than she could bear.

"And looks seventy-five," she threw back. "Anyway, bye Mum, look after yourself – or make sure Ada looks after you! – and if not before, see you twenty-fourth of June."

"Bye, darling," June said, and had to gaze in admiration as her handsome heartless daughter clacked out of the ward on her high heels, leaving behind a faint whiff of scent and a rather stronger sense of relief, both on her part and her mother's.

Thank God, the space she had till a moment before occupied seemed to declare. *That's* over.

June was sorry she would probably not see her elder daughter again until the day she married, though she knew how *frantically* busy she must be – even if she had never understood what it was that even at the best of times kept Soops so tied up she claimed to be scarcely able to breathe. She was more sorry, however, now she was alone again and had the chance to reflect, about the news that Soops had given her.

She had been afraid for the last few months, ever since Soops had introduced her to Stefano, that the rather unlikely relationship between a temperamental and frankly rather disagreeable English beauty and a quiet, serious and extremely agreeable Anglo-Italian academic might end in an announcement of marriage. But she had generally managed to dismiss her fears by telling herself that before it ever came to that, one or both would see the light.

Lovely Stefano, with his tweed jackets and deep quiet voice and sense of being heir to centuries of history and culture, would wonder why on earth he was associating with an at times almost unhinged virago, who even if she was a great beauty, was likely to turn into the sort of woman who, by all accounts, his own mother was. A farmer's daughter from Yorkshire who had rebelled against her family, gone to Italy and worked as a showgirl and stripper, met and married Stefano's father – himself a farmer of sorts – and proceeded to make his life a misery. She was reputed to have slept with every man she had met – she had considered it her *duty* to sleep with every man she met, Soops had defiantly told her mother that Stefano had told her – and was both mystified and scornful when her husband, unable to bear her promiscuity any longer, announced he wanted a divorce.

"I never realized I'd married a *petit bourgeois*," were, apparently, her parting words as, having won custody of a son she didn't really want, she returned to Yorkshire. Where, following the early death of her parents, she took over the running of the family farm, became somewhat surprisingly both an enthusiastic and successful farmer, and never again, it was rumoured, had sex with any man.

She was still farming, still by all accounts happy, and June couldn't help wondering how she viewed the prospect of having a daughter-in-law in many ways similar to herself. If, so far as June was aware, Soops's promiscuity was more of the spirit rather than of the flesh. Soops, as it were, embraced every new idea she came across, in the hope that this one might satisfy her, or at least relieve her torment. When, inevitably, it didn't, she moved on to the next. The idea of marriage was, it seemed, but the latest in the series, and when that in turn failed to have the desired effect, the consequences were only too easy to imagine.

Why Stefano shouldn't marry Soops was then quite clear to June, however much the young man thought he loved his fiancée and hoped to save her from herself – to save her from becoming like his mother.

Why Soops shouldn't marry Stefano was, though, even clearer. June, in the short time she had known him, had become extremely fond of the twenty-nine-year-old history don who taught at New College, Oxford. He was not merely polite, he was deeply kind, she felt, deeply decent, and while obviously intelligent, both unpretentious and good-humoured. In the three months since June's terminal cancer had been diagnosed, Soops had called her mother maybe four or five times – and one of those times had even forgotten to ask her how she was, preferring to moan about how disorganized the BBC was and how ill *she* felt. Stefano, on the other hand, having got on with June right from the start, once he had learned of her condition had taken to calling her two or three times a week – almost as often as Lizzie – and had been encouraging, soothing and, there again, good-humoured.

Nonetheless, impeccable in every way though he was, Stefano was gay. Obviously so to June's eyes, and she couldn't believe not equally so to the as-a-rule almost too sharp-sighted Soops. Yet it seemed that despite that – or, it occurred to June, precisely because of that – Soops wanted to marry the man.

Of course, Stefano's gayness in itself was no bar to his being a good husband, and possibly a good father. June knew a number of women who had married essentially gay men, and had had, on the whole, happy marriages. Indeed, her own husband, Owen, had preferred "driving on the other side", as he put it, which made it all the more ironic that he had died in a car accident in France while in the company of a male student of his with whom he was probably having an affair. He had, according to the police report, in a moment of distraction "been driving on the other side".

Yet it was this very sense of history repeating itself that made June feel so certain a marriage between Soops and Stefano would not just be doomed, but in some obscure way, *wrong*.

Stefano was marrying his mother; Soops was marrying her father. And both were marrying simply to do a favour to her; if not to give her something to live for, in the belief that by marrying they would make her happy.

But you're not going to make me happy, June wanted to cry out in her hospital ward. You're going to make me *un*happy. You're going to make me feel that history, with all its miseries, is bound to keep repeating itself, on and on "until the last syllable of recorded time". And you'll make me feel that however much you claim to love one another, you actually want to *save* one another – and thereby save your erring parents. But you cannot save other people, June continued to the young couple. Your mother *chose* to live as she did, Stefano – she still chooses to live as she does. And your father, Soops, much though I loved him, successful though our marriage was in most respects – he *chose* to drive on the other side. And even though it proved the death of him, I do not believe he ever regretted his choice. No, not even in his last moments, if he was aware of the truck that was about to hit him. All right, if someone has a physical disability you can give them a hand. But existential unease, gayness: oh, the former seems to me no more than an honest reaction to the world in which we live, and the latter – the PC police would probably arrest me if I even dared to suggest it was a disability. So please, my love – my loves – please, don't do it.

All these thoughts continued to run through June's mind over the next few days: as she was driven home from hospital by her younger daughter, Lizzie; as Ada, her sister from Manchester, came to stay and "not look after you, but keep you company"; and as Stefano phoned to say he gathered Soops had announced the good news, and he did hope – that is to say, he supposed he should have come himself to ask June for her daughter's hand in marriage, but under the circumstances he trusted she would forgive him, and hoped that she was happy about the engagement and would, as it were, give them her blessing.

"Yes," June said, "of course I forgive you, Stefano." And then, having paused to make it plain she was purposely not commenting on his second hope, she said, "But I would be grateful, Stefano, if, as soon as you can – I mean if you have a spare moment – you could come down to London. I should like to talk to you."

Stefano sounded a little apprehensive, and surprised. But he said, of course, "Of course," and went on to ask if the day after tomorrow, Saturday, would be all right.

"It would be perfect for me," June said. She smiled. "I've got nothing to do now. My sister's staying with me."

"Soops said."

"And she's treating me like a complete invalid. Though I have to say, apart from a little tiredness, I'm still feeling perfectly fine. Actually, rather better than I felt in hospital. Just one thing," June hurried on, "if you could, Stefano. I mean if you don't mind – don't tell Soops you're coming. I don't want her to think I'm interfering."

Again, Stefano sounded slightly surprised. But he agreed to this request, too. The dying must be indulged . . .

On Saturday, he turned up with roses for his future mother-in-law, who had sent out her sister for the morning; he kissed her on the cheek, and told her how well she was looking.

June, who had been to the hairdresser the day before, thanked him for the compliment and the flowers. "Come in," she said, and offered him a coffee. When it was made, and the two were sitting together in the living room, she continued, "I'm sorry if I've made this feel a bit like an interview. But – there are a couple of things I must talk to you about, Stefano. I must ask you."

No longer surprised or apprehensive, Stefano looked as if he had guessed what she was going to ask.

They were, in essence, those questions June had been asking herself in hospital. But if she had answered herself at some length, Stefano was altogether briefer.

Why did he want to marry Soops? He looked June straight in the eye and said uncompromisingly – though with a hint of melancholy, aware of what she was getting at – "Because I love her, June." He paused. "I could elaborate, but that, really, is the long and the short of it."

Why did Soops want to marry him? Again, pretty much the same reply, though this one delivered with a certain self-deprecation. "Because, I guess, for some reason – she loves *me*."

June took that without flinching. Her last question, however – "At least, I think it'll be my last!" – she refused to have shrugged off so easily. Meeting Stefano's dark serious eyes, and managing to make it plain that she was not asking this out of any sense of outrage – in fact, was sorry to be asking it at all – she enquired of her daughter's fiancé, "Stefano, forgive me, but – does Soops know you're gay?"

Stefano held her gaze. He was tempted for a second to ask how *she* knew. Then, accepting that it was irrelevant, he murmured, "I assume so."

June didn't move. She felt implacable, but couldn't help it. "Assume so isn't enough, Stefano." She was about to add, "My daughter's happiness is at stake." But since this was so obviously untrue – Soops would never be happy whether Stefano slept with men, women or budgerigars – she decided to spare the young man the platitude. What she did at length say was, "I think you should find out."

"Why?" Stefano replied, looking implacable himself now.

"Because – I don't know," June admitted. "It's absolutely none of my business. And not only am I not in favour of spouses telling each other the truth, the whole truth and nothing but the truth, I don't think they can if they want to. I don't think anyone can. We don't know the truth," she declared. "And the more we think we do, the more we . . ." She stopped, it hardly behoving her to make Delphic pronouncements.

"My husband was gay," she went on, simply. "I didn't know it when we got married – though I suspected – and Soops has never known. I've never discussed it with her, and she was only five when her father died."

"She told me – about his dying, I mean," Stefano said. He paused. "And was your marriage happy? Or as happy as any marriage can be?"

"Yes. I think so. I mean *we* were both happy, and yes, despite – I was going to say despite everything, but I mean despite *that* – I think we did have a very happy marriage."

"So why shouldn't Soops and I?"

"Because Soops isn't happy now!" June declared. "She's not happy even if, even though she loves you. She's never been happy, she never will be happy, I don't think you – or anyone else – can make her happy, and I like you too much to want you to be miserable."

"So my being gay – being anything – isn't really the issue?"

"No," June said. "It's not. But if Soops doesn't know, and if by telling her I could—" She paused, hardly daring to continue but knowing she must: "I could get her to call off the wedding, I would – I will."

"You won't," Stefano murmured. "You cannot. That would be wicked. And you're not a wicked person." He smiled, apologetically. "You might like to think you are, but – why?" he asked. "It can't just be to stop history repeating itself. Besides, it isn't. It won't. As you said, you were happy, Soops isn't. Your marriage was happy, and would probably have gone on being so if your husband hadn't died."

"And you are *not* happy? Your marriage *isn't* going to be happy? Yet still you want to go ahead with it?" June heard how appalled she sounded. "I think it's my turn to ask again, Stefano – *why*?"

"No, I think I am happy," Stefano corrected her. "I agree that Soops isn't and is never likely to be. But it seems to me hers is a – what can I say? A noble unhappiness. A justified unhappiness. And an unhappiness that she bears with grace."

"With grace!" June hooted. "She's a fiend! She's a horror! I mean, she's my daughter, and I love her, and I feel sorry for her, and I wish she were happy, but – please don't do it, Stefano. Please. I shall die in misery."

"Soops thought it would make you happy."

"No she didn't! She told me it was your idea. But I think she knew, knows . . . She's challenging me, defying me to try in some way to stop it. So she can blame me further. But I don't mind what she thinks. I don't really mind what *you* think, Stefano, fond though I am of you. I just want to stop you getting married because I think it's wrong, because I think Soops will destroy you—"

She stared at the handsome young man sitting opposite her, and continued, in a whisper, "Or you, in an effort to save yourself, will destroy *her*. Destroy her by holding out the possibility, the illusion of happiness, and then withdrawing it. And I don't want you to destroy her, Stefano. I *do* love her. I love her passionately. And I long for her, if not to be happy, whatever that means, at least to find some measure of peace. Not to see this world constantly as a park of monsters, a hideous vale of tears. And I do not believe that marrying you will give her that peace. Maybe not marrying anyone. But you, Stefano – it's not just that you're gay. It's also because of who you are, your family, your background . . ."

"Absurd though it is in this day and age," Soops had said when she first mentioned Stefano to her mother, "absurd though it would have been in any day and age," she had felt compelled to add furiously, "Stefano's father is a prince. Oh, it's more than absurd," she had roared on, fuelling her own anger. "It's grotesque, it's ludicrous, it's *obscene*. It's like some Jamesian novel, isn't it? The Italian prince . . . And of course Stefano doesn't use any title – though apparently in Italy he's entitled to call himself a prince, too – and he's always saying that princes in Italy are two a penny, but all the same – I bet later on in life, when his father dies, as he's the only son, he'll go back to Italy and take over the family estates – the family estates, indeed!" Soops had snarled. "And, 'how can you?' I keep asking him. But all he does is smile, and say 'let's wait and see' and – it's like someone becoming a cardinal who doesn't believe in God," Soops had concluded. "A prince of the church. A . . ."

It was the very fury with which she had spoken that had first alerted June to the fact that she might be serious about her Anglo-Italian don. At any rate, more serious than she had been about any of the other men with whom she had gone out and had affairs, all of whom she had openly – to her mother if not to them – despised. It had also alerted June to the possible danger of the relationship; a danger that now it seemed was being realized.

"Soops is violently – too violently – republican, atheistic, contemptuous of the past in general and Europe's past in particular," June went on to Stefano. "As you obviously know. Which makes it all the more peculiar that she should plan to marry someone who teaches history, and whose ancestors might have had more of a hand in the writing of that history than your average illiterate peasant."

"Yes, I think she sees my father's forebears as the villains of the piece," Stefano confirmed. "Or among the villains of the piece."

"Yet part of her – a childish part, the last remaining unspoiled, happy part of her, maybe – is clinging to . . . still believes in the fairy tale. And possibly some of her anger stems from the fact that she cannot believe in the fairy tale any longer."

"I'm sure it does."

"She's mourning the loss of her vision," June murmured, as if the idea had only just occurred to her. "She's trying to reclaim her innocence. Her ignorance. And for all her scorn, part of her still hopes to be 'The Princess'. And when, having married you, she is forced to admit that the fairy tale is not true – and if and when your father dies and you go back to Italy—"

"It's by no means certain that I will. I may just sell the family land, the family *palazzo*, and – continue to live as I always have lived." Stefano shook his head. "My mother believed briefly in the fairy tale, and—"

"Look what happened to her!" June couldn't help saying.

"Yes, indeed," Stefano agreed, with a smile. "But she's happy now. Actually, she always was. Too happy! But eventually my father forgave her even for that. In fact they sometimes speak on the phone together now. They've accepted each other."

"Soops will never accept you," June said. "And I'm sorry to keep repeating this, Stefano, but Soops will never be happy either. Not as a BBC producer. Not as a mother. Not as a don's wife in Oxford, a farmer in Yorkshire, or a *principessa* in Italy. Soops is doomed," June almost wailed, aware she was getting carried away but not caring. "My poor beautiful daughter is cursed, as surely as any child in a fairy tale whose finger has been pricked by a wicked witch is cursed. And – I cannot stop you getting married, Stefano. You're both adults. And if you really want to, you will. But I swear, though the time is so short, I shall do my damnedest to *try* to stop you. And if that means telling Soops you are gay, that her father was gay and died in a car crash with a young man he was having an affair with – I'll do it, Stefano. I'll do anything. I cannot save Soops. I cannot save myself. But just possibly, and though I've always believed that one cannot in fact save anyone, I may be able to save you, Stefano. And – what's the old Jewish saying? If one can save but one life, one becomes one of the righteous . . . Something like that. I don't want to be righteous, Stefano. But there's still time. Even now. Get out of it. Somehow. Or I'll get you out of it. Get Soops out of it, and—" June was crying. "I'm sorry, dear. I'm very tired. Will you leave me now?"

Stefano got up and kissed June on the forehead. "I really did think it would make you happy," he murmured. "*We* really did think it would."

"Oh, happiness, happiness," June moaned. "Please dear – go!"

Stefano went, and never saw June Robinson again. Nor did he phone her. He was waiting, June supposed, for her to do, as she had put it, her damnedest.

But June, when it came to it, couldn't. She would have felt treacherous. She would have felt low, dishonest, shabby. If Soops really wanted to marry Stefano she would, whatever he was like. Just as if Stefano wanted to marry Soops he would, whatever *she* was like.

If, however, they were only marrying to make her happy – that was a matter she did have a say in, June told herself. The doctors had given her three months to live? Fine, she would prove them wrong. Not by clinging on for another six months, or a year. Rather, by concentrating her mind, and with no backward glances nor a moment's hesitation, reducing three months to three weeks. She would will herself to die, June vowed. She would force herself to die. And after that – no one would ever again be able to make her happy, or unhappy, in this world.

Die, June commanded herself. *Die.*

And so, just eight days before the projected wedding, she did. She died without pain and in peace, and she died both proud of her achievement and satisfied that she had done all she could to prevent what she called to her younger daughter "the misalliance". Whether she had done enough and *had* prevented it, she couldn't of course know, and that was perhaps her one regret. But as she said to Lizzie, who came up from Cardiff to be with her in her final hours, "There are bound to be some untied knots, aren't there? And I suppose it's a bit presumptuous of us to think we can always know how the story ends."

The Parasite that Grew Bigger than the Animal
John R Gordon

———

At a grey plastic desk, on one of two grey plastic shell-chairs that faced each other, Tunde sat waiting. The room was windowless, and lit by a fluorescent ceiling strip-light in either end of which the dark speckles of dead flies had accumulated. The door – closed, not locked, but through which he knew there was no point in attempting to leave – was behind him. The chair was the one he had been directed to take. He considered swapping chairs so he would be facing the door, but he didn't want to antagonize his opponents.

He would pretend he hadn't noticed their psychology, their tactics.

Tunde was in his twenties, slender, dark-skinned, fey, with wide cheekbones and feline eyes. His sunglasses were pushed back on his head, perching like bunny-ears on his close-clipped, barbershop-fresh fade. Tunde lifted the small gold cross he wore on a chain around his neck to his full lips, kissed it and murmured a prayer. He replaced the cross inside his open-necked orange-and-turquoise silk shirt, resting it on his smooth, flat breastbone.

Waited some more.

Shifted on the sweat-inducing chair.

The zipper of his excessively tight white jeans jammed itself chafingly between his balls. The jeans were eye-catching party-wear: not the clothes he would have chosen to travel in.

But then he hadn't had a choice.

Elsewhere in the terminal, flight announcements were being made, their intonation audible if not the details; and, intermittently, the sounds of planes landing or taking off. London Heathrow was so grey after Lagos, its functionalist orderliness in one way a relief, but also implying a lack of humanity that was ominous. His hand went to the breast pocket of his shirt but no, they had taken his cigarettes from him, and his lighter. He drummed his fingers instead. He had no watch: his mobile was his timepiece, and that had got left behind. The walls were bare and there was no clock. What did it matter anyway? He twisted the sovereign ring on his left little finger restlessly.

Brief footsteps and the door opened. Tunde twisted his head round to see an African man come in, followed by a white woman. The man was stocky, shaven-headed, and wore a short-sleeved white shirt, a black tie with a gold clip to hold it in place and black trousers. Igbo, by his features, Tunde guessed, and his guess was confirmed by the name tag on the man's shirt: Chimsom Chike. Chimsom Chike was carrying a folder and a carrier bag with things in it.

The woman was white, hard-faced, slim, with straight fair hair, in a short, close-fitting black skirt, high heels, a white blouse and a cinched black jacket, and she carried a chair with her. This she set against the wall and sank down onto as Chimsom Chike took the seat opposite Tunde. She wore no name tag.

This woman is the referee, Tunde thought, maybe the judge; anyway, in charge. He didn't look at her directly. She too had a folder, and also a notepad and pen.

From the carrier bag, Chimsom Chike took out an expensive digital camera – a Nikon D3x with a large lens – and a block of British bank notes, wrapped in plastic. These he placed on the desk in front of Tunde, breathing through his nose as he did so. Tunde said nothing. Gave nothing.

Chimsom Chike was attempting to project authority, but still he shot the white woman a glance for her permission to begin the interview. She nodded slightly.

"You are Akintunde Akinsanya," Chimsom Chike said.

"Yes."

"I am Mr Chike of the UK Border Agency, your case owner. I am interviewing you today because you say your life is in danger in your country of residence, Nigeria."

"Yes."

"And you say this is because you are a – homosexual." Mr Chike made a noise in his throat before saying "homosexual".

Glancing at the woman, Tunde said, "Yes."

Mr Chike nodded. Looking down, he flicked through his folder, searching for a page. Finding it, he pulled a ballpoint pen from his breast pocket. "Do you have proof of this? For example," he went on before Tunde could answer, touching the first bullet point of a checklist with the pen's nib, "love letters?"

"No."

"Photographs of, ah, acts?"

"No."

"Film of acts?"

"No."

Mr Chike twirled his pen, indicated the Nikon with the clicker end. "This camera is expensive," he said, tapping it.

"I am a fashion photographer."

"For who?"

"I am freelance."

"It's true that is a job for a homosexual," Mr Chike said, and ticked a box. "There is also this money." He lifted the plastic bag. Tunde said nothing. "So, please tell me, Mr Akinsanya, what are the reasons to make you come here to the UK to claim asylum?"

"Yesterday," Tunde began, and how strange the word seemed, yet it *was* only yesterday. He tried to state the facts without emotionally revisiting the moment. "I forgot my mobile phone at the barbershop where I always go for a cut. A fellow customer looked in it and found photographs. Of me with – someone. A man. In a situation of intimacy. You couldn't see his face but you could see mine. My friend was there. He drove quickly to my apartment and warned, 'Tunde, they will come and kill you, you must go straight away.' So I grabbed my passport and ran. To the bank, to turn my nairas into these pounds." He indicated the banknotes. "To the airport. To here."

"Africans are not barbarians, Mr Akinsanya," Mr Chike said dully. "Do you really think these men from the barbershop would have tried to kill you?"

"Yes. Because of this anti-gay-marriage law—"

Speaking for the first time, the white woman interrupted Tunde: "Were you trying to get married?"

"What? No."

"I mean, to a man," she added. "Not a woman."

"It isn't about gays marrying," Tunde said, and an anger rose up in him then that he couldn't push down, and anyway it might be better to be angry, emotional. Didn't they say gays were full of emotions, like women? That might help convince this woman and this man. "That's just bullshit to put people into a panic and fire them up, as if we want all that when we just want to be free to be ourselves. This law, it's really about being gay in any way at all. You can even be jailed just for knowing gay people and not reporting to the police about their homosexuality."

"I think you are exaggerating," Mr Chike said, keen it seemed to at least partly defend his homeland to his white British supervisor. "The media often makes things out worse than they are, to get people worried and make Africans look bad."

"It is on YouTube for all to see," Tunde said. "People are being beaten with spiked clubs and stripped in the streets and driven like cattle just for being suspected of gayness. They are being killed."

"How do you know that is why these punishments are happening?"

"Because the people call out while they're doing it, 'We are doing President Jonathan's good work!'"

The white woman broke in again: "Why did you travel here, instead of seeking refuge in a neighbouring country?"

"Because here there are rights for gays. You can live openly, like a human being."

"But you're giving us no proof of your so-called gayness," Mr Chike said irritatedly.

"My word," said Tunde. "As a man. As a Christian." Mr Chike's eyes on his were gelid. "Look, I can't magic proof from thin air," Tunde went on, a sudden desperation lancing through him. "If you send me back to Lagos and they kill me that will be proof but I will be dead. That is not a joke or a technicality. Everyone has gone mad there. You have a duty as a fellow human being, as a brother!"

Mr Chike stirred uncomfortably in his seat, started to respond, stopped, then looked over to his supervisor: she would have to break this moral impasse, this conflict of duties.

"Mr Akinsanya," she said. Her voice was flat and harsh.

For the first time he turned to meet her eyes. Attempting a friendly smile, he said, "My friends all call me Tunde."

She didn't smile back. "During anal intercourse," she said, "what position do you prefer?"

Tunde's throat tightened: to be asked this was shocking to him; to be asked by a woman was worse, and to be asked in front of a compatriot worse still.

"Receptive or insertive?" the woman ploughed on. When Tunde didn't reply she added, "It's hardly a difficult question for a homosexual, Mr Akinsanya."

"I – it is just we never speak of such things," he stammered. "Not in such a way." Then, taking a breath: "Both. I enjoy both."

Mr Chike made a note, leaning heavily on the pen point.

"Fellatio," the woman said. "Do you enjoy performing it?"

"I—"

"Do you like the taste of semen?"

"I'm sorry?"

"Spunk. In your mouth."

"I, er, I . . ."

"What music do you like?"

Thrown by the abrupt change of subject, Tunde groped for a reply. "I suppose I like all sorts. D'banj. Seun and Femi Kuti. Banky W."

"Anyone else?" the woman asked, sounding dissatisfied.

The penny dropped for Tunde then: she had no clue who any of those musicians were. "Beyoncé, very much," he said. "Madonna is good too. Lady Gaga. What is that song, 'Born This Way'?" Falteringly, he began to sing the chorus, the words to which he couldn't remember properly. Mr Chike looked at him with pity and contempt.

As he wavered to a stop, the woman wrote something in her pad, then asked, "Have you had intercourse with women?"

"Yes. Well, in the past."

"Did you come?"

Awkwardly, Tunde replied, "Mostly I pretended."

"But you did come?"

"Yes, sometimes. But then I was with a man, and—"

"Was this for money?"

"No."

The woman's mobile started to ring, *Psycho* shower-stabs. Tunde and Mr Chike watched as she answered it. "What?" she snapped. Then, "Oh, for fuck's sake, do I have to do everything? No, no, leave it." She sighed. "No, don't do that: you'll only fuck it up worse. I'll come and deal with it." She turned to Mr Chike. "Can you finish up, Jimmy?"

"Yes, Mrs Rand."

"I'll come back in case you get stuck with something." Talking into her mobile as she briskly left the room, she went on, "Well, remind him we have targets to hit. Especially from Commonwealth countries."

The moment the door closed behind her Tunde leant in confidentially. "One Nigerian to another," he said, "perhaps we can help each other, eh?"

"I do not need you to suck my cock, Mr Akinsanya," Mr Chike said. "I am a Christian."

"No, no, I meant—" Tunde patted the block of banknotes.

"Eh, you Yoruba," Mr Chike said. "You think everyone is as corrupt as you are. This is the UK, Mr Akinsanya, not Naija. Here we apply the letter of the law without fear or favour."

"As a fellow-Christian—"

"As a Christian, my duty is to tell you your homosexual antics will send you straight to the fires of hell."

"Plenty, plenty Christians don't believe that nowadays," Tunde said. "They have moved on. They believe in rights."

"They are just afraid to piss off the white people in power."

"Unlike you, working in border control," Tunde said, unable to keep the contempt out of his voice. "Saying who can come in after you were let in. Saying what they tell you to say. A little god and a slave."

Mr Chike looked him over coolly. "I think you are lying about this so-called homosexualism," he said. "You seem normal to me."

"What did you expect?"

Mr Chike pushed his chair back. "My wife," he said, "she is Yoruba. Back in Lagos she was a – a socialite. She used to know gays. She told me they were all very flamboyant-type people. Colourful and loud. Womanish. She found them fun to hang about with. Go out shopping with for clothes and make-up. Then she embraced Jesus Christ and we became married."

"Not all gays are like that," Tunde said.

"Okay," Mr Chike conceded. "Okay. To be honest, I knew that. Because of what I've seen here in the UK. Some of them are all big and muscled. They call it 'hench'."

"Okay."

"But I will tell you what, Mr Akinsanya, it is all a big confusion. They don't love the gays here. They say they do, and they have these laws to protect them, but really they hate them just like everywhere. It is considered bad manners to say so, but—"

"Laws are not nothing," Tunde said. "Even good manners are not nothing."

"Then I'll tell you something else for free," Mr Chike said, and now he leaned in towards Tunde. "The gays here, they don't love the Africans. They say, 'Why doesn't he suck cocks at home instead of coming over here and taking our benefits and being a lazy asylum seeker?'"

"You know a lot about gays here," Tunde said.

"They're just like the other *oyibo*, that's all." Mr Chike grunted with contempt. "You are romantic, I think."

"How so?" Tunde asked. Pursue the connection, he thought: two Africans, two Nigerians, two men talking, perhaps as friends would talk.

"You think all the gays across the world hold hands. They don't. They don't give one fuck for the gays of Africa."

"I've seen protests."

"A handful among millions." Mr Chike waved a dismissive hand. "The rest would rather take drugs and go nightclubbing. They live in a dream where they are perfect, the perfect white people who never made any mistakes. Just like the rich who step over beggars and see only rubbish, not people."

"But these dirty, heartless laws we're stuck with in Naija are *oyibo* colonial-leftover bullshit," Tunde said hotly. "They are *their* laws. And now we have these fundamentalist pricks from America pushing their poison, and like fools we're shoving the needle in our arms and getting high on hate while the lights go out in our brains; and our so-called rulers nail gays to the cross because then the Muslims and Christians will be best friends for the next five minutes, until the next thing that calls for scapegoats comes along. And by then, all the gays will be dead or abroad so they'll have to find others to blame for why the country is broken and God isn't loving Naija. Why did you leave?"

Mr Chike didn't reply but clicked his pen. Clicked it again. Behind Tunde, the door opened noiselessly. Unseen by him, the supervisor re-entered.

"That woman who didn't say her name asked why I came here," he went on. "I came like you: to collect a debt. Blood money from the parasite that grew bigger than the animal."

Mr Chike cleared his throat awkwardly.

"Right, Jimmy," the supervisor said with forced brightness. "Are we done here?"

"Yes, Mrs Rand. I have concluded—"

"Mr Akinbanjo," the supervisor interrupted.

"Akinsanya," Tunde said.

"Your claim for asylum is dismissed on grounds of no evidence." The statement hit Tunde's heart like a punch. *No, no, no! What can I do to—* "You will at your own expense be placed on the next available flight to be returned to your—"

"Excuse me, Mrs Rand," Mr Chike said, "I didn't present my report yet."

"Jimmy." She turned on him with a slash of a smile. "You're here to show that the Border Agency has a diverse face, and that we follow best practice in developing BME employees, not present reports, okay?"

Mr Chike opened his mouth to say something, then closed it, his face masking over. Ignoring the woman, Tunde turned the full blaze of his attention on him. "Didn't you ever have a friend," he said urgently, "a cousin, an uncle who everyone knew was – different?"

"My uncle, one of my mother's brothers," Mr Chike answered distractedly.

"And did you like this person, your uncle?"

"I – yes. He was – is – a good person. Gentle and kind. He paid for my studies when my father's business was struggling."

"And what if he was sitting in front of you right now?"

Mr Chike dragged up a breath. Avoiding looking at his supervisor, he declared, "I believe Mr Akinsanya is a homosexual and is in danger. I consider he should receive asylum in the UK."

"We didn't fast track you for you to show favouritism along tribal lines, Jimmy."

"It is not tribal. It is what is right. What is Christian."

"Hitting removal targets is a key attribute of the successful case owner," Mrs Rand recited.

"I believe Mr Akinsanya should have asylum here in the UK," Mr Chike repeated stubbornly. "Where gays have rights."

The woman tilted her head back and pushed out her lower jaw. For a long moment she wavered, then she tugged a form from her folder and slammed it down on the table in front of Tunde. "This will initiate your claim for indefinite leave to remain. Welcome to the United Kingdom, Mr Akinbola."

"Akinsanya."

Giving Mr Chike a poisonous look, the woman stalked out.

The door swung shut behind her. Both men exhaled. "Thank you, Mr Chike," Tunde said. Mr Chike shrugged. "I don't think that will help you secure your promotion," he added, dredging up a half-smile.

Mr Chike handed Tunde his pen, clicking it to push the point out as he did so. "If I am not promoted I will file a complaint of racism," he said amiably. "Here, that is the system."

Tunde reached into the bag of money, pulled out one of the blocks of banknotes and offered it to Mr Chike.

Mr Chike shook his head. "You will need it. They won't give you anything to live on here and it's all very expensive. You must find some rich older gay to support you."

"Will you pray for me?" Tunde asked.

"I will pray for you."

Tunde extended a hand across the table. Mr Chike took it, shook it firmly. "Welcome to the UK, Mr Akinsanya," he said.

First Flush
Royston Ellis

———

In two hours, it would be dawn. He lay on his pallet on the flagstones of the floor and listened to the early morning sounds. A rat scurried across the room's tarpaulin ceiling, its family of young squealing in protest. There was a rustle beside him as a cockroach chased across the open book he had dropped on the floor as he fell asleep.

A branch scratched against the wooden shutter of the bedroom window, stirred by a gentle breeze feeling its way around the house. From the jungle hedging the glade, a jackal yelped, and then the silence of the dark, heavy dawn surged back, echoed by the almost imperceptible purl of the river that snaked along the eastern boundary of the plantation.

He breathed deeply, not a sigh but a conscious effort to drive away the last vestiges of sleep. A lamp burned low in the parlour, its glow seeping under the sacking draped from the transom to form the door of his quarters. He rolled off the pallet and pulled himself to his feet, his bare toes scuffing against the rough finish of the stone floor.

He hitched up his trousers, ignoring the agonizing erection that afflicted him as he rose every morning, and stepped over to the makeshift door. He held the sackcloth open while he dug his toes into the waist of the boy asleep on a mat at its threshold. He nudged him with his foot a second time, deliberately digging it into his crotch, and the boy murmured, scrambling to rise from the floor.

James Taylor grunted to himself and crossed the room, sitting down heavily on a chair. He reached for his boots, turning them upside down one by one to shake out any centipedes or spiders that might have lodged there overnight.

Satisfied, he pulled them on as the glow from the parlour brightened. The boy had lit a second coconut oil lamp and cautiously entered the room, wiping sleep from his eyes with a fist. He hung the lamp from a hook suspended by a rope from a roof beam.

Taylor glanced at the boy, who was trying to conceal his own arousal. He pretended to take no notice and finished lacing his boots.

There was a sharp crack from the parlour as the boy lifted the bar that spanned the veranda door, and released the bolts at its top and bottom. He heard the splash when the boy poured water into a washbasin before carrying it out to the veranda. Taylor stood up and strode across the parlour, stroking his beard vigorously. He was bare-chested and felt the chill that funnelled in through the open door, chasing away the musty warmth of the interior.

On the veranda, he plunged his hands into the basin and scooped up water, splashing it over his face and beard, letting it trickle across his shoulders and over the thick mat of black hair covering his chest. He cupped more of the water with his hand and slurped it up, swilling it around his mouth and spitting it out into the darkness of the jungly forest at the veranda's edge.

He drew himself up to his full height and raised his arms above his head, stretched, and touched the ceiling beam. He lowered his hands and scratched his chest in a practised circular motion, enjoying the feeling that it inspired as his nipples tingled. He peered beyond the half-moon of light cast by the lamp to the devilish darkness of the dawning.

He let out a loud roar to banish the night's demons, to expel bad air from his lungs, and to force his rigid body to relax. The boys curled up on mats on the veranda stirred as he clumped along the wooden deck among them, his loud voice ringing through the forest's misty stillness.

"Up! Up!" he roared, delighting in being the first awake.

Flames spluttered in the darkness in the cabin at the other side of the veranda where the cook was coaxing the kitchen fire to life from last night's embers. Another boy, barely awake, scurried low to keep out of his sight across the grass in front of the bungalow, bearing a pail of water freshly drawn from the well.

James Taylor pursed his lips with satisfaction that the day was beginning in good order, the breeze was mild and, judging by the stars that still lingered, the dawn would be cloudless. He wanted to raise the lamp and inspect the leaves of tea that had been set out in trays to wither during the night, but he restrained himself.

He was a man of habit, dedicated to the discipline of a daily routine he had developed since arriving on the plantation twenty-one years before. He had been sixteen when he left Scotland for Ceylon in 1852 and found himself posted to Loolecondera, a bleak expanse of wilderness 4,000 feet above sea level in the hills around Kandy.

When he arrived, there were just two fields of coffee bushes, dense forest and thick tangles of tropical jungle, a long escarpment of sheer cliff face that was the plantation's back boundary, and the sweeping curve of a river whose flow rose and fell according to the monsoon.

He had camped below the huge rock, hired lively local lads as labourers, chopped down trees, and opened up a vista that was God's own view. From his plateau he overlooked deep, fertile valleys watered by broad rivers and plunging waterfalls, and a range of hills called the Sleeping Warrior because of its profile, and the Knuckles Mountain that was the clenched fist of the Kandy countryside.

He was enchanted with the billet and, being young and foolhardy, had persevered to open up the forest as a thriving coffee plantation, ignoring those who said it couldn't be done. He had nothing to lose and, by his example to his gang, proved it could be done.

He was ruthless in driving himself, and expected no less of others. What he could do manually he expected every one of the boys he employed to do too, without a word of complaint. Slackers were dismissed and sent on the long road back to Kandy, the capricious were tamed, some were bedded, and the plantation flourished.

He kept himself in good shape through tackling every task on the plantation; he felled trees, split logs, ploughed fields, and became mason and carpenter to build a bungalow he was proud of. He was tough and fit – it was said that no one, European or native, could lick him in a fair fight – and he became the respected master of a plantation that yielded profits for its owners in Scotland.

He liked to think he treated his workers as family, although with a firm hand since he tolerated no familiarity. His workers, all natives, were like him, he reasoned: far from home, married to the land, and bonded to each other for company. He had watched what they did on the veranda at night, and spied from the wilderness by the river when they played naked under the waterfall.

"Coffee, master?" Ram, his number-one boy, was watching him inquisitively because this morning he had strayed from his usual routine by spending such a long time gazing out at the unseen plantation from the veranda.

He scowled, turned his back on the darkness, already streaked with strands of dawn's early light, and stomped back into the bungalow to finish dressing. Ram was patiently waiting with a mug of coffee when he pulled aside the sackcloth and emerged from his room into the parlour.

"Muster the men," he told Ram curtly, seizing the mug from his hand.

The boy nodded and weaved his way through the stacks of wooden boxes that were cluttering the neat order of the parlour. He opened the back door and leaned out, picking up a large bolt that hung from a rope. He banged it noisily on the yard of railway line hanging beside the door. With a peal like a bell, the sound reverberated around the glade, bouncing from the face of the rock escarpment and out across the valley, announcing that another day was beginning at Loolecondera.

However, this day was to be unlike the others. In 1867, five years before, James Taylor had planted tea seedlings in a twenty-acre field he had originally prepared for coffee. He had chosen the field with care as the ideal one for this experiment.

It was a mile walk from the bungalow, at a point where the great black rock sank like an exhausted wave to the shore. It was granite-strewn land, cleared of all trees, and dug with holes six feet apart to receive the plants.

He had first set out tea seedlings the year before alongside the trails that ran through the fields of coffee. They had grown well and so, with the consent of Mr Harrison and Mr Leake who owned the plantation, he had planted field number seven with tea seedlings instead of coffee.

He was encouraged to do so by Dr Thwaites, the superintendent of the botanical gardens at Peradeniya, outside Kandy, who helped him obtain the tea seedlings from Assam. This was the first crop of tea ever to be grown commercially in Ceylon.

Taylor had read avidly about tea growing in India, and had talked to many planters who had visited India and could give him advice on the production of tea. Tea from China, a green, smoky liquid drunk with plenty of sugar, was a popular beverage in Britain. Tea from India, said to have more flavour, was also gaining popularity. If tea could be grown successfully in Ceylon it could become a lucrative export crop for the British market, in support of the island's main export of coffee.

The tea bushes in field number seven, after five years of care, nurturing, fertilizing with buffalo and elephant dung, pruning, and watering, were now deemed by Taylor, because of the first flush of white flowers, to be ready for harvesting.

He and his gang of boys had plucked the young leaves and brought them in jute sacks to the bungalow. The leaves were shaken out and spread evenly in wicker trays placed on the veranda. There, they were left overnight so the cool air would reduce them to a pliant limpness, to be rolled and crushed, ready for drying.

Taylor, with Ram at his side, looked at the leaves in the trays as light began to seep through the trees. The boys carrying coconut shells as cups to be filled with sweetened coffee were lining up outside the log cabin kitchen.

"See," Taylor said to Ram with a note of pride in his voice, "how bright and green the leaves were yesterday. Now, just as I thought, they have withered and dulled."

Ram nodded, declining to comment, but Taylor wanted his favourite boy to understand the beauty of the process. He stuck his hand down into a nest of leaves and gathered some of them into his fist. He reached over and seized Ram's hand, pressing the leaves into the boy's palm.

"Don't you see? How easy it is to crush the leaves now they have taken the damp night air!" He looked around the veranda. "Take some boys and bring the dining table here. We shall use it for the rolling."

The day that began with that dark dawn was a long one. It was an unsettling experience having to work without a pre-set routine. However, Taylor was accustomed to trial and error; having taught himself to be a planter he would now learn to be a tea maker too.

He set the boys rolling the leaf by hand on the surface of the dining table, using the forearm from wrist to elbow for pressure to twist and curl each leaf. The boys muttered about this odd task but kept at it. Ram suggested utilizing the granite rolling pin the cook used to crush chillies and spices for curry, but Taylor knew that would be too brutal. He wanted to squeeze the leaf gently to release its flavour, not pulverize it.

While some of the boys rolled the leaves, getting their brown, sinewy arms stained a bright green, others were set to light braziers of charcoal. Large clay pots, the kind used to cook curries for festivals, were heated over the fires. The rolled leaves of tea were cast into the pots and baked, each handful drying for a different period while Taylor timed the process. When the leaves turned wiry and changed to a crisp, nutty brown colour as they cooked, he declared the process complete.

He sent Ram to the kitchen to bring a mug of boiling water. When it came, he threw in a pinch of the baked leaves and watched in fascination how the leaves slowly opened up, colouring the water gold. He waited, letting it brew, and then held the mug to his lips, inhaling deeply through his bushy black beard. Slowly he sipped the infusion.

"Och! It's water bewitched!" He guffawed triumphantly. "Ram, I've done it!"

He ordered some of his workers back to field number seven to pluck more leaves, others were instructed to pack the baked tea in the wooden boxes stored in the parlour. He would transport them to Kandy the next day to distribute in the market so everyone could try the new beverage he had created: pure Ceylon tea.

He was feeling so pleased with himself he was perhaps more relaxed than usual at the end of the day. Normally, he was a taciturn person and, although he had leaned to speak Sinhala and Tamil, the languages of the natives, he seldom conversed with them, only ordering them what to do. He liked Ram, which was why he had made him houseboy, entitled to sleep on the floor in the bungalow, be bedded from time to time, and to benefit from whatever privileges he decided to bestow upon him.

After bathing at the well to remove the lingering aroma of baked tea from his beard and body, Taylor sprawled in a planter's chair, its arms extended outwards to support his legs. He called Ram to bring a dram of whisky. Instead the boy sidled in from the veranda and announced softly that there was a stranger, a white man, climbing the hill to the bungalow. The boy paused at the threshold, biting his lower lip as though fearful of Taylor's reaction.

Taylor looked at him fondly, surprised he should seem nervous. Ram had been with him since he had planted field number seven. He was clean and pleasant-looking, recognized the value of a cheerful smile at the right moment, had nimble fingers, did what he was told, and knew how to keep him content.

He suspected that Ram was cleverer than he pretended; he seemed to understand his moods, his rages, even his dreams. He was happy to kneel unbidden in front of him after a long day in the fields, unlacing his boots, easing them off, and then massaging his feet tenderly.

He would listen quietly as Taylor expounded his theories on planting coffee and tea, on the health of his prized dahlias, on his problems with the workers. He was a silent confidant, the no-nonsense kind of companion a man needed in plantation solitude. He was a comforting release, too, when the fire raged in his loins and the warbling of the jungle night rang in his ears.

Taylor felt himself stirring as he looked at Ram; he planned to share his happiness with him later to celebrate the production of this first batch of tea. "Tell him I am not at home," he said gruffly, indicating with a nod of his beard that Ram should pour his mug of whisky.

"A planter not, sir," Ram said earnestly.

Taylor frowned at the excitement in the boy's voice. Since the visitor was white, he was probably a newly arrived creeper, a plantation apprentice come to seek advice. Yet Ram thought otherwise. "How do you know he is not a planter?" Taylor forgot about his drink and stroked his beard thoughtfully.

Ram's eyes glinted with a twinkle of mischief. "Please him see, sir."

His curiosity was roused by Ram's strange behaviour. "Very well," he sighed, hauling himself reluctantly out of the chair. "Coming at this hour he will expect to stay the night. He must sleep in the boys' hut, Ram. I dinna want a stranger in the house."

Ram bobbed his head and hurried out. Taylor eyed his untouched mug wistfully, annoyed that his evening with Ram was to be delayed because of the arrival of this stranger. He decided to hear what the person had to say and then send him to the kitchen for a bowl of soup. It was part of the planters' code to be hospitable to visitors, but he didn't have to be charming.

He strode out to the veranda. Even without his boots, he was tall and commanding and knew the impression he created. He liked to put the fear of God into people; it stopped him having to be sociable. He had no time for small talk.

The tables on the veranda were loaded with the wicker trays filled with green leaf set out to wither that night. It was the hour of dusk, when the tropic day fades suddenly, and night slips in so surreptitiously it is dark before the lamps can be lit.

One of the boys, obviously instructed by Ram, was hanging a lantern from a beam; it threw shadows on the veranda over the tables spread with freshly plucked green leaves of tea. Another lad was sweeping the deck free of fallen leaf and the wiry strands of baked tea. There was no one else there.

He frowned and looked beyond the veranda to the lawn he had himself planted blade by blade in front of the bungalow. It was an affectation he enjoyed as it gave a semblance of normality to his rugged, pioneering life.

In his youth in Scotland, he associated a well-laid lawn with the gentry. He was a farm labourer's son and had aspired to be a teacher, to be with boys he loved. Well, at least he had his own lawn even if he had become a planter instead of a schoolmaster.

He fingered his beard, wondering where the unknown visitor had gone. A flash of a colourful sarong beyond the flower garden caught his eye in the failing light. It was Ram, talking animatedly with someone hidden behind the dahlias. Taylor was proud at his success in growing those dahlias, their white blossoms a pretty counterpart to the enveloping verdure of the jungle.

By some freak of the dying light, as the visitor emerged, holding aside the flowers and stepping onto the lawn, he looked for a second like a dahlia come to life. His tousled hair was fair, long and flowing around his face, framing sterling good looks and emphasizing the youthful bloom of his smile.

To Taylor he seemed short, perhaps an inch taller than Ram. He was as slender as a sapling and carried himself with the leonine grace of a hunter. Taylor grasped the tip of his long beard in amazement as the youth approached.

There was something curious about him. Perhaps it was his clothes, a simple smock open to his chest, no jacket, and linen trousers tucked in stout walking boots; not the normal dress of a convention-bound expatriate Briton. Or was it the ease with which the lad moved, lithe and light like an athlete, that gave him an aura of easy affability? Certainly the familiarity with which he was talking to Ram in his own tongue, making the boy laugh, indicated this white visitor was a rare breed indeed.

The youth spoke before he even reached the veranda, heedless of the courtesy that required the host to speak first. "To see those dahlias, Mr Taylor, sir, is alone worth the trek from Kandy. No one told me that a man of your robust reputation has a poet's soul."

Taylor's narrowing eyes indicated his astonishment, and the youth seemed to sense that he had gone too far.

"Forgive me," he said, bowing his head. "I forgot my manners in my excitement at arriving at this veritable Eden. At your service, sir! Ned Barnes, born and bred here in these hills but I have never been privileged to see such dahlias in my life. Even those at the botanical gardens do not match yours. I shall tell Dr Thwaites."

"Thwaites?" Taylor was prepared to like the youth despite his cheek, but he was cautious. "Did Dr Thwaites send you here to flatter me about my dahlias?"

"No, sir. That is my own enthusiasm." The youth stood at the veranda waiting to be invited in. He sniffed with curiosity, taking in the wicker trays, the clay pots, and the charcoal braziers. His eyes – which were the green of a leopard as they sparkled in the lamplight – completed their scrutiny of the veranda and looked directly at him.

"You are a man of enthusiasms?" Taylor spoke dourly. He was still chary of this unexpected visitor, trying to place him. The way he spoke English gave no clue to his origins.

People of his complexion – he seemed as white as Taylor himself under his natural tan – who were born and bred in Ceylon could be burghers, as those with Dutch as well as native ancestry were known, or half-breed descendants of English planters long resident in the island. It was customary, upon meeting someone for the first time, to swap clues about one's family and background. It helped establish status.

"Forgive me for not asking you in," said Taylor firmly, waving his hand at the clutter on the veranda as an excuse for his poor hospitality.

"Tea, isn't it?" the youth asked brightly.

Taylor gasped. "How do you know that?"

"I am a wonderer, sir, as well as a wanderer. I was raised an orphan, of planting stock. I have become familiar with many things on my travels throughout this well-blessed land," he said, with a sly reference to Ceylon's Buddhist culture.

His calm confidence was impressive. It reminded Taylor of the cockiness of his own youth when he first came to Ceylon. He thought he knew everything then. Now he did.

"So what brings you here, son?" His use of the word "son" slipped out unexpectedly.

It wasn't wasted on the youth, whose smile broadened. "I have a message for you, sir. From Mr Lindsay White."

"You have walked from Kandy?"

"All twenty-two miles of the trail, up hill and down dale." He grinned again.

"*Dammit!* Come on in!" Taylor extended his hand. "It's not often I get visitors conversant with dahlias, tea and Dr Thwaites."

The youth's handshake was firm and Taylor could sense an inner decency of character even if, with the thick ring of gold he wore in his left ear, he resembled a Sassenach brigand. Before he walked towards the parlour, the youth paused to place the pack he was carrying on the veranda floor by the door.

"Bring it in!" said Taylor, urging him into the room. "Ram, bring whisky for my guest." He ignored Ram's glance of disapproval and waved the youth to sit down opposite him.

"Your name again?"

"Barnes. My friends call me Ned."

Taylor fingered his beard, wondering about the youth. He seemed no more than eighteen. As an orphan and obviously without regular employment he was probably a drifter, however engaging.

Ram brought in the bottle of whisky and, with a great show of importance, poured a peg into a metal mug, which he passed to the stranger, eyeing him carefully.

Taylor raised his own mug. "Yes, tea. You are right. I am celebrating the successful production today of tea, right here on my veranda."

"I am honoured to share the occasion with you, sir." Ned raised his mug, waited for Taylor to down his whisky, and then followed suit. He didn't choke, as many would have done taking the fiery liquid for the first time. Instead he smiled appreciatively.

Taylor was intrigued at how comfortable the lad seemed. He was aware that people meeting him for the first time were usually nervous in his company. He was not a tidy man; his unkempt appearance, his long black beard, his size, and his gruff manner intimidated people. He liked it that way.

Living so long alone he had no consideration for others, and never bothered with the niceties of conversation and social etiquette. Yet to this lad – Ned – sitting opposite him as though he were perfectly at home, apparently he did not seem to be the ogre most people assumed he was.

"So what has that whippersnapper Lindsay White sent me this time? Another petition to join a Planters' Association committee? Bah!"

"No, sir." Ned reached for his pack. "Here is a letter addressed to you. Mr White took delivery of it from the Queen's Hotel to where it is addressed. It had been there for several weeks, waiting for you to visit Kandy. He said that since it might be urgent, I should bring it for you."

"How strange of Lindsay White to be so solicitous about my affairs."

Ned smiled wryly. "Actually, sir, he wasn't. It was my idea. I saw the letter and volunteered to bring it here for you. In my situation one is hopeful that a favour will earn a reward. For me, the reward was to see your magnificent dahlias."

The whisky has loosened his tongue, thought Taylor, pleased that the reason for the youth's visit was revealed: *he expects a reward*. He ignored the remark; he would give him a tip in due course. He held out his hand and Ned passed the letter across without a word. Taylor took it and signalled to Ram to refill their mugs.

"Mr Ned will join me in a bowl of soup, too." He heard a swift intake of breath as though Ram was reproaching him for this change in his usually churlish behaviour.

He studied the letter. The handwriting was unfamiliar but he could guess it was a woman's. He was puzzled as he wondered who could be writing to him from England, which was where the letter came from. He turned it over and broke open the red seal, unfolding the single sheet of parchment while Ram poured two more pegs, not so eagerly this time.

Taylor read the letter slowly, toying with his beard, unaware that his expression conveyed his feelings about the letter. He tossed it aside and raised his mug with a sigh.

"Another supplicant for your advice?" Ned asked casually.

"You've read the letter!" Taylor was cross at the lad's impudence.

"No, sir." Ned sat back, opening his arms wide in a gesture of innocence. "I read only your face. You do not want to be troubled by a new arrival from England."

"Aye!" Taylor drained his mug and allowed himself to calm down. It was a change to have someone in the bungalow with whom he could converse intelligently, and in English.

"The pending arrival is the daughter of an old acquaintance, a planter now deceased. He was a foolish ne'er-do-well and, from the sound of it, his daughter is no better. She thinks she can make a go of the plantation where a man, her father, failed!"

"She?" Ned's eyes glinted. "That should not cause you concern. Many are the bachelor planters here who would be delighted to offer a lady advice on plantation matters."

"You amuse me . . . Ned." Taylor laughed. "You are right, of course. Especially as the bugger's plantation could yield a fortune if planted in tea as I have done. This will be Ceylon's new crop, my lad; it's this colony's future, mark my words!"

Ned's eyes brightened with interest but he didn't take up the implied offer to discuss tea growing. "I pray that the young lady falls into capable hands, so she does not sully yours, Mr Taylor."

There was an unnatural silence in the room while Taylor wondered what to say to Ned's odd remark. It was broken only by Ram filling their mugs a third time. He set out the soup bowls on the table and put a steaming clay pot of hot soup in the centre.

Taylor stared at Ned and blinked. "You can sleep here tonight," he said gruffly. "You shall share my quarters."

Ram dropped the soup ladle on the floor with a loud clatter. He retrieved it, placed it on the table, and scuttled out of the room, as though anticipating Taylor's shout of rage. It didn't come. Instead, Taylor stroked his beard, his eyes roaming over Ned's body as the youth stretched out his legs, gently sipping his whisky.

"Ye're a bonny lad."

"Aye," said Ned, his eyes twinkling. He stroked his thigh. "So they say."

"They?" Taylor felt a strange feeling come over him, almost like jealousy. He couldn't risk another word in case his voice betrayed his thoughts. He looked enquiringly at the youth.

"You know, the mothers . . ."

"Mothers?"

"Those looking for husbands for their daughters." He paused and Taylor felt he was being tested. "But that's of no interest to me."

"Indeed?" He felt his heart racing as though he had just climbed the mountain behind the bungalow. He stood up, intending to reach for the whisky bottle. He saw Ned slip deeper into the planter's chair, raising his legs so they hooked over the extended long wooden arms. He moved in a trance towards him. His hand dropped to Ned's knee. He patted it affectionately.

Ned raised his mug as he lay back in the chair with a knowing look. A smile tremored on his lips. "Gets lonely here, I'm sure?"

Taylor shrugged his shoulders, unable to speak. He placed his hand back on Ned's knee, waiting. He didn't know what for. He squeezed. Ned's smile blossomed into a glimmer of invitation.

Taylor's hand, as though with a life of its own, slid up Ned's outstretched thigh. "I've never . . ." he heard himself saying.

Ned reached up and Taylor felt the youth's hands clasping him around his neck. He sank to his knees in front of him, cupping his hand on the lad's bulging crotch.

The damp aroma of the leaves of tea withering on the veranda drifted like vapour on the gentle breeze, filling the room with a scent that Taylor would forever associate not just with tea, but with the first flush of love it inspired that night.

The Letter
Scott Brown

———

To you,

I hope you are well. Sincerely I do. I wanted to write sooner, so forgive that I haven't. The old saying of "it's not you, it's me" is true this time. There is so much to talk about and yet I don't know what to say. There is nothing I can say to make things different. We are where we are. I'm here and you are there. It's my fault. But you are to blame.

But this is not about blame. This is about me wanting you not to hate me. I hope you can find space in your heart to do that. I don't think I could cope if you hated me. But I'm working on that. Coping. On how I deal with other people's feelings towards me. I'm getting better at it. That's what they tell me.

I want you to read this letter with the knowledge in mind that I am only writing it so that you understand what happened. Why I did it. It's important to me. Important that you do that. Understand. Just remember I am sorry. Sorry for what you did. Not sorry for what happened after. Only sorry that it happened. Had to happen. And not sorry by way of an apology for it, but sorry in a sad way that we both went through that. Are going through that. We will always be living it in some way I guess. That was my doing. But you did it. And we know that and we move on. Or at least I know that and have moved on. I hope someday you will too. Maybe you have already. I have no way of knowing. We haven't spoken. I suspect we never will. I don't know what I have to say apart from what follows. So maybe this is closure. The last chapter. For me it is. I just need you to understand. And maybe forgive. One day.

I've wanted to write to you for months but I couldn't. Don't think you were ever out of my thoughts for one minute – you weren't. Quite the opposite, in fact. You were there every moment. Sleeping and waking. It was there. It will always be there. I know that. It will always be there with you too. Our time. This time. Now and for ever. I wanted you to notice me. I wanted to not just be another of your boys. I guess I've achieved that. I guess you will never forget me. Us. Not the us I imagined, but certainly a lasting memory. Maybe more than a memory. Probably more of a scar. A scar that will live with us both until the end of days. It's certainly not the us I wanted. But this is where we are. Me here and you there.

If I'm honest, then I'll tell you that I don't know where to start. I don't know what I want. I want you. I still do. I can't help that, even after all that has happened. Yet I don't. I can't. It's more than impossible. Could you still love me? No. You're not able to love. Certainly not able to love me. Maybe you'll learn to love. Someone. Not me. Not now. Probably not then either. When we were together. But then, even then, you weren't mine. Even though there was an us, it wasn't real beyond that moment. That moment together wasn't really an us either, it was you and me. Just then. Nothing more. You were someone else's. He was in your mind. He was the "us" you referred to. Not a you and me "us"; a you and him "us". You weren't mine. You never planned to be. Then. Now. You're not free. Not like that. Not in that way. Not in any way. I can't have you and that makes me want you so much more. Still. Perhaps I always will. I hope not. I hope that pain will someday go away.

Is there a beginning to this? A middle? An end? Was what we had even something significant to you? I suppose not. I'm not sure I was anything to you but a means to an end. And maybe that's what makes the pain so much worse. If pain is what I'm feeling. Maybe none of this is for me. Maybe it all is.

Part of me feels I used you. If use is what happened here. Between us. If anything happened that we could call something, then it was I who got something out of it. It wasn't what I was looking for but at least it was something. Something different. But then that's what we were; something different. Don't ever feel I didn't take anything away from this, I did. It wasn't all bad. You made me stronger. You made me understand how far there is to fall. You made me make mistakes and I have learnt from them. There is probably no consolation in that for you, but I wanted you to know.

I think I still love you. But I don't like you. I don't think it's hate. It could be. But love and hate are so very close relations that sometimes you can't differentiate between the two. At times I know I've wanted to hurt you. To punish you for how you treated me. I wanted to hurt you like you were hurting me. What is happening now isn't the punishment I wanted for you, but maybe it's poetic. Maybe it's good for you in some fucked-up way. But those moments of fantasized punishment were fleeting; more often I cried myself to sleep, alone, just longing for those arms around me. To feel your reassuring embrace. To feel your lips on the back of my neck as you hold me. To feel your hard cock nudging between my arse cheeks, pushing forward and joining us together as one. Maybe all of that is what passion is about. Love and hate. Pleasure and pain. Everything and nothing. It was a rollercoaster ride and it was out of control. I don't know how long it took me to realize that I was riding the rollercoaster alone. My mind wasn't right then, I was blinkered by love. Lust. Passion. Blinkered by you and it's only now it's over that I can sit back and acknowledge that you didn't even notice I was there. I was someone. Someone madly, desperately and deeply in love with you. All you had to do was hold my hand.

I hated it when you spoke of him affectionately. Or maybe when you spoke of him at all. His name makes me angry. Still. I won't write it here, I can't. I hate him and yet I don't even really know him. I hated him because I wanted you and I couldn't have you because of him. But that isn't really true. It was only true in my mind back then. I couldn't have you because you just didn't want me was the reality. In my mind it was him, in reality it was you. I know now that you were incapable. But you told me you wanted him, so it was easy for me to blame him. He stopped us being together. I'm sorry to say it, but I'm glad you aren't together any more. He wasn't good enough for you. Sometimes I think that if it wasn't for him then maybe I wouldn't want you. I talk of wanting you like I know that is what I'm still looking for. It's not. I don't think. Having you would be everything. It's not. Not now. Not then. I know through the way that you treated him how I could expect to be treated. That thrills me and scares me at the same time. After what you did I know what life would look like. That leaves me more scared than thrilled, I'd say. More scared that you have the ability to do that within you. More scared that I never saw it.

If I think about the "beginning", if that's the way to order my thoughts for the sake of this letter, then I suppose I first met you just before I'd allowed it all to fall apart. My love. My life. My world. It wasn't you, it was me; I was ready to fall. Fall down I mean, not in love. You entered my world when I was on the edge. You either pushed me off or pulled me in. I'm not sure which it is. Was. These things matter; it was a defining moment of my life and you were there to witness it even if you had no idea it was taking place. It's one of the amazing things in life how significant one person can be to another without that other person ever even knowing it. I'm not talking in a creepy stalker-type way. It's inspiration drawn from their strength. Some people are like that. They have that in abundance. You do. It's one of your beautiful qualities.

But I jump forward. I knew none of this then, that's all in the middle. I'm still at the beginning. The start of you. The end of my life before you and this thing that could have been something but really was nothing. Or it was everything and nothing all rolled up. You changed my life. My world. You changed me in so many ways and I never saw it coming.

There have been times recently when I've wished I were dead. When I wish I had been hit by a train rather than hit by the force of your world. I still have those thoughts, though less often. I can't help but think about how all of the lives touched by this would have been different if only I'd died. It's funny that I think about dying rather than simply saying I wish I had never met you. I don't think that. My life is enriched by those happy moments we shared. All the darkness in the world couldn't snuff out that light and I never wish I hadn't experienced that time. That's the power of you. The vulnerability of me.

I wonder if you did what you did because somewhere inside you were actually scared of falling in love with me. I smile when I write that. A fanciful throwaway line that would change my world if it were true. A tiny part of me has no idea if that is a good thing or bad. Probably bad. You are dangerous in every way. But maybe I like that. Maybe I'm drawn to that. I never have been in the past, but like our palate things change as we get older. Grow. Learn. Appreciate things we have never tasted before. And I tasted you. Sipped gently and gratefully from your cup. You on the other hand simply devoured me without tasting, and then spat me out. It's different. I liked it. I wanted it. But I now know that isn't good.

So I fell. Fell apart that is, not in love. My world was breaking up at that very moment when you walked through the door. I was alone. Then there was you. You didn't know it. I didn't know it. But I needed someone. Anyone. You. A perfect stranger who would steer me safely through the minefield of my life. Through the minefield of my mind.

It was only when I fell that I found there was no one to catch me. No one to save me. I hadn't expected that; I had never expected to be alone. For those around me to fade away into the mediocrity of their own lives. Scuttling away. The glorious me, the happy me, broken into pieces. It was too much of a mess. I had blindly counted on people who were friends to be there at my side for ever and then when I needed them they casually, quietly, turned the other way. Conspicuous in their absence, their silence was deafening. A huge white noise that stopped me sleeping and filled my days with terrible loneliness. I suppose right then I felt what the future might be like. What this life has the potential to be. The fun times are hedonistic but in those desperate moments, which thankfully have been rare in my life, I found no one there to help ease the pain and tell me everything would be all right. I fell. My fault. I was sad no one came to save me. I hated them for a while but in the end I don't believe they should have been there, why should they? My dependency said more about me than them. They have their own lives to live. My life falling apart was of no consequence to them. I would bounce back. Time. Space. The fun times would return and we would ignore the period in between. I suppose everyone assumed someone else would pick me up. But they didn't. I didn't know where the light was. I couldn't see anything. Anyone.

Apart from you.

I remember the first time I saw you. I knew right then that I wanted you. Back then when I wasn't me. I remember you got my name wrong twice. You don't know how much that hurt. But I wanted you right then in that moment in ways I never thought possible. Ways I have never ever felt before. And I couldn't have you. It was far too complicated back then. It is even more so today. It eats at my insides.

The confidence, the arrogance, the charm. Beautiful eyes and a beautiful mouth. How I wanted to kiss you. You were, are, wonderful. And all of that hidden under the thinnest of veils which masks the danger. The danger of you. The danger of getting to know you. The danger of allowing you to abuse me. Sorry, maybe that's strong, we were both adults, both drunk, both lustful – again that's for later, I'm skipping ahead. But danger indeed. Danger I ignored as I wanted to be wanted. Wanted by you. But I don't think it was me you wanted, it was sex you wanted. No strings. Just fun. Just a fuck. You didn't know. Not about me. Not about my shattered heart. My damaged mind. My dark thoughts. And why should you? I hoped you might mend my heart, but somewhere in that part of your mind where you put rational thought when you don't want to hear it I knew that you wouldn't. I suppose I always knew the broken bits of my heart, my life, that lay on the floor all around me would just be trampled on by you. Ground into the floor with your boots when you put them on after you fucked me and walked out of the door without looking back. Without saying goodbye.

I knew about him then. You told me. But the fact that you wanted me that evening meant that you loved me too. Didn't it? Didn't you feel it? I thought the fact we were going to do it meant that you wanted me, not just that you wanted sex. I was going to say that you wanted *sex with me*, but you didn't, I know that now; you just wanted sex and it could have been with anyone, it's just that I was the one in front of you at that time. I was there. It was as easy to fuck me as it was to not. Pure chance and circumstance. I confused wanting sex with wanting me. I know now they weren't one and the same. And in my mind if you wanted me then you didn't want him. You see how quickly I got things wrong? But you didn't correct me. You didn't lead me to believe anything else. You did want sex. And to be with him. How could I have known that? I had been out of the game too long. I had fallen for you and was following a love story. You were going to leave him for me and we would be happy; my strong man with the beautiful eyes and wonderful mouth. My protector. My lover. My saviour.

But it doesn't work like that, does it? Not now. Not these days. You only have to be off the ride for a short time for it to change direction and become something different. Where did dating go? What happened to sex leading to more sex? For that lust to turn to love? The learning curve was steep. People don't do that any more. What a sad world I've awoken to find myself in. It's not set up to deal with people like me.

I had fallen. You didn't catch me but you picked me up. That was OK. At least you were there; even if I couldn't count on you to catch me you were at least there to nurse me through it. All I wanted was someone there, someone there when I hit the bottom. I didn't understand then that even though you had landed, you might not have hit the bottom. Sometimes there is further to fall. Much further.

Do you remember when we met that night with Daniel? It was the second time I had seen you. The second time conjured up more emotions than the first. I had gotten my hair cut before we all met in the pub for a beer. You complimented me on my shaven look. You liked my T-shirt. You stroked my arm in that familiar way and I got goose bumps. I thought right then how right it was. I thought of what could be. The future. Us. It was perfect. Everything in an instant. I had eyes for nothing else but you. These were the next steps of my life. You were in my future already every step of the way.

I think we had known Daniel for the same amount of time but we hadn't ever met, not until that last time and this time, both within a week. Daniel thought we would get along. He was right. To a degree. We don't speak now. I blame him for this too. Not only you. Certainly not just you. Was he there when it happened? You still refuse to say.

That night, Daniel left after two drinks. He said he was unwell. Do you remember? We planned that. He wanted us to work. He thinks you are wonderful. I suppose on reflection he is infatuated with you too. Your personality, beauty and radiance means most people are. You ooze sexuality and sex. But you know that. It gets you what you want. And you wanted me. But I just imagine that you wanted me because you fucked me. I guess I'm old-school, that's how it used to work.

You called him after Daniel left, you told him you were working late that night and you couldn't meet him for dinner. You called him in front of me. That was the first of two calls to him that night. That first call was hard. I wanted you but he had you. You had a life, dinner plans, weekend plans. A love life, a sex life and here I was, some twat who was broken into pieces and hanging on to some faint hope that you would have the slightest interest in me.

But you did. Have an interest in me. Or at least in it. Sex. Which happened to be with me. I punish myself for joining up those dots. I said at the start that I've learnt from my mistakes and I have certainly learnt from that one.

And this is where I struggle. This is where I find it so hard. The sex. I'm not old, maybe more old-fashioned. But this casual approach to sex. The fact that you treat sex as one of your three meals a day. The fact that you can pick something up with the fluttering of an eyelid and leave it full of your cum an hour later distresses me. I thought more of you. More of me. But when I got to know that I was simply one of those meals of your life, devoured and forgotten, it upset me. Not me. How did I allow that to happen to me? It's because I wanted you. It's because I wanted to be loved by you. It's because I believed in love and you believed in lust. It's because you are a fucking animal who treats people like shit and you have no fucking respect for anything apart from satisfying your own needs. I hate you. But I don't. Maybe this is all my fault. Maybe I'm the one out of sync with the world I now find myself struggling to live in. I don't want casual sex. I don't want a stranger in my bed every night; I want a lover, a friend, a soulmate who will hold my hand throughout this struggle that is life. But I'm learning that doesn't happen these days. I'm learning it's about sex. I'm learning that it's about fucking people on your lunch break. I'm learning it's about knowing how many queers are within a twenty-metre radius of you at any time. It's about seeing if you can dangle the bait in front of some guy walking from the Tube home to his husband and sucking him off mid-journey.

I struggle in this place. You thrive. This was the awesome hedonism that you were born to embrace. I'm more romantic. Pragmatic. I think things should be cleaner, clearer. Better. But I think too much. I put too much stock in people. Is this what the riots were for? Is this why people marched? Is this why people got bashed and died? Back when we were looking for equality, was it so we could have a phone app that showed us how many people were available to fuck right now? If so then that, for me, is a sad end state. But it's the cycle, isn't it? It's the world we live in. It's the popular movement and, like most popular movements, there is little point in resistance. So yes, I join the sites, I have the apps, I find out who is around and who wants to fuck and I do it. But it hurts. Every time I come, I feel a little less like me and a little more like you.

I'm sorry. It's not your doing. This is a rant. It wasn't supposed to be. I understand that you, like many, are just another piece of the puzzle. You're a child of that generation. Different time. Different worlds. Different values. I don't think the gay world has moved on for the better with this advance. It's not for me. But I have no choice. I do it but it doesn't make me happy. Does it make anyone happy?

Us.

We got drunk. We chatted. You stared in my eyes and you made me feel like I was not only the most important thing in the world at that moment, but also the only thing in the world at that moment. Such intense attention on me. Only me. I felt amazing. Was it a game? Did you use the same approach with all the boys? I hope so. It's a gift. A talent. You made me feel amazing even though in hindsight I know it was all just a show. But thank you. Thank you for those moments where I was allowed to feel like that. To feel special. Moments like that, and I'm only talking about seconds, are wonderful and surprisingly far between in this life. It was the most liberating feeling after my fall to have someone pay attention to me. To my life. To what I wanted. What I needed. I spoke, you listened. I knew (mistakenly) right then that my instincts were right. You were a beautiful person. Wonderful. Life for us could be amazing. To have you on my arm, at my side. Right then I truly believed we had the potential to be the most beautiful couple in the world. I was at peace with you. With us. Already.

But you were already a couple. With him. Truthfully, I didn't feel bad about wanting to steal someone else's boyfriend. Sometimes people are coupled with the wrong one. We were not wrong. We were right. We had the world before us. I felt good. I felt really good.

You stroked my arm. Our knees touched. My cock was hard but you didn't notice. I don't think. Yours wasn't, I looked.

We went to your house. We watched a movie. I hadn't done this for a long time; laid in bed with someone who made my heart race as they stroked my hair and kissed me gently on the back of the head. We cuddled. I had the warmth of you radiating into me as we spooned on the bed fully clothed. It was electrifying in its simplicity. I just needed to be held and you instinctively knew that. It was intimate and perfect. I didn't know at the time but you had already fucked your boyfriend that morning and someone else at lunch. I was very much your evening meal. You were my whole world.

You told me about the other two you had fucked that day after you had come in me. That throwaway nature you have. An incidental aside that you spoke of like a badge of honour. A throwaway line which for me took everything we had just done and ripped it apart.

I was timid at first. I hadn't had sex with someone new for a long time. And I wanted you. You weren't just sex, you were everything. All I had been looking for my whole life in a shiny new box.

Your lips were soft. Your tongue was probing. You were gentle with me. Those hands so at ease, I should have known how practised you were at that point, but I didn't. It was about me. Us. I didn't notice that you weren't part of this in a real sense, just a participant who took what you wanted and then left while the going was good.

Sex wasn't wonderful. It was fumbled. Forced. You were rough, uneasy. But that was nice too; it shouldn't be perfect, this wasn't a movie. This was life. Leading to love. You have a wonderful cock. You licked my arse and then quickly fucked me hard and deep until you came. I couldn't come. I was too wound up. I wanted more and more and more. Not just your cock but all of you. In every way. I just wanted to be wrapped up in your arms. That was the bit I was looking forward to. The sex was my way of us getting where I needed to be; with your arms around me again, holding me tight and reassuring me that life was going to be fine.

You were looking in my eyes when you came. It was beautiful. But it wasn't. Not thinking back. You weren't smiling at what we were doing and looking into my soul, you were looking through me and smiling at adding another number to your book.

You came in me. You hadn't asked, but I didn't mind. You pulled out of me. You put your pants on. You lit a cigarette. You called your boyfriend and arranged to go over to his house. We were done. I played along. It didn't matter. This was sex. But inside I felt the floor moving and I fell a little further. I wanted to spend the night. I wanted to sleep in your arms, to wake up in the morning with your face the first thing I saw and then I wanted us to have breakfast together. A day together. A life together. You'd made it clear that wasn't an option and I should leave quickly with your cum inside of me. I felt cheap. I felt wrong. I felt a fool. But this wasn't the end, just a beginning. In reality it was the beginning of the end. For us. For you. For him.

I cried when I got home that night. I went to bed but there was no chance of sleep. All I could think of was that you were, right at that moment, in bed with your boyfriend. Inside of him like you had been inside of me. Then he would be in your arms. He would be where I wanted to be. He had you in the way that I wanted you and that made me sad. Sad and angry. So very angry.

I wanted you to want me in that way and you never did. Never have. Perhaps never will, but I hold out hope. It's crazy but it's true.

Now I write this, I feel that I want you so much. I do. I remember those beautiful moments and the pain is gone. I forgive it all. Have me. Have me and I will give everything for you. Everything for those few seconds where I felt like the most loved person on earth. Yet breaking those moments down, I realize how few of those seconds there were. How false every one of them was. And that hurts. A lot.

And so I think of the pain. Feel the pain. Feel sorry for him. For you. For you are flawed. You have an illness. But you can't see it. You will never be happy and there is nothing I can do to help you. When I think of that I feel better. I will be happy because I can be. You, like many, will never be happy. Can never be happy, because you don't know when to stop. Or maybe you do know when, but you just can't.

I've lost the start, middle and end structure to this letter. I'm sorry. I'm just talking now. To you. I've never been able to do that. Maybe it would never have happened if we had talked. Who knows.

It's important that you know that I really do want you to be happy. One day. However you manage that and in whatever form happiness takes. It's important that you know that I wish that for you, despite everything. You deserve it. In a way. And I want you to know I'm sorry. I am.

So we fucked. Had sex. Whatever. I wanted to write "made love" but we certainly never did that.

I remember calling you after. Well, the next day. You were cold towards me. That's when they all started coming together properly. The pieces. You didn't want me. You certainly didn't want us. It was sex. I realized then I think that that was always all it would be with you. But that felt bad. So horribly bad. Wrong. Misguided. You were. I thought I could fix you. I thought I could show you how much more there was to the world. I thought I could make it perfect. The perfect life. Me. You. Us. How amazing that would be. I still think it would be. Could be. Sometimes. I'm the misguided one now.

When I masturbate, it's you that I'm thinking of when I come. Still. Even today. I've had some of you inside of me and deep down I hope it stays there forever. I'm sorry if that upsets you.

You know what happened next. It's not something I'm proud of but, at moments in our life, we do things that are just wrong but we reason they are right. I guess we do it as human beings. Justify our actions. I've read justification is what paedophiles and murderers do. I guess in the grand scheme of things my madness was nothing compared to paedophilia and murder, a mere anthill against a mountain. But then to ants an anthill is large, so it depends on where you are coming at this from.

So we became friends on Facebook and I liked everything you posted. I followed you on Twitter and checked your updates by the hour. I wanted to be in your head and in your world. I stalked your boyfriend online. I looked at his pictures. I looked at the ones of you both together and I wished that I was there with you, at your side, and not him. The cunt.

I called you daily but you didn't answer the phone. I texted you a lot. I remember how carefully crafted each of those words was, every character strategically placed. I think one day I sent you sixty messages. You soon stopped replying. That just made me want you even more.

What was I supposed to do? You were that life raft to rescue me, there was no way on earth that I was going to let you go – I was drowning and you were my only hope of salvation. Why couldn't you see that? Why couldn't you see me?

When I saw that you were having your birthday party and had advertised it on Facebook it was clear to me that you had simply forgotten to invite me. There was no option open to me; I knew I had to be there for you. With you. At your side to celebrate. I had to come. There were people we had in common who would be there. There would be drinking and fun. I would be close to you. Wish you a happy birthday. Spend some time in your company, like it was supposed to be. It was the only way to see you; you had left me no choice. And I wanted to see him, to meet him. To present us both side by side to you. To show you I was the better option. The better man. You know this all made sense to me. It was as clear as anything; I could see no flaw in this plan. Hindsight is a wonderful thing and of course I would never had done it if I hadn't had those feelings for you. I would never have left the house that night and none of this would ever have happened. Regrets are not good, but that's my big regret. If only I had stayed home. I would probably still be hurting from losing you, but it would be hurting in a different way. And neither of us would have gone through this past year like we have had to.

If you were surprised when I showed up at the restaurant then you didn't show it. You smiled. You smiled at me. You had the waiter turn the table of ten into an eleven and you poured me wine. You included me in conversation and you touched my leg repeatedly. You touched me and he saw you do it. He didn't get angry. Maybe things were bad between you.

I was funny. I was charming. I did nothing wrong.

I went to the bathroom. You followed me in. You kissed me. You didn't speak. You kissed me hard. You had a piss and left me at the urinal with my hard cock in my hand.

The night was drink-fuelled. Drug-fuelled. I went to the bathroom with your friends and did coke. Lots. I saw you dancing with him. With others. I saw you rubbing against others, but that was just the mood, the moment. Your hands up their shirts meant nothing. Their hands dipping beneath your belt meant nothing. It was fun. We were drunk. He watched me watching you. He knew.

We went to your house, how many of us? I don't know, but lots. It was fun to be back there, to be where we had fucked. To be there with you at your birthday. Laughing. Joking. It was one of the happiest nights of my life. We all drank vodka, played music and took more coke. He spoke to me. "How do you know him?" he asked. I don't remember my reply. People passed out. You were drunk, you were swaying but very much with it. You took my hand and you took me to your bedroom. He came too. It was the first time for me with more than one person. I didn't know what to think. What to feel. I wanted you but the trade-off was clearly that if that was going to happen then he would have to be there too. I didn't care. I just wanted you so whatever else would have to happen to make that so was fine by me.

I was excited again. Excited when you took my clothes off. I kissed him. You sucked my cock. Kissing him was OK because that's what you did. Your mouth around my cock was wonderful. His mouth around it was fine while your tongue was in my mouth. I was part of the something you thought was amazing. I trembled with delight. You gave me more drugs from a key. "Coke," you said, and there was lots of it. Then you fucked me. You fucked me hard and quick. Your cock wet only from the spit you had in your hand. In me. Hard. It wasn't romantic; this was sex. Just sex and something went through me and I felt everything change. I came. Your strokes too deep, your force too hard for me to hold back. But you weren't in it. You weren't there right then; it was a process for you. No kissing, no fondling. No sensuality. You fucked my arse till I came and then you pulled out. You pulled out of me and into him. You took him in your arms and kissed him. You called him baby and it was intimate. You did this in front of me and you did this on purpose. I could tell. You let him ride you slow and easy and you filled him from the base of your cock full of that cum that had once flooded into me. You lay back. You gave me another huge bump of something that wasn't coke and I felt helpless. I couldn't move. I couldn't leave. Then you told him to fuck me. I couldn't say no. I wanted to say no. No. I didn't want to be fucked by him but I couldn't resist. You sat on my chest and forced your cock in my mouth. It tasted of shit and cum. My shit. His shit. Your cum. You leaned back and pulled my legs apart. He fucked me. He came in me. You both laughed. You made him do that. You made me do that. I remember you laughing. At me. And then I passed out.

Time flies. I came to briefly and couldn't move still. I saw you cuddling him while I was left on the other side of the bed, naked, alone and exposed. My raw emotions laid bare in human form. I could do nothing about it; the ketamine stopped me from being able to leave.

When I came to again, and I'm not sure how much later this was, you were stood over me with your hard cock in your hand. He was asleep and then I was aware that one of your friends was inside of me. I didn't know him. I hadn't spoken to him but now there he was, coming. Coming in me. I couldn't speak. The man pulled out. And another came in to view. He did the same. I couldn't feel it. I passed out. I don't know what happened after that, what happened to me in those following hours. I was unaware. Unable to protest. Unable to defend myself. My body there, naked and exposed, you encouraging people to use it. Eventually, I woke up. Eventually, I was freed from my paralysis. Freed from the drug-induced sleep and now awake to start slowly, frame by frame to remember the nightmare you had been a part of. I still don't know how many of your friends had fucked me. Maybe I don't want to know. Shouldn't know. But in that moment I just wanted to leave. Leave there. Leave your house. Leave you. I wanted to run but my legs were unstable. And so I left, left slowly and walked out while people lay around me in contented drug-laced sleep. I eventually got home and I cried for the whole day.

In my lifetime, I had limped from relationship to relationship. I had only ever had three long-term lovers in my whole life. That's four people in my bed. Four people in twenty years and then god knows how many in one night. That wasn't me. It wasn't fair to force that upon me. To force yourself upon me. To force others upon me. I wonder in my hazier moments if you thought it was all something that I might enjoy. Maybe you do think that. But you were wrong. So wrong. And if you got that feeling from the time we spent together then I realize that you don't know me at all. Didn't listen to me at all. And it's then I know for sure that I'm just part of your fucking game. You pulled me in to your fucked-up world and spat me out.

Aids plagued my thoughts and I tried to kill myself two days later. I'm sure you wished I had succeeded – would you have cared? Would you have noticed? If you did notice, would you have come to my funeral? Would you have felt the slightest tinge of guilt? I suspect no is the answer to all of those questions.

I withdrew from the world for six months. Counselling. Therapy. Doctors.

Then I came back.

I was me again. And I understood myself. I knew where I had been and what had happened to me. I rejoined the human race. I didn't have Aids. I hadn't caught anything but that bit of fortune doesn't mean I wasn't scared. I thought for so many hours how what you had done could have changed my life. How you could have given me something that would affect the way I had to act for the rest of my natural life. How different conversations with potential boyfriends would need to be. How different the end of my life had the potential to be. How much shorter my life could be. All because of you and your selfish games.

I thought about this a lot – how close you had been to changing my life. How much of a role you could have played in defining my life. But I was lucky. And it was only luck that saved me. You had no right to do that to me.

But you did change my life. You have affected it. I have two scars on my wrist to prove it and I have less visible mental scars that are very, very real and which will now stay with me for ever. People may not be able to see them but I can assure you that they are there.

You think I'm weak, I know. But I'm not. I'm stronger than you could have imagined and I'm a better person than you are. That much I know with certainty.

I wasn't a person from the world you inhabited back then. I was just an innocent who thought he had found someone he loved. I now know that love isn't something you have the capacity for. But it is something in my heart that I felt and feel for you.

But you abused that. Me. And you broke what was broken even further. I feel I am at the bottom now. There is only death that is below where I have been. And sometimes I think death may actually be above the many dark places that I have visited. I know I have completely fallen and that's why I know things can now only get better.

But there were things I had to do. It wasn't about vengeance – it was about what's right. It's about me feeling like I was able to look at myself in the mirror and know that everything that needed to be done had been.

I spoke with my therapist at length. It wasn't easy remembering and then reliving the pain that I went through in those months last summer. I need you to know the effect you were able to have on someone's life. It was painful. It was hell. You made my life a constant living nightmare.

None of what I did was easy given that it was all coloured by the fact I loved you. Love you. And still want you – but these are my own personal demons I still battle daily. You are still there always in my thoughts. I guess I am saddled with you for my whole life. I know that and have accepted that. Or started to.

Not that it is of any comfort to you but the police were really helpful. A queer going to the police to report this kind of thing is always perceived to be something that is going to be laughed away, but it wasn't. They took it seriously and I think they arrested you for assisted rape that evening. I heard you were in bed with him when they arrived to take you away.

The months between were difficult. Friends fell away again as they chose you over me. Your boyfriend saw me in the street and threatened to beat me up. They were not happy days, but I knew I had done the right thing. I'm pleased the police questioned him too.

The two friends who stuck by me were the people there with me in court. They held my hand and gave me the strength to tell my story to strangers. I looked at you when I spoke and you just sat there shaking your head. I could see how much you hated me. I hope that has started to recede.

Then you got sent to prison, which is where you now are, which is why I am writing to you. You have time on your hands to think and reflect. And I hope you do. I want you to know that I didn't set out for this to happen but you needed to know that what you did wasn't right. It wasn't just not right, it was wrong.

You did destroy my life. And getting you arrested and convicted wasn't about righting the wrong – it was about you knowing that people can't behave like that.

I wanted to also say thank you.

Thank you for telling the police what you did. Thank you for making our friends know that I wasn't a liar. Thank you for helping me rebuild the foundations of my life, although it wasn't in the way I'd hoped you would have helped me that day when I first met you.

I want you to tell the police who those other men were. Who were the people who fucked me? Fucked me. Raped me. I'd like to know their names as I need to exorcize those demons too. But I understand your loyalty, although I don't accept it.

It hurts me the most that I had undying love for you and yet all I was to you was a pawn in your game. I felt a fool and I still do. But I know we are very different people, and while it hurts it's not something I can blame you for. It was me that was stupid, not you.

I know he has left you now. I know many of your friends have too. And I'm sorry. I just hope you see this as a turning point in your life and hope too that, after your few short months in prison, you will be able to face the world anew and afresh.

I have forgiven you. I hope you understand why I've done what I've done and then learn to forgive me. It'll take time, but I can live in hope.

Please stay safe.

I loved you and I still do.

Yours for ever.

Me

Brown Manilla
Patrick Gale

———

Pregnancy suited Sylvia. Other women puffed and sweated through it, complaining incessantly, but all five of her pregnancies had seen her attain a state of charged wellbeing like nothing she had experienced in what she came to think of as her *empty* periods. Far from being a time of distortion, pregnancy seemed to her an all too brief perfecting, a sculptor's rounding-off.

Throughout her youth she had been restless, goaded by a sense of entitlement as indignant as it was directionless. She had worried that to achieve whatever it was that would finally satisfy her would take more money than her family possessed or more education than her father was prepared to purchase. When Richard found her at the regimental dance she had only attended to please a bossy friend, and proceeded to court her with quiet assurance, she decided it was marriage she had been craving.

And it did bring her satisfaction: the handsome guard of honour, the conferring of family jewels and silver, the charming of his widowed father and the muffling of her name in Richard's felt as flattering to her femininity as his borrowed greatcoat over night-chilled shoulders. And yet it was only with the sensation of a second life quickening within her that she felt at last a deep, calm fulfilment come upon her.

She adored each baby, marvelled at her cleverness in producing such perfection, wondered at the ordinary miracle that each should grow so alike and yet so distinct from its siblings, and she relished the small workshop of the nursery – its nappies, its bottles, its carefully selected toys and well-made clothes – and his acknowledgment of her expertise within it. She knew, however, that this child, warm and heavy beneath her pinny, must be her last. They had agreed to stop at four, with a tidy two of each, because, although he had made brigadier while still in his forties, they were comfortable rather than rich and Richard had a quaint horror of their being taken for Catholics.

He was not a passionate man and did not find self-restraint a challenge. She gathered from other regimental wives she should be grateful for this. Some men were beasts. When the need arose, he used condoms he bought from his barber, mysterious things she never actually touched or saw, for which he fumbled in his sock drawer and of which all trace had gone come morning. This fifth pregnancy, arising after a four-year interval, had taken them both by surprise.

She had been on the point of giving away the pretty cot and the Silver Cross pram outgrown by their four-year-old, and had long since converted all the nappies to dusters and floor cloths.

"It's utterly inconceivable," he exclaimed when she broke the news, then laughed at the unwitting witticism, which they had both repeated so often since it would surely enter family lore.

Without it being discussed, it seemed they had agreed to treat the fifth baby as a sort of blessing. No further condoms had been called for – in a moment of extreme boldness she had looked in his sock drawer that morning and found nothing but socks and loose change – and she detected him withdrawing from her as though fearing that, God-like, he could impregnate her by the bestowal of a glance or passing caress. The oldest children were of an age to be noisily excited at the prospect of a baby. The youngest was wary and unconvinced and cast grim looks at the bulge where her waistline had been, as though to blight whatever rival lurked there. But neither toddler's curse nor husband's withdrawal could wound her, cushioned as she was by the potent combination of birth hormones and profound satisfaction.

Her mind was not so bliss-fogged that she couldn't see the timing was dreadful: the baby was due in two weeks but in four they were due to move house. The regiment, together with attendant wives and families, was moving to Germany. They were to exchange a plain

Georgian officer's house in a Berkshire garrison town for a bungalow in a featureless army camp in a country where they had no friends and no language. It was a reversal of fortune but one she found could not trouble her. It was as though she were in shock.

As usual, her mother would come to stay a few days before the birth to supervise the others and keep house, the difference this time being that she would take the children away to stay with her in Ascot until after the move to Germany. Although Sylvia knew the pregnancy was not her fault, she had taken on herself the burden of preparing for the upheaval in the spirit of a penance. Her mother was apt to find fault and to treat Richard as a victim of wifely neglect. Sylvia was thus determined that, well before she went into labour, every wardrobe and chest of drawers, every over-burdened bookshelf, bursting toy cupboard and chaotic kitchen drawer should have been tidied and its contents winnowed so as to be ready for the packers. Any adult clothes beyond repair or redemption, any children's ones too tired to be worn by yet another child, had been bundled and tied for the rag-and-bone man. Bag after bag had been filled with rubbish they seemed to have been hoarding: incomplete jigsaws, knives with wonky handles, dolls that had lost their legs and balls that had lost their bounce.

She enjoyed herself. It was a task that called for a ruthless decisiveness that came easily to her. She worked at it in the mornings, while the toddler was at playgroup, and aimed to purge one room a day. She kept herself clean with a pinny and tied up her hair in a cheerily spotty cotton scarf. She tuned the radio to dance music and felt like an illustration in *Good Housekeeping*.

She had tackled their bedroom (which was how she finally knew the contents of his sock drawer). Today it was the turn of his study. Their quarters in Germany were a fraction of the size and certainly lacked either nursery or study. The study was tiny but it was attractive and an established child-free territory, and they would miss it keenly. The desk was a distinguished bureau bookcase inherited from his grandfather. The glass-fronted bookcase was still filled with grandfatherly books –

Kipling, Dickens, Scott and Thackeray. Apart from the *Just So Stories*, *Thy Servant a Dog* and *The Rose and the Ring*, which she had read to the first two children and would read to the rest in turn, nobody had disturbed them but she had pledged to start reading them to herself once the children were more grown up.

The bureau below had two large drawers and, above them, two identical but artificial drawer fronts which together folded down to reveal the desk section with its blotter and array of tiny drawers and compartments. She knew her way around the desk and used it more than Richard did, as he had an office elsewhere and she was a keen letter writer. She wrote to her mother and brother on alternate Monday mornings. It was easily readied for packing – the pens and pencils zipped into a pencil case, writing paper, envelopes and postcards tucked into a Three Candlesticks box. She made a note to remind herself to order stationery with their German address on from the local printers before they left, then she sat with the wastepaper basket close beside her and tossed in an empty ink bottle, an ancient sheet of blotting paper and a cache of the better Christmas cards she had hoarded with the thrifty intention of converting them to present labels or bookmarks. In the little drawers, she found an assortment of small things inexplicably retained – a stick of sealing wax, a farthing, a suspender clip complete with ragged scrap of flesh-pink ribbon – and tossed them into the bin.

It wasn't enough, however. Perhaps it was an effect of all the books but the room felt little emptier than when she had started. Standing with effort, she pulled her chair back a little then tugged open the first of the big drawers. She knew exactly what was in here: every reply dutifully written by her mother and brother to every letter she had dutifully penned. Why on earth had she kept them? In the dim hope they would acquire with age a piquancy they had not displayed on receipt? Or as evidence of virtue against some future inspection?

Humming along to the stupid Frank Sinatra song that had come on the radio, she fetched a big cardboard bag from Dickins & Jones she had been saving and began to fill it in a kind of fever, surprised that she felt so little temptation to reopen any of the envelopes. She filled the bag almost to overflowing, tipped the contents directly into the dustbin, then returned to the drawer and almost filled it again, astonished that there were so many letters to dispose of.

Tucked away at the drawer's back, she came across a large manilla envelope, its original address heavily scribbled out. She snatched it up and was about to toss it after the rest but checked herself when she felt it wasn't empty. She tipped the contents onto what the baby had left of her lap.

It was a clutch of letters and postcards. She knew at once they weren't hers because her habit had always been to store letters in their envelopes because they were tidier that way and the postmarks were a speedy guide to a letter's date and origin. She flattened out the first to come to hand. The paper was good quality, thick, pre-war stock, but unheaded. The handwriting was distinctive, italic, the ink a smoky blue. She liked to think she could tell a man's writing from a woman's but in this case she was quite uncertain. Then she started to read.

Dear Richard. This separation is a perfect agony. I work and walk and drive about and take commands. I go through the motions so well I doubt anyone notices anything out of the usual about me but all I think about is last weekend and you . . .

The date was 1944, reassuringly before he had first asked Sylvia to dance. He had mentioned no old girlfriends – the only past loves he had spoken of were dogs – and, uncharitably, she had always assumed this was because he had none. Now she saw he had simply been showing a well-bred respect for her feelings. Touched and obscurely flattered, she flicked the page over to glance at the letter's end and saw only, *All my love, your E.* Then, shamed into emulating his rectitude, she refolded the letter and tucked it back inside the brown manilla envelope with the others and returned them to the drawer, which otherwise was now quite empty.

She fetched herself a cup of coffee and a rock bun, trying to put it out of her mind, then tackled the drawer below. This turned out to be a graveyard of old bills he had pointlessly stashed there and stacks of the little yellow folders in which her photographs were returned from the developer's. Any pictures that came out well, she stuck in carefully annotated albums soon after they arrived (it was the nearest she had to a hobby). All the folders contained now were negatives and the photographs she had never stuck in. However funny or evocative, they were all more or less hopeless so she tossed packet after packet in the rubbish bag after briskly checking the contents of each. She sang along to the radio but all the time she was thinking about the stash of letters in the other drawer.

Honesty was always the best policy. When he came home for lunch, she would find a discreet moment in which to tell him, honestly, she had stumbled on the letters while tidying the drawer, and see if he told her anything in return. But what if he simply threw them in the dustbin and told her nothing more? It would be unbearable not to know. Who was the girl, this mysterious E? An Evelyn or an Enid? Was she an older woman, even, or married? What did she look like? Perhaps if she looked more closely into the package she would find a photograph, an inscribed one. A pretty face, smiling bravely in a WAF uniform or a nurse's one. Or a smoky vamp with a flirtatious half-veil. But vamps, she sensed, would never have been his type. Perhaps there was a tragedy? Had E gone off with some handsome American once the separation she wrote of proved longer than her heart could bear? Or had she stayed true but been killed in an air raid? The letter Sylvia had glimpsed had been maddeningly – purposely – denuded of clues. Not even a town or house name. Merely that reassuring date.

By the time she needed to tidy herself up and fetch the youngest from playgroup and set soup and rolls to heat for lunch, there was nothing left in the bottom drawers but files of bank statements, a shoebox full of precious school reports and, bomb-like in its insignificant brown housing, the testimony to Richard's romantic past.

She always made an effort at weekday lunchtimes because they were the only time, apart from sleepy late evenings, when she could be sure of having him to herself for a little precious adult conversation. The four-year-old was always grouchily ravenous after a long morning of playgroup so she would feed her the moment they got home then settle her down for an afternoon nap while she enjoyed lunch alone with him, hair brushed, a little lipstick on, a dab of scent and with her pinny firmly left in the kitchen. It was quite possible he was unaware of these details but she felt they mattered and was sure he would notice their absence.

Sometimes he was barely home for half an hour before he had to hurry out again but it was still half an hour in which they could speak quietly and calmly without the happy hubbub of childish demands and arguments coming between them. That day was one of the brutally curtailed lunch breaks. Even as he came in he was apologizing for having to rush. Some bigwig from the MOD was visiting unexpectedly in the afternoon and Richard was not convinced the barracks were ready for him. "I'm sorry, darling," he said. "We'll have to talk tonight instead."

He called her darling all the time now, she had noticed. When they were first married he called her by her name or by her nickname, Billy, short for Silly Billy. She tried not to dwell on it but sometimes she felt it sounded as though he were speaking from a script and encouraging her to do the same, as though they were Kenneth More and Kay Kendall and not themselves at all. *Dear Richard* was all the letter had said, not *Darling* or even *My dear*.

"That's quite all right," she told him. "Is everything bloody?"

"It is a bit."

"More soup?"

"Thank you, no. It's delicious but I must get on. How's the beastie?" He grinned as he gestured towards the ceiling, meaning the four-year-old, whom she suspected was his favourite.

"Oh. A bit teary. She'll be fine in the end. Nobody likes being an ex-baby. Mummy will probably spoil her rotten when she comes. That might help, actually. Don't you want pudding, even? Apple and cheese?"

He was on his feet again already. "No time. Anyway, the Minister will expect fruit cake with his tea so I shan't starve. Was that oxtail?"

"Mulligatawny."

"Very good. Bye, darling."

She washed up the lunch things then checked on the four-year-old, who was still fast asleep, still clutching the pink rabbit she would never let Sylvia wash, still frowning. She was such a thundery, passionate child. Sylvia hoped she would grow out of it. Thunder and passion rarely made for happiness or easy friendships. She woke her slowly by quietly drawing her curtains then tiptoed out and returned, without a moment's hesitation, to the study and the drawer and the brown manilla envelope.

There was no fighting it. She had to know everything.

She opened the desk again and tipped the letters and postcards out over the blotter. Resisting the urge to read immediately, she made herself sort them by date then began at the beginning and worked through to the end. She was dimly aware of time passing, of her daughter getting up and beginning to play by herself, talking to her rabbit then squeaking terrible, formless tunes to it on the descant recorder she had stolen from her oldest sister, but her conscious mind was on the pages before her and the vivid scenes they evoked.

At first it was a struggle to understand. The pair had clearly known each other a long time, known each other's families even, but something had changed all their former easiness in the course of a weekend where E had initiated a risky conversation. The first letter was written in a state of suspense. She had clearly said things to Richard in the conversation she could never take back, confessed her feelings for him, presumably, before they had been interrupted by her mother and sister and Richard was left no space in which to answer. The next letter made it clear Richard's response had been encouraging. Then the pair had met for a country walk. They had kissed in a barn.

Sylvia felt a spasm of jealousy at that. Richard had always seemed uncomfortable, even disapproving, at public displays of affection. He had certainly never been moved to kiss her in the day-lit open air, even when unobserved. Reading E's rapturous response to it she began to feel something like anger.

When you held me in your arms and kissed me like that, it felt like an unexpected homecoming. I know we can never speak of it, that for any hint to get out would be a catastrophe, but I'm afraid you've left me so excited and happy I want to shout it from the rooftops. I don't understand how people can say the things they do, disapprove as they do, when loving like this feels so entirely right, so meant!

So that was it! E was a married woman. Small wonder Richard had never mentioned her. Sylvia wondered more than ever who she could have been. If the families were friends, then there was every likelihood she had met her by now at a wedding or a funeral. Perhaps she had even been there when Sylvia married the man E loved?

She read on through the little pile, tossing aside a snapshot of some army friend of Richard's that had come among the letters by mistake. She read a postcard from Tenby which said only:

All day, all night (especially the latter) I think of you, your face, your hands. Your E, and another, of an elegant youth by Ramsay, which said, I think that was an experiment best left unrepeated. Don't you?

There was a letter largely taken up with memories of an adored older brother just lost in action. Another, inspired by an idyllic weekend the pair had just snatched in some friend's borrowed cottage, was full of a future life together. *Somewhere safe, where we can be unremarkable, unjudged. Can there be such a place?*

There was something odd, however. The letters were circumspect, of course, as all wartime letters had to be. Nobody was mentioned by name. Places, even, were rarely specified. And yet there seemed to be an extra caution at work, as though they were not just lovers but spies or criminals, as though not just reputations but lives were at stake. E's descriptions of her war work were especially opaque because she edited so much out with inky scribble and tended to refer to everyone simply by letters of the alphabet.

> *Yesterday was particularly hard to take. All morning I had to listen, and yes, join in as X was sounding off to Y about how all p------s should be sniffed out like rats and shot or sent to a camp somewhere to avoid infecting the ranks and depleting morale. I almost ruined everything when Y suggested there should be camps on Anglesey and the Isle of Wight (just imagine, darling!) and I got the giggles amongst my files and had to pretend to be choking on a biscuit crumb. I'm sure they suspect nothing, I know they don't, but still . . .*

The tone had grown less effusive by now. There was a sense, not of the affair petering out, but of its having achieved an equilibrium. Or resigned impasse. Presumably because leaving E's husband and family (if she had one) was out of the question. For the first time, Sylvia found herself wondering why he had kept these letters. Had he done it unthinkingly, the way he did his bills, simply amassing them as they came in the post but never rereading them? Or was this a cherished cache he returned to repeatedly? Most of the pages felt barely creased or handled. They certainly hadn't been kept under pillows or wept over.

There were just two letters left. As she unfolded the penultimate one, her name flared out at her from the page and it took considerable presence of mind to read from the beginning and not dart down to that line.

> *What can I say? Sylvia is lovely. Idealistic. Innocent. If you insist on marrying then I dare say she is perfect for you. I hope you will be happy. I know you long for fatherhood but . . . Oh Robert. Perhaps*

*I was naive? I had thought you were more courageous than this. I
dared to think that when this bloody war was finally over we could go
somewhere. Paris, maybe, or Tangiers. Somewhere we're not known
and could build a life. But I know you. I know your unswerving
moral compass. Sylvia represents the Right Thing and I've no doubt
you expect and trust me to re-embrace respectable normality in my
turn, as though what we have shared was nothing more than an
adolescent adventure. And I dare say you will succeed in shaming me
into compliant orthodoxy. But I know I will never entirely surrender.
I know that marriage, whatever its blessings, whatever the relief of
escaping from this constant subterfuge, will seem like a bare, grey
room after the garden we've been walking in . . .*

She had the letters out of order. This was the sad, quiet *adieu* – the
next letter came from a few weeks before and was far less interesting. The
phrase was so insignificant Sylvia almost read past it without noticing.

Blah blah blah, she read (E's style was frankly rather undistinguished
and a bit novelettish). *Blah blah blah, the other men, blah blah blah.*

She had read to the bottom of the page and was turning before its
meaning snagged her attention and her eyes flicked back to reread it.

*Z had suggested he spend the afternoon going over the plans with me
and the other men.*

The four-year-old had made her way downstairs and chose that
moment to say, "Mummy," suddenly from the doorway. Sylvia jumped
and, nonsensically stacking the letters out of harm's way before
attending to her, brushed the small photograph onto the carpet.

"Coming, poppet." Leaning to pick it up, she found it had landed
face down. *To R from E*, she read. No grotesque love or kisses. Nothing
untoward. A friendly gift from one soldier to another. But the
handwriting was unmistakable.

"Mummy!"

Trained that the room was territory forbidden to her, the child came
no further in for all her anxiety.

"Oh darling, I'm coming!" Sylvia said, more sharply than she had intended and the child began to cry in the over-dramatic, attention-seeking way she did when thwarted. Sadly, she was beyond the age of being left to cry herself out in a pram at the bottom of the garden. "I'm sorry, I'm sorry." Sylvia left the desk and, ambushed by emotion, scooped her up, kissed her and danced her around the hall in her arms, face pressed into her golden curls until the child was laughing hysterically and it was the mother who, for a few jagged breaths, was weeping out loud. "I know," she sniffed. "Let's play with the buttons."

"Yes."

"You want that?"

"Yes."

The child had a thing about the button box, perhaps because she had been forbidden to touch it unsupervised lest she swallow a button or suck one into her little windpipe. As they jigged to the sitting room, Sylvia drew a few moments of intense comfort from being able to hold her close.

"My precious," she said.

"Buttons," the child replied then shouted, "Buttons!" so loudly it hurt at close range.

Sylvia set her down on the rug by the fireplace, fetched the button box – an old Turkish delight tin – and, after teasing her a moment ("Ready?" "Yes." "Are you sure?" "Yes!") tipped its glittering, clattering contents onto the floor before her. She stretched past her to the shelf where, only yesterday, when she had been a kind of unknowing doll, she had tidied the photograph albums and arranged them by age.

The oldest and thinnest was his mother's – a haphazard assemblage of snaps from the twenties and thirties, mostly frustratingly small and unascribed. The next oldest, not much larger, was Richard's. He had been given a Box Brownie for his twelfth birthday but had taken so few photographs with it that the evidence of his entire life between then and his meeting Sylvia occupied less than two-thirds of its length. At that point, it became obvious that his young wife, much the keener and abler photographer, had taken up the duties of household chronicler.

There were lopsided pictures of his parents and dog (several of the dog) and of an unfeasibly large cat and a few pictures of boys at his prep school, uniformed or in cricket whites. Then there was a whole page of pictures of a strikingly handsome boy, fourteen or fifteen, grinning awkwardly in a cloister somewhere (a cathedral or their school). *Tim Endersly*, the still-childish hand announced, *came to stay all summer*. The answering page showed an array of adults and children in holiday mode, the boy among them. *Assorted Enderslys*, it said, *came to fetch him back*. Thereafter Endersly appeared almost to the exclusion of anyone else in a way she (Fool. Fool!) had always thought a touching proof of a deep and lasting friendship, evidence that, however undemonstrative, her husband was a man of enduring loyalty. Endersly was pictured on other holidays, up at Cambridge and then, before the blank pages ensued, in September 1939 as a member of a well-wrapped student reading party in the Lake District. There were young men and women in the picture, many of them obviously paired up for the camera. Endersly was standing noticeably alone, the only one not smiling as he met the camera's eye. Her husband's eye.

Of course she had met him. A smartly suited civilian, introduced as Richard's best and oldest friend which, naturally, he was – Richard never lied about anything – he had been best man at their wedding and delivered a short and extremely witty speech. Two years later, within the space of six months, he had been a godfather at their first-born's christening and boasted Richard as best man at his wedding in turn. She recalled a faintly hysterical occasion in the bride's home village in Hampshire, dominated by assorted Enderslys. The bride had been weepy and rather drunk and Richard, Sylvia remembered now, noticeably short-tempered. Since then, the wife had been fulfilling all the godfatherly duties, sending clumsily unsuitable presents with cards signed by her in her husband's name or not at all, and had missed the last birthday entirely.

"Sad," was Richard's only comment on the omission, which their son had accepted with a version of his father's stoicism. "She drinks, I gather."

Suddenly it was time to fetch the others from school. She tidied the remaining buttons away, stowed the four-year-old on the back seat and drove into town and back, feeling like a drunk herself, alarmingly detached and out of control as she negotiated turnings, zebra crossings and roundabouts with her precious brood noisy about her.

They washed their hands and sat around the kitchen table and she gave them glasses of milk and banana-and-honey sandwiches and heard from one then another about their day, stories of miniature endurance or injustice so crucial to them, so completely unimportant to her just now. When she could bear it no longer she lurched to her feet and left them to crumble hastily delivered slices of fruit cake.

The pile of letters was where she had left it. She seized it off the desk, scrabbled up the little photograph too and took them all to the sitting room fireplace where she tossed them into the grate and put a match to them. She waited, staring, until the pile had flared and was turning to curling ash. Then she stabbed it a few times with the poker before returning, heart racing, to the kitchen where the children had already abandoned a crumby chaos of tea things and school bags to race upstairs to watch *Children's Hour* in the nursery.

She would not tell him. Where, how could she begin? He had been a criminal repeatedly – if she had interpreted the letters correctly – committing acts that would see him thrown out of the army and into prison, if brought to light. This morning all was well. She cleared the tea things and made a start on supper. A few hours ago she knew nothing of this and all was well. When he came home she flinched instinctively but found he was the same man she had calmly loved and accepted at breakfast. She had changed, however, as surely as if his secret was something she had eaten that had stained her tongue and poisoned her.

If he should ever happen to ask what became of the letters, she decided, then they would have the conversation. Otherwise she would take the matter to her grave, as many a wife must have done before her. As she laid the table and opened a tin of pineapple rings, as she arranged gammon steaks under the grill and oversaw the youngest's bath, she fantasized as she often did about scenes in their future life. The German army base might be better than she imagined, with trees and a park and a library. She might make a new friend among the wives there, a soulmate of the kind she had not enjoyed since school. The children would grow up and she would have to endure the regular trauma of enrolling each in turn in boarding school. Richard and she would make the perfectly normal, even expected, shift to having twin beds. They would survive.

And yet, once she had them all gathered about the table again, the youngest and oldest on either side of her and he, so distinguished and reserved at the other end, so serious in his calm interrogation of the middle two beside him, she knew this was a secret she would have to share. Sooner or later it would bubble out of her or be drawn from her by some accidental imprudence. As they ate and talked, drank and argued, she looked at each child in turn and imagined the moment when she burdened it with the odd, unthinkable truth. The oldest boy and girl were so earnest, so correct, she could imagine them blaming her: either insisting she was mistaken or that the whole thing had been somehow her fault. She could not imagine them offering her consolation or relief. The youngest girl adored him entirely too much and would never forgive Sylvia for the perceived calumny. The youngest boy, her guilty favourite and licensed clown, would refuse to take it seriously and make her feel that her years of secrecy had been a wasted, delusional effort.

She eased herself back in her chair and briefly met Richard's gaze as she dropped a hand to her belly. Which is when she knew it was her unborn child's birthright, born past the period of its mother's innocence, to be the only one of them to know her utterly. It might not hear the full truth for fifteen or sixteen years but, boy or girl, for better or worse, she would make it hers, bind it to her with secrets and prepare it for life as she feared she could never prepare the others, with vaccinations of the bitterest truth.

"Everything all right, darling?" he asked her, and something in his tone caused the children to fall silent and turn to her with small questions on their faces.

"I'm fine," she said, abashed, and instinctively reached out to touch the youngest one's cheek to reassure it. "Just a bit of indigestion, that's all. Now. Who's for pudding?"

Handle with Bear
Lawrence Schimel

"It looks ridiculous," I told him, looking up at his head as we stood at the crosswalk at Gran Vía, waiting for the light to change.

"You need to relax and get into the Holiday Spirit," Aiden replied.

"But Christmas is over already!" I complained. Which was technically true: Christmas Day had passed two days ago. Not that you would notice here in Spain, where the holiday was still in full swing. From what Nacho had told us last night, Christmas was a drawn-out affair here, which lasted until 6 January, known as the *Día de Reyes*, the Day of the Kings. It actually made a lot more sense to me, giving gifts on Reyes, which is when the Three Wise Men did actually show up bearing their gifts, rather than on Christmas Day itself. But then, I couldn't imagine England practically shutting down for nearly two weeks of festivities and jollity; a demonstration of the difference between our Protestant work ethic and a Catholic country like Spain.

"When in Rome, do as the Romans do," Aiden said, unflappable in his good humor, as we joined the surge of pedestrians crossing the street.

"First of all, we're in Chueca, not in Italy," I grumbled. Chueca was the "gay neighborhood" of Madrid, which we'd just entered by crossing the street. It wasn't the source of my bad mood; on the contrary: with any luck, coming here would help me find someone to help perk me up.

I was somewhat jealous that Graham had abandoned us again, to go off to Nacho's place and have sex. Not that I wouldn't have done the same thing in his position. What I resented, if I was honest with myself, was not being in the position to abandon my mates.

"Second of all," I continued, "did you notice how only the heterosexuals engage in this sort of frivolity?"

To my dismay, just then, two incredibly hot studs wearing matching silver wigs, their arms around each other, turned the corner onto Calle Hortaleza and started walking toward us. Both Aiden and I watched them in reverent silence, and as one we both turned to watch them until they disappeared from sight, turning right when they reached Gran Vía.

"It's still inappropriate for a bears' bar," I insisted, a mix of embarrassment to be seen with him wearing that and all the free-floating general cussedness I was feeling. "Neither deer in general, nor reindeer in particular, have a place in the fauna of the bear subculture."

"Then I'll stand out. Since I don't speak the language, I have to do something to give me an advantage if I hope to hook up." And with that, Aiden pushed through the doors into Hot.

As I followed him inside, I was just glad he hadn't changed into his kilt as well when we stopped at the hostel to drop off our afternoon's purchases.

It had been something of a lark to come to Spain for our holidays. I forget if it was Graham or Aiden who'd broached the idea one day at lunch but, whoever it was, it quickly took hold as the plan for New Year. Graham had heard wonderful things about Madrid's club scene, and all of us enjoyed a bit of fantasizing about Spanish men.

The thing is, Graham had been a bit more proactive about it than the rest of us. He'd moved all his online profiles to Madrid weeks ago, so even before we landed at Barajas airport his dance card was more or less full. Although the first guy he met with, Nacho, seemed to be turning into one of those holiday romances, given that Graham had stood up the second guy on his dance card to spend a second night with Nacho, and from the way things were shaping up, he'd spend tonight with him as well. It felt almost as if Graham were spending his holiday with Nacho instead of with us, which was fine, I was happy for him, even if I was jealous. And Graham's beau was turning into somewhat of a boon for us as well, since Nacho had become our local guide. He was off from his job until after Reyes, so the times he wasn't having sex with Graham he was happy enough to take us out and show us the local nightlife, or other touristy things like shopping at the Christmas market in Plaza Mayor this afternoon, where Aiden bought that stupid moose-head hat.

Nacho had been the one to recommend that we come here, to Hot, which he said was one of the few places that had some sort of scene this early (early by Spain's standards: it was 8 p.m.) with its two-for-one drinks during happy hour. And there definitely was a lively scene: the place was pretty packed, with sexy hirsute men of all ages and sizes. I hurried to slip into the brief wake created by Aiden, some men shifting back to give him room as he headed straight to the bar while others took a step back to get a better look at all of him. By the time I caught up with him, he had already ordered a beer for both of us. *Cerveza* was one of the first words Nacho had taught us, and even I could count to *dos*.

"*Gracias,*" I said, as Aiden handed me a bottle of the local brew: Mahou. He had unzipped his jacket, but he hadn't taken off that damned hat, and it looked like he planned to wear it the entire evening. And nothing I could say or do seemed likely to have any effect on his decision.

I couldn't explain why, but it seemed that Aiden's good spirits only left me feeling even more Scrooge-like. Maybe it was the whole holidays atmosphere, with its relentless good cheer and the constant ·insipid carols, not to mention years of childhood frustrations: years of getting "appropriate" boy presents instead of the ones I truly wanted, awkward gatherings of the extended family clan, the usual stuff a shrink could have a field day with if I wasn't so averse to the idea of paying for the privilege of lying on a couch and spilling my guts to some stranger. I tended more towards self-medication, I reflected, taking another sip of my beer. Weren't trips abroad just another way to drown one's sorrows?

Or at any rate, to distract one from them? (With the hope that on one's return everything didn't seem even bleaker by comparison; it is my theory that this explains why so many people show holiday snapshots for months after they get home, as if that could let them recapture or drag out the holiday feeling a bit longer.)

"So here we are, three friends in Madrid over the holidays," I grumbled, highlighting Graham's absence.

"Lighten up," Aiden said. "You're on holiday. Try to enjoy yourself a bit. Live it up!" He spread his arms above his head in a wide, camp gesture, before letting them fall back to his side. "Besides, this is precisely what friendship is about: giving your mates space to do their thing without going all jealous. That's why they're friends and not boyfriends."

I opened my mouth to reply with some biting and bitter retort, but Aiden's comment (and no doubt the beer on an empty stomach) set me thinking. I already knew I wasn't jealous of Graham, not in a sexual way: it's not that I wanted to be having sex with him and resented Nacho for having sex with him instead, or even the reverse, that I wanted to have sex with Nacho (although I wouldn't have minded that) and resented Graham, competitively, for getting to do so. If I was jealous of anything, maybe it was Graham's sudden independence, whereas I was feeling almost nostalgic for our friendship, for things to be as they had been before, for nothing to change.

Friendship was such a curious thing, really; it was so much harder to understand than sexual attraction. That, at least, made perfect sense; even if I didn't share a particular kink or fetish I could more or less understand the basic concept, or accept that it floated someone else's boat even if it left mine high and dry. And that attraction could be there, even if it wasn't mutual, even if it was never acted on.

But friendships were another matter, much more tenuous and inexplicable. Sometimes they happened by pure chance, rather than any shared interest. In our case, it was almost from proximity more than anything else: we all worked in the same office for TNT in

Lount. Which could in theory have fit some gay-fantasy scenario (the hunky delivery man in his uniform) except we all worked in the back offices instead of making the rounds in our distinctive orange vans delivering packages. Graham and Aiden were both team leaders and I was a resource manager, something boring but necessary to keep everything flowing properly. But what did we really share beyond our jobs and our sexuality? The three of us had hit it off somehow, for some unknown reason. It's not that we were the only gays at the office; TNT had a special gay diversity group, on an international level, and while Lount was not a hotspot of gay life, there were at least a dozen other homos who were out of the closet in our office. So why only us three and not those others, who were just office acquaintances? They didn't have the intimacy we all did, and not just the three of us: we three were also part of a sort of clique within our little TNT world with a few (straight) women and even one or two straight men. We knew all about each other's lives because we were together all day at the office, using lunches and smoke breaks as a chance to gossip. Not to mention keeping up on all the gossip through Facebook and email.

Would we all still be friends when we moved on to other employers? Or was our friendship merely a convenience? Like regulars at our local, comforting because they were known and unchanging.

Carmen was still part of the group, even though she'd just gotten promoted to the head office in Amsterdam and now spent three weeks a month traveling between TNT centers. We just didn't see her as often. Of course, she still worked for TNT, so there was still that team-spirit bond. If she'd moved to some other company, would we all (understandably, naturally) just drift apart over time?

Here we were in another country (the others all had spouses and/ or kids to deal with, so only we three single gay men had decided to spend Christmas together abroad) and already the ties that bound us were beginning to fray. Or were they really? I asked myself. What was so different about the three of us heading in to Birmingham (Lount, after all, didn't offer much in the way of a nightlife, gay or otherwise) one weekend, and one of us abandoning the other two because he'd pulled?

The difference being that here I didn't speak the language and, as a result, I was clinging too hard to the world I knew: my two mates who were here in Madrid with me, or even just the memory of our group, lost in my head like this, thinking drunkenly about all of us and the mystery of our friendship. I determined to try to live in the now, to have a good time, even if it felt almost like a threat or an obligation: I would enjoy myself, whether I wanted to or not.

––––––––

"I think we should go over there and talk to those two guys," Aiden said, indicating two very young Spaniards. They were both gesticulating wildly and yet standing very close together; I couldn't tell if it was because of the press of other bodies around them or if it was something to do with their being Spanish.

"They look like they're barely old enough to drink," I said, already breaking my determination to enjoy myself. "I prefer men to boys."

"Well, I think they're kind of cute. And I think they might be interested. At least in me. But there's two of them, so I'm willing to share."

"Was your beer much stronger than mine or is this just wishful thinking?"

"They're talking about my hat."

"How can you hear what they're talking about from across the bar?"

"They're signing," Aiden said, as if it were self-evident. And as I watched them, I realized it should have been obvious that they were deaf, and they were not gesticulating to accentuate their conversation but rather conversing entirely with their hands.

"I can't believe this. You don't speak Spanish but you can understand Spanish Sign Language?"

"My niece is deaf. The whole family learned British Sign Language so she wouldn't feel left out when we got together for holidays and whatnot. I don't think it's so very different from signed Spanish."

And without waiting for my consent, he started heading across the room. Once again, I was pulled along in his wake. This time, though, I felt like we were a couple of some sort, instead of just friends: coupled together by both being strangers in a strange land. A moment ago, we had both been equals in our outsider status, but now Aiden had discovered that he could indeed communicate with these deaf Spaniards, for he was chattering away with them, it seemed, from how fast their hands were flying. It was fascinating to watch, and not merely because all of a sudden this friend I thought I knew so well seemed a completely alien being to me. Not that being able to speak sign language was the same as suddenly sprouting tentacles or something (although he did have those stupid antlers sticking off the top of his head), but it did feel almost like there were some new dimension to him, or rather, it underscored how even though we might feel like we knew everything about one another there was still all these hidden depths we didn't know anything about. Things that weren't necessarily secrets, it's not like Aiden actively kept his knowledge of sign language or his deaf niece from me (and presumably the rest of us): it had just never come up before. But I was still left somewhat blindsided by the surprise, not the least because I was now excluded from their chatting.

So I drank faster than I probably should have. Aiden gave me the drinks ticket and I pushed my way back to the bar to get our free second beers. While I was waiting, I looked back at the three of them, and for a moment I felt disoriented, as if I had gone back in time a few moments only now I was all alone, and Aiden had crossed over to become one of them. As if he had gone native somehow, whereas I was still a foreign visitor. I think it had to do with language, with being able to communicate, whereas all I could do was watch. Watch and think, although since my thoughts were becoming so somber and morbid I tried to just watch.

There were two of them, and they were both enough alike to make it hard to tell them apart at a quick glance. Not once you really looked at them, but in that cursory way that often makes people lump racial or ethnic groups together by broad obvious features instead of individual traits or personalities. Both boys were white without being too pale, with dark hair and dark eyes, and they were both dwarfed beside Aiden although they were probably 170 cm in height. Though it was a bear bar they both looked quite slender, even under the many layers of winter clothing. They were both in their very early twenties, though one of them had a sparse beard that only made him look even younger than his clean-shaven companion. They both radiated that youthful fresh-faced energy and earnest intensity. Or maybe it was because they were deaf, I realized, that they looked at everything so carefully, so strongly, so fully, because they were absorbing only through their eyes what we would take in through our eyes and ears. It was something we took for granted so easily, those of us with all our senses, even if in raucous and noisy environs like this bar the absolute quiet of being deaf might be a welcome relief. But that was just being cheap and facile, I told myself, since there would be lots of other times when I would strain desperately to hear something, if I were to suddenly lose my own hearing.

Even after the bartender gave me the two beers, I watched them from afar, trying to discern what differences I could see from here, before approaching and seeing up close the other differences. Aiden had his back to me as he chatted with them, so to start with I dubbed them Left and Right in my head. Because they both were looking primarily at him, glancing between his face and his hands, as his fingers moved through the words he was trying to say. (For all that Aiden offered to share, he was quite obviously the center of attention for both of them.) Right was the one with the attempt at a beard, something it would take him a few more years to grow into. Not to mention his assurance. Left seemed to be the much more dominant of the two, gesticulating (I mean talking) more (more often, more fluidly), grabbing Right by the shoulder to get his attention, or one of them would touch Aiden for the same reason. At first I thought he was just being pushy, but as I watched them I realized personal space must be so different for them, casual touching a necessary part of the conversation process.

I thought of Graham and Nacho, no doubt also touching right now, having sex or maybe in a post-coital tangle, and I felt even more isolated and alone, in that way that you can only feel when surrounded by other people at a bar where no one pays you any attention.

So it felt almost a like relief to go back to them, which was strange, since I hardly knew the two of them; even Aiden barely knew them, although he at least could talk to them. But they had taken on a sort of singular identity, this threesome, and my friend was part of it and yet also still my friend. I stood beside them, waiting and watching, not wanting to interrupt, but Right noticed me, and touched Aiden's shoulder, and he turned his head to look at me, with those goofy antlers on his head, and said, "Thanks, mate," as he reached out for his beer, and it was sort of a shock to hear him talk again; I had been thinking of him as part of their group almost more than mine.

He turned back to the deaf boys so I watched the crowd a bit and then watched them. I wondered if it was considered rude to watch a signed conversation if you weren't involved, if it was like eavesdropping. Up close, I could see that Left's face was more narrow than Right's, with a pointed chin that made him look dainty or elfin. Left also had a piercing under his lip, a little metal stud that caught the light from time to time. Right had stronger features: a squarer jaw, sharper cheekbones. I didn't really know Spain well enough to identify its regions, but I found myself wondering if maybe he was Basque or from some other northern region.

He has nice eyes, I thought, before I realized that I could see them so clearly because he was looking back at me, and not at the conversation. I glanced away, my face turning red to have been caught staring at him, and I saw that the conversation had been derailed. Or perhaps it had evolved to a new level: Aiden and Left were kissing.

———

There is something contagious about being in the presence of sex. It's probably biological. I think that's what makes so many heterosexual men so uncomfortable about seeing gays: confronting the fact that they recognize the desire before them as something they, too, share, even if it's just a glimmering, a little tiny tickle.

And the kissing going on between Aiden and Left was definitely sex, even though they were both fully dressed and in public.

I was suddenly nervous. Not because I was turned on by watching my friend make out with a boy he had just picked up, but because now Right was also excluded, and that left him and me alone. Alone in that way two people can be together in a crowded bar where their mates have just hooked up with one another.

It was an awkward situation under the best of circumstances, but to top it off, I didn't know how to talk to a deaf person.

I looked at Right again, and he was definitely watching me and not the two of them, not the bar in general: that intense look I had noticed earlier.

I opened my mouth to say something, to explain that I didn't know what to say or how to say it. Of course, almost immediately, I realized my instincts were all wrong, I couldn't just speak, I had to try to convey what I wanted to say through non-verbal means. Unless maybe he could read lips? Although that would only work if I could speak Spanish.

Right looked at me for a while longer with those intense dark eyes, and then he said aloud, in accented but passable English, "So you're Eric."

I was flabbergasted. Not so much that he knew my name (obviously Aiden must have told him) but by the fact that he could speak. I had just assumed that because they were deaf, they must be mute as well. And it turns out that he could not only speak, but speak English as well.

"Yes," I said, beaming at him. I could feel words bubbling up in me, all the conversation I had swallowed with my beer, feeling isolated and alone, while lost in my thoughts. I hated myself for feeling so relieved, but I began to feel sympathy and understanding for that kind of British traveler I had always disdained before (more for how it smacked of colonialism than for fear of recognizing myself in him, how little had I known myself before!) who suddenly become bosom buddies with any stranger merely because they could speak the Queen's English.

I realized I had answered vocally again without thinking. Maybe Right could read lips, I thought. Or maybe I had made the assumption he was deaf, when he was merely someone who could also speak in sign, like Aiden.

"And you are?" I asked aloud. "Aiden didn't have a chance to introduce us before, and it looks like he's otherwise indisposed right now."

Right smiled. "I'm Javi," he said. And he leaned toward me.

How forward they are in this country, I thought, closing my eyes before he could kiss my lips. But he merely kissed one cheek, and I remembered the local custom and quickly offered the other cheek for a second kiss. Only two here, as far as I recalled; I could never keep straight in which countries it was three, or which side to start on.

"Pleased to meet you," I said automatically, each of us falling back on the ritual pleasantries to smooth out the awkwardness of the situation. "And I am glad you can not just speak, but you speak English as well."

"Did you think I was deaf?" he asked. It would no doubt take me a while to think of him by his name, Javi, instead of as Right.

"At first I just assumed . . . and since Aiden didn't say anything otherwise."

He laughed. "I only learned it recently. I am an interpreter. Spanish Sign Language is now officially recognized as a language in Spain. Just like Catalan or Basque. But there are few people who know how to speak it. So when I lost my job, I started to study it. And now I work as an interpreter between deaf people and hearing people. And there is always work."

"That's a job that I had never stopped to think about before," I said.

"The world is always changing," he said. And as if to underscore his point, he pulled an iPhone from his pocket. "Excuse me," he said, and answered the phone, rattling off a stream of Spanish I couldn't understand at all.

I was amazed at how smoothly he moved from one mode of conversation to another, slipping between languages and media: from hand signals to high-tech gadgets.

"Sorry," he explained to me when he was done with the conversation. "Friend having a fight with another friend."

"It's OK," I replied.

Then he grabbed Left's shoulder, interrupting the kiss. A flurry of signing followed. Aiden grinned at me and winked. He was still wearing his antlers, even with all that tongue-wrestling. I didn't know if I was getting into the holiday spirit at last or if I was simply on my way to getting drunk and didn't care any more.

"Just one minute," Javi said, tapping away at the touchpad screen to write a message of some sort.

"No worries," I replied. "Why don't I get us another round?"

Aiden and Left were at it again, so rather than wait for a reply I made my way back to the bar and ordered and paid for two beers, then right away gave in the ticket for two more.

But when I got back with the drinks, Aiden was zipping up his coat. "Miguel has invited me back to his place," he explained. "In case I don't go back to the hotel tonight, I'll see you two tomorrow morning some time. I'll send you an email. Have fun."

Suddenly, Left swooped in and gave me a kiss on either cheek, though we hadn't even been introduced yet. Miguel, that was his name.

And with that Aiden and Miguel were gone.

I was still holding the four beer bottles, two in each hand. "Thanks," Javi said, as he took two of them from me. He put one on a sort of shelf behind him and drank from the other.

"*De nada*," I replied. I figured I might as well show off my few words of tourist Spanish. Besides, I was feeling dizzy by how fast things changed: now it was just me and Javi, who because he spoke English, felt more like a friend than someone I had known for less than half an hour in a bar.

And even though Aiden and Miguel had left, there was still a sexualized zing lingering in the air. Or maybe it was because we knew they were on their way to Miguel's place to have sex. But I felt now that when Javi looked at me, sex was more of a possibility between us than it had been before, even though he was still so young, still so fresh, and I tended to like men who were the opposite, a bit rugged, and in general older than I am.

"Everything OK with your friend?" I asked, thinking it was a neutral topic of conversation.

"Yeah, I sent an email to another friend who said she could stay there."

"You're probably too young to realize it," I said, although as soon as it was out of my mouth I knew how pompous that sounded; good thing I wasn't trying to pick him up, I thought. "But this whole email thing has really changed the world. When I was young, I used to have a pen pal. I don't know if you even know what that is: I used to write letters to a girl my age who lived in Johannesburg. We would send letters back and forth every week."

"Did you ever meet her?" Javi asked.

"No, we never did. I wonder what happened to her."

"You could probably look her up on the internet." He pulled his iPhone out of his pocket again and offered it to me.

"No, no. Thank you. I may try and find her. I hadn't thought of her in years, but I don't need to do it right now." I took a sip of my beer, feeling pensive again. "I know I must sound like a drunken old queen, but back then, communication was something special. It wasn't something we took for granted the way we do with emails or SMS, something just dashed off."

"I bet you're not as much of a dinosaur as you pretend to be. How old are you?" Javi asked.

"It's not just a question of age," I said, avoiding the answer. "The world has changed. And the whole gay world has changed, too. How people meet: these days, back in England, it's all on the Internet, it's like shopping by numbers. It's all so . . . de-humanized in some way. Like, what happened to real letters? Now we send little electronic blips of emails and SMS and tweets. Sometimes I feel like everything is in some secret code. And I only speak the old language. I can only speak one language, English. I don't even speak a second language, like you do."

"There's always sex," Javi said, suddenly tugging my hand and pulling me away from the wall, out into the middle of the room.

"What?" I said, my mind trying to make sense of what he'd said even as my body followed him.

"Sex. As a means of communication," Javi said.

He was now standing at the entrance to what Nacho had told us was the dark room.

"Come with me," he said. "I'll tell you a story."

I wondered, for a moment, how we had come to this. I was on the brink of sex with a boy I would never ordinarily look twice at.

Was this the sexual freedom that happened only when one was far from home?

What could this boy see in me?

Was this because I was a foreigner, something exotic?

Was this just a pity fuck because our friends had abandoned us and he was bored and why not pass the time together in a search for mutual pleasure?

Had this sexual tension always been there, between us, even if I didn't recognize it before? Maybe it had been dormant in me, something that was only set into motion by Aiden and Miguel, like ripples after the splash of their sexual charge?

If Miguel lived nearby, they might be having sex by now. But in a bed. Which is how I thought it would happen for me, if it were to happen on the trip. Not in a back room in a bears' bar, with a wisp of a boy who wasn't even a cub.

At the same time, I had to live my own life, my own story. I was being offered sex just when I had been feeling left out, both my mates having managed to hook up with guys they had chosen.

And even if this wasn't the guy I might have chosen, maybe this was one of those unexpected plot twists. Or maybe I was just drunk enough to be thinking all of this.

I could listen to how someone else told the story. Or I could maybe tell a story or two myself.

I reached out and took Javi's hand, and followed him into the back room.

Wolverine Cirque
Joseph Olshan

—

If you could be given your youth back, it might have true meaning for a few days, or maybe even a week. A month might allow you to forget that you were ever old, but the whole point would be to never forget – to understand that your visit back in time would expire almost as soon as it began. Sam is thinking this as he and Mike soldier the last ascent up a trail in the Wasatch Mountains of Utah, skis on their shoulders, notching their ski boots into steep snowpack, eyeing the flat table above where they'll soon stop and put on the rest of their gear. They've been hiking for an hour and a half in whirring, wintry silence, punctuated by groans and cackles of shifting snow and ice and by the soft wailing of the wind. The sun is high, and it's a bluebird day. Looming constantly to their left is Wolverine Cirque, whose headwalls are built up from ice melt that has gathered layers of snow; the slope looks almost vertical in places, dark dashes of rock to be avoided at all costs. It's an extreme descent that only solid expert skiers can drop into and be confident of surviving. The adrenalin blast of a run to the bottom of the canyon would, to those above them, be almost meaningless.

The night before, pointing to the image of the cirque on the computer screen, Mike had said, "You can get into it one of two ways. You can sideslip in, ski straight down the first headwall, then check your speed and pick your way for a bit until it gets wider" – then he grinned maniacally – "or you can just jump off the cornice, which I don't think either of us wants to do."

At forty-five, Mike is five years younger, a stronger skier. He lived for three seasons in Tahoe, tuning edges, adjusting bindings and skiing almost every day, and that has given him a confidence, a fluidity of motion that never seems to falter, even when his skis trammel the eastern ice. He's a tough little guy of French-Canadian background; one of his eyes is blue and the other is golden green. Last night he watched Sam staring slack-jawed at the screen.

"You with me, bud?" he said.

"Yeah, I'm with you."

"Don't overthink this, Sam. You overthink everything. You know the terrain. Now you just have to nail it. We've done the whole East Coast, we've done Tucks, we've done the West: Gunsight and the Baldy Chute at Alta, we've done Corbet's at Jackson. This is not far out of that league."

Sam disagreed; to him, Wolverine Cirque presented a higher degree of difficulty. Plenty of lesser skiers took on Tuckerman Ravine's 45-degree plunge, which was pretty short and could be dispatched with five turns. Corbet's Couloir in the Tetons was admittedly very steep, but still a marked trail in bounds – whereas Wolverine Cirque was miles and miles off-piste.

"But whatever you do," Mike spoke up again, "try not to think about him."

"About who?"

Mike knew Sam was being coy. "About you-know who."

But how could he not think about Luc? Doing the Cirque together was what they'd talked about from the very beginning, when Sam had shown Luc the YouTube footage accompanied by a heavy-metal soundtrack of skiers tackling it. "We'll do it; together, we'll do Wolverine," they had promised one another, hugging tight and cringing, as they'd watched Billy Poole's final moment – miraculously captured on video – when he was killed there in '09 at the age of twenty-eight. But Billy Poole was scouting for a ski film, and everybody said that had something to do with his demise.

Mike and Sam finally reach the top and, without acknowledging their arrival, look around at the sweeping expanse of summit vistas, sheets of snow draping the peaks and folds of mountains nestled close to them, and then begin the mindless drudge of putting on equipment.

Sam had been sure to ski several days at Solitude and Alta on his rented powder skis so that he was used to them. Mike, who'd brought his Atomics out from Boston, felt he would not need the advantage of extra-wide skis. They check their stowed avalanche gear (their probes and miniature shovels), turn on their transponders, secure their backpacks, and approach the lip of the cornice, staring down into what first appears to be a crevasse but is actually just a break in the fall line. As Mike has pointed out, dropping in off this major cornice is not an option because you'd begin with too much air and invariably hit rock below. You had to jet in from the lip at the side and, once in, ski straight down a headwall through a narrow gate of two squat boulders, then jump-turn down a slim ribbon of skiable terrain and continue jump-turning until you dropped lower into the bowl that would widen before you'd finally be free to turn widely. Nervousness and adrenalin were fine, as long as your brain didn't go numb.

"Okay, it is a little tricky," Mike concedes as they stand there, studying the slope like military strategists, "but just set your skis, aim for between the boulders. You'll probably be going fast when you get through. So start turning as soon as you clear those rawks." His South Boston accent sounds quaint in these western provinces. And for a moment Sam centers himself by taking deep breaths and looking out at the graduation of peaks in the distant part of the Wasatch that unfurl toward western Colorado, and the white parentheses of Solitude's downhill trails, where they hiked in from. Mike, who is always pretty laconic, seems slightly on edge, and Sam knows that even he is worrying about those first ten or fifteen seconds of the run. They've already debated who should go first; originally they thought Mike because he'd set the example, but then they reasoned perhaps Sam because he, being the weaker skier, should have somebody sweeping behind him. Their ultimate decision: Mike should lead.

"You're going to follow me. You're going to do it, right?" Mike asks softly, still scouring the Cirque. "You're not going to psyche out. Which means . . ." He looks at Sam shrewdly with his different-colored eyes.

"I'm not going to think about him," Sam fills in the blank. "And he wouldn't stop me, anyway. I will do it," he insists, still not quite sure that he will in the end.

Sam had placed the ad out of boredom, out of loneliness – a shirtless picture of himself posted with the stern warning that any response without a photo would be ignored. The image Luc sent was blurry, hardly revealing, and Sam, who calculated a twenty-six-year age difference between them, kept putting him off. But Luc emailed persistently until Sam gave in, thinking to himself: He's twenty-two, how bad can he be? He never anticipated the tall, strapping guy wearing aviators who drove up to the country store in his mother's Mini Cooper. And Sam, on his motorcycle, leaning in the passenger window and asking Luc to take his sunglasses off, awed by the pale-slate eyes against the dark hair, the blond streaks in his beard from spending the summer landscaping. And the very quiet moment when two people look deeply into one another and see something at once welcoming and disturbing.

"Your picture almost lies," he told Luc, concealing his delight.

"I have to . . . lie, because it's a secret," Luc said, the first words that Sam, of course, should have heeded.

"Well, I lied, too," he admitted. "I'm forty-nine, not forty-four."

"It's okay. I'm only into older guys," Luc said, then winked and admonished, "But tell the whole truth next time!"

Even then, Sam was still thinking it would be quick and easy, never dreaming he would be compelled to tell the young man how beautiful he was or would hear Luc say the same thing to him. Or that, back at Sam's house, when they were taking a breather listening to an Internet radio station that played classic hits, Luc would recognize songs like "Under Pressure" by Queen and David Bowie, able to sing the lyrics while they were lying in bed together.

"But this is so before your time," Sam remarked.

"Good music is good music," Luc said with a wise grin.

"I couldn't imagine growing up listening to my parents' music."

"Nobody did that . . . before the revolution," Luc pointed out. "After the revolution everything changed."

"What revolution?"

"Free love." Luc laughed, laying his head on Sam's chest.

Weeks later, they would playfully argue about how many hours they stayed in bed that first day. And it was only when they were showering that Luc revealed that he'd been recruited to Middlebury as a soccer player and had changed his major from economics to ecology and, after college, hoped to spend a few years working outdoors at a national park.

———

"You have nothing to prove to anybody," Mike now tells him sagely. "You've wanted to ski this since college." They'd met at Middlebury in a ski club when Mike was a freshman and Sam, two years graduated, was teaching an English class before going to architecture school. "And we're gonna do it!"

Now, time seems to telescope; no sooner does the grin on Mike's face fade, than he pushes out and grabs several feet of air off the lip before his skis hit and he's already rocketing down the narrow path toward the rocks. He's through the gate in a moment and adjusts his speed beautifully and then begins the quick jump-turns down the narrowest part of the face. Sam notices another drop that neither of them had anticipated, but Mike, who has remarkable reflexes, takes it in his stride and gets some more air before hitting the slightly flatter, wider part of the Cirque. And then he's turning great S's through the new snow – Sam can hear whoops of pleasure – making virgin tracks, as though writing words on a blank white tablet. And then, ever so faintly, "Awesome!" floating back up to him. As agreed, Mike finds a good place to stop halfway down and turns his face up to Sam. He yells something, but he's too far below now for Sam to understand it. Sam knows he's got to jump in, that he's going to do it, but hesitates just one last moment to collect his thoughts, to review what needs to be done, maybe even pray because he's superstitious.

"I'm afraid," he admits aloud to the blustering wind; he knows it's not just fear of the adventure – it's fear of losing his power, his athleticism, his attractiveness. Muscular and rugged throughout his life, he's reluctant to let it all go. Ever since he can remember he's been dreaming of mastering Wolverine Cirque, a notch in his belt before he gets too old to attempt terrain that often intimidates equally talented younger skiers. Shredding it all the way to the bottom of the canyon will hopefully slow his own decline down another arguably more difficult slope.

The hardest part is getting off the lip and making it down that first schuss, and to continue strategizing while doing so. "Come on," he imagines Luc urging him, and then he's in and knows with a flash of exhilaration that it's a good entry. He's following Mike's tracks, gaining speed down the headwall toward the stubby boulders, zipping through them until a jolt of his shoulder hits one of them, throwing him off his game for a second, but instinctively he bends his knees, checks his speed, and then enters phase two: the slightly less steep chute that's maybe two feet wider than his skis. Sam is making his way down, jump-turning to the right and then the left but, just as he's about to enter the bowl's wider field, one of his edges catches and, with a flash of paralyzing panic, he knows he's going to fall forward.

The second time Luc stopped by, he texted one morning at 11.30 and asked if he might visit at 12.30 that afternoon. It'd been raining and his landscaping company had called it a day. Sam had already spread some blueprints out on his drafting table: a house in Cornish, New Hampshire, that he was designing for a French couple, a minimalist building with walls of translucent glass, a whimsical structure that they loved. Due for a meeting with his clients at 7 that evening, he'd promised to have everything finished, but figured, When am I going to get such a chance again—with somebody like this, somebody so open, so youthfully unguarded in the act of love? Then, too, Luc was as yet undeclared about what he ultimately wanted – men or women

– and could very easily have decided that one tumble with Sam was enough.

When the young man walked in the door, his Adidas bag slung over his shoulder, a sheepish, slightly frightened look on his face, Sam guessed Luc had probably thought a lot about their first encounter and that sheer compulsion had driven him to the second. As they were passing Sam's home office, Luc noticed the plans on the drafting table and wandered in.

"What are these?" he said, gently caressing the blueprints with a finger.

Sam approached and fit his chin on Luc's shoulder. "House I'm designing. Done a lot for these people. Did their place in France."

"Where at?" Luc said.

"A town called Lourmarin, it's in—"

"I know where it is. We know a Canadian lady who has a house there. And that guy who wrote all those books about Provence was really describing Lourmarin. Now our friend says it's overrun; it's ruined." Luc glanced at him with a smirk, then regarded the row of sharply focused photographs above the drafting table and smiled goofily. "Would these houses be your designs?"

"Yup. All local. Except for the one in France . . ." Sam pointed to a photo of the old stone house whose remodeling he'd overseen. "I've never done anything on a national scale."

Luc shrugged it off. "So what? You make a living at it, don't you? Better than blood sucking on Wall Street or ambulance chasing, right?" He winked. "Plus, you're sexy, *mon*," he said with a Caribbean accent. "Too sexy, really."

"What does that mean?"

Luc laughed. "I don't know, but don't make me explain it. Just keep being it." And then he kissed Sam.

"His moon is conjunct your sun," said a close friend of Sam's who dabbled in astrology (Luc had mentioned a birthday in August and Sam had asked him what day). "I mean, if he's the age he says he is."

Sharply skeptical of this new-age perception, Sam nevertheless said, "No, he is – he showed me his driving license when he could sense I was nervous . . . that he might be younger, not that he looks it."

"With his moon conjunct your sun, you'll always know pretty much what he's feeling, even when he's trying to hide it," the friend said.

That second day when they were in bed together, there was a great deal of emotion in Luc's pale eyes, and he started to use the word love to describe what they were doing. "Oh baby, I love it when you . . . I love when you do this to me." And every time Sam told Luc he was beautiful, Luc would turn it around and say, "No, you're the beautiful one, Sam," with his face in a kind of religious rapture.

————

Sam wakes up to a sky that has cooled, a lower sun and the snowfields taking on rosy color. He's lying at a critical angle, his right leg folded beneath him. He gasps, realizing something is terribly wrong, then glances around and spies his right ski lower down, sticking out of the snow, jack-knifed over itself, snapped in half, shocking. He can no longer feel his leg and yet there is pain pulsing everywhere in his body, electric surprises radiating from a dead zone. But then it fades for a bit; thankfully, it's not constant. Soon it occurs to him that it's more than just the skewed limb, divining a deeper wound. He is losing something, and he's losing it quickly, and he doesn't know quite what it is. And then hearing Mike calling – he'd almost forgotten Mike was there with him. At last Sam tunes in to the litany, and he's in an echo chamber: "Sam!" Sam! Sam! "You okay?" You okay? You okay?

Shifting his head to the right, Sam sees Mike 100 yards down, skis off and crisscrossed at one side, trying to scale the shallower part of the Cirque, near an outcropping of rocks, having terrific difficulty. "Don't try to get up here. Just call Life Flight," he manages.

"So it's that bad?"

"I think so. Stay there, Mike. You can't make it . . . up here."

Mike had once been a gymnast, but this was one of the steepest slopes on the North American continent.

"Are you cold?"

Sam takes a moment to assess. "Nah, I don't think so."

They've rented avalanche satellite phones that have Life Flight's number programmed in. Muted tones of conversation float up to him and then he hears Mike yell, "Okay, they're on their way!"

Though the pain slams him again, he is able to consider that this is his first – and maybe only – moment of relief. Life Flight is coming; it's in their hands now. They'll know what to do. Sam leans his head back, admonishing himself to rest despite the intermittent screams of his injured body. When they rented the phones they were told Life Flight was pretty quick, so maybe he'll have to endure another half hour of this? At first he thinks, okay, I think I can handle it, but then panics as he did once far out in Grafton Ponds, when he was swimming between two coniferous islands, growing afraid of drowning, and then turning on his back and trying to relax and then hearing the sound of loons, the birds that mate for life, calling out in their haunting lament. And then he discovers wetness, and manages to unzip his jacket and almost passes out when he spies the tremendous pooling of blood. And dimly wonders: what could possibly be causing this? How much have I lost?

The times Luc actually could drop by were not so numerous over the summer; his predicted arrivals always amended due to the vagaries of his parents or his job. Sam made him promise two things: that he'd never cancel at the last minute and that they'd ski together. And Luc taunted him, "As long as you can keep up with me."

"I'm fast – I'm really fast but I'm not reckless," Sam told him. "So even if you wait for me, it will only be ten or fifteen seconds."

"I'm just having you on," Luc said with that dazzling smile, youthful but manly, his baritone voice that always sounded so reasonable. "I'll wait for as long as necessary. Or maybe you'll be waiting for me."

"I hope so."

"Nobody knows anything about this or about me," Luc admitted later on in that conversation. "I've told none of my friends or my family. Nobody knows but the people I've been with. And most of them probably don't even remember my name."

But one did, a college professor who wanted a lot more than Luc could give – Luc finally had to break it off. Sam considered himself a lot smarter, realizing that Luc might not be able to give anything at all for the moment, and he would have to be fine with that. Like other younger men Sam had met, Luc tried to describe his tastes as veering between girls his own age and much older guys. But unlike the others, Luc admitted his attraction to men could overwhelm him.

One lazy afternoon several months after the tsunami struck Japan, they were sprawled over each other watching the Women's World Cup. Luc, who knew chapter and verse about the disaster, was rooting for the Japanese team, claiming that the devastated country's morale needed it. Sam was still pulling for the Americans. "And they deserve to win," Luc said emphatically. "Look at how beautifully they're playing. They're hot!" he said almost lasciviously. Sam couldn't help it; he found himself plummeting into jealous silence.

They were watching the American team struggle against a disciplined Japanese defense, when Luc turned to him. "I guess I can't get married," he said wistfully.

"Oh?"

"Couldn't bear the idea of cheating on my wife." Luc moved closer to him, his lips now only a few inches away. "And I would, especially if there were somebody like you around," he said sweetly.

A roar erupted from the television and both of them instinctively turned to learn that Japan had scored a goal.

"Yes!" Luc cheered, pumping a fist and then turning back to Sam with a different, more confident smile.

"You're right, though," Sam said, picking up the thread of their discussion. "It wouldn't be fair." And then he watched clouds of confusion and conflict drift over Luc's face. And hoped that this wisdom and self-awareness might even come to bear on what was between them.

Yes, against his better judgment and against all the advice of his savvy, caring friends, Sam was already hoping for something that he knew was nigh impossible, that Luc would eventually come to his senses and Sam would be there waiting for him. But this would never happen in the end, Luc still pledging himself to be at the mercy of women he wanted to date, claiming he could still love them deeply, and Sam was desolated to think that in the end this might be too big a hurdle to clear.

"I was thinking we could spend the night together, if you're up for that," one of Luc's texts said. Reviewing the message on his screen months later, Sam would realize they'd never once spoken on the phone. In advance of that visit, and in honor of Luc's arrival, he cooked a chicken Provençale, and they sat over candlelight eating and polishing off a twelve-pack of beer, boisterous and merry, Sam saying they were acting like two frat boys and Luc saying he wasn't into fraternities, never had wanted to join one, wasn't on Facebook either, and had done his sophomore year without a mobile phone. He was a soccer player on scholarship, his parents dutifully educating him at private institutions so that he'd have a chance.

"I like the fact that this is uncomplicated," Luc said that same night at the dinner table, candlelight flickering illusively on his face, so that in certain moments he looked older, more mature.

"Is it?" Sam wondered.

"Relatively, don't you think?" Luc asked, looking momentarily bewildered.

"Yes, but only because we get together on your schedule – on your time, not mine," Sam pointed out.

"So are you saying I've inconvenienced you?" Luc asked with a nervous chill, carefully lining up the amber bottles of beer that he had drunk so far, not meeting Sam's eyes.

"Look at me," Sam said, and when Luc did, he declared, "No!"

"Okay." Luc sounded relieved and smiled his sweet, intoxicating smile.

"But this is the sort of thing that can only flourish in . . . a hothouse environment," Sam tried to point out. "We can't be seen together in public. You're not out and . . . the age difference is obvious. I'm nearly the same age as your parents, so they'd certainly never understand."

"I guess what I meant," Luc went on, slightly frustrated, "is that we get together, we have fun, but we don't ask anything of each other. And then we're back in our own lives."

This had a hollow ring to it. And yet Sam thought to himself: their arrangement must be a relief to Luc, as most guys his age probably had a lot of childhood freight that would interfere in their relationships until they grew old enough and mature enough to jettison it. "Yes, agreed, but there's an emotional bond here," he pointed out.

Luc looked surprised. "Of course there is. I couldn't do it if there wasn't."

"All I'm saying is that's where it can get tricky . . . unfortunately," Sam said. "And even when you don't want it to get complicated, it always seems to. Even when you remind yourself of all the pitfalls . . ." He hesitated, and then said, "Because in the end, the heart wants what it wants."

The weather had changed yet again in Luc's face; a look of deep affection was suffusing it now, and he reached forward with a large, chafed hand and took Sam's. "All I know is I really want you," he said.

That night, Luc wanted to be taken more fiercely than ever, coaxing Sam to go harder and harder so that it all began to feel like punishment. But Luc's face was slack in sublime pleasure. And then it arrived, his unqualified, "I love you, Sam," when Sam was still inside him. Carried away, Luc probably didn't realize he'd said it, and so Sam didn't repeat it back for fear of drawing attention to it and possibly startling the exotic bird from its perch into flight. But he carried it with him, the simple affirmation chanted over and over again during the life of love affairs, but which he'd heard only a few times in a whisper. And it had more meaning for him than all the people who'd ever loved him in his life, and all the people he'd ever loved, and all the people to whom he had repeatedly said exactly the same thing.

That night, Luc slept spooning Sam with his arm draped over Sam's chest. And fell asleep almost immediately. Sam knew he'd have to extricate himself to get any sleep, but refused to do so, not wanting to end the backward embrace, telling himself he could own it temporarily if only he just stayed awake. And he did, all night, until he could spy shadows on the walls of his bedroom, until the sky faded into light. All the while Luc slept deeply, innocently, his mouth slightly open, his breath souring. It was real life, albeit briefly, maybe even real love, named hours before in a sort of fever, a shiny token tossed into a deep well that still glimmered from far below. Luc was gone by eight in the morning, and listening to his car drive away with a crushing of gravel, Sam felt so alone.

Somehow, Mike manages to reach him; he's there looking at Sam with composed concern. The pain has preternaturally subsided again, and yet Sam can no longer move, can barely even swivel his head, and realizes, even before he gets alarmed, that his breathing is sharp and fast. And then recognizes he's gone into atrial fibrillation, something that happens only when he's under extreme stress, the episodes sometimes lasting a torturous few hours: his heart racing erratically, his blood pumping inefficiently, the beats scattering like discordant music, making it impossible to climb stairs, to lie down. When it happens, he feels like an athlete who goes down in the middle of a race that he's trained for studiously. Normally, he'd keep checking his pulse, hoping for sinus rhythm to resume, but now he can't even move his arms.

"How did you get here?" he says, breathless from his fluttering heart.

"I managed – I'm a gymnast, don't worry. I can climb anything. I couldn't be down there just looking up at you struggling. I had to reach you."

"Can't move very much," Sam groans, peering at Mike, whose distressed, different-colored eyes are glinting light off the snow.

"I know, Sam, I know. And you've lost a lot of blood. But maybe I shouldn't be saying that."

"Already figured that out." He forfeits the ability to speak for a moment. And then says, "Why did I?"

"I think you smashed into a rock. There's an open wound."

"Then don't . . . let . . . me . . . bleed!" Sam wants to add, "to death," but can't bring himself. Not yet. He debates telling Mike about his erratically beating atrium but decides not to.

"I don't think it's so bad now." Mike has unzipped Sam's orange shell and lifted his inner fleece to study the oozing wound. "But I just can't tell." He pivots around and checks the sky. "I don't see them. Where the *fuck* are they?" And the tough little guy shakes his head and Sam can see tears on his ruddy cheeks.

"It's okay, Mike," he says, finding himself doing the comforting.

Mike snorts a laugh and says, "Don't say that. I'm supposed to be telling *you* that."

"Well, I'm telling you. Okay?"

Mike's voice breaks again. "Okay, Sam."

And then the first of the shadows comes down like a bird of prey with a wide wingspan, or maybe it's a cloud dappling the sun, but it glides over the white parchment on which he lies, over the glistening gorges that have melted in the midday warmth and are, as evening comes on, cooling into quicksilver ice. He feels it in the part of him that can still feel, and thinks of his mother, dead now for a decade, whom he could have sworn was breathing on his neck the last time he was seriously injured: mountain biking. That was two years ago when he was lying in a hospital getting pebbles picked out of his road rash.

"Road rage," he says aloud and laughs, light-headed.

Damn, his heart again, beating like a fickle fiend. He wishes at the very least that it would just revert to normal rhythm; all of this would be much easier and the relief would be almost narcotic. Can't he just deal with one malfunction at a time? He feels stupid now worrying so much about trivial things, about aging, about being too old for guys he was attracted to, about being too old for Luc. What did it matter, the age difference?

Hadn't he read something somewhere that the frontal lobes of men younger than twenty-five were still developing, which meant their assessment of risk was evolving, their sense of responsibility, their dependability? But Luc believed Sam was the risk-taker because Sam rode a motorcycle and actually carried around a note in his wallet that spelled out where he lived and that he had a dog who would need to be let out, and whom to call in an emergency. Luc had always worried that news of a motorcycle wreck would never reach him, but refrained from asking Sam to give anyone his name and number. How ironic. But wasn't the point of these sudden switchbacks of fate to shed light on that which was never true and now needed to be made true?

Toward the end of August, a girl dawned into the picture, somebody Luc had dated who'd moved to the West Coast but returned to Vermont and surprised him and wanted to stay at his house. And of course, Luc's mother, who loved her, wanted this, and so he couldn't come. Couldn't visit. Or at least his texts said that and who knew the real story? In retrospect, Sam realized it didn't matter; what mattered was Luc had pulled back, probably because he knew he was returning to school, back to the regulated life of college athletes and – maybe his nascent frontal lobes just couldn't reconcile it. And his parents had to drive him back to Middlebury; he'd rented a car for the summer and turned it in a week before his departure. After that, Sam would receive texts, mostly late at night, and suspected they were sent when Luc had been drinking. The messages were often interrogative: "Why is it the way it is with us? Why can't I put my finger on it? Why can't I understand it? Why do I think you can see into me? Why do I hate that? But why do I love it, too? Why do I hear you talking in my head? Why do I love being underneath you? Why do I think about borrowing a car and driving down to see you, even if it's only for the night?"

Why only for the night? Sam wondered, puzzled; it was as though Luc were living under some self-imposed curfew. But then Luc broke down and borrowed a car and drove down from Middlebury.

In the meantime, Sam followed his soccer games, against Amherst and Williams and Cornell – all in all a mediocre season for Middlebury. Luc was a defensive full back so he had few opportunities to score. But there was one brilliant moment against Bowdoin, available on YouTube, when Luc had captured an opponent's pass and, from fairly far out in the field, slam-kicked one into the goal, his teammates crowding around him, hugging him, leaping on him, tousling his hair. He was taller than most of them and almost looked like a serious doting father overwhelmed by his exuberant children.

And for a moment Sam could imagine his younger lover not quite so young anymore and that made him terribly sad.

The last time they saw each other was a few days before Christmas; on winter break, Luc had shaved off his beard and arrived with a scrubbed face, wearing a red sweater with snowflakes and looking so retro quaint Sam had to laugh. And it was surprisingly easy between them, never awkward, and Sam thought: Maybe we'll just keep getting together on and off for the next five years, and maybe by then something will turn over in him. Surely, he'll realize . . . eventually?

That last night, when they'd achieved their rhythm and, soaring in his own pleasure, Luc looked longingly at Sam and said, "I want you to come inside me."

"I shouldn't," Sam replied. "I can't guarantee."

"Doesn't matter. I know you're okay."

It occurred to Sam that Luc had come of age when the plague was no longer so scary, and he'd read somewhere that very young people weren't taking precautions. "No, I can't, Luc."

"You have to, Sam. What happens if this is the last time I see you?"

Sam stopped his motions, frightened at the words. "But why, why would that be?"

"I don't know! But we can't be sure of anything. Can we?"

"But we have to trust that—"

"Just do it!" Luc cried. "Don't you want to?"

And then Sam burst into sobs, now believing that this actually might be the very last time, the only moment. His tears fell on the younger man's chest and Luc looked stricken. "What's wrong now?" he said with a tinge of impatience.

"I love you, is what's wrong now," Sam admitted.

"I love you too," Luc mumbled with less conviction, but Sam convinced himself that it was much scarier for him to say. "Fuck!" Luc exclaimed. "Just do it, please."

And so it happened, and then Christmas happened, and after Christmas Luc left for skiing in Wyoming. And then, he fell out of contact, no longer texted, no longer returned Sam's reasonably written messages. They never ended up skiing together and Sam never saw Luc again.

————

In his delirium, Sam actually believes that he sees the speck of the helicopter before Mike does and vaguely wonders how they're going to dig him out of the snow and put him on a stretcher. Surely they understand – his breathing is even shallower, but he's no longer afraid for some odd reason, sleepy rather, and it seems as though he sleeps with open eyes. The helicopter seems to arrive more quickly than he can imagine and he observes a kind of spider's web of rope drifting down, attendants in white jumpsuits floating toward him, and vaguely wonders why they're dressed this way, and if maybe the hospital garb is in winter pallor. It makes sense, doesn't it? Their hands seem so soft as they tend to him; miraculously, they are able to create a trench around him and effortlessly pry him out, and he has a halo of snow around him. He's like some weird, crooked angel who fell into the Cirque when he should've been flying overhead on some astral plane. Mike is smiling in stupefied relief; the ropes are finally attached to the stretcher and Sam is lifted gently, rocking in the air, rising like steam toward the whirring helicopter blade.

And during that imaginary ascension, Sam pictures an art opening in Lebanon, New Hampshire, noticing a plump woman with salt-and-pepper hair held in place with a girlish beret, a woman with a grave, florid face carrying a pitcher of red hibiscus tea with the name tag Eleanor Flanders, the name he recognized from his first Google search. He can't help but stare at her, desperate to see Luc's likeness in her face; could she really be out in this harsh world merely two months into her grief?

He shakes his head and then an opposing thought: surely she has to try and keep busy, so why not? But unfortunately he has stared at her for too long and she catches his gaze and migrates over to him.

"Do I know you?" she asks. And he thinks: grief has cracked open her soul, she'll talk to strangers now because she's distraught, she's wrecked, her life is ruined, it will never, ever be the same for her. As his own tears come, he tries to staunch them at first and manages to say, "I heard about your son. I'm so sorry for your loss. I was just thinking about . . . well, I lost . . . a . . . young . . . too," he hears himself say.

"Your son?" she asks quickly, incredulous at the possibility of such a coincidence.

He nods his head. "Yes," he says and immediately feels ashamed. In her fluted sigh he recognizes the exhalation of a soul that keens every time it breathes. "Then I'm sad for you," she tells him. "I just hope people have been as kind to you as they've been to me. I wish you knew him. I wish you knew my son."

"Me too," he says, conjuring up the girl who visited Luc at the end of the summer (and maybe there never was such a person) calling to say Luc had written his name and number down and made her promise both to relay the message if it ever came down to it and never to speak about it to anyone. Because Sam reads the *New York Times* instead of the local paper, he would never have heard the news until the faltering voice broke it. After she calls, he sees himself collapsing in his kitchen and retreating to bed, and his friends having to visit and plead with him to go on with his life. And having to keep explaining to them that when

Luc arrived that first afternoon in his mother's Mini Cooper, some lost part of him had . . . returned: Sam was young and hardy again with no lines on his face and a fierce determination to get ahead, even to make love without restraint. And even though their affair was painfully brief, Luc had resurrected him.

He's slowly drifting now, almost looking down on himself injured in the middle of the Cirque and sleep coming on in the second wave of shadows.

And then he actually fancies Eleanor Flanders calling him. Yes, that somehow she has figured it out, but mothers always do, so they say.

"We met the other night," she'll remind him.

"Ah, we did."

"I have this strange feeling that you know more than you're saying."

"Do I?"

"I believe you do."

"Why would you think that?"

"Because I was told that you don't have a son," she will say angrily. "So why would you lie about that? Why would you ever tell me such a horrible, awful lie?"

Why, indeed?

"But I think you knew Lucas," she will say, her voice stinging Sam with the sound of her son's proper name. "I think he was in your life in a way that I wouldn't understand. Except . . . well, I have to try to understand now, don't I?"

"I guess you do," Sam will agree.

"I think . . ." she'll falter and then proclaim, "I think he loved you."

"No," Sam will say, "I think I loved him."

———

"I think you've been dreaming," Mike says now, stroking his face, and in a final moment of clarity, Sam realizes this is true. He peers up through the deepening shadows, up at the darkening decline of Wolverine Cirque and then hears the sound of blades hacking the air. Mike tilts Sam's head so he can see the helicopter hovering above them; it's no longer a dream now. Somebody in blue surgical scrubs is appearing at the door, and his last lingering thought is: Mike might never be able to reach the college boy who, several months ago, broke his best friend's heart.

Past Caring
Rupert Smith

Andrew Adams awoke one morning to discover that he no longer gave a shit.

After so many deaths and disappointments, so many jobs left and lovers who had left him, he had run out of the small stock of fortitude with which the creator equipped him. He lay alone in a double bed, dry-eyed and sore-throated, and thought about starting the day with a martini. But one would lead to another and possibly the fatal third, and what was the point of pleasure if you only hurt yourself?

On a normal day, Andrew showered and shaved, had breakfast, ironed a shirt and left for work at eight o'clock, whether he needed to or not. Usually not. His career, as he laughingly called it, had not been crowned with success. He was currently a part-time tutor at a second-rate college, failing to inspire students with his stale knowledge, but at least he had a desk and an office and the illusion of purpose.

But this was not a normal day. Perhaps there would never be another normal day. Why go to work at all? He didn't need the money. Why bother with the students? They weren't interested. Why iron a shirt? Why shave? Why wash? Nobody got close enough to smell him. If he had everything delivered, he could take to his bed for good. Who would suffer? Who would even notice? Colleagues? No. Students? Sigh of relief, probably. Not even his mother, who at least had the excuse of being recently dead, depriving him in one fell swoop of his only confidante and his only restraint. No need, with her gone, to remain respectable, or even to work. She left enough to keep him for the rest of his life. The mortgage was paid off, and if he was careful he could feed and heat himself for another forty years.

By then he'd be ninety, the age his mother reached, and someone else could pay to bury him.

No more nightly phone calls, discussing the weather and the latest deaths.

No more weekend visits for cooking and cleaning and keeping the care workers in line.

Just an empty house far away, full of unwanted possessions and, when that was sold, all trace of her was gone. Distant memories of the mother she had been, firm of purpose, high of standard, determined that Andrew would go the right way. And then he became the carer, and everything changed.

He took a sip of water to relieve his mouth and throat, administered eye drops to separate eyelid from cornea, and blew his nose hard enough to clear blocked nostrils and stuffy ears. Every morning was a process of switching on failing body parts. In the kitchen he made up and swallowed a glass of fibre supplement to get his bowels working. In the bathroom, he stuck a suppository up his arse to relieve his piles, and took two paracetamol for the general pain of living.

And then, as he took off his pyjamas, Andrew experienced an urge he had not had since the age of fifteen.

He fancied a fag.

He replaced his pyjamas, put a coat over the top and left the flat in his slippers. There was a kiosk across the road where he sometimes bought a newspaper, and now, feeling an unaccustomed thrill, he asked for twenty Rothmans. They cost a lot more than he was expecting, and if this were to become a habit he would have to recalculate his finances.

There was a tiny park on the corner, just big enough for some unused children's play equipment and a clump of overgrown laurels which gave shelter to those who slept, injected, defecated and sometimes died there. Andrew sat on a bench, pulled the cellophane off his fag packet and dropped it to the ground. He felt a hot surge of delight. The foil insert was balled up and flicked into the bushes. And I, thought Andrew, who once campaigned for extended recycling facilities in the borough. But that was long ago in his optimistic thirties when he had a Green boyfriend and a passion for social justice. Gone, gone, gone.

The smell of tobacco took him back further, to a fleeting moment of camaraderie with his schoolfellows when they shared illicit cigarettes down by the castle ruins at lunch time, sitting under cherry trees, woozy from the smoke, talking about girls. It didn't last. They started going somewhere else and didn't tell him where. He went back to lunch times in the library.

But for a moment he remembered the pleasure and not the disappointment, and took the same pleasure in the pristine whiteness of the filters, the perfect roundness of rolled papers, bunched tight in three rows, seven, six, seven. He drew one out, smelled it, put it in his mouth, tasted it, anticipating the curls of smoke, the sense of belonging. And then he realized that he didn't have a light.

He shuffled back to the kiosk in his slippers, starting to feel ridiculous, and would have bolted for the safety of home until he saw, leaning against the wall, a young man in a grey tracksuit, hood up, smoking.

Well, why not? What could happen? A curse, maybe. It was too busy for blows, unless he was psychotic. He didn't look psychotic.

Andrew pulled his coat tight, and hoped that his pyjama trousers (a muted blue-and-white check) would pass for daywear.

"Excuse me . . ."

The youth fumbled in his pocket, drew out a green plastic lighter, handed it over without comment or eye contact.

Andrew lit his cigarette, inhaled, tilted his head back and exhaled a long, regular stream of smoke. "Aaaaah," he said, already feeling the intoxication. "Thank you."

He gave the lighter back. The boy had badly bitten nails, his brow furrowed as if in deep thought. Some guidance, perhaps, some advice from a more-experienced older man . . .

The boy separated himself from the wall and slouched away.

But it was a start. Human contact, and with a desirable, unsuitable human who gave him fire, the primal gift, the spark of life, defiance to the gods, oh the burden of over-education, the terrible crushing burden of knowledge, all lifting away now, floating up with the smoke. There would be another and, if that failed, another, just wait and they will come, you can pluck them from the streets, back to your flat, your bed, nobody to disapprove, and if they murder you, nobody to grieve.

He returned to the park to smoke. *It will kill you*, said a voice in his head – his mother's, perhaps. *You will get lung cancer. You will start looking old.*

He inhaled again, sucking the smoke so hard he could feel wrinkles forming as his face caved in. And he did not care. If I die early, thought Andrew, I can spend more money in the time I have left, and if I have money it doesn't matter what I look like because if I want it, I can buy it.

That boy in the tracksuit, for instance. What would he do for fifty quid? A hundred?

Prostitution is a cancer in society, an assault on the human spirit.

"I really *don't* give a shit," said Andrew, and wondered if there was anything else he no longer cared about. He looked at his watch. Eight thirty. He had a class at eleven, but he found he didn't care about that either, and sat back down to finish his cigarette.

He would not go in. Today, or ever again.

No job, no income, no status, no structure.

Don't care, don't care, don't care, don't care.

No mother to worry. It just doesn't matter.

"So what," said Andrew, and tossed his still-burning stub into the dry leaves around the railings. It had not rained for weeks – drought loomed, but Andrew didn't care about that either – and he might easily have started a fire, endangering life and putting extra pressure on the emergency services.

"Ha!" he said, and almost skipped from the park, light-headed with indifference.

He needed the toilet in a hurry and ran across the road, slippers flapping against the tarmac. Usually it took hours of unsatisfactory pushing and clenching to empty his bowels, but now it was coming with youthful urgency and vigour. Already he was feeling the benefits of his new lifestyle. He got to his bathroom with seconds to spare, and rose a minute later feeling half a stone lighter. All that money wasted on laxatives when he could have just taken up smoking.

A coffee, that's what he wanted, something to kick-start the day. A very strong coffee. Or really, a drink. He had a colleague once, a woman with a massive but well-managed drink problem, who was rumoured to have gin on her cornflakes and bring wine to her desk in a large styrofoam cup with a lid, disguised as tea. She seemed to manage. She was no less productive than her sober co-workers. Apart from the smell, you'd never have known, at least not until she was admitted to hospital with acute renal failure and never returned.

Heavy drinking also meant some financial recalculations and the possibility of early death, a prospect that Andrew faced with equanimity, even cheerfulness. To die, to sleep, and no fear of the afterlife to screw that up. He hadn't made a will; there were better uses for the few hundred quid it would cost: several bottles of supermarket own-brand vodka, for instance. If he died intestate, then his cousins would get a nice surprise.

Vodka. That was a drink for the morning. Clean and odourless. Gin at lunchtime, Scotch for the evenings. A very cold vodka, perhaps a squeeze of lemon for freshness and vitamin C, pop in a soluble aspirin and it could be the universal panacea.

There was a bottle in the freezer, almost held fast by ice, and it took a bit of chipping with a knife to get it out, snow on the floor, but there it was, thickened by cold, ready for the throat. Andrew poured two fingers of it into a tumbler, and stared into it as if he were looking into the very mouth of perdition, and then thought "sod it" and drank the lot in one gulp. It slipped down like jelly and as soon as it hit his stomach he began to count.

One . . . two . . . three . . . four . . . five . . . six . . .

By seven he felt the first inklings of inebriation, and by twelve he couldn't be fucking bothered to count any more and poured himself another.

And lit a fag from the stove.

It was not quite nine o'clock. At college, students would be assembling for their first lectures and tutorials of the day. Two hours till he was on. Time to sober up and put this lapse behind him.

He drank the second drink and, when that was gone, another.

No going back now.

By ten past nine, Andrew was drunker than he'd been for years. Any more and he'd be vomiting or unconscious. If there was purpose in his debauch, he must at least be conscious.

The walls were starting to slip and slide. Time for some deep breaths and cold water before the day ended prematurely. A shower, for sanity if not for hygiene.

Brush the teeth and dress. It's one thing not to care, quite another to give up.

He dressed to look young and carefree. Jeans, obviously; there was a pair he could still get into, relic of the days before he moved permanently into corduroy and flannel. A T-shirt? Did he own such a thing? He leafed through his wardrobe, work shirts, work shirts, work shirts, fucking work shirts, short-sleeved, long-sleeved, he threw them on the bed in a crumpled pile, and found a polo shirt, white with a bold blue stripe; it had been left behind by a friend who stayed disappointingly on the sofa bed, laundered and cherished for a while, harbinger of a hoped-for return and then forgotten. "A-*ha!*" said Andrew, with a note of triumph, even vengeance, "you will do."

And so, looking like any other unemployed middle-aged man, Andrew set off on an adventure, with nothing in his pockets but his keys, a wallet, eighteen Rothmans and a box of matches.

———

The streets that Andrew had walked in varying degrees of depression for the last twenty-five years now seemed fraught with possibility.

He felt like a fish entering water, a bird taking flight, absorbed and buoyed by his surroundings, eager to merge with the other luminous entities that swam or flew around him. Quick, he thought, before the low replaces the high and I see only dog shit and syringes and not the beauty and potential. The beauty, the beauty . . . him, him, him, swimming past him, that one, that one, they would all do, any of them, in any combination, they had only to see as he was seeing, feel as he was feeling, the oneness, the simplicity.

This feeling lasted until Andrew realized that he was weaving and staggering rather than swimming or flying, his mouth hanging wetly open, eyelids half-closed. People were avoiding him – prim, uptight people with places to go, straight, sober and disapproving, a thousand fragments of his mother's watchful spirit each in a new host to censure him.

He grabbed some railings and managed after a few attempts to come to a full halt. Just another drunk, and anyone could see him – employers, students, neighbours. *I don't care, I don't care*, he kept saying, but the tightening in his chest, the griping in his guts told a different story. How hard it is, really, to throw off the shackles, even when you have nothing to stop you. Whirling through space without brakes, slipping so easily out of the world, as easily as a razor blade across the throat, and suddenly Andrew wanted very much to live and be part of the world, and he was holding on by a thread. He screwed up his eyes and swallowed hard to quell the nausea. He gripped the railings so hard it hurt. Finally the whirling stopped, the panic subsided, and when he looked at his hands the skin was white and heavily indented where the metal bars had pressed in.

He belched, a sour, rotten smell bubbling up from his dying organs, booze and fags and decay, falling apart like a vampire in sunlight. Time to go home. Back to bed. Phone in sick, sleep it off, and when you wake up have a long talk with yourself. You're not the first middle-aged man to fall to pieces when his last surviving parent dies. You're dealing with grief. This is one of the stages. He'd read about them once, and didn't remember "three vodkas before 10 a.m." in the list, but he was pretty sure that was covered by "denial". Apply for compassionate leave. No one would object to that.

And so, with a pang of regret for his short-lived freedom, Andrew turned his slippers homewards. Just another disappointment, another "what if?" that would never be answered. What if someone had loved him? If he'd got a proper job? Published a book? Had children? But those avenues were closed now, nothing left but a long straight road to the grave.

He hadn't gone far. Just two streets away from his house. It took all of three minutes. So much for not caring. He didn't even have the courage to flee. What was life without courage? All he had was fear of failure.

"It's sad, believe me, missy, when you're born to be a sissy, without the vim and verve," he sang softly to himself, turning, as so often in times of difficulty, to MGM musicals for consolation. He even essayed a sad little step-ball-change as if he too were off to see the Wizard, but there was nothing behind the curtain for Andrew, not even a kindly old charlatan, and no Dorothy either. No brainless, heartless fellow-travellers. No faithful Toto. Nothing. Regular drinkers will recognize that Andrew had slipped into the self-pitying stage.

There was a supermarket delivery van parked outside his house, wheels up on the pavement which made it difficult to squeeze past, and he was ready with some disapproving comment such as "other people do live here, you know" until he saw the driver. Stepping out of the vehicle, six foot something and almost as broad with a long hooked stick in his hand, like something out of a Jean Genet novel, thought Andrew, who had flicked through those turgid volumes in search of the good bits when he was a bookish teenager. Shaven head, bad teeth, a face like an old boot, deeply lined. Arms like a gorilla, thick and hairy. Andrew felt the familiar flush of desire, took in the barrel chest, the outward curve of the stomach, the mighty thighs, and then looked away, fiddling with his keys.

"All right, mate!"

Andrew officially disapproved of "mate" as a form of address, but in this case he was willing to overlook it. "Morning," he said, trying to sound businesslike and not drunk.

"Lovely day." The accent was somewhere between London and Lodz, roughened by shouting and smoking.

"Yes," Andrew said in a way that hardly invited further conversation, but he found that the man was staring at him with a smile on his face. There was a gold tooth somewhere in there, stage right, upper circle, about row E. He held the stick upright at his side, like a soldier resting on his spear. One of the Germanic legions, perhaps, SPQR and a goatskin tunic.

"Lovely." A huge ham of a hand rubbed the bristly skull. There was a faded tattoo between thumb and index finger. A prison mark? What did it mean? Killer? Sex fiend?

"Well, I'd better . . ." said Andrew, and got his key in the lock as fast as his trembling hands would allow. He glanced back before closing the door. The man was still looking, smiling, waiting.

Andrew scurried inside, short of breath. He needed the toilet again. He wondered if he was going to be sick. From outside came the familiar clank and thump of groceries being delivered. The driver would be humping those boxes upstairs, muscles bulging, and the harassed single mother who lived up there with three noisy floorboard-thumping kids would barely give him a second look.

Andrew went to the front window, on a level with the door. A quick look, and Christ! There he was, three crates in his brawny arms, turning to meet Andrew's eyes at exactly the right time, zap, looks locked, again the smile, the gold tooth, the deep lines deepening, a slight nod as if in acknowledgement and agreement. Acknowledgement of what? What sign had passed between them? What contract had Andrew entered into with looks and words and smiles?

He retreated into the shadows and busied himself with a lever-arch file containing documents relating to his mother's estate, letters from solicitors, banks and a hefty correspondence with HMRC. He looked busy and purposeful, his presence near the window quite justified and natural. Near enough to see out, far enough to be a murky presence from without, especially on a bright day like this.

But no, there it was again, the locking of eyes – they were blue, a very bright blue – and the flashing of teeth, the raising of the eyebrows to say, "Okay mate, we both know what's happening, wait and I shall come."

Andrew nodded and felt so astonished by his own boldness that he buried his face in a schedule of assets. Only after a few seconds did he realize it was upside down.

The last crate was delivered, upstairs' door slammed and the driver was away down the front steps, intent on an electronic device, never a backward glance. Andrew closed the file and felt the relief of a great danger avoided. But then, unexpectedly, came anger, disappointment and self-disgust. Why had he not followed through? Why had the driver given up so easily? Could he not see what was there, on offer, everything that Andrew had, his bed, his body, his heart, his home, all there for the taking if only he had the balls to turn around and . . .

Rattle, bang! The side door of the van was shut, and here was the driver again, bouncing across the street, light on his feet for a heavy-set man, an empty plastic water bottle in his hand, pointing at the bottle, pointing at the door, at Andrew.

So easy to look away, to carry on reading, post office savings account, accrued interest, pension arrears, funeral account . . .

But instead he found that his feet were moving across the carpet to the door and into the hall, someone else was at the controls, not Andrew Adams but Mr Vodka, perhaps, or the new Andrew who didn't care any more, who would take risks for uncertain rewards. He watched his fingers opening the locks.

There he was, filling the doorframe, all dark-blue polyester silhouetted against the day, the clear plastic of the empty bottle a bright spot in the massive darkness.

"Can I use your tap?"

"Of course," said Andrew, as if it was the most natural thing in the world, a service that any stranger would ask of another, I thirst, you have water, I bring my pitcher to your well. "It's just down here." He led his guest to the kitchen, where at least there were no dirty breakfast things to embarrass him, just a half-empty vodka bottle and a still-wet glass.

"Ah, vodka!" said the driver, sounding distinctly foreign now. "Good!" A big smile and a huge hand patting the belly. He smacked his lips.

"Yes," said Andrew, trying to think up an excuse, but there was no need. The driver didn't care, and wouldn't tell. There was no one to tell.

The tap was running, the bottle filling.

"I get thirsty." The driver took a long drink, and went back to the tap.

"I'm sure you do. All that heavy lifting. Driving around in the sunshine." Andrew was babbling, and there were no railings to grab. "Must be very tiring. I mean, I hardly ever drive in London, not if I can avoid it, so I really don't know how you manage."

The driver nodded. "Day off?"

Andrew made a play of looking at his watch, but he hadn't put it on. "Just the morning," he said, unwilling to be thought unemployed. "Got to go in soon."

"Soon?"

"In a while."

"Nice." He drank again, wiped his mouth on the back of his hand. Stubble crackled. "In a while."

"Yes. I suppose so."

Silence, and again the nodding and smiling as if they were both in on the secret. "I drive around all day," said the driver, patting his stomach and lifting his shirt. "I get fat." It was a drastic change of subject but it seemed to justify the exposure of hairy flesh.

"Oh, I think you're in pretty good shape," said Andrew, and the die was cast. He patted his own stomach, flat at least, but saggy where the driver's was firm. "I should get more exercise."

"You do what I do." He bunched up the other arm, biceps stretching the fabric. "Don't need no gym."

Andrew reached out and touched, squeezed, held. How many words had they exchanged to get from there to here? So few, and none of them to the point.

"You like it?"

"Yes. Very much."

The driver's other hand moved down to his crotch. "Here."

Andrew hesitated.

"Go on."

He reached out and took what he wanted, a large polyester-wrapped handful.

"Never done this before," said the driver with a wink. "It's all right."

Neither have I, thought Andrew, but he wanted to seem more experienced, and it all seemed so easy, and he said, in his polite college tutor's voice, "Shall I?"

"Yeah?" A question, rather than permission.

"If you'd like me to."

In reply, the driver leaned against the work surface and pulled down his pants. Andrew knelt, neither caring nor even wondering whether he was overlooked.

———

When it was over, the driver wiped himself and left, still smiling. "No doubt you have many calls of a similar character to make in the neighbourhood," said Andrew once the door was shut. He had not touched himself, nor did he particularly want to. Save that for later, when the incident had resolved itself into a narrative. Now the panic of reality was all too acute. It was barely ten o'clock. Still time, thought Andrew, feeling stone-cold sober, to make it to class. He looked in the bathroom mirror. Apart from a little dried residue around his mouth and cheeks, there were no particular marks of dissipation. If he hurried now he could make it. He splashed himself with cold water and squeezed toothpaste on to his brush.

But no, he would not do that, he could still taste the driver and the vodka and the tobacco, sensory evidence of his lost morning, and would he now erase that with minty freshness? No. At last he had a secret life, and he was damned if he was going to relinquish it so easily.

The world that on waking seemed so worn out now throbbed with expectation. A daytime drinker, a promiscuous homosexual picking up rough trade in the streets, on his very doorstep, the breakfast vodka not yet dry in the glass, a few dying sperms still wriggling around his buccal mucosa. Neighbours said that Mr Adams seemed such a quiet, ordinary man. Colleagues and students were shocked to discover his secret life. His mother . . . ah, well his mother was unavailable for comment. "She must be turning in her grave," said distant relatives, angry no doubt that dear cousin Andrew left the whole lot to a supermarket delivery driver. The flat, the residue of his mother's estate, the savings, the lot. "I was so surprised," said Polish-born Vlad or Andrzej or whatever his name might be, "he was a nice gentleman but we barely knew each other," no mention of the weeks, months, years perhaps of regular visits that developed into something more, friendship, love even, tragically cut short by Andrew's early death, a green harvest.

He brushed away a tear as he changed into his work clothes. A clean shirt from the pile on the bed, slightly crumpled now, but that was nothing. Charcoal trousers with a subtle pinstripe, rather shiny on the thighs and seat, but they'd do for another year. Matching jacket in need of dry-cleaning. Black socks. One of his father's ties around his neck like a yoke. Back to the fold, back to the pen.

Unwashed, unshaven, hurrying out of the house, the hangover starting as he boarded the bus, but it was too early yet to take more paracetamol. Ibuprofen when he got to work, there was always some in his drawer. An hour's class, a three-hour wait before another in the afternoon, then home.

It was quite empty on the upper deck, now that rush hour was over. A handful of people all sitting alone, spaced evenly apart. Andrew sat four rows from the front. The bus laboured through traffic, the branches of plane trees clattering against nearside windows, sirens and engines and ringtones and the importunate voice of the bus itself announcing stops to idiot passengers. Andrew stared until he was blind, mouldy flowers blooming in his eyes, and wanted very much to die. There was so little to keep him here. Just routine. The expectations of a woman he could no longer hurt. A bright hectic moment with a stranger in his kitchen was all that he knew of love, and it was not enough to live on. He had failed in all respects in that matter, and saying "I don't care" wasn't going to change the fact; he was fifty years old, not fifteen, old enough to know that pain will endure whether you care about it or not.

There was a horse chestnut on the corner by the bus stop where Andrew got off, a tree that always gave him pleasure whatever the season, and now it was glorious, the leaves green, yellow and brown, the branches heavy with conkers. He looked up through the canopy and saw the bright blue September sky, felt the freshness of autumn air on his dirty face, and wondered if the illusion of oneness with nature might get him through another day, as it had often before. He stooped to pick up a conker, shiny and waxy and the richest of browns, a strange token from his childhood when things were vivid and hopeful, each day a lifetime, and little Andrew was cared for, carefree. He put the conker in his pocket and went to work.

Vasya (February, 1950)
David Llewellyn

He stepped out through the doors beneath the station's clock tower, his coat held around him and his hands clasped tightly in his armpits. He was forty years old but prematurely grey and uncommonly thin, even by the standards of the time and, as he exited the station, he looked out at Leningrad as if it still might be a mirage. The city was grey and the snowflakes fell like ashes after a forest fire.

From everything he had been told these last few years, Sergey Grekov was anticipating ruins – hollow buildings and charred timbers, streets strewn with rubble. Instead, he found it repainted and rebuilt, and yet the place felt strangely different, as if everything had been moved around in his absence, as you might rearrange the furniture in an old room, and he wondered if these changes were real, or if he had simply misremembered the city as it was.

From Vitebskiy Station to Nevsky Prospect the streets were all but deserted, the few people Sergey passed looking shabby, not at all how he remembered them. Moscow, to him, was always the peasant city, the place where everyone looked as if they'd just arrived from the country. Not Petrograd.

Nevsky was busier. There, he moved through a shuffling black mass of other people as a xylophone-ribbed dog shivered and kept pace with him along the gutter. Trams glided past, whispering through the slush, their passengers pressed against windows opaque with steam, and the bell of a nearby clock struck one.

The last time he had seen this street, it was through the windows of a police car, in the early hours of a Tuesday morning. It was August then, the air already humid, and stuffier still inside the car. He remembered one of the agents, a lad barely older than twenty, lighting his cigarette for him – his own hands were cuffed – and the way the car was filled almost immediately with smoke.

As a younger man, Leningrad's winters had seemed so much colder to him than this – too cold to stay outside for more than a few minutes, and certainly too cold to consider walking very far – but the last leg of his journey saw him sharing a cramped train compartment with ten others for a day and a half. He and his fellow passengers had taken it in turns to sit, but even then, even when it was his turn, he didn't get much sleep. Cold as it now was, it felt good to be outside, and besides, he had known far colder.

His papers told him to report to the tenement building no earlier than 3 p.m. and so, to pass the time, he found a café a short distance from Nevsky where he ordered coffee, a bowl of *rassolnik* and some black bread from the lanky, docile youth behind the counter.

Sergey had thought he might see more MGB agents, secret-service men, both on the train coming in to Leningrad and in the city itself. In the north there had been so many of them it often seemed as if all those who weren't prisoners were secret service. Perhaps here in the city they preferred to remain hidden. Perhaps that toothless fool behind the counter was MGB, or the old woman taking tiny spoonfuls of some grey, indeterminate mush from her bowl. Perhaps everyone in Leningrad – except for him – was in the secret police.

The soup, when it arrived, was mostly barley and carrots, with very little in the way of meat and, as Sergey dipped some of the bread, he became conscious of someone staring at him from the far side of the room: a small man with hunched shoulders, his face drawn, pinched and beetle-browed. On the stranger's table lay a plate of crumbs and, soiled with coffee rings, yesterday's *Izvestia*. Though as threadbare and hungry-looking as everyone else in the city, this man *could* have been secret service.

After studying him with considerable intensity a moment longer, the stranger rose to his feet, tucked his newspaper into the inside pocket of his long, grey overcoat, and crossed the café.

"Seryozha?" he said, with a smile of yellow teeth and greyish gums. "Sergey Andreievich?"

Sergey nodded slowly, waiting for the stranger's smile to fade, and for him to say there had been a mistake, that Sergey should never have been released, that his rehabilitation was incomplete and that he would be placed on the very first train back to Komi, by orders of the MGB.

"Do I know you?" Sergey asked.

The stranger laughed. "Know me? Sergey! Of course you know me! It's me! Vasily Nikolayevich. Sidorov! Vasya!"

Vasily Sidorov. A name he'd neither said nor spoken nor even thought about in a very long time. When had they last seen one another? He couldn't recall. Perhaps the night of the premiere, or in the days that followed. No, his memories were too clouded to picture the exact scene.

When he had *first* laid eyes on him, however . . . this he remembered clearly. A rehearsal room, backstage at the Kirov. Secretary Remizov taking him on the grand tour, introducing him to everyone as "our latest genius". Echoing against a polished wooden floor, the sound of a piano playing "The Young Prince and the Young Princess" from *Scheherazade*. In the studio itself a young man, eighteen or nineteen and with dark, lightly curled hair performed a series of nimble *fouettés*, stopping only when he noticed the presence of a stranger.

Now, in the café near Nevsky Prospect, Sergey felt his stomach lurch, as if his innards had turned upside down. Like a nightmare in which one's family or friends are replaced by imposters, the face he saw bore only the vaguest resemblance to the person he remembered.

"Vasya?"

The man nodded, drew out the chair opposite Sergey's and sat down. "I knew it was you!" he said. "I come here for my lunch every day, every single day, and I know everyone who comes in here. If not by name, then by face. I see them every day. But you, as soon as you walked in, I thought, 'Hold on, he's new.' And then I looked at you again, and I realized it was you."

"Yes," said Sergey, smiling almost painfully. "It's me."

"But how long has it been? Ten years? Fifteen?"

"Twelve."

"Twelve years. Well. Can you imagine? Twelve years. Incredible. I heard you were up in Archangel, writing music for a theatre company. That's what everyone was saying. Is it true?"

Sergey shook his head.

"Oh," said Vasily. "Well. They must have got it wrong. But you're here now."

Sergey nodded.

"And it is so good to see you! I hardly see anyone these days. We were, well, you know . . . One oughtn't say such things when out in public, but people like us, us artists, we weren't exactly front of the queue when the rations were being handed out. Were you here at all, during the blockade?"

"No," Sergey replied.

"Of course not. Silly question. But you were lucky. Say, are you going to eat all of that bread?"

"Yes."

"Only, if you weren't, I have some wood in my flat that I could swap with you. It's good, too. It won't burn too quickly, not like some of the cheap shit that's going around these days."

"No, I'm quite hungry, so—"

"Where are you staying? Do you have a place to stay?"

Sergey told him that yes, he had a place to stay, in Kirovskiy.

"Nice, nice," said Vasily, without conviction. From what Sergey had been told, no one in their right mind would consider Kirovskiy "nice". "And have you moved in yet?"

"Not yet, no," said Sergey. "I got here only an hour ago."

"Oh, well," said Vasily. "If you've not moved in yet, they might not have wood. In your rooms, I mean. They don't always give you fuel, when you move in. Some places, it takes weeks for them to get around to it. So, you know, if you don't have any . . ."

Sergey drew his plate closer and dunked all that was left of his bread into the *rassolnik*.

"You must be hungry," said Vasily. "I know they don't always have much bread on the trains. I've heard, a friend once told me, if you want a bigger ration of bread . . ." His voice dropped to a whisper. "If you want a bigger ration of bread, you have to give the ticket inspector a blowjob. Is that true?"

Sergey smiled. "I wouldn't know."

"Then you must be hungry," said Vasily, laughing and coughing at the same time. "Say, listen. I live near here. When you're finished, let's go to mine. I'm on the third floor, so it's not too cold, and I have some vodka."

A loaded invitation, but Sergey had nowhere else to go and two hours till he could report to his tenement and so, when the bill was settled, he and Vasily walked the short distance from the café to Vasily's building.

Twelve years ago, Vasily Sidorov had lived much closer to the theatre, in an apartment complex on Sadovaya Street, and Sergey remembered summer parties there, when they would congregate on a terrace overlooking the square, and drink champagne – Soviet champagne, of course, but still ice cold, and sparkling, and as crisp as a fresh apple.

Vasily's new building had no terrace. One of its two entrances was sealed shut by a frozen snowdrift, and the other opened only when Vasily barged into it with such force that Sergey worried he – and not the door – might break.

Once inside, they were taken up to Vasily's flat by a gloomy hallway and a flight of stairs that smelled strongly of piss, while his rooms smelled mustily of tobacco smoke, mildew and dust. Sergey recalled Vasily having a small collection of illicit Persian rugs, and a mantelpiece crammed with ornaments, but this new place, if it could be called new, was sparse, decorated only with a few pieces of German furniture, dating – he guessed – from the turn of the century. The floor and walls were quite bare.

"Please, sit," said Vasily. "I'll get us some vodka. I only have one glass. Do you mind having yours in a teacup?"

"Not at all."

"What am I saying? You have the glass, I'll have the teacup. As you may be able to tell, I don't entertain very often . . ."

Moments later, he returned from his kitchen with a small bottle of vodka, a chipped teacup and a cloudy tumbler. He moved across the room with an awkward, scuttling motion; bug-like, a spider creeping along a skirting board. Vasily Sidorov was once the most graceful man Sergey had ever met. Small in build, without being feminine. Women and men alike considered him beautiful. Now he reminded Sergey of a gargoyle, or some grinning demon, a *didko*, from an old folk tale. He took to the sagging armchair opposite Sergey, and for a moment they sat in silence, Vasily still smiling at him, scrutinizing him.

"It's incredible," he said, at last. "That you came here. To Leningrad. It isn't often men come back. Usually, well, usually they're sent to some other place. You remember Remizov?"

As if the room had grown a degree or two colder, Sergey flinched. "Yes," he said. "I remember him."

He remembered Remizov, and a late-night telegram, and a taxi cab across town to the man's office. He remembered the union secretary telling him there would be no further performances of his ballet; that its formalism had angered someone senior in the party. He remembered the anonymous review in *Pravda* which echoed almost every sentiment, as if either Remizov had written it himself, or was quoting the nameless reviewer – perhaps that "someone senior" – in advance. He remembered this being the beginning of an end.

"Well," Vasily went on. "He ran into a spot of bother. Not long after you went away. Last thing I heard, he was teaching ten-year-olds in Vladivostok."

"Is that so?"

"Well, you know how it is. That's what people say. But no one's seen him since . . . well . . . long before the war."

A better man might have stifled his own pleasure at knowing Remizov had joined the ranks of those taken away to places cold and unforgiving. As it was, this news felt like a small victory, so that when Vasily lifted his teacup and said, "Peace and happiness to all men," Sergey mentally excluded the former union secretary, wherever he might be. Then the two men, Vasily and Sergey, clinked their cup and glass together and drank their toast, and the vodka tasted raw, as unfiltered as white spirit, and it made Sergey wince.

"He knew about us, you know," said Vasily.

"Who?"

"Remizov."

"He *knew*?"

"Oh yes. No idea who told him. One of the boys from the reserve troupe, I imagine. Little bloody gossips, the lot of them. I hear he wasn't best pleased. Still, I suppose at least he didn't tell anyone. Well . . . he didn't have the chance. No sooner had you gone, than so had he. And then the war happened, and everyone was gone. At least, that's how it felt."

"So you were here?" asked Sergey. "During the war?"

Vasily nodded. "You were lucky," he said. "To be elsewhere."

"Was it so bad?"

Vasily began to chuckle, his laughter bubbling up out of him as if he couldn't quite control it, but tears were welling in his eyes. "Was it so bad? Was it so bad? Oh, Sergey Andreievich. Like you wouldn't believe. Everything . . . everything just fell apart. I don't remember the Civil War, I was too young at the time, but my father told me this was so much worse. The sense that everything was coming apart at the seams. And then, in that first January, he died. We still had some money left to pay for his burial but, when we took his casket to the cemetery, the corpses there were just piled up on the roadside. Like so much refuse. There must have been hundreds of them. And the bodies on top of each pile had been stripped. First of their clothes. Then their flesh.

"They looked ridiculous, these corpses, with their oversized heads and bloated bodies, and their arms and legs nothing but bones. Like marionettes."

Vasily laughed again, and Sergey felt a surge of nausea, salty spit filling his mouth, his shoulders and forehead tingling with cold sweat.

"What happened to the place on Sadovaya Street?" he asked. He wished to hear no more about the blockade. "Why aren't you living there?"

"Oh, Sadovaya Street!" said Vasily. "Well. First, it was damaged. A mortar attack, or some such. Fucking fascists. Not a direct hit, you understand, but a shell landed in the square. Blew out every last window. They said I had to move, so they could fix it up. Moved me across town, to this place. I think the previous tenants had all starved. Or perhaps it was typhoid. Anyway. The place was empty, so I moved in. And then, when the apartment on Sadovaya Street was all fixed up they told me I couldn't have it back. Some party member wanted it, after his house was destroyed. Charming. Anyway. I've been here ever since. I know it's not much, but it's home."

"And you say you don't see anyone else?" said Sergey. "No one from the Kirov?"

"They're all gone, I think. Either like you, or during the blockade. Tatiana Ivanovna, well, she flapped her wings and flew off to Paris and then America. All very scandalous, of course. We don't talk about *her*."

"But you're still here."

Vasily grinned, baring ashen gums and the small black spaces where he'd lost one or two molars.

"Yes," he said. "I'm still here."

"And the dancing?"

Vasily began to laugh again, a nervous giggle that escalated into something braying, almost hysterical.

"Dancing?" he said. "I haven't been a dancer in a very long time. Oh, Sergey Andreievich! Do you remember a dancer called Vasily Sidorov? If you do, you have a far better memory than me. No. I haven't danced in years. The Kirov was damaged during the war, so there was nowhere to dance. And besides, after we had gone hungry for so long, well . . . look at me."

He sighed, waving one bony hand before his shrunken frame.

"But do you remember how I danced?" he said, rising clumsily from his chair and taking another sip of vodka. "Remember your ballet?"

"I remember," said Sergey.

"I was Pechorin. The hero."

Then, placing his cup on an otherwise empty mantelpiece, Vasily performed an exaggerated march across the sitting room, humming a melody Sergey hadn't heard in many years; the dance a parody of what it was when Vasily first performed it at the Kirov. Sergey struggled to hide his distaste.

"It was a wonderful ballet," said Vasily. "Such a shame."

"It was a long time ago," said Sergey. "It doesn't matter."

Short of breath, Vasily braced himself against the back of his armchair and looked down at Sergey with that same appalling fascination with which he'd studied him in the café.

"I've just remembered!" he said. "I have it here somewhere."

He paced across the room to a small bureau and began opening and closing its drawers, rifling through the papers in each one before producing a manuscript bound with a cover of purple card.

"Here!" he said.

"What is it?" asked Sergey.

"Your ballet."

Vasily handed him the book, and Sergey began thumbing through its pages, seeing, written in his own hand in both pencil and ink, snatches of melody that were both surprising and immediately familiar.

"You kept this?" he asked. "Even after everything that happened?"

"Yes," said Vasily, beaming. "Even then. I thought someone should. You left it here. After the party. Do you remember?"

He remembered.

They were, as Remizov put it, "celebrating the launch of a great endeavour"; a new Soviet ballet that would be the envy of Europe. Let the bourgeois composers of other cities experiment with ugly noise. Sergey Grekov's ballet, based on the novel by Lermontov, would prove for once and for all the primacy of Russian – no, *Soviet* – culture. This was not a time for understatement.

In the theatre, the cast and crew assembled on an otherwise empty stage, lit up with spotlights, the auditorium's empty seats lost in the dark. They drank Soviet champagne, and everyone was happy. They told him that his music was sublime. They called him the true heir to Mussorgsky – bypassing all those other recent composers who had been named Mussorgsky's heirs before becoming unmentionable.

Upon leaving the theatre, a group of them went on to a nearby café where they drank Georgian wine well into the early hours. Their company was boisterous, singing songs that annoyed the other clientele, but they didn't care. They were all far too happy. Eventually, when the owner had grown tired of their songs and wished to lock up for the night, Sergey and Vasily found themselves staggering alone in the vague direction of Vasily's rooms. Sergey lived on the other side of town and so Vasily invited him in, ostensibly to sleep on his couch.

There, they spoke about Sergey's music, and about how Vasily should portray the lead role of Pechorin. He is a hero only in the broadest, most ironic sense, Sergey told the boy, and as for the title, well, that was Lermontov's most cutting joke of all. The author looked upon his own time as one of vanity and self-regard. He saw in his generation only a self-serving arrogance, a kind of hubris, which was far from heroic. Sergey tried to explain all this using language that had been drilled into him at the academy, with talk of Pechorin's "wicked individualism", and he and Vasily talked and drank vodka until it began to get light, but with increasing frequency their conversation turned to the subject of sex.

"It's been so long for me," said Vasily. "I can't remember the last time I was fucked."

Sergey coughed and spluttered and told Vasily not to be so scandalous.

"What is so scandalous about that? It's the *truth*."

"But saying 'fucked'," said Sergey. "You shouldn't say such things. Not at your age. Not at all, in fact. You don't know who's listening. Say 'fucked', and people know exactly what you are. And you can be jailed for that, you know."

"Locked up with lots of other sex-starved men. Sounds like a strange punishment, if you ask me."

"Well, that's as maybe, but you should be more careful."

He now struggled to recall just how this exchange had moved on to something physical; whether it was he or Vasily who had made the first move. Certainly, he remembered Vasily's hand on his crotch, and the tentative way in which he had unbuttoned Sergey's trousers, checking for his approval with each button undone. The next thing he recalled was fucking the youth with an aggression that frightened him; though what disturbed him more was Vasily's breathless "thank you" when the act was over and they had collapsed, shaking and cold with sweat, back onto the couch.

Sergey had thought what happened that night – or rather, in the very early hours of the morning – remained a secret between them. He left before the first workers took to the streets, and crossed the city in a mood that shifted turbulently from pride to shame and back again. He had left his score for *A Hero of Our Time* at Vasily's flat, but there were copies at the theatre. Having had the boy, he saw no reason to return.

Now, in this other, far more squalid apartment, Sergey offered the manuscript back to Vasily, but Vasily told him it was his, that he should keep it.

"I can't do that," said Sergey. "You've had it all this time, and besides—"

"Oh, I insist. I can't imagine they let you keep any of your work, where you were."

It was true; they had not. For a while he had played in a band that stood on the camp gates, performing rousing marches as his fellow prisoners filed out for another day in the mines. Many times, fewer men filed back in at the end of the shift. Otherwise, there had been very little music in Komi. Occasional peasant tunes, but nothing like the music he'd once written or listened to. It never seemed the place for it.

Sergey took back his manuscript and held it tightly against his chest. "This could have got you in a lot of trouble," he said.

"I didn't care," said Vasily. "I thought that if I kept it here, you'd one day come back to collect it, and that perhaps . . ."

"Perhaps what?"

Vasily shrugged and, for a moment, Sergey saw in his expression something of the boy he'd first met in the Kirov's studio; that same wounded longing, threaded through with something far more calculating.

"How are you here?" said Vasily. "In Leningrad, I mean. The others, when they get out, they're sent elsewhere. They're never allowed *back*. What is it Akhmatova says about Dante? '*Even after death he did not return to his old Florence*'? And yet here you are. How come?"

"I don't know," Sergey replied. "When I first got there, they said there had been a mistake. Something to do with my paperwork."

"A mistake? They don't make mistakes."

"Well, I don't know," said Sergey. "They said there was another Grekov. A thief. They thought perhaps he should have been sent north, and that I . . ." His voice trailed off. He knew how to end the sentence, but also knew that some sentences should not be finished. "You're right, though. Most people are sent east, or they're moved on to other cities."

"But you came back."

"I came back."

"Why? What was here for you in Leningrad? You have no family. And as I said, our friends, our old friends, are all gone. Why did you come back?"

Sergey drained the last of the vodka from his glass, and suppressed a brief, stomach-bracing heave.

"Leningrad is all I know," he said.

"Perhaps you thought you would see some of your old friends?" said Vasily, leaning forward and folding his emaciated arms across the back of the chair. "Is that it?"

"I didn't know who would be here," said Sergey. "I didn't know if anyone was still alive."

"Did you think perhaps you would see me?"

"As I said, I didn't know who I would see."

"Did you miss me?"

Sergey rose suddenly and crossed the room to Vasily's coat stand. His was only the second coat hanging from it, and taking it away left the thing looking spindly and bare.

"Where are you going?" said Vasily. "I thought you might stay a while."

"I have to go," said Sergey. "But thank you for the vodka, and for your hospitality."

Vasily followed him to the door and Sergey awaited an ultimatum, an offer caged inside a threat. Stay a while, or else. Stay a while, or as soon as you step outside this building there will be men waiting for you, men who will put you on the first train back to Komi.

Instead, Vasily called after him: "I'll see you around, yes?"

Sergey nodded, descending the staircase quickly and without saying another word.

There were no men waiting outside the building, nor was he followed at any point between Vasily's street and the place where he caught the Kirovskiy tram, which was crowded and smelled of damp coats and cheap booze. Standing beside him in the aisle, a young woman cradled her small boy, two or three years old, against her shoulder. The boy smiled at him, and Sergey smiled back. Sergey poked out his tongue and crossed his eyes, and the boy laughed, but on seeing him pull faces at her son the boy's mother scowled and Sergey turned away, blushing.

He had forgotten just how much the people here had changed, those last few years before he was sent away; the hardness they'd acquired. No sense of anything but proximity binding them together, and a kind of caustic animosity hanging in the air between each person, as if it would take very little for them to turn on one another like dogs.

The tenement building was new, built since the war; one of countless identical grey blocks on a grid of streets surrounding the Kirovskiy plant. The whole neighbourhood smelled acrid – a claggy, chemical tang that seemed to gather and cling to the back of his throat; a smell he could taste. In the cold, drab lobby he was met by the building's commandant, an older woman with greying black hair hacked close around her ears and sticking out from beneath her peaked cap.

"You're Grekov?" she asked, glancing at his paperwork.

Sergey nodded.

"And you came from Komi?"

"Yes. From Komi."

"That's unusual. We don't get many from Komi. How long were you there?"

"Twelve years."

"And you were in *Komi* the whole time?"

Her expression, previously so hard, so unflinching, softened, as if the force of resentment behind it, whatever it was that made her dislike him on some deep, fibrous level, was beginning to dissipate.

"No," said Sergey. "Not the whole time. For a few years, during the war I was in Kotlas. I worked as a clerk, on the railroad. Then they sent me back."

"Still. Twelve years. Come. I'll show you to your rooms."

Sergey wondered if the woman had ever married. He imagined that she might once have been quite pretty. Perhaps her husband had died during the war, either here in Leningrad or on the Front. He could picture her with neither children nor grandchildren.

She took him to the fourth floor of the building, where he had a small bedroom and a kitchen. The bathroom and toilet, a short way down the narrow corridor, were shared with four other rooms.

"You will report to the factory on Monday, at 8 a.m.," she said, handing him a piece of paper that was printed with the factory's details and the name of his overseer. "Don't be late." When she left him and he had closed the door behind her, Sergey felt truly alone for the first time since the morning of his arrest. Instinctively, he placed the manuscript, the score to his ballet, beneath his bed, and into a shadowy corner of the room.

He slept heavily that night, exhausted by his journey and the day, and his dreams were crowded with sex, images and sensations that drew on distant memories, as if the part of him that crafted his dreams had been given permission by some higher authority. Sergey had dreamt – and even thought – of sex very rarely in the North. Like music, there had seemed so little point. There was neither a time nor a place for intimacy in Komi. What little sex there was happened either through desperation or by force.

The following day was a Saturday, and Sergey woke wondering if he had been rude to Vasily, if his paranoia had made him treat the man unfairly. Few in his situation had the good fortune to go back to their hometowns, let alone be reacquainted with old friends. As the day went on, he thought about this more and more, until he was unable to do much else.

Sergey remembered Vasily telling him that he went to the same café, the café where they had met, each day, and so he took the tram across town and headed straight to Nevsky Prospect. There, at the café, he ordered coffee and a bowl of *rassolnik*, and he waited. In the coming months, as winter faded verdantly into spring, he would visit the café many more times, and in vain he would search the neighbouring streets for a familiar building, but he would neither see nor hear from Vasily Sidorov again.

He's Funny that Way
Alfred Corn

———

That I both did and didn't want to go to San Francisco only added one more conflict to the chaotic swirl of emotions surrounding a departure date. I'd agreed to do a teaching gig there because funds were running low, and Gene was between acting jobs (nothing new in that). Besides which, he grew up in California and feels expatriate boosters of the Golden State should revisit it every year. Four months away from home is nothing, really, but my New York parochialism always asserts itself before we take any trip. I have this funny, unexplainable reluctance to deal with. Dread and queasiness lead people (like me) who are normally easy-going to behave badly. We pitch hissy fits with people we love and concoct insults that never would have crossed our lips if we didn't have a thousand practical telephone calls to make and several hundred pounds of sundry schlock waiting to be loaded into the car. Past experience had taught my main-man Eugene that, when those moody winds swept in, anyone within range better watch it – he was in danger of sustaining blows about the face and eyes. Lucky for Gene, he also knows how to dodge and feint like a kung-fu black belt and, what's more, to land a few pulled punches now and again.

Another convenient brunt for my bad temper was Teddy, our doorman. Hefting the unwieldies out of the elevator so I could load them into the car, I lobbed several tart comments his way, at which he grinned his idiot grin – one corner of the mouth going up, the other down – and said nothing, the most likely method of squelching the tenant confronting him. On a blazing day in August he should have been overheated, too, in his tight-fitting gabardine uniform (Teddy is fat) and cap. Oh no. Unflappable efficiency kept opening the door of the air-cooled lobby and sending this hapless Okie tenant out into the swelter. As much as I'd let him, Teddy would help me with the bags, somehow never losing his baby-elephant complacency. My physical clumsiness, which I try to see as an endearing fault, today felt like one of the afflictions visited on poor slobs that Miss Happenstance likes to oust from their comfortable slots – why? Because she gets bored, wants to be amused, and thinks a homo on a hot tin roof would make an interesting spectacle.

Gene and I had never lived in a doorman building before. Here's how it happened. An older well-heeled friend of ours named Ralph Dunhill, who has several chi-chi addresses scattered around the globe, heard our apartment building in Chelsea was about to succumb to the wrecking ball, and offered to sublet us a co-op he owned up on the East Side (at a nominal rent) until we found a new place. Was Bette Midler ever right when she sang, "You got to have friends!" There was just one problem: after plumping ourselves down at Ralph's, we totally failed to find new digs so that we could move out again. Our gracious living requirements and our bank account were singing in a different key. Actually, they still haven't managed to play in tune, so we've come to regard the clash and jangle as modern music. We looked and sniffed and turned down everything in our bracket that was shown to us. Our interim sublet continued on and stretched out into a residence pure and simple. Ralph didn't seem to care. Those times when he wanted to spend a few days in the city, he stayed with us. No longer young himself, he was nevertheless (unheard-of trait) a fan of youth and beauty. But he didn't like going out to trawl for it. We'd invite a few stud muffins from our gym over for dinner to meet charming, silver-haired Ralph. Some of these, as we'd guessed they would, turned into projectile rent boys at the mention of a London flat or an April jaunt to Sicily – the usual upshot being that a match for the night or the month would be made. Everybody came out ahead, whether on the giving or receiving end.

When we first settled in at 77th Street, we congratulated ourselves on the new perk of enjoying doorman service. It was nice to have a soft-spoken, efficient man in uniform take your packages, send visitors up after a polite intercom message, and whistle down a cab when you wanted one. Actually, there were three: two reliable elder statesmen to handle these tasks, and then Teddy, the younger, less formal third. None of them really approved of us, though, not even Teddy. Quite clearly we didn't fit in with the genteel atmosphere of the building, wearing jeans and even Ts, our guests in equally informal attire. It takes an experienced Eastside doorman about five seconds to decide whether you own municipal bonds or not. Gene and I sometimes came in carrying plebeian sacks of groceries, whereas the building's "nice" co-op owners had theirs delivered – through the service elevator, of course, according to civilized practice. Furthermore, although some few of the other residents were secret friends of Dorothy, our behavior was way too "out" to suit the tone of this particular enclave. Gene and I pretended not to notice the ironic smiles that went with the elaborately polite words greeting us as we waltzed in and out of the lobby every day. Despite which, Teddy began to cross the invisible line that protocol establishes in such situations. Given his obvious conviction that we had no class whatsoever, why did this one doorman want to be friendly? We didn't know, but he clearly was angling to punch through those ice curtains his co-workers always closed against us. It made for a pleasant contrast. I mean, at first.

"Now when do we expect you back, Mr Caswell? Early December? I'll mark that in my book." (The one formality Teddy stuck to was the "mister" bit, which was even more preposterous than usual, pronounced in his museum-quality Brooklynese.)

"Right, and if you'll just hold the junk mail. Thanks, I've got this one."

Heat volleyed up from the pavement and glared from all the black and silver cars double-parked on 77th Street, including my Stratus, which needed a wash. I unlocked it and threw in an inordinate number of bags, the question of whether we'd need quite so much paraphernalia flashing through my mind one last time as I tried to fit everything in.

Then, right behind me, up stepped my hubby, a freshly pressed Empress Eugénie, with his little black duffel, plus picnic basket with a carefully wrapped bottle of Prosecco protruding from it.

"The duffel can go anywhere, but why don't we keep this within easy reach." He put them where he thought best and returned my do-what-you-want-to-sweetie look with a snippy smile. A lean, blond icon in sunglasses and sandals, he's an object lesson in how to be sultry-sexy at thirty-seven – which probably explains why he has the upper hand in our particular tandem. All I ever need do in order to push myself into a stimulating episode of self-denigration is look at us side by side in the mirror. It's not possible not to wonder what he sees in me. But I don't *ask* him because the question might introduce a hairline fracture and break the spell of downwardly mobile enchantment. Renewed awareness of my amazing luck, of the imbalance between his visuals and mine, didn't, even so, help me get a grip, not at that moment. My cool cucumber of a spouse turned and walked back to the door being swung open for him, me muttering under my breath and following after.

Thanking Teddy, Gene swirled around toward me, flipped off the sunglasses and said, "Listen, Matt, I'm going to telephone and say goodbye to Ralph. Do you think you should stay down here and keep an eye on the double-park?" It wasn't a real question so I didn't answer. The *clip-clap* sound of his sandals on the tiles as he walked to the elevator reminded me of summer a year ago in Greece, where he'd first bought and worn them. Now that was a trip. We *were* capable of having a good time together. Today, not. I slouched down on the lobby sofa. Through the grillwork shadows of the doors it was fairly easy to make out the car. Nobody likes waiting, but at least here inside you had shade and A/C to assist while you cooled your heels.

Teddy was my junior by about seven years, a fact no more reassuring than the thought that most policemen are younger than I now am. Authority figures, people in uniforms, should be as old as your father, or so an ironclad sense of suitability tells me. Teddy was the same age as my kid brother. And since most of the building's tenants were in their sixties or seventies, an odd complicity had grown up between him and me, as representatives of a newer crop of humanity. Eventually, though, I began to discourage the chumsy tone. The tack I usually took was to breeze past each morning's fresh-served joke, nod, and then stride forth into imperturbable sunlight. Once, when Gene and I were going out together, Teddy gave us a leer and said (to the partner he figured as the "woman"), "Oh. Mr Downey, are you carrying Mr Caswell's baby?" His double-barreled "mister" in the context of pregnancy really pushed the envelope, but that's our boy. I glared at him and said, "Drop it, Teddy," flicking him off my lapel, so to speak, like a crumb of pizza crust, as we fled the precincts and set out in search of company less crude. But that was then; on moving day, the routine MO didn't hold. As long as my loaded car was double-parked, Teddy had a captive ear for his ready wit.

Which he figured out immediately. Eyes dark brown and face round as a mushroom cap, he approached me, his fists dangling at his sides. "Mr. Caswell, did I tell you about my aunt?"

"Did you?"

"My Aunt Martha died. This is the one my mother didn't speak to anymore. Well, because: One night, this was back in the fifties before I was born, they were going to a New Year's Eve thing, a big fancy party over in Kew Gardens. Like I said, I wasn't born yet, this is like my mother telling me the story. She got all dressed up – you know, she had on her fur cape with the squirrel heads biting each other – and they drove by first to pick up my aunt. Mother took one look at her and says, 'What'sa matter, your lipstick is crooked.' And when Aunt Martha tried to answer, my mother says, 'You're drunk, Sister.' Didn't I tell you this? Aunt Mart was really kind of plastered already 'cause it was New Year's. They went ahead to the party anyway, and at the party they had some kind of party punch with vodka and creme de cacao I think in it. So it was party time, and my aunt drank a lot of the punch and started asking all the men to dance. So finally my mother said, 'We're taking you home,' and then Aunt Martha *insulted* her, and—"

"Hold on a second, Teddy, they're going to give me a ticket." I went out to the curb and talked, in that volcanic heat, to the unconvinced young woman in cap and uniform. The car would have to be moved. Now. No ticket, just this once, but I've been warned, so get moving, sir. I circled three blocks up and down and then, the meter Nazi having plodded farther along on her daily rounds, slid into the same exact illegal space. But Gene still hadn't come down.

Almost before I was inside, Teddy restarted his story. "So anyway, after Aunt Martha insulted her—"

"Um, Teddy, let me phone upstairs." I did. On the house intercom, our voices staticked like cellophane. Gene had been comforting Ralph, who wanted to communicate the news that his mother had gone into intensive care. Ralph was devoted to his mother, so his trip to Finland and St Petersburg would be a no show. Gene had done his best to find the right assurances and was sorry he'd taken so long. If I could just be a little patient, he'd be there in a jiff. The first thing my eyes alighted on when I put down the phone was Teddy's face, brimming with narrative lust.

"So anyway, Mother wouldn't speak to her after that, not until she apologized for saying what she did. Except that Aunt Martha never *would* apologize, she just moved out to California – this ain't where youse guys are going, it was LA. But nobody had her address, and they didn't know what she was doing out there anyways. But then my mother got word from a mutual friend that Aunt Mart was dancing in a nightclub show. See, she'd always been very talented; she could sing, and she'd taken tap and modern. Aunt Martha was the kind of person who always got a kick out of showing off for people, like, at parties and things. Mother claims I take after her." Teddy laughed, both pleased and self-deprecating, then went on. "But Mother was, like, real upset when she heard her very own sister was performing in a nightclub, to *her* that was just like if she'd a been a – a criminal pervert. And she felt guilty about it, like maybe she was partly responsible because Aunt Mart might not a gone to LA if Mother hadn't stopped speaking to her so nasty. You know what I'm saying?"

"Excuse me, Teddy, I want to check something." I'd seen a delivery van backing up to the car. I wasn't sure if they were going to block access, so, safer to ask. Out into the furnace. I went around to the driver and talked to him and his assistant. They scratched their beards and said they'd appreciate it if I could back up, say, a few feet. There was a furniture delivery for the Josephsons. The seventh floor, was that right, did I know? I said I thought it was, moved the car, and stepped back into the lobby, my hands sticky from the steering wheel. Cool air washed over me.

"They want to make a delivery, Teddy."

"Oh? OK." He looked outside to where the two men were wrestling a big carton out of the van. Then he turned back to me and picked up his thread. "So my mother felt guilty, and then she felt even *more* guilty, you know why? Because one day she went out to the cemetery to put flowers on my grandmother's grave. It was Gamma's birthday. What she found when she got there was Gamma's tombstone had tipped over flat on the ground, face down. She got to thinking about it and figured it was my grandmother being so upset about what happened to Aunt Mart. You know, from beyond the grave. *Woo.*" I saw a shiver run through Teddy, then he recovered and plunged in again. "My mother felt so bad about it, she got, *man*, like, real sick. The doctor put her to bed for two weeks. And she got my aunt's address finally and wrote her. She told her she was very, very sorry and would she please come home. But Aunt Mart never answered. Never heard a single word. And after a while the family lost track of her completely and just gave up trying to get in touch."

He scuttled over to hold the door for the two deliverymen, who were piloting a big brown carton into the lobby and then back to the service elevator, toward which Teddy shepherded them in a series of flitting but authoritative gestures. By now I was curious to know what had happened to his aunt (such is the tyrannical enchantment of story), and when he came back I asked him.

"I was going to tell you. See, last New Year's my mother went to another party, also in Kew Gardens. A different house this time, but just like before, a classy level of people. Actually, she said a few of the same guests were there as at the other party, just kind of more decrepit now. A lot of them had died since the first party. Anyway, just as they were about to leave the party, my mother had a mental experience, like. She heard a voice that was saying her little sister would be dead before next New Year's. And she busted out crying right there, because she and her sister had been real close when they were kids; it was only later they got sore and stopped speaking to each other. So my father asked her what was the problem, but she wouldn't tell him, so he thought she'd had too many cocktails. He said, 'Let's go home, Tess.' And she didn't even tell him what it was until last Friday, when they got the news."

"You don't mean your aunt *died*."

"Yeah, Aunt Mart was dead. And some friends of hers got in touch with us."

"I'm sorry."

"Thanks. I didn't really know her, she left before I was born, but she was a terrific person, and she was my aunt, so I loved her." We blinked at each other silently.

"I'm going to call upstairs again," I said.

Gene came down. We said goodbye to Teddy, who waved from under the awning outside. At some point during his story the car had been ticketed; there was the slip under the windshield wiper. I released an appropriate profanity. Gene let this dereliction of duty on my part balance off his dawdling upstairs. As we buckled ourselves in, the delivery men came out of the building, visibly thrilled to be free of that heavy appliance or whatever. They looked at Gene and nodded goodbye to me. They must have figured out that we were (to borrow a 1950s bit of gay slang that Ralph pipes up with occasionally) "as queer as Dick's hatband". One of the men started whistling like a canary, the other one volleyed a gob of spit into the gutter. (But don't they always, the Cold War among demographic categories being what it is. Say what you like, none of us passes for straight when sized up by construction workers and delivery men. They seem to have better gaydar than the middle class. Oh sure, I realize that their gestures are as much come-on as insult. But my tactic is always just to whistle back even louder and let fly my own gob, so that they know I'm not fazed in the least.)

As we thrashed our way through traffic toward the Lincoln Tunnel, I began to retell Teddy's story, which at least got us out of our grim, set-jawed mood. There was also the relief of finally having got the trip underway. Oddly enough, during the week-long drive, Teddy's name kept cropping up, for no special reason, in a thousand haphazard contexts. And because that old standard came on the radio one afternoon while we were analyzing his weird, moony innocence, we started adding the refrain, "He's funny that way." It was almost as though he became the mascot of the trip. "He's funny that way . . ." Some of his choicer comments have entered the private, ironic phrasebook that every couple develops over the course of their years together. For example, whenever we get gussied up to go to some fancy soirée, one of us usually says, "Now don't forget to put on your fur cape with the squirrels biting each other." And so forth. Of course, Teddy's contributions amounted to only a small percentage of the rococo lingo and wry inflections at our disposal, but still.

As I mention this, it occurs to me to wonder why it is that folk on the gay side of the fence develop and deploy so much special idiom while working out our aberrant destinies. I specialize in interior design, not sociology, but I can theorize that we use clever verbality as a first-line defense against . . . well, you know, all the walnut-brained lunks who think they've pronounced words of thundering originality as soon as they've called us fags. We tweak and hone our blithe condescension and stiletto put-downs as a way of proving, if only to ourselves, I AM SOMEBODY: tony bitchery as self-affirmation and survival technique. And once we've seen how effective it can be when used on the dire straight world, we can then direct it at our own kind, staging a festival, a reciprocal orgy, of personality roasting. Put two or three Queer Eyes in the same room and within six minutes at least one of them is going to have his beads read in agonizing detail. Do I need to point out that we're all capable of aiming the same *Star Wars* ray guns at ourselves while we're at it? Why else do we all strive so insanely to be flawless on every front? If we weren't perfect, our inner *Mommie Dearest* would reach for her correctional coat hanger and get to work.

Anyway, Gene and I beguiled the long hours of the driving day by retelling all the old stories from our past, interjecting an occasional Teddyism for comic relief. As soon as the drive was over, though, we relieved our daffy doorman of his tour of duty, and never thought to call him once while we were in San Francisco.

———

Now it's December and our West Coast interlude is over. We've been driving the reverse route back through all kinds of weather, and I'm ready to resume my former existence – as much as anything future can be former. As we turn onto 77th Street, Gene gives me a quick, excited smacky. The city's been subject to several transformations since we left. The air is cold, it's night now, and all the avenues are blaring with the lit-up fanfare of the last few days before the chimney drops begin. From a dozen apartment windows on our block, half a dozen Christmas trees in silver-tinsel drag are winking and flashing their sugarplum-colored lights into the darkness. We slip on our jackets before beginning to unload. Who should come out to help us but – our very own Teddy! Strange, because he never works the night shift. But he's been transferred – at his own request, he tells me, when he shakes my hand.

"Welcome home, Mr Caswell, Mr Downey," he says. "Just in time for the holidays." Well, sure: He's due his bonus check any second now. You can see, though, that he is sincerely glad we're back. And I feel a helpless, sickening rush of homecoming warmth toward him as well, which I *will* overcome eventually, just not tonight. Co-operating, we get everything smoothly into the lobby. Gene surveys the pyramid of cartons and bags and says apologetically, "Hope you can manage this. I'll put the car up." He twinkles a "ciao" at me and steps outside.

I'm waiting for our 1930s-vintage slow-boat elevator. Shaking his head at our "stuff", Teddy catches me by the sleeve and brings me up to date on the building gossip. Until I interrupt him: "How's your mother?"

"Oh, well, she's getting along OK. She and my dad are going downta Florida right after Christmas Day."

"You're not going with them?"

"No, it's not my vacation. I'll stay and take care of the house. While they're gone."

"Won't that be lonely? But you can throw a big party." *Bingo*, Teddy blushes a big bright red, and it's obvious that I'm on target about his plans.

"Mother wouldn't like that, not in her live-in room. She'd be afraid of cigarette burns on the live-in-room suite." But practiced detective skills tip me off that he's just going to ignore those restrictions and throw his party anyway. We're looking in each other's eyes; he knows I know. Wait a minute, is that . . . ? Yes: He's exuding a floral, musky roach-spray aura. No, it can't be, but it is: Aramis. (I have a Proustian flashback to 1975, an era when the little tot I am knows something is *different* about himself, just not what exactly. A little tot who can name any perfume he smells.) There's more. Teddy's left ear now sports a little gold ring. Aha, bet 77th Street doesn't like *that*. Now what do I imagine he'd say on being asked, "Oh, Teddy, have you *gone gay* since we left?" A plan I instantly reject. He's sure to say YES, and then we'll *really* be defenseless against those volleys of sassy cheer delivered in the lobby every evening. I will happily join other building residents as we muscle him back into the closet, at least for the hours when he's on company time. (With a certain amount of concern in his voice, Gene will report, a week later – the morning after Teddy's unauthorized wingding out in deepest Brooklyn – that our debutante has a black eye and a cut on his chin. But that will be only the beginning, only the beginning . . .)

At last, here it is, the slowest elevator in captivity. It opens and, as I step into it, Teddy beams his big, space-dish grin at me and waves, "Merry Christmas, Mr Caswell! Happy New Year!"

The Bargain
Damian Barr

———

David planned a good hour of gallery cruising after finally finishing his Autumn Term marking. Only one more to go, although he'd mentally doomed it to a middling 2:2 purely for the use of Comic Sans.

Penzance was close enough to St Ives that he allowed himself to dream of finding a Ben Nicholson that had sailed off course or maybe even just one of the less lumpen Troika vases that he could then eBay. As he neared his fortieth birthday, Sunday-afternoon 'tiquing had replaced Saturday-night clubbing. A relief, really.

He'd nurtured such magpie hopes since bagging a Maggie Hambling seascape for £1 during a dawn raid with Paul on the Brighton Marina car-boot sale. Paul, as usual, trailed behind moaning that he wanted coffee while David walked a few paces ahead, tugging at an invisible lead. He'd spotted the Hambling propped tipsily between two brass candlesticks in the boot of a rusting Mondeo and felt the familiar surge of pre-find adrenalin. Although only postcard-sized it somehow managed to contain a whole roaring sea, foaming white horses. Knowing what a prize it was, David bought the candlesticks too but binned them on the way home – he would have put them in the recycling but wasn't sure they took brass. They fought about that. They'd fought about everything.

David still had the picture but Paul, his unlikely talisman, was a year gone, up to London for his second, or was it third, career. He'd muted him on Facebook but not unfriended him – this way he could cyber-stalk him during late-night bouts of Merlot and maudlin. Luckily, the Landmark Trust place he'd rented for the dead days between his first Christmas and New Year alone had no wifi – the welcome pack boasted about this like those couples who purr about not owning a telly.

As much as he loved Radio 4, David did enjoy a secret box-set binge. He looked forward to getting back to *The Good Wife* on Monday. He was to be up and out by 10 a.m. "latest" so, even with Bank Holiday trains, he'd be back in Brighton by evening – time for a good few episodes. At least early starts were easier without Paul, who'd taken every morning as a fresh insult.

Marking done, he carefully popped the lid back on his marker pen, imagining the heritage outrage if it bled onto the little orange armchair. Seized by the fear that someone else might be about to find the bargain waiting just for him – his bargain – he wriggled his feet into his brogues, threw on his Barbour – patting pockets for keys and phone – and helter-skeltered down the spiral staircase and out into a cold, empty street.

Even with no one else here to admire it, David felt proprietary pride about his temporary abode. The Egyptian House was a candy confection of pink and yellow pillars topped by buxom caryatids with drag-queen make-up and iced with garlands of golden stucco. Eccentric even when it was built in the 1880s, it now looked bonkers. It was split up into three flats but he hadn't heard anyone above or below. The organic cosmetic workshop on the ground floor was closed for the winter but its pleasantly medicinal smell lingered. It was all his, if only for a long weekend out of season.

Lunch beckoned but David couldn't bring himself to eat in a pub alone. A pasty and a walk by the sea, let's see if the waves really are different from Brighton, filling his eyes with the Cornish light he evangelized about to his Beginning Art History students. Then another night in for one. He wondered briefly what Paul was up to and fingered the phone in his pocket, considered checking Facebook but then thought better of it. Phone now in hand he eyed Grindr – surely the regional gays would be grateful for fresh meat. But it refused to load – no Internet connection, barely any signal at all down here. Not that he really wanted to meet anyone.

Chapel Street sloped gently down to the sea, which he realized he could actually hear. Brighton was always so noisy, his flat besieged by a DJ above, a piano teacher below and children either side. The sky hung grey and low like the suspended ceiling in the staff room. The sun was up there somewhere but wasn't staying long.

Every gallery he passed had a passive-aggressive little note taped in the window: "Closed for Christmas". *You should have better things to do at this time of year,* they taunted. Most showcased just one eye-rollingly terrible piece by a doubtless local "artist". There were lots of flat faux-naïve seascapes and many highly smashable ceramics. One place did have what looked like an early Henry Moore sketch and he cursed them for not being open, not that he could afford it anyway.

Up ahead, a lozenge of amber light spilled out on to the pavement and David picked up his pace until he found himself spot-lit in front of a tall, slim Georgian terrace, stucco pore-perfect like a glamorous dame who'd just finished putting on her face. The glossy black door had no number. *Galerie Revenir* said the sign over the door – the overwrought wrought-iron art nouveau lettering seemed to writhe before eyes tired from marking, and he promised himself he'd never visit Vienna. The opaque yellow film staining the big bay-fronted window was doubtless to stop the sun from fading whatever was inside but it was now as out of season as him.

The sign in the window was flipped to *Fermé* but the lights were on and, pushing the heavy door, he found it open. Distantly a bell tinkled. The floorboards were painted high-gloss black, the dark of unfathomably deep water. He hesitated to break the surface, to cause any ripples. As he stepped in, clammy air enveloped him and he remembered suddenly his mother's one attempt at baking bread and how she'd left it proving in the airing cupboard for days and how it had almost filled it by the time they'd tracked down the smell.

He unzipped the neck of his jacket and, quietly because he was in a gallery, uttered an enquiring "Hello?" He realized he'd not spoken aloud for days.

Silence. He looked out through the yellow cataract, noting that he could see the still-empty street quite clearly from this side. There was no furniture of any kind, no till or anything. There was nothing at all to distract from what was hanging on the teeth-white walls.

In front of him floated a huge Hockney swimming pool, bigger than any he knew of. Thousands of interlocking Polaroids, each an ocean. The vast collage, taller than him, held all the blues he could imagine, was bluer than the eyes of any man he'd ever kissed. Fringing the pool were Rousseau-green palm trees and beneath these basked hunks in trunks, boys really. They reclined, confident of being looked at. Rent boys, David reassured himself. This was 1980s LA, they'll all be dead now, he realized not unhappily. He leaned in closer than he would have dared in real life. At this scale they were all doll-sized and he remembered the smooth bump of disappointment between the legs of the Action Man he'd been given one Christmas. He stood as close to the picture as gallery manners allowed and when he'd devoured all the men at eye-level he hunkered down for the rest. Minutes passed, hours maybe, his knees stiffened, his mouth felt dry. It was so hot in the gallery that David wanted to dive in to the picture or maybe just dangle his feet, as he'd never really been one of life's divers. Not spontaneous enough, Paul said.

From above came the sound of slippered feet shuffling. So he was not alone. Reluctant to lose his place by the pool, David walked to the back of the room where a wrought-iron spiral staircase snaked up. Clearly commissioned from whomever had made the sign out front, it bean-stalked with tendrils and leaves. He half-expected it to rustle when he put his foot on it and called up: "Hello?"

Silence. What if there was more up there? Another Hockney he'd never seen? Perhaps a print he could convince the owner to pretty much give away on this otherwise dead day?

Taking the coffin-narrow stairs two by two, David ducked to avoid hitting his head on the dainty brass bell that had announced his arrival and had to turn sideways at the top to squeeze into the room above. Up here the ceiling was lower, and there was no window. Light seemed to come from the pictures themselves.

Here was an orgy of Duncan Grant. He'd not seen this many since his last visit to Charleston. There had to be twenty of them, rushed charcoal sketches of naked men each trapped in horribly rococo gilt frames. God save me from becoming an old queen, David thought. As he moved closer to the pictures, he realized they were all the same man, probably a gardener judging from the size of his thighs and the strength in his arms. He was what his students would call "fit" and he reclined expectantly like the boys downstairs. He looked familiar somehow. David went from picture to picture observing minute changes in posture as if watching a film frozen into frames. If he ran around quickly the man would move, Muybridge back into life. He was glad to be able to look without being looked at. Nothing put him off more than a needy gallerist asking if there was anything in particular he was hoping to find. Peace, he always wanted to say, quiet. The eye must travel and David found his gaze straying down, he was so close he could lick the yellowing paper. He found himself wondering how big the model would be hard before remembering that this man was long dead. Unzipping his jacket fully, David loosened the collar on his periwinkle blue Oxford shirt, wiped sweat from his brow.

Again a noise from above but this time the unmistakable rustle of something being unwrapped, a child tearing open a Christmas present already guessed at. "Hello?" David called, less tentatively. The gallery was, technically, closed and he didn't want to be mistaken for a thief and find himself shot by a *Daily Mail* vigilante. He relaxed a little, remembering this was not *Daily Mail* art, but, still, what if he gave the old queen – because that's what the owner had to be – a heart attack?

Silence. Then, the tap-tap-tap of an audibly small hammer striking a fine nail – a picture hook going in, the sound of a successful acquisition. "Helloooo?" he called up into the gloomy absence above.

Silence. Telling the Grants he'd be back, David hauled himself up the final spiral into a tiny attic room lit only by a filthy skylight. Outside, the afternoon was almost over. There would be no walk today. Like all the others, it was empty of furniture. It did not feel like anybody had been here recently or for a long time. As the eaves sagged towards him he stooped. Feeling dizzy now, he took his jacket off and it slid to the floor. It didn't seem important to pick it up. His shirt stuck to his back and would be see-through. Steadying himself in the centre of the chamber, he found he could almost touch the walls.

Each of the three walls in front of him held one picture framed in what looked like ivory. He narrowed his eyes in the murky gloom, unsure of what he was seeing. Each picture showed a different man's face gouged from a palette of pulmonary, private reds. No neck or shoulders, just heads. Life size. Bacon, Frances Bacon. They had to be. They couldn't be. They couldn't be anything else. Their mouths were open wide, twisted in an emotion too extreme for David to have ever felt. Their eyes, he realized, had no lids and they seemed to be imploring him. David was aware of his hand reaching out to touch one. His fingers brushed the canvas.

Far below, the bell tinkled.

David turned towards the noise and as he did he saw, above the spiral stairs, a fourth frame. Empty.

The Good Butler
Tony Peake

————

Ralph Goodall started swimming the morning after his fortieth birthday. He'd always planned to avoid the clichés of ageing but, as the years proliferated, so the attraction he felt for younger men intensified, and in helpless thrall to this burgeoning obsession, so he began, unfavourably, to compare the sleekness of their hard, enticing bodies with the progressive softening of his own. Not that anyone else – least of all his regular drinking companions, John and Henry – shared his disquiet. Still enviably lean, and always dapper, Ralph looked to them as slick and trim as he'd always looked. Yes, his barbered beard was now flecked with grey, and yes, the primness of his mouth was bracketed by lines, but the clean, sharp cut of his face and figure belied any need to worry.

"Hyper-sensitive, dear," John would murmur, casting a rueful, downward glance at the Falstaffian swell of his own ungovernable body. "Neurosis. That's what you have to guard against. Not blubber."

And Henry, who had, in addition to all the major musicals, the entire Gilbert and Sullivan canon by heart, would hum in camp reassurance: "She may very well pass for twenty-nine in the dusk with a light behind her."

But Ralph knew otherwise. Lying full length in the bath, he would roll what excess fat he had between finger and thumb and note with dismay the way it puckered; and when he stepped out of the tub, he had only to turn to the mirror for further, more spiteful proof of the advancing years: the striated sagging of a once-pert bottom.

"Maybe it is neurotic," he pouted at his reflection, "but those who only serve have a duty to do so decorously."

So, at ten-thirty on the morning after his birthday, armed with a photograph and proof of his address, he presented himself at the Victorian baths round the corner from his flat.

Although he'd lived in the area fifteen years, and passed the baths every day on his way to and from the houses where, in the course of duty, he waited table, he'd never ventured inside. Wisely, too, was his first reaction. After the Victorian swank of their Gothic exterior, the foyer was a distinct disappointment. Modernized some time in the sixties (and probably not renovated since, thought Ralph), it seemed intent on distancing itself from the building it inhabited, on disclaiming its provenance, and thus providing an appropriately seedy setting for the tatty vending machine, the rows of fly-blown notices, and last but not least, the woman behind the ticket desk, who, if her thinning beehive was anything to go by, dated from when the foyer had last enjoyed the attentions of a decorator. Such was the air of desolation about this woman that Ralph felt impelled to chatter brightly about the weather as she filled in his details on the form. Not that he need have bothered. She didn't appear to hear a word he said, and as soon as she'd issued his card, returned her tired attention to the dog-eared paperback at her elbow.

"And the changing room?" queried Ralph.

Without lifting her eyes from her book, but in tones made mercifully precise by her obvious reluctance at having to impart this information yet again, the woman said: "Down the corridor and on your left."

The corridor was narrow and badly lit. Halfway along its dim, oppressive length, Ralph came to a swing door made of heavy plastic and, pushing it open, found himself in a high-ceilinged room that, for all its unexpected loftiness, was every bit as cheerless as the rest of the building. The tiled floor was grimy and cracked, there was a scattering of sodden towels on the line of slatted seats that dissected the room, and half the metal lockers that stood against the walls were keyless.

Ralph grimaced, and skirting the puddles on the floor, stepped past the only other occupant of the room – a man in his eighties struggling into a pair of underpants designed for someone twice his size – and made for the bank of lockers against the far wall, where he quickly undressed and, with a pleased sense of aptness, put his neatly folded clothes into locker 40, only to find a moment later that he had to take them out again and feel through his pockets for a 10 pence piece with which to close the locker and release the key. He pinned the key to his swimming costume, then, towel in hand, gave a wide berth to the eighty-year-old (now flailing about inside his shirt), and emerging into the corridor, turned left and followed the signs that said "Stanhope Pool".

After the preceding seediness, the pool itself was a pleasant surprise: a cube of enticing blue set like a jewel in a vast and vaulted room that boasted a raised gallery at the far end, a tracery of metal girders across the ceiling, and, on a chair against the opposite wall, a rather sexy little lifeguard playing the mouth organ.

Ralph hung his towel on the row of hooks along the nearest wall and approached the edge of the pool. Apart from a knot of splashing children in the shallow end, there were no more than half a dozen swimmers churning their way up and down its length – for which, as he lowered himself gingerly into the water, Ralph was profoundly grateful. A textbook homosexual sired by a dominant mother and retiring father, he'd never been remotely sporty. As a boy he'd shied away from the playing field, preferring the quiet of the library to the hurly-burly of soccer, stamp collecting to cadets, and had come to think of exercise as inimical to his particular sensibilities.

Imagine, then, his amazement on finding himself welcomed rather than chilled by the water, and discovering that although he didn't attempt more than ten unhurried lengths, sticking to a rather cautious breaststroke lest he collide with the other swimmers, he could emerge from the pool a quarter of an hour later feeling invigorated and refreshed.

Back in the changing room, he opened his locker, retrieved his clothes and began to towel himself dry. He was just slipping into his trousers when he heard the swing door open and, looking up, saw a young man, towel strung negligently across his hips, make his way to the locker opposite. The young man had a bar of soap and a bottle of shampoo in his hands, which he placed on the seat next to Ralph before removing his towel and beginning to draw it vigorously back and forth across his back.

Trying his best not to let his eyes stray too obviously in the direction of the young man's body, Ralph sat down and felt for his shoes. A wave not exactly of lust, but more accurately of lust and sadness combined, engulfed him. In his mind's eye he was taken back to his swimming classes at school and the sight of Mr Eedes, his swimming master, pulling on his trunks and heedlessly tucking what the other boys sniggeringly called his tackle into its pouch of clinging nylon.

"You got the time?"

"I beg your pardon?" Startled out of his reverie, Ralph instantly, and hotly, began to blush.

"The time," repeated the young man. "You got the time?"

"I'm sorry. The time. Yes, of course." Ralph fumbled with the cuff of his shirt and consulted his watch. "Just gone eleven."

"Eleven. Right." The young man had finished drying, and now he stretched languidly, throwing back his arms and pulling in his stomach, so that his cock, surmounted by its dense bush of hair, hung proud of his muscular legs.

This time Ralph was unable to tear away his eyes, and when the young man looked down again, it was directly into the older man's gaze. He let his hand fall to his cock, and with a slow, knowing smile, said: "I always swim mid-morning. It's quieter then. Later you get the school kids, and at lunchtime the business men."

"I suppose," said Ralph. "Of course. That would make sense."

"And in the evenings," continued the young man, "you can hardly move in there." He had a faint stubble, and his hair, curly on top, was cut short at the sides.

"I really wouldn't know." Ralph forced himself upright and began folding his swimming costume into his towel. "This is my first time."

The young man's hand was lightly caressing his stomach. "Good exercise," he said. "Swimming. The best."

Ralph cleared his throat and pointed at the young man's soap. "Tell me. Is there a shower?"

Again the young man smiled, and again there was, in his smile, a hint of teasing, taunting complicity. "Sure," he said. "At the far end of the baths. Under the gallery."

Then, turning his back on Ralph, he opened his locker and pulled out a pair of expensive-looking boxer shorts.

Back at the flat, Ralph dropped his towel on the table, collapsed onto his sofa bed and had to wait a good ten minutes before his excitement subsided. Then, going through to the kitchen, he put on the kettle, made himself a cup of coffee, and took it into the living room.

He'd bought the flat in the early eighties. Although tiny, consisting merely of a living room that doubled as a bedroom, a galley kitchen, a bathroom and toilet, he had, with the help of John, who was an interior decorator, made it so stylish that visitors never noticed its size. The bathroom they'd painted an opulent maroon, the kitchen they'd done in lemon and white, and in the living room the functional furniture was offset by dove-grey walls and curtains of the palest mauve.

Sometimes Ralph wished the flat looked more homely, that there was a touch of chintz somewhere, a battered old chair, or that he wasn't quite so obsessive about keeping it clean. But that wasn't in his nature, and it had to be said that no matter who visited the flat, be they friend or one-night stand, it was always and extravagantly admired, even down to the last of his carefully chosen ornaments.

Only his mother expressed reservations – but then there was nothing about his life of which she did approve, and never had, ever since George.

He took his coffee to the window and, with the image of the young man from the baths flickering in a recess of his mind, thought back across eighteen years to the madness of those two months with George. Just twenty-two, he'd been in his final year of college and living in a bedsit in Kennington. He could no longer remember exactly where he had been, but it was returning from some party or other at one in the morning that he'd seen, coming towards him along Kennington Lane, a sheer Adonis, a blond and fiery god, who'd caught his eye as they passed, looked over his shoulder at the same moment Ralph had done, and lingered at the next corner, exactly like Ralph, the one a mirror image of the other, both wanting . . .

Ralph sighed. He knew what he'd wanted. He'd wanted that beauty, that perfection, and the promise it held of reciprocity. But George? George, it transpired, had wanted only the mirror that Ralph held up to his beauty. "All the better," as Ralph had spat at his departing back, "to admire yourself in." Oh, he'd gone along with Ralph, allowed Ralph to make plans for the two of them, moved in, even, for a couple of weeks, but it had all been a dream, an illusion, that most predictable of traps set for the lonely, a fantasy. George was in love with love, and when Ralph's love proved altogether too constant, too reassuring, George had, of course, shrugged him off and gone in search of other, more arbitrary, and therefore more stimulating loves.

And Ralph? Ralph had been left to pick up the pieces and cry, literally cry, for two solid weeks, until John and Henry, bored by this excess of grief, had dragged him to Mykonos and arranged one night for a young Greek to wait in his room so that when the three of them got back from their night on the town, there he was, this Greek, this other, lesser god, spread-eagled on his bed.

Except that not even then had Ralph got over George, not properly, nor the awful thing that George had taught him, that love between men was, by its very nature, transitory. Nor, and here a bitter smile played about his lips, would he ever get over that other legacy of his weeks with George, the loss of his mother's love. For when George had moved into his bedsit in Kennington, so certain was Ralph that this was for ever that he'd gone joyfully, gaily to see his mother and tell her he was, in every sense of the word, gay. Except that wasn't the word he'd used. He'd used her terminology: queer.

Nothing in his relationship with his mother, who'd always been so proud of him, so certain he was marked for something special, had prepared him for the vitriol she loosed on him that weekend. After the tears and hysteria, after the "What have I done to deserve this?" and the "Where did I go wrong?" came the "I've read about your sort. It's dirty and unnatural. You're fooling yourself if you think it can last."

He'd protested, of course, told her he wasn't like that, that he and George were going to live together for ever, just like a married couple, and that anyway, it wasn't something he had any control over, he'd always been like that, ever since – and here he made the mistake of telling her how Mr Eedes's body had branded itself on his adolescent consciousness, pointing the way forward. Then she'd really given way to her horror and, lunging at him across the room, had ordered him out of the house.

Of course she loved him really, he knew that, just as he loved her, and eventually they'd started spending Christmases together again, had even gone motoring in the Lake District the year before last. But it wasn't the same. Her disapproval hung over everything they did, although now it no longer manifested itself over his sexuality – that, as a subject, was taboo – but opted instead for the size of his flat, the fact that he wasn't making enough of himself, that she couldn't for the life of her understand why he'd given up his studies to become, of all things, a butler.

He brushed away the tear that had formed in his eye. What he could never tell his mother was that if she hadn't reacted as she had to the news of his sexuality, then perhaps he would have continued his studies. But when, the week after his mother's attack, George had announced he didn't want to cope with Ralph's emotional baggage or be dragged into his relationship with his mother – that wasn't what being gay was about, for that you might as well be heterosexual – Ralph had started to neglect his work, and when, at the end of the year, he'd failed his finals, what option had he had, when you looked at it, except to run away, to start travelling, in search not just of places where he wasn't known and could therefore be himself, but of the boys who were to be found in those places, in the bars and on the beaches of Greece and Italy, the Caribbean and South America. Not that it did to knock his years of travel. They'd taught him all he knew about serving others, not only as a waiter and butler, but also – and here he smiled crookedly – as celebrant of the male form.

He finished his coffee and, taking his cup into the kitchen, washed it and put it back in the cupboard. One shouldn't complain. So what if he hadn't planned on becoming a butler? It gave him a reasonable living, and besides, he had fast friends in John and Henry, not to mention Claire from across the road, who, when it did get to him occasionally that there'd never been another George, would invite him into the post-feminist chaos of her flat and console him with her own accounts of the horrors to be suffered at the hands of a man.

And as of today, going hand in hand with the promise of a trimmer body from the swimming, as of today there was this youngster from the pool, fine fodder – what finer? – for fantasy. Again Ralph smiled. By now George would doubtless be fat or balding or both, and he'd always left a lot to be desired in the cock department. The boy from the pool, with his muscular legs, his inviting smile and neat little ears, the boy from the pool was as close to perfection as it was possible to come. More, reflected Ralph, at the age of forty and after only one visit to the baths, it would be indecent to expect.

That night he had a dinner in Mayfair for Lord Cartwright, one of his more demanding regulars, and he didn't get home till after two. He made sure, though, to set his alarm for nine. He wanted to wash and shave before his swim so that he was looking his best when he put in his second appearance at the baths.

He entered the foyer at ten-forty sharp, and knew when he got to the changing room that he'd timed things perfectly. There at the bench was the eighty-year-old, struggling into his underpants. Ralph made for the locker he'd used the day before, and as he began to undo his buttons, noticed with surprise that his hands were trembling, and that the sensation in his stomach echoed the sensation of all those years before, when he'd stood on Kennington Lane looking back to his Adonis on the corner. "Ah," he could hear John murmur. "*L'amour, l'amour!*" Without bothering to fold his clothes, he bundled them into his locker and fumblingly retrieved the key.

At the poolside, he scoured the handful of swimmers to see if he could pick out the boy. It was, though, impossible. His could have been any one of the submerged, churning bodies. So, slipping in at the deep end, Ralph forced himself to concentrate on his breaststroke; and found, to his surprise, that the swimming so calmed him that his stomach had returned to normal by the time he emerged from the pool and made for the door under the gallery marked "men".

The showers were empty, and something of a shock after the pool. If the changing rooms were shabby, the showers were worse. The paint hung in unsightly strips from the ceiling, there was mould on the walls, and on the floor in the corners of the room, under the blue plastic matting, accretions of hair and soggy paper. Not, thought Ralph, shuddering, an ideal setting for seduction.

Picking his way across the mat, he chose the shower by the window, and stepping under its torrent, slipped out of his swimming costume.

He lost track of the time he stood under the shower, but when, quite superfluously, he'd finished soaping himself for the third or fourth time, and was still alone, it dawned on him that maybe the boy, knowing that he hadn't showered yesterday, had skipped the shower himself, hoping to meet Ralph in the changing room – and without losing another minute, he switched off the water, snatched up his towel and ran for the door.

A burst of noise greeted him as he approached the changing room and, pushing open the swing door, he found himself besieged by a throng of shouting, screaming schoolboys. A weary master, too weary to return Ralph's startled nod of greeting, stood by the wall, every so often barking at the more rowdy of their number to keep the noise down. No sign, though, of the young man.

Miserably, Ralph fought through the boys to his locker and, facing into the corner, began swiftly to dress.

It was the same the next day, and the next, no sign at all of the young man, and on both occasions the gauntlet to run of a dizzying horde of school children who, when they weren't stealing each other's towels or reporting each other to their master for swearing, would stare pointedly at Ralph before dissolving into gales of laughter.

He began to wonder if he should give up the swimming, and then, more sensibly, decided to give up his fantasies about the young man. The swimming was good for him – better, certainly, than any fantasy – and given the state of his body, he owed it to himself to concentrate on doing that extra length each day, so that by the end of the week he would be up to fifteen and a good deal less puffed when he emerged from the pool.

So, in his mother's phrase, he knuckled to, managing by the Thursday, and not too breathlessly, to complete his target of fourteen lengths. Except that he hadn't, of course, forgotten so much as a follicle of his fantasy – and when, on the Friday, the shower door swung open, and through it, as stunning in the flesh as in memory, came the young man, Ralph realized that powering his every length up and down the pool had been the hope that the young man would, as he was doing now, materialize again, and pause on the threshold to close the door behind him, step under the shower next to Ralph's and slip off his trunks. Ralph waited for his breathing to return to normal. Then, not daring to catch the young man's eyes, he retrieved his soap from its container and began very carefully to lather himself a second time.

"Do you mind if I borrow some shampoo?"

Ralph looked up and found himself confronted by that remembered, knowing smile.

"Of course. Here." Fumbling behind him on the windowsill, he handed the young man his shampoo.

The young man poured a generous dollop of shampoo into the palm of his hand and returned the bottle to Ralph.

"You haven't been swimming," said Ralph. "Since the last time."

"No," said the young man. "Work."

"Been busy, then?"

The young man nodded.

"What do you do?"

"I'm a writer."

"A writer? Really?"

Again the young man nodded.

"Books?"

"Scripts."

The young man closed his eyes and began to lather his hair. His body was angled towards Ralph, and as he worked at his hair, his eyes still closed, Ralph was able to devour its every detail. He felt himself starting to harden and turned away.

"And anyway," he heard the young man say, "you sometimes get the school kids on Wednesday and Thursday. Nasty brats."

"Don't tell me. Noisy lot."

"Exactly."

Unable to look away any longer, Ralph once again turned to face his fantasy. Cock in hand, the young man was lathering between his legs. He looked up and saw the direction of Ralph's gaze, then looked down and saw the extent of Ralph's excitement. His eyes went hard and, twisting sideways, he muttered something under his breath.

For a moment, Ralph couldn't think what to do next; then, his panic subsiding, he decided it would only compound matters if he didn't acknowledge the mutter.

"I'm sorry," he said faintly. "I didn't hear."

The young man swung round. "I said it's a good thing you've got a towel. You're going to need it." And with those hard, ungiving eyes, he held Ralph's gaze until Ralph, near to fainting, snatched up the aforementioned article and, shielding himself behind it, fled from the showers.

For the next three days, Ralph didn't go to the baths at all. He was simply too frightened; too frightened and too hurt. Never in his life had he made such a fool of himself. Then, as rationality returned, and because Claire stopped him in the street to say how well he was looking now that he'd started swimming, he took a deep breath and set out once more.

After all, it wasn't as if this was the first time he'd been given the brush-off, nor was it likely the young man would report him to the pool authorities. No, as long as in future he avoided the young man's eyes, no harm – no lasting harm, that is – had been done. He'd even been made to re-learn a valuable lesson: that if he wanted a man, well, the trick was to keep it simple, as simple as the tricks themselves, and to hunt for them only in the clubs, where the manner in which they displayed themselves wasn't open to misinterpretation.

He was relieved to find, as he entered the changing room, that the young man wasn't there – nor, for once, the perennial eighty-year-old – and it was with a light, determined step that he crossed to locker 40 and began to undress. He'd only got as far as slipping off his shoes, however, when another young man came swinging into the room, a young man every bit as heart-stopping as the first. For a moment, despite himself, Ralph gasped: gasped and was tempted to gawk. But he'd learnt his lesson, and even when the young man commented on what a nice day it was, Ralph kept his head averted. He couldn't, of course, help a quick sideways glance as the young man peeled down his jeans, but no sooner had he seen what he wanted to see than he looked away again and, scooping up his soap and shampoo, made for the pool.

There, pacing himself carefully, and emptying his mind of thought, he managed to swim as many as twenty lengths, and one for luck, before getting out and making for the shower. To his amazement (for he'd still been ostentatiously naked when Ralph had left the changing room) the young man was there before him, under the shower by the window. Ralph opted for the shower in the opposite corner, balanced his soap on the tap and began, with particular absorption, to wash himself.

It was some moments before he looked up again to discover that the young man was staring at him.

"Knackering, huh?" The young man's eyes were decidedly mischievous, and that wasn't all: his hand was making another kind of mischief with what hung between his legs.

Ralph turned quickly away and reached for his soap.

A second later, and much to his relief, he heard the door open, though when he glanced up to see who it was, he found to his horror that he was looking straight into the taunting eyes of the very man he'd been avoiding. His first instinct was to bolt, but something – he didn't know what – made him hold back, hold back and watch with growing amazement as, stepping casually under the shower midway between Ralph and the first young man, the newcomer slipped off his trunks, and taking out his soap, began with slow, luxurious strokes to apply it to his cock. Unable now to tear his eyes away, Ralph watched mesmerized as both young men began to soap themselves until their cocks became wholly erect. Then, shooting a look half of defiance, half of disdain at Ralph, the young man nearest him leant over and reached for the other man's cock. It didn't take the pair of them more than a minute to come. Then, as if nothing more untoward had happened than an exchange of shampoo or a request for the time, both men returned to their separate ablutions. Ralph looked down at his own, pathetically eager member, and powerless to prevent himself, came on the spot in a series of short, sharp spurts.

"No kids today," said the young man in the middle.

Ralph, in the panicked process of gathering up his things and preparing to leave, was forced to hesitate. "I beg your pardon?"

"No kids," repeated the young man, fixing him with a look of quite devastating neutrality.

"No, indeed," stuttered Ralph. "No kids."

"Yeah, don't you hate those fucking kids," supplied the other young man. "Really hate them."

That night, at the club, Ralph confided in John and Henry.

"I mean," he said, "isn't it bizarre? What is he playing at?"

"What young men like to play at," said John. "Each other."

"But why lead me on like that? He flirts with me, then he cuts me dead, then he comes in front of me."

"Narcissism, dear," said Henry. "Young men like that get a kick out of being admired. I should know. I've done enough admiring in my time to satisfy whole armies of them."

"No," said Ralph, "it's more than that."

"Oh really?" said Henry. "In what way?"

"I don't know. Something in me, perhaps. Some reaction I invite."

"If you want a partner," said John, "don't go looking in the locker rooms of London. Ring a dating agency."

"Who said I wanted a partner?"

"Sorry, I could have sworn you did."

He hadn't, of course; he'd never confided that to anyone, not even Claire. But John had been right. He did want a partner, it was what he'd always wanted, and always would – except, and this was the problem, his partner had to be a man, and men weren't made for permanence.

He didn't go swimming for a week after that, and when he took it up again, it was first thing in the morning, when the pool was full of commuters on their way to work, men in hock to their mortgages and their marriages who, if they noticed Ralph at all, took him as one of their own.

And then, when he was least expecting it, he met the young man again – not at the pool, but at Mrs Bartholomew's. Mrs Bartholomew was married to a financier, and every couple of months she held a dinner, either to oil the wheels of her husband's current deal, or else, more frivolously, to flaunt some media personality before her friends. On this occasion, her find was an elderly American film star who'd been rescued from obscurity and a more or less permanent suite at the Betty Ford Clinic by a triumphant revival, first seen on Broadway and now transferring to Shaftesbury Avenue, of a Kaufman classic written as a vehicle for the star's mother.

"Ralph, angel!" Mrs Bartholomew had cooed when she'd phoned to book him. "I want to push the boat out. You know Americans. They love a touch of the Jeeves. As formal as you can make it, yes? Let's give the old has-been the works."

It was, accordingly, a Ralph as crisp as his wing collar who marched to the door on the third or fourth ring and, throwing it open, saw at first glance a man in a white linen suit, all twined about by a dark-haired beauty in a sheath of red, and then, on closer inspection, seeing through the social disguise at the same moment as the young man penetrated his, recognized the eyes.

Keeping his voice level only by the most mammoth effort, Ralph stepped back from the door and said: "Good evening, sir. Madam. Whom shall I say?"

Charmed by this apparition from a bygone age, the woman whispered something in the young man's ear. The young man, however, didn't take his eyes from Ralph's as he drew his partner across the threshold and replied, in a voice every bit as level: "Mr and Mrs Parker."

"Just a minute!" The woman flashed Ralph a winning smile and, turning to the mirror on the wall, began fussing expertly with her luxuriant tumble of auburn curls.

Ralph closed the door and, without daring to glance again at either of them, led the way to the drawing room and made the announcement: "Mr and Mrs Parker." In an instant, Mrs Bartholomew, in a swirl of unsuitable pink, was upon them, and with a cry of "Laura, my dear, and Charles, how well you both look!" hustled them off to meet the film star, who'd been propped, like a piece of statuary, against the fireplace.

If he could have left then, he would have – but although he'd become a butler by chance (in spite of himself, and perhaps, also, to spite himself) Ralph had over the years come to take a certain pride in his work. So, drawing himself up to his full height, he returned stiffly to the hallway to await the next guests.

He didn't see his nemesis again until dinner, when, much to his discomfort, far from avoiding his eye, the young man seemed to lose no opportunity in catching it and allowing a flicker of amused recognition to play about his lips.

Then, after the main course, and as Ralph was clearing the dishes, the young man caught him by the sleeve and whispered in his ear: "I'm absolutely bursting. Can you show me where it is?"

Instinctively, Ralph shot a look across the table to the young man's wife. Mercifully, she was deep in conversation with the man on her left.

"Of course, sir," he said. "If you'll follow me." And pulling back the young man's chair, he ushered him from the room.

"Heavy duty stuff, eh?" smiled the young man as they reached the hallway. "Old Amy certainly knows how to lay it on."

Ralph didn't pause in his progress towards the passage that led to the downstairs loo.

"Don't look so bloody uncomfortable," said the young man. "I won't tell if you won't."

Whereupon, to his horror, Ralph felt a hand on his thigh.

"Here it is, sir," he said. "Through that door there." Averting his eyes, he stepped aside to let the young man pass.

"In here, you say?" The young man opened the door and stepped into the loo.

Ralph made to turn away, but he wasn't quick enough. No sooner had the young man slipped inside the loo than, already erect, he had his cock out.

"Come on," he whispered. "It won't take a minute."

"I really think, sir," began Ralph – and then, drawing himself up: "I really must be getting back."

The young man merely ran his hand with enticing deftness up and down the length of his shaft.

"Come on," he said again. "I know you want to." And, hitching up his shirt, he revealed a wedge of hard, flat stomach.

Surprising himself with the force he used to utter the words, Ralph put a finger inside his wing collar to loosen its stranglehold on his neck and said: "I'm sorry. You had your chance."

The young man let go of his cock and his eyes went hard.

"I beg your pardon?"

"I think you heard."

"But isn't this what butlers do? Serve?"

"Some butlers, maybe," said Ralph. "Not this one."

And, swivelling sharply, he retraced his footsteps down the passage. When he reached the safety of the hallway, he turned and saw that although the young man had at least had the grace to put away his cock, he was still standing in the open doorway of the loo. He looked almost exactly as George had looked, standing on the corner of Kennington Lane all those years ago, and it came to Ralph suddenly that what had been wrong between George and him was not, as his mother had said, that it was two men, and therefore transitory, but that they had made it so. For although George had been in love primarily with love, and with any admiration of his body, what Ralph hadn't realized till now was that all he had been able to offer George in return was precisely that: adoration. It wasn't enough to hold up a mirror to another, or to ask them to hold up a mirror to you. True love happened only when the mirror was smashed and together you stepped through it to the other side.

"Sir has a most beautiful body," he said stiffly. "But even so, I think sir would be better served by that."

And gesturing to the rococo mirror that hung on the passage wall, and in which sir was reflected, so that if you removed Ralph from the scene, it would have seemed as if the young man was coming on to himself, Ralph returned to the dining room, where Mrs Bartholomew, beckoning him to her seat at the head of the table, said: "Thank heavens, Ralph. For a moment there I thought we'd lost you. Dessert, I think." And as he turned away to organize it, she caught him by the arm and murmured in tones of extravagant but genuine appreciation: "Tonight, Ralph, you've excelled yourself. You really are the most splendid of butlers. I don't know what we'd do without you."

Sexploitation
Brent Meersman

I thought Jürgen had been foolish. What had he expected from a relationship based on such disparity – a rich German from Hamburg and an urchin from Cuba?

"I have never met a people more keen to give themselves, you know, to sell themselves," he said. Jürgen spoke English with ease, but with a thick German accent, conflating "t" and "d", and clipping his vowels. "No, it is true," he continued. "Men, women, boys, girls, they're all the same here in Cuba."

I assumed it had worked to his benefit though.

"You know, I found out my João was getting money from my friends, sleeping with them right under my nose! There is no excuse for that kind of betrayal."

What about the betrayal by Jürgen's friends? I thought that should have been of greater concern to him.

"It is a beautiful island. I used to visit every year. In all, I have probably five years here. But now, since João, I don't come so often."

We were huddled together beneath an umbrella, the subtropics drumming down around us, forcing us to sit closer than we would have normally. Our knees bumped. Bad-weather friends, I thought.

Jürgen was thickset. He had a jowly face, but was not unattractive, except that his mop of black hair had an oily look to it. I had been aware of him for some time. I'd watched as three old Cuban men sat behind him, eagerly sharing a copy of *Rebel*. They had scraggly beards and wore berets, as if they were partisans just emerged from the woods, but fifty years after the revolution. Cuba has hoodwinked time for decades now. They didn't order food or drink, but shared between them one of those nine-inch Presidente-sized parejo cigars. From the way Jürgen had watched me, I'd thought all along he might be gay.

When the thunderstorm broke, I'd gallantly beckoned to Jürgen to come over to my table, the only one equipped with an umbrella. Huge drops were falling. Jürgen's plate filled with water; we watched the fish skeleton swim off the deserted table and into the patient jaws of a bedraggled grey kitty.

Jürgen told me he was a freelance journalist working mostly for a Catholic newspaper based in Hamburg.

"I found the Cathedral of San Cristobal quite cruisey," I told him. I'd received more than one scabrous gaze when I entered. And from others a quick look away – as strong a sign of gay recognition as any long stare. I was asked to remove my hat, but I thought it an odd mark of respect in a country with state-mandated atheism, and a big Cuban flag firmly perched on the altar. But Jürgen corrected me. "Not at all. Even the Pope has visited, and Fidel welcomed him."

Jürgen spoke Spanish and was knowledgeable about the island. Apparently, the Castro government had felt compelled to close the gay clubs, ostensibly for reasons of prostitution, not homophobia. Homosexuality was illegal before the revolution. In the decadent days of Batista, a blind eye was turned for the elite who trafficked in boys.

Homosexuality became associated with gangsters, the drug mafia and the worst American political corruption, like J. Edgar Hoover and the sinister debauched plotters behind Nixon. I suppose, for macho Fidel, it must have been a sort of national insult to have filthy-rich capitalist foreigners come over and screw your young socialist cadres for a few dollars. Yet times changed, and the Cuban Ministry for Arts even sponsored a gay film called *Strawberry and Chocolate*, which went on to international acclaim; a significant departure from the 1970s, when *maricones* (effeminate boys as opposed to machos) were denounced as imperialist perverts.

The irony of it: while McCarthy in the fifties destroyed the lives of homosexuals in America for suspected communism, the Castro government in the seventies was incarcerating homosexuals as capitalists and counter-revolutionary agents. Homosexuals seem always to be caught between political factions and religious leaders looking for scapegoats or competing for so-called moral high ground.

When I first visited Cuba, only public homosexuality (in theory at least) was illegal; "ostentatious displays", as they were called. But the discos were closed on various spurious grounds.

Jürgen said, on weekend nights, the boys pitched up outside the local cinema called Yara, and by word of mouth found their way to the gay party, always at a different location. Someone would remain behind each time to invite the next group, as individuals slowly straggled in to cruise the steps of the infamous movie house.

"Sometimes," he continued, "these *fiestas de diez pesos* are good, sometimes not. Last weekend's party was bad. The floor was concrete and full of holes. There was no light. You could not dance properly. You would twist your ankle.

And the rum was some local brew – pure poison." Jürgen gulped down the last of his rosé, the red wine rescued too late from the rain. "But you must always be careful. It can be very dangerous to pick up boys here." And he dramatically made the gesture of a slit throat.

It seemed he was offering himself as my safe alternative.

"Yes, I got scammed by a young woman today. She had a baby in her arms and she begged me to buy milk for it. I knew better, but I thought, it was only some milk. Seventeen US dollars later for a half-pint!"

Jürgen laughed. "You were charitable at least."

"I was empathetic, the charitable bit was involuntary."

"Where are you staying?" He was popping the question.

"In Vedado," I replied vaguely.

"I always stay here, in Vieja, the old city." His tone turned nostalgic. "I love the beautiful colonial feel. It's the only restored section. We can share a taxi along Malecón, as far as Paseo Martí."

"I'm still waiting for my change."

Jürgen now laughed. "That waitress, she will not bring it. You must ask again. Tourists give up and the staff put it in their pocket. It's always the same. That's Cuba."

Eventually, I saw the waitress peeping from the window, probably checking to see if we'd gone yet. Jürgen hissed through his teeth, startlingly, like a note on a tin whistle.

"That is how you get people's attention here," he said. "Try it in a Latin club in Europe and all the faces that look round at you, they'll be Cubans!"

It worked. She came over. He spoke in Spanish to her. She clapped her forehead pretending she had forgotten, rushed off, and didn't come back.

The rain eased, but only until we reached the Malecón, the broad boulevard that follows the shoreline. There was no shelter and we were soaked in seconds, frantically waving at taxis that ploughed through the water, wheels submerged. A bus carriage drawn by a truck slowly rolled by, belching fumes like an oil fire, crammed to capacity with standing people, armpits pitted with sweat.

"I thought if you owned a private car in Cuba you were obliged by law to stop and give anyone a lift."

Jürgen laughed. "On the highways, not in Havana, and not for tourists. Even on the highways, people are reluctant to stop. That's why private cars have different number plates, and there are officials to stop cars. They wear yellow, or as they pronounce it here, the "jello" people. You'll see groups of people waiting beneath the bridges on the national roads."

Eventually, a taxi did stop for us. The driver, an old man with a straw fedora and an extinguished cigar, calmly announced the fare: triple the normal rate thanks to the rain. With my jeans sticking to my skin, and my wet clothes making me itch, we got him down to double the usual fare before we surrendered.

The taxi had a damp vegetable smell, as if he'd been boiling yams inside it. Its grubby windows quickly fogged up, obscuring any view of the seafront buildings. The windscreen wipers flicked frenetically from side to side like metronomes gone haywire, but didn't seem to connect with the windscreen. The driver could hardly see where he was going. He was hunched, peering forward, his face just millimetres from the windshield, helping to mist it up further. He kept wiping away with an old red handkerchief.

"I'll be at the Yara tonight, 11 p.m. Hope I see you there," Jürgen said as he climbed out. He meticulously paid 50 per cent of the fee to his stop.

The driver had by now chomped through half his dead cigar, yet I hadn't seen him spit or swallow. Maybe it was some act of wizardry. At least he wasn't smoking it in the cab. He dropped me at the bottom of the Calzada de Infanta. The rain stopped and patches of blue appeared as I made my way up the hill, my back steaming as the sun peeped out.

A dance school was practising in the street, undeterred by the threat of cloudbursts. I'm used to people in Africa spontaneously singing, whether at work or walking in the street; the Cuban equivalent seems to be to burst whimsically into dance, whether out of love, sadness or excitement. The class master, in his early seventies at the very least, but still dandy with a spring in his step, was tapping his leg and counting out loud. The young students in leotards, their skins shining in the vapour-filtered sunlight, concentrated hard, working on poses for a paso doble, I think: the boys prancing gallantly in one long column, the girls enticing them from another.

Turning up Habana Libre, I stumbled upon a pleasant tourist-class restaurant with a covered terrace, not far from my hotel. The waitress was voluptuous and scantily dressed, but unusually self-effacing for a Havanan. It was as if she wanted to smile, but hadn't given herself permission.

What I hadn't noticed until I sat down was a reed partition that stood hip high and a young man on the other side of it brooding in the corner. He was staring intently at the waitress; in front of him, an empty glass in which some ice had all but melted.

I felt self-conscious, as one usually does opening a guidebook or a map in untouristed areas. I soon became aware of another two pairs of eyes staring at me. These belonged to two boys, both in their twenties, also on the other side of the reed partition. One wore a military green cut-off T-shirt and his friend a tight-fitting, shiny viscose top. They were eating drumsticks with their hands, grease all around their mouths, bits of chicken skin on their lips. Simultaneously, they both gave me huge, toothy grins.

I smiled. At once, they took this as a cue, gesticulating wildly for me to come over. I hesitated, not sure what they wanted from me; then I felt slightly disgusted by myself for being thankful for that little reed partition, the economic apartheid that separated me, the tourist, from them, the locals. Had they come to sit on my side of the terrace, they would have been shooed away by the management.

I went over and sat at a table against the partition, bringing my coffee with me. We shook hands over the reeds. The possessive young man smouldering away in the corner, debarred from even sitting in the restaurant where his girlfriend worked, now stared straight through me.

"Where you from?"

"South Africa."

They looked at each other, and laughed. They had obviously both guessed wrong. Their names were Giovanni, who spoke English, and José, who didn't.

"José's father fought you in Angola," said Giovanni.

It seemed now an incomprehensible scenario: that in the 1970s, South Africa was at war with Cuba. Over 2,000 Cubans died in that conflict. It was heartening to hear that his dad survived.

Giovanni was a dancer and José a lifeguard. Both were proud to exhibit their muscular arms and shoulders, their skins like polished Zimbabwean soapstone.

"So what do you like to do in Cuba?" José asked. "Meet the people? You like boys," he concluded.

I smiled. They both looked at each other briefly before turning their heads back to me, smirking openly. From the way they wordlessly communicated with each other, I guessed they had known one another for a while, which at their youthful age probably meant since childhood. I was sure they'd had this kind of encounter with foreigners before.

"What kind of boys you like? You're not racist? Black, white, you no worry?"

Was it because I was South African that they had asked?

"You're both very nice, both." I looked each of them in the eyes as I said it. They giggled.

At this point, the waitress stepped out on to the veranda. She shook her head disapprovingly at them, said something apathetically under her breath in Spanish, and went back inside.

One of Havana's many troubadour collectives sauntered over to our terrace, having spotted me – the European. They sang from the street. A group of schoolchildren with red revolutionary scarves around their necks passed by, winding their way around the band. The music was pleasant, with a güiro keeping rhythm. The boys started swaying in their seats. The ceiling fans also seemed to be wobbling to the tempo.

"Tonight, we take you out," said Giovanni.

I took the precaution not to tell the boys my room number or my surname.

"I am at the hotel on the corner," I told them. "Meet me downstairs in the lobby at 10 p.m. If you're not there, I am going out. Si? I don't wait." I left a few dollars on the table and turned to leave.

"Adios, amigo!" they called after me.

I tipped the band and ended up buying a CD they thrust upon me. The only way to get by in Havana is to wear thick sunglasses; the moment you make eye contact with a stranger, you will be engaged.

As I turned the corner, I looked back. José and Giovanni, smiling, waved exaggeratedly to me.

Not far from the hotel, I saw two men dressed up in sort of protest-camp: tight-fitting, see-through tops with effeminate sequins; jeans dyed bright purple, and tied with pink scarves instead of belts; colours and cultures clashing. It all hung together surprisingly well. It reminded me of the gay scene back in South Africa during the apartheid regime.

Small, incestuous and underground, but generally allowed to carry on, as the powers that were, disbelieving and ignorant, wondered: "What do they do in bed?"

———

Back in my hotel room, sipping a disgusting blend of scummy instant coffee and insoluble powdered cream, I switched on the small black-and-white television. There were speeches giving lip service to revolutionary slogans: "comrades in arms", "the revolutionary masses", "workers unite". It was a developing-world solidarity conference with the usual calls for justice, equality, condemnations of the rich nations' economic bullying, trying to preserve some dignity while having to beg and plead for food, debt relief and financial aid. Then the television blinked off and the air-conditioner wheezed its last. It was yet another power outage.

After ten minutes, the hotel generator kicked in. The conference came back on; the air-conditioner didn't. With all the rhetoric, I soon dozed off.

———

I awoke from my afternoon snooze feeling thick and heady. I opened the window for air. From my room, I looked out onto the squalid balcony living of Havana, where washing lines, bicycles, broken-down appliances, and families all vied for space. In that climate, a veranda acted as an extended living room. The spectacular Art Deco block of flats across the way had no glass. Makeshift shutters had been added. I could glimpse original light-fittings and furniture from the 1920s. On the exteriors, paint bubbled and peeled off in large sheets, while the railings and pipes dripped earthy shades of rust down the walls.

Across the street, a huge man with grossly enlarged, veined biceps, like phallic semaphores, was leaning on the railing, smoking a cigar, puffing out his broad chest with each inhalation, then expelling the fumes in a cloud around him.

The body beautiful cult was here too, and having half the country's men in uniform at any one time didn't help ameliorate the macho culture.

I had to decide to either trust in Giovanni and José, or to head for Yara and the German. I decided that if the boys made the effort to meet me, I should pursue this for as long as I felt safe. After all, Jürgen had duly warned me.

I took the stairs to the lobby, in case there was another blackout and I'd end up spending the evening in the lift. The elevator was eccentric enough with electricity; stopping level with the floor depended on the number of people in it. On my floor, which was the third storey of the building, the fourth-floor light would go on, so whether you used the British or American system, counting or not counting the ground floor as one, it still didn't make sense. Somewhere between the ground and my bed was at least one ghost storey. On the elevator was a sign: "No Use in Case of Fire".

There was no one waiting for me in the lobby.

"Any messages?" I asked at reception. The concierge shook his head from side to side, and ever so slightly shrugged his shoulders. As he made no effort to look in the actual pigeonholes, I began to wonder whether he had understood me.

Stepping out of the musty hotel, there was a refreshing gust of air. The earth had cooled down substantially, and it was a pleasant, inviting night.

I passed the restaurant where I had met the boys, and was within sight of the Yara when a beaming Giovanni blocked my path and threw his arms around me, laughing, as if I was his long-lost friend. There were three of them now. José introduced me to Santos, a student. He looked like a thirteen-year-old. His long blond coif kept falling in his eyes, and he constantly flicked it back with thin, tapering fingers.

"I waited for you," I told Giovanni rather brusquely.

"The hotel security, they threw us out. The police want to know why I am waiting around," he explained.

I at once felt sorry for him. He however did not appear too upset by the experience, as if it never occurred to him how unjust it was. I felt a pang of guilt. There were rules for local people and special allowances for us rich capitalist foreigners. As a Cuban, you couldn't step into a Western hotel with dollar rates. On the streets, I'd met people clandestinely selling cigars for *divisas* (hard currency).

The four of us headed for a local *paladar*. These were small restaurants of up to eight tables run in private homes. The rules required them to be family run, and to cook only Cuban food, except lobster and chicken breast, which were strictly reserved for tourist hotels.

The Cuban economy goes through waves of reforms and rescissions. When I returned a couple of years later, tourists couldn't use pesos and the *paladars* were all closed.

We went to one of the fancier of these eateries in an old colonial mansion. It had a romantic feel, but on closer inspection, the tablecloths were greasy and there was congealed dirt stuck to the salt and pepper pots. Not feeling terribly hungry, I ordered a bottle of beer. The waiter brought it already opened.

I'd been foolish. The food looked far superior to anything I'd seen in Cuba thus far. The boys wolfed down a plate of spicy chicken wings, the meat falling off the bone. Then they ordered a platter of succulent chicken thighs, followed by yet more chicken, this time crispy drumsticks. I began to wonder how much chicken anybody could possibly eat in one day when, with a satisfied burp, José excused himself from the table. The feast was over. Between smacking their lips and stuffing down dinner, they had spoken mostly to one another and in Spanish. Although I was enjoying the spectacle and the overall ambiance, I had begun to feel somewhat spare. We don't speak about it, but whenever there is a new casual encounter, there is always a quick, silent financial computation.

Meanwhile, the waiter, a tall, pretty lad and the cleanest-scrubbed thing in the restaurant, made little effort to hide his hostility. At first, I thought it was because of the usual misunderstanding service personnel have of their function in socialist countries; whether in old East Berlin or Shanghai, waiters and bank tellers behave like bureaucratic functionaries to which you are their supplicant. But then I realized he was homophobic, and he resented waiting on my decadent new friends who now had a foreign purse to dip into. We must have disgusted him.

It didn't help that Giovanni and José kept making vulgar jokes about cocks and chickens, jokes the waiter clearly overheard.

"Some people are still too Catholic," said Giovanni.

With their hunger satiated, the boys at long last turned their attention to me. They wanted to know about South Africa, more specifically whether we were rich or not. I told them about all our Cuban doctors and trade exchanges. But conversation was a struggle. My Spanish was almost non-existent and their English was basic. Giovanni would keep translating what I said into Spanish for the others, but I increasingly felt he was misconstruing most of what I said.

Our surly waiter interrupted us by banging the bill, scribbled in childlike handwriting with red ink, on the table. As I'd anticipated, Giovanni, José and Santos folded their arms, and stared at me. I paid. The boys broke into great smiles and started to samba in their chairs once more. Throughout dinner, they had been constantly in motion from the hips up.

"We must take you to Fiat," Giovanni declared, glancing at Santos's watch, which kept slipping halfway down his skinny arm. They conferred in machine-gun rapid Spanish.

As we were leaving, I saw José pocket the tip I had left. "Ah, fuck him!" he said, catching my eye.

———

Fiat was an old car showroom on Malecón converted into a bar. It still had floor-to-ceiling display windows, and posted outside the old sixties version of the four-cubed white-on-blue Fiat logo.

In the parking lot, a saggy transvestite was surrounded by a dozen boys. Some were drinking from paper cups, costume rings on their fingers glinting.

Inside were two haggard women serving drinks. We sat down at a small, round, white plastic table. There was a crush of patrons against the bar, flapping notes and shouting their orders at the two *señoras*. The music was playing at full volume and several boys were gyrating in a corner.

José motioned to me, opening and closing his hand. "Six dollars," he said.

I gave him the money and he headed off to the counter. Santos started to play with my feet under the table. Giovanni was contentedly dancing in his chair. I had noticed at dinner he didn't smoke or drink alcohol.

José returned with a bottle of white Club Havana rum, two cans of Coke and four cups. He decanted a round of rum, measured by placing his fingers next to the cup, as is customary, and pouring how many fingers' worth you wanted. We all had four fingers, topped up with cola, and we toasted each other by touching cups and drinking fast. José drank Giovanni's too.

The evening grew progressively rowdier, and the conversation in Spanish more volatile as José poured rum. I noticed he consistently filled his cup more than anybody else's. It was not long before we needed a second bottle; this time, we splashed out on the three-year-old Gold Club.

An argument and scuffling started at the neighbouring table, training shoes squeaking on the showroom floor. Two local boys were arguing over the only other foreigner in the bar that evening. He was sitting with his shirt off, flaunting an underdeveloped chest, badly sunburned. His vest straps had left albino white stripes on his body and now he resembled a Union Jack. He looked plastered. Yet a third boy tried to engage him but was set upon by the two quarrellers.

As the rum held sway, I felt as if I was at some burlesque romp. Boys kept sitting down near me and trying to engage me in conversation, only to be shooed off by Santos and José, more possessive than protective.

Not a spirit drinker of habit, and combined with the humidity, the heat and not eating, I was soon intoxicated. Everyone was laughing. Santos had worked his way up from my feet and was now stroking my inner thigh under the table. I began to insist he show me his identity document, repeating drunkenly that he looked about thirteen years old. Finally, he produced his driver's licence. He was on the cusp of eighteen. The legal age of consent, he said, was sixteen.

The bar was emptying out when José decanted the last of the second rum bottle into his cup. Looking blearily up from the table, I was confronted by a line of half a dozen boys leaning with their elbows on the bar, every one of them with their eyes fixed unwaveringly upon me. The minute I looked up, they sprang into action – prancing, posing, flexing in an erotic *pas seul*.

One of the boys winking at me clutched a wooden crutch with a bandaged hand, his leg in a plaster cast. Another one of these *pingueros* – hustlers – stripped off his shirt and puffed out his enormous pectorals, like a sage grouse in mating display.

In my inebriated condition, I found myself being dragged towards the quayside promenade. Everyone from Fiat had gathered here, together with those too impecunious to enter the bar. The boys were singing, dancing the rumba, doing the lambada for themselves, getting steadily smashed on raw rum. My chaperones, while keeping a watch over me, were engaged in several energized conversations with their friends, who eyed me longingly. Everyone, it seemed, was speaking simultaneously. My head had started to spin. I was unsure which way led back to the hotel.

———

It was in the small hours of the morning when we arrived at Giovanni's home, on the upper storey of a suburban house. I noticed a shiny new SUV in the driveway, the first and only modern car I'd seen in Cuba.

"Politicians," José spat disparagingly.

The mistress of the house emerged in a luminous pink nightgown. From the way her hair stood, I could see she'd been sleeping on it. After some Spanish, she presented us with several huge bottles of beer, and after lots of good nights in English and *buenas noches* we headed upstairs. I gave Giovanni some more dollars for the drinks.

Giovanni ushered us out onto the cement roof of the garage, which served as a large terrace. I remember us collapsing with laughter and behaving like schoolboys. They had drunk substantially more than they were accustomed to. A brief altercation with José followed and I saw Giovanni defiantly down a large beer and angrily throw the empty bottle off the roof, landing with a dull thud on the lawn below.

Feeling unsteady, having drifted once too often to the edge of the flat roof, which had no railings, I sat myself down on the concrete.

José was waving his shirt above his head and dancing licentiously for Giovanni's entertainment. They started sucking each other's nipples while Santos, standing behind me, began to play with my hair. We all linked hands and with Santos tugging, heaved ourselves into the bedroom. We were rocking together on the bed when Giovanni raised his hand over his mouth and made a dash for the bathroom.

"He doesn't drink," said Santos.

José followed and I could hear him soothing the retching Giovanni. I was disappointed. Santos kept yanking at my belt and clambering over me. I heard the hot water tap squeak open, the plumbing give a great groan and shudder, followed by an explosion. There was a stunned silence. Santos burst out laughing, like a kid astonished with a shred of popped balloon in its hand. After fumbling in the dark, the lights came back on. Giovanni reappeared, now wide awake and awfully sober.

"It's never done that before."

José muttered something about the Miami Mafia and we crashed back in a heap on the enormous soft bed, flinging our shoes so that they cannoned off the walls.

Santos was still determined to get my pants off. My fingers could encompass any one of his thin limbs. From behind, he looked even more like a young boy, with his chicken thigh-shaped shoulder blades jutting out, his buttocks square-edged, his narrow hips grinding under me.

José had now stripped off as well and was begging Giovanni to screw him, parting his buttocks with his hands. Giovanni was groaning and saying no, teasing José with his glans, and without a condom; José all the time watching Santos and me.

―――――――

When I awoke from a series of confused and disturbing dreams, details of which I cannot remember, except the image of a child's limbs protruding from the rubble of an earthquake, Giovanni was conscientiously tidying up the room from our night's debauchery. Santos and José still lay in drunken torpor. I kissed their sleepy foreheads.

Half an hour later, Giovanni and I piled into the back of one of the old 1950s Chevrolets, part of the retro-fleet of Buicks, Studebakers, Plymouths and Cadillacs that ply the streets of the Cuban capital, from the days when cars still had faces. Hooters often ring out the first bars of "La Cucaracha". When I returned a few years later, they had all been given metallic paint jobs.

On our way back to Vedado, people climbed in and out of the car, dressed in casual summer clothes. We stopped every few kilometres, money changing hands with the driver.

Giovanni pushed my head down when we passed the police. I didn't ask why. The foam stuffing was escaping from the seats. Every time we pulled away, the car filled with fumes, and if the trip had been any longer, I feel sure I'd have died from plumbism.

As a courtesy, I invited Giovanni to breakfast. It consisted of grapefruit and spaghetti with ketchup – I am not kidding. It was served by a waiter with squeaky shoes; a young adult, who appeared to still have deciduous teeth. We discussed what I should see and do while I was in Havana, and I scribbled comments on my tourist map.

"I'm sorry I was so drunk, but I don't have alcohol," Giovanni explained forlornly.

"Do I owe you anything?" I asked.

"Here it is the custom. You go with boy, you make a gift. No, not prostitute, just polite, you understand?"

"For the taxi and the tour, then. And please give to Santos," I said, and slipped some folded dollars into his hand under the table.

We made plans to meet later in the day, but I never saw him again. Then I changed hotels. The food and service problems, and the fact that their credit-card machine was never working, finally drove me out. I moved into the expensive Hotel Nacional, the 1930s palace where people like Churchill and Ava Gardner had stayed. In its heyday, it was the equivalent of Singapore's Raffles.

I decided to sequester myself for a few days, to read and relax, in an enormous, comfortable cane chair in the beautiful grand portico of the veranda.

Outside, Cuba was crumbling, and it would either carry on crumbling for another fifty years or change overnight. Peacocks and guinea fowl strutted on the lawn; four tired-looking green parrots sat bedraggled in a light drizzle, protesting in mournful, almost human screeches, from their bamboo cage.

———

At the bar in the airport lounge, cherishing my last genuine Havanan cocktail while I waited for my flight to be called, I fell into conversation with a Swedish journalist.

"I feel sad that the revolution has failed so miserably," she said.

"Has it? Perhaps ultimately, but far from entirely. I'm afraid I may have undermined the revolution too." It just slipped out.

She looked at me thoughtfully. "You mean you had sex with some poor girls, I suppose."

"After all that bravery and sacrifice, everything and everyone is up for the dollar. Just as it was under Batista."

"Of course, a lot of tourists come here for the wrong reasons, to have cheap sex, but I don't think you undermined the revolution any more than Hemingway could be said to have delayed it."

"Sexploitation," I quipped. Or sexploration?

And we sat in silence, sipping our mojitos, staring at a giant full-colour poster of an umbrella on a tropical beach, which hangs invitingly in the departure hall.

A Dry Past
Richard Zimler

————

The island of playground vibrated with the disjointed popping sound of basketballs. Waves of traffic hugged close to the shore of fencing, their reassuring monotony giving the days inside a protected feel, as if the city itself were agreeing that it was much safer to play pick-up games than to venture into the outside world.

Tony Silva leapt upward towards the basket in his faded jeans and torn black sneakers, the ball arched over his head, keys and coins and disposable lighter jangling in his pocket. He was seventeen years old and he didn't want to be taken for one of the Anglo punks who needed to change into special clothing to sink a running hook in the face of some lanky homeboy cultivating his first, tentative shadow of moustache.

My brothers and I noticed black dots of stubble peppering his upper lip when he was lying in the dark wooden casket at the back of the Fonseca Funeral Home. We tried not to peer over the lid, but his nose was poking out and didn't look human and everybody in line was looking at us with these great big marble eyes the Portuguese have. Tony's icy skin reflected the creamy, polished folds of blue satin lining. Big white lilies with sharp crests popped up all around, but he smelled like dust. And he looked like he was packaged for a long trip.

Not even in his nightmares would Tony have ever sported a suit like the one he had on then. It was charcoal grey with yellowish pinstripes. Like in a big-budget gangster movie musical. Looking at him on the basketball court, you'd have thought his muscular shoulders and arms would have ripped through the seams of any sport coat. But bodies are deceptive like that.

The game was argued over. While heads shook away curses, Tony grabbed the ball and positioned himself at the foul line, tossing in shot after shot. The players on the sidelines kept eating peanuts, were waiting for either J.K. or Harold to give in. And all the while the traffic drove by the island.

We wouldn't have admitted it, but we were jealous of Tony. We couldn't sink so many foul shots while everybody was arguing. And we couldn't dunk in one of the rebounds. He'd have been given a chance at the point guard spot on the school team if he weren't already an anarchic legend. Sometimes, after he made an impossibly off-balance fifteen-footer or driving reserve lay-up, he'd look at you with those green falcon eyes of his, just waiting to pounce on you if you couldn't censor some smart school-yard comment. Then all of a sudden his lips would twist into that loopy lopsided smile of his meant to charm everybody. At school, he'd grab your lunch with an inflamed threat about ripping your head away from your neck and, after he'd wolfed it down, buy you a replacement. He'd grin with his rubbery lips while he was patting you on the back. Like it was all a game. And you could either appreciate it or risk getting walloped.

Sometimes he'd open his mouth and stick out his tongue and there'd be your food all chewed into a brown ball.

Whenever Tony noticed a pretty girl walking by the playground, he sang Prince's "Gotta Broken Heart Again". His tenor was rough, scratchy, as if he retained sand in his vocal cords, but he could keep a tune. If he was waiting for a game, he'd sing the whole song and maybe J.K. or Big Ben would slap the bleachers for percussion. Tony knew all the words. He had a memory like that.

He confessed once that no matter how desperate he ever got, he'd never follow in his father's footsteps. Spitting through the fence and looking us up and down to make sure we believed him, nodding that he was planning on becoming a rock star. Or if things didn't work out, he'd be satisfied just being a cab driver or maybe a waiter. Didn't really matter.

His mother had made him swear on the Bible that he'd stay in school and live at home till his eighteenth birthday. My father said it was more for her own protection than anything else. At the time, I didn't understand and thought it was a bad English translation of whatever he was really thinking.

There were twenty-two rows in the funeral parlor. I counted them over and over. The air-conditioning had given out and the Puerto Rican and Portuguese women were wiping their foreheads with lacy handkerchiefs like the doilies the sparrowish ladies cover pastries with at the Lisbon Bakery on Jericho Turnpike. Rumor had it that Gregory Gill was out on bail by then, $50,000 paid for by an anonymous donor. But he'd never stand trial. There'd be a plea bargain and he'd get a suspended sentence.

Even after he was cleared, Gregory's parents treated him like he was tainted with a blood disease nobody ever dared name. So at age seventeen he stuffed his Flaubert and Victor Hugo novels into a canvas bag and grabbed the E subway train into some neighborhood of Manhattan where either nobody noticed such illnesses or everybody had one or another of them. The West Village maybe. That was the rumor at least. We had never been there so we wouldn't have had any idea where to begin looking. Many years later, I ducked under the awning of an art gallery in Chelsea during an impossibly bright sun shower and there he was behind a desk in a fancy suit not so different from the one that held Tony at his funeral. They were coming back in style then.

In the casket, it looked as if whatever invisible ether had made Tony Tony had evaporated without a trace. For one thing, he wasn't glaring or smiling. His lips were sculpted into a kind of contented pucker, as if he had caught his breath before saying something angelic. His long eyelashes fluttered out like perfect cilia above crazy, pink, bulging eye sacks. His face was too long, like maybe they had trouble getting his mouth to close or certain parts of his jaw to fit just right. Apparently that's what happens when all your bodyweight crashes against a tile floor with your face in between. Thinking about that too much is why I started counting those pews.

Tony made pocket money by driving his Uncle Manuel's taxi for a couple of hours on Tuesday and Thursday evenings. A rich young stockbroker in Brooklyn Heights with a thing for barrel-chested Latin immigrants waited for Manuel under her black sheets on those nights. They screwed for an hour then watched *Seinfeld* reruns.

———

You couldn't see where the knife had made the opening which allowed life to swirl out of him, of course. But we guessed that below the green paisley tie the wound was patched and powdered and refrigerator-cold like the rest of him.

Gregory Gill was the only black kid in the French Club. He had the club's advisor, Monsieur Miller, in ninth grade. I overheard him saying to Mr Coleman, the driver's ed teacher, that Gregory was a brilliant student, one of a kind. The only one who ever used the subjunctive correctly. Was going to sojourn in France one day, too. And the French liked black people: Josephine Baker, Miles Davis, Michael Jackson.

The way he said it made me think that nobody in our neighborhood liked them even a little bit.

Gregory walking down the hall with a pile of monster textbooks and notebooks balanced on his hip, held back by the spindly buttress of his bowed arm. A tyranny of footsteps lurking behind. Solemn eyes bearing shame. Daring not to turn till books and papers explode forward. The triumphant laughter of manufactured amusement. Got him again! Back-patting boys disappearing into the crowd of shuffling students. A teacher stooping to help.

All those disjointed notes across the dirty restroom-yellow vinyl of the school floor made you wonder why he bothered.

Most of the basketball players called Tony "Tony-S". It was better for shouting across the playground. And the rusty-haired old man, Belden, who held court when he wasn't complaining about rent control at City Hall, could use it in his raps. Nobody got in Tony-S's way, on or off the court. Kind of gangly and crazy even with all those muscles, like he was made for dancing some macho lambada all his own. With a jangly, bobbing walk. Always moving, jumping, twisting, like maybe there was some gyrating spark at his centre that would never be cooled. You couldn't imagine he'd turn up so perfectly confined in that casket. Falsely perfected by all that powder and make-up. I was tempted to smear my finger across his cheek or maybe poke his chin to see if some lingering nerve would make him twitch even a little, like those sliced frogs in biology class. But all those Portuguese eyes behind us . . .

Tony's floppy brown music-video-messy hair always slapping over his forehead when he walked, of late greased around the sides with something smelling like caulking. His hands stank like that, too, from wiping his fingers through his hair. You sniffed it in when he popped you on the chin, daring you to say that there was something you wanted from him.

His eyes would bug out when he ate, like he was asking himself some daring question or was just barely stifling a shout. He liked the school's spaghetti and grilled hot dogs and veal parmigiana. And the square hamburgers with grey dribblings of fat, which the posted menu had the nerve to call Salisbury steak.

Maybe Tony could have become a model if he'd learned to walk with less energy and fit neatly inside a 35-mm grid. The Portuguese and Latino girls, some of the blacks, too, thought he was *louco* but handsome.

Teachers sent him into a trance. He'd slouch back in his chair and suck on his pen like the ink was honey. Boredom paled his face until he latched on to a daydream of basketball. The bell was the only way to get him back from that. When it rang, he'd kind of slither out of his chair, yawn and pretzel his arms behind his back to get his circulation going and to show us just how sick he was of daily incarceration. Once, in history class, he must have dreamed the period was over. He swirled up, wriggled around and cracked the vertebrae in his neck by cocking his head all the way forward, Egyptian-dancer-like. Mr Trainer snapped off his glasses and furrowed those white caterpillar eyebrows of his. Did

Tony have a pressing problem he wanted to share with the class? When the bell rang for real that day, Tony, sat up, gripped his chair and looked around till we had all popped up and he knew it was safe. It was the first and last time I saw him intimidated. Only gym gave him pleasure. But it was only three times a week.

How he passed through school each year without being left back was a mystery that could only be answered in the school boardrooms of large American cities.

The game never did get going again. Harold wouldn't give in and left with his ball. J.K. sat smoking on the bleachers.

Tony left the playground and started to walk home the long way, by Miller Avenue so he could buy some Camel Lights at the Italian deli. A pack with one cigarette missing slipped out of his pants pocket with some change when he later fell to the kitchen floor. Getting them meant that he could cut back towards his house by the high school. Occasionally, you know the right way to go, but most of the time you haven't got a clue.

Reading *L'Éducation Sentimentale* by Flaubert with the help of a tiny purple dictionary, Gregory was by himself; sitting cross-legged on the field behind the school gymnasium, down near the steps into his home street, Greenway Drive. Afterward, people all said they knew. Had that plaintive, cottony voice, was always turning away like you had the secret he needed to reach adulthood but was afraid to ask about. His parents should have tried some cure when he was little, before his habits were imprinted on his brain. The public school had had psychiatrists on staff, and maybe it's true that they weren't that good but they were free.

Mr and Mrs Gill claimed they didn't know. Sure, he mumbled French idioms to himself during dinner, but was that any indication? Mr Gill stopped paying attention to him early. Not the kind of boy a father reaches without a long and lonely uphill climb. Early on, there were constant sideways looks exchanged between mother and father. Assurances held back, enthusiasms stifled. Frustrations ending in beatings when Gregory was little. Neighbors said he didn't scream, he screeched. Like a tropical bird. Nobody knew what it was he was trying to say in that avian language. Or who he thought might answer him.

Nights afterward my father could hardly look at me. I'd say good night and he'd sort of lift his night-time glass of hot milk and rum above the back of his *Newsday* like he was toasting an invisible guest. Or, if my mother had settled nearby with her crocheting, he'd make an extra effort to finally look me in the eye to show her he wasn't afraid of our connection at all. Before bed, my mother would hold my face in her cold hands and give me clinging kisses on both cheeks, like the ones she gave her orphaned nieces from Porto, meant to watch over them when she wasn't there. You didn't need to hear her or understand Portuguese to know she was whispering to God to protect her strange little boy from all those things that could get him in New York. In 1981. Not like back in her mythical, whitewashed ivory crown of a village perched on that serene mountaintop overlooking the Spanish border.

Imprisoned by her hands, I'd close my eyes tight and make believe the darkness confirmed that none of this was happening. I knew that my parents were trying, but the words wouldn't form and I'd have to do the talking for all of us sooner or later.

Mrs Gill explained that Gregory had always been "a little nervous and shy" to anyone who brought the subject up. She'd hesitate, fawnlike, before disclosing her description, then shrug like it wasn't of any use to speak. When pressed further she'd offer an awkward smile, like maybe if you looked at him from some upside-down angle you might see that Gregory possessed an incipient charm.

Gregory – thin, naturally coordinated, gifted with a streamlined, foal-like musculature, but compelled to hide himself below woollen sweaters even on the hottest days. Green almond-shaped eyes that led to questions about a possible Afro-Asian heritage.

He wore insect-eye tortoiseshell glasses and, even when you were talking to him, had a tendency to slip one or two carefully studied steps behind you. He never laughed or swore or ran; he'd had his overt enthusiasm trained out of him. He touched the backs of chairs before sitting down as if he had to constantly verify the presence of the real world. Strange fantasy secrets seemed to seal his forever pact with silence. Like when we all learned over the school intercom that Mrs Olivetti, the girls' gym teacher, had given birth to a boy and he started humming "La Marseillaise" real softly to himself while curling his lips towards a bemused smile.

Sometimes at night, reading in bed before sleep, when death is only a single page of darkness away, I wonder why his mother abandoned him after all those years of uphill struggle.

Just after I got my learner's permit, we were driving around near Jones Beach when the car next to us crushed a terrier of some sort. Gregory hid his eyes in his hands and sobbed.

He opened up once to me and said in his carefully moderated voice that he daydreamed about growing up in South Africa or Namibia and fighting for a country. On my fifteenth birthday, he gave me triangular stamps from Mozambique because they had brilliant pictures of iridescent honeybirds and he knew that I occasionally went birdwatching with my brothers. He spoke French to people who teased him. He knew they didn't understand. But that, I suppose, was the point.

In a corner of my basement, I goaded him into looking at pornographic photos for the first time, men bowed back, hoisting up powerful erections. I was calculating and casual. He stared at me with a criminal look in his eyes, then dashed home for the safety of his familiar regrets. I felt the weight of our solidarity at the back of my throat. Affirming an identity to yourself can have unforeseen consequences for somebody like Gregory. We didn't talk much after that.

Tony's family lived in a big old clapboard house behind Vito's Restaurant on Mineola Avenue, and the baked ziti and pizza scents that had come to inhabit their walls and furniture would never be exorcised. Mr Silva hailed from the arid city of Beja in the southern interior of Portugal and Mrs Silva from Fajardo on Puerto Rico's northeast coast. It was the climatic differences that produced their arguments, even the bruises and burns on her arms, Mr Silva claimed. How could he be expected to get along with a woman born in a rainforest? They had four children, Tony the oldest. Their limbs were all too long, and the protruding, bug-eyed, questioning face that Tony made when he ate had solidified in varying degrees in each of the younger Silvas as their normal, resting expression. Mrs Silva's fidgety anxiety in her children's presence, her lowered eyes, her yearning gentility all gave you the feeling that her family embarrassed her. A long depression following the birth of her youngest took her appetite and left her with skeletal arms and wrinkled, turkey skin. Waxy blue veins shone through on the undersides of her wrists and she often gazed around as if astonished to still be in this world.

Mr Silva was a plumber for the town of Hempstead. He went bare-chested in summer, the black hairs on his chest and shoulders matted and sweaty. He never learned any of our names and frightened us all. Tony used to say you could hear the Miller and Super Bock beer sloshing in his stomach whenever he came near. And that it was a good thing, a jungle drumbeat of warning.

Mr Silva didn't come to the funeral. Nobody knew why but we all tacitly acknowledged that it was because he was drunk. Mrs Silva sat with her three youngest, clutching with those bony, shrunken hands onto her black leather bag like it was going to fly away at any moment, the kids' faces all asking those protruding questions. It scared me the way she gripped Tony's head and whispered conspiratorially to him. My mother stood at attention behind her and led her away when the ceremony was about to begin.

Was it significant at all that the game had never really ended at the playground? And if it had gone on would Tony have sauntered home a different way, and the funeral and Gregory Gill's arrest and my mother hugging Mrs Silva would all have never happened?

Those questions meant a lot to me for about a year, conjured up repetitive nightmares. Then the spectrum of tempting possibilities faded away and the past became dry and sepia-toned and varnished –

what it was and what would never be changed and what we'd tell other people who hadn't been there.

Our damning secret was that we treasured the one meaningful event that had ever happened in our neighborhood. This unspeakable admission played like an anxious, unacknowledged pedal point for weeks, and when it was finally covered by the normal droning melodies of school and home, the single date of Tony's death was highlighted in thick red on our timeline of forever boredom: 6 May 1981. Life was always a little safer afterward. As if a powerful necromancer who had threatened all our futures had been vanquished. But we were at an age when we craved danger. The year crept slower towards graduation without his excitement.

Gregory Gill remembered most all of it. In the hospital emergency room, holding his hand over his ripped, bloodshot eye, he repeated over and over to the resident on duty that it was self-defence. It was his mother who must have gotten him the cardigan-sweatered lawyer from Manhattan with the long blond hair tied in a ponytail. Who else would've called?

A few years later, Gregory's sister Linda informed me in an adamant voice that the lawyer was just like Gregory, one of them, you understand. She flipped her wrist and batted her eyes to make sure we'd get her meaning. Like me, you mean, I said. She blinked her startled eyes and looked around for someone to nudge. That was how my youngest brother found out. My father had wanted him to be spared the burden till he was eighteen.

There Gregory was, sitting in the field behind the school, pencilling translations from his dictionary onto the margins of *L'Éducation Sentimentale*. He saw Tony from a long way off, fought his urge to stare. But the tugging pace of his heart pulled his eyes from his book. He said "Hi" to fill in the castigating silence. Tony nodded towards him. Who you saying "Hi" to? You, just to be friendly. Me? You want to be friendly to me? Gregory was saying that he'd just go back to reading and was that OK – *ca va*? What did you say? Just was it OK? Yeah, it was fine, but if he really wanted to be friendly, something else might be better. Tony cupped his hand under his balls so that there'd be no doubt.

Mrs Gill had taken Linda shopping to Macy's at Roosevelt Field. Gregory's room was in what should have been a kitchen pantry. People said they could've added on another real room, that they had the money since Mr Gill's direct-mail business had taken off, but that they treated Gregory like a temporary visitor whom they didn't really want but had a religious obligation to accept. It had a small window that looked out on the side yard where Mr Gill had parked the old Rambler for the last time. For spare parts it was to be. After a while, when its wheels had been stripped and it had rusted beyond hope, it settled into its neighborhood role as an urban sculpture.

The bedroom door was shut and locked. Mrs Gill had suggested the lock because she preferred not to accidentally find Gregory with something she shouldn't see.

Nobody in the neighborhood said they heard a sound. But the window in Gregory's room had been shattered. Tony's hand, palmed over Gregory's face, had prevented him from screaming through the open frame. There were blue and yellow bruises on his cheeks for a week afterward. His collarbone and a rib were broken. The cornea on one of his eyes got torn pretty badly. Human tissue is surprisingly fragile when not made-up for primetime television.

The knife was on top of a yellow plate next to the last slices of cake Mrs Gill had baked.

Afterward, Gregory would say he didn't know where he got it. Deflated, panicked, he sat at the edge of Tony's stain of blood, so silent that it was hard to tell what kind of voice might come out. His crusted fingers knotted together as if he was praying or locking inside his stomach the knowledge of whatever had happened. He never cried. Two big white medics, both with moustaches, walked him into the ambulance.

Mrs Silva was visited by the police. She said she knew it was terrible news. Tony had been conceived before her marriage and drew bad things to him. He wasn't ever gonna live a long life. Afterward, on those muggy New York summer evenings when it seems our lives are endless, we sometimes saw her sitting on her porch. But she never talked to anyone except her three youngest.

Though all the city tabloids called it a racial incident, she was all too aware of Gregory's reputation and formed her own scenario.

Mr Silva stopped drinking and managed to find his wife's image of God, coming to believe that Tony's death was a message from Him on the need to live a righteous life. He now does all the plumbing and some of the carpentry for the Our Lady of Grace Church in Floral Park and only charges half for labor. Despite his wife's inattention and his own inclinations, he neither raises his voice nor lifts a hand against her. I guess you can change sometimes if it's a question of survival.

The Gills' house is still there, and Gregory's room is back to being a pantry for a Thai family from the Bronx. Pungent ginger and lemongrass smells come from there now, at all hours of the night and day. One morning when we walked by, we found that the Rambler sculpture was gone. In its place was this gawky plant with orange tubular flowers. Nobody knows where Mr and Mrs Gill went. My mother sees Linda now and then at the Pathmark supermarket, but doesn't talk to her.

I brought Gregory some French literary magazines, which I found at an Italian bookstore on Fifth Avenue, when he was out on bail and staying with his lawyer. He said *merci* but would only let me into the foyer. His attorney had said not to have guests. We stood talking in hushed, awkward voices for a few minutes. A black patch covered his right eye. He'd have an operation. It was feeling OK.

After I had a lover for the first time, we'd go to the old neighborhood sometimes and I'd show him to the island playground. On nights when we'd secretly make love in my old bedroom under my childhood quilt, I'd daydream about those days and not be able to recognize the kid I was, as if that iron bind on my heart had never really been there because here I was in love now, lying with a lifelong friend, safe and secure. People forget how it was. It's like a kind of grace maybe that they do.

In front of the playground, in our car, I'd think of Tony and Gregory, what happened that day in the kitchen of the Gills' house. And the ripped body hugging the floor, covered with both their bloods mingling together and as mixed up as everything else except the local newspaper headlines. That ghostly scene infiltrated my mother's and father's thoughts, too, every time they looked at me from my darkened doorway. But parents are powerless after a certain point, and they never spoke about it.

My lover and I would invariably watch a game or two at the old island playground, and I'd remember Tony's loopy smile. It fled his face for a moment as he tugged his hands back through his hair, hesitating on the Gills' steps so he could look around for those watchful Portuguese eyes. Inside, behind the closed door, his walk was wild, confident, and he discovered his grin again, because letting go for the first time and playing for real was going to be a relief. Gregory's hands were dangling by his sides, and his beseeching, expectant expression was asking this basketball star for the secret, the password he had always wanted and never received. He closed and locked the door to the pantry. A blow hammered his back. He gripped the ground, turned. Tony was shouting that he was no faggot's friend, so he'd better suck it, choke on it now, and there was no getting away till he got what he wanted no matter how much it hurt and how much whimpered begging he heard. Gregory gave a dry shriek till Tony tossed him against the wall by the window. His collarbone and rib snapped under the force. His terrified glance caught a rivulet of blood snaking across his wrist. A hand palmed over his face cut his eye and held his screams, and a feverish voice was shouting for him to take it, take it, take it now, till the grip was loosened and a slap was stinging his cheek and Gregory was racing into the kitchen and holding the knife with both hands and thrusting it as hard as he could into Tony's chest when he leapt into the air after him.

It felt horribly right in the moment afterward, Gregory told me before he caressed the lawyer's door closed. Like a golden regret you'd polish for ever because it meant you had a right to be alive.

Speak My Language

*A Tale of Seduction, Corruption
and Abandonment in Three Parts*

Jeffrey Round

———

I

THIS IS NOT YOUR COUNTRY

It was the usual Friday-night crowd, sipping beer and complaining about the heat. The Americans had taken over Bar Magenta, a watering hole for expat models and anyone who wanted to sleep with models. Tired of all the metrosexuals, Matt finished his beer and left.

Outside, the sidewalk was mired in a squabble of tables and parked motorbikes. The scent of cologne and cigarettes lingered. Across the street, a figure stood framed in a pool of light. Dark curls blew across an oval face. A white T, chinos with rolled-up cuffs and a leather jacket slung over one shoulder completed the uniform. He seemed to have stepped onto the corner from some far-off world.

A group staggered out of the bar and Matt felt someone brush against him. He turned to see a boy he'd worked a show with earlier that week.

"Sincerely sorry," the boy said then he recognized Matt. "Matt! How's it goin', dude?"

"Great, Kent – looks like you're off for some fun."

"Gotta make the most of the weekend! Hafta face that old sidewalk come Monday morning." He gestured vaguely toward his companions, who had stopped drunkenly to watch the exchange.

"Catch you later, then," Matt said.

"Awesome, man – keep well."

The group staggered into the street, oblivious to passing cars and other mortal dangers. When Matt looked over again, the boy with the leather jacket was standing next to him, lips wrapped around a cigarette. He took it from his mouth and let it fall.

"My name is Giorgio," he said.

Matt stared into green eyes framed by a grove of dark lashes.

The boy waited. "You don't know yours?" he asked with mild sarcasm.

Matt laughed and extended a hand. "Sorry – it's Matt."

"*Piacere*. Pleased to meet you." Giorgio pointed across the street. "And that is Paolo."

Matt looked over but saw no one. "Where?"

"There – my motorcycle is called Paolo." He looked slyly at Matt. "If you are free, Paolo and I will take you for a ride."

Matt liked his humor. He felt drawn to the boy's dusky presence.

"All right," he said. The soft night air and beer had dulled his thinking. He agreed without considering where this might be heading.

Giorgio slipped on his jacket as they crossed the dark street. They passed a fence topped by dangerous-looking spikes constraining a garden. Giorgio took a penknife from his pocket, reached through and freed a blossom.

"What's the rose for?" Matt asked.

Giorgio looked at the blood-red flower as though he'd just discovered it in his hands. "I think it is for you," he said, handing it to Matt.

Matt took the rose and considered it.

"You have a problem?" Giorgio asked.

"No," Matt said, inserting it through a buttonhole in his vest over his heart. "It's just that in my country, boys don't give other boys flowers."

"This is not your country. It is mine." Giorgio stood over the motorbike and gunned the starter. It roared and shook with life. "Climb on!"

Matt slid a leg over the seat and sat unsteadily behind. Giorgio turned to give him a sarcastic stare.

"If you sit this way you will fall off. You must put your arms around me. Are you afraid?"

"I'm not afraid."

He gripped Giorgio's torso, feeling the flanged ribs beneath his jacket. The bike rolled onto the pavement and picked up speed. Warm wind lifted Matt's hair as they passed under stone archways and along winding streets. The facades of ancient granite buildings flew by until they seemed to have left the twentieth century behind, vanishing into the cool face of antiquity.

Matt held on tightly, leaning in with the curves. Smooth leather grazed his cheek as they weaved in and out of traffic. The bike veered onto a narrow roadway following a shadowy canal.

"There is the *naviglio*," Giorgio shouted over the noise of the engine.

The bike glided to a halt and they dismounted.

"I will take you to my favourite bar," Giorgio said, leading them along a dark cobbled street pursued by the echo of their footsteps.

Water rippled to the right, reflecting the pale street lamps lining its edges. They came to a building with a flashing sign – Scimmia Jazz – that lit up the block.

"What's it say?" Matt asked, looking up.

"Shee-me-yah," Giorgio pronounced. "It means the animal that lives in the trees and likes bananas. How do you call it?"

"A monkey?"

"That's it – Jazz Monkey."

The bar bristled with music as they entered. A saxophone made clipped squawking sounds like coins tossed across a tabletop. A singer poised in a pin-spot of light broke into song as though she'd been waiting for them.

"I will buy the beer," Giorgio said, taking out his wallet as a waitress came up balancing her tray.

Giorgio held up his fingers in a V-formation and she pushed two glasses across the water-beaded surface of the table. He fanned a collection of bills at her, allowing her to pull several from between his fingers. She said something in rapid Italian. Giorgio turned to Matt.

"She says you are a very handsome American boy."

"*Grazie*," Matt said. He removed the rose. "May I?"

"Of course."

He laid it across her tray.

"*Per me? Grazie!*" she said, laughing as she went on to the next table.

Matt relaxed beside Giorgio, their bodies gently nudging one another. Whatever was happening between them felt slow and easy.

"I did not think you would come with me," Giorgio said. "Most American boys do not talk to the Italians."

"I'm not American – I'm Canadian."

Giorgio shrugged. "Is it not the same thing?"

"Not to a Canadian."

"You are quiet and more polite."

Matt laughed, thinking of his well-mannered and order-loving compatriots back home. How happily they queued up for anything, how politely they behaved even when they went on strike or protested the government.

"But you have the same country," Giorgio persisted. "The American president is your president, no?"

Matt shook his head and laughed again. "We share the same continent, but we're a separate nation with our own government."

Giorgio regarded him curiously. "What is it like to be a Canadian?"

Matt had to think about it. "It's very clean back home. Canadians believe in fairness and respect for the individual, and protecting the environment, and we're . . ." But he couldn't think what they were exactly. "It's a big country, so it's a lot of things." He shrugged. "What's it like to be Italian?"

"The best, of course!" Giorgio said, laughing. "Italians have passion and we love beauty and our country. But you are a lucky country, I think. It was never a big war in Canada."

Matt recalled the train station he'd emerged from on his arrival, a long crypt-like monument fronted by prancing stone horses erected to the glory of Mussolini and his *Fascisti*.

"No," he agreed. "Not a big war."

The music flowed, shifting moods with the crowd. It was well past the oasis of midnight when the band stopped playing, disregarding the stamping and cheering of patrons hoping to extend the night for just one more number that might possibly stretch on to eternity.

Outside, it had cooled slightly from the day's oppressive heat. The evening was deflating like a balloon, in small degrees. They mounted a footbridge over the *naviglio* and stopped midway. The moon, half-light and half-shade, reflected soggily on the water, rippling with the slight breeze.

"It's nice here," Matt said, his gaze following the river.

"Yes, I thought you will like this place."

Matt glanced over. Dark ringlets framed Giorgio's face. A smile flickered, faded. Giorgio moved closer, breath held. Matt shivered as their lips touched – moist, warm – then parted.

He stood there, becoming aware of certain things – a taste of salt in his mouth, the smell of flowers in the air, the infinitesimal distance between stars. Things that had been there all along, but which he'd never noticed before. It was like looking over the wall into an unknown country.

He'd just been kissed by another man. In the world he'd inhabited until that moment, such a thing would have been impossible. *Tabù*. But here was a boy in a black leather jacket wearing a white T-shirt with curls fawning around his neck . . .

Giorgio's lips pressed forward again, retracing their eager route. Matt felt a sense of trepidation, as though he'd broken some inviolable rule. He pulled back.

Giorgio's face wore a look of bemused intoxication. "I think this is another thing the boys in your country do not do."

All at once, the feeling of trepidation vanished. "No – none that I know of," Matt said.

"I had to kiss you – you were so beautiful." Then, almost apologetically, "I do not kiss other boys very often."

"You could've fooled me," Matt said.

Giorgio grinned. "You have a problem? Are you afraid?"

"No," Matt shook his head. "Not any more, I guess."

They laughed at the same time. Matt felt Giorgio's hand steal into his, their fingers intertwining.

II
A SACRED PLACE

The boat rounded the escarpment as Domenico stilled the motor. Wooden masts filled a small harbour like rows of crosses in the slicing blue afternoon. A tree-dotted terrain rose above, rheumatic and inaccessible, a handful of buildings rooted to the black slopes.

"This is San Fruttuoso," Domenico said in his softly accented English. "It is a fishing village. There are no roads over the mountain, so it may be reached only by boat."

This was the surprise he'd been promising Matt once the round of fashion shows was over. Although Italy was Domenico's home, and the centrepiece of European fashion, most of the models in Milan's fashion houses were non-Italians. While some resented this, others took advantage of the opportunities for international sex-capades.

Matt and Domenico had flirted with one another since meeting at a disco the previous month, but so far nothing had happened between them. Matt suspected Domenico had brought him to this out-of-the-way spot in the hills of the Italian Riviera for seduction.

"I want to tell you this place is sacred," Domenico continued in his dreamy voice.

"Why is that?" Matt asked, looking up into Domenico's suntanned face and gleaming brown eyes.

"Once there was a big storm when all the men of the village were on the sea. When they returned safely, the people made a sign of thanks to God. Under the water is a statue of *Gesù Cristo*. He is covered in gold and is very tall. He stands on the bottom blessing the boats that pass out to catch fish."

"Cool!" Matt said. "Where is it?"

"Over there somewhere," Domenico replied, pointing to an area that took in half the bay. He handed Matt a pair of swimming goggles. "Put on these glasses and dive. You will see it."

Matt fitted the goggles over his head and dove. Shafts of light split the underwater gloom. Schools of silvered fish meandered by. There was nothing that looked like a statue, only sand and a few rocks. He kicked back up and broke the surface.

"I can't see it," he said between gasps.

"I remember! It is over here," Domenico said, swimming away.

Matt followed then kicked his legs and dove again. To his right, face upturned and hands lifted in blessing, a dark silhouette reached up from the bottom surrounded by rays of sunlight transformed into a chalky moonlight.

Matt kicked down further. A dull weight pressed at his temples as he touched the tip of an extended finger. It felt surprisingly mild, as though it might warm him in the cool depths. He turned and pushed upwards, exploding into the air, coughing and spluttering.

"You have seen it?" Domenico called out.

"Yes!" he choked out. "I touched it!"

Domenico took the goggles and dove. Other seekers had reached them now, diving and coming back up subdued.

They returned to the dinghy, resting on the hot seats while the sun dried them. Domenico was the first to stir. He took up the oars and guided them to shore. Once on land, he grabbed the basket of food.

"We must take the oars for someone not to steal the boat," he announced.

Matt hoisted the oars across his shoulders. After a fifteen-minute climb, Domenico called a halt. Small, twisted trees extended branches of fattening figs and olives, the over-ripe fruit corrupting in the air. Matt laid his burden down and turned to look back. The village lay far below. At the horizon, sky and sea poured into one another with an ineffable blueness.

They stripped off their bathing suits and settled under the shade of a crabbed fig. The boys laughed to see their faces and limbs coated with salt, their hair sun-dried and dishevelled. Matt rubbed a hand over his chest and grimaced at the sharp, dry sensation.

"I'm getting a burn," he said.

"You are not used to our sun," Domenico chided. "You are only an honorary Italian, my friend."

Domenico reached for the basket, retrieving a bottle. He uncorked it with his teeth then lifted his head and drank until the wine spilled out his mouth and down his neck. He looked slyly over at Matt as his cheeks expanded and he spewed a shower of red.

Matt smiled and wiped the drops from his face and chest, then held out his hand. Domenico passed the bottle to him. Matt raised it slowly and sipped. He swallowed once, twice, three times. Then with a quick flip he inverted the bottle, pouring a stream over Domenico's head. The two burst into laughter.

"Now we are baptized!" Domenico exclaimed.

Within minutes the sun had dried them, as though its merciless kiss could tolerate no moisture. Domenico reached for the basket again. He grasped a flask of oil and tipped a long, thin stream into his hands. He rubbed his palms together and placed them on Matt's shoulders. A pungent odour rose as he kneaded flesh that beaded and knifed with pain.

Matt leaned his head on Domenico's chest and felt a delicate weaving of desire. The air was dense with scents and the sounds of insects and birds. Amber flowers nodded among the greenness and the solitary murmuring of bees.

Domenico raised the flask again and let the oil spill over Matt's chest. He traced a finger across his pectorals then down between Matt's thighs. Matt's cock lengthened and swelled in his slippery palm. Their lips met. Purpling fruit hung like dark flesh under the coronal of the fig tree.

Domenico straddled him. Matt pushed upward without penetrating.

Domenico laughed at his clumsy efforts. "No, like this, bambino," he whispered, grasping Matt's erection, guiding him in, unfisting him once he was secure.

Matt fell back as Domenico's body began to buck and grip. The struggle embarrassed and excited Matt, making him gasp until he felt a sensation like an iris dilating, beams of light discharging into the other's body.

The sky leaned forward. Clouds dissolved as everything stopped for a solitary moment before time began its ineluctable spread around them again, inconspicuous, in tiny endless waves of consolation.

III
ABLE WAS I ERE I SAW ELBA

It was midnight when they reached the campground. The trek had taken them on a long winding route over the mountains in the dark, past Napoleon's prison-home during his exile on Elba, while the defeated emperor regrouped his flagging ambitions before staging his second attempt at conquering the world

Gian Carlo and Matt set up the tent where the attendant indicated. He hadn't been happy to see them arrive at his gate, possibly because they were two young men without women or maybe just because they'd woken him up. He scowled as if he might refuse them entry, then nodded and let them in. Lucky, as they were low on money and couldn't afford a hotel.

The campground was full. Silhouettes of palm and cypress trees towered over the soft tarpaulin erections of tents dotting the hills, the smell of sea everywhere. In the morning, they woke to the Mediterranean's cool green vista viewed from the far end of a horseshoe bay. The water bobbed with colorful sails hemmed in by a silver strip of sand. They spent the afternoon on and off the beach crowded with swimmers, getting burned and trekking into town at day's end.

Gian Carlo had offered to pay for the trip as a token of their affair, knowing Matt was flying home in a week. The modeling season was nearly over, and, although it had been his best year for earnings, he'd overindulged in Milan's social life, spending too much on booze and drugs and hanging around with the glitterati. You had to do it to boost your career, but this time he'd overdone it. He'd be going home with little to show for his efforts.

That evening they had an argument. It was a silly argument. They were in a bar on the beach when two German boys entered. The older was about twenty-five and very fit, the younger twenty, if that. They'd looked around before settling against the patio railing across from Matt.

The younger boy was attractive: clear skin with a hint of freckles, blue eyes and pale lashes, his finely shaped hands held down beside firm thighs. Matt drank in the boy's physical details, thirsty for the tiny bits of knowledge they offered about him while Gian Carlo sulked.

The boy knew Matt was watching him. His sprawl became a pose, as if to make himself more desirable, though he could hardly have been more so. As he stood there, he kept shifting and re-shifting his thighs that seemed to be offering to swallow Matt whole.

Gian Carlo stomped off indignantly, but soon returned and began dancing wildly with two Italian girls he'd met at the bar earlier. The older German watched him, calling him a gigolo to his young friend who leaned against the railing, glancing over at Matt from time to time.

Matt laughed to himself, thinking Gian Carlo deserved it. That was when the German boys began talking to him. He answered in their language, telling them he was Canadian. They switched to English then and said, "But you are one of us, yes? Your background is German?"

"Yes. Somewhat."

That was all.

Gian Carlo was mute on the way back to the campground, refusing to acknowledge Matt in either Italian or English. They trudged silently over the sand, from time to time stumbling across embracing couples whose skin glinted like pale fire in the moon's light.

Matt knew what was coming. He was used to Gian Carlo's sulky outbursts, waiting for the bitter, delicious fruit of his anger like sudden unexpected sex. He also knew he would miss Gian Carlo when they parted. Strange to say, but that was what he longed for – not the affair itself, but the tangible ache of loss that followed once it was over and the feelings of abandonment set in.

At last, Gian Carlo spoke. He demanded payment for Matt's half of the trip, accusing him of taking advantage of his affection.

"That's fine," Matt said. "I can pay you, if that's what you want."

"Does it not make you angry when I say that?" Gian Carlo demanded.

"No."

Matt smiled. He didn't want to make Gian Carlo mad. This wasn't how he wanted it to end, with tempers rubbed raw and egos flayed.

"You North Americans are so cold," Gian Carlo sneered.

Matt wasn't sure if Gian Carlo was jealous over the Germans or upset that he was leaving for good. Not that he could have stayed. In any case, it was almost over now. It was time to return to the real world. Way past time.

Matt opened his wallet and removed two bills. He shrugged and handed the notes to Gian Carlo, who took them with a frown.

"Do you have anything left now?"

"No – nothing," Matt said. Which wasn't true.

Gian Carlo hesitated then held out one of the two bills. Matt stuffed it back in his pocket. Nothing more was said. At last, they crawled into the tent and undressed silently.

They lay together side by side for a long time without touching. Matt felt the tension, the unspoken resentment. He reached out and draped an arm over Gian Carlo's hip, waiting for him to throw it off. When he didn't, Matt pulled him closer.

Gian Carlo rippled with suppressed tears. He was a silly boy – twenty-four, though he still lived at home with his parents. A dutiful son.

Gian Carlo nudged his ass against Matt's crotch and wriggled in that wordless way he had of saying he wanted to be fucked. They had sex one last time, Matt's firm, lean body arching over Gian Carlo's softer brown flesh, the canvas taut above them.

It wasn't the sex Matt desired so much as the feel of muscles poised and pressed against the places where they encountered each other's bodies. The piston-like strokes of Matt's flesh entering Gian Carlo's excited him, while the palindrome "Able was I ere I saw Elba" kept pulsing through his brain.

Afterwards, they lay side by side without touching. This time there was no tension, just a soft unwinding of muscle.

Matt waited till he heard Gian Carlo's deep breathing before he allowed himself to relax fully. In the morning, he would leave before Gian Carlo awoke, catching first the bus back over the mountains and then the ferry down at the harbour, returning to the mainland alone.

Flags of the Vlasov Army
Ian Young

London in the Thatcher years – from the late seventies through to the eighties – had seen better days. And Finsbury Park, the working-class district where I lived, was especially shabby. Its grim, crumbling Victorian terraced houses and the eerie silence of its evening streets gave it an atmosphere of decrepitude, neglect and gloom. But when I look back on that early time, I remember best the people I came to know – most of them good people, all of them struggling to get by, as I was, some of them living day to day, others lost in memories, nursing dreams. When you are young, you imagine you have nothing – yet you take so much for granted. Only later in life do you realize how lucky you've been. But one thing I appreciated, even then, was the old, green-painted shop near the high street, Boris Mostoyenko's stamp shop – with its slightly faded sign that said HOME & OFFICE – STAMPS FOR COLLECTORS, and the light that shone from the back kitchen through the glass of the front door and onto the street. We were lucky to have a place where we could always be sure of a welcome on a cold evening, a warm stove to sit by, and an enamel mug of hot, sweet tea.

It was at Boris's that I first met Henk Sonderhausen, a lanky, temperamental Dutch daredevil whose pugnacity and streak of exhibitionism were always getting him into scrapes. Henk was one of the few true bisexuals I've ever known, and his rosy cheeks and mop of blond hair endeared him to teenage girls, old ladies and boy-fanciers wherever he went.

I met Henk on the night of the big fight. Tommy Noakes, an aging local boxer who was everyone's friend, was scheduled to fight the Finnish middleweight champion at the Park Road Boxing Club. The

Finn's scheduled opponent (who had knocked Tommy out a few months before) had broken his hand, and Tommy had been drafted to take his place at the last minute. It was the one big break of Tommy's less than glorious career, and all his friends from the neighborhood were eager to see him fight the Scandinavian, who was in line to try for the European championship later in the month. Tommy himself was so excited he was having trouble sleeping and his trainer was getting more worried by the day.

The bout was scheduled to start at eight in the evening, and the stamp shop usually stayed open late. So when I walked in the door at about half past six, Boris was especially glad to see me.

"My prayers are answered!"

"Yes, God sent me, Boris! What can I do for you?"

"First, you sit. Get warm. Then, while you relax, I will assign duties."

Boris's shop was a hodge-podge of three or four different shops in one. Signs taped to the front window announced BOOKS, STAMPS, STATIONERY and APPLIANCE REPAIR. One side of the shop was piled with broken toasters, used record players, old electric typewriters, antique radios and parts of unidentifiable machines. The other side was fitted out with brown-painted bookshelves. Some of these held envelopes, staplers, notebooks, packets of coloured writing paper and rolls of stout brown parcel wrapping. The rest were crammed with second-hand books, mostly of pre-war vintage. On Boris's shelves I found Madison Grant's *The Passing of the Great Race*, Winwood Reade's *The Martyrdom of Man*, Elinor Glyn's *The Philosophy of Love* and Nicholas Roerich's *Shambala* – all of them half-buried among dusty, broken sets of the works of Henry van Dyke, H. de Vere Stacpoole, Charlotte M. Yonge, Warwick Deeping, and other bestsellers of long ago, now yellowed, foxed, chipped and forgotten.

Towards the back of the shop was the counter and, behind it, five-foot high walls of labeled wooden drawers in rows, holding stock cards and packets of foreign stamps, as well as coins, badges, buttons and an assortment of other bits and pieces. Beyond was the spacious kitchen with its large round table, unmatched wooden chairs and long, overstuffed couch, all surrounded by precarious piles of encyclopedia volumes, magazines, comics, outdated roadmaps and much-thumbed copies of *Gay Times* and *The Catholic Worker*. A narrow staircase led upstairs to the living quarters, and a heavy, metal door to a small, weed-covered yard and a shed that served as a workshop. Taped to the wall above the gas stove was a yellowing sign that said, in printed red letters, THE TEA IS FREE. Underneath, someone had written "Sandwiches 10p". Posters, advertisements and portraits covered the walls. An ornate gold frame held a slightly damaged painting of the Infant Jesus of Prague, crowned and solemn, hand raised in benediction.

Boris was working at the counter as I closed the shop door behind me. Dressed, as usual, in grey flannels and a ratty cardigan, he was a small, wiry man of indeterminate age, balding and rather birdlike, with an erect, military bearing, and (I knew) surprising strength and stamina. A sardonic smile was his usual expression. Behind him in the kitchen I could see the identical figures of Elliot and Lionel, one of them sitting at the round table sorting through piles of old envelopes, the other standing at the stove stirring furiously.

"Elliot, it won't hurt that soup at all if you should stir it a little more slowly. Thank you. What was I saying? Oh yes. When I first got to this country I could not properly say the letter 'W'. I would say 'Voolvorts' instead of 'Woolworths'! So – I taught myself by repeating every day over and over, 'The Wormy old Wolverine of Wolverhampton' – you see, I was living in Wolverhampton at the time."

At the stove, Elliott giggled and shook his head, and Lionel sitting at the table did the same. Handsome, disheveled boys in their late teens, they were Boris's helpers and companions, uncannily identical, with thick, dark curly hair and long eyelashes. Somehow Boris seemed to have no trouble telling them apart but no one else ever could and how he did it remained his secret. They were apparently twins but if you referred to them as that, you would be treated to a standard short lecture from one or the other of them (or both). They were not twins, you would be told, but triplets. There had been a third-born, so the story went, their "baby brother" Theodore, who had died at birth, and whose brief existence on the planet they refused, on principle, to overlook. Baby brother's spirit was even represented, on special occasions, by an old, handsome and much-loved teddy bear. This being the night of the big fight, Teddy was now in evidence – parked on top of the fridge, his fuzzy head sticking out of a battered green Aer Lingus flight bag with a broken zipper.

"The wormy old wolverine of Wolverhampton . . ." Boris rolled his tongue around the consonants again, accompanied by more giggles from the triplets. "I repeated that linguistic mantra over and over so many times until I became the wormy old wolverine of Wolverhampton! And then I moved to Finsbury Park where I speak English as perfectly as she can be spoke. Almost! That tea is Tesco's special blend, a particularly good lot if I may say, so drink up."

I sat myself down across the table from Lionel and sipped the hot sugary tea, flavored with the peculiar metallic taste of condensed milk, and asked Boris what I could do for him. He held one finger in the air to indicate *Time Out*, reached into a drawer for his tobacco-rolling machine of green canvas and rusted metal, and proceeded to create a fat cigarette. As his tongue flicked along the gummed edge of the paper, he looked over his rimless glasses and winked at me. It would help immeasurably, he said, if I would watch the shop tonight and close up at the usual hour so he and the boys could get to the fight on time. I said I would.

"Lionel, when you come to a cover that's torn," Boris instructed, "put it in waste paper and keep just the stamps. The market for torn covers I have not yet discovered. So anyway, where was I?"

"You were telling us about the war," said Elliott, who was ladling out the soup.

"The war! Pah!" Boris raised his voice, spitting flecks of saliva into the air. "A nightmare from beginning to end, the war! Well, the whole of Europe was experimenting with government by the mentally ill! I was . . ." he said, lowering his voice and turning in my direction, "I was in the Polish army. Then Stalin invaded Poland and I was in the Soviet army. And then I was captured by the Germans and put in a bloody camp. And I wanted to get out of the camp any way I could and ended up with General Vlasov. You know who was General Vlasov?"

Elliot interrupted to point to an old framed black-and-white photo of a horse-faced man in rimless glasses and a military uniform. "That's him, isn't it?"

"That's him. If ever there was the right man at the wrong time, that was him!"

Apparently, Boris and the other Russians could get out of the camp if they joined General Vlasov's turncoat Russian army.

"Vlasov was one of Stalin's best generals," Boris told us. "And not many of them survived the purges. He kept Hitler out of Moscow and then was too daring for his own good and got captured. The Germans let him head up a Russian liberation army made up of all us rag-tag and bobtail and flotsam and jetsam from the conquered territories. What Vlasov had in mind, you see, was to fight Stalin and Hitler – and Russia would be free again. Again? What am I saying? Anyway, that was the idea and we had about one chance in a thousand of pulling it off."

Now Elliot was spooning bits of carrot out of his soup bowl into Lionel's, and they were both watching Boris.

"By that point, Hitler was getting his behind kicked good and hard and Stalin's armies were driving the Nazis back into Czechoslovakia. And we went with them and ended up in Prague in the spring of '45." Boris glanced at the clock. "Prague was held by the SS and the Russians were advancing fast. That's when we Vlasov men surprised everyone. In May, we rose up and attacked the SS, drove them out of Prague Castle, ran up the Imperial Russian flags we'd made, and chased the Germans out of the city. And that was the only day of the whole bloody war that I actually enjoyed . . . Come on boys, eat up. I refuse to be late for the fight."

"Someone said you were a war hero," one of the triplets said cheerily.

"They were most ill-informed! I was no such thing!" Boris answered. "I was a hunted man. I, Boris Mostoyenko, was chased across Europe like a rat and only escaped by the skin of my teeth. History issued one of its wicked decrees – and instead of heroes we were traitors! Churchill and Roosevelt did a deal with Stalin, you see. And Stalin insisted that all the Vlasov men be handed over to be shipped to Siberia in the boxcars they were no longer using for Auschwitz."

Of course, we all wanted to know how Boris got away.

"Fortune smiled on handsome young Boris." He tipped his head back and smiled. "I had a tiny affair with a rather good-looking English officer. And the Englishman got wind of what was up and warned me. To him and to God I owe my life. But I found out later that there were Vlasov men on the run all over Europe – with every soldier and policeman on the lookout. So much for our great enterprise to save Mother Russia! We ended up scurrying like rats in the ruins! I, Boris Mostoyenko, lived in a pigpen! In a pigpen! For a week! And your old Boris ended up in Vienna where Marcus Grumbacher was with the Allied Control Commission – and he got me out, thank God."

So that was where Boris had met the distinguished Marcus Grumbacher. I had met Marcus several times – a portly, well-dressed Liechtensteiner with silver hair, an evaluator of rare coins and (Boris had confided in me one day) the silent partner behind Boris's shop.

"What happened to General Vlasov?" I wanted to know.

Boris Mostoyenko looked right at me, paused for dramatic effect, and slowly spoke. "General Vlasov," he said, "was one of those men who made a wild, brave gamble with history – and lost. Stalin hanged him."

The soup bowls were piled in the sink and Boris and the triplets headed off to the boxing club, carrying Teddy in his flight bag. And I was left alone in the shop to look through the bookshelves and stamp packets, to stroke Tom, Boris's mouse-catching housecat, to browse through the musty old books and make cups of tea. There were few customers.

As I was standing behind the shop counter toward closing time, I came across an old leather-bound album with photos of a younger Boris in what looked like a tiny chapel, stripped to the waist, and enacting each of the stations of the cross. Then the little bell on the shop door tinkled, I looked up, and in came Henk Sonderhausen.

He was a tall, slim youth with a mop of blond hair, a wide mouth and a fair, apple-cheeked complexion. He wore a long army greatcoat that came down to the top of his Doc Martens, a slightly wilted yellow rosebud in his lapel, and a long, striped woolen scarf. When he saw me, the little frown on his face turned into a grin.

"Is Boris here?"

"No, he's gone to a boxing match. I'm sitting in for him. Can I help you?"

"I come to pay my debt," he said, and took a handful of change from his pocket. "I bought one of Boris's famous Cinderella packets and didn't have quite enough. So here's the rest." He placed a pair of 20p pieces on the counter.

"I'll make sure Boris knows you came in, " I said, slipping the coins into an envelope. "What's your name?" I wrote it on the packet. "Those Cinderella packets are great, aren't they? What did you get?"

"Some Touva triangles and lots of South Moluccan birds and flowers – and these, I don't know what they are."

From the pocket of his greatcoat, he took Boris's paper and glassine envelope with the drawing of Cinderella trying on the glass slipper, and removed three small, simply printed rectangles.

"I know what these are. Reproductions of old stamps from the Papal States."

"Are they forgeries?" he asked. He appeared to like the idea.

"Not forgeries exactly . . .reprints." I told him my name and stuck out my hand, which he pumped vigorously for a few seconds.

"It's getting cold out," he said.

"How about a cup of tea? It's time for me to close up."

He wrinkled up his pert little nose, which was slightly red. "I've got a better idea," he said. "I'll buy you a hot cider at that pub around the corner."

"Oh, you've discovered that! You're not from around here though, are you?"

"I'm from Holland," he said. He had only a trace of an accent. "But I'm living in Ilford. I work in the riding school in Wanstead."

I imagined him atop a horse, galloping across the countryside, hair and scarf blowing romantically in the wind.

"A cider sounds good! Let's go."

As we walked to the pub, Henk unbuttoned his coat, in spite of the chilly evening air. Beneath it, he had only a flannel shirt and a very tight pair of skimpy cotton shorts showing an ample bulge at the crotch. His thighs were milky white with little blond hairs. He grinned at me and I noticed the wide gap between his gleaming front teeth. "I like to show off!" he confided, and we both laughed. Well, I thought, he's certainly different as well as cute. And friendly!

To my surprise, the Four Kings was already packed when we arrived. Everyone seemed to be talking and laughing, and the place was full of smoke. As we pushed our way through the customers, I heard my name called loudly from one of the booths.

"Me fellow poet!" I looked in the direction of the booming voice and saw Seamus Moore, surrounded by the triplets and a few other locals. "Here he is, and a friend with him as tall as hisself!" Seamus roared, though he was a head taller than both of us. Seamus Moore was a local poet, a frequent and enthusiastic performer to captive audiences at the local launderette. He reminded us all, from time to time, that he was descended from "the famous Thomas Moore, the Irish man of letters" whom none of us had heard of. A large, raw-boned man with a beret, a grey beard and a full set of menacing yellow teeth, he was a pub regular who would only occasionally allow me to pay for my drink, and never minded that I ordered Coke.

"Boys, you missed the fight of a lifetime!" he shouted over the din. "Tommy took a terrible pounding from the Finn for the whole of three rounds but he would never go down. Then half a minute into the fourth, someone in the other corner yells out and the Finn turns and answers back. Answers back, he does! And as he turns his head, old Tommy sees his opening and takes it, by God! Tommy never could fend off the blows so well but he's got one good punch, that fine left hook on the rare occasion he can find a chance to use it, and he used it tonight, boys! Down went the Finn and never got up till the count was over! Oh, it was beautiful, I never seen anythin' like it! What are you boys drinking?"

"Cider!" Henk and I both said together, and joined in the general jubilation as Seamus made his way to the bar.

Henk and I wanted to talk and it was difficult to hear ourselves in the pub so after about twenty minutes we decided to make our exit. We said hello and goodbye to Boris, and to the battered Tommy, who was breathlessly asking everyone, "Did you see me, did you see me?" and stepped outside. At some pubs, the life inside overflows onto the street, but at the Four Kings, as soon as the doors shut behind you, the noise and light and warmth all suddenly cease, and there you are again, back in the dark, damp silence.

We were just about to head out when Seamus Moore clambered through the pub door and wrapped a huge arm around my shoulders.

He leaned toward me conspiratorially, his beard tickling my neck, his breath smelling of beer and tobacco. "You know, me friend," he whispered, "we're all glad our Tommy won tonight. But how many of them actually put money on him? Eh?"

It hadn't occurred to me. Very few, I'd suppose. As the local boy, Tommy was the sentimental favorite, but the odds against him had been long indeed.

"Well, I did!" confided Seamus, and took a roll of bills out of his coat pocket. He peeled two off. "You and your tall friend have a few on me to make up for missing the fight!" And, giving me a wet kiss on the ear, he turned away and aimed himself at the pub steps.

We hadn't walked more than a few blocks when Henk decided he had to take a piss. Instead of finding an obscure spot, he just stopped where he was – in front of the concrete wall of Latif's Service Station. He unbuttoned the appealing khaki shorts and leaning on the wall with one hand, took aim with the other, all the while grinning at me and talking about how to get to Ilford. We were a few yards down the street when we heard a shout behind us. Running from the service station were its owners, the Latif brothers, Winston and Mohammed. Winston, the older, larger and less unpleasant of the two, was bringing up the rear, and little Mohammed was charging ahead along the street yelling, "You piss on my wall! You piss on my wall! I charge you to the police!"

And so we ran as fast as we could through the empty streets, hopping over puddles and dodging around corners, past the cemetery wall and the closed stores, Henk's greatcoat flapping in the wind around his delicious naked legs, until we knew the Latif brothers would never find us. Then we collapsed on the little wooden bench outside the dusty windows of Mrs Singh's launderette, out of breath, laughing, and holding each other's arms.

We were there for a while, getting our breath back, and talked for a bit about the pub and the fight, and then just sat quietly, at first gazing across the street, then looking at one another.

"You dropped something," I said, and picked up a bit of paper – the torn-off corner from an envelope – that had fallen out of Henk's pocket.

"Oh, thanks. That's off a letter from my pen pal in Czechoslovakia."

I looked at the stamp – an engraving of the same Prague Castle Boris had helped liberate from the Nazis years before. I was about to say something when Henk put his hand lightly over my mouth, reached inside his overcoat and pulled out a little bottle in a brown leather cover.

"Rum!"

I took a sip and felt it warm my insides as I watched this tall, handsome boy perform a delicate pantomime. As we sat close together, Henk flung open his coat; I could see the wooden slats of the bench gently flattening his naked thighs. I brushed my fingers against the little blond hairs on his legs and wondered why he didn't have goosebumps as the night air was getting cold.

He took my hand in his big, smooth, long-fingered hand, and cupped my palm over his crotch. As he leaned back against the grimy window and took a swig of rum from the little bottle, the soft warmth in my hand stiffened under my fingers, his eyes closed, and a long, satisfied sigh drifted from his pink, parted lips and floated out to dissipate in the drab darkness of the street.

We were halfway home by the time it started to rain.

Potholes in the Yellow Brick Road
Neal Drinnan

The circumstances by which Randall Stout came to be checking out the décor of Redfern's Centrelink offices were curious but not unusual. He clung to whatever debris he could salvage to stay bouyant on the sea of despair. Once a man of a cheerful if cheeky disposition, fortune had been dealing from the bottom of the deck in the closing months of 2006. He'd finally been dealt the grim reaper he remembered from the 1980s. The gothic spectral figure that had attended his deflowering and hovered ever present, ever since.

Contracting HIV at forty-something is embarrassing to say the least. Upon notification, every hard-wired voice in Randall Stout's subconscious echoed the finger-wagging reproach, "You're old enough to know better you filthy sod!" And he was . . . "Mea culpa, mea fucking culpa," chanted that hoary old hag in his head. "Let's see you turn this into a musical and pull busloads from the 'burbs!" But whatever the tut-tuts and no-ninnies in the chorus might say, Randall's lapse of caution was a very human one, gothic in its denouement and Greek in its classicism. After all, unprotected sex happens; you've only got to open the newspaper . . . or your legs!

Twenty-five years of safe-sex indoctrination and more copulation, safe and otherwise, than might be considered respectable by his peers. Heaths and houses, this way and that, he'd not left too many stones or rotting logs unturned. And, say what you like, the spirit of the libertine has been present in the world since long before Stout's snout got whiff of it. No one could say he hadn't been warned.

Being HIV-positive meant he had to think positive, live positively and experience each day to the full. That's what the brochures and blogs said. Randall decided it was a wake-up call from the universe and frankly he'd been living a reckless life for far too long. These epiphanies happen after forty, someone had told him, and thinking back on his mentors they were all scoundrels, hedonists and whores who turned their debauchery into adventures, and memoirs just in the nick of time. It's worth living through anything if you can get a good story out of it and even the most appallingly louche have to clean up their act or pay the price. It was that price Randall was yet to reckon with.

The prognosis was good if he behaved. What he didn't count on was a ten-week seroconversion illness that began on a holiday abroad. Initially he thought it was dengue fever, the symptoms corresponded and he'd tested negative not four weeks prior. When the test trumpeted HIV, a mosquito could have knocked him over because he'd been tested three or four times a year for the past twenty-five years. Seventy-five times in total, according to his little book of facts and delusions. After that many tests, any number of which flirted with fate, it was difficult to sustain that mortal anxiety he'd affected as a younger man waiting for results that at the time did mean life or death.

So it was then, that seventy-fifth time, Randall limped into the doctor's surgery without so much as a butterfly in his gut to receive the news. "With the medication available today, you'll probably die of something else."

"Great," sighed Randall-poz-Stout. "I still get a shot at cancer and heart disease after all."

Two months of sickness slowed time down to a crawl. In hospital with a raging fever and pneumonia, Stout was close to out! IV antibiotics put the latter to rights but the rest of the time he lay on the couch. Nothing but DVDs of Nip/Tuck to watch and maximum doses of paracetamol to reduce fever and the curious aches and pains inhabiting his marrow like gremlins. These invading foes kicked like foetuses in the womb but they were no babies – these were the minions of the HIV virus endlessly replicating themselves in his system: destroying the being that apparently invited them in. Pain was Stout's valiant, yet futile, struggle against it. His viral load was "as high as we've ever seen, sir," according to the doctor while his T-cell count slipped down to a dangerous 220. A sturdy 64 kilos slipped in four weeks to a grim, skeletal 57. Fashionista weight, perhaps, but he looked more like Donatella on a bad day than Gianni on a good one.

Stout was no stranger to HIV in theory, or reality. He knew dozens of people infected and had lost others to its formidable end product. He'd written about it, researched it and ironically enough worked on safe-sex awareness campaigns, but he never realized how bad or long its overture might be. He was Stout by name, not by nature. For him an illness was ideally a random misfortune, borne with courage and made easier by the sympathy of loved ones. When it sneaks through the back door as it doubtlessly had in his case, it felt unseemly, no matter how loving or forgiving those around were. More humbling than the sea and leaving a similar taste in the mouth.

Randall's seroconversion lasted months and left him wondering if he was not slipping into the ghostly footsteps of departed friends who'd shrunk and trembled and been as brave as they could, until all that was left was their huge extraterrestrial eyes before they vanished behind the veil. Feeling like death had been one thing but the cold reality of financial survival was quite another. Without support, he wondered how anyone would cope with this. The licentious lure of his filthy former self had turned on him. He'd become a spectre at the ruin of his own feast.

His mother always said, "You want to make good and sure you've got plenty of money behind you after you're forty, because no one's gonna look twice at you otherwise!" Clearly, as his predicament indicated, that was not strictly true but these cheerful suggestions were echoed large in his subconscious, especially when the well did run dry.

Unable to work, he prevailed upon Centrelink and applied for Newstart. They sent glossy brochures with pictures of smiling, optimistic people on the front and when he phoned for information, the customer service people weren't in Mumbai; they were in Adelaide.

All in all, the process was much less painful than he had expected. He was prepared now to get some of his tax dollars back, gradually, at a cool $213 a week. He swallowed his pride with his Panadol and signed up.

The next week his doctor issued a medical certificate citing depression and fatigue as the malaise. Lame but adequate at that stage. This allowed him to forgo signing on for a couple of months. Nor was he compelled during that time to attend compulsory job interviews for positions he was wildly unsuited or unqualified to do. He nodded dutifully and cowered obsequiously as they ticked all their boxes. Then succumbed to the citation that should he still be ill in two months' time, he would require another certificate and need to undergo an interview. He brushed it all off; after all, he'd be much better by then, probably working as well.

Fortune, sly hound that it is, had him foxed. He'd no sooner shuffled to his feet and gained a couple of kilos, when shingles came a calling; a volatile virus that is one of the horsemen of HIV's quiet apocalypse. Furious that the summer had passed and he had played it out like a scene from *Camille*, he called upon his doctor for another certificate. We have to be honest with these people. "I'll need to mention you've got HIV and had pneumonia as well as shingles."

"Whatever," Randall muttered. Far too involved in morbid self-pity to consider the implications at that moment. It seemed all roads led back to the dole queue.

The Centrelink office was no Shangri-La. They dealt daily with conflicts most would cross the street to avoid but Randall's dark day beckoned and he was still ill. He turned up looking as sick as he could and was given instructions to wait until called for his "interview". While Centrelink might use the term "customer service", he was cautious. They could say what they liked in their literature but it was one of those places where he got the impression "the customer" wasn't always "right".

Bizarrely, he was far more nervous awaiting this consultation than the one in the doctor's three months prior. "What will they ask?" he thought to himself as his colleagues in limbo shifted uncomfortably on their chairs, each running their own silent incantations of woe. Here they all were, minorities together as one, native-title holders, Torres Strait Islanders, the disabled and the diseased. Coffee-coloured people by the score sitting about like long blacks and flat whites.

Would they want to know how he got HIV? He shivered while watching a very young customer-service consultant negotiate something unpleasant with someone unstable. Would they say stuff like "haven't you heard of safe sex?" or "if it was up to me, people like you wouldn't get a cent". He took a deep breath like it said to do on his meditation tape. He asked himself if all this was really worth it for $213 per week. At that moment prostitution seemed a less demanding option but that window of opportunity had slammed shut now. The breath didn't work. He was catastrophizing, which caused more stress – he shouldn't have stress because that could contribute to HIV turning into Aids; then where would he be? What if they asked if he knew who gave it to him or for a list of all the people he'd slept with? What if there was a panel of interviewers like in *Trainspotting*, one of them asking if he'd ever had unprotected anal sex while the others ranted about oral lesions, infectious bodily fluids, mucous membranes and IV drug use. Just what were they allowed to ask and just what did he have to tell?

Forty-five minutes passed. His mouth dry, his tongue feeling like the Nullarbor Plain. He looked at the man beside him, his face quietly dignified and uncannily reminiscent of David Gulpilil. Could it be him? At least this was not Sub-Saharan Africa, he told himself, with all that female genital mutilation and no hope of drugs or treatment. Always look on the bright side of life, he hummed. He thought about the articles he'd read on combination therapy, natural complementary therapies, the endless websites, links and conspiracy theories that stretched into the virtual never-never: Aids was introduced to eliminate blacks because they have no resistance to it. Homosexuals felt guilt – that made them susceptible. He sighed. Bizarre conspiracies, inexact sciences brewed up by an unfathomable agent with an unfathomable agenda. He thought about his Muslim neighbour who warned him with a smile that if they keep having Mardi Gras, there'll be another tsunami.

The doctor told him not to read up too much at this stage: "It will only confuse you." Perhaps he was right. Maybe it was the African monkeys who started it or that promiscuous Air Canada flight attendant or the Reagan administration. It hardly mattered where its seeds lay.

Now that it had been tamed, it was a gravy train for pharmaceutical companies in the West and a gruesome culling tool for the Third World. He was just a minor, elite symptom of a global sickness so vast he couldn't begin to contemplate it.

Time, like Centrelink's mustard-coloured carpet, stretched on while he felt shingle bumps on his shoulder and goose bumps from the air-conditioning.

You can only get shingles if you've had chicken pox. People who haven't had chicken pox, however, can catch it from someone with shingles. Randall felt irresponsible being in public with it and hoped those beside him didn't catch anything. In spite of all assurances to the contrary, he felt tainted. Ugly. Sexless. It took more confidence to kiss people now. He feared they'd pull away. When he cut himself, a plague issued forth. One he was sure could be seen by all.

He remembered in the eighties, offering a colleague a cup of tea in his kitchen. "Oh, no I won't," she said. "I know you can't get Aids from sharing cups but it'd be just my luck to be the first one who did!"

In the nineties, when he'd got fit at the gym, another associate spread "concerned" rumours that he had lost weight because he had Aids. After all those years of ignorance and prejudice when he didn't have HIV, he thought he must have outmanoeuvred it, bypassed it and triumphed, but it was always one step behind. Old Randall Stout was not as quick as he used to be.

"Stout." The name echoed like a guilty fart through that chamber of bureaucratic despair. His trembling hand gripped the doctor's certificate. His Waterloo had come and this young "customer-service consultant" standing before him was here to whisk him away to those sombre, bureaucratic authority figures who would assess his culpability and calculate his fate.

He was directed to sit and it seemed it was just the two of them after all. No authority figures to be seen. He relaxed a little. They smiled at each other like coy new lovers as he handed the certificate over.

"Don't you hate doctors' handwriting?" she asked.

Randall smiled. "I know, it must be part of the training."

He relaxed more to the gentle tap of the keyboard as he waited for the program containing the appropriate questions for the interview.

"HIV . . . Mmmm . . . It says here you can have three different types: HIV/Aids, secondary infection Aids . . ." There is a pause while a bottom lip is bitten and the third type considered.

"You're not in the final stages of Aids, are you?"

"Do I look like I am?"

"No, but with some of them you can't tell. One week they're fine, a fortnight later they don't sign on and you never see them again."

"Perhaps they've found jobs?" Randall offered hopefully but the mouse was clicking and she'd moved on to other business now.

"I just put HIV/Aids, OK?"

"Sounds good to me."

"Now, pneumonia . . . I can't seem to find it on the list . . . I'm not sure you can have that with HIV."

"Oh, believe me, with HIV you can have anything. It especially loves pneumonia."

"Nup, I can't find it. It's not on the list."

"Let's have a look." He turned the screen towards him and suppressed a giggle when he noticed the diseases listed.

They all started with "n".

"Oh, pneumonia starts with 'p'; it's silent like the 'h' in Chardonnay."

"Oh I love *Kath & Kim*, they're a pisser . . . It's not under 'p' either."

"Let me see that," he said cheerily, because his mood had definitely improved with this slapstick turn of events. It's true, there is no "pneumonia". There were all sorts of other more complicated things, conditions Randall had never heard of but no good-old three-times-and-you're-out pneumonia. Eventually he settled on something between an acute respiratory illness and bronchitis, loath though he was to underplay the seriousness of his condition. Shingles was found without a hitch and he was released with a smile, not required to report back for twelve weeks.

Randall Stout took his leave. Dizzy with love and gratitude towards his customer-service representative. He would have loved to give this sweet woman a big kiss, but with HIV . . . you never really know.

Key West Funeral
Michael Carroll

―――

The funeral for Harlan Douglas, Cherry de Vine, was New Orleans jazz-style. His body was cremated and his ashes locked in a safe in the offices of St James Church until his last wish could be fulfilled and his lawyer in New York had released money from a special account to pay for it. He wanted no images of himself displayed, which confused mourners like Dan who'd never met him. Was he going as a guy or a girl, Harlan or Cherry? Maybe he was playing a joke on his final audience, trying to confuse them, playing a gender-fuck game or performing a sort of academic exercise. Or maybe he just wanted to be remembered as an entertainer who went home at night and took off his drag and was a regular guy: a man who'd graduated in engineering from Cornell and been a marine in Vietnam before his discharge in 1972 – when he'd runner-upped in the first-ever Miss Gay America Pageant held at the Watch Your Hat & Coat Saloon in Nashville, losing to Arkansas state representative "Norma Christie". This was according to the single-sheet program Dan got from a card table set up on the sidewalk near the Aids Memorial at the foot of the White Street Pier. You could also take one of the Mylar balloons taped by their tails of violet ribbon to the edges of the table, although the same balloons were going faster from a tan shirtless boy handing them out under a knot of sabal palms that shaded a mic stand and one speaker. Dan recognized this kid as Blair, a fishing-boat mate he'd spent fifteen long minutes kneeling in front of in the back bar of the Duval Saloon. A construction worker on the lam from Fort Myers, Blair was straight, with a cheerfully reliable weed habit. Either way, Dan decided against a balloon.

He was jogging when he spotted the crowd of two dozen or so

gathering at the foot of the pier, remembered the occasion and decided to stop, hanging back reading the hand-out so that his sweat wouldn't offend anyone. He had once been fascinated by drag queens. Growing up in the South, he'd been encouraged, entering a club underage, by their forthright outrageousness. The club had been owned by the Mafia, he'd been told, and his first worry about trying to get past the doorman (that an Italian bodybuilder would be called in to kick his ass before throwing him out) disappeared when a giant in line wearing a victory-rolled wig and a flounced satin gown grabbed Dan's hand, blinked her black moth-wing lashes, and said, "You're coming in with me, Private!"

Later he'd found out that minors never got kicked out of the Old Plantation. The owners of the OP knew they needed window dressing – at forty-five Dan couldn't believe he'd ever been considered decorative – in order to keep the regulars loyal and give the heavy drinkers and closet queens something to look at, before they got cut off or lost heart making passes at the "chicken".

In the heavily judgmental, surprisingly uncharitable gay world of before, you were either a chicken or a chicken hawk. At the time, at least no one that Dan knew dared believe that a gay man really wanted to settle down with another homosexual his own age. A straight man his own age, maybe. The inner world of queer exile had been as presumptuous and full of stereotypes as the larger one they were all trying to escape. Dan rather missed the old slang. He supposed that if the self-loathing lingo had survived to today, he would now be considered a chicken hawk. He also knew that he probably had more in common with the deceased than with Jackson. The night before, he and Jackson had argued about Dan's drinking – and it was anyone's guess who'd won.

Jackson was young, but it was hard to judge him naive. He knew the importance of hard work. The twenty-four-year-old's savings outstripped Dan's five or six times. He was a cute and fetchingly self-assured youth, but he should go a little more easily on himself. Also a little easier on Dan. After their love-making, Dan had enjoyed two glasses of white wine. Dan had checked: the alcohol content of the California plonk he'd bought at the drugstore was under 10 per cent. It was the same practically soda-pop-grade stuff he'd had three or four glasses of while summoning his thoughts on Marion earlier that afternoon, before Jackson returned from quitting his shitty job at Fantasy House, "the best gay resort on the planet", according to the gay travel magazine in which the resort prominently advertised. Jackson had more work elsewhere on the island. And he lived with his mom and wasn't going to starve. But he was keyed up after the sex (which Dan thought was good and dirty, a pleasing new low), and after catching his breath and lying under the covers in the quiet after the thundershower, had calmly said, without turning to face Dan while he said it, "Do you need that stuff to feel normal?" Normal? Because what was normal? Was to be normal not to feel in a constant state of fear, cognizant of not only death but imminent penury? And how was "penury" pronounced? Marion could have told him. Dan had given Jackson a pass and said nothing. He realized how frightened of his own homosexuality Jackson was. And if it wasn't his sexuality he was frightened of, then he sure should be. Dan was lonely, profoundly lonely in this temporary place of endless summer; he'd tried not to start a fight. He'd considered telling him in a complex tangle of syntax and comic periphrasis to mind his own fucking business; instead he'd kissed Jackson's white polished-marble shoulder smelling of talcum powder. He'd said, "You're a lot smarter than I am. Smart as you at your age, I wouldn't be relying on it now." Jackson had kissed him then – God knew why. It was almost obscene. His mouth was a pale little strawberry erupting with leaks of juice. Why should it crave Dan's dry, cynically curved, loathing-deformed lips? The world held multiple mysteries. Jackson cared about him. Frightening. He'd then told Jackson, "I want you to start thinking about junior college again. You'll do great." That got him. Before they fell asleep, Dan heard a languid, yawny, "And I know about your secret smoking."

Today there was a bright Florida haze, the air humid and breezy.

Father Bill wore a black short-sleeve shirt and collar and dark glasses and strolled the crowd creakily but in his usual nice mood, no doubt eager for the reception back at the vicarage, where right now Jackson helped his friend Nicole set up. Father Bill, the vicar, had long thin white hair pulled back in a ponytail.

Off to the side, a brass quartet played lively music. They were kids from the high school, all in their uniforms, crimson trousers, stingingly radium-white jackets. Dan didn't recognize the tune, but it was lively. He thought he picked out an undertow of disco, but without strings disco meant nothing to him. An orchestra defined a disco classic. There was a trumpet, flute, sax, and jabbing trombone, and the beat behind them was wan and not especially danceable. There was a bass drummer drumming, but the snare was a precise roll of hissing – like an emission of gas that kept growing – and the young ensemble filled in with their electric, Vitusian party moves. Father Bill took the microphone, grabbing it from its stand like a principal at a prep rally, saying, "Good afternoon! Harlan, I think, would say you've done him proud."

At first it seemed that most of the crowd hadn't heard. Those who'd heard filled in those who hadn't, and then there was applause.

"I'm about to speak in the words of my dear friend, Harlan Cherry de Vine Douglas, who it must be said struck himself down recently in the line of duty, which is to say Cherry was about to go on and entertain us all. I for one respected Harlan or Cherry's choice. I loved Harlan, or if you like, Cherry. He or she was my friend. I'm feeling a little emotional now. To his words . . ."

The crowd was restless. So far, Dan thought, it all seemed literary with a twist of tartness some might have interpreted as archly gay. Don't be so queer, he thought. Go with it.

Father Bill rattled the pages of the prepared goodbye speech, glanced down at them, and said, "'In the words of my Meemaw, it's shit-or-get-off-the-pot time. Meemaw, what a gal.'"

The band had suddenly quit, making it easier for the priest to be understood.

"'I have words of advice. Date a Frenchman, Spaniard or Italian, but marry a German, if marriage is compelling to you. Germans like things neat and clean and don't mind pitching in.'"

The crowd swayed. Tan bare-chested Blair snickered appreciatively and mutely.

"'So to speak, I married a German, and that was good until I made an error of taste. But I won't bore you. The most important thing is sex. Without that chemistry, everything dries up.'"

Cheers.

"'Love everyone. Be ready to. Anyone in the world can surprise you. Love is beautiful. It holds the world together. I never hated anyone, even in Nam. I hated my superior officers but that was because they didn't get it. But the other guys? Gold. Treat everyone like gold. I was a stupid grunt crawling in the mud and still I knew to love. That's why I wanted out. I got out and I missed my buddies, who were gold. I have no wisdom. There's no wisdom. I almost died two or three times. I lost count. But when they flew me home? I was never the same . . .'"

The crowd got restless again. A man in a silver lamé jumpsuit sipped bottled water.

"'Love like there's no tomorrow. A long time ago Goldie Fresh, that was her name, said to me, Bitch, go out there tonight like it's your last. Goldie was great. Colorectal. Eat roughage and get exercise. I'm serious. Sunshine is the best source of vitamin D on the planet. Enjoy!'"

Father Bill nodded jocularly. The band struck up a ragged, faithful "When the Saints Go Marching In" and formed a line choogling toward Atlantic Boulevard and proffering their joyous and dully glinting instruments in the air against the oblivious nickel sky.

Owing to police regulations, they stuck to the sidewalk.

———

Jackson thought suicide was wrong. It wasn't much better than abortion, but still.

You lived with your choices, no matter how shitty the things they brought were. Or you made a plan to get 'er done and set another course.

He suspected that Nicole didn't care about these issues. Catholics. They were so jaded. He was putting out the crudités. The bar was set up. Why drink to the dead? Why eat? He didn't believe in ghosts or souls but he suspected some of the people about to show up could. Why turn death into a party? After they showed up, were they expecting Harlan to make an appearance?

Father Bill wasn't a Catholic priest, but in his religion (Jackson supposed he should think of it as a denomination), some of the old-fashioned formality applied.

Jackson lived at the intersection of his own personal beliefs and crass commerce. He was supposed to turn away when he saw something that bothered or insulted him or otherwise got his goat. Key West weather was humid, which was a perfect symbol of the social life here, everyone in everyone else's hair, hair matted to your forehead and sticking unflatteringly to your crown.

And another thing. People fell apart on this island believing in the eternal party set-up.

About a half-hour before Harlan Douglas's OD, Jackson had said, "Anything else?"

Harlan, nibbling a sandwich and sipping a tumbler of bourbon, had lifted his nose serenely.

He wished now that he hadn't said it so snottily. Really, the man was nice. But he hadn't been looking forward to going on stage. Jackson had told the police all of this and he thought he should give it to them from his angle. The investigating officer had fretted, saying, "Did Douglas say or in any concrete way indicate he wasn't looking forward to going on and performing?"

"It was in his attitude," Jackson had said. "I don't know him but when I picked him up at the airport he was in a mood I wouldn't describe as, I don't know, jolly or, I don't know, pleasant or friendly. Maybe he was trying to impress me. And I thought he was drunk to boot."

"Let's stick to the facts. Give me more facts. What'd you watch happen or hear?"

"He slumped in his seat. He hid behind sunglasses."

"Sunglasses. And a cap or hat of any kind?"

"What? No. When we got to the complex here and we settled him in the cabana, he got suddenly quiet. He'd been chattering nonstop, and like I said, we didn't even know each other."

"All right, chattering." The detective scribbled. "How's your mom? It's Linda, right?"

"Really? I mean, excuse me? Really?"

"Just tell her Teddy said hi. Teddy and the police department ought to do. Now, did you see him using or holding any prescription medications, or any controlled or illicit substances?"

"I thought he'd already taken care of that before getting off the plane when I met him. I wasn't too surprised when I was across the street at the sister bar a while later and then heard."

"He didn't tell you anything odd? When you say he was chattering, do you mean talking in a loose or what one might characterize as a rambling fashion, unconnected by topics?"

"Oh, there was a lot he said that was odd, just not unusual for somebody in Key West. He talked about his life and I suppose too what you'd call his philosophy – giving advice, whatever."

"Did he mention recent problems that had cropped up in his life, sustained tragedies?"

"I'm kind of confused. He talked about himself. A lot. He yammered on."

"Thank you for your time." Teddy pulled out a card. "Detective Theodore Carver."

"Uh-huh."

Jackson read it. It had the official seal of the city on it. In slanty letters along the bottom under his detective title it also read Sports and Public Entertainment Liaison. An image came to Jackson, a couple or so years ago: his mother staggering out of a Key West squad car in front of their house. The siren and blue light were activated and his mother suddenly giggled, tripping on the weedy lawn. Jackson was poker-faced, but he felt Officer Teddy's look hard-fastened to him.

"Anything else you remember, any salient details – that's any concrete, conspicuous—"

"I know what salient means."

"Tell her Teddy's been wondering what's up. What a fun gal, your mom, and solid."

He hadn't made use of the number. He assumed they had everything they needed to rule it a suicide. Why should they be wasting their time? Jackson knew depressed when he saw it.

Harlan had requested a full procession, going from the garden bar of the French Quarter complex up Duval toward the Atlantic side and swinging out past Higgs Beach, but there hadn't been enough time to clear it. The city would have to barricade every street on the way like it was Fantasy Fest or New Year's, probably making it a bigger spectacle than it deserved to be. Drying up taxpayers' dollars. The night before, Dan had said, "Do you think that's out of homophobia?"

And Jackson could get so exasperated. "No, Daniel. It's an expediency, nothing more."

When he heard himself say, or think, Daniel – Daniel the Biblical prophet, the angry one, who predicted great changes for the Jews, for the People of the Book – Jackson felt dissonant.

He no longer believed but he had the aspirations still of someone with faith, an optimism. He looked around the room. It was the perfect Key West room, dilapidated and romantic.

Nicole found a mirror, a mirror like a huge gold-framed painting where her portrait came at the center of silvery clarity, and adjusted her bow tie. She looked into the mirror at him.

She smiled over her shoulder and said, "Do I look all right?"

"You look perfect, my darling."

He was going to lose Dan. Dan was better than anyone he'd ever slept with, flawed as he was. Then Glen came in. He was the first guest, and what a motherfucker. Jackson was furious.

He went over to Glen, not fussing with his uniform, feeling confident in his cinch-waisted black vest and his blindingly bleached-white shirt – the bow tie, he sensed, straightly aimed.

"Why are you here?" Jackson said.

"I realize I love you," said Glen, tilting his face, his glasses crooked and smudged, and he shifted the long black shoulder strap of his colorfully woven, humble and small Andes hip bag.

"That's interesting."

"Don't you love me?"

"It's just interesting to hear you say that."

Glen looked pretty beaten-up, which was great. He looked unkempt, uncareful.

Glen said, "Why is that interesting?"

"I don't know, it's interesting – that's all. You not answering my phone messages for ever, then you did and it was all lame. Whatever."

Glen contorted his face into a series of reactions.

He said, "I've been in bad shape, you know that. Baby. I've been a wreck."

"What about me, Glen? And how childish is that, just running away without telling me?"

Nicole undid the caps on a series of tonic and soda waters. This crowd was all hard-core liquor drinkers, Jackson supposed. The vicar himself, Father Bill, could put away the cocktails.

Seriously, Glen needed to check himself and get back to Jackson later.

Glen said, "Angel Bear, I'm in love with you!"

Nicole looked up from her barkeep ministrations, raising one admonishing eyebrow.

Jackson found something to do. The surfaces in this house, a pretty good example of the Queen Anne, were appallingly dusty, and he kept tearing off double sheets of paper towel to rub at the filthy places. He thought Nicole would whore herself to any man who made such a protest of love, and how embarrassing. Exactly why he was glad he wasn't a girl. Girls gave it up fast.

He said, "Who cleans this place? The man's a minister. Doesn't he have a maid?"

Glen hovered, saying, "Can I see you later?"

"God, no. Will you just – I'm trying to work, honey."

"Can I have a glass of wine before I go?"

"Did you know the deceased? No, you're too uptight about drag queens and stuff. You left town the day I had to chauffeur her around, and then she killed herself. How do you think I felt when that happened and I found out?"

Glen studied him knowingly, a smirk trying to break through. It was disconcerting. He had a way of suddenly going cruel, not often, just every once in a while, going un-Buddhist for an instant and looking at Jackson hatefully. Next, he'd be calling Jackson's anus by dirty slang words to feminize and subvert him, the pig. Jackson felt the beginnings of a woody in his black pants.

Glen hadn't washed his hair in God knew how long. Had he swum down from Marathon?

Glen said, "Since when do you like female impersonators?"

"I didn't say I did. I said I'd met him, I was his driver. Just for a little while."

"I saw his show once," said Glen, "at La Te Da. He was talented. It was all right."

"I never saw him, but I would have. Oh, you can stay. On the porch, until they come."

"I'm banished to the porch."

"Put that bag under a bush or something. You look homeless. Have you bathed lately?"

"You want me to go somewhere and shower?"

"It's a religious event, silly."

"It's all a social screen," said Glen, accepting a clear-plastic cup of wine from Nicole.

"Out of respect," said Jackson, "and to get you out of my hair, please go sit on the porch."

With Glen gone, Nicole said, "That was too firm. He looked so sad shuffling out."

"I'm not in love with him anymore."

"Sure you are. Or you're still attracted, I can tell."

Jackson hated lying. Everybody in his family had taught him to be honest, and he had a certain amount of pride, an almost erotic one, in this superiority.

"No one's ever made him grow up," he said quietly, and got bored dusting.

The people started coming. He stepped out into the street when he heard horns playing a saggy tune and a slowly thundering off-stage bass drum being beaten. He stepped back up onto the porch, being sure not to look at Glen sitting there, sure his expression would be smirky, huffy and pathetic. "Honey Angel," he then heard, in a lightly strained tone. "Oh, Angel Bunny . . ."

Sandrine, who ran the catering company, came out from the kitchen with a silver tray. On it were miniscule delicacies widely spaced. She was French but had shed most of her accent; she had been here so long. She was never going back to France, she said – not until her mother died. But after that she was taking her money, turning around and coming right back, trying to civilize Key West one pointlessly underloaded salver of tiny goat-cheese-and-mushroom puff pastries at a time. No one knew how old she was, forty or sixty being the usual range people would speculate within, though her mother, she said, was eighty-two. Sandrine said she worked to live and didn't live to work, but could handle as many as three caterings a day in season, complaining the whole time. Jackson was too wise to believe in her grousing. He romanticized her, her skimpy clothes and simple manner. It added up to some kind of elegance. Sometimes he wished she'd ask him to be her business partner. Sandrine was the only one whose personal criticism and fussing after Jackson he could stomach. He loved flirting with her. He didn't know if she liked guys or girls, though from behind with her chopped brunette hair and pencil figure she looked like a teen boy.

"Sandrine," he said (raising his voice so Glen was sure to hear twenty steps away), "why don't you move your catering to the French Riviera, and Nicole and I will come work for you?"

"There I could not afford you."

Her mood was good. Sometimes when she dispensed sourness, it amusingly sang. She added, "I cannot go back to France, unless it's either to Paris or Normandy, and even then . . ."

She didn't specify. She didn't seem to care. Sandrine's great gift was indifference, a cool apathy that sounded like a playful warmth. She was wonderful. Jackson liked her sailor blouses.

Nicole said, "But if we all went, Jackson and I could learn French."

"You would do better to stay here and use your Tagalog in useful, beneficial ways, so you could help some of your own people. Start an employment agency for Filipino immigrants."

"I don't think so," said Nicole, "and besides, there aren't so many Filipinos around here."

"You could go somewhere else. Go to Maryland. You could make a fortune."

"Maryland?" said Nicole. "Where do you get that?"

Jackson said, "Sandrine, you're the one who's always saying money isn't everything."

"I meant that as an incentive. It's not good to stay for ever in the place you grew up."

"Maryland?" said Nicole, giggling. "Um. My Tagalog sucks."

"I see. Well, you should learn while your mother is still alive."

"Not for much longer, she isn't."

Sandrine was shocked by the matter-of-fact, almost cheerful way Nicole announced this. Personal matters were not to be mentioned among colleagues, or in most social climates.

"You're a naughty girl. They're coming. You hear all the car doors closing? Why do the Americans drive everywhere? It's a small island. Even here, there are shockingly few bikes."

"Bikes are for tourists."

"This is what I'm talking about – these attitudes. Where do they come from? If you went on a bike, Nicole, you would lose an extra ten pounds easily. And if you stayed away from rice."

"I'm happy with the fifteen I already lost. I'm always hungry for the rice I don't eat."

When Sandrine had placed the platter of puff pastry on the long cloth-covered table and gone back to the kitchen, Nicole said, "Have you noticed, she doesn't like being contradicted?"

Jackson said, "Just tell her you already have one mother."

"Yeah, but not for much longer."

She said it distractedly. She lived to work, to stay away from home.

———

She'd left Zach at home with his brushes and paints. He was starting to get deadline-frantic.

Once, when she'd said something awful to him about someone she knew he loved dearly, he'd drawn her a Venn diagram of their relationship. She was a triangle and he was a blob, or an imperfect oval. Where they overlapped, one of the corners of the triangle pierced him just where the oval was slightly crimped. He had done it on a scrap of heavy sketch paper with a brush and black paint, just the two shapes, and posted it on the fridge without labeling or giving it a title. He didn't have to; it was obvious whose pointy corner was going into the soft, vulnerable blob. That night, she'd refused to cook. They'd gone out for crab cakes instead. When he offered to order a bottle of her favorite Chablis, she'd said, "Nope, not tonight, I don't believe." She'd dared him to default to his usual glass of Scotch and ice, silently, with a proud stare. The next morning they'd fucked harder than usual. Funny how these things turned around overnight. After the restaurant, she'd gone home to bed and he'd sat up drinking Scotch, waking with the hangover hots. Like it or not, Zach was always the one in control – when she wasn't the one in control. She loved him.

Now she thought about turning around before stepping onto the porch of the vicarage and walking briskly home, letting herself in quietly to read. She thought about a lot of things.

Jane was a writer, after all, and the observations and ideas that drove her writing kept her head in a state of constant agitation. In the past she'd done volunteer work for Father Bill during periods of fallow creativity, and she thought now that she'd gladly paint this shabby porch in any scheme the diocese deemed appropriate – a soapy lavender, psycho purple trim, hippy colors.

Ahearn, Priscilla Jane (1948–)

"Priscilla Ahearn" would have made her sound like a romance novelist, God help her.

When she and Zach had first moved down, she'd liked Key West because it reminded her of San Francisco, if San Francisco were cleaner and had better weather. Key West was said to be part of the redneck riviera, was its out-to-sea unofficial capital, but she found it far more tolerant than their old neighborhood in New York, where the original ethnic families and poor artsy types had been chased out by yuppies. Young working couples with fertility-drug twins pushed around during the day in double-wide strollers by tired West Indian nannies – puzzled-looking kids who were sometimes old enough to walk. Even the gay men (who Jane would have thought had fled the heartland to escape the Family) were getting in on the act, adopting orphans of wars or floods and earthquakes, or hired down-on-their luck girls to smuggle their sperm into, before the babies came out of them and they were gotten rid of. She'd known Zach was for her, not because Zach was self-sufficient, which thank God he was, but because the last thing he wanted was a child to compete with his other creations. Together they shared a distaste for squalling brats – or maybe they were not brats, they were perfectly intelligent, imaginative youngsters who might very well grow up to become reasonable, productive citizens, but who the hell had the time to find out?

Jane's students were her children, meaning they could be lazy with low attention spans.

Her main literary subject was spoiled adults, whom she liked to catch acting like children. And she considered herself spoiled (see above stream-of-consciousness). Her mother had hoped for a grandchild. Before going howling into the night (quite literally, the nurse had attested), her mother during her most lucid moments would say, "You were always a grown-up, even as a little girl, but a terrible, terrible sensualist. You crushed cut flowers to your face. Slurped your soup."

She and Zach came every year for the sunshine and bougainvillea, but it did seem like her allergies, along with the mosquitoes, were getting steadily worse. She couldn't stay away.

She'd seen Cherry de Vine at a piano bar here on Duval caterwauling torch standards and, the best part, tearing the hecklers apart. It was too strong for Zach, but although she'd never met Harlan Douglas or offered her expression of arch gratitude after a Cherry de Vine show – she had never laughed so hard or felt that grateful to be alive (as an "unconstructed woman", a gay friend called Jane) – she'd gone back each night all through Cherry's engagement, and felt this affinity.

The good novelists didn't fit squarely into any place, but here she could get work done.

She'd been sixteen when she went to her first protest but, as an older boy had pointed out, she'd looked about twelve. She'd looked around at the others in their sandals and jeans; she was the only one there in heels. Yet everyone had been nice. Her father was disappointed in her, and her mother embarrassed by her. The other night, she and Zach had watched a documentary about the folk-music festival in Newport, something in black and white that at the time was considered the last word on the power to change the world by singing in a syrupy quaver. She and Zach had not known each other at the time, but he'd been doing similar things in other parts of the country. He'd gone to Alabama and Mississippi, gotten busted, and spent the night in jail. Just before the commercial break, Jane had then looked over at him. The footage was gripping. Such attractive boys. She noticed that most of the festival-goers shown on screen and interviewed saying loopy, abstract things were cute, clean-cut boys, any one of whom she would have gladly dated back in the day. But the stuff they were saying. At the first commercial break, Jamie Lee Curtis selling a yogurt that was supposed to make you more regular than the usual brand did, she turned to Zach and said, "Were we really that self-assured and on top of things – and so fucking self-righteous?"

Zach's messy-haired head was still in the studio, mixing pigments, and he'd said, "It's all in your books. Isn't that what your writing's all about, always has been?"

"I know," she'd said, getting up, "I was being rhetorical. But amazing, huh?"

He nodded, sipping an iced vodka. She'd gone then into the kitchen, but why would they have any yogurt? She didn't like it especially, and rarely bought any. But still she had looked.

"Can you, can you," she heard across the crowded front room of the vicarage, as though a postmodern confessional poem was being steadily recited, "could you possibly gimme a dollar?"

In the background she heard Grand Funk, an old fave, overlaid with a rap refrain: "We gonna whip yo booty!"

The rap fit the beat, an odd variation of "We're an American Band", and a fitting update.

Vilda was a go-go dancer, inscrutable and straight. He was tall, muscular and golden, his skin almost the same shade as his hair, his nose like a smooth, perfect hacking instrument, curved and mean. His whole body looked like it would prefer to be naked – and of course he hadn't finished putting his uniform on, was still attaching his bow tie. His vest was unbuttoned, while the house was already half full, and he stood in the middle of the party getting himself together. Cherry de Vine, from beyond the grave, had requested they call this a party. Adjusting his tie, ineffectively, Vilda, late as usual, scooted up beside Nicole laughing, saying, "Hey, how are you guys doing?"

His idiomatic English was always a tad off. He said, "Having a good time, you guys?"

To Jackson, he sounded like a beach-bum vampire, unaware of the night-feeding sharks as he surfed through life. You never saw him at noon, but you always heard him coming, his loudly adenoidal voice making light about something he might not have even understood as it was being said. He laughed about nothing and got on Jackson's nerves – getting on them now by nudging Nicole aside behind the bar and saying, "I'm here, so I can take over. Sorry I've been late . . ."

Nicole stepped sanguinely over, grinning embarrassedly, her high flat cheeks flushing.

Jackson came hotly up, hissing into her ear, "Are you going to let him do that again?"

Vilda had already fixed his stare into the crowd, foolishly saying to Jackson, "What?"

Jackson fisted his hand on his hip. "Nicole set this whole fucking bar up, and now you?"

"I don't understand."

"You come late, don't do any of the set-up, you expect to collect the same amount as—"

"I don't have to make the same amount. Take more than me. Money, who cares?"

"All right, we'll see about that with Sandrine."

"I am fine," said Vilda, "truly fine. You should maybe pull your head out from your ass."

"Is that a gay thing, a cute little wry, sly slur? About my head and my ass being gay?"

"It was anything you imagine. It was nothing. I don't care, I do my job."

"Interesting," said Jackson, looking at no one. "He thinks he's doing his job. Wow."

Vilda said to Nicole, "Your friend likes talking to himself very much. Wow."

Nicole snickered and headed for the kitchen, picking up an empty tray on her way.

Vilda eyed the room for the priest, one of his best tippers. Never groping, though the old guy did like to have Vilda bend as he stashed the bills in his G-string right along the hip.

Jackson found Dan, hugging him and saying weirdly, "I'm sorry, but Glen's here."

"Was that him on the porch?"

"How did you know?"

"He just looked so lonely."

"I think the woman behind you knows you."

It was Jane and he smiled queasily, but at the same time he was glad to see her.

He'd been reading her since college, first hearing about her in a survey course. She was in all the modern and contemporary anthologies, including the Norton. He'd heard a rumor that she was depressed about her declining sales, numbers that Marion would have killed for.

"I meant to write you a condolence," said Jane. "Are you all right?"

"I'm okay. Obviously, being here has it coming back to me. It's been four months."

"I heard the day it happened. I wanted to call. Funny how sometimes we just can't get around to doing what we know are the most important things."

They both wondered if they should hug, but the right moment might have already passed.

"I hated Marion's stupid tiff with you. I never got it," he lied. "And I never had a chance to get your side of it. I didn't know if I should call or write."

"Probably for the best," she said. She offered Jackson her hand and said, "Hi, I'm Jane."

"I know who you are, you're a writer here. We did that benefit, where you talked?"

"This is Jackson Stone."

"I probably made no sense whatsoever. But how can you, talking about us and Haiti?"

Jackson said, "I heard the donations overall were pretty generous."

"White upper middle-class guilt," she said and laughed.

"Maybe," said Jackson, who wanted to experience such guilt. "Anyway, back to work."

Jane said, "Good luck with this crowd, right?"

"I can handle them," he said, suddenly more cheerful. He stared smiling at Dan.

"Nice to meet you."

"Nice to meet you."

"A friend of yours?" she said.

"I'm not always sure."

"Are you ready for guys again?"

"Oh, sure. It's not that."

"Lucky you. You can choose from both sexes. Forgive me for butting in where I have no business, but maybe it's time. They say it takes a year, but I think there are shortcuts."

The Czech dude Dan knew from the Odyssey came with a tray of different drinks.

"How are you guys doing?" he said, flashing that wallet-loosening smile.

"Just mineral water," said Jane. "I'll never make it home otherwise."

"Who said you should even go home?" said the Czech. "There are other things to do."

"Did he just say that?"

"I think he did," said Dan, who took another white wine. "You just had a moment."

"I'm lucky I know which side my bread's buttered on."

"I didn't until I met Marion," he said.

"Aw!" She reached over and patted his hand. "Sweet pudding, you'll be all right."

"I miss her. I know you two had words, whatever they were. I'm just sorry for that."

"So were you at the pier before? Was it a scream? I was late coming from something."

———

While young, he'd struggled with alcohol, then drugs, and then a combination – going solely back to drink again as he entered middle age, when he'd begun reading and understanding from the Fifth Precept that intoxication was the only thing holding him back from becoming a Bodhisattva. An up martini with olives, this was his cross, so to speak. The Buddha had obviously taught that life was struggle, and that the only way for it not to be a struggle was to surrender to struggle. It had taken him eight days sitting under the pipal, his beloved Bodhi, to figure that out. It was all myth or allegory, but you couldn't find a better or more realistic teaching. The problem was desire, the most human of problems. The Buddha, quite the character, from what Glen had studied, anyway, just before he died had told his followers: "Strive on." Like, thanks, Gautama Buddha! He was a joker somewhat, and a vegetarian, but ironically may have eaten bad pork merely to be polite. A desire to please others, not be rude, had gotten the best of even old Siddhartha. Glen didn't give full release, not even when they asked. He'd already said so in his ad and on his card: "Sorry, no 'happy endings'." That most tragic and Western and common of self-delusions. They'd ask and he'd just laugh corporeally. Nothing much else to say, except that Christ had had less of a sense of humor, apparently. Or else his disciples were more gullible, taking the Messiah at his word when he'd led them to believe he was coming back – and soon. Still waiting! Salut, Jesus. Or, that other thing. Where he supposedly had foresight, but if he'd seen what was coming and told the others what to expect, even guessing Peter's denial of him, why did he act so surprised up there, for crying out? Dramatically, the Passion had to work two different ways to work at all.

Glen worked as a masseur. At home he did yoga, meditated, read the enlightened texts, all of it, but it didn't mean he couldn't have fun. He felt playful, the old mischief creeping in.

Lightning flashed, not so nearby. The sky had been darkening. The wind had picked up. And when it flashed Glen counted two or three seconds before he heard thunder. The rain hadn't begun falling, but you smelled ozone. It was rich in the air. Across the street he saw the red soft-top antique Corvette with its top down. He stirred in the wicker chair on the porch and got up.

He was thinking about the time in his uncle's Corvette, his sexually abusive uncle whom he'd loved, riding to Memphis. They were riding away from the Ozarks and that tacky Passion Play, everything that was tacky in his life. And what a beautiful machine, such attachments!

He went inside, yelling, "Whose Corvette is that? Whose Corvette with the top down?"

The hot bartender, whatzisname, hollered, "What's going on? Does it rain now? Crap!"

Father Bill, tilting a cocktail to his lips, said, "Who wants to see my banyan tree?"

Several people in the room including Glen said, "I do. You have a banyan?"

He remembered a summer in Europe; not this eternal, infernal summer of here, but one where morning and evening skies were blue, and all below was green. There were cherries and apricots, such fruit. The light at the extremes was blue yet during the day so mellow and golden.

He was running from the Ozarks and the Passion Play in Eureka Springs, where he'd first tasted herb. He preferred to call it herb. And then he was running with his horny uncle. But the past, all of it (though better), was completely gone. The future was pale. You died, being reborn.

Among his other failings, he was claustrophobic. He went up the cramped stairs.

Someone said, "I hope no one farts!"

The covered deck was packed. The tree was magnificent. You felt like leaving this town, then you'd have this view. Saw magical things. Considered suicide then changed your mind.

————

A homeless man was here. People made room for him, owing to his odor. He was wearing a peach Izod shirt with a broad diagonal streak of bleach stain down the front, plaid bermudas and a pair of leather-thonged flip-flops. He'd shaved cleanly for the occasion, yet his cheeks and neck were nicked and in places gashed and flayed from the razor. A scrap of toilet paper with a dull lozenge of blood at its center patched a spot over his Adam's apple. He held his clear-plastic cup of white wine delicately from the bottom, rotating it at eye level as though to inspect the color and clarity.

Dan and Jane stood near the open front door and Dan heard the man say, "Cherry was my buddy. He used to come out and visit me in the mangroves and suck me off. I let him for free."

Jane said, "I'm not proud of the way I reacted. I always loved Marion. It's just that—"

"I know," said Dan. "She wasn't the easiest to be with. It was odd, how I loved her."

"But everyone knew you loved her. I think only here could people understand that."

A gay man, worshipping a woman, but a talented woman. A fiercely independent woman. He wasn't bi. He had just loved Marion. Now he had the opinions of others to deal with.

Jane said, "Actually, I had lunch with Lily today. That's why I didn't make it in time for the memorial. I hope you don't think it was inappropriate, but I asked about you. Lily acted like she wasn't sure but she'd look across the deck at the little cottage and everything seemed hunky-dory to her. Personally, I'm glad you're here."

"Lily never got me."

"You can't go through life like that, worrying about other people's opinions. Who cares? People wonder about Zach and me. We just knew. Marion knew. You knew. Screw the others."

And he thought about his life. He'd loved a woman. He, a homosexual man, who never before would have been able to believe he could love a woman – he'd loved one who'd just died.

He said, "And now I'm alone, which is odd too. Being here's half-paradise, half-torture."

Jane said, "Did you know, Marion's the reason I'm here, and that Zach and I are here?"

"I can't imagine what it was like for you guys, the original crew, back in the old days."

"It wasn't that great. There were laughs, but you were always looking over your shoulder."

"You guys just drifted apart."

"Dan," she said, "in your opinion, was Marion an alcoholic?"

How did most alcoholics answer a question like that? By covering, or by dissembling? He was in danger of revealing himself, but revealing what wasn't exactly true. He had time left. He wondered if he shouldn't have taken mineral water from the Czech, whose name he remembered was Vilda. He could always drink back at Lily's guest cottage. Marion had loved it there.

He said, "Marion went through periods."

"Wet and dry, you mean."

"Periods where she didn't touch the stuff, not one drop. Weeks. Months, for a while."

"Who am I?" said Jane. "Look at me. I don't drink a lot, but I drink a little every day."

She was used to two glasses a night, what people in recovery called maintenance. She'd never gotten out of control. Marion would get out of control, start handing out insults, grinning.

Dan excused himself to the restroom and Jane blinked twice, an affectionate Morse code.

The homeless man laughed fruitily at a remark a woman wrapped in bands and layers of tulle and velour was making. Seeing that a line had formed at the bar where the hot Czech go-go boy had left it to go raise the top on his car, Nicole hurried over with a tray of crudités arranged on a bed of coarse sea salt, its dip contained on the side in a ramekin like a pool in an oasis. The homeless man said, "Oh," and Nicole stopped. He reached for a radish and dunked it and Nicole smiled awkwardly. Already the colorfully dressed woman who'd made him laugh moved out of his zone, but he didn't notice. Nicole turned and the homeless man made little kissing mouth sounds.

A large black dog came out of the driving rain, bounding up the porch steps. It paused on the porch and shook its coat violently, three good hard times, then stepped confidently across the threshold and toed more tentatively into the crowd. He was a mutt, with all the spirit mutts had, the kind of dog Marion had liked – Marion, the New England pure-breed. He was less an omen than a reminder. She'd gone the way her father had. Jane heard that it had started with a pain in her side, hard and throbbing and radiating to the back. She'd put it down to drinking too much liquor; she would go back on the white wine. White wine, a post-sixties panacea. But that was all Jane had heard, though she wanted to hear more from Dan. She'd made crass snark at his expense but she could see, from his hunched-forward shoulders and saggy eyes, that he was now paying a penance for wanting to steal fire from Olympus, and he'd gotten burned. He was taking his singed hands to the oracle now, asking what was left, what was ahead. Likely, nothing. He'd come down to see what the old crew had to say, and of course they all had been polite to him, loving a loser more dearly than the competition. Cozier company. It was said that when he'd met Marion he was a writer himself, but that in her work he'd seen everything he was incapable of doing. He could either now believe he'd been released from that burden or say goodbye to the old dream, a dream that fewer and fewer anymore believed in. What was so good about words on a page? He looked older now, certainly not aged but seasoned. He'd had and lost his companion black dog.

————

Dan needed him, he knew, but who was Jackson? Young, scrawny, without discernible skills – unless you counted experience in the hospitality industry. That's what they called this shit here.

He'd often entertained apocalyptic visions, the island consumed by electrical fires – fires started by lightning, of which they had plenty. A dry lightning threatening a rain that didn't quite come in time, before the island burned down and the storms came, perhaps a hurricane. It wasn't hurricane season, playing hell with his idea. The idea was Dan and Jackson fleeing the holocaust visited on a sinful place. He liked that part of Genesis. It wasn't just about gays, apparently.

But Dan wandered in his mind, holding things back. Marion, for example. He wouldn't talk about her, yet Jackson wasn't judgmental. It was okay that he'd been with her. But how did a gay guy leave his gay life behind then come crawling back to it? Sex was like washed-out hair color or calves that didn't respond to repetitions at the gym. It was, if not a curse, then a reality of genes, he'd thought. Jackson had spent most of his life believing he was ugly, then found out he was beautiful but only to the most despicable characters, and he was stuck here. He hadn't fallen into a maybe representative sample. Dan lived in New York, where Jackson longed to be. There, he'd have anonymity, no one making presumptuous remarks just because they were drunk – or if they did then they weren't the only ones you encountered on the street. Here the streets were this open book. Everybody knew your business. No, he was pretty enough for Dan. But Glen would never grow up and was afraid of intimacy. Jackson needed to be dominated and a little degraded, erased temporarily, reset, rebooted. He wanted to be reminded that he was trash.

He was twenty-four and done feeling bad about being gay. Other gays were the problem.

_____

"Are you my rival?" The guy was tipsy and teetered slightly left. He smirked superciliously as though awed by his own powers of confrontation and resolve. "You're my rival, aren't you?"

"I don't think I'm anyone's rival. I don't think I could be."

"Yeah, you're that guy, the one everyone sees in bars. Liking homosexuality again?"

"What's that supposed to mean?"

"Oh, you know. Going back out, picking up boys, stealing lovely young youths from the guys that don't hide and know what side our English muffins are buttered on."

"I'm still confused."

"I don't think you are. I think you know that I know precisely what I'm saying."

"Okay. I won't refute that."

"Refute. Refute. Mighty fancy words, but you're that guy in bars saying he's a writer."

"I never said that."

"But you lived with one, that woman from down around here, and you know big words."

"Homosexuality is a lot longer than refute. Now you're not going to refute that, right?"

"Are you finished with my boyfriend? I found him first, chicken hawk. Going from the beard back to boys you couldn't have in school, hiding from the Western bias against the erotic."

"Look, Glen. You're a masseur, right? It's Glen, isn't it?"

"I'm man enough to say it is."

"Good. So Glen, you already know what it's like to love and then lose someone."

"You're a wit. Oh, yes. I can see it in your witty, silly eyes. I guess he likes looking into them, all nice, brown, dark and mysterious. I've got to say, you're not some mystery to me. You like to go to bars and pick up all these boys, and I've heard you like karaoke. Sing, don't you?"

"I'm not very good at it but I enjoy it. It's fun. Have you tried it? I sing my heart out."

"So now I'm a bad person."

"I'm not saying that. You seem like you're probably a nice person. Jackson's said so."

"So now you know all about my life, and my lover's life. Met the grandmothers?"

"Not yet."

"Well, they're a hoot. A real stitch. Good, decent, I'd say overall open-minded ladies."

He teetered there some more. Jackson came over. Dan wondered if he'd said anything that would get back to him. He wondered if from the smirk Glen was going to ask him to sing.

"Come on," Jackson said, "let's go talk, sweetie. No, just talk."

"I'm in distress."

"You're sensitive to alcohol. How much have you had? Don't answer that, I don't care."

"He doesn't care. You don't care. No, you just said you don't. I could make you care!"

Jackson guided him out to the porch and Dan heard, "I'm in distress, angel mouse."

They were out there for a while and Blair, the gay-for-pay first mate, approached.

"Hi," said Dan.

"Having a good time?"

"Not really."

"Then I'll leave you alone. You want me to leave you alone, I bet. Seriously."

"Seriously."

It was five minutes before Jackson returned, his eyes ringed in red. He was shaking his head with a controlled-burn fury. He said, "What did you say to him? Were you shitty?"

"I wasn't shitty."

"Jesus. He said it happened when he was up under the porch on the second floor looking at the banyan tree, when the hard rain came. He said the tree looked fierce and holy. Whatever."

Vilda came in from the rain, his pale hair slicked and exposing pink patches of his scalp.

Good, thought Jackson, he's starting to lose it. Bald in no time.

Blair was mixing for himself a Captain Morgan and Coke, looking contentedly guilty.

Nicole approached and said, "Is Glen all right? Did he have too much to drink?"

"Doesn't he always?" said Jackson. "Jesus."

"No," she said to Dan, "because my father always did – and you couldn't tell. We had to push him around in his chair after they took off the second leg. But then he got an electric one."

Heavy on the Captain Morgan. And Vilda sitting in his car, a wake-and-bake. Trash!

In the kitchen, Sandrine laughed, graceful rills of high descending notes. She'd just made a special hors d'oeuvre for Father Bill, starting with a thin, curved, finely waffled potato chip, on top of which she'd stacked a dollop of tarama, fresh chopped cilantro, minced shallot and caviar. Really, sometimes the fish here was a scandal, with not at all the exacting French standards. She had grown up with the best of it, before the oceans had become a sewer. You made the best of it.

"Vod damn it," said Father Bill after crunching into it. "Hi nush mroke an imray!"

"You just broke an inlay?" said Sandrine. "Well, hell. But do you still have it?"

He spat out the pink and green and beige mush and began picking through it. "Here."

"So take it to the dentist," she said. "He'll just insert it right back in. No one died!"

Halfway across town, Zach Hooper listened to Fats Domino's "Kansas City". It bomped and carried him bumptiously forward as he mixed titanium white, cadmium orange and Naples yellow, leaving out the ultramarine as the foot was the one feature of the girl not in the shade. It was a local scene, lovers picking up their things around the pool. They were about to go in for a cocktail mixed by the man who was mostly a violet wraith nowhere near the dappling of late-afternoon honey sun. They were closed in by green and blue and black, the tropical foliage that rioted about them. Fuchsia pops of bougainvillea blossoms. But the foot. It stepped out. Zach waited for Jane to return, but pray tell not before he'd palette-knifed it on and smoothed it into a narrow, if not quite detailed, flesh loaf of expectantly extended femininity. An impression of her pretty foot, which he'd lived with happily for ever. Glanced at out of the corner of your eye, just as you were recalling something, or someone, else.

It was like that here. Heaven and hell. You learned to guide yourself or you were lost.

The Railings
Ronald Frame
___

He'd been expecting to find himself, literally, behind bars. But the building was modern, remarkably bright and the only screens were of plate glass. An "open prison" was a contradiction in terms, but apt: his adult life had been a succession of contradictions, after all.

Instead he dreamed about metal bars when he was in his room, with the door unlocked, his spartan but unprison-like room. Or, rather, he dreamed about metal railings. The ones they'd always had in front of the house. Absurd things: a screen to protect their privacy from the road. Iron, painted black, each rod tipped with a clumsy fleur-de-lys motif. Their wee corner of Carnbeg had had aspirations beyond its location but, because he'd lived there since he was two years old and grown up with its values, he had failed to observe its pretensions.

Then at a certain point, during the war – a couple of weeks before his seventeenth birthday – the railings in front of the house had been requisitioned for the war effort: melted down to make a tank, or a portion of a gunship, or a fresh supply of rifles. The day they lost the railings was the hottest of the year. The team of workers arrived to do their work, equipped with torches and clamps and saws. A lorry load of men: not army types, but labourers from the cities, excused service for some reason. They all seemed able-bodied enough. One, in particular: just about the same age as himself.

He was studying for his exams that morning, and had been granted a few hours off from the timetable at the grammar school. His bedroom was at the front of the house, the small bedroom above the front door, next to his parents' room with the bay, now his mother's room. His desk was placed directly in front of the window. He was sitting at the desk, looking out.

The conditions were all wrong for exams. The heat and the war. His father was stationed out on a ship, somewhere about Malta, although it was hush-hush and Dad wasn't allowed to say, even to them. His mother was worried about that, as she worried about most things. She had been worried about losing the railings too, on to the road, and became more worried when the neighbours told her she could plant a hedge next to the low wall that would be left.

Hedges took a lot of growing and the house, meantime, would look bald and – well, more common. Their sandstone house had benefited from the appearance of the railings. They had pulled the terrace up in the world, never mind that the railings had only been erected a few months after the house was built, in Edwardian times, to help make them a more attractive prospect for potential purchasers. Now, with the railings gone, they would be reduced to privet, or beech, or laurel – acacia maybe, and it wouldn't be the same, not at all.

He sat at his desk watching the workers – watching the boy especially. The youth took off his shirt in the boiling heat. The muscles flexed in his shoulders, his arms, his back, all in harmony, as he helped a colleague saw the remaining resistance out of the railings.

He was watching the youth so closely that he realized he'd forgotten to be sorry about what was happening, the indignity being done to his home.

Moments later, Mrs Harkness passed by, accompanied by Jennifer. Jennifer must have had the morning off from her school, too. She looked over and spotted him at the window and waved a white-gloved hand at him. He hesitated for a few seconds before lifting his arm, opening his hand, slowly spreading his fingers like a fan. An immobile little wave. Maybe Jennifer was puzzled by that because her cheery smile seemed to slacken. He didn't smile back at her.

That was bound to set her discussing him again in earnest with her friends. He knew he was a frequent topic of conversation: about how he wasn't more demonstrative when Jennifer asked him to dance with her at the tennis-club socials. He was aware that some of the girls were trying to match-make, pairing him off with her. He wasn't sure why he wasn't able to respond more openly. Stupid, really. But he just felt that he couldn't. It hadn't to do with Jennifer, who was nice enough. He didn't dislike her. But sometimes he felt intimidated by her: the smell of talcum and shampoo, the paleness and warmth of her skin. Menaced, even. And not curious, not itching as some of his own friends were, to discover what lay concealed beneath the buttons of a girl's blouse.

He read a few more sentences from his history textbook. English history, about Francis Drake and Walter Raleigh and the southerners' adventuring spirit. He read until he knew Jennifer and her mother would have passed. Then he raised his eyes again. He stared out at the youth: at the ease of his movements. He had grace, for all his what his mother would have called commonness. He imagined him dressed in doublet and hose and ruff, gaze turned towards an Atlantic horizon, face in profile. Not a *fine* face, but handsome, in a rough and ready way.

He realised too late that his eyes had fixed to a stare and that the youth was now watching *him*. How long had he been looking while mentally making the resemblance to Walter Raleigh? He lowered his head, red-faced, scalp prickly with embarrassment . . .

———

When he had to go out after lunch, to return to school, the railings in front of their own house and their neighbours' had gone. Only ugly iron stumps were left, which would have to be filed down. The workmen were now at the other end of the terrace. His mother was inspecting the damage.

"Whatever would your father have to say, Roy?"

Dad wouldn't have let it worry *him*, because he wasn't the type to: in that respect he was a careful foil to his mother.

"It'll be all right, Mum."

He touched her arm sympathetically. She smiled, sadly, but was grateful nonetheless. He had a knack of knowing what would give her comfort.

"Wasn't that Mrs Harkness who passed by?" she asked.

"Was it?"

"What on earth will she think of us now?"

His mother favoured Jennifer Harkness, because her parents lived in a detached house with a third of an acre of garden. She kept telling him that good exam results would take him to university, that he would become qualified to enter a profession. She might have been expected to view Jennifer Harkness as a distraction to him, but quite the reverse. She seemed to belong to the scenario of his life that his mother had in mind for him. His glittering future.

He said goodbye to his mother and walked along the terrace. When he reached the end and turned into the lane – the shortcut to the grammar school – he heard a quiet but distinct whistle from the verge. The youth was sitting in the shade of a thorn hedge. He was alone. His shirt was still off; his body seemed to have browned since the morning.

"Saw you looking," he said, "from your window back there. That your bedroom?"

The voice was oddly coarse and sweet at the same time.

"Like what you're looking at, then?"

Roy turned away, so he wasn't looking, but the voice followed him.

"A quid, how'd that suit you? A quid, and you and me could go for a walk by the river."

His head reeled. He shut his eyes. He heard the din of more railings being thrown on to the back of the lorry. Everything now – in a matter of moments – was being turned upside down, inside out. The voice was saying something else, under the screeching of metal. About its taking one to know one . . . But he wasn't listening. Somehow he found the will to move off. To start walking. To put some distance, any distance, behind him.

Our privacy's gone, he was thinking, the world is opening up. This is not how I want it to be. Suddenly, he understood his mother's worry over the railings. About the vulgarity. About displaying themselves.

At the end of the lane he was vaguely conscious of a familiar figure, Mrs Harkness without Jennifer, walking by on the opposite pavement. He smiled like a maniac, not towards her but into the middle of the road. What had the words spoken from the shade of the hedge *meant*? He knew, of course he did, but he wasn't thinking, wasn't thinking.

———

After that, Jennifer's friends began to look on him more indulgently as he allowed himself to show willing.

He partnered Jennifer at tennis doubles. They practised together and notched up a few significant wins for the club. He let her show him how to kiss. It felt awkward, unnatural even. But he learned how to, despite her talcumy smell clinging to his clothes and the clutch of her hand on his sleeve paralysing his arm. From novels and a film or two he mastered the right words to say to her. He memorized and rehearsed the nice remarks of no consequence that would cause Jennifer's mother to smile whenever he was invited to their house. He taught himself to swallow Mrs Harkness's monstrous dry-as-dust saffron cake between swigs of hot tea from the good china cups.

One Friday afternoon, in the month Everest was conquered, he married Jennifer Harkness – like a mountaineer in the high ether, not thinking. Not thinking.

———

The big red sandstone church on the high street had kept its railings. On the day, children poked their faces between the bars and old women offered the newly-weds sentimental smiles.

But now, his private dreams and ambitions ended.

Their life together was to prove a quiet one. He did decently well in the tax offices, but not outstandingly so. To the complacent eyes of the town Jennifer and he settled quite predictably into domesticity, the childless sort, and in the fullness of time Mrs Harkness's home became their own.

Half the garden they sold to a builder, and then they were obliged to raise quick-growing conifers to minimise the hazard to their privacy.

———

Following Jennifer's death he had given more attention to those temptations he had kept so hidden from her for nearly forty years. In the loosened-up 1990s, and with his days his own, he felt freer. But the predatory aspect was a long-standing habit by now. Unfortunately, he took less care in how he went about the business of picking up.

He was apprehended by the police in a public place, a park in Perth. He told them, panicking, that it had never happened before and he knew they didn't believe him. The police reminded him that the youth was young enough to be his grandson. Did he have a family of his own? He answered no, and he considered it a blessing, although to Jennifer it had been a constant sorrow. Then he told them his bereavement had sent him off the rails. He supposed Jennifer would be turning in her grave to hear his lies, but he wasn't thinking any more. He wasn't thinking.

———

The prison is new, but nobody calls it that.

He has been promised counselling. A psychiatrist breezily informed him that the problems lie inside, deep inside, and it's there they will find the solutions, too. Mr Hamilton hopes there will be no barriers to understanding, to truthfulness.

All the time the man was smiling, he was emptying his pipe into a brass ashtray—

Suddenly he's back there, he's turning that corner again, from the terrace onto the grassy lane, past the lorry of dead railings. The boy under the thorn hedge smiles up at him, slyly, as if he foresees the end of everything: *you have to be honest or else*. The railings go tumbling into the lorry's hold. Everyone's talking of a better world ahead, one day when the war is over, talking of liberation, while all the time – clinkety-clank – a cage of iron is being cast and riveted around him.

MovieLand
Drew Gummerson

——

I was supposed to be the authority, but it had to be said that they were probably right: the duck did appear to be dying. It wasn't a spectacular death, not like last summer when Ed had slipped from turbine seven and skewered himself on the radio mast of this very ship, *The Best Foot Forward*, but it was a death nevertheless.

"It's an eider duck," I said, in what I hoped was a calm and distracting manner. "Their feathers have great insulation qualities and were traditionally used in bedding, hence eiderdown."

"Jesus H. Christ," cursed one of the mothers as she peered down into the foaming waters. "It's got blood coming from its freakin' beak."

Giving me a remonstrative look she slid a gloved hand over her child's eyes. This was the same child I'd caught earlier throwing our complimentary refreshing mints at one of the feral shore cats in the Pre-tour Holding Area while waiting for the next trip, or "Wind Farm Experience", as Doug liked us to call it. When I'd questioned the child he'd stuck two fingers up, called me "beaky" and carried on launching his sugared missiles.

"Aren't you going to do something?" This from the same mother.

I looked into her eyes like we'd been taught during our two-and-a-half week training period. One forty-minute module had been entitled "Guest Psychology". Doug had said that by looking into someone's eyes you can usually tell what they want but, whether this woman wanted me to dive in and save the duck or hit it with a spade or something to put it out of its misery, who knew?

I was rescued by Captain Skarsgård poking his head out the wheelhouse and shouting that a squall was coming in and we had to head back to shore "'pronto pronto". He said there was room for the mothers to come and sit up in the wheelhouse with him while I entertained their kids with a wind-turbine installation and activation hand-puppet display. Captain Skarsgård had a rugged jaw, deep eyes and a chest like Charles Atlas. I'd had something of a crush on him once, but that was before I realized he was only out for himself. When I'd done the collection for poor Ed's widow and son he'd patted his pockets and said he was awful tight this month and then that very same evening I'd spied him down at the Moby Dick Lobster Grill with Mavis from accounts. And she wasn't a cheap date!

Some people don't know the meaning of personal responsibility – and that's a fact.

———————

Doug was waiting for me at the Guest Reception and Welcome Centre, arms folded. He was wearing his life jacket, which was point six on his health and safety aide-memoire, although as he was on dry land I didn't see the necessity. That was the thing about Doug: he was a stickler. He asked me to step into his office. I thought it might be about the duck.

"If it's about that duck," I said.

"How many offshore wind turbines have we got at this facility?" Doug's chair uttered a short motivational phrase as he sank down into it. He had got the idea from one of those toys on which you pull a ripcord to make it say something and married it with a whoopee cushion.

"Sixty-eight," I said.

"And how much electricity can they produce?"

"Seven megawatts." I eyed the chair opposite Doug's, but remained standing. If it was about the duck I wanted to deny responsibility and exit quickly. "As long as it's reasonably windy."

Doug nodded. I was yet to be lulled into any false sense of security. This was how most of Doug's meetings started. He liked to check his tour guides were on the ball. Or tour guide, I should say. Ed had yet to be replaced.

"We had a call today." Doug narrowed his eyes and frowned slightly. Behind him, on the wall, was a huge framed picture of the whole wind-farm facility, taken from a helicopter or something else really high up. Maybe a satellite. The effect really was quite something. Spartak liked to joke that Doug fancied himself as one of those Bond villains, and all he needed to complete the effect was a cat or a tank full of sharks, but I told Spartak to keep it down. Things had a way of getting back to Doug.

"From your wife."

Doug blew a mouthful of air out of his mouth like he couldn't believe it. That made two of us.

"She says there's been some trouble and she needs you to help out." He shook his head and said the words slowly. "She's told me to tell you she's sending your kid, James, here tomorrow."

He pushed a piece of paper across the desk towards me.

"I've written down the time of the train. You're supposed to be on duty but I've pulled some strings. You can make up the time on Friday."

I picked up the piece of paper. The words and numbers on it spun before my eyes.

"She's not actually my wife," I said. "It was a long time ago. We were best friends at school and then . . . you know?"

As I was making my exit, Doug coughed behind me and I knew something else was coming.

"We'll deduct James's accommodation charges direct from your wages. Cut out the middle man, if you like. Like I always say, we're all one big happy family here. *Mi casa es su casa*, and so on."

The accommodation area is called Palm Beach. There's no palm and no beach, just twelve portable Quonset huts lined up on what was once a car park.

It was rumoured that the huts had formerly been used to house troops over in Iraq. I didn't believe this until one day under my mattress I found a porno mag, stamped with the insignia of a military base in

Basra and a letter from a soldier to his mother. He told her he missed her and was sorry for all the grief he'd caused when growing up. Then, he said he'd killed a man, shot him in fact, and every time he closed his eyes he could see the bullet entering this man's head, how the head had literally exploded into all these pieces, and how his comrades had whooped like it was a video game but all he could think was that that man was someone's son and now his parents would never see their baby again. He said he didn't think he could take any more. I didn't like to think why the letter had never been sent.

The car park the huts are on used to be used by guests at the neighbouring MovieLand Theme Park, but the park only opens for one month a year now as they don't have that many guests.

After the park closed its doors for most of the year, six local youths broke into the *Night of the Living Dead* Fun House. It might never have been discovered, except for the fact that one of the boys caught sight of himself in the distorting mirrors, thought he had seen a ghost, and threw himself out of the nearest window, breaking his spine and both legs in what was quite a fall.

It was because of this that Doug hired Spartak and stepped up security here. Doug is not a touchy-feely person. He doesn't care about anyone hurting themselves. It's the litigation he's scared of.

Stepping into my hut, I found Spartak sitting naked on the sofa, watching *Jeremy Kyle* on the old TV we'd found miraculously washed up on the beach one morning. On the screen, a sallow-faced girl was saying how she'd been having a sexual relationship with her brother for the past seven years. She hadn't even stopped when she had become pregnant and found out that there might be certain health implications for the baby. The crowd was booing her, waving their arms in the air like the Romans did in that film *Spartacus*. Then, the girl's mother appeared from the wings. She took a seat and explained how the girl's brother wasn't her brother after all. She had kidnapped the boy from outside a supermarket when he was just a few months old and so everything was OK.

"It isn't incest," she said. "You're fine. I'm sorry I didn't tell you before."

"My son is coming to stay," I said to Spartak. English wasn't his first language and I'd learnt it was best to put things as directly as possible. "No more nights of wild and noisy sex for us and you're going to have to start wearing some clothes around here."

Spartak lifted his leg and let out a long slow fart before scratching at his arse. "Don't you love your Spartak no more?" Then his eyes widened as the complete translation must have sunk in. "You have a son?"

Spartak's story had come out in dribs and drabs over the six months we'd been together. From the age of ten, he'd been incorporated into a ruthless Muscovite gang. Having started out drug running, he'd quickly progressed to extortion, protection, handling fake goods and finally to the security of the big boss himself.

It was on a trip to St Petersburg that he'd been found in bed with the bellhop of the exclusive hotel they were staying in.

Homosexuality not being particularly well looked-upon in the Moscow gangland milieu, Saprtak decided to make his escape as soon as possible. Which goes some way to explaining how he'd ended up here watching *Jeremy Kyle*.

His story was so fantastic, so full of dramatic twists and turns and exotic foreign places, that I'd kept quiet about mine. It seemed boring in comparison. And besides, I felt ashamed about James. I'd let him down. I hadn't been much of a father to him.

"You should have told me you had a secret love child," said Spartak. His eyes lit up. "Are you sure it's yours or do we need to arrange a DNA paternity test?"

"You've been watching too much *Jeremy Kyle*," I said. "Now will you help me tidy up? And put some clothes on. Please."

We collected three bags of rubbish – mostly old beer cans and mildewing pizza boxes. I was making up a bed in the spare room, fitting a sheet over the cushions I'd taken from the chairs in the kitchen area, and then throwing a duvet over the whole lot when I heard Spartak shouting from the living room.

He was bent at the wall, pointing at something with a finger.

"It's bullet hole," he said.

Sure enough, there was a hole in the wall. Whether it was a bullet hole or not, I wasn't sure. I was no expert.

"And this," Spartak said, moving his hand down the wall, "looks like blood-splatter pattern.

"It's lucky none of us believe in ghosts," he said.

I wasn't so sure about that. It was five years since I'd last seen James. I'd not imagined him dead, exactly, but absence can soon be indistinguishable from nothingness, nothingness from a possibility of supernatural form.

———

Captain Skarsgård's squall turned into a full-blown storm. Back in the early days, when there was a storm, Spartak and I would go out to the sea wall. Even though the turbines were seven kilometres out you could see them, especially when there were background flashes of lightning. You couldn't believe they were man-made, these towers, and their solidity and unlikely presence said something deep about humankind's ability to harness nature. But you can get bored of anything if you see it enough and these days we only hoped that the storms would be deep and long enough to stop any guests from coming the following day. We didn't mind the guests per se, because after all weren't they the reason our wages got paid? But if they didn't come, Spartak and I could spend more time together. This seemed especially important now, what with James coming. So we lay in each other's arms, feeling both loved and protected, and each of us made the same silent wish: no guests.

———

The following day, we had three guests. They were bunched together, huddling for warmth, in the Pre-tour Holding Area. All three were dressed in similar thick black coats with hoods pulled up: a woman and two young boys. The rain was trundling down as the wind whipped at their faces.

"I promised them," said the woman. She had a strained grin fixed to her face as she held out the tickets, which were already turning to mush in the downpour. "After everything else, I couldn't let them down, could I?" She gave a nervous glance towards the chopping waters. *The Best Foot Forward* was rocking violently up and down on its moorings. "Is it safe to sail?"

I glanced towards the flag. It was down.

"The flag is down," I said. "It's safe to sail."

I usually filled the journey out to the turbines with a brief history of wind farming, starting off in 200 BC – Heron of Alexandria's windwheel – before taking in vertical-axis design, growth and cost trends and finishing with the imminent spectacular collapse of the carbon economy. Doug insists on no deviations, whatever the external circumstances. He calls this "'the tour guide's 'show must go on'" but, when two minutes out the woman put her hand to her mouth to stifle a sob and one large tear rolled down her cheek, I handed each of the boys a Wind Farm Activity Book with Attached Pencil – which isn't usually given out until the very end of the tour – and asked if she was OK.

"Not really," she said. "You know?"

I did know. I was all too well-acquainted with pain. Informing Captain Skarsgård it was an emergency, I asked to borrow his flask of rum and, sitting the woman down on the bench normally reserved for elderly or infirm guests, I poured us both a shot.

"Down the hatch," I said.

"You actually do have a hatch," she said, pointing, "but I think I might drink it myself. My need is greater than a lousy hatch's."

We grinned at each other as the fiery liquid went down.

"It's a long time since I've genuinely smiled," she said.

"Have another," I said.

She laughed this time, which seemed to break the ice that was already beginning to crack. So while the two boys shaded in the wind turbines in the Activity Book with Attached Pencil, the woman poured out the deep recesses of her heart. Her husband, the shipbuilder. A worldwide recession. Shipyards mothballing major new construction projects. The bottom falling out of the shipbuilding business.

"Every day he came home with the same defeated expression," she said. "And it was the way he looked at the boys that was the worst. Like he had failed them or something. The evening he didn't return home I feared the worst. He'd been depressed, we all had. When he was eventually found washed up on a beach outside Carnoustie by a pair of elderly dog walkers, it was almost a relief. Except it wasn't. It never is. His pockets were filled with ratchets. That's what he used to do, fix ratchets onto boats. Maybe he was hoping it would look like an accident. You know, ratchets had pulled him under. It's the boys I worry most about. All boys need a father. I've been trying to do everything I can to cheer them up." She shrugged her shoulders. "Hence today. All right, Sammy! All right, Pete!"

The younger of the two held up his activity book. He had shaded in his wind turbine, almost perfectly keeping within the edges. If truth be told, it didn't look like much, kind of dark and foreboding. We used to give out a set of colour pencils, but Doug had got a deal on these packs: Ten Shades of Grey. Pencils for all Occasions. At the staff meeting, where he had announced it, he had claimed that "shading is the new colouring" – but that was just Doug putting his own spin on things. None of us believed it.

At the end of the tour, as I stood at the gangplank wishing the guests a safe and pleasant onward journey, the woman put her arms around me and gave me a tight hug. She said it had been wonderful to talk and then Sammy, he was the younger of the boys, tore out the page displaying the wind turbine he had shaded in and held it out towards me.

"This is for you. You can pin it on your wall. That's what Daddy always used to do."

I watched them cross the car park to an old battered Fiat. For a moment, I thought about calling them back and asking them to come with me to the train station. The woman could tell James what a great person I was. Plus, if James saw me with a woman, then perhaps that would make things easier. I wasn't sure if he knew about me and it seemed like another thing to deal with on top of everything else. But what was the point in lying? How did that ever help anyone? If you put your heart on the line and then it got trampled, at least you'd put it on the line. You can't go through life with your heart never on the line. That would be a life half-lived, a quarter lived, even.

I raised my arm and waved towards the departing Fiat. I waved until the car had disappeared from view. I don't even know if the woman had seen me. Or those two little boys either.

———

I'd seen this film once. Someone meets someone at a train station. The train looks like its last stop was *The Railway Children*, and as it pulls in, steam billows from the smokestack, obscuring everything from view. As the steam clears, only the hero and the person he is there to meet are left. They run into each other's arms.

James's mother and I had ended badly. I could have perhaps got away with the condom she'd found in my trouser pocket after a business trip to Glasgow, or the flyer for Pump – with its promise of dark areas and even a "watersports" dungeon – but not the two together. She confronted me with them clutched in her hands and asked if they meant what she thought they meant. I broke down at once, glad at last for a chance to confess, and agreed with everything she said in return. I didn't like myself, or what I was doing. I agreed I was scum and, even at the height of my self-abnegation, admitted that in Pump I had let grown men urinate on me and enjoyed it. Or not enjoyed it but felt at last that I had got what I deserved. Which was a kind of enjoyment. I packed a suitcase and that was that. Ten years of my life over in one afternoon. I never saw or spoke to her again. She knew how to find me because every year I put my address and phone number on the back of the envelope in which I put James's birthday card, containing £500 in £20 notes. I had been doing it for so long I almost didn't connect it to any physical reality. That was why the phone call had come as so much of a shock. Like Doug had advised at the emergency staff meeting the morning after Ed died, I had put my feelings in a box, put a lid on the box, put the box in a cupboard, closed the door and walked away.

I worried I wouldn't recognize James – after all, it had been five years. But there was no mistaking the young man on the bench. He was slouched down, legs apart, eyes glued to a copy of something called *Nuts*. He looked like he'd lost weight, which was a concern as the last time I'd seen him he'd been nine.

As I stood there watching, he plucked a suppository-shaped object out of his ear and said, without even looking in my direction, "Before you ask, I don't want to be here. It wasn't my idea."

All the way back in the taxi I could hear the music coming from his ears. It was like being at a rock concert but also being far away. I thought about Ed's son. After Ed had died he had threatened to wonk Doug on the side of the head with one of the stainless-steel replica wind turbines we sold in the gift shop. Later, I'd found him sobbing in the guest restrooms. That was serious. Staff, and relatives of staff, weren't allowed in there. If Doug had found him, there would have been serious repercussions. But Ed Junior didn't care. He missed his dad. Ed was a great bloke. You get the children you deserve. That's what I thought now.

On entering the Quonset hut James prowled around, picking up and putting down objects as if I'd brought him to a shop and he was looking for something worth buying. Spartak was sitting on the sofa. He'd taken my advice and for once he was fully dressed. With all his Moscow Mafia tattoos covered up, he looked quite respectable but, after I introduced him, James didn't even ask him who he was or what he was doing there.

When James disappeared into the bedroom we'd prepared for him and closed the door I almost felt a sense of relief, but seconds later he came straight back out.

"WHAT'S THIS CRAP?"

He was holding out Sammy's greyed-in wind-turbine picture. I'd tacked it above the bed in an effort to make the place look more homely.

"YOU KNOW WHAT?" James shouted. "YOU DISGUST ME. I DON'T WANT A PICTURE OF AN ENORMOUS PENIS PINNED UP OVER THE BED."

With that, he screwed up Sammy's page and tossed it towards me and stormed back into the room, slamming the door behind him.

Spartak fixed me with a stare.

"In Russia, son speak to father like that you break his legs. You want me to do business? Or maybe just slap him about a bit?"

———

I walked out, past the other Quonset huts. One had a row of underpants hanging in the window. I wasn't sure if they'd been put there as decoration or to dry in the weakening afternoon sun. The way they were so neat and held by brightly coloured pegs made me think the former, but what kind of judge was I? I was disgusting. James had said so.

The last of the Quonset huts abutted the fence of MovieLand. It being a barrier to any further forward motion I followed it around, stopping only when I came to the tall and imposing iron gates.

Behind the initial bank of closed-up concession stands, coloured lightbulbs popped or dusty, loomed the lifted-up cars of Wonka's Flying Marshmallows, tarpaulin covers stretched over them, and behind these rose the bare tracks of *Indy's Last Crusade* Coaster. If the park had been open, I could have brought James. He might not have liked me any better, or thought me any less disgusting, but at least he might have thought it a cool place to live. I remembered him as a baby, his arms and legs waggling uselessly in the air like a turtle turned on its back. I remembered how, shortly after his birth, his mum had gripped my hand tightly and said we had done it, me and her – we had made this beautiful and spectacular living thing.

Past the theme park, on a patch of otherwise deserted land, was the only other building within a three-mile radius: a garage with a 24-hour mini-mart attached. A bell rang above my head as I went inside. It was then that fate took over.

Although it was getting on for the end of March, they had some Christmas stock set out jauntily on an end-of-aisle merchandizer. A string of lights twinkled off and on around it, and on a sign someone had handwritten in a thick red felt tip, "Last chance to buy! 20 per cent off."

I knew what I had to do.

Quickly, for you never knew what other eager bargain hunters would appear with grabbing hands behind you, I chose a plastic tablecloth with fat Santas marching over it, a candle in the shape of the Virgin Mary, some disposable plastic plates with snowmen regaling the edges and a wind-up Yule log that played "God Rest Ye Merry Gentlemen" over and over until the spring ran out. Gathering up all these items in my arms, I took them over to the checkout, along with six frozen microwave meals nearing their sell-by date. We didn't have a microwave, but from past experience I knew you could put these things in a pan and they wouldn't taste any worse.

The plan was simple: James, Spartak and I would have a Christmas dinner together. It would both make up for all the Christmases I'd missed with James, and it would also show him what a normal and loving family unit Spartak and I had formed.

Back at the Quonset hut, James was still holed up in his room. I explained my plan to Spartak and as quietly as we could we set to work.

When everything was just perfect – it really was quite a scene – I shouted for James.

It had grown dark and we had turned off the lights so the room was lit only by the glow of the TV on mute and the Virgin Mary candle. The Santa cloth had fit perfectly on the table and Spartak had had the idea of making an extra chair from an upturned beer crate. The *pièce de résistance* was the Yule log. As I brought James in, it was belting out, "In Bethlehem, In Israel, This Blessed Babe was born, And laid within a manger, Upon this blessed morn". The whole thing formed quite an effect, better even than I had hoped.

James looked one way, then another, his eyes growing wider and wider and just when I thought he was going to say how brilliant it all was and how sorry he was for calling me disgusting, he shouted, "I NEVER WANTED TO COME HERE. WHY COULDN'T THINGS STAY AS THEY WERE?" And without touching his Specially Selected Lasagne with 50 Per Cent Real Beef on the snowman plate he was out the front door.

Spartak said he would be back when he was hungry, but at midnight there was still no sign of him and he must have been hungry by then. At 2 a.m. I went to look for him, but the truth was that he could have been anywhere. He had a five-hour headstart and he was just a thin boy and this was a big place. At 4 o'clock I came back.

"He'll be back in the morning," said Spartak.

"It is the morning," I said.

Spartak pulled a face. "Later in the morning."

Later in the morning, he wasn't back.

Nor the next morning, either.

On the third morning, Doug asked me how I was getting on with my son. I said, "Fine." When he said he had taken the accommodation charges out of my next week's wages I said, "Fine."

After all, I didn't want to tempt fate.

———

On the fourth night after James's disappearance I drank too much sambuca and decided I would go to ask Ed.

Ed didn't have a grave or anything – Ed Junior having tipped his ashes into the sea – so at just past midnight I cast off *The Best Foot Forward*'s mooring ropes and stepped purposefully into the wheelhouse.

The thing was, just as I blamed myself for James's disappearance, I also blamed myself for Ed's death. It was a sorry tale.

The way some people are bent as all Holy Hell, Ed was straight up and down. We'd started at the Wind Farm Experience on the same two-and-a-half week induction course and we'd hit it off straight away, although I understood right off that Ed was something of a rebel. Every time Doug said something contentious, Ed would surreptitiously dig me in the ribs with an elbow and say, "Jeez," or "What a sucker," while pulling this awful pained face. Ed really believed in all that new-age kind of stuff: renewable energy, saving the planet and so on. He thought Doug was a fake.

"Doug crawls down my pants and bites," he said to me one time, after Doug had spent twenty minutes demonstrating to us the correct way to wear out tour-guide hats. "He's all Mr Corporation and Money, Money, Money. What he doesn't understand is that right here is our last chance to save the planet. It's real."

When Ed wasn't working he was sending off letters or making up little badges that he would hand out to schoolchildren, "Turn out a light today", "The Earth is our best friend – Treat her right", and so on.

In the end, it was me who came across that blasted article. I found it tucked away at the back of the town's bi-monthly free newspaper and I knew straight off it would be exactly the kind of thing Ed would be interested in. Some researcher based at Leicester University had discovered that it was the white colour of the wind-turbine blades that attracted insects. In turn, the insects attracted birds or bats. Then the blades killed them. This same researcher found that insects were a lot less attracted by the colour purple. Ed was straight on the bandwagon. The blades had to be painted purple. It was a no-brainer. That's why birds and bats had always been flying into them. Hadn't we all seen it ourselves?

We heard Doug's reaction and we weren't even in the room. He wasn't going to paint the blades purple. Did Ed have any idea how much that would cost? Ed pushed a piece of paper across the desk. He had got a quote. Doug pushed the piece of paper back. He didn't even look at it.

Ed was not a man to be beaten. If Doug wasn't going to help him out, then he'd do it himself. One morning, he rowed out to turbine seven, hoisted himself up to the blades with a rope and pulley system of his own devising and set to work, a pot of paint dangling between his legs.

It was me who'd found him. It was during the first of the morning tours.

"Get down, you idiot!" I shouted. "You're going to kill yourself!" It was as he was looking down that he fell.

My fault.

There are some things that are difficult to live with. It's not a question of getting over them, more of accommodation: finding a place inside yourself where they can live. It made it easier that I knew Ed would forgive me. He was the most decent person I'd known. That's why I wanted his advice.

I glided the boat to a halt. Looking up, although it was too dark to see, I knew one of those spinning blades would still be half purple. Doug said we'd leave it that way as a memorial to Ed. That getting it repainted white would incur a cost, of course, hadn't entered Doug's mind. What a toerag!

"If you can hear me, Ed," I said. "I need some help. You've got a kid, you know what they're like. Did you ever go through any bad patches with Ed Junior? Not that this is the same thing. You weren't an absent father. Nor were you a homosexual. If I'd have been there and loved his mother in a regular way, things might have been better. Although I would have still screwed up. That's the only thing I'm good at. Screwing up. I know. You'd tell me I'm being hard on myself, but that's why it was easy to go when Tara told me to go. I looked deep into my heart and asked myself if I would be a good dad. I don't have to tell you what answer I came up with. I went into James's room before I left. He was asleep. He looked so perfect like that, in his pyjamas, hair spilling across the pillow. I put my hand on his head, said, 'You'll be better off without me, son. I'll bring you down. That's what I do. I'm like a disease.

I'd infect you. I'm like a mirror you look in and see everything that's bad about yourself. So I'm going. It's a cliché, but I will always love you. It's because I love you that I won't be around to screw up your life like I screwed up mine.' Then I left.

"It wasn't until I saw him at the train station that I realised what love is. It's a mess. It's imperfect. It does screw you up but what's the alternative to not being screwed up? Emptiness? Alienation? Long nights alone? I wanted to reach out my arms to him, but I didn't know how. Now he's gone and I think it might be too late. What do you think I should do?"

I knew Ed was dead so I hadn't expected an answer. Not really. Just talking had been a help. I had started at some place and wound up someplace else. That was all I needed really, just a kick up my own backside. I fired the engine and headed home.

———

Spartak was sprawled out on the sofa asleep in front of the TV. What I hadn't told Ed was that it was Spartak who had taught me how to love. How it could be messy and difficult, but also perfect and heart-affirming. I loved him. I put a hand on his shoulder and shook him awake and said I wanted him to help me find James.

"We used to track people down and break their bones," he said, rubbing sleep from his eyes.

"Go with the first part," I said.

"OK," he said. "Have you got recent photograph?"

I pointed towards the door. I scrunched my face up in an imitation of James the last time we'd seen him.

"You've seen him," I said. "He was standing right there."

"To show other people."

I shook my head, ashamed suddenly that I didn't have a single picture of my son.

"Don't worry," said Spartak, "we can draw."

The following day, we had a group of trainee hairdressers taking the tour. I thought I was being cheeky when I asked for a haircut but they were more than up for the idea.

"I can only do one length," said Amanda, the one who had volunteered herself and produced a lethal-looking pair of scissors from her backpack. "That's all we've learnt so far."

"That's OK," I said, "I only want it one length." And she laughed as if I'd said something funny.

The deck of the boat rocked. Over our heads the blades of turbine sixteen swooshed. The truth was that when we found James I wanted to look my best, to make him proud.

"Are you going anywhere nice on your holidays this year?" Amanda asked.

Another of the hairdressers laughed. "Day one, lesson one: Entertaining the Clients."

When I got home Spartak said he had some news.

"They didn't recognize him at the train or the bus station. That narrows it down."

"To what?"

"To other forms of transportation."

I hadn't been asleep long when I felt Spartak shaking me awake. He had a broad grin on his face. Some people don't like gold teeth, but I do.

"I think I have breakthrough."

In his hands he was holding a single sheet of paper.

"This is statement from owner of garage shop. Every day boy who matches description of drawing comes into shop to buy food and cigarettes. This mean he is not far away. Then tonight I see something and – *how do you say?* – bingo!"

He led me by the hand through the door of our bedroom and then outside. Lifting an arm he pointed over the roofs of the Quonset huts.

At first I didn't know what I was looking at. It looked like nothing, but then I saw it. High up, a light.

"MovieLand Theme Park," said Spartak. He gripped the roll of flesh at my waist and pinched.

"One word. Person who shows light at night wants to be found. Trust me."

Even in Russian, I didn't think that could be one word but who cared? Spartak was telling me exactly what I wanted to hear.

We went together.

The security fencing was no match for my former Russian gangster. Spartak pulled out the multi-tool he always carried with him and within seconds it was toast.

With its discordant shapes and moon-cast shadows, the theme park was eerie at night. When James was three years old, he always made me check under the bed before he went to sleep. And in the cupboard. And behind the curtains. He told me once that I was his hero, his big blue eyes wide open, just like that.

"You're my hero."

Sometimes we lost sight of the light, but then it would reappear again over the roof of a concession stand or through the angular struts that supported the roller-coaster track. But it was obvious where we were going. Spartak had worked it out. To be that high up he had to be in the very highest gondola of *The Living Daylights* Big Wheel.

The wheel stood right in the centre of the park and the regulars said, back when there were regulars, that it was possible to see its massive structure from the other side of the channel. Or the moon. It loomed and groaned above us in a way that sent shivers down my spine.

"Oh James, be safe."

"We find engine room," said Spartak, gazing upwards towards the twinkling light. "Then we bring him down."

I put a hand on his arm. I could feel his taut muscles through his shirt. "I rather think I'm supposed to go up." I attempted to sound brave. "Let me do this. It's important."

I felt like a character in a Biblical story as I climbed. Or Cary Grant in the climax of *North by Northwest*, scrambling up Mount Rushmore. I knew the trick was not to look down, but I wanted to look up anyway. I thought of Ed and how he had died for what he believed in. I would do this for Ed. And me, of course. I would do it for me. And I wouldn't die.

The door of the gondola had been wedged half-open with a broken-off sign from one of the concession stands. James had made the inside cosy enough. He had a sleeping bag in there and there were some pictures pasted up on the inside of the glass of impossibly beautiful women who set you up for disappointment in later life. From their raggedy edges, I guessed they came from that magazine he had been reading the first time I'd seen him. *Nuts*. If he was surprised to see me, he didn't show it.

"That climb scared *The Living Daylights* out of me," I said.

To my surprise this rather feeble line was answered with a laugh.

"I've told myself the same joke every time I've climbed up here." James was sitting with his knees pulled up to his chest and he had his arms wrapped around them. "What happened to your hair, Dad? It looks weird."

"It was cut by a trainee hairdresser," I said. "She asked me what I was doing on my holidays. Apparently that's in the very first lesson."

It came to me that this was the first time James had called me dad. Taking this as encouragement, I hauled myself fully inside. It wouldn't do to fall just when I had got so close.

"Of all the gin joints in all the world, I should walk into yours," I said. And then I said, "*Casablanca*." And then I said, "I've let you down."

James turned away and gazed out of the window. Somewhere out there, the blades of the turbines were turning, powered by the Earth's own energy.

"I'm sorry, son," I said.

When James turned back to me there was a tear in his eye.

"It's not because you're gay. Mum told me about that years ago. And I've got a friend at school, John. Although he prefers to be called Vivienne now. He's having gender-corrective surgery." James lifted an edge of the sleeping bag, dropped it again. "Actually, that's why I'm here. Mum said Vivienne and I were getting too close. She caught us

Skyping together. I was only helping her choose some shoes, but Mum was worried I'd end up like you."

"And so she sent you to me?" The words snorted out of my mouth.

James smiled. "I know. That's Mum's logic for you." He paused. "Spartak, is he your . . . ?"

I thought about explaining what I had said to Ed out on the water, but sometimes when you say words out loud they don't have the same meaning as they did when they were in your heart. And besides, James was James and Ed was Ed. They were different people. Shuffling over until I was right next to my son, I lifted an arm and put it around him.

"I love you," I said, and he kind of fell towards me and he was crying.

After all that had happened, it was as easy as that: a simple contraction of skeletal muscle and three small words. I had left James and then he had left me. He had wanted to be found. I had found him. Insecurities and self-hatred could only take you so far in life. There came a point where you had to make a choice. We couldn't all reach for the stars but we could reach for something.

After a time, James bent forward and lifted an object from under the blanket. "I hope you don't mind. I borrowed this. Although it might not have seemed so at the time, I thought that what you tried to do that day was actually kind of sweet."

In his hands was the wind-up Yule log. I hadn't even realized it had gone. James gave the key some twists and pressed the button that started the music.

In the distance was the Quonset hut I called home. Beyond that were the wind turbines – toothpicks pricking the horizon. I imagined their blades, invisible from here, spinning in time to the music.

"O tidings of comfort and joy, Comfort and joy, O tidings of comfort and joy".

"Happy Christmas, son," I said.

"Happy Christmas, Dad," James said.

About the authors

JAMES ROBERT BAKER was an American author of sharply satirical, predominantly gay-themed transgressional fiction. A native Californian, his work is set almost entirely in Southern California. After graduating from UCLA, he began his career as a screenwriter, but became disillusioned and started writing novels instead. Though he garnered fame for his books *Fuel-Injected Dreams* and *Boy Wonder*, after the controversy surrounding publication of his novel *Tim and Pete*, he faced increasing difficulty having his work published. According to his life partner, Ron Robertson, this was a contributing factor in his suicide in 1997. Baker's work has achieved cult status in the years since his death, and two additional novels have been posthumously published.

JOSHUA WINNING is a film journalist and author of dark fantasy series *The Sentinel Trilogy* (available through Peridot Press). He is a contributing editor at *Total Film* magazine and co-founder of the *Night Terrors* book series, which launched in 2014 with gay murder-mystery *Camp Carnage*. He lives in North London and can be found online at www.joshuawinning.com

DAMON GALGUT is an award-winning South African playwright and novelist. He has been nominated for many awards for his writing. Most notably, *In a Strange Room* was shortlisted for the Man Booker Prize in 2010. *The Imposter* was nominated for the Commonwealth Writers Prize (Africa Region, Best Book) in 2009; and *The Good Doctor* was shortlisted for The International IMPAC Dublin Literary Award in 2005 and the Man Booker Prize for Fiction and the Commonwealth Writers Prize (Africa Region, Best Book), both in 2003.

VESTAL MCINTYRE is the author of the novel *Lake Overturn* and the story collection *You Are Not the One* – both Lambda Literary Award winners and *New York Times* Book Review Editors' Choices. His work has appeared in *Tin House, The Boston Review, Open City* and several anthologies. Originally from Idaho, he now lives in London and teaches at the University of Northampton.

NIGEL FAIRS is a British actor, writer and composer. He trained at Bretton Hall College and as an actor has worked in television, theatre, radio and film, performing everywhere from the West End to HM Prison Holloway. As a writer, he has had more plays produced than William Shakespeare, and six musicals. He has also written a large number of murder-mystery scripts, which are performed throughout the world. www.nigelfairs.com

DIRIYE OSMAN is a British-Somali short story writer, essayist, critic and visual artist. His critically acclaimed debut *Fairytales for Lost Children* (Team Angelica Press) won the 2014 Polari First Book Prize and was named one of the best books of the year by the *Guardian*. His writing has appeared in the *Guardian, Time Out, The Huffington Post, Attitude, Prospect, Poetry Review, AfroPunk, Kwani?, Jungle Jim, Under The Influence* and *SCARF Magazine*.

DAVID ROBILLIARD was a London-based poet and painter. He first met Gilbert & George in 1979 and was described by them as "the new master of the modern person". They would remain good friends until his death in 1988. Throughout the 1980s, Robilliard published books and postcards of his poetry, as well as contributing to publications such as *The Fred, Square Peg* and *The Manipulator*. Robilliard had no formal training but produced paintings, drawings and eight volumes of poetry in his short life. The collection of poems in this anthology was weaved together by Robert Cochrane.

TIM ASHLEY was educated at Oxford and Cambridge universities. After ten years as an investment banker, he left to start an Internet company in 1996. After a series of mergers, the company was floated on the Stock Exchange in 1999 and Tim was free to leave full-time employment in 2000 to pursue his real interests: writing and photography. As a writer, Tim's first novel, *The Island of Mending Hearts*, was published in 2004 and since then he has also seen a number of short stories published in anthologies and collections. His longer narratives tend towards the optimistic whereas his short stories explore darker themes.

SEBASTIAN BEAUMONT is the author of *On the Edge, Heroes Are Hard to Find, Two, The Cruelty of Silence, The Linguist* and *Thirteen*. He has contributed short stories to several anthologies, and lives in Brighton, England.

PAUL MAGRS is the author of *Marked for Life* (1995), *Does it Show?* (1997) and *Could it Be Magic?* (1998). Magrs's first children's book, *Strange Boy* (2002), prompted controversy due to homosexual content involving its 10-year-old protagonist and a 14-year-old neighbour. Magrs's other novels include *Aisles* (2003) and *To the Devil – a Diva!* (2004). His novel *Exchange* was shortlisted for the 2006 Booktrust Teenage Prize and was longlisted for the 2007 Carnegie Medal. Magrs has also written several novels, short stories and audio dramas relating to *Doctor Who*. His current ongoing novel series is *The Adventures of Brenda and Effie*. A stand-alone novel, *666 Charing Cross Road*, was published in October 2011. He lives in Manchester, England.

JERRY ROSCO is a New Yorker and author of the biography *Glenway Wescott Personally*. He also edited books of Wescott journals and stories, including *A Visit to Priapus and Other Stories* and the Lambda Literary Award winner *A Heaven of Words: Last Journals*.

COLIN SPENCER is an English writer and artist who has produced a prolific body of work in a wide variety of media. His work includes novels, short stories, non-fiction (including histories of food and of homosexuality), cookery books, stage and television plays, paintings and drawings, book and magazine illustrations. He has appeared in numerous radio and television programmes and lectured on food history, literature and social issues. For fourteen years he wrote a regular food column for the *Guardian*.
www.colinspencer.co.uk

FELICE PICANO is the author of more than thirty books of poetry, fiction, memoirs, non-fiction and plays. His work has been translated into many languages and several of his titles have been national and international bestsellers. He is considered a founder of modern gay literature along with the other members of the Violet Quill. Picano also began and operated the SeaHorse Press and Gay Presses of New York for fifteen years. His first novel was a finalist for the PEN/Hemingway Award. Since then he's been nominated for and/or won dozens of literary awards. Picano teaches at Antioch College, Los Angeles.
www.felicepicano.net

ROBERT COCHRANE is a Manchester-based writer, poet and journalist. He has contributed to various magazines, including *Attitude* and *Mojo*, and his poetry has appeared in numerous magazines and anthologies. He has had a long involvement in the publishing and promotion of the work of the late poet and artist David Robilliard.

CLIFF JAMES is the author of the gothic novel *Of Bodies Changed*, which was inspired by his year-long stint in an Anglican monastic house in the South Downs. After leaving the Church, he became an active campaigner against religious privilege and was the Secretary of the Gay and Lesbian Humanist Association (GALHA). He has been engaged in the Occupy and anti-austerity movements, and is a founding member of the new Socialist party Left Unity. As a columnist for 3SIXTY and GHQ magazine, he has written on social justice and human rights issues and has published poetry and short stories in anthologies.

NICK ALEXANDER is the author of eleven novels, including the five-book 50 Reasons series featuring gay hero Mark, and a number of number-one women's fiction bestsellers. His most recent novel, The Photographer's Wife, is out now. Nick lives in the southern French Alps with his partner, three mogs and a complete set of Almodovar films. www.nick-alexander.com

MATT HARRIS is an actor and writer. His last notable role was the character Daniel in Channel 4's Metrosexuality, aired in 2001, after which he was inspired to try writing his own work. He has produced numerous plays at the Oval House Theatre in London and various festivals, and formed resident company TheatreKit at The Rose Theatre, Bankside. He is currently working on a variety of new plays.

FRANCIS KING was born in Switzerland but spent his childhood in India, where his father was a government official. While still an undergraduate at Oxford, he published his first three novels. He then joined the British Council, working in Italy, Greece, Egypt, Finland and Japan, before he resigned to devote himself entirely to writing. For some years he was drama critic for the Sunday Telegraph and he reviewed fiction regularly for the Spectator. He won the Somerset Maugham Prize, the Katherine Mansfield Prize and the Yorkshire Post Novel of the Year Award for Act of Darkness (1983). His penultimate book, The Nick of Time, was long-listed for the 2003 Man Booker Prize. He died in 2011.

JOSEPH LIDSTER is a television writer best known for his work on the Doctor Who spin-off series Torchwood and The Sarah Jane Adventures. He also writes the content for the tie-in websites relating to the fictional world of the television series *Sherlock*. He has co-produced Big Finish Productions' dramatic reading range of *Dark Shadows* audio dramas since 2011. In 2011 he script-edited the short film *Cleaning Up*. In 2012 he won the "Audience Favourite Writer" award for his first play, *Nice Sally*, in the Off Cut Theatre Festival.

NEIL BARTLETT is a writer and theatre director. His first book, *Who Was That Man?*, was published in 1988; his most recent, *The Disappearance Boy*, was published by Bloomsbury in 2014 and won him a nomination for Stonewall Writer of the Year. You can find Neil, and contact him, via www.neil-bartlett.com

HUGH FLEETWOOD published his first novel, *A Painter of Flowers*, in 1971, for which he also designed the jacket. As he did for his second novel, *The Girl Who Passed for Normal*, which won the John Llewellyn Rhys Memorial Prize. His fifth novel, *The Order of Death*, was made into a film (aka *Corrupt* in the US) starring Harvey Keitel and John Lydon (Johnny Rotten). He continues to write and paint, and currently lives in London.
www.hughfleetwood.com

JOHN R. GORDON lives and works in London, England. He is the author of six ground-breaking novels of black gay British life: *Black Butterflies*, for which he won a New London Writers' Award; *Skin Deep* and *Warriors & Outlaws*, both of which have been taught on graduate and post-graduate courses in the United States; *Faggamuffin*, *Colour Scheme* and, in 2014, *Souljah*. He script-edited and wrote for the world's first black gay television show, *Noah's Arc*, and co-wrote the screenplay for the GLAAD Award-winning *Noah's Arc* feature-film *Jumping the Broom*, for which he received an NAACP Image Award nomination. In 2007 he wrote the autobiography of America's most famous black gay porn-star, *My Life in Porn: the Bobby Blake Story*, and his short film *Souljah* (directed by Rikki Beadle-Blair) won the 2008 Soho Rushes Award for

Best Film. As well as mentoring and encouraging young gay and lesbian and racially diverse writers, he also paints, cartoons and does film and theatre design. He is also a student of Vodoun. With Rikki Beadle-Blair he is the founder of Team Angelica Publishing.

www.johnrgordon.com

www.teamangelica.com

ROYSTON ELLIS left school at sixteen, determined to be a writer. Two years later, his first book, *Jiving to Gyp*, was published. In 1961, his book *The Big Beat Scene* was first published. At twenty, Royston left England for Moscow, where he read his poetry on stage with the iconic Russian poet Yevtushenko, and then to the Canary Islands where he acted briefly as an Arab with Cliff Richard in the movie *Wonderful Life*, and wrote three novels. Later, he lived in Dominica and wrote the bestselling *Bondmaster* series of historical novels as Richard Tresillian. He is the author of more than sixty published books (guides, novels, biographies and volumes of poetry), and has lived in Sri Lanka since 1980.

SCOTT BROWN has worked as travel correspondent for a number of magazines. His short stories have appeared in several anthologies, including *Bend Sinister, Death Comes Easy, Serendipity, A Casualty of War* and *What Love Is*. He recently completed his first novel.

PATRICK GALE is a British novelist who lives on a farm near Land's End, Cornwall. His first novel, *The Aerodynamics of Pork*, appeared in 1985 and his most recent books are *Notes from an Exhibition* (2007), *The Whole Day Through* (2009), *Gentleman's Relish* (2009), *A Perfectly Good Man* (2012) and *A Place Called Winter* (2015).

www.galewarning.org

LAWRENCE SCHIMEL was born in New York and writes in both Spanish and English. He has published over 100 books as author or anthologist in many different genres, including the short-story collections *His Tongue, Two Boys in Love* and *The Drag Queen of Elfland*; poetry collections *Deleted Names* and *Fairy Tales for Writers*; the graphic novel *Vacation in Ibiza*; and numerous anthologies. He has won the Lambda Literary Award twice, for *First Person Queer* (with Richard Labonté) and *PoMoSexuals: Challenging Assumptions about Gender and Sexuality* (with Carol Queen) and has also won the Spectrum Award and the Independent Publisher Book Award. He lives in Madrid, Spain and New York City.

JOSEPH OLSHAN is the author of nine novels, the most recent of which, *Cloudland*, was published by Saint Martin's Press and Arcadia Books in 2013. His first novel, *Clara's Heart*, won the *Times*/Jonathan Cape Young Writers' Competition, a prize judged by Ian McEwan, Doris Lessing and Peter Stoddard. The novel went on to become the feature film *Clara's Heart*, starring Whoopi Goldberg and Neil Patrick Harris. Olshan is currently the editorial director of Delphinium Books/ HarperCollins. He lives in Vermont.
www.josepholshan.com

RUPERT SMITH was born in Washington DC, grew up in Surrey and moved to London in 1978, where he's lived ever since. After a few years pursuing an academic career, he enjoyed a twenty-year career in journalism, writing for a wide variety of dailies, weeklies and monthlies in the UK and elsewhere. He is the author of numerous novels, including *Man's World* (Arcadia Books 2010) – a story of gay life now, and gay life fifty years ago. Rupert also writes under the name James Lear (erotica) and Rupert James (blockbuster chicklit).
www.rupertsmith.org.uk

DAVID LLEWELLYN is the author of six novels, including *Eleven, Everything is Sinister* and *Ibrahim & Reenie,* and has written for BBC Books' *Doctor Who* range, aimed at young adults. He lives with his partner in Cardiff.

ALFRED CORN is an American poet, essayist and writer. His first book of poems, *All Roads at Once*, appeared in 1976, followed by *A Call in the Midst of the Crowd* (1978), *The Various Light* (1980), *Notes from a Child of Paradise* (1984), *The West Door* (1988) and *Autobiographies* (1992). His seventh book of poems, titled *Present*, appeared in 1997, along with a novel titled *Part of His Story*. He is the recipient of numerous awards and honours, including the 1982 Levinson Prize by *Poetry* magazine, an Award in Literature from the Academy of Arts and Letters in 1983 and a Guggenheim Fellowship in 1986. In 1987, he was awarded a Fellowship of the Academy of American Poets. His latest novel, *Miranda's Book*, was published in 2014.

DAMIAN BARR has been a journalist for over ten years, writing mostly for *The Times* but also the *Independent, Telegraph, Financial Times, Guardian, Evening Standard* and *Granta*. He is the author of *Get It Together: A Guide to Surviving Your Quarterlife Crisis*, featured on *Richard & Judy*, and has co-written two plays for BBC Radio 4. He is a Fellow of the Royal Society of Arts, on the Faculty at the School of Life and host of the infamous Literary Salon at Shoreditch House. He was named Writer of the Year at the 2013 Stonewall Awards. Barr's second book, *Maggie & Me*, a memoir of growing up in small-town Scotland during the Thatcher years, was published by Bloomsbury in April 2013. He lives in Brighton.

TONY PEAKE was born in South Africa but has lived most of his life in London. As a short story writer, he has contributed to four volumes of *Writer's Tales*, *The Penguin Book of Contemporary South African Short Stories*, *New Writing 13* and *Seduction*, a themed anthology which he also edited. he is the author of two novels (*A Summer Tide* and *Son to the Father*) and a biography of Derek Jarman.
www.tonypeake.com

BRENT MEERSMAN was born in Cape Town, South Africa. His first novel, *Primary Coloured* (Human & Rousseau) was published in 2007, followed by *Reports Before Daybreak* (Umuzi/Random House) and *Five Lives at Noon* (Missing Ink, 2013). He is a compulsive traveller. His latest book, *80 Gays around the World*, was published in 2014.
www.meersman.co.za

RICHARD ZIMLER was born in New York but has lived in Portugal for the last twenty-four years. His novels have been translated into twenty-three languages and have appeared on bestseller lists in the UK, Australia, the USA and many other countries. Four of his works have been nominated for the International IMPAC Dublin Literary Award, and he has won literary prizes in America, France, Portugal and the UK. His most recent novels in the UK and America are *The Warsaw Anagrams*, *The Seventh Gate* and *The Night Watchman*.
www.zimler.com

JEFFREY ROUND is a writer of contemporary fiction, equally at home in different genres. His first two books, *A Cage of Bones* and *The P-town Murders*, were listed on AfterElton's Top 100 Gay Books. His most recent title is *Lake on the Mountain* (Dundurn), a literary thriller. He is author of the Bradford Fairfax comic mystery series, whose style has been described as "a cross between Oscar Wilde and Agatha Christie". He is also a director, television producer, and songwriter. His blog, "A Writer's Half-Life", has been syndicated online.
www.jeffreyround.com

IAN YOUNG was born in London. His stories about Finsbury Park in the 1980s have been published in the anthologies *The Mammoth Book of Gay Short Stories*, *Boys of the Night*, *Serendipity*, *A Casualty of War*, *What Love Is* and *Best Gay Stories of 2012*, and in the periodicals *Jonathan* and *Chelsea Station*. His books include *Sex Magick*, *The Stonewall Experiment*,

Out in Paperback and *Encounters with Authors*. He lives in Toronto with his partner Wulf.

NEAL DRINNAN was born in Melbourne, Australia. He has worked in publishing and journalism for many years, and is the author of five novels: *Glove Puppet*, *Pussy's Bow*, *Quill*, *Izzy and Eve* and *Rare Bird of Truth*, as well as *The Rough Guide to Gay and Lesbian Australia* and numerous short stories.
www.nealdrinnan.com

MICHAEL CARROLL was born in Memphis, grew up in northern Florida and lives in New York. His work has appeared in *Boulevard*, *Ontario Review*, *Southwest Review*, *The Yale Review*, *Open City* and *Animal Shelter*, as well as in such anthologies as *The New Penguin Book of Gay Short Stories*. His first collection, *Little Reef and Other Stories*, was published in 2014.

RONALD FRAME is a prize-winning novelist, short story writer and dramatist. He was educated in Glasgow, and at Oxford University. *Unwritten Secrets*, a novel and his fifteenth book of fiction, was published in 2010. He has written many original plays and adaptations (most recently *The Other Simenon* for BBC Radio). His serial *The Hydro* (three series) was a popular success. A radio memoir of growing up in fifties and sixties Scottish suburbia, *Ghost City*, transferred to BBC Television. His first TV film, *Paris*, won the Samuel Beckett Award and PYE's "Most Promising Writer New to Television" Award.

DREW GUMMERSON lives in Leicester, England. His first novel, *The Lodger*, was published in 2002 and became a finalist in the Lambda Literary Awards. His latest novel, *Me and Mickie James*, was published by Jonathan Cape in July 2008. He works for the police.
www.drewgummerson.co.uk

Acknowledgements

Individual stories remain the copyright of their respective authors.

This is Serious © 1997 James Robert Baker, was first published in *The Mammoth Book of Gay Short Stories* (Robinson, 1997) and is reproduced by permission of Ron Robertson.

Dead Air © 2014 Joshua Winning

Shadows © 1988 Damon Galgut, was first published in *Small Circle of Beings* (Constable & Co, 1988) and is reproduced by permission of the author.

Men Without Men © 2014 Vestal McIntyre

Nelly's Teeth © 2014 Nigel Fairs

Shoga © 2013 Diriye Osman. First published in *Fairytales for Lost Children* (Team Angelica Publishing, 2013) and is reproduced by permission of the author.

Tonight's Hope Shattered-Never and other poems © David Robilliard. Poems written over a number of years collected into one new story by Robert Cochrane in 2014. Reproduced by permission of Robert Cochrane and Chris Hall.

W.G. © 2014 Tim Ashley

The Gang © 1997 Sebastian Beaumont, was first published in *The Mammoth Book of Gay Short Stories* (Robinson, 1997) and is reproduced by permission of the author.

Imaginary Boys © 2014 Paul Magrs is adapted from a BBC Radio 4 play of the same title by Paul Magrs.

Ghost, Come Back © 2014 Jerry Rosco

A Night with Mr Goldstein © 1973 Colin Spencer is published here for the first time.

Best Tasted Cold © 2014 Felice Picano

Eric in Retirement © 2014 Robert Cochrane

The Halfway House © 2014 Cliff James

What You Left Behind © 2014 Nick Alexander

Déjeuner sur l'herbe © 2014 Matt Harris

The Man Who Noticed © 2010 Francis King, was first published in *What Love Is* (Arcadia Books 2010) and is reproduced with permission from A.M. Heath and Company Ltd.

Royale with Cheese © 2014 Joseph Lidster

Caesar's Gallic Wars © 1997 Neil Bartlett, was first published in *The Mammoth Book of Gay Short Stories* (Robinson, 1997) and is adapted by the author for this collection.

How the Story Ends © 2014 Hugh Fleetwood

The Parasite that Grew Bigger than the Animal © 2014 John R. Gordon, first appeared in *Offline* magazine (2014) and is reproduced by permission of the author.

First Flush © 2014 Royston Ellis

The Letter © 2014 Scott Brown

Brown Manilla © 2010 Patrick Gale, was first published in *What Love Is* (Arcadia Books, 2010) and is reproduced by permission of the author.

Handle with Bear © 2010 Lawrence Schimel, was first published in *What Love Is* (Arcadia Books, 2010) and is reproduced by permission of the author.

Wolverine Cirque © 2013 Joseph Olshan, was first published in 2013 by Open Road Media and is reproduced by permission of the author.

Past Caring © 2014 Rupert Smith

Vasya (February, 1950) © 2014 David Llewellyn

He's Funny that Way © 2014 Alfred Corn

The Bargain © 2014 Damian Barr

The Good Butler © 1994 Tony Peake, was first published in *Seduction* (Serpent's Tail, 1994) and is reproduced by permission of the author.

Sexploitation © 2014 Brent Meersman, was first published in the collection *80 Gays around the world* by Brent Meersman (Missing Ink, 2014) and is reproduced by permission of the author.

A Dry Past © 2008 Richard Zimler, was first published in *A Casualty of War* (Arcadia Books, 2008) and is reproduced by permission of the author.

Speak My Language © 2014 Jeffrey Round

Flags of the Vlasov Army © 2014 Ian Young

Potholes in the Yellow Brick Road © 2010 Neal Drinnan, was first published in *What Love Is* (Arcadia Books, 2010) and is reproduced by permission of the author.

Key West Funeral © 2014 Michael Carroll

The Railings © 1992 Ronald Frame. An earlier version of the story first appeared on BBC Radio 4, and was first published in *Telling Stories* (Hodder & Stoughton, 1993). This new version adapted by the author, 2014.

MovieLand © 2014 Drew Gummerson

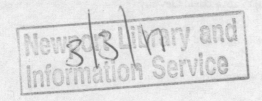